The Kingdom of the Wicked

Anthony Burgess

The Kingdom of
the Wicked

מַמְלֶכֶת

רְשָׁעִים

Hutchinson

London Melbourne Sydney Auckland Johannesburg

Hutchinson & Co. (Publishers) Ltd

An imprint of the Hutchinson Publishing Group

17–21 Conway Street, London WIP 6JD

Hutchinson Publishing Group (Australia) Pty Ltd
16–22 Church Street, Hawthorn, Melbourne, Victoria 3122, Australia

Hutchinson Group (NZ) Ltd
32–34 View Road, PO Box 40–086, Glenfield, Auckland 10

Hutchinson Group (SA) Pty Ltd
PO Box 337, Bergvlei 2012, South Africa

First published 1985
© Liana Burgess 1985

Set in Paladium by Colset Pte Ltd

Printed and bound in Great Britain by Anchor Brendon Ltd,
Tiptree, Essex

British Library Cataloguing in Publication Data

Burgess, Anthony
The kingdom of the wicked.
I. Title
823'.914[F]   PR6052.U638
ISBN 0 09 160040 5

Per Paolo Andrea, non martire

ONE

I take my title from the name the Jews have traditionally given to the Roman Empire. You may expect to meet all manner of wickedness in what follows – pork-eating, lechery, adultery, bigamy, sodomy, bestiality, the most ingenious varieties of cruelty, assassination, the worship of false gods and the sin of being uncircumcised. So you may lick your lips in anticipation of being, as it were, vicariously corrupted at the hands of your author. It is all too possible that the practice of literature is a mode of depravity rightly to be condemned. But, as is well known, literature ceases to be literature when it commits itself to moral uplift: it becomes moral philosophy or some such dull thing. Let us then, in the interest of allaying the boredom of this our life, agree to our complementary damnations. My damnation is, of course, greater than yours, since I am the initiator and you are merely the receptor of evil recordings. Moreover, you may throw this book into the fire if your disgust becomes too great; I am committed to writing it. Take another cup of wine and accept that we human beings are a bad lot.

My father was Azor the son of Sadoc, and I am Sadoc the son of, necessarily, Azor. In our family there has always been a feeble alternation of names, grandfather tossing the ball to grandson, and the custom goes back to time's mists. Looking like want of imagination, it probably has more to do with ancient spells, taboos, threats, conditions of inheritance, pacts with gods. I have no legitimate sons, nor have I much respect for tradition, but, were I to be a wave of the onflowing family river and not its ultimate dam, I would feel a certain superstitious fear about breaking the binary heritage. Names in our family, anyway, have always been the dull meat which we have left to others to sauce with sobriquets. My short fat father, in many ways the unluckiest man alive, was called Psilos, tall, Leptos, thin, and, which means primarily fortunate, Makarios. I have been nicknamed in my time Megas, big, and Onigros, donkey, both in reference to an endowment it would be unseemly to specify here. Having spent much of my life as a shipping clerk, headachy with manifests, squinty with the damnable green sea our wicked stepmother beyond the godowns, my spare time consumed in the, alas, overly promiscuous exploitation of

7

the endowment and another activity, more of a passivity, which earned me the nickname Dipsa, I have come, my yapping pack of diseases in tow, to retire far inland. I live in a rundown villa on an upland over a lake in the province of Helvetia, where the agencies of Domitian's bad version of empire leave me alone, save for an annual visit from the tax collector. For him I must convert one of my sheep or goats to sesterces and slaughter another for his entertainment.

I spend these last painracked days gazing on the misted Alps or else their hoods of snow and setting down what my father, before he died of the bite of a pack of ailments more vicious than my own, imposed as a filial duty – namely, the completion of a chronicle he began with his tale of the career of Yehoshua Naggar or Iesous Marengos. Both these names mean the carpenter Jesus. I write in Greek as he did, though you may be reading me in another language of the Empire. My Greek is not the tongue of Homer or Aeschylus but a sloppy ungrammatical sabir lacking Attic salt and tending to a saccharinity which sets my teeth on edge. This property is not in the writer but in the language. I could have written in Latin or even Aramaic, though my spelling of the latter is shaky. I know also a debased kind of Punic, but the things of Carthage have long gone under the earth or the sea. Whoever translates this, if it is ever to be translated, may be rendering me into the barks of the Goths or the cooings of the Celts, by grace of the alphabet of Rome. Latin itself is too cold and legalistic: even the pornography of Petronius reads like a series of court depositions. I have never had much love of Latin – all, in my life, orders and requisitions and rebukes, cold as executioner's steel.

Some of you may know my father's book on the giant who claimed to be God's son and thundered or wheedled, according to circumstances, of the new way. This new way my father sought to follow as an ethic while rejecting the theology behind it. I have inherited his scepticism concerning such doctrines as eternal punishment and reward, holding it as monstrous that any human enactment should be deemed worthy of either, and, more than anything, the tomfoolery of physical resurrection and life after death. Who, I ask you, wants to drag his bones out of the earth, reclothed in flesh which, in some foul magic of reversal, is regurgitated by the worms, in order that his eyes may see God, who, unless he is really the Emperor Domitian, is by definition unseeable? Who, I ask you, wants to live for ever?

We are not important enough for such transfiguration, nor, wicked though we certainly are, are we wicked enough for eternal fire. I have lived enough and am ready any time for the grand quietus. Life has had its moments of keen pleasure but there has been far more pain. The pain, in what you may regard as my perverted theology, is the work of God, and the pleasure, which all God's scriptures ban, is the benison of some demiurge too slippery for God to seize and choke. When Jesus spoke of God's love I do not think he could have been referring to the burly and capricious Jehovah the Hebrews worship in fear, for the scriptural record of his participation in man's affairs shows much vindictiveness but little charity. Jesus was referring, conceivably, to a God who could, as it were, be forced into existing by the pressure of human belief in him, a spiritual counterpart of himself. Or perhaps his God was a metaphor of the only thing that will save the world – the exercise of decency, tolerance and humorous scepticism.

You will find, I expect, recurring through my narrative the fine phrase *una nox dormienda*, which I take from Catullus. Only the poets seem to be able to lend humanity and sweetness to that rigid language of the law, but the poets have not been well liked by the guardians of empire, unless, as with Virgil, it was empire that they pretended to sing. Ovid was sent into exile for poeticizing about pleasure, and Catullus died too young for the full force of Roman *virtus* to punish him for singing of kisses. *Una nox dormienda* means that one final night that has to be slept through after a few score years of pain and its palliations, of pleasure and disgust after pleasure. This life of the body, perhaps tolerable for a senior clerk in a shipping company, is a torment for the enslaved, the captive, the deformed and the chronically sick, and it has been chiefly these who have drunken most thirstily of the Nazarene doctrine of a new life. Let them believe what their wretchedness bids them believe: they will find the *una nox dormienda* like the rest of us. In their eagerness to reward themselves and punish their enemies (of which Nature herself is one), they miss the essential truth of the new way, which has to do with the foundation and growth of an earthly society called somewhat extravagantly the Kingdom of Heaven. The members of this society pledge themselves to play what my father called the *lusus amoris* or game of love, though he considered *agape* or *ahavah* a more appropriate term than *amor*, which sounds like Roman patricians taking exercise after a day in camp or court. The game of trying to love one's enemies is the only practical response to injustice and cruelty. The insight which was responsible for propounding this truth was, one is tempted to think, superhuman. The claim of the primal gamesman of love to be the son of God represents a fine metaphor, but the assertion may contain a literal signification that time, with man's help, has yet to realize.

I propose, on this grey and unseasonable day of a month that has so far done homage to its presiding goddess Maia with soaked greenery and shrewd winds, the Alps shrouded and the thrushes silent, five dripping ewes and a heavily ballocked ram nibbling forlornly in the scant shelter of my poplar and my arbutus, to begin to set down what I can of the story of the spreading of the ground rules of the love game in

9

the kingdom of the wicked. I shall start with the events that followed upon the supposed death of its founder and end with the terrible time of the Vesuvian eruption which, destroying two fine cities, reminded us all that, though there may be a mother empire and even a mother church, there is an older and more capricious mother who nourishes her children without love and without enmity bids them perish. From the ashes of Pompeii there appears to be no resurrection. When man dies in the body his soul dies too. The temples go down and the tablets and scrolls of the various faiths, and the gods are shown to be impotent. Men, however, must try to live against all the odds and set up rules for living. Nature does not understand these rules, nor do human tyrants. Perhaps what cannot be wholly understood cannot wholly be destroyed. This is a feeble article of faith to begin with, but it helps to push my pen through this exordium and what now follows. Those of you who already yawn at what seems to be a moral tone will get your wickedness soon enough. One never has to wait long for wickedness.

Concerning the resurrection of Jesus, everyone must believe what he can. For my part, I will not accept miracles if the rational lies to hand, and I have no proof that Jesus died on the cross. He was, by all accounts, a man of immense stature and strength with huge lungs rendered the more powerful by the practice of a kind of oratory. He was certainly nailed to a cross by the wrists and feet, his body left to leap like a stranded fish to gasp in what air it could, but when exhaustion came death was still some way off, for those vast lungs, in the control of the muscles of a powerful midriff, still held enough air to sustain life. His legs were not broken, as we know, and the spear that pierced his side seems to have ruptured no inner organ. It was as a whole man that he was removed from that tree of shame, with full vitality in brief abeyance but ready to be restored after a healing sleep. It was no great act of strength for such a colossus to shove aside the stone that served as a door to his tomb, and it was like his humour to replace that stone. To speak of his resurrection, as all his followers did, was to abet no trickery: tombs are for dead men, and when a man seemingly dead is lain in one his lively egress may be termed a resurrection. A prophecy had been satisfactorily fulfilled, the Son of Man or of God had rebuilt his temple after three days in the sepulchre. But if death is defined as the cessation of breathing and the stilling of the heart, with the consequent onset of fleshly decay, then no man has risen from the dead, not even Lazarus. Lazarus's sleep was exceptionally long and sound, and to restore him to animation was an act of thaumaturgy of a kind, but the breaking of the seal of death, even if it were possible, would surely be a blasphemy against the Creator–Destroyer who inexorably stamped it.

10

This resurrected or reawakened Jesus appeared to many – first to a common prostitute, next, so some say, to Pontius Pilate in his cups, and then to two of the least of his followers, Cleopas and Zachaeus, the latter a Jerusalem fishmonger who smelt of his trade. Jesus was always close to fishmen, catchers and buyers and sellers, and soon became identified, through typical Nazarene wordplay, with a fish. Cleopas and Zachaeus had been thrown into jail for a brief spell during the Passover that was just ended on a charge of making ugly faces at a Roman decurion. In fact, Zachaeus had been showing Cleopas a bad back tooth that ached and Cleopas had been making a rictus of sympathy. One of the prison guards knew Zachaeus well enough, or at least his fish, and release, though without apology, had, at leisure, followed. The two humble Nazarenes, as the followers of Jesus of Nazareth were beginning to be called, had missed the crucifixion and were in time only to witness the dismantling of the great cross and its two smaller fellows by a Roman workforce, the wrenching out of nails and hurling timbers to the Jerusalem dust with coarse soldiers' cries of *Pone in culum, fili scorti* and the like. Cleopas and Zachaeus saw also a blind man being led by a boy to the site of execution, a beggar not too sure whether to retain blindness as his trade or consent to have a healing act performed upon him. He had come, in his blessed innocence, to Golgotha or Skull Hill to discuss the matter with Jesus, having heard that he was the centre of attention there. But now, 'God knows best,' he kept saying, 'God wants me blind, all is providential, blessed be the name of the All High. Pity the poor blind, fair gentlemen and lovely ladies.'

Another beggar, one in rancid rags and with a halo of flies, sidled up to the two, nodding. He lived mostly on stews of fish heads and guts donated by the kindly Zachaeus. He said:

'Your man's dead and your man's alive again. You missed it all.'

'Alive again?'

'Shoved him in one of those tombs cut out of the rock and he's not there no more. The corpse got lifted out during the night, bribery, some of those oneeyed Syrian guards will do anything for money, and now the story is he walked out large as life grinning all over his beard and they've got him hidden somewhere. Stands to reason. The priests would get him for coming back to life, which is against the law, and the Romans would nail him up again and make a better job of it next time. That's the story. Of course, it's a trick and a good one, like all his tricks was. He's dead all right.'

'Do you know,' Cleopas asked, 'where the others are?'

'Others? The one for each tribe bar one, you mean? Some say one thing and some say another. They reckon five or six of them went off to Emmaus, that's that dungheap seven miles out of town. Lying low,

11

sort of. The rest are sort of scattered. A sort of council of war, making up their minds what to do. It's not too healthy here in Jerusalem for those that knew him. They want that dead corpse and they want it quick.'

A cart was being loaded with the uprights and crosspieces and a titulus with IESVS NAZARENVS REX IVDAEORVM scrawled on it. A bucket of water sluiced the area. A sponge, an empty wine flask, the skeleton of a fish, blood, evidences of life to be cleared away by the Roman passion for order. They yelled for free passage for the cart through the city gateway. Cleopas and Zachaeus took the road. They left the city in light rain which became briefly heavy, pushing through the crowds, jostled by police and crying chapmen with handcarts, avoiding donkeydroppings and cowdung and horsemerds, coming out into sweeter air and, soon, weak sunlight. On the road a Roman maniple swung by, *sin dex sin dex*, with a couple of chained and bloodied prisoners. Cleopas and Zachaeus hid, till it passed, in a clump of dead olives. It was more than halfway to Emmaeus that a big man in a hood and cloak came out of nowhere and gave them a cheery shalom. Where going then? I too. Walk together? Why not? What news then in the great city?

Cleopas and Zachaeus looked warily at the man and at each other. A Roman spy, deliberately chosen for his bulk, face hidden, talking Aramaic like a foreigner. But knowing the scriptures as no foreigner should. They trained them well these days.

'Well, if this was truly the Messiah prophesied in the sacred writings he had of necessity to rise from the dead. The prophecies have to be fulfilled. Believe he was what he said he was and you have to believe that he went into the underworld for three days, there to ransom the good men who died before he came to redeem them, and then in the flesh returned to the world of the flesh.' Cleopas and Zachaeus now knew that this was no spy but the man himself. How were they supposed to respond? This was one of his games, in which you were to pretend to be ignorant of his identity until he gave you the key. But he had given the key already. In his hood and cloak, marching towards Emmaeus at a pace they panted to keep up with, the stranger gave them many chapters and even more verses, citing all the prophets until the brains of Zachaeus and Cleopas whirled enough to make them forget the pains in the soles of their hurrying feet. But Zachaeus's bad back tooth did not forget its master and shot a twinge at him coinciding with Jeremiah IX iii. The stranger saw his grimace and said: 'This citing of scripture gives you pain?'

'It's a back tooth, a grinder. I have to have it out.'

'You seek a tooth surgeon in Emmaeus? You would have been wiser to have it drawn in the big city.'

12

'In Emmaeus,' Cleopas said, 'we seek the chief of the companions of Jesus. Might we ask why you're going there?'

'Country air and a country meal in an inn and a night's meditation. I am what you might term a thinking man.'

'A reading one too,' Zachaeus winced.

'You have to load your brain with the thought of the past before you can hatch thoughts about the future. So. Here it is.' Meaning Emmaeus, a miserable small town of naked children chasing scrawny hens. An old man sat outside a cottage door whence floated garlicky oil fumes. He watched their arrival, sucking few teeth. The inn had a collapsed thatch. The last drops of the late rain made the surface of the water in the bucket in the eating room set for the rain's indrip gently shimmer. Anybody from Jerusalem been around? Not that I know of, the landlord said. Had some troops in taking prisoners, spitting good wine on the floor and not paying for it. You say from? These were going to. What will it be then? A jug of red and fish on the coals. Bread's brick hard with there being no baking these last days. Take what comes is what I say.

The three ate their supper not in the eating room with its melancholy raindrip but at a table set in the garden, a weedy neglected affair full of mewing kittens, the sunset a free show of crimson, green, purple, spilt eggyolk. It was when the talkative stranger reached for the winejug that Zachaeus saw. His tooth was not shocked into quiescence by the sight of the dark red wound. They had both known, of course. Cleopas said: 'So it really happened.'

'Oh yes, it happened.'

'And we.' Cleopas began to choke on a fishbone. The stranger who was no stranger hit him kindly thrice on the back. Cleopas spat out the bone on to his trencher. 'Thanks. We, I was trying to say, are the first to know. We're the least, we're nothing, and this place is on the road to nowhere.'

'Casualness, you can say,' Jesus said. 'Life being a matter of the casual. You're not quite the first to know. There was a reformed prostitute first, and then – never mind. No trumpets, so to speak. No flamboyance, except in that sunset over your shoulder. There's something Roman about a sunset. Never despise the casual. You are custodians of the truth and sowers of the word as much as any of them. You, your toothache is a warning of worse pain –'

'Zachaeus is my name, Zachaeus.'

'I know your name and I know your trade, you smell of it. The bad time's coming, the time when you'll be questioned about love. Let's finish this jug and have more.'

'Love?' Cleopas gulped.

'Of course. You will preach love to the world and the world will

13

think there's a catch in it. For love you will be whipped, flayed, clawed, burned, nailed to a tree. I preached nothing but love.'

It grew dark. Zachaeus shivered as the night wind rose. 'You had skill in it,' he said. 'Preaching the word, that is. Have skill still, I mean, in preaching, that is. What will you do? Lord,' he added.

'I've done my work,' Jesus said. 'I leave the world soon. Your world. A whisper of encouragement, there is no death and so on, and then – best not to ask where I go. Go, yes, but in a manner stay. I am on this table.' They saw that his hands were but saw that he meant more. 'In the bread, brickhard though it is, and in this wine where, see, the vinegar-making mother is already at work. It's all quite simple. Believe, when you take both, that I am in them. I am on this table, in your mouths, dissolved in your stomachs, becoming your flesh and the spirit the flesh serves, excreted, yes, but daily renewed. When wine ends and bread ends the world ends. Till then I'll be there. That is a truth as love is a truth, but more important than the truth is the game you will play. The game of taking bread and wine and tasting me in your mouths. The game of trying to love, because love is not easy. But it is the only answer.'

'What now?' Zachaeus asked. His tooth sang viciously. 'Tonight, I mean. I don't like the look of this darkness.'

Jesus understood. 'Yes, the enemy lurking in it, the eyes of bad beasts in the woods and carrion birds untimely awake in the branches. Nothing to fear. The beasts will roll at our feet to be tickled and the enemy will know love. Stay the night here and then go back to Jerusalem. I have to go, there are others to see. They too must be sent back to Jerusalem.'

'So they *are* near here?' Cleopas said.

'Yes, in an old farmhouse. I must have words with them. They are to go to Nicodemus's house in Gethsemane, if they can bear the smell of treachery there. I will pay the reckoning for you and go. Though, as I told you, I also stay. In that bit of hard bread that is left and these red dregs. So take my blessing while I take my leave.'

Both Cleopas and Zachaeus felt that the night whose falling had all their lives been a friendly summons to sleep had now become a malevolent visitation bearing no seeds of sunrise. 'Stay with us,' Cleopas said urgently. 'Don't leave us, Lord.'

'I stay and I go.' And he went, paying the reckoning on the way. Who had given him money? The reformed prostitute?

It seemed to Zachaeus, though he recognized the unworthiness of the thought, that it would have been a good gesture on the part of the resurrected to ease that flaming tooth. Meditatively and with his fingers shaky, he probed his dry mouth. The tooth was loose and, as he finger and thumbed it, it grew looser. He rocked it like a screaming child in a cradle. He felt confident that by morning, if morning were ever to come, he might well have it out. There were things that a man could sometimes do for himself.

'Questioned about love,' Cleopas brooded. 'I don't like it.'

The kinds of love enacted on the island of Caprae were not of a sort that anyone durst question. This refuge of the Emperor Tiberius was also called Capri, but it was nicknamed Caprineum, meaning a place of goatish lust. Here let us meet Tiberius Claudius Nero, called from his youth Biberius Caldius Mero, meaning boozer of neat hot wine. A man of orgies, who would hardly accept a dinner invitation unless assured that the waiting girls would all be naked, who promoted a nobody to the quaestorship because he could down a quart tankard without taking breath, who made Flaccus governor of Syria and Piso prefect of the city of Rome because they were all-night guzzlers and swillers, he is, in his seventies, aware of failing appetites, especially in the area of what he would call *love*, and needs a variety of stimulants.

See him now waking late in the presence of a large picture of Atalanta and Meleager performing the rite of fellatio, whimpering because he cannot attain a swift fore-breakfast emission with a catamite whom he has lashed for his failure to arouse the requisite rush of lust, gulping cheese, wine and the feathery bread his baker has learnt from the Arabs, then going to look upon his *spintriae*. These are boys and girls garnered from all over the Empire for their skill in unnatural coits, and he sets them to copulating in triads to whip up his difficult desires. Then he visits the woods and spinneys, where there are Pans and Syringes beckoning him into their caves with the lewdest gestures. Now he goes to the sacrifice, there to conceive instant lust for the bearer of incense and his brother the holy trumpeter, haling them out of the temple before the end of the ceremony so that he can bugger them both. It is a dry and fruitless process and he groans. The brothers protest feebly at being so ill used, so he has their legs broken. He hears then that his chief cook's wife has had a baby, so he has the blind suckling brought to pull on his flaccid penis with its boneless gums, what time the mother wails and is beaten for wailing. Then it is time for him to swim in his warmed marble piscina, with the little boys he calls his minnows darting between his spread legs to nibble at his shrunken genitalia. This, O Romans, is your Emperor, successor to the great Augustus.

Dried and wrapped, he sits in the imperial garden, full of stony magnificence. Naked boys and girls from all the provinces save one serve him cooled white wine and morsels of salt fish. Curtius Atticus, an ageing and respectable patrician, comes and is permitted to sit with his Emperor. Curtius has always averted his eyes from Tiberius's excesses. He is here on Capri to exert what good influence he can on the old goat, but he knows the task is hopeless. It is above all things necessary, in his view, that there should be a ruler in Rome, but there is none, and the Senate is corrupt and impotent. Curtius has recently taken to Stoicism. Tiberius says:

'You have some more gloomy wisdom for me?'

'I wouldn't call it gloomy. The aim of the Stoic philosophy is to dispel gloom.'

'Only the pleasures of the senses can ease the pains of the spirit,' Tiberius says in the Greek of Rhodes, where he was once in exile. He nods to one of his secretaries, a freshfaced clever Greek slave who smiles inwardly at the Doric accent. He has transcribed this same trite maxim at least a dozen times before. The attendants, boys and girls, now strip naked and, to the music of the thrushes in the pines, perform a chaste enough ballet. PNS F TH SPRT, writes the slave.

'The senses fail,' Curtius says justly. 'At your age, our age.'

'Speak for yourself. And I think you may keep your philosophy to yourself. I was looking at my *spintriae* earlier this morning, and I note that there is only one race unrepresented among them. I mean the Hebrews. Why,' he quavered petulantly, 'does not our procurator at Caesarea send me little presents like the other governors?'

'Last month there was a shipment of dates and a couple of camels.'

'The Hebrews are all for truculence and incorruption. That isn't human, Curtius. I've a mind to see some of the younger incorrupt corrupted. We have enough corrupting agencies here. I would like to see some little handsome Jews, boys and girls, wrested slowly of their incorruption. That would be a new pleasure.'

'May I mention the word duty, Caesar?'

'You may not. I'm not going back to Rome.'

'Well, at least perform some of the essential duties from Capri. There are no governors of consular rank in Spain and Syria. The Dacians and Sarmatians are plucking Moesia like a ripe plum. The Germans are in Gaul. In Armenia the Parthians –'

'Shut up, Curtius. I forbid you to mention these things. Talk to me of the duties of rule when you've experienced the burden of rule and the nightmare of treachery. My only concern now is self-preservation. That's why I'm here. A natural fortress of rock with one well-guarded landing beach. I'm safe. I've made sure of that.'

He was indeed safe, but the rocky island was not so impregnable as he thought. Down below, rocking on blue calm, on the other side from the Villa Jovis, a small fishing boat rode a chain's length from the wall of rock. A hardworking fisherman, gnarled and lean and black with sun, was dragging his netted catch inboard. It was a huge sea perch or *morone labrax* being nipped by angry crabs. 'Row in,' the man said to his boy.

'Why?'

'*Why?*' He slammed with his fist at the mad despairing eye of the bass, which leapt in its confines like a man on a cross. 'Have you ever seen anything like this afore?'

'It's a big bastard right enough.'

'Well, it's going up to him. His worship the Emperor. I'm off up that rockface with it. Plenty of tufts to cling on to. That'll give him a bit of a surprise that will. What I'll say is this: From the god of the sea to the god of the world. That'll show him I'm book read too. There's many a small man been made big by doing the unexpected. It's the spirit that made the Empire what it is.'

'It's like intruding,' the boy said. 'There's soldiers all over.'

'Row in, boy.'

Not knowing he had a gift coming, Tiberius was saying: 'You've not seen your own son, heard him howling in his blood while the knives struck and struck and she there, grinning –'

'With respect, Caesar, you did not see it either.'

'I see it every night. I wake sweating.' Drusus, his own son, sitting at the cleared supper table, his wife Livilla playing the game of holding up fingers quickly for the guessing of how many. And then Sejanus, the one man in Rome the Emperor could trust, prefect of the Guard, came in with his killers, and Drusus crawling under the table while Livilla laughed. They dragged him out by the hair and then stabbed and stabbed. Livilla laughed because now she was going to marry Sejanus, and Sejanus was going to be Emperor. Sejanus, trusted master of Rome while his ageing master tasted an earned repose on Capri.

'And what satisfaction did you find in revenge?'

'It was retribution, it was –'

'The whole family?'

The daughter was a mere child, crying: 'I didn't mean to be bad. I won't do it again. Please don't hurt me.'

And the captain of the detail said to the executioner: 'This girl's a virgin presumably. We don't execute virgins. That's the law.'

And the executioner: 'I'll rape her. Then we can follow the law.'

Tiberius now shakily drained his cup of white wine. Curtius said: 'Calm, Caesar. Refuse to be moved. Take a calm mind back to Rome. Rome has become a filthy shambles. Macro is worse than Sejanus was. Rome needs its Emperor.'

'I will not go back to Rome. I will die here. In my bed.'

'And the succession?'

'The succession is assured. Gaius has the army behind him. Nobody is going to kill Gaius.'

17

'A *fish*?' Curtius said. They both looked towards a grinning man, approaching with a monstrous sea perch in his arms. It was kicking still. He was between two guardsmen. They too grinned. The fisherman said:

'From the divine Neptune a gift for the divine Tiberius.' He had been practising the new and improved form all the difficult way up the rockface. Tiberius approached, saying:

'Not so divine if mortal men can climb his Olympus. You guards, you forget your instructions. Throw this man where he came from, fish and all. Then report to your commanding officer for disciplinary action. No – wait. For me, you say? A gift from Neptune? Strange that he doesn't deliver it personally.'

And he took from the arms of the fisherman the huge fish, staggering under its weight but, despite his age, strong enough to bear it. He smiled, and the fisherman smiled back. Then Tiberius took the fish by its tail in his hands like a flexible club and began to lash the man with it. Sharp scales struck his face like flakes of flint. He screamed, he was wearing blood like a moving mask.

'If fishermen can get in, so can hired murderers.' He threw down the battered fish, panting. 'What's he saying?'

'He's saying, sir,' said one of the guardsmen, 'that he's glad he didn't give you his crabs as well.'

'Take him,' Tiberius ordered, with a promptitude that bespoke well the imperial gift of swift decisions, 'to the fish tanks and set all the crabs upon him. Then throw him back the way he came.' Curtius held on to his stoicism and his breakfast. So, howling, the fishgiver was hauled off. Tiberius sat. Curtius remained standing. A servant came on flat bare feet bearing a black snake from Sabatum on a velvet cushion. 'My darling Columba,' cooed Tiberius, taking it to his bosom. 'My little pet. The only living creature I can trust. She's hungry, Metellus. Bring some frogs and mice. Make sure they're properly alive.' The snake hissed happily.

Having hurled the screaming fisherman over the rocks, the crabs clinging to his face and head in indifferent viciousness, the two guardsmen reported to their centurion, Marcus Julius Tranquillus. He was a young and decent man, his family of the plebeian branch of the Julian line, in the army as a career, like his father before him, a junior centurion on detachment from the Praetorian Guard. He listened gravely to what they told him and delivered judgment.

'He expects me to order your execution,' he said, 'so we will take it that this has already been done and that your bodies have been at once buried in the communal dump because of the great heat. Take over guard duty near the beach. I will arrange your immediate replacements. You realize, I hope, that you were very foolish.'

18

'We knew the man, sir. Drunk with him in the bars. Not an ounce of malice in him. Climbing up those rocks at his age with a struggling fish on his back. Out of respect and love for the Emperor, as he put it. It strikes me nobody can do right these days, sir.'

'That's how it strikes you, eh? So that's how it strikes you. Strikes you that way, does it? All right, dismiss.'

He was a lonely and troubled young man, well built and not unhandsome. He had tried, throughout his brief career, to hold on to certain principles of *virtus*. A congenital incorruptness had brought few rewards. He had been fortunate enough to be one of the first to pick up certain hints that Sejanus had been responsible for the murder of Drusus, despite Sejanus's own eager prosecution of a case that at first preferred no solution – the Emperor's son hacked to pieces and found, a feast for flies, in an alley near the Tiber. Well, great men always had enemies. Farcical trials and executions, no shortage of informers and perjurers. And then a slave had said something to another slave – slaves, having nothing else, had become depositories of honesty; being in theory insentient machines, they heard and saw more than was available to free men – and a love note from Sejanus to the Lady Livilla had been found crumpled under the pillow of a bed that a slave was making, and one thing had led to another. Julius, as acting mess secretary, had been offered this note by a slave in the officers' kitchen for a hundred sesterces. One thing had led to another, including the rape and execution of an innocent child. The whole of the Praetorian Guard had been rewarded – ten gold pieces a man – for not following Sejanus in his revolt; the legions in Syria had received equal sums for refusing to set specially blessed effigies of Sejanus among their standards. And he, Marcus Julius Tranquillus, had been honoured for his loyalty by this present appointment, forced to warm his hands at the central fire of corruption, madness, danger. But Tiberius could not live much longer. The son of Germanicus was, it was certain, to inherit the purple. Germanicus, adopted son of Tiberius, great soldier, fine man, unfortunately dead untimely in Syria and everyone knew why and how, had no bad blood to transmit to the boy who had been the darling of the military camps. Always in soldier's boots; they had nicknamed him 'Little Boots'. Caligula, which meant that, was a name that already made one smile in referred affection. There could be nothing but good in a son of Germanicus.

In one of the outer courts of the Temple, upon which Syrian guards looked down indifferently from Antonia's Tower, the Rabban Gamaliel discussed with his senior class the dangers of zealotry and the virtues of compromise. 'Compromise,' he said. 'Some of you

19

wrinkle your noses and curl your lips, as though compromise were a dirty word. But it is only through compromise that we may keep the faith alive. We have ruling here in the holy territory of Israel an infidel race with unclean habits and an undisguised contempt for our religious laws. With one stroke of the sword they could sever the silken cord that binds us into one people. With their battering rams they could destroy the Temple. We live uneasily with the Romans, but at least we live.'

'That is Sadducee talk.' So spoke Caleb the son of Jacob.

'What,' said Seth the son of Zachaeus not the fishman, 'is wrong with Sadducee talk? If it weren't for us Sadducees you'd be kissing the little toe of Tiberius's statue. You'd be burning incense before Jupiter and Mercu.y and the rest of the godless crew. Rabban Gamaliel is right. Diplomacy is the way. Jewish intelligence can always defeat Roman stupidity. You Zealots would have us all strung up on that hill over there.'

'Nailed up,' Stephen shuddered. He was a Greek Jew.

'Look,' Caleb said. 'The Zealots ask only for a restoration of the Jewish birthright. Jewish rule in a Jewish land. Rome grows weak and Rome grows frightened. An old mad Emperor and a Senate full of squawking chickens. Interim rule in Syria, and how long can they hold Syria? Strike at Rome in Palestine and the provincial structure would collapse. Rome wouldn't send out any legions. The Roman Senate would say good riddance to Judaea and then go off to dinner. Let the Jews rule themselves, they'd say; they were almost more trouble than they were worth.'

'I think,' Gamaliel said, 'that you underestimate the Roman appetite for power. I see no sign of debility in Pontius Pilatus. His Syrian troops would rush in and eat your Zealots for breakfast.'

'Some say,' Stephen said, 'that he saw the light.'

'If you mean the Galilean,' Caleb said, 'it was a very shortlived light.'

'A shortlived light for all his followers.' This was Saul, a young man already growing bald, his eyes in dark caves, the frontal lobes unnaturally bulging. 'We've had a succession of these false prophets, almost one a year in the last ten or so. Most of them knew the scriptures, I'll say that. The scriptures drove them mad. But this one was an ignorant carpenter burbling about love.'

'A carpenter's trade,' Gamaliel said slyly, 'is not inferior to a tentmaker's.'

'If I make tents,' Saul said, 'it is in accordance with our Jewish tradition. We must all work with our hands. But I think of myself first as a scholar.'

'He was a scholar too,' Stephen said. 'The scriptures were never out

20

of his mouth. And what was wrong with burbling about love, as you put it?'

'I'll tell you what was wrong and what *is* wrong,' Caleb said. 'By love he meant submission, turning the other cheek, putting up with foreign injustice. He countenanced tyranny. He said nothing about a free Israel.'

'Caleb, my son,' Gamaliel said, 'admit there was something in what he preached. We must change ourselves before we change our systems of secular rule. Man's soul comes first.'

'A soul in chains,' Caleb said, as was to be expected, bitterly.

'The chains are personal sin, not foreign oppression. Don't disparage love. Love is a thing we all have to learn, and through hardship and bitterness too. On a practical level, it may well be that love will save us. We Jews play into Roman hands by hating each other – Pharisee against Sadducee, Zealot against both. Sect against sect, tribe against tribe, division not unity.'

'So you,' Saul said, 'are becoming a Galilean?'

'Like you, Saul,' Gamaliel said, 'I belong to the Pharisees. At least I accept the doctrine of resurrection. As for the narrowness, the xeno-phobia of small farmers – that's another matter. But God forbid that I should approve the blasphemy of his desperate claim to be – the very thought of the words makes me shudder – I cannot utter them.'

'The Son of God,' Stephen said. 'The Messiah. Well, a Messiah was prophesied.'

'*Is*, Stephen,' Saul said. '*Is* prophesied.'

'An endless is, I see. We believe in the coming of the Messiah, but anyone who claims to be the Messiah is condemned and put to death. Must it always be so?'

'Yes,' Caleb said. 'So long as you live under a foreign power that puts down free speech. So long as the holy Jewish council is in the control of a sect that loves the Romans.'

'You will take that back,' Seth said with heat. 'That is a lie and a calumny. That is a gross insult to the guardians of the faith –'

'Enough, enough,' Gamaliel said mildly. 'Can we discuss nothing in rational calm? Let us think always in terms of the things that unite, not divide. We are all Jews and we must stop these dissensions. You may sneer at love as you sneer at compromise – but find me some other answer.' And he dismissed the class.

The class became a little mob of highspirited youths as soon as it touched the secular life of the street – a roaring camel, a donkey bonneted in flies, hucksters. Seth and Caleb wrangled still, however. Caleb said: 'You licker of Roman arses. God bless the Emperor Tiberius and all the little boys that he buggers. Kick us, your exalted divinity, lay it on real hard.'

21

'That's stupid, and you know it,' Seth said. 'Do you really think I like these foreign louts with their spears and eagles and hairy legs? I stand for a free Israel too, but we won't get it by spitting at their shadows –'

'May the Roman eagle spread its wings,' Caleb jeered.

'Till it splits its –'

'Sycophantic Sadducee.'

'Xenophobic Zealot.'

And then they began to push each other in high good humour. They started to wrestle. Saul held their coats, cheering on neither. A weary noncommissioned officer from the Italia legion in Caesarea, posted to Jerusalem to keep the Syrian troops in order, paused with his dusty maniple to watch the wrestling match. Disturbance. Jewish noise. One of those two Jewboys had got the other on the ground in the dust. What they called public disorder. There were onlookers roaring and cheering. Time to step in. He stepped in.

'All right, enough of that,' he said in bad Aramaic. 'If you Jews want to fight join the Roman army. Not that we'd have you. Come on, get off home. You, get up.'

He meant Caleb, but Caleb had twisted his ankle and made the ascent slowly and in pain. The noncommissioned officer grabbed him by the collar of his sweaty robe. Caleb spoke unwisely. He said:

'Keep your filthy Roman paws off, you uncircumcised pig.'

'Uncircum – whatever it was. Pig I know. *Chasir* means *sus*, doesn't it? Nasty, very. Dirty lot, you Jews, aren't you?'

Caleb unwisely hit out. He was encouraged by the sight of a little gang of known Zealots in the crowd. Action. You had to act sometime, no good just talking about action.

'All right. You're under arrest. Disaffection, disorder, insult to the occupying forces. Come on.' Saul intervened. Saul said:

'Excuse me, officer – he's a little overwrought. See, he's in pain. Surely an apology would be enough.'

'And who and what are you?'

'*Who* doesn't matter. But I'm a Roman citizen.'

'You're a Jew.'

'Yes, a Jew. But also a citizen of Rome. Lucius Saul Paulus, if you must know my name. The name is enrolled in the praetorium –'

'Look, sir, if that's what you're to be called, we have our duty. This one has to be taught a lesson. He'll learn it while he's looking down from that hill up there. Come on, you.'

As he started to drag Caleb off, the little gang of Zealots thought they might as well erupt now. Five Syrian privates and a fattish redhaired Roman. Seven Jews more than a match. Then a bucina grated from the watchtower. Reinforcements on their way. Fists and clubs against swords and spears. A rangy Zealot clubbed the noncommissioned officer briefly. Then a panting maniple got its spears to work. A quieted riot, not much of a riot.

'You're here in time for some rough justice, sir,' Quintilius said. Pilate had just arrived from Caesarea. Dusty, hot, tired, he took a swig from the winejug kept cooled under a statue of Mercury, patron of thieves. 'A Jewish riot to celebrate your arrival.'

'Started again, have they? Been suspiciously quiet for too long.'

'A synagogue student spat on the uniform, used insulting language, blasphemed against the Emperor, resisted arrest. Then it started. None killed. But a Roman soldier severely wounded.'

'Yes yes yes yes yes yes. That last letter from the island of Capri said something about our skill in maintaining tranquillity in Palestine. Have we, in your informed opinion, Quintilius, shown such skill?'

They surveyed each other without warmth. Pilate had to go carefully with his deputy, who was, Pilate knew, intriguing in long letters for the governorship of Syria. Too friendly with the Jews, to be construed as a capacity for cooperating with men of compromise who would help keep down a growing dissidence. A bribetaker, but one who regarded a bribe as a gratuity for which he would do nothing in return. The givers of bribes retained their innocence, hopelessly believed you could bargain with Rome. He, Pontius Pilatus, had been a protégé of the late Sejanus. He had written friendly letters to Sejanus, wishing him all that he wished himself. Those letters would be on file. He, Pilate, had not made himself indispensable. The procuratorship of Judaea was no plum. He was due for retirement soon. He wished to resign into a sinecure, a numinous Roman presence in a mild climate, one who did not even have to sign papers. He felt hopeless. Quintilius was, as ever, smiling and foxy, saying:

'Well, procurator, there's been no call to bring in reinforcements from Syria. It's been a matter more of policing than of invoking martial law. Of course, the ill-smelling gentlemen of the Sanhedrin have helped –'

'Not from any love of Rome. Those Jewish priests like a quiet life. They know where the best wine comes from. They like their seaside villas.'

'A foxy lot,' Quintilius said foxily. 'The best of both worlds.'

'We played into their hands,' Pilate said. 'Over that Jesus of Nazareth affair. That still rankles. They made us crucify the wrong man. It won't happen again.'

'Assuredly not, procurator. About these Zealots –'

'There's a Jewish feast coming up, isn't there? Pentecost. A Greek name for a Jewish carnival.'

'Hardly a carnival. Feast of the first fruits or something. Pentecost means fifty days after the Passover.'

'I know what it means, Quintilius. I think it might be a good time for reminding them where the power lies. They had three crucifixions for Passover. We let one of those damned Zealots go. Because the *people* wanted it that way. Then he murdered one of ours.'

'Lucius Publius Strabo.'

'Never mind the name. It was one of our people. This time we'll nail up three Zealots. And if the mob howls, let it.'

'Including this Caleb bar something? He's no more than a boy, procurator.'

'A student, you said. All the better. Get them young. Destroy them in the egg. Which reminds me that I'm hungry. Shall we dine together?'

'I'm invited out, procurator.'

'By Jews?'

'The maintenance of good relations with the subject people. You taught me the importance of that, sir.'

'Don't get too close, Quintilius. Remember who we are, what we are.' Saying it, he felt hopeless.

'Oh, I never forget that, procurator.'

Pilate grunted and went off to his quarters. Quintilius looked out from the terrace to the street, where a Jew of wealthy appearance was hurrying, as if late for an appointment. Busy people, a busy town. They believed in money. They sometimes seemed more solid, some-how, than the Roman Empire. It was sustained by soldiers, and soldiers didn't make much money.

In the upper room where that last supper had been eaten, in retrospect it appeared with little appetite, but the mutton had been carved to the bone and the last of the sour herb sauce scooped up with the last of the hard bread, the eleven were assembled. Simon Peter and Matthew, once the sorely taxed and the sorely taxing, stood with Thomas, the dour North Galilean given to scepticism, hard to please and pessi-mistic. Philip hummed a tune and Thaddeus breathed it on his flute, so that Thomas said: 'Ach, for the Lord's sake –' Bartholomew silently nursed his dyspepsia, big James, called Little, performed the muscle flexings of the country wrestler he had been. The other James was biting a hangnail. Andrew and John and Simon, who had been a Zealot, were talking quietly to a nervous man named Joseph Barnabas, Simon saying: 'Well, if he doesn't come the place is yours, that stands to reason –' But then they heard feet arriving rapidly up the outside wooden stairway and then the door opened and the Jew of wealthy appearance whom Quintilius had been idly watching came in, breathless.

'I'm sorry to be so late. My nephew – Caleb – he's under arrest. I

24

was trying to make an appointment to see the procurator –'

'Well now, master,' Little James said to Peter, 'we can start.'

'Don't call me master, Little James. I am no master.'

'Peter. Here are the – Are we right to use them?'

Peter took them in his left hand and clicked them together. He then addressed the assembly with some diffidence, saying:

'Friends, brothers, when the master was with us he had many followers but only twelve disciples. He chose that number as you know because it is the number of the tribes of Israel. One of the twelve died – shamefully, by his own hand. He is buried in the potter's field that is now the burial ground for strangers who die in Jerusalem. The Field of Blood, it is called. I will not mention his name. Nor, so I may hope, will his name ever again be mentioned when we are met together. Well, today we are met together for a happy purpose. It is to complete our number, choosing between Matthias and Joseph Barnabas, equally good men, equally worthy – though who of any among us can be called worthy?' He bowed his head as though to wait for a cock to crow, but they were far from any fowl-run. 'We may add only one to the inner brotherhood. Chance, they sometimes say, is one of the toys of God. Toys are for children, but the master told us we had to become like children. Chance shall choose for us then. We have dice.' He showed them. 'I think you all know where they come from. A certain Roman soldier diced for a certain garment and regretted what he did. Joseph Barnabas, take the dice and roll.'

Joseph Barnabas was a swart young man with a round trimmed beard. His eyes were large and liquid. He took the dice timorously and shook them in the cup of his right hand. He threw. All looked at the table surface. Three and two.

'Matthias.'

Matthias rolled in both hands, shaking their clasp in what looked like premature self-congratulation. He let fall rather than threw. Two and four.

'There is almost nothing in it,' Peter said. 'Welcome, Matthias, to our midst.' Joseph Barnabas was goodhumoured in defeat. A matter of luck only. Matthias was taken to various bosoms and thumped on his back like a baby with wind. He was, they all noted, the first as well as the last of the well-dressed disciples: a gold chain round his neck and his beard not only trimmed but oiled, his single long garment embroidered at neck and hem with a Greek key pattern. Well, he would have to become ragged and unkempt as befitted one close to the Lord God. They could certainly use his money, solid clean money made out of land.

'We will sit round the table,' Peter said. 'And if Little James will be so good as to go down to the cookshop and fetch up our dinner, not forgetting the wine, we can have the first feast of our new our new –'

'Dispensation?' Bartholomew suggested.

'I was going to say something like lonely responsibility,' Peter said. 'I'm not good at words, as you know, and we're all going to have to spout a lot of words. Look, Joseph Barnabas, there's no need to fidget as though you shouldn't be here. If one of us gets picked up by the Romans or the Sanhedrin and stoned and crucified it's you who'll take his place. How many of us are there now in Jerusalem? I'd say about two hundred –'

'More like a hundred and fifty,' Matthew said.

'Well, we're all brothers together, and there's nothing secret about what we're going to try to do. So in future there won't be many meetings of just the twelve. We'll need all the help we can get from the others, and that means you more than anybody, Joseph Barnabas. It's only a pair of dice that says you're not one of the twelve.'

'Very good, sir.'

'Don't call me sir. Peter's the name. Go and get the dinner, Little James. They said they'd have it ready.'

James got up in his burly way and swung towards the door. A dry wind peered in as he opened it.

'He's back in the world,' Peter sighed, 'but to us he leaves the burden of the word, so to speak. We're not well prepared to shout the glory of his rising from the grave and the truth of his message. I dreamt last night I was back on the lake working at the nets. It was fine to be – well, what you might call ignorant and peaceful again, not to have any responsibility. But I have to accept the burden as you do too. The trouble is that we don't know well how to carry it.'

The door opened and Jesus came in carrying a jug of wine and a bread basket. James followed with cold broiled fish and cups and platters on a square tray. He kicked the door shut and the wind out. They all stood clumsily. Those who sat by the wall had difficulty getting up at all. Jesus waited till they were all standing and then said: 'Sit. Thirteen of you? Of course, I understand. You're Matthias. You take the place of poor dear Judas, who was killed by his own love and innocence.' They all looked at each other uncomfortably. He had always been one for mentioning the unmentionable. 'And you, Barnabas it must be, are the unlucky thirteenth. Well, there'll be trial and tribulation for everyone, no shortage of that.' He grinned at Thomas as he sat next to Barnabas on the rocking bench, saying: 'And how are the doubts today?'

'Ye know what I thought,' Thomas growled in his rough North Galilean accent, 'and I was in the right to be thinking it. There's too much trickery about these days. There's not many as comes back from the grave. I know there was Lazarus who got himself killed in a tavern

26

brawl three days after, something of a waste of effort I always thought. And there was the girl where I was working and ye first dragged me into the fellowship, saying ye needed what ye called a sceptic. Well, we've seen enough of false prophets about, and what was to stop one going the rounds with a dab of red paint on his wrists and ankles. I was in the right to say seeing is believing.'

'I say again,' Jesus said mildly, 'blessed are they who believe and have not seen.'

'Ye'll no convince me of that. Well, not all the time.'

'Listen. And eat while you're listening.' The wooden trenchers clattered dully and the cheap winecups clanked. Matthew's knife made heavy arithmetical work of dividing the fish into fourteen pieces. 'You must all try and impart this power of innocent belief to those who hear the word. My word but now also yours. This is the last time you will see me in the flesh but do not forget I stay with you in these simple gifts of God. I will start the ceremony, you must finish it. I take this bread and break it. This is my body. Do this in remembrance of me.'

He tore at the loaf roughly. The wrist wounds seemed nearly healed. He threw the pieces to the farthest, handed them to the nearest. Peter said, chewing Jesus's body and then gulping it, 'The last time, Lord?'

'Yes, I leave you tomorrow at dawn. Don't ask me where I'm going.'

'We're well aware of where ye're going,' Thomas said, 'and we don't have to see it. Ye're going back to your father.'

'Difficult,' Jesus said, picking out the bones from the piece of fish in his hand, 'for this flesh to become spirit. But take it that that is what is going to happen. I will take none of the flat roads out of Jerusalem. I'll climb Mount Olivet and disappear at the top, and that will be the last of me. You may come and wave farewell if you wish. Then you have to wait for a particular visitation. You won't have long to wait. I'm going now to have a word with my mother. Complete the ceremony, Peter.' He stood and put his fingers to his lips. With the other hand he motioned that they remain seated. He opened the door, letting in no wind, and closed it. They could not hear his feet going down the outside wooden stair. Silence. Peter sighed very deeply, took the winejug, filled his own cup, said:

'Now his blood.' He passed it round. They all sipped.

'A matter of waiting, is it?' Thomas said. Nobody else said anything. That last brief sight of the living God, capricious, unhelpful, gave them little comfort. They needed comfort badly. The dry wind grew stronger and rattled the catch of the window shutter.

'A young man, your honour,' Caleb's mother was saying, 'and you know what young men are like – full of wild ideas. He has no father to keep him on the right path. A mother can do nothing when a young man's head is filled with mad notions. Freedom and suchlike nonsense.'

'So freedom is mad,' Quintilius said. 'Freedom is nonsense. What do you think – *you*?'

He meant the elder daughter Sara, eighteen years old, paleskinned, tall, unveiled, who looked steadily at him, without sexual appraisal, rather with a kind of quiet polar challenge which he found hard to interpret. Judaea against Rome? One generation against another? The upholder of a rigorous scheme of social conduct against its careless violater? For Quintilius had insisted that the interview take place in his dining room. He ate while they stood. Ruth, sixteen, her veil over all but her eyes, watched each mouthful of meat with what could be horror. A barefooted Syrian mixed wine with wellwater. It was against the Jewish law for the faithful to enter under the roof of the infidel. Matthias, who had brought them hither, insisted on waiting in the courtyard, though that left the women unchaperoned. They considered that the need to plead for a son and brother absolved them from a taboo which, being women, they could not anyway take seriously.

'There are two kinds of freedom, sir,' she said. 'It does not matter if the body is in chains so long as the mind is free.'

'Free to do what?'

'To think. To believe. That is a freedom that cannot be removed – not even by –' She had perhaps gone too far.

'Not even by the oppressive forces of Rome – is that what you wish to say?' He began to work on a bone.

'It's a thing we accept,' Sara said. 'Roman rule, I mean. We in our generation have known nothing different.' Then she said: 'You seem to have difficulty with our Aramaic. Would you prefer that I spoke in Latin?'

'I neither have nor have not difficulty with your Aramaic,' he said in Latin. 'It is not a language I wish to master. To render unto Caesar the things that are Caesar's. You know the saying?'

'And to God the things that are God's,' she said in Latin with a strong Judaean burr. 'It's a common saying.'

'And a saying that your brother spits out like a bad fig. Where did you learn your Latin?'

'At home. We Jewish women stay at home. But I can see the world through books.'

'She is a clever girl,' her mother said, as in apology. 'It's the way some of the young are these days. Asking questions and so on. I don't hold with it, sir.'

'Well, woman, see where asking questions has got your son. For him I can do nothing. He defies the Roman state and he must take his punishment.'

The mother began to wail.

'Wait,' Quintilius said, 'I hadn't finished. He's not alone. There are others of his kind. To me indeed he's not even a name. What would you give to see another in his place – carrying the punitive cross?'

Sara said cautiously: 'What do you mean, sir – give? You mean we can – *buy* his freedom?' They were back on Aramaic; her mother knew nothing else.

'Crudely put – *buy*. A very crude word. Shall we say that his punishment could be commuted into a fine. A heavy one, of course. There is money in your family?'

'My husband worked at the potter's trade, sir. He left nothing. There is my brother, though –'

'Uncle Matthias,' Ruth said, 'has joined the Nazarenes, mother. He is going to give his money to the Nazarene poor.'

'Aren't we the poor?' the mother wailed. 'Isn't his own sister's son more deserving than the – unwashed beggars of the town? We'll speak to him, your honour. Give him an hour and he'll come back with the money?'

'Shall we say fifty *aurei* – gold pieces?'

Sara said firmly: 'It's impossible, sir. I know it's impossible. And we have no –' She looked for the word and could not find it.

'No guarantees, you mean, I think. You have no trust in Roman mercy? Or in the word of a Roman officer?'

'Just half an hour, sir,' the mother cried. 'I know he can get the money.'

'Alternatively,' Quintilius said, 'you ladies are now, I suppose, destitute. You are hereby offered posts in the household of the deputy procurator of Judaea. Unpaid, of course.'

'You mean,' Ruth said, very wideeyed, 'to be *slaves*?'

'Come, mother, Ruth,' Sara said. 'As the deputy procurator says, Caleb has defied the Roman state. He must take his punishment.'

But Caleb's mother was on her own knees and clinging to those of the deputy procurator. A small dog, almost hairless and with eyes like small lamps, looked up from his bit of gristle with surprise. Quintilius kicked her off and calling the waiting guard:

'Get these Jewesses out of here.'

Matthias, waiting in the courtyard, now in a very plain and, it appeared, artfully torn and soiled garment, asked how things had gone. Badly. 'There was never any hope,' Sara said. 'I've heard of his ways before. He takes money but gives nothing in return.'

'Save him, Matthias,' the mother wailed. 'Fifty gold pieces.'

'No,' Sara said firmly. 'Caleb knew this would happen sooner or later. He talked of being a living torch burning for the cause. I knew there was no point in going. All we can say is that we did what we could.'

'You're a hard hard girl. All this booklearning.'

'But he's not dead yet,' Sara said harshly. 'He's not even been whipped. It's not over yet.'

Matthias, before going to his widowered home, escorted them to their single-roomed lodging in the house of Elias the mad. This Elias was a second cousin, bequeathed his house by his wholly sane brother Amos, and was mad only in the sense that he believed the world would soon be taken over by rats, *achbroschim*, and that the Romans, who spoke what he called rat language, were the harbingers of their coming. Matthias himself had a large house not far from the Temple. He was now in his thirties but had been made a widower in his twenties, when his wife Hannah had died of an infection from cutting her finger along with the evening loaf. The *achbroschim*, according to Elias, were the responsible ones. On their way in the early evening the little party saw with gloom the festooning of the housetops in the narrower streets in celebration of coming Pentecost or Shabu'oth, the feast of weeks or the day of the first fruits. Young men were climbing ladders to affix strings of dried leaves to roofs, and these were lifted across the street with pronged poles to be affixed to the roofs opposite. Whole streets were so festooned. The Greek Jew Stephen saw the three women in black and the ragged rich Matthias from the summit of his ladder, interpreted their gloom and cried: 'Don't worry. It's not finished yet.'

On his way home Matthias passed the Temple, behind which a sunset of splendid though as it were casual lavishness glowed in a sort of benediction. Was it, Matthias asked himself, still properly the house of his faith? Yes, more his Temple than that of the many who would not accept that the history of the race had reached its fulfilment. It was the solid and immovable tabernacle of the living numen whose son he had known, though but briefly and not intimately, in the flesh, and whose message he accepted with all his heart. Why then, this sunset, did the Temple seem faintly hostile? Because it was in the hands of the custodians of a past already dusty; it had nothing to say to the present. The task of the Nazarenes was to take over the Temple, slowly, slowly, through the infiltration of belief. It was to be the Temple of fulfilment, but not yet. It had, in a sense, to be loved more than ever, as a dumb but living creature gently to be taught that it was the house of the Christ as well as the immemorial Father. Yet hard hearts would set themselves long against the truth.

Here was one hard heart, though a young one, one prematurely indurated to dogged ancient priestly intolerance. Quite near Matthias's home the young theological student from Cilicia lodged in the house of his sister. He sat crosslegged outside this house in the dusty unwalled garden, working with hard fingers at tent-stitching while the light lasted. He nodded somewhat menacingly at Matthias, who nodded more amiably back. 'So,' Saul said, 'you are become the replacement of the man who hanged himself.'

'The twelfth of the inner group, yes. How did you hear of it?'

'I see it as a duty to keep my eyes and ears open to all things that would impair if they could the serene fortitude and sempiternal truth of the Jewish faith.'

'You speak pompously for so young a man. But much study will often make a young man pompous. Why do you look so bitterly at me?'

'Is my look bitter? It's meant to be pitying. You have fallen into terrible error. Error, they say, must be burnt out quickly before it takes root. Don't you fear the burning?'

'I am a good Jew who, by God's good grace, have been granted a vision of salvation. Very well, I am in error as the world sees it. There is hardly one prophet in the holy record who was not stoned and reviled because he caught a gleam of the truth. We were promised a Messiah, in time not eternity. In the reign of Augustus he was born, in the reign of Tiberius he was put to death. Because he wore the robes of human history does he defile the eternal by induing the temporal?'

'Now it's you who talk pompously. You know as well as I that these last years have seen too many of these false saviours puffed up with their mad inner visions. They are all as bad as each other. We shall have more yet. Some of them have been sane enough not to spit defiance at authority. Your man blasphemed against everything – even the Temple.'

'I have just come from seeing the beauty of the Temple in the glow of this sunset. He never blasphemed against it as the house of God. He loved it as we all love it. But just as the presence of the Lord himself can inhere in a bit of bread, and bread is no more than flour and water, so the Temple is, without God's presence, no more than bricks and stone and slime and a little gold and silver. It was made by human hands, as bread is. But the body, he said, is a greater Temple, because it was not made by human hands. If we must choose between the two Temples, even an erring man is more sacred than what Solomon built and Herod, to his own vicious glory, improved upon. Do not say: *even* the Temple, young man. There are greater things than Temples and Sanhedrins and high priests.'

'You see.' Saul seemed to marvel. 'He's been adept at leading you into dangerous error.'

'I'm a simple man, not a theologian like you. His simplicity spoke to

31

my own. But it isn't only theologians who have to be saved.'

'Well, hug your *simplicity* to yourself, or it will be the worse for you.' And he dug the strong sharp needle into the tough canvas.

'You, a mere student, have the power to threaten?'

'The law speaks through me, and through all of the true sons of the faith.' His sister then called him in to supper. He put his needle with others into a little wooden case and nodded a fierce good night at Matthias.

I am, like many, somewhat confused about the events that, we are told, transfigured the sixth day of the month Siwan. Early in the morning the disciples, along with Mary the mother of Jesus, who had been telling them some story of the early youth of the man who had disappeared in the dawn mists on the peak of Olivet, had assembled in their upper room with the intention of going to the Temple to witness the first fruits' offerings. Thomas, tetchy, tired, sat at the table while the rest stood around the mother. He dozed.

'He was climbing to the roof of our house and the ladder collapsed when he was near the top. He fell – oh, it seemed a terrible fall. He was so young and we thought he would cry. But he didn't seem to be hurt. He got up and laughed, then he shook his little fist at the ladder. Then he seemed to comfort the ladder, embracing it as if it were a kitten that had scratched him and couldn't understand why it was being scolded –'

At this moment Thomas woke with a harsh shout as of terror. They turned to him. 'Did ye no see it?' he panted. 'It was the mouth of God ready to swallow me and in the mouth was a tongue all red and the tongue split in two and all fire came out of it.' Then he knew it was a dream. 'Ach, I've a wicked taste in my mouth. Pass that waterjug, James, one or other of ye.'

Peter's story later was that Thomas spluttered his water out, for a wind rose suddenly, in the room not without. Without there was no stir of flag, leaf or garment. They saw each other's hair and beard lifted by this wind. It sang at them like a choir and, exerting huge force, drove them in a huddle to the door.

The streets were full of people of the separation: Parthians and Medes and Elamites, citizens of the other provinces of Palestine, of Cappadocia, Pontus, the territories of Asia, Phrygia, Pamphylia, Egypt, Cretans and Arabians and even men and women from Rome, all Jews come to the sacred city for the ritual of the presentation of the first sheaf of the barley harvest. Many of these people saw twelve men come tumbling laughing down wooden stairs and many more saw and heard them in the streets that led to the Temple. Thaddeus the fluteplayer had, it seems, found a ram's horn or shofar, and he was blowing this not in the normal manner of an angry summons but so as to produce a melody of four notes, like a camp call to dinner or parade. The laughter of the others was like drunkenness or inspiration, which have something in common, and, in the way of all people seeking diversion, even at a solemn time, people followed the dozen, smiling, shaking their heads, mockcheering.

At this time Caleb was being prodded down one of the narrower lanes towards his crucifixion. His wrists were roped to the crossbar he bore on his shoulders. He was naked except for a cloth round his groin which would in time be pulled off to underline the obscenity of his execution. On his back were visible the bleeding stripes of his statutory flogging. Behind him were his two nameless Zealot victim companions, and a Syrian maniple thrust spears at all three and at the murmuring crowd in the street. The Syrian under officer had chosen this street rather than the main road in the innocent belief that the little grim procession would thus attract less public notice, and he feared, being a somewhat timorous Syrian, Jewish violence. In fact he got neither; he got worse. Knots of people followed the tuneful shofar against the current of the cortège and bumped against speared small Syrians with little fear. Caleb interpreted the great noise as the alleluias of zealotry. His mother and sisters, weeping, accompanied by those goodhearted ladies of Jerusalem who tried, against Roman opposition, to give drugged wine to the crucified, attempted to join his death march, wailing and weeping with the loudness considered proper on such an occasion, and Caleb cried:

'You hear them, mother? This is the noise I wanted to hear. I regret nothing. Leave me.'

At this moment young men leaned from the roofs of the houses and set torches to the festoons of dry leaves and flowers that stretched across the street. Acrid smoke got in eyes and nostrils, as much those of the Syrian escort as of the crowd, most of which read this as a new and somewhat brutal mode of rejoicing. Young men, cushioned from yelling Syrian military by staid and bewildered visitors to the city, got at Caleb's roped wrists and freed them with a pair of knives, and the crosspiece fell and caused stumbling. A rope ladder rolled down from a roof. Caleb began to climb. The Syrian under officer yelled and prodded with an impotent spear, whose shaft had been grasped by two youths who showed fine white teeth. Burning and smoky festoons still fell. Caleb reached roof level, the ladder was drawn up with remarkable speed. By Jupiter, there was going to be trouble for somebody.

By now it could be said that a great part of Jerusalem, natives and visitors, had found its way to the open courts of the Temple, where

33

Peter, as leader of the twelve, had fixed on a pillar with a plinth that afforded room for two bare feet and volutes on the column that granted a handhold. From this he was to speak. The Syrian escort, holding on to the remaining two prisoners, were diverted from the straight road to execution by their need to find Caleb. He had got on to a roof, meaning that he could now be anywhere. The under officer frankly wept, waving his spear in gestures of desperation. By Castor and Pollux, there was going to be trouble.

Priests in the courtyard were chanting: 'We offer you, Lord God of Hosts, these first fruits of your planting and nurturing, as also this holy bread baked from the first of the new barley grain –' But they had but a small attendance. They turned at the babble of many voices. A brawny Nazarene, no longer young, was bawling:

'Men and women of Judaea, and all that are dwelling in Jerusalem, give ear to my words.'

What language was he speaking? Some say that a miracle had been performed, whereby he spoke the primordial Adamic tongue and his listeners had been granted an instant course of highly skilled lessons in it. It is safer to believe that he spoke not Aramaic, nor a bizarre amalgam of all the tongues of the dispersal, but a pure Hebrew with no Galilean accent (the Galileans always had difficulty with the gutturals). That the language of the sacred texts should now become the medium of immediate discourse may be taken as miracle enough, as also an eloquence Peter had not previously possessed and, indeed, rarely possessed thereafter. A Thomasian kind of sceptic (I refer to what Thomas had been; there was danger now of his becoming over-credulous) stood near to Peter and, hearing the careful enunciation of one who must consciously control the movement of tongue and lips, as well as the tonalities of enthusiasm, was heard to say:

'He's drunk. They're all drunk. They've been at the new wine.'

I must cast some doubt on the *new* of his accusation. The vintage of the year was still some months away. He may have said *sweet* instead, knowing, as we all know, that if you put new wine in a jar and cover the stopper with pitch and then place the jar in a fishpond, your removal of the jar after thirty days will ensure that your wine will stay sweet the year long.

Peter laughed and said: 'I heard that. I'm not drunk, nor are any of my friends here. It's only the third hour of the day and the taverns are hardly open. No, this is no drunken talk but the giving forth of the good news. You know, some of you, what was said by the prophet Joel: "I will pour forth my spirit upon all flesh. And your sons and your daughters will prophesy. And your young men shall see visions. And your old men shall dream dreams. And I will show wonders in the heavens overhead, and signs in the earth beneath, blood and fire and the vapour of smoke." ' Some there had certainly seen that. ' "The sun shall be turned into darkness, and the moon into blood before the day of the Lord comes, that great day, that notable day." Well, that great and notable day is upon us. Jesus of Nazareth, approved of God by mighty works and wonders and signs – Jesus, crucified, slain by lawless men – him has God raised up, having loosed the pangs of death.'

Dangerous talk. Priests listened grimly.

'This Jesus,' Peter repeated, 'did God raise up. Of this all we twelve assembled before you are witnesses. Being therefore exalted by the right hand of God and having received of the Father the promise of the Holy Spirit, he has poured forth these words which you hear and of which I am the vessel. Let all the House of Israel therefore know assuredly that God has made him both Lord and Christ – this Jesus whom you crucified.'

Some of the Sanhedrin were now present. Saul, who should not have been here but tending his fellow student Caleb, hovered near them, showing a proper horror.

'Save your souls,' Peter yelled, 'men and women of Israel – for the wonders and signs are upon you.'

The impressed ones in the crowd cried: 'How?'

'Repent. Be baptized every one of you in the name of Jesus Christ for the remission of your sins. And you shall receive the gift of the Holy Spirit. Save your souls – save yourselves from this crooked generation.' And, the die finally cast, he pointed towards the back of the crowd, where the priests were. Some of them stalked off. Saul, blazing and silent, stayed.

Matthew, the former tax collector, trained in practicalities like sums due on what dates, cried to the crowd that baptisms would start next day at dawn on the banks of the Kedron.

On a rooftop which granted a distant view of a huge gathering being addressed in tones that, their words being indistinguishable, had a flavour of zealotry and showed also a lack of retaliatory preparation on the Tower of Antonia, the Zealot Caleb was having his wounds washed in white wine and then soothed with a grassgreen ointment. Stephen, no Zealot, performed these tasks while six true young Zealots, Joshua son of the Sabbath, Tobias, the younger Elias, Joseph bar Joseph, Jonathan Levi and Abbas Barabbas, watched for Roman action. There was none save for the due and unusually vicious execution of the two who had not escaped. They had not been theological students. Stephen said:

'Wait for nightfall. Then go to Qumran. You'll get there by dawn. I have a friend there, Ananias. He'll take care of you.'

'One of us?'

'He's no Zealot, if that's what you mean. He's trying to become an Essene, but he's not sure about it. Whatever you'll think of the Essenes, and you probably won't think much, they're against the Romans.'

'The smoke and the ladder – all that was your idea?'

'It wouldn't have worked without that crowd. It looks, by the way, as if the Nazarenes have come out of hiding. You ought to be grateful to Jesus.'

'You're not one of us. And yet you did it. Now *you'll* be in danger. Let's go to this place together.'

'No. I help you as a friend, not otherwise. I think the Zealots are wrong, or should I say impractical. You won't prevail. The true road lies somewhere else.'

'The Sadducee way? The Pharisee way? The – who are these people I'm to go to?'

'They live the life of the spirit. Cut off from the flesh. That's as impractical a way as yours. I'm a Greek Jew, Caleb, not a Palestinian one. We think differently. My idea of God isn't yours. I can't accept a bellowing tribal Jehovah protecting his own – rather inefficiently, if I may say so.'

'Saul would call that blasphemy. I suppose it is.'

'Let Saul call it what he likes. Saul, by the way, wasn't very helpful. Other things to do, he said, than confirm fools in their folly. I notice you show no concern about your womenfolk. Something vaguely Nazarene about the Zealots. Give up your family and follow the right. Very unjewish.'

'I know. I thought about them too late. But the Romans don't know them, won't find them, unless somebody like Saul gives them away.'

'Saul's Roman citizenship doesn't go so far. Quintilius knows them. They visited Quintilius but got nowhere. But Quintilius won't find them. They've already gone to my place. Besides, I have a feeling that Pontius Pilatus isn't going to last much longer. The Romans are supposed to be an *efficient* people –'

Caleb smiled faintly at that.

In the praetorium the procurator hit out at the flies with his whisk. The flies seemed busier today, bit more. They were like Jews who did not disdain to enter a Gentile dwelling nor suck at honey unblessed by priests. When Quintilius showed in prisoner and escort, Pilate did a thing unseemly in a Roman officer: he struck the wretch twice on the face with his flywhisk. 'You're a damned Syrian but you're still in the Roman army. You're going to answer for your crime in the accepted Roman manner, so get the point of your sword sharp. There'll be songs tonight in the taverns about an eagle that lost his claws. You

36

have disgraced my procuratorship and disgraced Rome. Don't botch your suicide as you botched – Ah, get him out of my sight.' The guards led him off wailing in the Syrian manner. 'I presume,' Pilate said to his deputy, 'that you've found the man by now.'

'Totally impossible, procurator. These Jews all look alike, and the town's crammed with tourists. How could we ever find him, and what would be the point of making an arbitrary arrest and saying that was the man? Best to talk about last-minute mercy if there's to be any talk at all. Two of them are hanging up there on Golgotha, and that ought to be enough to show the authority of Rome's ah plenipotentiary. Of course, we could declare war on the city, but that would mean bringing in legions from Syria and the sudden interest of the Emperor. They got the better of you, so best, sir, just to shrug it off. It's not the end of the world.'

Pilate gave Quintilius a good long look. 'Got the better of *me*, did they?' he said. 'I left all that business in *your* hands.'

'Yes, sir, but I remain merely the one who takes orders.'

'I smell insolence.' Quintilius shrugged and said nothing. Pilate said: 'I take it you've already delivered Roman justice to whatever family that Jew has.'

'Not yet, sir. A mother and two sisters. The girls presumably are virgins. Roman law doesn't allow –'

'Well, get them deflowered, man, and then shove the sword in. Go on, what are you waiting for? No, wait – lash them till the skin comes off and then put them on the next boat to Puteoli. Tiberius may relish a little Jewish flesh for what he calls his love games.'

'Do we,' Quintilius asked, '*have* to report this – unfortunate humiliation to Syria? Or to Rome?'

They looked at each other. Pilate said:

'I don't think, Quintilius, anyone will care one way or the other. A very minor incident, such things happen. On the other hand, you may be already preparing your report for the authorities, suggesting that the procurator of Judaea is ripe for replacement –'

'I would never dream, sir, of so disloyal an act.'

'Of course not, Quintilius. But, listen, Quintilius, if I fall, you fall with me – remember that. Now – get on with the prosecution of Roman justice.' Quintilius rather ironically saluted, then marched away slowly, as from a funeral.

It was a long day, unseasonably warm, with full taverns but not many arrests. The twelve disciples stayed quietly in their upper room, some of them lying on their pallets, while they unpicked the fabric of the morning. Euphoria had passed and there was a slight sense of crapula. Peter said little, having already said enough. Bartholomew the country doctor, learned in little except medicinal herbs, was yet enough of a thinking man to raise the business of the Holy Spirit, a term used freely by the oratorical Peter but not yet defined. 'As I see it,' he said, 'this is the wind that blew and the fine Hebrew Peter spoke and everybody understood, and I would say it was also Thomas's nightmare of a tongue split and on fire.'

'Those,' Simon the former Zealot said, scratching his cheek, 'are what you might call appearances of this Holy Spirit. This Holy Spirit seems to be the power coming out of the two of them. The Father and Son get on with the business of whatever has to be done up there, and they leave this Holy Spirit down here.'

'Ye fail to see,' Thomas said, 'a very peculiar change that's come over things. There used to be one God, and now it looks as if there were three.'

'There can't be three,' John, so mild and yet with so inordinately powerful a voice, put in. 'The Father and the Son are the same, and so is this Holy Spirit.'

'The same as what?'

'The same as these two that are one. Three in one. So tomorrow, if anybody turns up for the mass baptizing, we have to say something like "I baptize you in the name of the three." That's going to upset some people.'

'There'll be a lot turning up,' Matthew said. 'Especially from those who've come from a long way off. Something free to take home with them. You're right in a way, John. Things have got a bit complicated. God has a son now, and they've sent down a sort of bird.'

'Bird?' Peter said, rousing himself from counting over his narrow stock of pure Hebrew. He was also watching his performance of the morning as though he were one of the crowd. 'Let us have no nonsense and no blasphemy. What has a bird to do with anything?'

Matthew turned in surprise. 'I saw the bird up on the ceiling when the wind started blowing. Like a pigeon only big as an eagle.'

'What wind?' Andrew asked.

'Is everybody going mad?' Peter cried.

'Well, yes, it could be put that way,' Matthew said. 'We were all a bit mad this morning, else we wouldn't have done what we did. And that's how it's going to be in future. It's another name for being touched by the Holy Spirit.'

They ate little and went to rest early, for the next day would, they thought, be a busy one. Nor was the Kedron, set in its steep ravine, at all like the Jordan. Steep banks, no true shore, and the river flowing fast and hostile. A difficult day beckoned, and after it a difficult future, what with the Holy Spirit descending and withdrawing with the capriciousness of the Jesus who had promised it or him or her, a wind or bird or the fiery tongue of Thomas's dream. It is said that

John, once the beloved disciple, woke everybody before dawn with his loud voice (to be accounted a curse to him, according to the Book of Proverbs) and said he had invented a sign, or rather a sign had come to him in a dream. This sign, made with the thumb on brow, breastbone and shoulders, combined the cross Jesus died on with the Father, the Son and the other one. It made things clearer. It also imported into the simple faith an element which the fisherman Peter, who had never heard the word *mustikos*, considered dangerously fanciful. But let them now all ride on chance, dreams, visitations from the Holy Spirit, and the actions of their enemies. Amen.

At dawn, while the new faithful or merely curious were picking their various ways over stones, roots, dry ground towards the ravine, the Zealot Caleb arrived at a hill on which simple stone dwellings had been roughly reared. He was cloaked and staffed and boneweary. In his ears faintly sang certain words of Stephen: 'I pray you'll rethink your philosophy while you're there. If God made the world, he made it for more than the Jews. The end of life isn't the proclamation of the free Jewish nation.' Caleb had said: 'The end of *my* life.' Stephen had responded: 'It nearly was.'

It had been a rough night journey under the moon, with God's night creatures rasping or barking or hooting signals, words from some unreadable book that God could read well enough, along with owls and foxes. He had sat on a stone and munched some bread and salt fish, washed down with Jerusalem water. If I forget thee, O Jerusalem, let my right hand lose her cunning. Now, with the sun starting to wash white stone, he heard a thin hymn: the faithful of the sect that had abandoned Jerusalem, Temple, Sanhedrin, all, were saluting another day presided over by the solar spirit. Caleb climbed rocks among which a few thin goats pulled at yellowing grass and saw an open gateway. Within were men in bleached garments ready to sit at an openair breakfast. Water was being called up from a well and new bread was being borne in in a basket from a bakery. There was a man who had clearly been expecting him. But how had a signal reached here? Had this all been foreseen at the time of the Pentecostal festoonings? The man was in early middle age, and he wore a white robe that was dingier than that of the gaunt Essene who summoned Caleb to break his fast. Caleb said: 'Anias?'

'Ananias. I was told you might come here.'

'When? How?'

'The young man who gave me lessons in Greek in Jerusalem said there was some scheme afoot. I came here only four days ago. I am not yet one of the brotherhood.'

Caleb sat at a thin feast of bread, water, roots, dried figs and shrunken grapes. His presence was neither questioned nor welcomed.

He had come from Jerusalem because he had rejected Jerusalem, and that was enough. Caleb could not understand the prayers said over the breaking of the bread. A kiss on the cheek was passed about the table from left to right. Caleb kissed the shaven cheek of a bloodless epicene youth without relish. After breakfast Caleb was permitted to visit Ananias's cell and wash in a ewer, wiping himself after on a bleached towel. He said:

'Everything white. No blood in it. Even the bread's white.'

'The very elixir of the faith,' Ananias said. 'Here it attains the limits of purity. Dung and make water, and you must bury the ordure in the ground, wearing white gloves. No marriage, no fornication – bodily pleasure is sinful. The body is made of dirt and red mud. Men must transcend it and live in the spirit.'

'It's not easy to forget we have bodies,' Caleb said. 'So these men never take a woman in their arms. How do they breed?'

'They don't breed. After all, the end of the world has been prophesied and soon it will come. Not much point in breeding. What is needed is purification.'

'I was taught that the world was beginning, not ending. The new world of the free Jewish nation.'

'A flippant dream, they would say. Purification is the one serious thing. Then pure soul is lifted up into heaven.'

'And you're joining them?'

'Well, I've been doing a certain amount of searching for the right way. That's why I wanted to read Greek. I see these Essenes as the final posting house on the journey. John the Baptist was one of them, you know. And then he was led to something different. I don't believe the world is going to end. I think it's wrong to be cut off from a world in which much wrong has to be put right. I'm here to ponder the new doctrine. You've met the followers of Jesus?'

'My uncle Matthias has just become the twelfth of the dead man's disciples. Absurd, isn't it? A disciple of a dead man.'

'The message is only just beginning to be born.'

'And it says you have to submit to the Romans. It won't do.'

'The point is that the Romans will burn themselves out sooner or later. We ought not to waste breath or muscle on them. The important things happen outside the *politikon*.'

'Stephen taught you that?'

'Of course, Stephen. I'm bad at names. No, I read that in a book.'

'They say,' Caleb said, 'that John the Baptist is buried in Samaria. They say that he appears to them and cries that the hour of deliverance is at hand.'

'And what do the Samaritans think deliverance means?'

'What *I* mean by deliverance. Herod the Great built solid fortifications

40

there. It may be in Samaria – not Judaea, not Galilee – that the great blow is struck. That came to me in the night, wandering, missing direction, finding it and the thought of Samaria at the same time. You know Samaria?'

'I know that the Samaritans are supposed to be a bad lot. They shovelled shit once on to the steps of our Temple. And dead men's bones. They're not real Jews – halves and halves –'

'Does that matter?'

'Oh, I don't doubt there are good Samaritans. There's even a story about one.'

Caleb's morning of rest was a time of labour for the disciples, listening to sins, degged with tears of repentance: there was enough water about. High above, on either side of the ravine, troops from Jerusalem stood. There was even an Italian centurion from Caesarea, the real thing, no Syrian nonsense. Beware of Jewish crowds was a fair Palestine watchword. All that these Jews seemed to be doing there in the river was saying a few words and then getting ducked. Some of them carried leaves and fronds of the season. There seemed to be no harm in it, but you never could tell.

Thaddeus, a clumsy baptizer, had composed a song based on the prophetic words of Joel:

Daughters with a prophet's tongue,
Visions, visions with the young,
Dreaming dreams for the old,
And dreams and visions will have told
Of Jesus Christ
Sacrificed.

He taught this but, teaching it, held up the baptizing business. It was strenuous work. The heads of the disciples swam with other people's sins, most of them to do with cheating and robbing and having sexual desires for the wrong person. Meanwhile, in a Jerusalem quiet after Pentecost, a maniple searched for Ruth, Sara and their mother. They eventually found their lodgings, where a potter's wheel and dried clay were kept still in widow's remembrance. Elias the mad greeted the troops with laughter and spoke of the coming of the whiskered *achbroshim*. They tried to knock him about, but he was spry and wiry. His lodgers, he said, had been eaten by rats. The soldiers asked people on the streets where the three women were, but none knew.

They were, in fact, now lodged in the house of Stephen and his parents. The father, a retired schoolmaster called Tyrannos, had given up the Jewish faith but was tolerant towards his son's learned devoutness. Tyrannos had decorated the house with scenes out of Homer and was eager to teach the girls Greek. Sara, who had the seeds of scholarliness in her, was quick to start tracing the alphabet and was soon reciting *autos, auton, autou, auto*. Ruth and her mother helped Maia, the crow-haired lady of the house, with the cleaning and cooking. They sobbed sometimes in fear. Stephen said:

'You'll be safe enough. We have this deep cellar. Safe, that is, if you can talk of safety these days. You'd be safer still with the Nazarenes.'

'With an uncle,' Sara said, 'who's giving his money to the poor. Not to his own family.'

'The Nazarenes have a different concept of family. They say their family's the world.'

'Are *you* becoming a Nazarene?' Sara asked.

'I'm sick of the wrangling of the sects,' Stephen said. 'I'm sick of the shrieks of the Zealots.'

'Yet you saved Caleb.'

'In spite of his zealotry.' Outside the dining room where the three young people, their elders already having eaten, lingered over dates and olives and flat thin bread, came the wailing song of an old beggar being led somewhere by a boy who said, bored: 'Alms for the love of heaven.' He was being led to the Temple because the ninth hour was coming up, time for prayer and oblation, and a few coins were regularly thrown to the blind and crippled by the worshippers – less real generosity than a token of it.

Peter and John were also going to the Temple for the ceremony of the ninth hour. The other disciples were sleepy; the baptizing of a thousand or so had been hard work. So Peter and John mounted to the Court of Israel through the Court of the Gentiles, passing the notice which said in Greek and Latin that the unbeliever would be stoned to death if he went any further. There were nine gates from the outer court to the inner, and one of these, which led to the Court of the Women, was called the Nicanor Gate or the Gate Beautiful. It was made of Corinthian bronze and was skilfully crafted. It had, of course, cost a pretty penny. As Peter and John approached this gate, they saw a cripple on a cart, a boy with him. The beggar had a strod or thumb-stick with a crossbar. He said to Peter and John:

'In the name of the Lord, give. For the sake of the love of the Lord –'

Peter saw the cruciform shadow of the beggar's stick on the square right post of the gate. He was being told something. Peter looked the beggar in the eyes and waited for the capricious Holy Spirit to rush in. 'Look at me,' he said. And then: 'We have no gold nor silver, being poor men like yourself. But what I have I now give you. Get out of that cart. In the name of Jesus Christ of Nazareth, walk.'

The beggar made a grotesque mime of walking, to show that he could not, and then, to Peter and John's surprise as much as his, got up on his useless feet. Peter held out his right hand and he took it. Then he found he could walk.

'Always knew he was a cheat,' a Sadducee said. 'The same with too many of them here. He's certainly kept it up for a long time.' The beggar allowed indignation to usurp the place of fear, wonder, gratitude, regret at the loss of his trade: ask, and you always get too much or too little, never enough. He said:

'I know you, Zadok the fat, and you know me. I'm coming up to forty-one and I've had no use of the ankles since I was born. Now, look at that bone and muscle and praise the Lord's goodness before you start sneering.'

'You'll have to dance for a living now,' the Sadducee sneered.

'Watch me.' And the beggar began to leap and cavort. A Pharisee nodded in awe and said:

'Isaiah thirty-five six. "Then shall the lame man leap as a hart".'

'Come in with us,' Peter said, embarrassed. 'Pray. Attend the sacrifice.' So the beggar leapt the way along to the candled gloom within and merely walked in a decorous fashion down to the place of sacrifice. When he and Peter and John came out again, they were followed by a large crowd towards Solomon's colonnade. Peter knew he had to say something, so he waited for what he took to be an inflation from the Holy Spirit, a bird fluttering in his lungs and fire on his tongue, and he spoke.

'People of Israel, what you see you truly see, no trickery. What has happened to this leaping beggar here has not come out of any power or goodness that I have, or that John here has. The God of Abraham and Isaac and Jacob who is the God of our fathers has glorified the Lord Jesus his servant. Don't forget that it was you who delivered him up to what you called justice in your mealymouthed ignorance. You had him stretched on a tree and jeered at while you let a murderer go free to commit more murders. The Prince of Life is what he was and is, for we saw him rise up from the grave. Faith in his name turned into the strength which made this man whole. Now you see that what was prophesied was no foolery. Repent and be baptized in the Holy Spirit. Set your feet on the new road.'

'Trickery,' muttered some of the Sadducees, 'for all his fine blasphemous talk. Ah – now we'll see.'

For the crowd and the flying rumour of a miracle had brought to the colonnade of Solomon the chief of the Temple police, the *sagan* or *segen*, the man of the mountain of the house, whatever that means – *'ish har ha-bayith*, I can render it no other way – leading a body of muscular Levites. The Sadducees and some of the chief priests, the lowlier ones keeping out of it, laid the usual charge – preaching resurrection, practising mountebank trickery, collecting a crowd and causing a disturbance – and the *sagan* or *segen*, in his fine breastplate and helmet, said: 'Under arrest, you and you and this leaping one also.

43

You're to be locked up for the night. You'll be tried at dawn.'

'We've things to do at dawn,' John roared. 'Baptism of the newly faithful.'

'Well, you won't be available, will you? Come on.'

The *'ish har ha-bayith* and his dozen or so Levites with their ornamental daggers took Peter, John and the healed cripple to a small and holy prison (necessarily holy: it was not Roman) near the eastern end of the bridge that crossed the Tyropoeon valley. There they were shown into a cold cell with a heavy door and locked in with a heavy key that ground squealingly into a rusty ward. There was a seven-barred wind eye above standing headlevel. The beggar leapt up to see if he could see out of it. 'Stop that,' Peter said wearily. John bawled through the doorbars:

'Food!'

'If you want food,' a guard said, 'you'll have to pay for it.'

'Have you any money?' John asked the no longer leaping one.

'I've not taken much today. And here's a question for you: how do I earn my living from now on?'

'We always get that question,' the tired Peter said. 'Learn a decent trade. Pottery, carpentry, something.'

'At my age? Who'd take me on as an apprentice now?'

'Have you money or have you not?' John bawled.

'Oh, all right then. But you won't get much with this bit of tinkle.'

They got stale bread and musty water. They slept uneasily on the cold stone floor. When the dawn cock indiscreetly crew (who of us is worthy, who?) they were let out and led to the council chamber, not far from the jail, the place called the *lishkath ha-gazith*, or hall beside the Xystos, this Xystos being the polished stone gathering place in the open air on the western side of the hill of the Temple. The beggar leapt most of the way to confirm that his cure was genuine, and Peter in his fatigue said: 'Please. Walk like a man.' Outside the chamber they were kept waiting for over an hour. A man was selling baked fish nearby, and the pungent reek was a torture to their empty bellies. At length they were admitted and they gaped at what they saw. Most of the Sanhedrin was assembled for them, though there were more Sadducees than Pharisees. You always stood a chance with the Pharisees.

Annas was there, appointed high priest by Quirinius, the legate of Syria some twenty-six years back, deposed nine years later but the main power still of the priesthood, which was all in his family anyway. His son-in-law, Caiaphas, made successor to the old man by Valerius Gratus, procurator before Pilate, they knew too well. There was the son of Annas, Jonathan, and a mild little man named ineptly Alexander. There were priests and laymen muttering in their beards. Caiaphas, president of the court, opening the proceedings by saying:

'It is claimed that you cured a man well known to be incurable. Is he in the court? Yes, I see he is. This leaping is unseemly. So. By what authority and in whose name have you effected this cure?'

Peter had prepared no words. Jesus had always insisted on the advisability of keeping one's head and mouth empty so that the bird of inspiration could flutter in, or wind blow in. Peter's tongue felt fire blaze at its root and he said:

'Rulers of the people, elders, it seems that John here and I are charged with the crime of doing a good deed to a poor cripple who is, by God's grace, a cripple no longer. Power and authority? These come from Jesus Christ of Nazareth, whom you crucified, as you will remember, and whom God raised from the dead. Now there is a line in one of the Psalms of David, which one I cannot recall, not being a man of book learning, and it goes like this: "The stone which the builders rejected is become the head of the corner." There is salvation only in him. There is no other name under heaven by which we can be saved. The making whole of this beggar here is a testament or testimony, I am not sure of the right word, being ignorant, of his glory. I say no more.'

There was a good deal of muttered arguing and ocular daggers aimed at Peter and John which missed their targets. Then Caiaphas ordered that the two disciples be put outside so that the muttering could be augmented into open, though secret, plain speech.

'Well, look, holy fathers and reverend gentlemen,' old Annas said, his parchment face scored as by claws and his wattles wagging, 'I can give you only the fruits of my experience in this sort of business. I have, as you know, no authority here.' He beamed hideously at them all. 'Belial and Beelzebub and the rest of the devils don't cure cripples, they make them more crippled, so you can get diabolic power out of your heads, it won't work. The whole city, I gather, is talking about this piece of thaumaturgy. Of course,' he said, appraising the limbs of the beggar, who could not remain still and so walked the length and breadth of the court without rebuke, 'we could always have his ankles broken and say that the cure never happened, but I think that would be gratuitous cruelty.' Some of the Sanhedrin nodded agreement. 'The God of our fathers sometimes effects prodigies which no man of learning is able to explain. What we have to do is to separate the act from the alleged spiritual force behind it. The thing to do is to say to these men that they have to stop propagandizing in the name of the Galilean. My son-in-law here didn't actually put him to death, he left that to the Romans, but he must find it acutely embarrassing that an amateur rabbi carpenter should now be proclaimed as the resurrected son of the Most High.' He grinned maliciously at Caiaphas. 'And the source of undeniable miracles.'

'You won't stop them,' Jonathan said. 'They either should not have been arrested at all or they should be stoned now for blasphemy. But that means stoning all of them, and the converts they're making will turn against us more than they have already. It's an awkward situation. What is needed is somebody like Rabban Gamaliel – why isn't he here by the way? – who can spin new words and theories and make out that this Jesus was a genuine minor prophet acceptable to the priests and the people.' He was shouted down.

'You must be careful,' Caiaphas warned. 'No compromise is acceptable. It's the claim of messiahship that's dangerous, along with what many will take to be proof of it. One thing at a time. Threaten them with dire punishments if they preach the Galilean again.'

'*Apeile apeilesometha,*' Annas mouthed with relish. 'Threaten with threatening. Not really a tautology. All we can threaten with is threats.'

'Let them go then? With a warning?'

'That's right. Till the next time.'

Peter and John arrived for the day's baptizing late. Peter relieved Bartholomew, who needed to seek his own relief behind a bush. The Roman bucklers to the west drank the new sun. 'Your name?' Peter said to the young man before him.

'Stephen.'

'And what sins have you committed, Stephen?'

'The ordinary human sins. Lust, though lust unenacted. Impatience and anger. Prolonged failure to see the light.'

'But now you see it?'

'I see it.'

'I baptize you, Stephen, in the name of the Father and of the Son and of the Holy Spirit.'

Now began the setting up of a Jerusalem community with no private property. Matthias turned his lonely house into a mart where furniture, plate and titledeeds to fields and messuages could be brought, evaluated, and transferred to the hands of the primal twelve as administrators. Cunning merchants willing to turn personalty and realty into liquid cash came and offered as little as they could. Matthias had not yet become a totally feckless Nazarene and inaugurated a system of auctioneering. The pens of clerks drove hard. Saul, hearing the crash of the hammer, came to see in his uncharity and anger.

'Monstrous and unclean. To throw away hardearned money on snotnosed beggars and stinking cripples.'

'And yet failing to buy the release of my nephew from the hands of the Romans. Unnatural – is that what you wish to say? Well, God took charge. God knew as well as I that the Romans are unbribable.'

'First things first, Matthias. Family. The company of the faithful. But of course you're no longer of the faithful.'

'I call myself a Godfearing Jew to whom a new grace has been added. You're an intelligent young man, Saul, as well as a learned one. You must see the signs of the times. The old way is finished.'

'I will protect the old way, as you call it, with the last breath of my body. And I will attack the new.'

'Simply because it *is* the new?'

'No, because it is blasphemous. God is a pure spirit and all above the decaying flesh of humanity.'

'We believe differently.'

'Believe then to your sorrow and destruction. The stones of justice are already grinding.' And Saul elbowed his way irritably through the press of bargainers and appraisers, hearing the voice of Matthias pursue him into the street.

'May the grace of the Lord Jesus Christ bring you yet to the true way.' Saul spat, then jostled the weaker members of the street crowd. He was in no mood for tentmaking and, besides, he had a sore thumb. He came to the grounds of the house which Joseph Barnabas had formerly owned and saw a new thing: there were awnings, and under the awnings litters, and on the litters the bodies of sick people. Stephen and Bartholomew were binding a wounded knee. Ananias was taking from bed to bed a breadbasket and a wineflask. He smiled when he saw Saul. He said:

'You've come to us at last? This is a good place for easing a stiff neck.'

'So,' Saul said. 'How long will this continue? You leave the Pharisees and join the Essenes. And now you belong to this blasphemous sect. Stephen too, I see. Folly. Have you too sold everything for the sake of the drooling cripples?'

'Everything, Saul.'

This was not strictly true. Later that day, in the former house of Matthias, Peter repeated, though with more grace, the words of Saul.

'Everything, Peter. Count the money – it's there on the table.'

'And the bill of sale?'

'That,' Ananias uncomfortably said, 'is not strictly the affair of the community. I was not bound to sell my farm. That was a voluntary act. Surely all our acts are voluntary? We live, surely, under no compulsion?'

'As we vow to live without possessions of our own and share all things in common, you, as one of us, were bound to give everything. I ask again, Ananias – everything?'

'Everything.'

'What does your name mean, Ananias?'

'My name? Why ask about my name? It's properly Hananiah, I'm told. Something about Jehovah giving graciously –'

'You mock what God does and you mock your own name. I see to your soul, Hananiah. And you, Saphira, you abet the lie?'

Saphira was Ananias's wife, her name properly Shappira, meaning the beautiful one. It is a dangerous thing to give girl babies names they may not live up to. Saphira was small of eye and thin of lip, her hair lank with an excess of God's own oil. She said, in some confusion: 'The farm was my father's. It's my father giving from the grave, but he made no promise to the Nazarenes. The Nazarenes did not exist when he died.'

'The money is nevertheless that of you and your husband to give. I ask again: do you abet the lie?'

'I am no liar,' she said. 'Were we not entitled to some small place of our own? Where are a man and his wife to live? There are things a husband and wife must do in private, they cannot sleep as in a jail with strangers who call themselves brothers snoring around them or keeping awake to watch what is forbidden.'

'So some of the money has been kept back. Yes, Ananias?'

'Nothing has been kept back. This I swear.'

'We're enjoined by our master not to swear but to say plain yes and no. Are you a liar, Ananias?'

'Whatever is meant by liar. We were granted a small messuage of the farm, no more than an outhouse. But the money from the sale is all there.'

'So,' Peter said, 'Ananias the liar finally speaks the truth. Go now, and Saphira with you. We're not like the Romans or the Sanhedrin. We exact no punishment, leaving that to God. For now the knowledge of wrongdoing should be punishment enough. Savour your crime alone, the two of you.' And he turned his back on them.

'Give me a little water,' Ananias said. 'I feel faint. My heart is not strong.' Nobody gave him anything. 'I see. The giving is all on one side. This shall be a curse to you, you will see.' And he left tottering, supported by Saphira. Matthias said to Peter:

'Forgive my presumption – I know I am the newest of the company and so understand least – but I can't see how Ananias was wrong. I had the opportunity to have my nephew freed – I mean Caleb. It was a matter of paying out money. How if I had kept back money that was really my own?'

'Was,' James the other, son of Zebedee, said. 'Was, remember that. Now you are in a happy position. Before you were in confusion, for you knew that bribes did not work and yet you had the faint hope that one might. It's always best to be without money. Turn money into what can be consumed and consumed quickly. That rids a man of confusion and greed and many another vice.'

48

'You would have lost your money,' Peter said, 'and, if things had not worked out differently through God's grace, your nephew would have lost his life. The Romans don't make bargains, James is right. Things have worked out for the best. Always look for the hand of God.'

'As now?' Matthias asked. He was looking out into the street, where Ananias had fallen into the dust. Saphira was bending over him, her hand on his bared chest, feeling for the heartbeat. She raised her head and her voice, crying for help. A laden camel went by, roaring out of its own inner dissatisfaction, and it was led by a man who, though not roaring, had troubles of his own. A dry wind bestowed more dust on Saphira and her husband. Two fat women passed with baskets loaded for the market, chattering.

'I thought we preached charity,' Matthias said. 'Or should I say that there is a gulf between preaching and practising?'

'God hates a liar,' Peter said doubtfully.

Caleb arrived at Sebaste, the capital city of Samaria. This, which had once borne the name of the country itself, had been rebuilt in the Greek style by Herod the Great and named for the Roman Emperor Augustus, who was styled in Greek Sebastos. Caleb saw in morning sun the hill Gerizim, on which the Samaritans had built their own temple to rival that of Jerusalem. It was not so fine to look at, though its eastfacing gold and silver doors were as brilliant in the sun as those of the city of true holiness. There could be no real holiness here, so the Judaeans taught. A lot of halfbreeds. Assyrian blood, blood of the Hasmoneans, a bad lot. But the people looked much like Caleb's own. They wore dirty robes, chaffered at fruit stalls, spat, scratched. An unveiled girl of rare pale beauty looked down wistfully from a high window and was then roughly dragged in to darkness by a scolding voice. Beggars cried for alms in the name of Jehovah. A man in whiteedged black with an Assyrian beard performed conjuring tricks before an idle knot of citizens the police rudely beat from the thoroughfare of burdened donkeys and camels, a closed litter in the Roman style borne on tough poles by nearnaked men who looked like Ethiopians. There were, as in Jerusalem, Syrian troops but more decurions of Italic blood. Caleb had a few coins stamped with the head of Tiberius Caesar, given to him by Ananias when he left the thin pale community of the Essenes. He found a small tavern and broke his fast. The bread here was baked hard in thin slabs on oiled iron. The wine was more pink than red. The girl who served him noted his accent. From where? Jerusalem. She was not impressed.

It was near noon when he met Samaritans of his own age and

something of his own fire. This was in the bathhouse attached to the temple on the hill Gerizim. When he stripped to sluice himself they saw the fresh scars on his back. They called an older man who, combing his wet hair with five tines of iron, came over and looked at the scars before properly engaging the eyes of their possessor. 'Who are you?' the man said. 'What are you doing here?'

'Caleb from Jerusalem. One of the Zealots. Scourged by the Romans. Escaped crucifixion.'

'We don't hold much here,' the man said, 'with the people of Judaea. The Romans did a good thing when they freed us from Judaean rule.'

'But now it's a Roman Judaea that rules you. Is that any better?'

'We don't hear much from your Pontius Pilate. It's all left to the prefect. He's a bastard called Gracchus who's got his eye on this temple here. The usual thing. Loot, loot, more loot.'

'I take it you head the freedom force.'

The man gave a single guffaw. 'That's a pompous way of putting it. No, I'm not a leader or anything like it. Call me more of a spy. I work in the prefecture as a sort of clerk. One thing I've found out is that they're reducing the garrison here. Increasing it in Judaea. What's going on there? Is it to do with you?'

'There's this new sect, the Nazarenes. I gather there's been a miracle or something like it, and there's a lot of enthusiasm. It won't last, that sort of thing never does, but the Romans get worried when the Jews get enthusiastic.'

'What are you after here? We're not your people.'

'I should have thought this was the wrong time for division. Zealots are Zealots, I should have thought, wherever they are. It's time to strike.'

'And what do you get out of striking?'

'We get rid of the Roman presence. It's been around too long. We get the House of David ruling the kingdom of Palestine.'

The Samaritan stroked one cheek then another. He said: 'We're not too sure here whether we want to be back under a Judaean king. But we certainly don't want the Romans here. You'd better have a word with John.'

'Who's John?'

'His father named him after John Hyrcanus. He dropped the Hyrcanus for obvious reasons. You know who John Hyrcanus was?'

'He took over here over a century ago, didn't he? Destroyed your temple as a blasphemous parody and so on.'

'John's father had this mad idea that there was conqueror's blood in the family. John and he havĕ come to blows. John's just John, a good Biblical name. John wants to kill Gracchus.'

'The prefect?'

'Gracchus had John whipped. Like you were whipped. Some charge to do with embezzlement, false of course. John used to carry money from the treasury to pay the troops. We know who the real embezzler was.'

'Well, why doesn't he stick the knife in?'

'Not easy. Are you used to fighting?'

'I led a raid against a desert camp once. The time's come to strike nearer the centre now, I think. The point is this, as I see it. It's not a question of winning pitched battles against the Romans. It's a matter of convincing the Romans that there's nothing for them in Palestine. It happened before. They'll be ready to take their governors out and let the Herod blood back in again. It's bad blood but it's native blood. And it's the beginning of something better.'

This John whom Caleb met was nearly all black beard and total baldness, though young enough. He sat crosslegged mending sandals on the city's outskirts. His hovel was dusty. He said:

'We've had strangers like you here before. Sadducees in the pay of the Romans.'

'Of course,' Caleb said. 'And I laid on the whip myself. I enjoy that sort of thing.' He showed. John whistled. Caleb said: 'How many men do you have?'

'I can gather two hundred. Good raiding material. Trained in knifing, garrotting. Outposts mostly, of course. We've been quiet lately. We're a bit slack. A raid on the prefecture, the city barracks is next door. Not ready for it. I don't know, though. We can't wait for ever. Gracchus has to be crucified.'

'You mean that?'

'A knife in his throat – too easy. Crucified and then burnt.'

'You're a hard man, John,' Caleb grinned.

The raid was daring and God, or something, was on their side. They invaded the city barracks before daybreak, strangled the guard, knifed a sleeping centurion and a couple of decurions who were already awake. They attacked naked men fearful in barrack dormitories, then they set the wooden building afire. They had difficulty in firing the stone prefecture, but they smashed all within, burned documents, killed the watchmen and set off for the suburban villa of the prefect. Gracchus appeared in his nightgown. A Samaritan succuba tried to escape, still warm from his bed, but she was held and her hair set alight. The guards had their throats slit. Then Gracchus was hauled sobbing down the road to the city centre. The entire town was awake, and men with buckets of water were trying to stop the spread of the barracks fire to innocent homes and shops. Smoke and flame made a good background for the enactment which John personally supervised. The Samaritans had found enough wooden crosses –

the new kind with crosspiece already nailed to upright, upright
sharpened to a stake's sharpness at the foot end – in the barracks yard.
Gracchus was lovingly nailed naked to one of these, and he sobbed
and howled in a dialect which none present knew – a form of Oscan or
Umbrian, perhaps, from his native village. He cried at one point for
his mamma, and everybody registered the word without compassion.
The hole was speedily and sweatingly dug for the crosspoint, and the
burdened cross was set in, swaying, unfirm, but that did not matter.
Before the casting of burning pitch on the still living body, John cut off
the genitalia in a single swish with a cobbler's knife. Caleb to his shame
vomited.

Tiberius's scream was less desperate but it inspired fear. The messenger who had brought dispatches from Syria through Rome stood
sweating in the manner of all who bring bad news. Tiberius's pet
snake, wreathed round his shoulders, responded to her master's mood
by hissing. Tiberius dinged with his fist on the wooden table of the
arbour and sent winecups flying. Curtius Atticus stood grimly by.
Tiberius got words out at last.

'How much more shall we tolerate? Have I not done more for these
Jews than than than –'

The repetition of *quam* became manic. Curtius said:

'Yes, Caesar. You gave them back their own property. Some of it.'

Tiberius hissed like his snake. 'Don't try your stoic sarcasm on me,
Curtius. Your white hairs grant you no immunity –'

'Have me killed, Caesar, if it will ease your frustration. Frustration
you've brought on yourself. This revolt in Palestine is only one symp-
tom of a total sickness. Armies in revolt on the Rhine. Thugs in the
Senate. I say again though I am sick of saying it –'

'*I will not go back to Rome*. Let's see what the fool has done.' He
read the dispatch once again. 'The Third Legion moved in from Syria.
He wants the Miliara division recalled from Egypt. Roman rule.
Roman order. Roman blood spilt in Samaria – wherever Samaria is.'

'It's a part of your Empire, Tiberius. Read on and you'll see what his
real foolishness was. A raid on a native temple. Wagons loaded with
sacred vessels. The temple treasury ransacked. He officially entered
Samaria to restore order, not provoke more disorder.'

A couple of naked boys, playing and giggling, got unawares into the
path of the tigerpacing Tiberius. He tore at them with his bare hands.
A servant shooed and beat off the children but was himself beaten.
Another servant proffered a refilled winecup (a beautiful one made in
Herculaneum, the handles naked bronze bodies and the cup itself like
a pregnant belly) and had it knocked out of his hand. 'Fetch more, you

clumsy fool,' he cried. He cried to Curtius: 'Pilate has to go. Send an immediate dispatch recalling him –'

'He comes under the Syrian governor. We should leave that sort of thing to Flaccus.'

'Get Marcellus sent out in his place. Another fool, corrupt and incompetent. Who *can* we send?'

'The Empire,' Curtius said, 'is forgetting how to breed administrators. Perhaps you'd be wiser to put the whole province under one of the native princes.'

'Another fool, if you mean this Herod Agrippa. A whole family of corrupt and cruel idiots –'

'Well, they've been brought up on the Roman example, Caesar.'

'My heart,' Tiberius whispered dramatically. His lips had not turned noticeably blue. 'The palpitations are coming back. Are they trying to kill me, the fools and ingrates? Take me to my bedroom. Fetch me a litter. And you're the biggest fool of them all. I can hardly crawl, and you want me to go back to Rome.'

On the other side of the island Gaius Caligula and Prince Herod Agrippa played ball. It was a simple game of throwing and mostly missing. Lithe naked female slaves retrieved the taut silk globe stuffed with duckdown. A wasp alighted on Gaius's bare arm. He cried extravagantly, much in the manner of his imperial great-uncle: 'It's bitten me, it's stung me, I shall die. Got you.' He held up the insect to the setting sun and carefully tore off its wings. Herod Agrippa wearily fell on to a pile of cushions. A slave's breasts swung over him as she wiped his sweating forehead. Gaius limped over to join him. He took a breast in his left hand and examined it curiously, as for blemishes. Then he withdrew his hand and let it bounce to rest. Gaius was not handsome. His neck was thin and his legs spindly. His brow was broad but his scalp very nearly bald. He made up for his lack of headhair with a thick pelt over his chest and big belly. His complexion was of the colour of rancid lard. As he reclined he kicked off his little boots. Herod Agrippa said:

'You need a larger size.' And Gaius said:

'The Emperor Littleboots.' He giggled. 'The army loves me, Herod. They'll never be disloyal to Littleboots.'

'Emperor sooner than. Judging from.'

'It's his heart, Herod. An old man's heart. He's lived too long. Still, we'll leave it all to nature, I think. It's your people that brought this on, you know. The talons of the imperial eagle shall dig into the heart of the Jewish nation. Hard words, Herod. And then he had to be put to bed.'

'Only a Jew understands a Jew,' Herod said. 'You people made a big mistake. Roman procurators hardly willing to mouth a syllable of

Aramaic. Telling the Jews about Jupiter and Venus and Mercury and the divine Emperor. No wonder the Jews laugh when they don't cry.'

Gaius gave him a steady look and spoke very softly. 'So,' he said, 'you don't like the idea of a divine emperor?'

Herod Agrippa grinned but felt, as it were, the single kick of a little boot in his entrails. 'For you, my dear, of course I become a true Roman with all the right pagan attitudes. I shall worship at your altar. I shall make your divine divinity cough with excess of incense. But you can't blame the Jews for finding all these *little* gods rather childish and tiresome. After all, we thought of it first. One God, the creator and sustainer of the universe. The Romans and the Greeks as well are rather slow in grasping that concept, aren't they?'

'Oh, I'm not slow,' Gaius said, 'your royal Jewish lowness. I think the idea of one God a very attractive one. To be totally totally totally in control.'

'Meaning?' The little boot kicked harder.

'You see, once the universe has been created, what is there left to do?'

'The universe must be maintained. God watches over it.'

'Very tiresome and boring for God, I would say. The act of creation was his great thrill, and he can find a what's the word commensurate one only in destroying it. Wouldn't you say that's reasonable? Pull it to pieces and then start again. Got you, you silly thing.' He meant another wasp, Capri was full of them this season, which had made itself drunk on a patch of spilt wine on the marble table. He squinted at it, dewinging it with care. 'Oh, we'll have great games when I'm installed in Rome and you're in your palace in Jerusalem. Visiting each other, you know, playing games. But I shall have to win always, Herod Agrippa, because I'll be Emperor, you see, and you'll just be a little king. But a little king is bigger than even a big prince, isn't that so? I hope you'll be duly grateful, your prospective Jewish majesty.'

'Lord of the universe, I abase myself.' But Herod Agrippa felt a certain nausea, playing these games with an Emperor designate he was fairly sure was moving swiftly from silliness to dementia. After all, he was in his forties and growing paunchy and grey. It was unseemly to be playing games with a boy of twenty-five or so, even though this boy was soon to become lord of the, if not the universe what the Romans thought of as the universe. He should be back there with his people. It was all his mother's fault, sending him to Rome as a mere infant, there to be brought up as a Roman. His father Aristobulus, whom he had never known, brutally and perhaps unjustly executed. Look to the safety of the son. For what end? He would not be king, of that he was sure; there would always be a Roman governor in Judaea. He felt weary, overfed, coated with honey that had a curiously fecal smell. Gaius said:

'You told me once there's a secret Jewish name for the Lord of the

54

universe. The ineffable name. What is it, Herod? Do tell me.'

'I can't.'

'Tell me, tell me, tell me.'

'I can't. Only the priests know that name.'

'Well, you must beat the priests till they tell you, mustn't you? And if they won't tell you, you must line them all up, then off with their heads, eh? Oh, we shall have great times together.'

He then began languidly to pummel Herod Agrippa with his feeble fists.

The whole twelve of them were now lined up facing the Sanhedrin. Annas grinned terribly at them and said: 'Let's have those names again. You two I know already, here before, weren't you, never listened to the solemn words of sacerdotal admonition, most disobedient, very unwise. Point them out, you, one by one.' He meant Saul, temporarily appointed, in the absence of Ezekiel, who was sick with belly cramps, a sort of clerk to the court. 'Two Jameses, I see. Who's that old frowning one? Don't frown at me, sir, we do the frowning here. Matthias I know well, you were a secular pillar of the faith, Matthias, sorry to see you arraigned on this charge, the charge being the same as before. A very ordinary-looking crew, I would say. Let's get on with it.'

'One moment,' Rabban Gamaliel said. All prepared to listen with grudging respect to the great Pharisee, chief of the school of Hillel, rabban, no mere rabbi. 'There has been too much talk about the allegedly disrupting influence of the Nazarenes. I think it ought to be made clear that, though they are undoubtedly a cause of the impaired tranquillity of the leaders of the Jewish people, they have been in no wise an inflammatory element in our public life. There is too much talk, I say, about their supposed connection with John the Baptist and zealotry. They have not been shouting the need for the breakdown of the established order and the need for insurrection. What happened in Samaria and could happen here, I mean insurrection and the brutal frustration of insurrection, has been wholly political. The followers of the man Jesus seek the cultivation of charity to all, what we may term a quite unpolitical quietism.'

'Nobody has made the connection,' Caiaphas said.

'Are you sure? Am I not right in saying that the Sanhedrin has become very eager to convince the Roman power that it is the willing agent of the *pax Romana*, and that it abhors both zealotry and the Nazarene cult as cognate manifestations of unrest and unreason?'

'The Romans,' Caiaphas said, 'are unable to see much difference between the enthusiasm of religious heretics and the ah *furor* of political activists. However, let us stick to the point at issue, which is that these twelve here arraigned have been preaching heresy and performing blasphemous acts.'

'Healing the sick, for instance?' Gamaliel said.

'Whether they heal the sick or not,' Caiaphas said, 'is hardly to the point. They foment superstition. There are some who seek to have their ailments cured by standing in the shadow of this man Peter, a common fisherman. As for their teaching, they have already been warned not to preach in the name of the proven criminal Jesus. Can you,' he said to Peter, 'deny that you have gone contrary to our ordinance? You have filled the synagogues with your blasphemies.'

'They want to bring that man's blood upon us,' muttered a Sadducee named Jonah.

'Enough of that,' Caiaphas rasped. 'You,' to Peter, 'what do you say?'

'This, sir,' Peter said. 'We must obey God rather than men. The God of our fathers raised up Jesus. As for you, you killed him. You nailed him to a tree.'

'We did not,' Jonah cried. Others cried too, others murmured, some went aaargh as though blood were mounting into their throats.

'God,' Peter said, 'exalted him at his right hand to be a prince and a saviour – to give repentance to Israel, and remission of sins. And we are witnesses of these things, and so is the Holy Spirit, whom God has given to those who obey him.'

'With such blasphemy,' Caiaphas cried, 'you put yourselves in peril of the final penalty –'

'The final penalty, as you call it,' Peter said, 'is in the hands of the Romans. As you know well. The Romans find no fault in us.'

'In that you challenge the authority of this sacred assembly, which is answerable to the occupying power –'

'That,' Peter said, 'is not good thinking. All you can do is to set men with stones on us. Kill us if you want to. As you killed *him*. You can't kill the divine word.'

'Look,' Jonathan said. 'You've been telling everybody that an angel opened the door of the prison and let you all out. And you said that anyone who's lawfully put in jail may expect the same, God help us, angelic intervention. That strikes at the very roots of order and law and legal punishment.'

'Nobody said that,' Thomas growled. 'Ye're too quick, the lot of ye to put words in folks' mouths. Somebody opened that door in the dead of the night and nobody knows who. It might have been one of yon prison guards that had come to the right way of believing. It might have been some decent quiet man that got the message of the Lord.'

'A messenger of the Lord, you say? That's blasphemy.'

'I did not say messenger of the Lord.'

'*Mal'akh*, you said. We all know what that means.'

'In my youthful days,' Annas said, 'it meant a messenger. The same as *angelos*.'

'Used of the spiritual attendants of the Most High.'

'Not necessarily.'

'Look,' Thomas cried, 'if the Lord sent a messenger to get us out of yon jail the Lord and his messenger both need their heads looking at, for it was clear we'd be back to the preaching and curing of the sick and get ourselves picked up by yon captain of the Temple guard or whatever he's called and where would be the reason in it?'

'You can't help blaspheming, can you?' Jonathan said. 'Blasphemy is stitched into your very skin.'

'A good phrase,' Thaddeus said. 'Sacrilegious sin. Stitched in your very skin.'

'Stop this,' Peter cried, as though he were chief of the Sanhedrin, 'and keep to the point. Somebody opened the door and we got out. But here we are, calm,' roaring, 'in our innocence. Let's get the business over with. We have work to do.'

'Ah no.' Caiaphas shook his head. Rabban Gamaliel said:

'Listen to me.' They listened. 'It has been said, and it will be said again, that every assembly formed in the name of God will stand established, and every assembly not so formed must needs perish. Now we have had in recent years two notable instances of selfstyled prophets. Theudas rose up some thirty years ago and won four hundred followers, but where is he now? He did not have God on his side and so he perished. Then there was Judas of Galilee, whom some of you may remember well enough. That was at the time of the Roman census to assess the amount of our tribute, and this Judas said that God alone was king of Israel and it was both blasphemy and high treason to pay tribute to Caesar. Rome crushed him, and now he is no more than a name. We have had many failed insurgents and many false prophets. Now take these Nazarenes. My advice is that you leave them alone. For if their counsel or their work is merely that of men, it will of its own nature be overthrown. But if their counsel or their work is of God – if – you will not be able to overthrow it. And those who attempt to overthrow it may find themselves in a very unhappy position. Even all unknowing, they will be fighting against the Lord our God.'

There were murmurs at that, but most of the Pharisees nodded at the good sense. John, little James, Thaddeus and Bartholomew cautiously beamed, but Peter and Thomas frowned, considering: good sense but had to be a catch in it somewhere. Caiaphas deliberated with his father-in-law. At length he said: 'Thus speaks the spirit of moderation that is a legacy of the great Hillel. Sometimes we may be moderate, sometimes not. Now is such a time. Our judgment is that you cease your preaching and practice alike –'

'So,' Thomas said, 'those that lie sick in our spittle have to take up their beds and walk? No more doing good works? Ye're flying in the Lord's face.'

'Oh yes,' Caiaphas said, 'one other thing. For insolence and stubbornness and truculence you will receive the punishment laid down in the book of Deuteronomy. A flogging. Forty strokes less one.'

'Ye mean,' Thomas said, 'thirty-nine? Why not say what ye mean?' The other disciples made noises of rejoicing not well understood by the holy assembly. Jonathan said:

'We'll hear less of your alleluias when they bring out the whips, my friends.'

'You've played into the Lord's hands, bless you,' Peter called. 'Now we share in what you did to *him*.' And, without waiting for a word of dismissal, he led his eleven towards the enclosed punishment yard near the *lishkath ha-gazith*.

'Weakness,' Saul said to his master. 'You see the weakness. And you, rabban, abet the weakness.'

'I hear the harshness of authority in your voice, Saul. You seem to be outgrowing your studentship.'

'Oh, I respect and honour you as ever, rabban. But I must be permitted to make my own judgments.'

'Read more. Judge less.'

'The whole of Israel,' Saul said, 'is imperilled by false doctrine. And they're to be given a lick of the whip and told to go.'

'Look, Saul, I find little fault in these men. I was not uttering mere rhetoric.'

'They subvert truth. They preach a known Messiah, rejected by the high priests who are the voice of Israel.'

'Read your scriptures, Saul. We were promised a Messiah. It's wrong to accept without further evidence, true, but it would be foolish wholeheartedly to reject. They do no evil. They do nothing but good. You've seen it.'

'Sheer cunning. They buy followers with good works. They cram the poor first with bread and then with false doctrine. You must speak against them.'

'Must, Saul? *Must?*'

'I'm going to see the flogging. I want to hear them howl.'

'A moment, Saul.' Gamaliel pulled at his party beard, troubled. 'I'm interested in you. Not in your devotion to the faith but in the strength of vindictive feeling you bring to those whom you consider are its opponents. The feeling is excessive, obsessed. You snarl. You frown as if you had a perpetual headache. Are you well?'

'Well enough. The *epilepsia* has left me alone these eighteen months and more. God keeps me well.'

'You have a powerful persecutory instinct in you. Remember that the desire to persecute is negative. It promotes fear. It promotes it even in myself. You make me wish to search my conscience for smuts of heresy or unpurposed blasphemies. This, dear Saul, has little to do with religion.'

'But,' Saul said, 'the undoing of centuries of endeavour. To come out of the desert at last and set up the Temple. The Temple is our home and our stability. And this man sneered at it. The human body is the true Temple. Destroy it and it can be rebuilt in three days. You ought to shudder as I shudder.'

'These days,' Gamaliel said, 'I shudder only with the cold. Well, the Temple may be our home and our stability and it may house the Holy of Holies, but it's still a work of human hands. The body is God's work and very wonderfully made. Old as I am, I glory in my flesh and anticipate, as you do, resurrection in it. That belief makes us Pharisees what we are. Now I see you really shudder. Most unpharisaic. Do you dislike the human body?'

'A tent,' Saul said, 'for housing the spirit.'

Gamaliel forbore to say something about the tentpole: Saul deserved to be shocked, but not perhaps with an unprepared obscenity. Instead he said: 'What is your view of a text we have never considered in class, I mean the Song that is Solomon's?'

'A well-made epithalamion. Somewhat vulgar. He strips his beloved and shows her flesh to the world. Like a slave market. The flesh is best kept hidden.'

'Except, of course, for flogging.'

Saul had no capacity for blushing. But he did not go to the punishment yard, where the disciples were being lashed in threes. James the Little stood with folded arms awaiting his turn while Peter and Thomas and Bartholomew had their wrists tied in a posture of embracing as with love the stone post of punition. A little wiry man named Esra was, out of supposed deference to the criminal's age, whipping halfnaked Thomas but feebly. 'Go on, man,' James bellowed. 'Lay it on. Do you want me to do it for you?' Thomas said:

'Ye're Esra, right? The brother of Jephtha. Jephtha's doing well with us. Join him, ow, that hurt. This seems a poor way of earning a living.' Thaddeus improvised a whipping song like a sea shanty, and all who could sing sang it with glee and false notes:

Beat us and bash us
Lick us and lash us
Forty less one

Then when you've done
Give us one more
Making two score.

Whipped, Matthew said: 'We'll have to sleep on our bellies tonight,
lads.' All laughed at this typical piece of Galilean fortitude, humour,
whatever it was. But they had to sleep on their bellies, and they did not
sleep much, for more than one night.

The Emperor Tiberius had slept this night on his back, and he woke
before dawn with his mouth open and his throat dry with snoring. He
wondered at the wetness of his hand, agleam in the tiny nightlight.
Then he knew that he had been scratching at the running sores on his
face. He had been dreaming of his dead son Drusus, whom he had seen
for the hundredth time lying in dried blood and a feast for the Roman
flies in an alley near the Tiber. And yet he was not sure now whether
he had died from dagger wounds inflicted in a kind of animal candour.
A story had at last emerged about a eunuch named Lygdus, dead now
of course, garotted and his penis sliced off first, who had been admin-
istering small potions of some Egyptian poison to the Emperor's son he
served, year after year, on the orders of Sejanus. Who was alive to tell
the truth about anything? Running sores. The marble body of Rome
pitted and scored. Truth was dead along with honour and honesty,
and history was a battle of lies. He, Tiberius, had begun well enough,
though aware always that his stepfather the divine Augustus had
chosen him as the dim foil of his own brightness. A bad fanfare to the
reign, though, Augustus's grandson Agrippa Postumus murdered.
That had not been on the orders of him, Tiberius, but he would have
done better to institute a larger inquiry, have the assassin centurion
questioned under torture rather than given the immediate axe. That
was Livia, of course, the imperial mother, hated the boy, dull and
slow though he was, as a possible focus of disaffection. He, Tiberius,
should have spoken out, not preserved a grim silence which seemed to
many like the dumbness of guilt.

There were a large number of things he should have done and had
not done. Looked after the army in Pannonia, paid those justly growling veterans at least as much as the Praetorian Guard. Inhibited his
jealousy of Germanicus. Not appointed Gnaeus Calpurnius Piso as
governor of Syria. Germanicus had been right to censure Piso for
mismanaging the province. Piso had been wrong to think that he,
Tiberius, would be delighted to learn that Piso had had the dagger put
in, or poison dripped in slow droplets into the clawfoot cup from the
Rhine that had been Germanicus's childish pride (the Germans good
craftsmen, intelligent, worthy the conquering). No, when a man rose

deservedly high and was dangerously loved of the multitude his destruction had to be encompassed by subtler means: the amassed false documents of bribery and conspiracy, gross evidence of sexual irregularities. Germanicus had been obscenely pure and incorruptible, as well as sickeningly competent. Such men were dangerous.

And yet what manner of men were required in a state which had been swift to deify Augustus and not slow in muttering 'Tiberius to the Tiber'? Men like Sejanus (dead), Macro (still alive), Piso (drainer of the wealth of Syria)? The provinces were atrociously governed. He, Tiberius, had joined with the divine Augustus in considering a dirt heap like Palestine hardly worth the exportation of administrative competence, and yet one could not close one's eyes to the massive inefficiency of this Pontius Pilatus, a man Tiberius did not know, a protégé of the butchered, rightly, Sejanus. Not enough to have this Pilatus tonguelashed in Syria and let him sneak off into opulent retirement in Corinth or Ephesus. Bring him back to Rome, lay bare before the Senate and the judges evidence of peculation, disloyalty, the cynical fleaing and clipping of the aquiline *potestas*. That deputy of his, Quintus or Sextilian or some such name, *not* appointed by Sejanus, had sent sly letters forwarded to Capri, unread by him, Tiberius, but mentioned occasionally by the stoic Curtius, wearisome voice of imperial conscience, as further evidence of provincial mismanagement. Well, he, Tiberius had done his share of judicial investigation and had been adjudged impartial and unvindictive. He could still flare briefly in the imperial firmament as a just princeps before retiring into the, what was the phrase, *una nox dormienda*.

Well, that was all there was. There were gods and avatars in the provinces which promised eternities of bliss for the just as well as the victims of injustice, but Rome sternly commanded a brief daylight of *virtus* and then the brave march into endless blackness. The just and unjust alike slept together in the *nox* that was wide as the universe but narrow as the grave. There was, it had to be admitted, a certain injustice in this shovelling of the unjust and the just under a common mound: not literally, of course, since the unjust usually had the final injustice of funerary magnificence. There perhaps ought to be compensation after death for living misery: he, Tiberius, had had misery enough, the gods knew, and he was to be bundled with filthy slaves who had never known the agonies of responsibility into the *una nox*. The gods, of course, were a quite farcical invention, though necessary for the as it were marmoreal exaltation of the civic virtues. You sacrificed to Jupiter after or before the bath or the games or the fruitless wrangle with debauched and asinine senators. Chance was the only goddess. He saw Chance looking down on his lonely bed, shaking dice but not yet throwing them. She had the lineaments of his detestable and detested imperial mother. He said aloud:

'Mother, you unkillable bitch, I am going to Rome.'

Lonely bed, yes, with no healthily snoring catamite sprawled across it. Banished, banished, all. He grasped the imperial penis, flaccid as a depleted kidskin moneypurse, and it did not awake to the prospect of its stimulation. His mother looked at it very sourly. Unkillable but officially dead. Dead in her bed at eighty; he had refused to go to the bitch's funeral. She had caught him at the age of twelve in the act of mastupration. Unseemly, unroman, Greekish, Jewish. Well, in a sense he had done nothing but mastuprate since taking the purple. The amatory images of boyhood, becoming ever more extravagant, had been transubstantiated into flesh and blood, but the wraiths of the heated brain above the frotting right hand had, in retrospect, more reality. Inadequate, eh? You are inadequate, Biberius Caldius Mero.

'I am going to Rome, you dead bitch, and I am going to spit on your grave,' he said to the dawn inching up over the mainland. He snuffed out the nightlight, and the imperial penis settled back to its torpor. On the table was a bell. He raised it and the little clapper gave its regular morning tongue. It was answered by a bigger bell and then a bigger bell still, somewhere off. A couple of naked slaves, Felix and Tristis, came running with his morning potion, a chilled posset of wine and goatmilk. Then he got up.

On the terrace of the Villa Jovis he saw the guard being changed. The junior centurion on his dawn inspection checked the dress of the incoming maniple. That sandal badly buckled. You need a haircut, Balbus. Tiberius watched. The junior centurion saw and stiffened and handed him a morning *ave*. 'Here,' Tiberius called. The junior centurion ran towards the terrace on light feet. Handsome enough, brawny, well made. 'I knew your name,' Tiberius said, 'but I have forgotten it. An old man's memory, as they say.'

'Marcus Julius Tranquillus,' the young man said, 'Caesar.'

'Julius? Julius? *Julius?* This is some joke. It is too early in the day for jokes.'

'No joke, Caesar. I belong to the plebeian branch.'

'There is no plebeian branch of the Julian line.'

'That may be so, Caesar, though my father and grandfather believed otherwise. Julius is certainly my middle name.'

'Well then, Marcus Julius, you have much to do today. I leave to you the details of the embarkation.'

'Embarkation, Caesar?'

'Yes, we are going to Rome. In a day or so. I must, of course, consult the sacred entrails. But the sacred entrails are a mere formality. And I suppose you ought to find Apemantus for me.'

'Apemantus, Caesar?'

'Yes yes, my astrologer. Apprise your men of the need for the utmost efficiency in the carrying out of their duties. We have enemies. They must be on the alert. I am going to Rome. Caesar is going to Rome. There is much to do. Messages must be sent. Every possible precaution. These are dangerous times we are living in, Marcus Julius.'

'Indeed, Caesar.'

'And tell me, young man, you may speak in all confidence, a dawn converse between man and man, what is your view of the future of the Empire?'

'A very large question, Caesar. I wish continued life to Caesar and rejoice that he is to show himself in Rome. Rome, after all, is the Emperor.'

'Come now, boy, you know I cannot last much longer. Your duties here have made you acquainted with my grandnephew?'

'I have seen him occasionally. But only from a distance.'

'And you have no opinion of him? I mean – as the imperial successor.'

'Caesar has chosen him. What else can I say?'

Tiberius felt anger spurt like bile. 'And if I said to you that I have been nursing a viper?'

'Caesar's devotion to his pet serpent is well known.'

'I've bred a race of sycophants and dissimulators and evaders of the truth. I can blame only myself. You can say what you wish to me, man. I won't order your crucifixion.'

'The prince Gaius,' the junior centurion said, 'is the son of the lamented Germanicus. We naturally expect the best from him.'

Tiberius wished now to void his morning posset. 'Oh, get out of my sight. Fetch Apemantus. You Romans will get what you deserve. You always have.'

His snake Columba was sleepily coiled on his left arm as he sat listening to the astrologer's interpretation of the stellar configurations. They would never be more auspicious.

'They will never be more auspicious,' Curtius said.

'I catch your sardonic tone, Curtius. I listen to soothsayers but not to stoic reason. But you ought to be pleased – the result is the same.'

'Praise be to God or the gods,' Curtius said. 'When do we start?'

'The winds are set fair,' the astrologer said. He was a sly man in middle age, Graeco-Roman, his eyes unwavering when trained upon his charts but shifty in human contacts. He had contrived a distinctive dress for himself to show the world that he was an astrologer – blue robe with cutout golden stylized stars sewn on and, also to hide his baldness, a turban in the eastern style. He wore seven rings, one for each of the major heavenly bodies. Onyx, amethyst, moonstone, ruby, opal, sapphire, plain gold. 'And the auguries for Caesar's health are truly excellent.'

When Tiberius took his midmorning swim in the piscina one of his minnows took a vicious bite at his shrunken testicles. Tiberius naturally had him whipped, though not to the point of extinction. Then, as the whip was handy, he had the astrologer whipped. He trusted nobody.

Bartholomew came out of the darkened bedroom to tell the two girls that their mother was fast wasting, unresponsive to herbal decoctions, unable, indeed, to keep even water on her stomach: they had better prepare for the worst. But, of course, if they required another opinion –

'We trust you,' Sara said, sighing. She put down her piece of stitching and added: 'No Nazarene miracles, then.'

'One never knows. They can never be predicted. And sometimes it's hard to distinguish between a miracle and an act of faith in the confidence of the healer. Nobody will ever properly understand the human temple.'

'The – ?'

'Human temple. A metaphor. I'll come again tomorrow. But I think you must –'

'We know,' Ruth said. She looked at a painted cloth hanging of Odysseus straining his bound muscles to get at the sirens. A naked man anxious to add his bones to a mound of others. Greek. There was loud Greek being spoken in the neighbour room. 'If only,' she said, 'mother could see Caleb once more.'

'It's enough,' Sara said, 'for her to know that Caleb is still alive. She clutches that little note like life itself.'

'She's not overanxious to live,' Bartholomew said. 'And that has to mean no miracle. I'll leave you now.' And he went, a little man with a neat beard, dressed in rusty black.

'You should have asked him,' Ruth said, 'about that poor woman.'

'Saphira?' Sara said. 'That would have been embarrassing. Her husband dead and she left all alone to die and be eaten by the rats. These Nazarenes are just like everybody else. Preaching love and charity and letting one of their own be eaten by rats.' She added: 'Most of them.'

'Will we ever be back in our own little room with Elias going on about the rats taking over the whole world?' Ruth said. 'I don't like these Nazarenes.' She added: 'Except Stephen and his family.'

'One religion's as bad as another,' Sara said. 'Religion is a lot of nonsense. What good has it ever done? Beatings and crucifixions and sanctimonious balderdash. Men make religions so they can threaten other men. And women too. Hypocritical rubbish.'

Ruth looked at her sister with fear and awe. 'That's terrible, Sara. God could strike you down. He hears everything. He could turn you into a pillar of salt.'

'Let him. Anyway, he's too busy at the moment. It must be hard work splitting yourself up, even if you *are* God. One bit for the Jews, another bit for the Nazarenes. And then there are all the other religions in Egypt and Syria and the other places.'

'You can't say that about the Jews and the Nazarenes. The Nazarenes say they're good Jews,' Ruth said. 'They don't say anything about a different God.'

'Oh, it's not really worth discussing. One God has a son and the other one hasn't. It's as simple as that.'

Loud Greek was still coming through from the next room: many voices, something important from the sound of it. 'Something important from the sound of it,' Ruth said. 'What are they saying?'

'I don't know enough Greek to tell you,' Sara said. 'Something about religion.'

'They're Greek and yet they say they're Jews.'

'So they are. Greek Jews.'

'How can that be?'

'Oh, it's a long story, Ruth. Israel has been all split up. The diaspora, they call it.'

'Where do you learn all these big words?'

'Some Jews went to Rome, some to the Greek islands. And then a lot of them decided to come to Jerusalem. Coming back home, they call it.'

'Listen to them.'

In the next room Tyrannos, the father of Stephen (I am convinced that his name was really a nickname given by the students he had taught), Stephen himself, and other Greek Jews – Prochorus, Nicanor, Timon, Parmenas, Nicolaus, others – were conducting a hot discussion over an amphora of resinous wine from Mytilene. Philomena, the only woman present, poured it into stone cups with an incised Greek key pattern. Nicanor was saying:

'As I've always said. They think themselves to be the only real Jews. And Aramaic the one true Jewish language. So we speakers of Greek are left out of it. Very well, we can accept that. But when it comes to a matter of genuine injustice –' Nicanor was in early middle age and was, by trade, a maker of metal, mostly silver, candlesticks. To say that he had Grecian features would be to assert that such features were measurably different from those of the other children of the Middle Sea. For all the sons and daughters of its mild sun (mild, I should say, in comparison with that which has burnt black the children of Ham) are alike in possessing skin that is of the hue of the olive, swart hair that in men defies the comb, a shortness of stature not to be found among the pale tribes of the north and west, and a generosity of nose that, so says the myopic Hebrew folk legend, was granted by God for the sniffing out of evil and fleshmeat not ritually slaughtered. Yet

65

sometimes among these Greeks gold flared in hair and body flue, a gift from Aphrodite a pagan might say, and Philip had such a metallic crown, and the sun nested in the thick brothy tangle on his bare forearms. It was Philip who now said:

'Neglect more than injustice, Nicanor.'

'Very well,' Nicanor said. 'Take the case of poor Philomena here. Widowed for six weeks and not one leaden *as* out of the fund. And yet they were quick with the showy funeral of what's her name –'

'Saphira,' Philip said. 'That was inevitable. Shameful at their neglect. So with the money paid out to that crippled daughter living with the aunt up in Galilee.'

'I could give you other instances,' Nicanor said. 'And not only as regards money. But the money part is the most blatant and shameful. It's time the Greek Jews spoke up.'

'Would,' Stephen said, 'you like Philip and me to speak to –'

'Do that,' Nicanor said. 'Lash out with it. Speak fishermen's language. And remind him of something in the Book of Genesis. "God shall give beauty to Japheth, and he shall dwell in the tents of Shem." '

'Meaning?' Parmenas of the heavy oiled beard asked.

'That the word of God is as good in Greek as it is in Hebrew.'

So Philip and Stephen went out into the hot noon and walked two streets to the house that had formerly belonged to Matthias but was now, in place of the upper room that had smelt of betrayal, the headquarters of the twelve. They kept the premises, the fastidious Philip noticed, in a state of dust and disorder; unlike their master they feared the distractive presence of women. It was old Thomas who was bringing a dish of beans, sliced onions, olives, oil and vinegar to the table as the two Greeks entered. Bartholomew, the two Jameses, Matthew and Peter were seated at the greasesmeared board; Little James was carving a loaf so stale it required much of his muscle. 'Come to eat, have ye?' Thomas beetled at them. 'Good Galilean fodder, none of your Greek fripperies. Come on, get seated.'

'Beans,' Bartholomew said, shaking his head sadly. 'A terrible maker of wind.'

'An Aeolus among vegetables,' Stephen flippantly said, putting his leg over the bench. 'May we discuss an important matter while we eat?' He addressed Peter. Peter said:

'It's about the widows, is it?'

'So you heard.'

'Hard not to, with you Greeks jabbering away about injustice. All right, such things are bound to happen, though I'll be the first to say that it's wrong.'

'Bound to happen,' Philip, fingering the beans and finding them underboiled, said, 'because you Palestine Jews think that we people of the dispersion are a race set apart and inferior. I'd remind you – What's that out of Genesis, Stephen?'

' "God shall give beauty to Japheth, and he shall dwell in the tents of Shem." '

'Meaning?' Thomas asked.

'It's up to you to tell us what it means,' Philip boldly said. 'You're the great explicators of the word. But I'll do your work for you. The language of Japheth is not like the language of Shem, but if we read the word of God in it God blesses us as much if not more than he does you when you read it in Aramaic. In other words the Hellenized Jews, as you people call us, are not inferior in rights to the Jews of Palestine. But this is daily flouted in the handings-out to orphans and widows. We want matters put right.'

'What ye mean,' Thomas said, 'is that the Hebrews are favouring the Hebrews.'

'He's right, God knows,' Peter sighed, letting a sliver of onion blow out on to his beard. 'And there's only one solution. Let's see how you Greek Jews get on with the day's handreaching. I'll wager all the complaints will come now from the other side. Besides, the twelve have other things to do than serve tables.'

He spoke Aramaic. Philip said: 'What's that phrase?'

'*Diakonein trapezais.*'

'He means,' Thomas said, 'that we're spending too much time dishing out bread to the poor and clanking down bits of hard money. We've other things to do than be, to speak your own language, what do you call them, *diakonoi.*'

'So the Greeks become the deacons?' Stephen said.

'Put it that way if you like,' Peter said. 'If a *diakonos* if that's the right word is a servant, then we're all servants or deacons, but you can be this special sort of deacon. So now there'll be no more trouble from the Greeks.'

'How many of us?' Philip asked.

'Well, not twelve, but there are other holy numbers, seven, for instance. Can you name seven?'

'Yes,' Philip said. 'Myself and Stephen here. Then Prochorus, Timon, Parmenas, Nicanor, Nicolaus.'

'They're very outlandish names,' Little James said. 'They don't sound a bit Jewish.'

'That ought to mean something,' Stephen said. Peter said:

'Yes, it means the Greek Jews look after the money and the Hebrew Jews look after the gospel.'

'Doesn't it really mean,' Stephen said, 'that Greek and Jew and Hebrew have no more meaning? That we're all united in the Christ and forget what we used to be? That the gospel is ready to be heard by men

67

and women with names more outlandish than ours?'

'We're not ready for that yet,' Peter said.

'The Samaritans are ready,' Philip said. 'The Romans have been teaching them the gospel of suffering. The next stage is to teach them the meaning of suffering.'

'That will come in time,' Peter said. 'The Samaritans are a sort of Jews, and they're entitled to hear the word –'

'And this Greek is a sort of Jew,' Stephen smiled. 'Ready to go to the Greek islands and speak the word in Greek.'

'Not yet,' Peter said. 'If you want to preach, preach in the synagogues here. Go to that synagogue where the Libertines go –'

'Libertines?' Philip frowned. 'Fleshly sinners?'

'No no no no. I don't know why they're called Libertines.'

'A *libertinus*,' Bartholomew said, 'is a freedman or the son of one. They like to keep together. They're from Alexandria and Cilicia and such places. You can talk to them in Greek.'

'Cilicia,' Matthew said. 'That's where Saul comes from.'

'There you are,' Peter said. 'Try and convert this Saul. You'll have your work cut out, I can tell you. Ah, gentlemen,' he said, rising, 'brothers. You're heartily welcome.' To the surprise of Stephen and Philip two men in priestly garb walked in. 'Forgive the clutter of the table here. We're humble men who have to fend for ourselves.'

'We'll go,' Philip said, 'giving thanks for what you've granted.'

'Bring the others here tomorrow,' Peter said. 'We have to perform a little ceremony. You'll have the hands of blessing laid on you in the sight of a houseful of the faithful, and then you'll know you are officially what you are. God be with you. Sit, brothers.' The two priests, astonishingly to the two Greeks, bowed to Peter before sitting. Conversion of the enemy? Well, these priests were poor men by the look of them, ready to give up what little they had in the Lord's name. It would be different with men like Annas and Caiaphas. Still, the new faith had breached the stone wall of the orthodox. Miracles, less spectacular than giving sight to the blind perhaps, but miracles none the less were proceeding quietly in the realm of the spirit. Yet Stephen felt a prick of unease. The faith was being kept in the family whose house was the Temple. Surely it had been intended that it should be part of a ship's lading, breathe new air. The Temple sat complacently at eternal anchor.

Tiberius had spoken of starting for Rome in a day or so, but the preparations for the imperial journey took more than three weeks, time enough for the fretful princeps to change his mind thrice and once again. At last, on a glorious day with the sea and sky mirrors of each other's serenity, the trireme sent from the mainland weighed anchor to return thither, the huge eagled mainsail bellying due east in the warm wind and assisting the labour of the three banks of slave rowers who, in their illsmelling dark with its brutal whipwielders and timekeeping drummers, heard the bucina up there in the world of the living signal the boarding of Tiberius and his entourage. There was a considerable staff, including three physicians, for the Emperor was far from well, though his running sores had been cleansed and his cheeks farded into a semblance of health. Gaius was insincerely solicitous. Herod Agrippa, to whom even the calmest of seas was prides of toothy lions, kept to his cabin and wondered all the time whether the Emperor designate would keep to his promise: he thought not. Not numbered in the ship's company were the minnows of the imperial piscina, nor the young schooled perverts of the venerean grots. These stood silently upon the beach and the headlands to watch the vessel leave, knowing their future more clearly than Herod Agrippa knew his: fresh slavery, their youth abused till bones broke or youth passed. The more innocent dreamed of a manumission kindly bestowed by the new Emperor as one of a number of acts of justice and clemency proper to a new reign. Those who had caught sight of Gaius rejoicing in the bumping and trundling of maimed bodies down the cliffside hoped for nothing.

The voyage to the mainland was brief. Puteoli, the port adjacent to Neapolis, was normally crammed with shipping, but all had been sent out to hover in the roads that the imperial trireme be unencumbered. As it put in, festive music of horns, trumpets, drums and cymbals erupted on the quayside. It made Tiberius's head throb, but Gaius greeted it with waves and smiles. Dockmen caught flung hawsers and drew the ship into the wharf, making fast their lines to stone bollards. Others rushed with a gangway empurpled and gilded and eagled with tacked cloth, others again with Alexandrian carpeting that should soften the brief imperial walk from ship to waiting litter with its tall and brawny German slave bearers. From a great height near the godowns the statue of Tiberius looked down on the arrival, its heroic cast bronze mocking solemnly its all too frail original. The Praetorian Guard saluted to braying brass and thumping drums, and Tiberius raised a feeble arm in answer. Under the dutiful cheers he could sense the undertone of satisfaction that he was sicker and had aged more than most had thought. For the son of the loved Germanicus the greetings were without doubt more robust. He, Tiberius, should not have come back. He had come back once before, many years ago, then merely to sail up the Tiber and view the city walls from a distance, troops stationed along the banks to warn off the populace, and then swiftly departed back to Capri. Now he was committed to a slow and solemn progress up the Appian Way, a noisy entrance into the city, ceremonies, addresses, banquets. He could not do it; he was a dying man, seventy-seven years old; he had earned his peace. No, he had not; hence he had elected this final suffering. No meanest slave sweeping the quay could be more wretched.

He was carried in procession then along the leafy Appian Way, the ornate cushioned litter swinging gently like a cradle. On his left arm his pet snake Columba slept: it was torpid, perhaps made sick by the voyage. 'My beloved,' he crooned, 'hiss your love for me,' but it coiled loosely in lethargy. At the seventh milestone he ordered a stop. He pulled the curtains aside in time to see Gaius whipping a slave who had dropped the roped impedimenta he had been entrusted to carry into the road's dust. 'Nursing a viper for the Roman people. Who said that, Columba?' The consuls Gnaeus Acerronius Proculus and Gaius Pontius Nigrinus appeared at the little window. Tiberius said: 'I will go no further today.'

'As Caesar wishes,' Pontius Nigrinus said. 'We are close to the villa of Pomponius Naso. Caesar may wish to repose the night there.'

'Is Pomponius in residence?'

Proculus looked strangely. 'Pomponius Naso was executed five years ago. On your imperial majesty's orders.'

'Is there – some other place?'

'A mile back. The former hunting lodge of the late Sejanus.'

Tiberius trembled as with ague. 'Pomponius's villa will do. Will all be ready for me there?'

'The imperial household anticipated your imperial majesty's wishes.'

'What do you know of my wishes?' he said with sudden anger. 'What do any of you know of my needs?'

There was a crowd of people, mostly rustic folk who gaped at the trembling lord of the world, standing near the gates of the villa. A bearded man in gooseturd homespun, carrying a wand, boldly spoke out as Tiberius alighted from his litter:

'Beware the power of the mob, Caesar.' Then, schooled in needful agility, he ran away before a lictor's whip could reach him. Tiberius went straight to a bed that had been warmed with hot stones wrapped in wool. He asked for gruel. Then he slept, and he dreamed an old dream, one that had maimed the drunken repose of his last birthday. The gigantic statue of Apollo of Temenos, which he had had brought from Syracuse to erect in the library of the new temple to the deified Augustus, spoke to him from a mobile mouth:

'You, sir, will never dedicate me.'

He woke to thunder in the middle of the night. He feared lightning. He called feebly and asked that he be given a laurel wreath. A slave at length brought one (there were several in his baggage), and the

Emperor tremulously donned it in wretched and pitiable apotropaic defiance. The lightning did not strike him; the trick had always been efficacious.

He woke finally at dawn to find that his pet snake Columba was not coiled on his arm but lying stiff on the floor. Not all of it; at least half had been eaten by ants. He screamed at the tiny milling army and stamped on it with his bare foot. *Beware the power of the mob, Caesar.* He called: 'We are going back to Capri! Cancel the journey to Rome!'

So the cortège turned about and snakeless Caesar went back to Campania. At Astura he fell very ill with bellycramps and dry vomitings. His chief physician Charicles gave him a posset of wine and milk and opium. He slept three days and awoke feeling stronger. Caesar was well. Caesar would show his recovered health at the garrison games of Circeii. Cheers but some murmurs for Caesar as he took his place in the hastily rigged imperial box. A wild boar was let loose in the arena, horrent and snorting. Give me a javelin. A javelin, Caesar? A javelin, curse you. And, to demonstrate his recovery, he hurled the proffered weapon at the beast, missed, hurled another, another, while some of the garrison cheered. Then: 'Aaaargh.' He had twisted the muscles in his side and seemed to bow grotesquely to the tiered assembly. He sweated with the pain and the brief exertion, then a cold wind started up and chilled him. 'Let us go,' he said hoarsely.

The party moved on the next day to Misenum, where a banquet was prepared. He knew few of the faces but smiled on all. It was a false rumour; see, Caesar is well. Another slice of the roast boar. Some of this gilded wheatloaf. Fill the cup to the brim; see, friends, I pledge you. Charicles the physician said: 'Caesar, I must go to tend the potion in its crucible. Permit me to leave.' Charicles took Caesar's hand to kiss it. Tiberius whispered:

'It's my pulse, isn't it? You're feeling my pulse because I do not look well. Stay here with me, Charicles. Tell me, Charicles, tell the truth: am I well, do I seem well to you, can I last this evening out without collapsing?'

'Take this powder, Caesar, in a little water. You will be sustained sufficiently. Do it covertly, let none see.'

Gaius, very drunk, shouted across: 'My dear and great great-uncle, how well you look. You will outlive us all.'

He was given next day in his litter the transcript of recent proceedings in the Senate. He read that the three patricians he had ordered to be brought to trial for treason had been discharged without a hearing: they had, said the report, but been named by an informer. 'Contempt,' he tried to yell. He missed sadly the comforting squeeze of his serpent on his left arm. 'It is contempt. Back to Capri.' Then Gaius Pontius

71

Nigrinus came with strange and terrible news. There had been a brief earthquake on the island, brief but powerful enough to send tumbling the lighthouse on the headland. 'The eye of the world is out,' Tiberius moaned. 'Who played that trick with the fire at Misenum? You are contriving bad omens, all of you.' For in his bedchamber at the villa in Misenum the dead fire had leapt to sudden life and watched him with its diffused vermilion eye the night long.

'The country house that belonged once to Lucullus,' Pontius Nigrinus said. 'It is but half a mile off. Will your imperial greatness rest there?'

'There is no rest anywhere,' cried Tiberius.

All of the above would seem to have little pertinence to the life of Jerusalem, but the state of Tiberius's health was known in Caesarea, and a rumour spread from there to Jerusalem that Gaius Caligula was soon to succeed to the purple, and that among his first acts would be the elevation of the prince Herod Agrippa to the kingship of Judaea, all this as a prelude to the liberation of the land from the eagle and the restoration of a Solomonic monarchy. It was time for the unity of the Jewish faith, the glorification of the Temple not merely as the house of the Holy of Holies but as the symbol of rule of the sacred soil of Israel. It was no time for the young Stephen to be standing up in the synagogue of the Libertines and preaching the new way. He stood and said to the frowning bearded:

'Of the new gospel of love and forgiveness you must know two things before you know any other. First, that it supersedes the law of Moses.'

Saul was there. Saul stood and said:

'Nothing supersedes the law of Moses.' Stephen said smiling:

'My old friend and fellow student Saul, I am glad to hear your voice. Let us argue the matter in amity as in the old days we disputed under our dear rabban. Would you not accept that the law of Moses was fitting for its time but not for the new age? For the people newly freed from the prisonhouse of Egypt needed the harshness of the *lex talionis* – an eye for an eye, a tooth for a tooth. They were yet in no state to hear the milder doctrines of forgiveness and love of our enemies. Then there was no forgiveness for even minor infractions of the covenant. The desert life was brutal and the law brutal too. Moses would have scoffed to hear that we should forgive not merely seven times but seventy times seven. The time for the gospel of love was not yet, but now that love is revealed – love that proceeds from the love of the Father for his Son, the love of both for all mankind.'

'You said there was another thing,' Saul said. 'What is this other thing?'

'This,' Stephen replied. 'That the law rests not in the Temple nor in the ministers of the Temple. The true temple is not one made by human hands. I do no more than repeat the words of our Messiah, who was as devoted as any of you here to the holy edifice raised by Solomon but recognized a greater sanctity in a temple no human hands had designed and fashioned – a temple that such hands may indeed destroy but, as he himself showed in this very city, God's grace may bid rise again.' There were mutterings: *He blasphemes against Moses. He puts the Temple and hence the nation in danger*. Saul said with calm:

'Proceed.' Matthew and Bartholomew, who had been sitting silently as self-appointed monitors (here was the first Greek Jew to proclaim the gospel) silently got up and left the dark airless square building to gain God's blinding air. They said nothing to each other until they were seated in the small dried up garden at the back of the wineshop of Zechariah the Sober. Here they slaked their drouth with water and then cheered their doubtful hearts with wine. Matthew said:

'He does it better than any of us. It's the Greek in him.'

'How?'

'The Greeks push things through to the limit. I've read a little in Greek, the old Greek, a tough language, and there was this Socrates who went to the limit with his logic as it was called and he was put to death with hemlock. No compromise in him. So with this Stephen. But the light was there, heavenly approval if you like. He was shining with more than sweat.'

'He's not a Greek,' Bartholomew said. 'He's a Jew like the rest of us. He knows his texts better than this damned Saul who was looking daggers.'

'It's hard for me to explain,' Matthew frowned. 'We were brought up on the Jewish faith and nothing else, surrounded by Jehovah so to speak. In the Greek islands they've got to God, some of them, the hard way, arguing from first principles. All our writings are sacred, theirs not. They've got to God through logic. Another thing, there's no real answer to his arguments, and they know it. Moses was good for his time, but not for ours, and they're scared to admit it. As for the Temple – well, that's where his logic is going to undo him. There's too much vested in the Temple – priestly position, money, trade brought to the city. What he doesn't have is discretion – Socrates didn't have it either – and we lot, we Hebrews have learnt that you can't preach the gospel in this city without being at least a little discreet. Wise as serpents, harmless as doves and so on. Christ fulfils Moses and makes his horns shine with a deeper gold. We preach at the Temple because the gold of the Temple door is brighter burnished with the messianic fulfilment. Damn it, we have two score priests in with us now. Stephen would scare them off.'

'So what do we do – recommend that he stop preaching?'

'We have to let God have his way. There's nothing to be done. But I fear we're going to have a death on our hands.'

Saul went straight from the synagogue to the house of Caiaphas. He said what he had to say and added: 'It's out of duty that I come, of course.'

'I appreciate that. Though, to be honest, duty is too often, forgive me, my son, a cloak for vindictiveness. You *boil* at these Nazarenes as if you bore some personal grudge. Pardon my candour.'

'It's your duty to be candid,' Saul calmly said. 'I've examined my conscience on this matter. Stephen was a fellow student, even a friend, though never a close one. A first duty might well be to talk to him as a friend – point out his errors, lead him back to the right way. But, you see, he voices the belief of a whole sect. He's encouraged to speak as he does. Also he's eloquent, even in Aramaic, a language he regards as inferior to Greek.'

'How,' Caiaphas asked, 'can one language be superior to another? All our languages were born out of the fall, equally confused in the destruction of Babel.'

'The tongue of Shem, so he once said in the presence of our master Gamaliel, is tribal, enclosed, unwilling to meet the impact of the world of the pagan.'

'God forbid that it should.'

'He says that Greek has struggled to get at a truth unrevealed, and the struggle has made it subtle and muscular. However, this is not the matter at issue. See him, and you'll see that he's taken on the shining look of the fanatic. What the man Peter says can to some extent be tolerated. Indeed, did not my master Gamaliel preach tolerance to the entire assembly in respect of the heretical proclamation of the Messiah? But Stephen – he strikes deeper.'

'How deeper?'

'You had best hear for yourself.'

Caiaphas heard, standing at the back of the synagogue of the Libertines in the shadows, Saul standing beside him. He heard Stephen's clear voice, weak on the Aramaic gutturals, rise over the murmurs of the orthodox:

'Our fathers had the tabernacle of the testimony in the wilderness, even as he appointed who spoke to Moses – which also our fathers, in their turn, brought in with Joshua when they entered on the possession of the nations, that God thrust out before the face of our fathers, unto the days of David –'

'Now it comes,' Saul muttered.

'But King Solomon built him a house – the golden house that is the glory of Jerusalem. Yet the Most High dwells not in houses made with hands. What does the prophet say? "The heaven is my throne. And the earth my footstool. What manner of house will you build me? Or what is the place of my rest? Did not my hand make all these things?" '

'Now you hear,' Saul said.

'Yes yes, now I hear. God help the boy.'

'I myself am prepared to bear witness.'

'No need. There are enough here to do it.'

'Shall I call in the captain now?'

'You're always too eager, Saul. I don't think you quite realize the implications.'

'With respect, holy father, I've thought of nothing but these implications. You wish to have clean hands. There are times when the Jerusalem mob is useful.'

Caiaphas looked on his shadowed eager face with a certain Sadducee loathing. Fanaticism was always a bad thing.

Saul strode up to the desk of the synagogue. Stephen said: 'The people of God are not in one place, nor is the home of their worship.' Seeing Saul, smiling he said: 'I welcome argument. In the Greek islands we prized dialectic as the zigzag road to the throne. My friend and fellow student Saul has something to say.' Saul said:

'Indeed I have something to say. This man Stephen, who was once a friend but is a friend no longer, who learned little when we sat together at the feet of Gamaliel, clothes in Greek eloquence a subversion terrible in its simplicity. He speaks against the law. He speaks against the holy place. I cannot put it more simply. This synagogue is defiled by his utterances. You know what action to take.'

Caiaphas was appalled. Fists shook, the nearest to Stephen let the sleeves of their garments fall back to show arms with tensed muscles ready to seize. Stephen merely smiled. Saul cried: 'Not here. This is holy ground.'

Outside the synagogue it was the chief priest himself who had to hold off righteous anger while Saul hurried off for the *'ish har ha-bayith* and his armed Levites. For, naturally, Stephen's protection. A mob had collected by the time the police arrived. What has he done? Nothing, but he's said a lot. Said what? That the Temple is a rubbish heap and the priests of the Temple a lot of timeservers. That's bad, is it? Bad, you say bad? Stephen was marched off to jail. The two Jameses, carrying figs and bread for the brethren, saw. They saw but knew better than to interfere. They ran home, that is to the confiscated house of Matthias.

Peter shook his head in great sadness. Thomas said: 'I had a feeling deep in my bones that there'd be nothing but trouble once ye gave in to the Greeks.'

'We're all one, all one,' Peter moaned.

'Ye'll not deny that he's been saying the wrong things. Just when

75

things were going so well. Ay, too well I've been thinking. What will ye do about it?'

'Things,' Thaddeus said, with the prophetic insight he, the small artist, sometimes showed, 'will proceed to their end. He's in God's hands. Things will be done that have to be done and they'll cry to heaven for vengeance. But there'll be no vengeance, only a greater glory.'

'Go on, make a song of it,' Thomas jeered. 'Play it on yon flute.'

There was a considerable crowd outside the council chamber the following morning. Said the Temple was a load of rubbish, cursed the priests, said that Moses was a juggler, I always said the Nazarenes were a bad lot, a Godless load of bastards, here he is now, a Greek, the Greeks were always a rotten crowd, my sister married a Greek and where did it get the poor bitch?

Annas wrinkled at Stephen, a clean-looking boy despite his night in a dirty prison, his beard sparse, his eyes wide but unfrightened. He stood in the heart of the halfcircle the seated Sanhedrin made. The morning sun from the wall of high windows bathed him. Annas said: 'More trouble from you Nazarenes. I quote.' He quoted from the papyrus handed to him by his son-in-law, quoting: ' "This man does not cease to speak words against the Temple and the law, for we have heard him say that this Jesus of Nazareth shall destroy it and shall change the customs that Moses delivered unto us." Are these things so?' Stephen looked at the grim assembly, noting a preponderance of Sadducees. One Pharisee, clerk to the court, leaned against the wall without windows, grimmest of all there. Stephen smiled at him and spoke.

'Brothers, holy fathers, this is a grave accusation and perhaps I may be permitted to answer it by means of a recapitulation which to many of you will seem supererogatory, but I beg your patience: my logic will, granted a little time, shine clearly enough with God's help.'

'We do not require logic,' Caiaphas said. 'We can manage without such Greekish importations.'

'Very well, nothing Greekish. Merely the truths of the holy texts. As you all know, God in his glory spoke to our father Abraham at the time when he dwelt in Mesopotamia, before he moved to Haran, saying to him that it was to Haran that he must move. So he left the land of the Chaldaeans and dwelt in Haran in the upper valley of the Euphrates, staying there till the death of his father Terah. Thereafter, under God's direction, he travelled as far as Canaan. Note that this was not his land, nor did he have any part of it. He was, as it were, a resident alien there.'

'Come to the point,' Jonathan said. 'We know all this.'

'The point is already before your eyes,' Stephen said boldly, 'if you will but look. Abraham had no land but believed the Lord's promise that there would be a land for his descendants. There would be oppression, exile, slavery for many generations, but the exile would not last for ever. In time God would avenge the injustices done to his children and bring them back to the land of Canaan where in peace they would worship him. A sign was given to Abraham, the sign of circumcision, the outward emblem of an inward grace and a divine promise. When Isaac was born, Abraham circumcised him on the eighth day, and this sign was passed on from generation to generation, from Isaac to Jacob and from Jacob to his twelve sons, these twelve being the ancestors of the twelve tribes of Israel.'

'Look,' Alexander said, 'we're priests and sufficiently, I believe, instructed in the scriptures. We await the answer to the grave charge that has been made.'

'Patience,' Stephen said patiently. 'For those with ears to hear the answer is already unfolding. I shall not, I promise you, detain you long with this recital of ancient history. Now note that even in those old days of the patriarchs there were men opposed to God's will in the guiding of the children of Abraham. For Jacob's sons sold their brother Joseph as a slave in Egypt. But, by God's grace, he did not long remain a slave. He rose to be grand vizier to the Pharaoh and, when famine struck Canaan, he was able, through his foresight in hoarding corn in the granaries of Egypt, to sell a sufficiency of grain to his brethren. Joseph saved men who at first did not even recognize him as their own brother. They had dealt harshly with him but he forgave and there was a reconciliation. Surely there is a lesson here. As a result of that reconciliation the whole seventy-five members of the family of Jacob came into Egypt to settle and prosper.'

'The correct number is seventy,' Annas said. 'You are citing a corrupt Greek text.'

'Pardon me,' Stephen said. 'Not corrupt. Your text mentions Jacob and Joseph and the two sons of Joseph. Ours omits Jacob and Joseph but mentions Joseph's nine sons. If you wish to spend some time with me now on the comparative arithmetic –'

'We want nothing Greek,' Caiaphas bawled. 'And we want no arguments with the high priest.'

'As Father Annas well knows,' Stephen said, 'his title is honorary. An arithmetical interlude would be a fitting irrelevance. Pardon me for that unwilled pertness. May I continue?'

'Keep it short, man,' Annas cried, though grinning.

'Very well. The Israelites prospered in Egypt, but there was still the question of reaching the promised land. It was necessary for God's purpose that a tyrant arise in Egypt, to persecute them, to make them long for deliverance. By God's grace and human cunning the child

Moses, who should have perished with the rest of the male children of the Israelites, was saved and brought up in the house of the princess. His sense of justice, whereby he slew a brutal Egyptian overseer of the Israelite builders, drove him into exile. Now note this carefully: his exile took him to the northwest of Arabia, to the wilderness of Mount Sinai – far far far from the holy land. Here God spoke to him and rendered that piece of Gentile territory holy. Now you will see, I trust, an important truth: that no place is holy of itself, that sanctity comes where God reveals himself. You may now legitimately question the claim of the city of Jerusalem to possess an innate holiness.'

There were the expected cries of *blasphemy* and *heresy*, but Annas held up his hand for silence. 'He is cutting his own throat,' he said. 'Why do you hinder him? Let him continue.'

'Another thing,' Stephen said, unflustered. 'As Joseph's brothers repudiated Joseph, so the children of Israel repudiated Moses. There came in each instance a second time when they were forced to accept their saviour. There they were in the wilderness, far far far from any promised land, but they had the covenant, the living oracles which spoke through Moses, the Angel of the Presence. They had the *qahal* or *ekklesia*, there in the wilderness, but they were not content. They wanted a visible tangible god of gold. They refused the authority of Moses. I am accused of speaking blasphemous words against the prophet, but who accuses me? The children of those who rejected the prophet. They longed to go back to Egypt to chew onions and leeks and garlic and breathe foul air in the invisible face of the Most High. And, once out of Egypt, their idolatry continued. Prophet after prophet was rejected, stoned. As the prophet Amos puts it, they took up the tabernacle of Moloch and the star of the god Rephan. But there was not lacking the tabernacle of the one true God, the trysting tent of the wilderness. Yet they disregarded, in their rebellion, the shrine which spoke to them of God's indwelling presence – not in one place but wherever their wanderings led them. I speak of the ark of the testimony, which we Greeks term *skene tou martyriou*, in Hebrew *'ohel mo'ed*, which may be rendered the tent of God's meeting. My old schoolfellow Saul, chief of my accusers to my sadness, knows all about tents. The place of the Most High is a tent. David spoke of building a mere habitation, a bivouac, a tabernacle. It was left to his son Solomon to erect an immovable *bayith* or *oikos* of stone faced in gold and silver, but this did not fulfil the intention of his father. Solomon himself spoke of the insufficiency of his edifice, saying: "But will God in very deed dwell on the earth? Behold, heaven and the heaven of heavens cannot contain him, how much less this house that I have built." '

'We respect your learning,' Caiaphas said with some sarcasm, 'but you have not deployed it to make your point.'

'Have I not?' Stephen cried. 'Is not my point now clear? I do not blaspheme against the Temple that is Solomon's, but I inveigh against the stiffness of mind that can grant a special holiness to a building of stone and forget the glory of what was housed in a tent of skins. For was not such a tent as pleasing to God as the temple that Solomon built? Is not the faith the faith of a pilgrim people, scattered by the winds of oppression all over the earth, scattered often in the past and without doubt to be scattered again? What will your Temple here avail you when you join, as my own people joined, the company of the dispossessed? The earth is the Lord's and the Lord's people are of the earth, not of a fixed and stony place in a populous city. I say again what I have often said, citing the Lord's own word: "The heaven is my throne, the earth my footstool." When he makes his own temple with his own hands, what right have men to mock him by saying: This that we have built is the Lord's place?'

Caiaphas raised both hands to quell the rising gale of fury and said: 'So the Temple is nothing and the priests of the Temple are less than nothing?'

'Now,' Stephen said, 'you put words into my mouth. There is no need. I have words enough of my own.' Then he raged, for the first time, lionlike, yelling: 'Stiffnecked leaders of the people, uncircumcised in your hearts and in your ears, you resist the Holy Spirit now as your fathers did before you. Which of the prophets did not your fathers persecute? Any that prophesied of the coming of the righteous one you slew without mercy. You received the law as the angels ordained it, but you did not keep it. Did you not saw Isaiah asunder in the reign of Manasseh? Did you not slay Jeremiah by stoning? Oh, there will be some of you to say: we are not our fathers; had we lived in their day we would not have partaken with them in the blood of the prophets. Yes, you now honour the prophets you killed and build monuments to grace their memory, for those prophets being dead cannot stir you to thought or right action. Now your fathers did no more than slay the messengers of the Righteous One – but you mocked the Righteous One himself and delivered him to the slayers. You accuse me. It is you who stand accused.'

Annas and the other priests had great difficulty in restraining the outraged fathers of the law who, having no words but *blasphemy* and *outrage* and *to the death with him*, made up for their bawling dumbness by putting out their long claws and stumbling in their blindness to seize and tear Stephen. Then Caiaphas, seeing the matter was outside control, said to Annas: 'We can do nothing. It is as well it is happening like this. His blood is not on our heads and hands.' Stephen, seized and rent, raised his eyes in ecstasy and cried:

'The heavens are opening. I see the Son of Man standing on the right hand of the Almighty.'

Now the doors had been pushed open and Stephen was pulled and clawed by the mob waiting outside. Peter was restraining the muscular

James. Stephen, seeing the group of disciples, cried that they should withdraw, there was nothing profitable that they could do. And then he roared in anguish as he saw his father Tyrannos and his mother Maia and, insisting on coming too to their evident danger, the two sisters of Caleb. 'Away,' he cried. 'Go home and pray for those who have reverted to the beast. Let them be forgiven. They do not know what they are doing.' This was both true and untrue. The Jerusalem mob gloated at the prospect of an act of righteous violence, though they did not know why it was righteous, the pious mental state which ennobles briefly the bestial act usually referring itself to sources it would be dangerous to examine, since this would allay the awakened brute. Saul was there with a rope, and with this he bound the hands of Stephen behind him, so that the victim could not wipe the spit out of his eyes. So bound, Stephen was hurried towards the city gates, outside which was a patch of ground hallowed by custom to acts of punition fulfilled, God being in the people, by the people. Stephen's friends and fellow workers in the faith were thrust to the periphery, where they moaned and prayed, though some cursed. A few Roman soldiers looked on, at first with apprehension and then in relief that this was a wholly Jewish matter, they could keep out of it. But a man that had once been crippled and now earned his bread as a leaper and dancer, his boy assistant playing unhandily on the flute, pointed out to the under officer of the maniple the two Jewish girls that had once lived near him, in the house of Elias the mad, saying that at last they had come to light, these were the ones that had been sought on the orders of the procurator, seize them quickly and (hand out) do not forget those that are on the side of the law. He had a few bits of metal thrown at him which he scampered under feet to pick up. The two girls saw what was coming and tried to run, but one of the mob hit the praying Stephen on the mouth and Sara, seeing the blood, could not forbear hurling herself at the grinning fool and beating him with her fists. Thus she was easily taken and her sister Ruth with her. Thank God their mother was dead.

When Stephen had been delivered to the rough place of punishment outside the walls the mob began with righteous eagerness to pick up the stones that lay there in a heap, ever convenient for the chastening of prostitutes, women taken in adultery, alleged blasphemers and the like. Saul expressed himself willing to hold the coats of the throwers; he would not himself throw, having fulfilled his own act of piety and being no vindictive glutton. Stephen said:

'Untie my hands, Saul. A small request from a friend. I do not propose to defend myself. I merely wish to join my hands in prayer.' Saul surlily unbound him and then, a stickler for correct procedure, spoke to the mob:

'According to Deuteronomy, the hand of the witnesses shall strike first, and afterward the hand of all the people. Seventh chapter, seventh verse. Back, all of you, ten cubits, for that is the law too. Now, four cubits from the place of stoning, let him be stripped.' So Stephen's garments were ripped off and he stood naked, thin, his body not much more than a boy's, his shame, according to the obscenity of the custom, exposed. A worshipper and disputant of the Libertines' congregation was glad to come forth as chief witness. He took a sharp flint and hurled. Stephen's lip was split and it bled. Then came the other stones. Stephen's nose broke and blood drained on to his joined hands, deforming the words *Lord Jesus receive my spirit*. That praying mouth had to be closed, as also the eyes that drank the sky and the birds in it that were blessedly above the enactments of men fired, as they would say, by faith. Soon the whole face was a bruised ruin, and an ear drooped unsecured by its cartilage. Stephen fell to his knees and cried, though only Saul could hear: 'Let this sin not be laid to their charge.' Those were his last words, for his skull was split thrice and the spirit left its seat or perished with the bone and tissue whose workings had seemed to raise it. But the stoning continued. Stephen lay quite motionless on his belly. Following custom, he should now be rolled on his back and three or four men should raise the greatest of the stones and break the ribs as an emblem of smashing the heart. But it was certain that he was dead. Saul put out a hand of authority (that of one who could cite the Second Law verse and chapter about the ritual of holy killing) and the mob looked with some awe at its handiwork. He handed back the coats he had held while Peter, John, Andrew and the two Jameses came forward. Peter said:

'I take it that nothing in your interpretation of the holy law hinders our taking the body of our brother and preparing it for burial?' Saul sneered and said:

'*Skene tou martyriou.*' None understood his reference, but John caught the last word and said:

'Protomartyr.'

'There will be others,' Saul said. The poor torn body with its mouth open showing broken teeth was raised on four shoulders and carried off to the house of the grieving parents. Saul walked away towards his sister's house. On the crowded Street of the Loaves he fell. He was lucky that Bartholomew, whose morning had been busy with the splinting of a broken arm, was hurrying towards whence Saul came, to what he was appalled to have heard was proceeding and could hardly believe. Recognizing Saul, he divined that all was over, and then Saul became merely one who had collapsed with the falling sickness. He saw the twitching limbs, heard the high scream. He took from his robe a small wand he used for depressing tongues and examining ulcerated throats. This he quickly placed between Saul's teeth lest, in the spasm of the muscles of the jaw, this particular tongue be deeply bitten. Around him were people talking of possession by devils, but Bartholomew said:

'Nonsense. This is called *epilepsia*. Help me to lift him. It's a few steps only to the place of healing.'

Saul shortly after opened his eyes to wonder what he was doing here on a rickety pallet, one of a row of a dozen, all laden with the broken and sore. Two men were talking about him, so he shut his eyes to listen.

'You know the man?'

'I know him. And I know what he has done. But the physician may have no feelings. Remember that, Joseph Barnabas. He must desire merely to make his patient well.'

'Well enough to do evil again?'

'Or good. Men can always choose. Look at the face. There is a strong pressure behind the forehead, like dammed water trying to break loose. A great power for good or evil, and to this brain it perhaps does not matter which. It is the power that matters. Nothing lukewarm there.'

Saul opened his eyes, raised himself from the bed, said: 'Doing good to your enemies. I see.'

'Do you?' Joseph Barnabas said. 'You're welcome to stay longer. But also well enough to go home.' Saul, weak but standing, saw a number of Nazarenes around him. They looked at him with wonder and a certain pity. He scowled in bitter humiliation and tried to stalk off with the gait of authority. But he tottered somewhat.

It is not certain where the body of Stephen was entombed. His parents had a family plot, but an artist's inspiration welled up in Thaddeus. Joseph of Arimathea, no longer in the city, had left a tomb to the brethren, and that tomb, though cheated of its freight, was available still. Nobody thought that Stephen would rise again, but no tomb could be more appropriate for the first martyr or witness in blood of the faith. But whether Stephen's body, made fragrant with ointments and wrapped in clean linen, was placed there is a thing unknown. It is, however, known that his interment took place that night, under a full moon that set the desert dogs to baying. There was, in the perhaps admirable perverseness of this new faith, more rejoicing than mourning.

Under that same full moon, or another, the junior centurion Marcus Julius Tranquillus patrolled the borders of the estate that had belonged to Lucullus, keeping the seven guardposts alert, untrue to his

cognomen, troubled, most unquiet. He had that day requested a posting to one of the active legions, in Gaul or Pannonia, but the *tribunus
militum* had rejected his application outright. He was to remain with
the detachment of the Praetorian Guard responsible for the security of
the imperial person, whether here in Italy or elsewhere. Why, you
young idiot, the tribune had said, you are in the first cohort of the
Guard, and in a year or so, despite your youth, you will be promoted
primipilus if you do nothing spectacularly foolish. Not of course (smiling somewhat contemptuously) that you will. Yes, he knew: integrity,
oldfashioned concern with burnishing *virtus* like a piece of his equip-
ment, something passed on by his centurion father who had never risen
to *primipilus*. He was derided, this he knew too, for his primness, for
what looked very much like unmanly chastity. But there had been
enough unchastity on Capri, enough vomiting with excess of wine and
grape syrup added round the imperial table: it had not been hard to be
both chaste and sober. The corrupt laughed at him, the stiff centurion of
old legends, without opinions, unskilled in exchange of wit and
scurrility, but they had to be thankful that the corrupt had such guardians. A soldier's duty was to protect the civic order, however rotten it
was. But such hypocrisy had become more and more difficult. He had
hoped, serving the hateful Tiberius at a distance, that all would change
with the accession of the son of Germanicus. A young man, scorning a
craven exile, ready to slice with the thrust of a young man's muscle
through the snaked roots of disease at the centre. This was, or should
be, Gaius. Now Marcus Julius was not sure. He did not believe that
Gaius was, like his dying great-uncle, a meditator of evil in deliberate
and conscious choice, but he was beginning to believe that Gaius was
mad. Was a mad emperor worse than a craftily malevolent one? Of the
madness he had, he thought, been granted evidence this very night.

Walking among the cypresses, he had heard a voice from above. He
had looked for the source of the voice and, keeping well in the cypress
shadows, had seen Gaius stark naked in full moonlight on the balcony
of his suite on the second storey of the villa. Gaius, raising his arms to
the moon, had cried: 'My beloved, come to me. I love you, why do you
not return my love? I want you so much. I want to embrace your shining
body. Divine moon, soon I too shall be divine. An emperor is a god as
you, my love, are a goddess. Do I call you too early, my beloved? Will
you come to me only when I am in purple as you are in silver?' And then
he had taken his large upright member in both his hands and begun to
frot it, crooning all the time of his passion for Cynthia, the pocked
planet that gave the light of three large candles. Marcus Julius had
watched in fascination and fear till the end. Gaius shivered in joy as he
spurted lavishly into the silvered night. Then he giggled and went to
his bed.

It seemed certain to Marcus Julius that Gaius would kill the moaning Tiberius who, mortally sick, yet could not die. For Gaius refused to permit a guard to be mounted outside the imperial suite, saying that his beloved great-uncle had told him, the Emperor designate, that he wanted now none of the trappings of power, a naked man whom death would take in his own time, he would go when called on a plain bed, alone with his conscience. Marcus Julius had heard the colloquy of the physician Charicles and the patrician Curtius Atticus, walking together gravely under the figtrees:

'He has nightmares about the earthquake on Capri. He seems to identify the ruined pharos with himself. The eye of the world. This troubling of the imagination weakens him.'

'And the voyage to Capri?'

'Too feeble. And the sea is far from calm.'

'How long?'

'A week at most. The eye of the world is out. Hm. Very poetical.'

'The dying snake can't hide himself in the greenery of Capri. The ants are waiting.'

Saul was with Caiaphas and Gamaliel in the high priest's chambers leading from the great hall of the council. Saul talked with sharp eloquence, walking up and down while the two older men, seated, watched him. When Saul was silent Caiaphas said: 'Your zeal is, of course, commendable. But it is a zeal wholly destructive.'

'We are taught to destroy evil. The tares choke the wheat. The tares must be pulled up.'

'And some of the wheat with the tares,' Caiaphas said. 'I believe your dead enemy the carpenter said something about waiting for the harvest. Never mind. You seek a destructive commission. What does your master Gamaliel say?'

'I say first that I regret I was not able to be present at the so-called trial of the Nazarene Stephen. He was, I remember, a good student. The rough transcript of his defence – if it is accurate – shows that his learning did me credit. I am shocked by what happened to him. Very well, blame the stupid mob. But do not let that happen again. Remember my former words. We don't yet know whether we're dealing with the work of men or the work of God –'

'The young man Stephen,' Caiaphas said, 'spoke against the Temple and the leaders of the Jewish people. Some of the assembly was rightly angry. Things got beyond our control.'

'Regrettable, very very regrettable.'

'You are the great advocate of compromise, rabban,' Saul said. 'I myself propose compromise in dealing with this sect. I don't seek its wholesale destruction, since I feel that many of its Palestinian members will, in good time, perceive their errors. Peter, Thomas, Matthew, others, are still good sons of the Temple, diligent at attending the services, active in healing and charity. It is the Greek Jews who worry me. The followers of Stephen.'

'Had followers, had he?'

'In the sense that he articulated a peculiarly Hellenistic heresy which appealed and appeals more than ever to his fellow Greeks.'

'More than ever – that was inevitable, wouldn't you say? You created a martyr, Saul. And don't tell me you had nothing to do with the stoning. I know that a martyr is no more than a witness, but the term has taken on a new and dangerous meaning. You propose further handings over to the mob?'

'No, rabban. Not at first. I propose rather a course of – may I call it re-education?' Gamaliel smiled without mirth. 'These Jews from the Greek islands could never have much reverence for a Temple that was so far beyond the seas. Here, living in Jerusalem, they have had time enough to learn that reverence. But they believe the Jews are still a wandering people with a travelling tent of the covenant, as Stephen put it. They will not learn. They have little respect for the priesthood since they have so little for the house of the Most High where the priesthood officiates. The Nazarene cult drives them much further from orthodoxy than is the case with the Palestinians.'

'We had forty years of wandering in the desert,' Gamaliel said. 'The Greeks want to send us back to the desert. Is that what you're trying to say?'

'You speak my words for me, rabban.'

'What precisely,' Caiaphas asked, 'does Saul of Tarsus propose?'

'Saul of Tarsus,' Saul of Tarsus said, 'does not propose anything so brutal as a general massacre of the Greek Nazarenes. He merely proposes that they be prevented from spreading their heresy. Sequester them. Imprison them. Bring them back to the light. And, but only with the most obdurate cases, give them to the rough justice of the people.'

'Meaning stone them,' Gamaliel said.

'We have our precedent. The people approved.'

'The people, I gather, were even enthusiastic,' Gamaliel said. 'The people are always enthusiastic about destroying things. Even when they don't understand what they're destroying.'

'I shall need,' Saul said to Caiaphas, 'a special detachment of armed Levites. And men skilled in interrogation.'

'Meaning torture,' Gamaliel said.

'A great and holy end justifies the roughest of methods. That is laid down somewhere.'

'Not anywhere that I know of.'

'Go then,' Caiaphas said. 'State your requirements to Zerah. We will see if your zeal works on these stiffnecked Greeks.' Stiffnecked: he caught the Greek voice of Stephen saying it. 'Go.'

'In the name of the Most High,' Saul said.

'If you must have it so.'

On the sixteenth day of the month of the wargod, thirty-seven years after the birth of, as he was called by many, the prince of peace, Tiberius breathed his last. He was seventy-seven years old and had reigned for almost twenty-three years. The manner of death is still unknown. Some say that Gaius gave him slow poison in possets he insisted on serving himself; others that Tiberius whimpered perpetually for food but was denied it. The philosopher Seneca, whom we shall meet later, writes somewhere of the Emperor, aware that his end was coming, removing his sealring as if to give it to another, clinging to it for a time and then replacing it on his finger, clenching his fist to hold on to the emblem of imperial power, then calling faintly for a servant to come. No servant answered, so he got out of his bed, staggered, fell, and died on the floor. Other tales tell frankly of Gaius stabbing Tiberius with a damascened dagger in the presence of a horrified freedman whom he then strangled with his own hands in the anger of a discovered assassination. More probable is the story of Gaius's smothering his great-uncle with a pillow he had just polluted with semen offered to the glory of the moon goddess. We are, remember, in the kingdom of the wicked.

The wickedness of Tiberius was not quickly forgotten. In Rome joy at the news of his death was qualified by a hatred and anger the more lively for not having to be stifled by fear. People prayed to our mother the earth and to the gods beneath it, Dis and his bride Persephone (or Pluto and Proserpina) to grant him no rest after death, rather to create a special hell for him furnished with fire and serpents less docile than his pet Columba. There were cries that his body should be dishonoured and quartered and the bloody bits flung on to the Stairs of Mourning. It seemed to many that his cruelty was able to flourish posthumously. The Senate, aware that his death was approaching, granted a ten-day stay of execution for all condemned criminals, assuming that his end would occur within that period, but Tiberius died on the very day of expiry of the term of grace. As Gaius had not yet been formally declared Emperor (it has to be remembered that in Tiberius's will Gaius and Tiberius Gemellus, son of Drusus the younger, were named co-heirs; the Senate had yet to execute this testament in favour of the son of the loved Germanicus), there was nobody to whom an appeal could be made, so the criminals who had been filled with hope and were now drained of it were duly strangled and thrown on to the Stairs of Mourning. Rage abounded, and the mob attempted to seize the corpse when it was carried towards Rome for the funeral ceremony, but the guard, with Marcus Julius Tranquillus not alone in whitefaced attention to duty, bore the already decaying body safely to its incineration. Soon the eyes of the Empire looked not to a bad past but to a shining future. And in Palestine there were strong hopes that, Gaius being necessarily a friend of the Jewish people since he was a friend of Herod Agrippa, the days of Roman extortion would soon come to an end and holy independence ensue. Herod Agrippa was no Solomon, but he was of the sacred royal blood, and that was everything. The kingdom must be cleansed of its heretics: Saul would help bring an Israel united in its orthodoxy neatly boxed in ornamental gold to the feet of the newly crowned monarch. Alleluia.

So let us see Saul busily at work. One evening a number of Greek Jewish Nazarenes sat at their love feast in the house of Nicanor the maker of silver candlesticks. Parmenas was there, with his wife and children, and also Philip. Philip was, as it turned out, lucky that he was a three-year widower without children. We can all tolerate persecution for ourselves. Nicanor, as head of the household, took bread and broke it, saying in Greek:

'For the night before he was put most cruelly to death, hanging on a tree that the sins of man be absolved through his sacrifice, he said to his disciples: This is my body. Take and eat. Do this in remembrance of me. And likewise he said: This is the blood of the new order, which shall be shed for the redemption of many. Take and drink.' And then, while the broken bread and the single cup of wine were handed around, the door of the house burst noisily open, and Saul appeared with six Levites in polished light breastplates, armed with swords. The celebrants froze, some with bread still in their mouths. Saul said with great smoothness:

'I apologize for disturbing your ceremony – with, if I may say so, so little ceremony. On behalf of the holy council of the priesthood and watchers of the Temple, there are certain inquiries that have to be made. You – what is your name?'

He was looking at Parmenas. Parmenas answered: 'Parmenas. You, of course, need not introduce yourself more than you have already.'

'We can dispense with Hellenistic wordplay,' Saul said. 'I ask you one simple question. Would you say that it was idle and idolatrous to worship in a temple made by human hands?'

'There is no harm in such worship.'

'But no great good?'

'If,' Parmenas said, 'you expect me to contradict the words of our brother Stephen –'

'Yes?'

'The truth is the truth. Do you wish to arraign us, as you arraigned him, before the council of the priests?'

'We can dispense with a trial. You condemn yourself out of your own mouth.'

'I have said nothing.'

'You have said enough.' He turned to his guards and said: 'Arrest this whole assembly.'

The chief of his Levites said: 'The women and children too?'

'The women and children too.'

The children were easier to seize than the adults. There were three of these present, the two sons of Parmenas and the daughter of Nicanor. The girl screamed piteously when the rough men handled her. Parmenas said:

'These children are innocent.'

'But their parents are not? So you admit crime. Take them all.'

The Levites drew their swords and began to herd the sheep towards the way out of their pen. They meekly submitted, but then Parmenas cried: 'Now!' They had, it seemed, prepared for such an eventuality. Nicanor seized the sword fist of one of the guards and tried to wrest the weapon. Saul sneered:

'So this is how you turn the other cheek?'

Nicanor was pinked in the left arm. He cried: 'Good. The others are coming.' As Saul and his Levites looked towards the open front door Philip broke free of a hand brawny as a smith's and ran towards the rear of the house. The chief guard cried *after him*, but Saul said:

'No. He won't get far.'

Philip ran out of the back door, into the working yard, then leapt to the top of the wall. The street was empty, but the clump of his weight on the street cobbles set a dog to barking. He ran in the direction of the Temple, turned off near the house of the disciples and entered by their back door. The whole twelve were there, unusually. They had performed their communion ceremony and were mostly gnawing at bones. Philip sat, exhausted. They gave him a cup of wine. He said:

'Saul. The persecution's started.' The disciples said nothing; they waited for more. 'Men with swords. They've arrested –'

'Who?' Peter said.

'It seems they're after those who speak Greek.'

'Aye,' Thomas said. 'Like Stephen.'

'Nobody's safe,' Philip said. 'Leave Jerusalem. The Greeks first, the Hebrews after.'

Peter shook his head. 'They can't harm us. Not yet. They've no case against us, not while Gamaliel's around. It's different for you people. It's you who must leave Jerusalem. Well,' he said to all, 'you can call this the prompting of the Holy Spirit. He uses the persecutors to make us carry the word abroad. This is the meaning of *God bless our enemies*. You, Philip, had best go to Samaria. Fertile soil, a battered people. The time for us here is not yet. Sleep in the cellar tonight. Leave at daybreak. We'll give you money.'

'So it's the Greeks who carry the word,' Thomas said. 'Who would have thought it?'

'God works in strange ways,' Matthew said. 'God's a great joker.'

So Philip cheated Saul, but Saul was not cheated of others. He seized the house of Nicanor, though that house was due to be conveyed to the whole company of Nazarenes, and set up a centre of interrogation in a workroom whose floor was blobbed with points of silver. He had Timon there, a man vigorous but old. He had him, already bruised, upheld tottering in the arms of two halfnaked Levites: torture was warm work. He said:

'Ready to recant? Is Jesus the carpenter the Son of God?'

'Yes.'

Saul nodded. Timon's right hand was seized and his arm twisted almost to breaking point behind.

'Yes yes yes.'

Saul with a gentle hand motioned that the torment should, for the moment, cease, saying:

'Timon, this torture is unseemly. It is also unreasonable. But faith has so little to do with reason. You are a Greek Jew who has abandoned the faith of his fathers. You must be brought back to that faith. How can we best bring you back?'

Timon panted for a half minute, then he said: 'I have not abandoned the faith. It is you who have baked the faith and said the cake is done.' Timon's trade spoke in the image. 'That was before Jesus the Christ came from the oven. I am a good simple Jew who has found the Messiah.'

Saul nodded. The armtwisting was renewed. Timon gasped and then cried aloud.

'The Messiah has not yet come. Has he, Timon?'

'Yes yes yes.' The arm broke and he fainted.

'He's a hard one,' the torturer said.

There is no name in any language for the openair centres of detention which Saul devised for his dissident Greek Nazarenes. Rough palissades were erected on Temple land outside the city gates, and within them were herded whole families of Christ-following Hellenes. There was no shelter from the sun, save for that afforded by arms and cloaks, brief tents sheltering the sick and old. There was not enough water and the only food was stale bread. Families with wailing children were quick to defect from the new faith and could hardly, even by the most rigorous Nazarene patriarch, a kind of Saul of the new, be blamed for their denial of the Messiah. When they were freed again, their faith could be tested by willingness to suffer exile or by the ingenuity of subterfuge. But some children died and very many of the old. The Temple shone in the distance and none expected a voice of protest to come from beyond the veil.

TWO

I began this chronicle in an unusually rainy late spring and have laboured at it, with what little result you have already been able to judge, through an unusually hot summer. I have suffered bitterly from the bite of the insect we call in Greek *kounoupi* and in Aramaic *yitusch*, so that my right hand, scratching its Greek and Aramaic letters under the lamp, has swollen to a red ball and my bare ankles have bled with the scratching of my left. I have had difficulty in breathing, waking gasping in the dark and begging for some god or demon to fell me with a heavy club, quelling not so much life as the agony of trying to sustain life with lungfuls of invisibility. My stomach has been out of order too, so that wine, the stomach's cheerer, has turned sour on me, sending me off groaning to a particular bubbling fountain in Savosa that, as I should have expected, has dried up this dry summer. I have eaten little except broiled lake fish and honey and black bread bought in the market at Lucanum, and not much of that simple diet has stayed down. Today the ninth month, termed the seventh, starts in a ferocity of heat with no promise of autumnal mellowness, but doubtless soon I shall be complaining of morning and evening chill. Neither heat nor cold pleases us; afflicted with the one, we long for the other. I dream of opening death's gate on to a quiet green field under a mild April sun, there to lie undisturbed for ever with a donkey grazing companionably by.

It is without doubt unseemly for an author to impose on his readers reports of his bodily condition, since the writer's hand is to be considered a mere abstract engine, along with the complexities of nerve, muscle, blood and digestion that have some part in the driving of that hand. The writer's words alone count, though even they may be begrudged as a barrier (though, in grumbling concession, a necessary one) between the reader and what he is reading about. The writer as a living and suffering being is set, as it were, in parallel to what he writes. We do not inquire into the condition of Virgil's bowels when he wrote this or that line of *The Aeneid*, nor do we seek to relate the love poems of Catullus to the love pangs of Catullus. Still, the engine can break down, as the *hydraulis* broke down last year in Rome at the games, to the fury of Domitian. Any author who has undertaken a lengthy enterprise must wonder if he will see the end of it. If he has sense, he will put himself out of the way of danger for the work's sake, refusing to swim lest he be caught by cramps and drown, avoiding tavern brawls and shellfish. But death, somewhat like God, is a great joker and can lurk in a speck of dirt on the table's edge. The unwary author, shut safe in his writing cell, chokes on the stone of the plum he sucks for refreshment or finds that life, suddenly grown bored with the monitoring of the drum of his heart, leaves him as he stands to stretch. He falls for ever, seeing bitterly as his head sinks below the level of the desk an unfinished sentence that will not now be finished.

This is gloomy stuff, and I apologize for it. I would do better if, instead of expending an hour's writing on the prospect of leaving this chronicle incomplete, I pushed on with the chronicle itself, seeing all time as precious. But, as I observe now, I am reluctant to write of the Emperor Gaius Caligula (whose birthday yesterday was, I should surmise and hope, universally forgotten or, if remembered, remembered with a shudder). I have summoned my own dyspepsia, philosophical gloom, disenchantment with an oppressive summer as a pretext for deferring a necessary account of a wretched reign. Let me then postpone until tomorrow our first visit together to the bloody city on the Tiber, rendered bloodier still by its new master, and swelter with you briefly in a village not far from Jericho, where two decent young men, fired by opposed ideals, by chance or not chance encounter each other.

Philip the flamehaired Greek Jew Nazarene was ready to start his evangelical mission in Samaria. He arrived weary at the village of Mamir, a league or two from Jericho, shortly before noon, the day a scorching one, glad to find shelter under a widecrowned raintree near a small tavern. He sat, dropped his scrip to the dust and, from the largebreasted serving girl who came from the open kitchen, ordered a small loaf and a mug of wine. She wondered at his golden handsomeness and at his accent, which combined Judaea and the ancestral Greek islands. While he broke his bread and sipped his wine, conducting his own service of unity with his divine master, Caleb the Zealot came from the interior of the tavern, saw Philip, thought he knew him at least by sight, walked boldly up to the sunwarped table and bench and, after a shalom, sat. The two looked at each other with some wariness. Philip at length remembered the name. Caleb's reported work of subversion in Samaria had been driven out by more recent and privier events. Caleb had seen Philip around in Jerusalem but did not know who he was or what he did. Jerusalem was a great city crammed with citizens. 'What news in Jerusalem?'

'Persecution,' Philip said, 'of the Greekspeaking Nazarenes. I was lucky to get away. I'm taking the gospel to Samaria. By that twisting of your lips I guess you disapprove."

'Who are persecuting – the Romans? No, of course not. The Nazarenes bow down to the Romans. The other cheek. Love your enemies.'

'One particular Roman. Who is also a Jew.'

'Saul of Tarsus. My old fellow student. He was hot against the Nazarenes. And now he's persecuting them. Well. Do you know a man named Stephen?'

'I knew a man named Stephen.'

'A good man. I suppose I owe my life to him. Knew, you say *knew.*'

'Stephen is dead. He was stoned to death. For being a Greekspeaking Nazarene.'

'Saul did this?'

'Yes. You could say that.'

'And what happened to Stephen's family?'

'The mother and father are good children of the Temple.' Philip spat out the word with some bitterness. And then: 'Ah yes, ah yes. You ask very obliquely and discreetly and with fear perhaps. You mean your sisters. The soldiers took them to the procurator Pilate. Pilate sent them as a gift to the Emperor. Along with camels and horses and dried dates and figs.'

'And,' Caleb said, his colour not yet changed, 'my mother?'

'I heard something from Stephen about the mother of Caleb being dead. And very quietly buried. Your eyes and changed colour tell me you blame yourself for all this.'

'I should have thought.'

'If thought always had to precede action there'd be little done in the world. Though most of the things done are hardly worth doing. We heard of your inciting the Samaritans to rise. And of the crushing of the rebellion. The outcome of which you will know, perhaps. Pilate's no longer procurator of Judaea. Vitellius summoned him – '

'Who's Vitellius?'

'The legate of Syria. Pilate's been forced into premature retirement. It was a mistake, apparently, to try to sack that temple on Mount Gerizim.'

'You've been learning something about Samaria.'

'It's as well to know something about the people one proposes to convert.'

'Your friends or overseers have made a good choice from one point of view,' Caleb said. 'You don't look like a Hebrew.'

'Whatever a Hebrew looks like.'

'They detest the Hebrews. They accepted me because of the stripes on my back. They spit at mention of the Temple in Jerusalem. Go carefully.'

'It's a strange thing,' Philip said. 'And I wonder if our master foresaw it.

The Nazarene faith is already splitting into two. Stephen was condemned because he diminished the worth of the Temple and the whole hieratic order of the Temple. But Peter and the rest still look like good sons of Abraham and Moses.'

'You split already,' Caleb nodded. 'You will split more yet. There's no health in you, no unity. There's no grip at the centre. You react to Rome in the wrong way. You're as bad as the Sadducees.'

Philip smiled, though thinly. 'And your way is what, now that you're rid of Pilate?'

'Not to be caught by the next procurator, whoever he is. That, for a start.'

'There's talk of your dream being fulfilled without knives or fuss. A client king, Herod Agrippa. No more procurators.'

'A client king is only a procurator in fancy dress.' Caleb gazed at the lively street scene without seeing it: a camel haughtily dropping its sandcoloured dung; the basketcarrying women, veiled to the eyes but the eyes lively; a girls' quarrel about the precedence of waterdrawing from the well, eyes and teeth a flash of toy knives; an old man drunk asleep under a clump of dusty palms. 'I have,' he said, 'to strike at the centre.'

Philip, with Nazarene tenderness, rescued a wasp that was trying to swim, against a current of waspish drunkenness, round and round in his halffull winecup. 'You mean,' he said, 'go to Rome?'

'First things first, you're right, go to Rome. I take it my poor sisters will have been sent to Rome, capital of a slave empire. The first strike at the centre is the stroke that frees my sisters. If they're still alive.'

'Slaves for the Emperor will, I think, be immune from rough treatment,' Philip said in his cool Greek manner. 'I refer to the voyage under hatches and the clanking of the chained gang from Puteoli or wherever they land. I mean that there will have been no whipping or rape. The slaveowner expects whole skins and a look of health. What happens afterwards depends on the temperament of the slaveowner. And the slaveowner is the Emperor. No longer the wretched mad Tiberius. The sane and well-loved Gaius of the little boots.'

'You seem to get good fresh news in Jerusalem these days.' The wasp staggered with feeble wet wings about the tabletop. Caleb saw himself in Rome, a city he knew only from fantastic visions: marble palaces with flights of laborious marble steps, gardens of planes and pines and oleanders closed to the rabble, ladies with predatory unveiled faces, wooden tenements quick to burn down, gigantic effigies of false gods. Caleb wandered the streets of Rome, a stranger speaking moderate Greek but bad Latin, living off bruised fruit and wormy cabbages discarded by the stallholders of monstrously huge markets, drinking at ornate fountains. The Jews gathered on the Sabbath at the many synagogues, and Caleb was ready to harangue about a free Israel: strike, spare the Emperor for the moment, but kill the Greek civil servants, metaphysical enemies of the Jews. It all seemed hopeless. Men in chestmoulded armour stood around, speaking all the tongues of the bad Empire, alert for dissidence. Hopeless, yes. But he was glad to have a small focus of action: to free his sisters, bangled and ankleted in slavish copper, was an act of piety that even the Romans might approve though forced brutally to punish. First things first. Philip said:

'Strike at the heart. Stephen's way was better.'

'Any fool can die,' Caleb said, seeing his own death, five or six Roman spears lunging. 'You Nazarenes will achieve nothing.'

'Has it ever struck you,' Philip said, 'that the Empire is already decaying? Decaying because force breeds nothing but force. There's a terrible emptiness that has to be filled.'

'We're the only ones who can fill it,' Caleb said. 'It took a long time to arrive at the fulfilled vision of a single God. The whole world will have to worship Jehovah. Jerusalem is the capital of the real empire to come. And in the heart of the capital the empire's heart, which is the Temple. This has to happen.'

'Battering rams,' Philip said. 'Pilfered gold and silver. Human hands can destroy what human hands have made. I think we're right. I'm sure.' But he delayed finishing his wine and trudging through the dust to the Samaritan capital.

I met an old man named Livius Silanus who, cautiously at the centre of Roman affairs as an efficient but not brilliant court advocate, had seen the whole of Gaius's brief reign and noted the point at which madness supervened on moderation. 'I remember,' he told me, 'the day when Gaius escorted the corpse of Tiberius to Rome from Misenum. He was dressed in full mourning and maintained a countenance of great sadness, but he was so greeted by the plebs that one would have taken the funeral procession for a military triumph, as if the young weeping Gaius had subdued some kingdom of darkness. They yelled mad endearments at him – our little pet, our own imperial baby, our son who is yet our father, star of the east and the west, our chicken who shall yet be an eagle, and so on, all quite nauseating to look back upon. I was one of those unauthorized citizens who pushed their way into the senate house to witness the setting aside of Tiberius's will and the conferment of absolute power on Gaius, rendering totally invalid the claim of the joint heir Tiberius Gemellus. The celebrations were of a dangerous extravagance, what with the public sacrifice of nearly two hundred thousand beasts and, it was said, human beings as well, slaves naturally, in his honour, in the space of no more than three months. Extravagance of one kind condones extravagance of another. The wonder is that Gaius did not yield more readily to the intoxication of absolute power. The adoration of the people was demented. When Gaius fell briefly ill of a surfeit of turtle's eggs, there were people ready to give their own lives – they went round the streets bearing cards lettered to that effect – if only the gods would grant his recovery. With Gaius recovered they forgot their pledges quickly enough.'

The September heat has somewhat abated. Last night there was much rain and, as I write, my two slaves Felicia and Chrestus are busy mopping up its inflow. Livius Silanus continued:

'Gaius endeared himself to the Romans by showing filial piety to what I thought an excessive degree. He sailed to Pandataria and the Pontians in very rough weather to transport back to Rome the remains of his mother and brother Nero (a name not at that time redolent of evil: all names are neutral, to be smeared with faeces or honey according to the temperament and acts of their possessors). He honoured their ashes with prayers and tears and placed them in their urns with his own hands. He organized days of funeral sacrifices and of circus games to the glory of his mother. As for his father, he renamed the month September Germanicus, a change about which many of us have ambiguous feelings, for we approve the honour while loathing him who bestowed it. Need I go on in this recital of acts altogether worthy? His uncle Claudius, the limping stutterer, the Balbus who built no wall but erected an ill-written pile of dubious Roman annals, was at the time of Gaius's accession a mere knight, but he was swiftly elevated to the rank of consul, fellow to the Emperor himself, while poor Tiberius Gemellus, who had as good a claim to the imperiate, he adopted and gave the title of Prince of the Young. His sisters, with whom he was soon to commit incest, he associated with his own glory, bidding consuls and senators end their official proceedings with the prayer "Good fortune go with the Emperor Gaius and his sisters".

'He cleansed the city of its perverts, called *spintriae*, wishing to drown them in the Tiber but restrained from an act of such excessive virtue. He abolished censorship, resumed Augustus's practice of publishing an annual budget, revivified the electoral system, pleased the plebs with new games – panther-baiting, boxing and wrestling with the best of the African and Campanian professionals, nightshows with the city illuminated, with lavish throwing of gift vouchers for the people from his own hands. The greatest of his shows was presented in no arena but on the stretch of sea from Baiae to Puteoli. He anchored all the merchant vessels of the west coast in two lines, and then he had mounds of earth laid on their planks. Wearing an oakleaf crown and a cloak of cloth of gold, sworded and bucklered, the Praetorian Guard behind him and some of his friends in chariots brought from Gaul, he rode on a richly caparisoned stallion from one to the other end of this fantastic bridge. This, I gather, was to give the lie to a prophecy of Thrasyllus the soothsayer: "Gaius has no more chance of becoming Emperor than of riding a horse dryshod across the Gulf of Baiae." Here, perhaps, you see the first public manifestation of his madness.

'He seems first to have proclaimed his divinity in a discussion with certain foreign potentates, including Artabanus, the king of the Parthians (who hated Tiberius but did everything to ingratiate himself with Gaius). At this time he had already insisted on being named by such titles as Father of the Army and Best and Greatest Caesar, but, in the kingly argument, conducted in the friendliest terms, as to which of the monarchs there present was the most nobly descended, he cried that he outranked them all. He was greater than any king, he insisted, and the greater than a king must of necessity be a god. From that moment on he began to forge proof of his divinity. He extended his palace as far as the Forum, so that the shrine of Castor and Pollux there became a mere annexe or vestibule. Standing beside the statued brethren, he put himself in the situation of one who had to be worshipped along with them. Some worshippers went too far and called him Jupiter Latiaris, but he was soon to regard himself as greater than the whole pantheon lumped together. He had a shrine built, with a lifesize golden image of himself, the clothes of which had to be changed every day to be identical with those which the divinity wore in the flesh, and there were sacrificial victims of great cost and rarity – peacocks, flamingos, pheasants, guineahens. He would converse with the statue of Jupiter of the Capitol, threatening to cast the heavenly father down to hell if he did not raise himself, the divine Emperor, heavenwards. It goes without saying that his ritual copulations with the moon goddess continued, though no longer in secret. All the statues of the gods he had decapitated, and an effigy of his own grinning head placed above the muscular stone or metal. A conversation with a Greek craftsman is reported from this first phase of his mania:

' "All these gods – you know what the Jews believe?"

' "No, Caesar."

' "That there is only one God. Clever people, the Jews. You understand my instructions about placing the head of the one God on this multiplicity of divine bodies?"

' "Yes, Caesar, but what do we do about the goddesses?"

' "Easy, you fool. Put my head there, but also hair, hair, hair in abundance." And he made the gesture of conjuring a sprouting of lavish locks from his own bald scalp, at the same time giggling manically. Gaius Caligula – the name still makes me shudder. It even induces a physical nausea. Ask me no more about him.'

It was to a Rome ruled by a still reasonable and indeed benevolent Gaius that the two sisters of Caleb were marched, though not lashed, in light chains. They had both been violently sick on the voyage from Caesarea, huddled under the hatches with too many other slaves, some of them Samaritan captives, but the *Cytherea*, a sailing ship wholly dependent on the winds and not on banks of wretched slave rowers (who were indeed only employed on the biremes, triremes and quadriremes of home waters at that time), was often becalmed and put in at many ports of the Roman Levant, thus granting periods when the tossed stomach might recover. Both Ruth and Sara had become thin, unable to eat salt pork and drink foul water though they later devoured broiled fresh fish with the hunger of animals, fighting for it. Ruth wept much but Sara set her beauty to a fierce grimness which, even when, as you shall hear later, she was manumitted, she never entirely lost. She was determined to live and dreamed much of revenge. She had also a sense, perhaps perverse, that it was better to learn about the great world even through slavery than to sit muffled at home in the metaphysical servitude imposed by the Jewish law. There was nothing metaphysical about Roman whips; there was indeed a kind of brutish honesty in Roman doctrines of buying and selling: no hypocrisy about the Romans: you knew where you stood or lay or tottered. It was a three days' march along the Via Aurelia, with an exhausted flopping-down in the fields under guard when nightfall had brought its tubs of water and its hurled bread ration.

And here at last was Rome: the Janiculum, the Marine Theatre of Augustus, the bridge over the Tiber that led to the Palatine. In the streets low people jeered at the slaves and some spat; Sara, unveiled now for ever, spat back, but the wind blew from the east. There north were the Forum and the Temple of Jupiter and the Circus Flaminius and Pompey's Theatre, but the slaves were to see none of these things: they were split into groups and impelled according to their imposed functions to this or that part of the slave quarters that lay beyond planted groves to the north of the imperial palace. Sara and Ruth were to be put to kitchen duties. They were greeted by a slavemistress from the Rhineland who barked at them. Sara barked back and was cuffed. They were herded with other women, many of whom wailed, to a window-less barracks filled, like a monstrous stable, with straw. Ruth lay down and wept for Jerusalem. Sara saw there was no way of escape.

'Our master said that we should be his witnesses in Jerusalem, and in all Judaea and also Samaria,' Philip told the Samaritans in one of the syna-gogues of Sebaste. 'So I am here.' The sun from the high window enflamed his hair and made it seem a sign of something. 'You have a word which you use much, and that word is *ta'eb*, meaning him who shall restore. What shall he restore? He shall restore health and wholeness after sickness and wounds. He shall restore the lost vision of the faith as a faith of love. The *ta'eb* appeared in Judaea and I bring his message. A message of tolerance, forbearance, charity. A glib and useless message, so some of you will say, smarting as you are from the fury of the Romans, the predations of an unjust procurator. Some of you dream of vengeance and a new rising of the people. We Nazarenes do not dream. We offer instead a practical answer to tribulation and pain. We must love our enemies, and such love, which it would be foolish to believe capable of gushing spontaneously from the heart, has to be learned as any other skill is learned. You burn your finger in the fire, and the throbbing finger causes you pain. Do you then hate your finger? No, for it is part of yourself. So when men cause you pain, blame the fire that is in them, but remember that such men are your brethren, are part of the body of God as much as yourselves. Love is a hard thing to learn, but if we do not learn it we are lost.'

The members of the synagogue listened not because they found great sense in the words but because Philip had been showing a certain therapeutic power which the simpler of the folk deemed thaumaturgical. A couple of cripples had been healed, and in public too. The imputation of the miraculous troubles me, as it must trouble any rational person, and I insist, along with my old dead sadly missed physician friend Sameach, Efcharistimenos in Greek, that certain conditions of the body have a basis in the soul, and that a cure may consist in unlocking the soul and plucking out the cause. Thus, a man who had struck his mother in rage found, as he thought, that God struck that hand and rendered it paralysed. He repented of his act, but that repentance was unheard by the deaf and dumb organ of grasp and touch. Philip apparently soothed him to an acceptance of his human lot, the unexorcizable devil that got into man with Adam, presented his own unfilial rage and violence as part of an ineluctable condition, and released him from an inner tension that, by some inexplicable traffic of the nerves, had stiffened his hand to an unbreakable stoniness. Alleluia, cried the man, wagging his fingers, Christ Jesus is great.

After his discourse in the synagogue, Philip was engaged in effecting what looked like a cure at a street corner in Sebaste. An old woman had fallen in a faint and lay as if dead near, but not on, a heap of uncleared camel dung. The Samaritans always had the reputation of a dirty people and employed no municipal streetcleaners. Philip knelt near to the woman, put his ear to her breast, heard a faint but rhythmical heartbeat. He knew she would recover so, with Greek cunning, used the circumstance to the advantage of the faith. 'Ponder on the goodness of God and his Son Christ Jesus,' he told the surrounding crowd, including a couple of uneasy armed police on its fringe. 'To God all things are possible. Let us pray.'

Two men, with staves and bundles, heard the prayer which Philip was teaching the crowd – 'Our Father in heaven, may your name be blessed,' and so on – and praised God that the work was proceeding. When the old woman was shakily on her feet again, though shrieking at the sight of camel dung, they pierced the crowd to greet Philip. Philip cried:

'Peter. John. You come in a good time. There's plenty to do in Samaria.'

'A bad time in Jerusalem,' Peter said. He was white as a baker with the dust of the road, but John, of an exquisite frail body that accorded oddly with his thunderous voice, had cleansed and brushed himself in a tavern at the town's end.

'Saul?'

'Having suppressed the Greek Jews he starts now on the Hebrews,' John said. 'As Peter's always saying, we never thought we'd be *kicked* into preaching the word abroad. Have you room for us?'

'I'm staying,' Philip said, 'in the house of a certain Simon. The Great Magician he calls himself, or used to. A performer of tricks that make the mob gape. He called them Egyptian miracles. He's reformed now. I baptized him last week. I think you'll be welcome there.'

Simon had made much money from his street and theatre performances and his house was large and furnished with Alexandrian bad taste. At the moment he was in the main room of that house, a neatly dressed man with a beard trimmed and greased in the Assyrian mode, looking gloomily at a dead sparrow that lay, legs up, on a salmonpink cushion. The girl who was his mistress as well as his conjuring assistant sat on the floor beside the little bird, weeping. She was a pretty girl in blue silk, her hair a black lustrous river, and her name was Daphne. She sobbed:

'It hasn't helped much – your joining this new faith.'

'The subject has to *believe*. You can't expect a sparrow to believe. Although, according to our friend Philip, God watches even over sparrows. No use. I'll buy you a new one at the market.'

'But it won't be the same. Death's a terrible thing. Even the death of a sparrow.'

'My sweet Daphne, you're too tenderhearted. Only animals know death. Men and women live for ever. That's the new teaching.'

'You believe that?'

'It's a consoling thought. We die – but then we start a new life – somewhere. I've never much cared for the *una nox dormienda*.'

'You know I don't know Latin, if that is Latin.'

'One long night to be slept through. With no awakening. Catullus wrote that. He also wrote a poem on the death of a sparrow.'

'Poor little thing.'

Philip arrived with Peter and John. 'Peter,' Philip said, 'John.' Daphne looked up at them, drying her tears with her hair. 'Simon. Daphne.' John saw a pretty girl with black lustrous hair like a river and felt an all too manly response. Was it right or wrong to respond thus? This girl might be that man's wife, though he thought not. There had been little time for feeling just glandular responses to female comeliness. It had been a hard time, no doubt of it. 'We would all be grateful,' Philip said, 'if you would allow my friends to share my room. These are very exceptional friends. They were the first followers of the Lord Jesus.'

'Most welcome,' Simon said, now on his feet. 'Friends of Philip are friends of mine and of my ah helpmeet here.' John had been right to think not. 'So,' Simon said. 'You are come here to add to the miracles Philip has already wrought?'

'That's not the main task,' Peter said. 'The main task is preaching the word of salvation. That poor bird there looks dead.' Daphne renewed her weeping. 'There, there,' Peter said. 'Best bury it and get a new one. I had a pet thrush when I was a boy in Galilee. When it died my mother cooked it. There was not much meat on it.' Daphne wept.

A man walked in, a stranger to Simon. 'Open house,' Simon said with sarcasm. 'All welcome.' The man was chewing, as if he had run here from his midday meal. He swallowed and said:

'It's my brother. He's leaping like a fish and making strange noises. The man Philip has to come.'

'Has to? Has to?' Simon rebuked. 'He'll come when he's ready. The fowls should be cooked by now,' he said to Daphne. Fowls of the air. She wept. 'Unseemly,' Simon said, 'to cry in front of our guests. Go to your duties, girl.' So she went to the kitchen.

'We'll have a look at your brother,' Peter said.

He was in the house round the corner. Baked fish lay cooling on the table, and there was a great spilth of wine on the floor. A large family ranging from a great-grandfather to a wondering thumbsucking child kept to the walls, allowing a young man, naked with a hairy body, to leap about the floor, crying words like *nagfalth* and *worptush*. He had evidently torn his clothes off. Peter, John, Philip and Simon watched. Peter growled: 'Out of him, quick.' He meant devils. He cried, more formally: 'I conjure you in the name of the Lord Jesus Christ to depart from him. Leave. Torment him no more.'

I suppose that some doctrine of possession by evil spirits will serve to explain, at least for the unlearned, such phenomena as we often see in our cities: men and women, usually young ones, who thresh around, froth at the mouth, emit what sounds like strange language

101

but may be merely the mechanical grinding of organs of speech which are out of control. I would refer this ecstasy or riot of the limbs to some physical cause such as faulty diet. It does not last long. The sufferer becomes exhausted and lies still, exorcized as the exorcizers would say. After Peter had growled or shouted further objurgations, the young man's open mouth gave out a stream of filthy language which made the women of the house tut and shut their ears. Then he snored in his exhaustion.

'Another miracle,' Simon said as he led his guests home to eat.

'Beware of that word, Simon,' Peter said. 'I too am named Simon, by the way, but that's another story. We did nothing. The grace of the Lord did it all.'

'But,' Simon said, 'the power is in you. And in Philip. It's a kind of magic.' He led them in and to the set table, where the scorched fowls already sat, legs in the air. Peter sat, looked at him sternly, said:

'And what do you mean by magic?'

'The power to change things that are not changed in the course of nature. I once had the appearance of that power. I called it magic but it was trickery. I learned it in Alexandria. Moses too learned this trickery in Egypt. You can take a drugged snake that stiffens itself to the appearance of a stick, then you throw the snake down, it comes out of its trance, it wriggles and hisses.'

'We learned this nowhere,' Peter said. 'The power is not in us. The power is in God.' And, famished, he began to work at a chicken leg, showing strong brown teeth.

'I'd like that power,' Simon said.

'Why?' John asked. 'Why would you like that power?'

'Well,' Simon said, 'to do good in the world. To show the world that I am one of God's favoured people. Like you.'

'You mean perhaps for your own glory,' Peter said, licking his fingers.

'I did not say that. I did not mean that. I was once a magician. Then I learned, with Philip's help, to follow the Christ and abjure all that trickery. Now I am no longer Simon the magician. I am a man without a skill. But you three have a skill, and a very precious one. I would like that skill.'

John had found the wishbone. He smiled at the redeyed Daphne, who stood by the table in the manner of a servant. He offered her the wishbone to pull with him. But she would not. Peter said:

'The curing of the sick, the healing of the lame and the blind – these are nothing, Simon. They're but sparks out of the flame of faith in the Lord. They show God's power, yes, but it's more important that we learn of God's mercy.'

'Bob's buv,' Philip went, his mouth full. Then Simon said:

'I want the power. I can pay for it.'

They all looked at him, silent over the ravaged fowls.

'I can pay well. I made much gold and silver out of duping the people with my tricks. Now that money can go to you – to do with as you will or as God wills. But I ask that in exchange you give me the power.'

Peter turned to Philip, who sat to his left. 'You've not taught him much, Philip. He understands nothing at all. Nothing of the mission or the faith.' To Simon he said: 'You want to buy God's grace, power, mercy?'

'I wish to do only good – to heal the sick, to bring the dead back to life –'

'To your own honour and glory,' Peter said.

'The power is in your hands. I have seen that same power in the hands of Philip. I wish, to the glory of God, to have that power in my own hands. I can pay well – ten thousand sesterces, twenty thousand –'

'To hell with you,' Peter said. 'To hell with your money. Repent of your wickedness while you still have time.'

'Wickedness?' Simon was genuinely puzzled as well as hurt. 'What wickedness?' John said, with unaccustomed faintness:

'You perceive no wickedness in trying to buy God?'

'A question to be asked is this,' Philip said. 'Is there as much wickedness in wilful ignorance as in wilful sin? Is sin a kind of ignorance, as ignorance is a kind of sin?'

'Let's have none of your Greek nonsense,' Peter said. 'We have a hard case here. I don't know whether to be sorry or glad that I've eaten his victuals. I can't cancel the hospitality he's already given us, but I don't think I want any more.'

'But,' Simon said in his bewilderment, 'Philip taught here in Sebaste that Jesus Christ himself made a bargain with God. He sold himself on the cross. He bought our redemption, isn't that what you said, Philip? The whole of life is buying and selling. Again I say – sell me the power.'

'It's been a brief stay,' Peter said, 'and I thank you for the offer of free lodgings. But we must go elsewhere.' He got up and made a clumsy bow in the direction of the girl with the black lustrous river and the red eyes for the loss of a sparrow. The two others got up with him. Simon was still bewildered.

Marcellus, the new procurator of Judaea, had already landed at Caesarea. The ship, named *The Heavenly Twins*, with a wooden painted effigy of Castor and Pollux embraced on its prow, lay at anchor, its cargoes human and mercantile discharged, new cargoes of furlough and time-expired troops, as also of sweet Palestinian wine and dried fruits of the country, to say nothing of tax money in strong-boxes, ready for boarding when repairs to the hull had been effected as well as a torn topsail resewn. Caleb the Zealot was in Caesarea, his hair cropped in the Roman fashion and his beard shorn. He spoke Greek in this town of Greeks and offered himself at one of the port offices as a trained ship's cook whose papers had been stolen by dirty Jews. He wished, he said, to work his passage back to the Italian mainland where his family lived. He was told there was no berth available. In conversation with the boatswain of *The Heavenly Twins* in a dockside tavern, he discovered who the undercook was – a Syrian, sweaty and of great girth. With no compunction Caleb knifed him in one of the streets of brothels, not mortally but enough to ensure that he would undertake no voyage for a time. On presenting himself again for employment on a seagoing vessel he learned that he was in luck. He gave his name as Metellus.

'If you're Metellus,' the overcook said, 'I'm Pompey the Great.' He was a small wiry Calabrian whose first language was Greek. The ship's stewards were insolent, and their insolence was prized as a comic speciality of Caesarea by the ship's officers.

'Isn't the fish ready yet?'

'It's being caught now. You said you wanted it fresh.'

'Watch your manners.'

'Aaargh' (leaving, clearing his throat).

'I wouldn't have that man's temper for ten thousand sesterces.'

Let us now look at this new Caleb, with his Roman crop and strong blue jaw, bare legs plentifully flued, bare feet firm to grip the deck, girt like a scullion, tending the wood fires in their iron prisons in the galley, frying eggs taken aboard at Tyrus, gutting fish caught off the coast of Cyprus, slicing the hard bread of Aspendus. He is wide of shoulder and very muscular. He is a temporary cook, and soon he hopes to earn his bread on Italian soil as a wrestler. He knows Greek holds, Judaean feints, points on the human frame which, if pressed, can induce temporary paralysis. He has always seen himself as a frustrated warrior, training for the day of liberation. He has worked at the use of dagger, sword and rope for garotting. He has a clear mission, the liberation of his sisters, and a cloudier one, the liberation of the Jews from the Roman heel. What he can do in Rome to further this he is not yet sure. He has vague dreams of collecting bands of young Hebrews who will so terrorize the Roman population that they will cry out to the Senate to let God's people go. But the fulfilment of such dreams lies very much in the future, for he tingles with quiet excitement at the prospect of seeing and living in Rome. He sees himself wrestling to Roman applause, hailed as the great Metellus. This, of course, is unworthy, since as a good fighting Jew he wants nothing from Rome except the withdrawal of the armed tax collectors (procurators are nothing more) from the sacred territory. But, like his sister Sara, whom temperamentally he much resembles, he feels it is better to be impelled by great misfortunes to the seeing of the world than to sit at home immersed in the narrow universe of Jewish law and custom. Our glands take precedence over our ideals. It was ever so.

'Hurry up with that fish soup,' the overcook cries. 'The captain's belly's arumble. What did you say your name was?'

'Metellus.'

'If you're Metellus I'm Marcus Antonius. You look like a Jew to me.'

'How,' and Caleb shows all his teeth, agleam in the marine sun as they draw near to Crete, 'would you like this fish soup poured all over you, you insolent bastard?' And he takes the handles of the iron pot in ready hands. The Calabrian sees the snaking of the muscles and says something about some people being unable to take a joke.

In the Aegean Sea a storm strikes up and drives the vessel towards the Achaean coast. Caleb is sick in his bunk and is jeered at. He recovers on the smoother run to Syracuse and wrestles with the bulkier of the jeerers, a man of mixed ancestry from Pergamum. Roman order converts the snarling violence into a formal match on the foredeck. Caleb hurls the Pergaman overboard. He cannot swim but Caleb can. He dives with grace and to cheers, and both are hauled up in a net. A patrician named Aureus Gallus or some such name, a treasury official who has been inquiring into allegations of peculation in Alexandria and Petra, speaks words of praise and admiration to the dripping Caleb. He seeks to work in the arena? Can he memorize the name he is now to give him? His is a manly trade; sybaritic Rome, that is becoming effeminate, needs to see muscle at work, recalling more primitive glories. I thank your honour, says Caleb.

They spend three days in Syracuse, where Caleb and the lout from Pergamum get drunk together. Then they sail north through the straits and hug the Italian coast. Soon they meet in the roads of Puteoli a mass of mercantile ships awaiting orders to ease in to the quays and start unloading. There is much grain from Egypt; Rome is forgetting the agricultural arts memorialized in Virgil's *Georgics. The Heavenly Twins* has a lading of troops and imperial functionaries and thus claims priority. Soon Caleb steps ashore; his now sandalled feet grip the earth of Italy. There is a grinning statue of the Emperor Gaius looking out to sea. Bales are rolled massively in and out of the godowns. Vessels strain at the lines secured to the bollards. Standing on a heap of bales a bearded man seeks the attention of sailors from Israel. He cries out in Aramaic:

'You who sail the seas, you have come to your harbour. But what of the harbour of the soul which all men seek? It is to be found in the

105

bosom of Jesus Christ, Son of the one God, Saviour of mankind, who died and rose again.'

So, thinks Caleb, the new faith is spreading already. Strange that so passive a cult should show such energy. Then he bethinks himself of what he has heard of Saul's work: it is Saul pushing the Nazarenes on to the sealanes, Saul, the pagans might say, doing the bidding of two opposed deities. A third deity, the grinning Gaius, seems to point his thumb towards Rome, so Caleb the Zealot takes a deep breath and the road to the heart of the kingdom of the wicked.

The new procurator of Judaea rode with the senior centurion who was his temporary deputy from Caesarea to Jerusalem. A courtesy visit, call it. Marcellus, who had modelled his visage on masks and busts of Julius Caesar, frowned at something he saw on the Street of the Smiths – respectable seeming citizens being dragged from their homes by armed Jews he took to be Temple guards. Mothers and children crying, men bruised. His horse snorted, as at some dim memory of battle under another owner, as the flats of swords smacked on backs and howls of pain rang. Marcellus heard the word *meluchlach* and asked the centurion what it meant.

'It means dirty,' Cornelius said, 'and it's being applied to these Nazarenes here.'

'What are Nazarenes?'

Cornelius forbore to say that it was the duty of a procurator of Judaea to have picked up at least a smattering of recent Judaean history.

'They follow a new prophet and they're being punished for it.'

'Ah, the slave Chrestus who said he was a god?'

'Not Chrestus. He was termed Christus, which means anointed. A confusion of vowels. And because Chrestus is a slave name it got around that the cult is a slave cult. These people, as you can see, are not slaves.'

'Disorder in the streets, Cornelius. Roman discipline has got slack in the ah interregnum.' He meant the period between Pilate's dismissal and his own accession.

'This is a religious matter, procurator, and we're instructed not to interfere in religious matters. The Jews are permitted to exercise their own discipline.'

'I don't like it, Cornelius.'

'He said he didn't like it,' Caiaphas said later, as he took wine with Gamaliel and the priest Zerah. 'He pointed out that his duty was to keep the peace here. He wouldn't interfere for the moment, he said, leaving the restoration of order in our hands. But I can foresee his eventual interference.'

106

'Which, in a way, would be right,' Zerah said, pulling out single hairs from his black beard; this fired a brief pain which to him was a pleasure: he was not a married man. 'The Nazarenes are troublemakers. Let the Romans subdue them. If, as I suspect, there are some false arrests – that old Ezra turned out not to be a Nazarene, after all – that was a pity –'

'He died of natural causes,' Caiaphas said.

'If,' Gamaliel said, 'you can call death by thirst and heat exhaustion natural courses.'

'What I'm saying is,' Zerah plucked, 'that it's always better to leave disciplinary action to the Romans, when, that is, the situation permits it. It leaves our own hands clean.'

'Unfortunately,' Caiaphas said, 'the procurator Marcellus doesn't see it that way. He sees Saul and his little army as the real troublemakers. After all, they spill blood. That camp he's set up is, I must say, an affront to anyone with humanitarian principles.' He did not smile, but Gamaliel did, acidly. 'I watched an old man die yesterday. His family droned out the Nazarene formula about forgiving one's enemies. Then they prayed rather a good prayer, nothing heretical in it, the one that begins *Our Father*. I think Saul has to be stopped.'

'Thank God,' Gamaliel said.

'And yet,' Zerah said, 'his work may be glossed as good and holy. You will not persuade him to see it otherwise. Why not send him to do his good work somewhere else?'

'That,' Caiaphas said, 'is rather a brilliant idea. Samaria, for instance?'

'The Samaritans would tear him to pieces.'

'He would be torn to pieces,' Caiaphas said, 'in a good and holy cause. But you're right, to denazarenize the Samaritans would not necessarily mean that they'd grow closer to the heart of the faith. We need somewhere with a large Jewish settlement where the Nazarenes have achieved a proselyting success. How about Damascus?'

'On foot, of course,' Zerah said.

'Oh yes, there need be no hurry about his getting there. On foot, certainly. But he ought to start soon.'

'He will need a lot of persuading,' Zerah said. 'But the Jews of Damascus are children of the Temple here. They must be saved from themselves.'

'By having their blood spilt?' Gamaliel said.

'I see no great harm in physical molestation,' Zerah said. 'It's the salutary shock that matters. If these Damascus Nazarenes won't listen to the warnings of the priests – well, Saul's way is a good way.'

'Efficacious,' Gamaliel said. 'Hardly *good*.'

There were few of the original disciples now left in Jerusalem. No one knows whither they dispersed, though I am fairly sure that the preaching Jew Caleb saw on the wharf was Matthew. James, son of Zebedee, stoutly refused to leave his post; he was almost pedantic about his attendance at the Temple, he was scrupulous in his refusal to distinguish between true Jew and Nazarene in matters of charitable bestowal, he preached not at all, he dared the forces of persecution to arrest him but Saul was wise enough to leave him unmolested. The night before Thomas was due to be seized, the news broke concerning Saul's new mission. Thomas left for Samaria none the less, having promised Peter and John he would join them there. It was he who, though difficult to understand because of his fierce North Galilee accent, planted unwittingly in the minds of the converted Samaritans the conviction that Christ had chosen them before he had chosen the Judaeans. 'Ay, mark that, all of ye. The travellers from Jerusalem to Jericho ignored the poor bleeding man by the side of the road, the Levite ignored him, all ignored him except this Samaritan merchant. The good Samaritan, the Lord called him, and no doubt had he not been done to death by yon hypocritical forces of law and order, the Lord would have brought the word here himself, instead of leaving the duty to us his humble followers.'

On a rainy morning Peter decided that Samaria could now look after itself. He had appointed an *episcopos* or overseer named Justin and a number of deacons. If what Thomas reported was true, there could soon be a general church assembly in Jerusalem to discuss the allocation of missions and also – There was a problem Peter found difficult to articulate. With a burst of sun Simon the magician appeared on the street. Peter, John, Philip and Thomas watched him from the open door of the tavern where they had broken fast. He had set up a small rectangular tent, and the girl Daphne, her eyes no longer red but her hair still a river of lustrous black, had entered it through a flap that Simon ceremoniously held open. 'Now see,' Simon told the crowd of idlers. He had a fistful of daggers which he drove into the canvas from all its four sides. Ample blood poured from the incisions. He reopened the flap and the girl reappeared unharmed.

'Miracles, miracles,' Simon cried. 'Every day here you will see miracles. Can the Nazarenes bring the dead to life? No, they cannot.'

'At least they don't ask us for money,' a oneeyed man in the crowd called. Then the rain poured out of a cloud, and the crowd ran. Simon sought shelter in the tent, but it was far from rainproof. Daphne, standing in a doorway, laughed at him. John felt the stirring of his glands again. Peter said:

'A thing that troubles me, lads, is this. What are we really supposed to be doing – preaching the word or healing the sick? It's the healing of the sick that the people take to be the proof of the truth of our preaching, but shouldn't the preaching be enough in itself? I mean, the truth is the truth and the doctrine's either sound or it's not sound. I mean, they'd believe anything you told them if you followed it up with what they call a miracle.'

'It's God's truth,' John said, loud over a thunderclap, 'and he had to show them that he was the Son of God. No use in just saying it. The only way he could show it was by going against nature.'

'Is healing the sick going against nature?' Thomas asked.

'Of course it is,' John said, 'if nature does nothing to cure the sickness.'

'But we,' Peter said, 'are very far from being the sons of God. And a lot of the things we've done – like that withered arm that began to fatten out when the girl said she believed – a lot of the things could be explained. Bartholomew said so, and he's a man of physic. What I mean is I'd be a good deal happier if people didn't bring their dropsical grandmothers and paralytic nephews along to the preaching. It's not the preaching they care about. The real changes of heart are when nobody asks for anything. You see how that Simon over there, I'm cursed with having the same name, you see what he thinks it all is. And he's one that worries me. I'd better go and have a last word with him.' So Peter, a man used to water, strode sturdily into the vertical lake and put his head into Simon's poor shelter, saying: 'Your heart isn't right with God, Simon. I can't leave you like this. Repent of your wickedness and the Lord may forgive you.'

Simon, wretched in the rain, began to snivel.

'You,' Peter said, quoting something he had read, he could not remember quite what, 'are in the gall of bitterness and in the bond of iniquity.'

Simon began to shake with hysteria or ague. 'Pray for me then,' he said. 'I don't want to go to hell.'

'You won't if you repent. Do you repent?'

'All I wanted was to do good in the world. All I wanted was the power.'

'Ah, to hell with you,' Peter said. He went back to his companions, soaked and sighing. 'He still doesn't understand,' he said. 'I wonder if he understood what I was saying. How is it that everybody could understand what I was saying at Pentecost and now I have trouble? I don't know anything now except my mother speech, and there are plenty who don't care for the Galilean twang. I'll have to go around with a whatyoucallhim.'

'Interpreter,' Philip said. 'I'll give you Greek lessons on the way back to Jerusalem.'

'I'm too old for it, that's my trouble. Well, the rain's clearing and we'd best move. There's a fair number of Samaritan villages to visit on the way back. Then you, Philip, you're a young fit man, you ought to go west to Gaza where Samson had his eyes put out.'

'It's all desert there,' Philip said.

'Then go north to Caesarea, where it's all Greeks. There's plenty for you to do.'

I now (on, thank heaven, a September or Germanicus day of most grateful cool, with the first prickings of a delicate fall melancholy) have the agonizing task of presenting to you a mad Gaius presiding over a mad imperial banquet for which few of the hundred or so guests have much appetite. Imagine the great hall of the imperial residence on the Palatine (whence the word palace is derived), with its pillars festooned with flowers and foliage, all the strong noonlight shut out with heavy samite curtaining to give a semblance of night (the Emperor is powerful: he has conquered the sun) and thousands of lamps reeking of oil scented with ambergris. A grinning statue of Gaius, or rather of muscular Mars with Gaius's head, is garlanded as in triumph in the centre of this field of marble, but there are lesser ingenuities of the sculptor's craft, all foully erotic: a donkey thrusts its member into the antrum amoris of a howling boy; two fat naked women, set head to tail like the fishes of the zodiac, suck at each other's vulva; a virginal girl chokes on the phallus of a laughing Priapus; the goddess Venus, with Gaius's head halfhidden in a flood of stone hair, is pedicated by a Gaified Jupiter. The huge marble table, C-shaped for Caligula, has strewn upon it, like casual sweetmeats, Alexandrian pictures showing specialities of the Alexandrian brothels – copulation with dogs and goats, with corpses newly beheaded, with corpses halfrotted, and other enormities that make my gorge rise sufficiently to make me forbear to list them. The food served, seen let alone tasted, would induce a vow in a reasonable man to live henceforth on bread and water. Nothing is what it seems. Dog faeces and horse globes have been moulded to the appearance of delicate cakes with silver icing. Stewed pallid veal has been sculpted to the shape of human hands. Human hands, conceivably, are to be found nesting, along with more orthodox meat, inside huge smoking pies. Boiled lobsters crawl up an effigy of a crucified man. Rolled beef slices are crudely phalloid. Sucking pigs are, of course, sodomized by other sucking pigs. Wearisome, wearisome. There are limits to the most scabrous ingenuity. Here and there a guest may find a dish banally honest, though he little knows what sudden minor horror may lurk in the depths of the confection. The bread is gilded, but it tastes of bread. The wine at Gaius's part of the table is served in small gold chamberpots. He reclines, the grinning Emperor, already tipsy at the

110

start of the banquet, with his sister Drusilla on the same couch (her whom he ravished before he came of age, whom, when married to the consul Lucius Cassius Longinus, he openly abducted), while the Empress Ennia Naevia (whom he stole from Macro, commander of the Praetorian Guard) is couched ignominiously alone below the salt. Lollia Paulina, starrily bejewelled, the wife of Gaius Memmius, a governor of consular rank not present, is there, though discarded, forbidden by imperial decree ever to sleep with another man. Opposite Gaius sits Herod Agrippa, bloated and sulking. Gaius says to him:

'Never satisfied, are you?'

Herod Agrippa is bold enough to say: 'An emperor should keep his promises.' Gaius says, though not dangerously:

'Don't you tell *this* emperor what he should and should not do. The whole point of being an emperor is the total freedom it confers. *Total*. And that includes the freedom to break promises. Be satisfied you have what you have, King Herod the Little.'

What Herod Agrippa has is the title king and the tetrarchies that once belonged to Philip and Lysanias in southern Syria, as well as, newly bestowed, the territory comprising Galilee and Peraea, once the domain of his uncle Antipas, now, with arbitrary wielding of a stylus, deposed by Gaius. But Herod Agrippa says:

'My throne should be in Jerusalem.'

'Oh, don't be tiresome,' Gaius says. 'Judaea remains a Roman province under Roman rule. The Senate says so and sometimes I listen to the Senate. Don't I, Uncle Claudius?'

Claudius sits some way down the table: sits, I say, since he is too tense to be able to recline. He is in middle age, with a shock of hair prematurely white. He nods at his nephew's question tag.

'*Don't I, Uncle Claudius?*'

'Occccasionally.'

'Entertain us, Uncle Claudius. Stand up and recite us some poetry. A little Quintus Horatius Flaccus.'

So Claudius tremulously stands as well as he can, since his couch is right up against the table, and emits the following:

'Pppppone sub cccccurru nimium pppppropppppinqui –'

'Oh, sit down, you old fool,' the Emperor cries. 'My friend King Herod Agrippa the Little will oblige us with a little Hebrew poetry. Won't you, your majesty?'

'All our Hebrew poetry is sacred, Caesar. The Psalms of David are not to be recited over lobster and sucking pig.'

'Why is everybody so *tiresome*? Why is everybody so *glum*? Why are the musicians silent? Aufidius,' Gaius says to a nearnaked freedman who stands ever behind him, 'lash those pipers and drummers into life.' Aufidius always carries a whip, the imperial

111

whip, manythonged and with lead pellets, its handle of the most chaste elephantine ivory. The players hear the threat and, though they finished their last piece a mere three seconds ago, at once throw themselves into a galop of Parthian provenance. There are four flutes, a harp of twenty strings, a mournful shawm, and a number of drums of oxhide, some to be struck, others spanked.

We, in our secure invisibility, may look with pity and a certain contempt on the great halfcircle of guests, who peck at the food, drink sparingly, and fear for their lives. Is life so great a gift that a man or woman should so feast in humiliation at the feet of a mad emperor? They are no better off, any of them, than the slaves who scurry in with new dishes, or the Praetorian troops who, in festal kirtles which hide protective daggers (what madman may not rush in to kill a mad emperor?) stand watchful on the marble staircase that leads down to the great vestibule or line the corridor that connects the banqueting hall and the imperial kitchens. Some of these troops remember an occasion when, in public too, they were ordered to strip naked and then line up to bugger the imperial person. The first buggering was enough. The Emperor screamed at the third or fourth thrust and cried that he was being murdered. But the buggering was being done on orders, the senior centurion insisted, and punishment of the overthrusting guardsman was out of order. Oh, very well, but don't let it happen again. That slave there has an undeferential smirk on his face. Whip him, whip him, Aufidius. The senior centurion was, and still is, Marcus Julius Tranquillus, who has again applied for transfer to a fighting legion but whose application has been rejected. Let me thrust (ha) all that is now to happen into the perfect tense. It is done, it is long finished, it belongs to the bad past.

Marcus Julius Tranquillus was much, though distractedly, taken by the looks of a Palestinian girl who brought dishes from the open fires and ovens to the servery counter. She was handsome but, more, she was unsubdued. She wore no anklet of servitude on, as it were, her fierce spirit. She had equal contempt for the screaming cooks and the timorous popinjays whom they fed. She was, however, most tender in her solicitude for another Palestinian girl, like her, younger, tremulous, totally subdued. This bangled fellow slave seemed to be her sister. Marcus Julius did not understand the language they spoke, but he caught the passage of charming exotic names – Ruth, Sara, as brief as birdcalls. The elder girl was Sara. She wore the grey of slavery with an apron cynically over it. Ruth, the younger, was, as a waitress, more becomingly dressed in silverpainted sandals, a white smock to the ankles but her thin brown arms bare, her black hair in a fillet. Marcus Julius's gorge rose, as mine rises in the telling, to see the object, presumably esculent, that Ruth had to bear to the table. It had the look

112

of a human head, moulded pastry of some sort with Jupiter knew what filling, hardboiled eggs with grapes set in them for eyes, hair of spun candy, and it was set on a dish awash in a fruit sauce that looked like blood. There were twelve of these monstrosities all told, and all the faces were different: one or two of them looked familiar to Marcus Julius – surely that was Cremutius Cordus and that the lady Lollia Paulina?

'If,' Gaius was saying, 'you will not entertain your Emperor, then your Emperor must entertain *you*. The imperial whip, Aufidius.'

He took the whip at the moment when the girl Ruth was nervously approaching the table with her swimming head of pastry. With glee and some skill Gaius let the lash fly and trepanned it. There was a gush of what looked like heavy brown cream which bespattered three grave senators. Gaius laughed high; some of the guests laughed too, though low. The frightened Ruth dropped her dish. Dropped her dish. Smashed head and crimson gravy and a heavy silver dish on the marble. Gaius spoke with great kindness, saying: 'Clumsy, clumsy. Where are you from, my little pigeon?' The girl did not understand. Herod Agrippa translated.

'*Ayeh?*' she repeated. And then, in Latin, 'Judaea.'

'Jewish,' Caligula said, 'but not one of your subjects, Herod Agrippa of my heart. Tell me, your majesty, what was the name of your grandmother?'

'Salome.'

'I thought so. She was a dancing girl, was she not?'

'That was another Salome – stepdaughter of my uncle.'

'She danced naked, did she not?'

'In a manner of speaking, yes.'

'And she was given a prize for dancing, was she not?'

'The head of –'

'Somebody's head, yes. Good. Princely entertainment. Dance, girl. Whose head shall it be? We will decide after. Dance, girl. Music.'

Drums began to thump in a variety of rhythms. The flautists were not sure what to play. The shawm began to skirl. Ruth stood bewildered. '*Rikud*,' Herod Agrippa said. Gaius climbed over the back of his couch and confronted the girl at the mouth of the tabled C.

'*Rikud*, as his majesty ordered. Dance.' And he whipped her to it. She began tearfully and clumsily to move stiff limbs. 'Faster, girl. Faster.' He stood back, granting her space and his whip too. He lashed.

At the servery counter Sara saw. She went over to the carvery and grasped a knife. Marcus Julius was ready. He took it from her. 'No,' he said. 'It will do no good.' Her ferocity was astonishing. Her eyes lamped the scene and her mouth snarled deep gutturals. 'No,' he said, and he held her. 'We are living in madness, we can do nothing.' Dangerous words from a servant of Caesar.

113

'Dance, Salome. Ah, I see. Your dress hampers you.' Gaius very neatly whipped off the upper part of her garment. She shrieked in more shame than pain, her arms protecting her breasts from eyes more than from the whip.

'Dance, Salome. Like this.' And Gaius clumsily turned and turned, crying: 'Applause! Applause! *Plaudite!*' There was some feeble clapping. 'Dance, girl.'

'*Lo, lo,*' she howled.

'Very well. I will make you dance.' He lashed her about the floor. She was all rags and bloody weals. Marcus Julius was strong, but soon, he feared, he would not be strong enough. The girl in his arms raged like a lioness in toils and, like that beast, bit at her constraining ropes, the tense muscles of Marcus Julius.

'You can do nothing,' he wished to cry, but instead he uttered a Roman obscenity at the sudden pain and the welling of blood. He impelled her to the safety of the seething kitchen. The Greek eunuch officer of imperial catering saw his territory invaded by one of the military clutching a fighting girl and squealed protest. 'Out of my way,' Marcus Julius snarled. Then, the sardonic Roman supervening, he said with taut reasonableness: 'This girl's sister is being whipped to death. Part of the imperial entertainment.'

Ruth now lay quite still on the floor, not yet dead, weals and blood and rent garment. Gaius handed the imperial whip back to its warden, saying: 'Now, dear Salome, you shall have a severed head as a reward for dancing so well. Whose shall it be? Whose? Whose? Whose? Choice is so tiresome a thing. Whose? Ah, *yours.*' He meant an old senator who had seen everything and was now a retired student of the Stoic philosophy. He had been surprised to find himself on the guest list, probably some mistake, his younger brother perhaps, now in exile at Mytilene, had been intended, but the guest list was a very arbitrary compilation. He had been, during the whipping of that poor slave girl, trying to induce in himself a coldly stoical attitude: life is evil, we cannot change it, to show compassion may result in more evil. He had been meditating earlier on the nature of absolute power: no power can be absolute if it is expressed solely through the enactment of evil, since there has been a limitation of choice self-imposed; in becoming a mere agent of evil the Emperor Gaius had forfeited his own freedom and was no better than a slave. 'When shall it be, you, whoever you are?' Gaius was baying. 'At the end of our banquet? Or perhaps now, as the crown of our entertainment?' The old senator showed no fear. He raised his cup to his lips and, with a straight face, pledged the Emperor. Whereupon the Emperor said: 'Oh, I'm so *bored.*' The boredom of forfeited choice, the senator said to himself. 'You,' Gaius suddenly said, pointing at a young officer of the municipal board, who was protectively embracing a handsome young woman clad in simple linen with a rather ornate headdress in the form of a thickly populated thrush's nest, bequeathed by her dead mother. 'You – take your hands off my wife.'

'With respect, Caesar,' the young man bravely said, 'she is *my* wife.'

'Oh, she can be yours again tomorrow, if the gods – I mean the god – kindly permits her to live. But tonight she's for me.' And he advanced grinning on the young woman, more a bride than a wife. She could not forbear screaming, nor her husband, or groom, tightening his protective arm. Gaius, with the swift changeability of a dog, seemed to lose interest in her. 'I've forgotten who it was we decided to behead. Never mind,' he smiled pleasantly at the young man. '*You'll* do.' He clicked his fingers for the guard, crying: 'The banquet's over. Thank you all for coming.'

Let us breathe a sweeter air, though the air of Jerusalem is as it were baked, the flesh of the city seething under a crust of heat and the pie brutally spiced with the odours of the unwashed and of camel dung. We are in the city only to observe certain personages leaving it. Saul, with an entourage of four armed men, one of whom is his old fellow student Seth, is at the market buying some fruit for the journey to Damascus. The Greek Philip has evaded Saul's last spectacular arrest of Jewish Hellene Nazarenes and is on his way to Gaza. In a day or so he is to meet a man on whom Saul and his companions are just now looking with curiosity. The man is big, muscular, very black, brilliantly dressed in the Ethiopian manner, and he is riding in a covered carriage drawn by two bay horses. He has a driver black as himself in costly livery, and the driver does not hesitate to use his whip to clear the way through the gawping crowd. The Ethiopian, if that is what he is, ignores totally his surroundings. He has a scroll from which, in the manner of that day, he is reading aloud. There are indeed, even now, very few who see reading as a silent activity. Saul catches certain words. Greek. He catches a whole phrase: *As a sheep led to the slaughter or a lamb before its shearer is dumb* – Saul grins at Seth and says: 'So one of the black tribe reads the prophet Isaiah. You see how the holy word may spread. Come. Ten miles before sundown.'

Philip was on a road opposed to that of Saul and his escort. He was on his way to Gaza, and had spent a flybitten night in Eleutheropolis. The Gaza he was going to was not, despite what Peter had said, the town where blind Samson, dreaming of old circuit judgments and abiding the regrowth of his shorn locks, had, under the lash, ground corn for the Philistines. That town had been destroyed a century before the birth of Jesus by the Hasmonean king Alexander Jannaeus.

Its ruins were still to be seen, an abode of snakes and lizards, and the name Desert Gaza applied to them. There was a new Gaza by the sea, erected some thirty years after the razing of the old by Gabinius. It was to this Gaza that Philip, his hair near white with sun and dust, was sorely trudging. The road was empty and so was the sky, except for far wheeling vultures, and the view on either side was of sand.

When Philip heard an octopudium of hoofs and a rumbling of wheels behind him and, turning, saw a nimbus of dust, he at first thought that Saul, expensively equipped from the high priest's own stables, was in extravagant pursuit. He shrugged (the game is up) and waited by the side of the road. Soon the carriage drew up with a snorting and stamping of two sweating bays. A black man dressed in crimsons and purples hailed Philip cheerfully in Greek of, considering his muscular bulk, a strange shrillness. His round face shone with sweat and amiability. On his head was a scarlet cap intricately patterned with gold thread and in his hand a fan of peacock feathers. He was sheltered from the sun by a white linen canopy. On his knees was an unrolled scroll. 'To Gaza,' Philip said. He was invited to climb into the carriage and sit on yellow cushions. Black but comely. Philip sat smiling.

'Gaza is on my way home. I go to Napata in Ethiopia. I have been visiting the holy city.' He waved to the driver and they clopped on.

'Holy,' Philip said cautiously, 'surely not for your people?' The text on the man's knees was Greek. Philip read: *Hos probaton epi sphagin ichthi . . .*

'You know my people?'

'I know that your king is worshipped as an offspring of the sun. That he is too holy to be permitted to rule. That rule is in the hands of the queen mother. Whose name is always the same. I have forgotten it.'

'Candace. It is always Candace. My uncle served the old Candace and I serve the new one. He was court treasurer and so am I. My nephew will doubtless follow me.'

'You do me great honour.' And then: 'So the office passes through a nepotic line? Not from father to son?'

The Ethiopian gave a laugh like a neigh. 'The court treasurer must always be a eunuch. You did not know that? Court officials must not breed and thus form dynasties. But we have learned to think of our nephews as surrogate sons. My nephew has already been castrated in expectation of his succeeding me. He becomes barren like me to serve a barren commodity. As Aristotle said, money does not breed.'

'You seem, from your scroll here, to be a Greek scholar. This looks like the prophet Isaiah.'

'I wondered whether you might not be a Gentile like me. You look Greek. And yet from a few words you know it is the prophet Isaiah.'

'I'm a Greek Jew who follows the new law of Jesus the anointed. I go to Gaza and thence to Caesarea to spread the word.'

'I saw this new way being persecuted in Jerusalem. I took it to be an aberration from the true faith.'

'You worship the scion of the sun and yet you talk of the true faith? Tradition says you're one of the children of Ham, cut off from the family of the chosen.'

'Well,' the Ethiopian said, whisking his peacock feather fan. 'This doctrine of heliolatry is a mere convention with most of us. We're an ancient people and not foolish. I cannot be a Jew but I can be what is termed a Godfearing Gentile. According to the twenty-third chapter of Deuteronomy eunuchs are not admitted to the society of the faithful. But Isaiah seems to promise a change.'

Philip closed his eyes and quoted: ' "To the eunuchs who keep my Sabbaths and hold fast to my covenant, to them I will give within my temple and its walls a memorial and a name better than sons and daughters." '

'Good,' the Ethiopian said. 'You are a better scholar than I. I know little by heart. I do know, however, what the priests of your temple have hammered into my skull: "No one who has been emasculated by crushing or cutting may enter the assembly of the Lord." They say that Isaiah merely fantasizes and that stern edict of Moses cannot be superseded.'

Philip took the scroll from the Ethiopian's knees and said, smiling: '*Ara ge ginoskeis ha anaginoskeis?*'

The Ethiopian laughed and said: 'The Greek language is graceful. It makes the word *to read* almost the same as the word *to understand*. The tongue of the Romans captures the same grace. *Intellegis quae legis?* But in my coarser language it would be bluntly: "Do you understand what you read?" Well, my answer is simple: No, I do not. Read the passage to me, and I will see if in your Greek mouth it makes more sense.'

So Philip read to him about the suffering servant. ' "He was oppressed and afflicted, yet he did not open his mouth. He was led like a lamb to the slaughter, and as a sheep before her shearers is silent, so he did not open his mouth." '

'Who does he mean? Does he refer to himself or to somebody else?'

'The prophet,' Philip said carefully, 'is being truly a prophet. He is speaking of someone who, in his day, was yet to come. But now he has come. Killed, as Isaiah predicted, three days silent in the tomb, then alive again, the marks of the executioners upon his body to show himself truly suffering man, yet also the Son of God and the everliving witness to – But the story is long to tell.'

'There's time enough. There's nothing to see except desert. Tell me all.'

There was a wadi northeast of Gaza. Children playing by it at sunset, women filling their pitchers with water squinting against the dying blaze, saw with some surprise a young man with hair like a flame and a large black man in robes as of the sunset alight from a carriage drawn by two bay horses and walk together to the place of running water. They had not heard the words spoken before the drawing tight of the reins and the grinding of the wheels: 'Here is water. Is there anything to prevent my being baptized here and now?'

'If you believe with your whole heart nothing hinders.'

'I believe the Son of God to be Jesus Christ.'

Philip baptized by aspersion not immersion, murmuring the words of the ceremony. Then the Ethiopian, now a Nazarene, resumed his journey towards the first cataract of the Nile and Philip walked towards Gaza. It was fitting, both felt, that they part now. They did not wish an anticlimax of either talk or prayer or exegesis of Isaiah. Both hearts were full. But that night in a wretched inn in Gaza Philip awoke from deep sleep clutching a pain in his side. Had he done the right thing? This stoneless man was uncircumcised, unacceptable on two counts, said Deuteronomy (and both centred on the genitalia), in the company of the faithful. Christ had come to redeem Israel, not Ethiopia. And yet to assume circumcision before baptism – was not that a manner of grim joke to play on one who had known the knife of a more demanding if less spiritual covenant? Come, cut all off while your hand is in. And why had God decreed that the snipping of the foreskin, and not say the tip of an earlobe, should be the condition of entry into the army of the chosen? Because the foreskin capped the tree of generation, human procreation being the moon that reflected divine creation's solar light. This eunuch born in Meroe and travelling to Napata (and Philip had already forgotten the name he had mur-mured in the ceremony of baptism) possessed no tree of procreation, only a limp conduit for the discharge of bodily waste, unworthy of the blade of the covenant. Uncircumcised, uncircumcisable, hence unbap-tizable? As he trudged from town to town northward on his mission, Philip half expected some gesture of displeasure from God, a bolt for the blasphemer (for to conduct a surely empty ceremony was – surely – blasphemy?), yet God did no more than he usually did, that is hauled the sun to the zenith and then let it slide slowly down, let grass grow at the rate of the growth of a fingernail (which he also let grow), killed some and allowed others to live.

When Philip arrived in Caesarea, he was half inclined to vow never to set foot in Jerusalem again, except muffled and anonymous for Passover, for he did not dare put the question to the leader of the Nazarenes. He did not know that the baptizing of an uncircumcised Ethiopian eunuch would later be seen by some as God's first intake of

118

breath for a gust of silent laughter. For the sons of Ham and Japhet were to partake of the patrimony of the sons of Shem, and many of the sons of Shem were to be excluded. It was not by coincidence that Saul was, a day or so after Philip's chanceseeming encounter with a black eunuch, to suffer an epileptic revelation and, a month or so after, Peter have a shocking dream about food.

Philip married one of his converts in Caesarea, a handsome girl named Deborah whose father was a ship's chandler. Philip entered the trade and preached the word now only in his spare time. God denied him sons but granted him four daughters with black married brows, all of whom became most talkative proponents of the new way.

About three miles from Damascus, one of Saul's escort, a glum wiry man named Esra, had a vivid dream in which an angel of the Lord told him that his wife and daughter were to be ravished by Syrian troops of the Roman procurator and that he had better hurry back to Jerusalem to forestall the outrage. In agitation he recounted this dream to Saul, who nodded and nodded impatiently over the morning breaking of bread in a frowsty inn. He said:

'Your heart doesn't seem to be in this mission.'

'They should have given us horses. Or camels,' one of the other men said, Enoch, who had limped ostentatiously all the previous day. 'It's not a question of heart, it's a matter of feet.'

'I heard the voice clear as the chirp of a grasshopper. *Go back, for the heathen will shoot seed straight as an arrow into the vessels of election.*'

Saul said: 'You three have grumbled ever since we left Jerusalem. Doubtless Seth and I will find honest Jews enough in Damascus. Men whose hearts will be in the holy work of persecution. You three may go back, though it baffles me why you should wish to go back now when you have come so far.'

'We were told we had to get you to Damascus free from harm, since you have enemies who might be lurking in the bushes, not that we see many bushes. Well, Damascus is there ahead, quivering in the haze of the heat. We have performed our mission.' This was Jethro, a longfaced man whom the flies got at.

'That was not the way your mission was put to me,' Saul said. 'Nevertheless, go back. Enoch will limp but Jethro will support him. You, Jethro, have had a face that would turn milk sour all through our journey. You, Esra, had better run.' And he and Seth turned their backs on the three and proceeded in good heart to Damascus.

Neither had ever visited the city before, but the priest Zerah had briefed Saul sketchily on its history and present condition. It was a very ancient city, having been the capital of the fierce Aramaean

119

kingdom until its overthrow by the Assyrians some eight centuries back. It had been part of the Roman province of Syria since Julius Caesar's time, but the Romans more or less left the rule of the city to the king of the Nabataean Arabs, whose realm stretched from the Gulf of Akaba to the outskirts of Damascus but who insisted, because of the large number of Nabataean nationals within the city walls, that he possessed full rights of dominion there. The Romans did not seriously contest this claim, but they showed a fresh polished eagle occasionally and demanded friendly tribute. This was sometimes the Roman way. Zerah had emphasized to Saul that it was by Godgiven right that he, Saul, was going to harry and torture the Nazarene heretics among the Damascene Jews, he being an agent of the high priest, but in truth it was by virtue of a treaty made by the Romans with the Jews in the ancient Hasmonean times that the high priest in Jerusalem could claim the right of extradition in respect of Palestinian breakers of the laws who had sought refuge in other Roman territories. The Romans, well over a century and a third thereof before the birth of Jesus, had given instructions to Ptolemy Euergetes II of Egypt and other allies in Asia to hand over to the jurisdiction of the high priest, Simon as he was then, all such offenders, and this privilege had been freshly ratified by Julius Caeeeeeeeeee

Seth was shocked nearly out of his skin by the high scream, the sudden eruption of froth at the mouth, the going down of Saul on to the dusty road at high noon. The falling sickness. He saw that the open mouth would soon close and the teeth bite off the blade of the tongue, so he fell to his knees and placed lengthwise in Saul's mouth the thin staff he had been carrying, so that Saul now had the ludicrous appearance of a dog struck with hydrophobia while fetching the thrown stick of his master. Saul tossed to and fro as in desperately uneasy sleep, but the ends of the staff set a limit to his rolling. Soon he was still, eyes closed, staff gripped in strong teeth, snoring and when not snoring groaning. *God help us* Seth kept muttering over and over in distress but also in a kind of relief, for Saul might take this when he came to as a sign from heaven that he had better intermit his persecutory activities, of which Seth had always had a qualified approval. He went too far too often, and there was, when you came to think of it, something a little unseemly about haling dissident Jews out of their beds in a strange city where one could claim no right of residence nor even possessed a minimal knowledge of topography, custom, or secular law. To Seth it was an embarrassing commission, but his admiration of the energy of Saul, let alone his devoutness, had led him to a vaguely reluctant acceptance of an invitation (which, if unaccepted, might soon have turned into an order) to help him haul back Jewish Nazarenes from Damascus to Jerusalem, there to consider their crime

120

in an already crammed camp of other wailing defectors.

When Saul came to he said nothing: all his attention was being given to an aftermath of the attack that he evidently could scarcely believe. His eyes were dead as stones. They rolled about as though sight had been snatched from him only to be playfully hidden in one quarter or another of the fierce noon sky, thence to be with ease retrieved. Seth said: 'Saul, Saul, how are you?' The staff fell from Saul's mouth.

'You heard? He has brought the night on me. Help me to rise.' On his feet he turned and turned clumsily as though, in some game, the withholder of vision were ever slyly at his back. 'You saw nothing? Heard nothing?'

'I heard you scream and saw you fall. It was an attack of the falling sickness.'

'There was thunder and lightning and a voice said *Sha'ul Sha'ul ma'att radephinni?*'

'It spoke Aramaic?'

'And in Aramaic it said something about a horse and a rider. God has the reins and he dug the spurs in. You must lead me, Seth.'

'Back to Jerusalem?'

'To Damascus.'

'Are you sure?'

'The voice said Damascus.'

'Well, then, if I tie this girdle of my robe to yours –' Seth did it with trembling hands. 'Perhaps the blindness will not last. Perhaps it's just part of the falling sickness.'

In total blackness Saul, led by the tautness of a cord, a dog on a leash, saw, as in a preternatural sunlight, the rooms and corridors of his own brain. It was the same brain as before, though the voice still echoed in it. The knowledge was the same, as also the banked ferocity, but the knowledge was presented as it were from a new angle of vision, which cast light and shadow not seen before. The ferocity was still in the service of destruction of great wrongs, but the wrongs had changed. He was everything he had ever been, except that now he must promote where formerly he had persecuted (the voice had thundered the accusation with a kind of glee), and yet he recognized now that the fury of persecution had always been the fury of belief. He had always known that no compromise was possible, and he had been the chief agent of Stephen's bloody witness against compromise. He was the same man that he had always been, and he recognized that the blindness was the bandage of some game in which he was turned about and about, finally emerging sighted as before to confront the world from a new angle. The same world and he who viewed it the same, but the light different. The God of the new faith wanted the zealot of the old but, with a flick of divine thumb and finger, the cause had been transformed. Yet in a way it remained the same cause, for between the old and the new there was no true division, one flowed into the other.

So, pulled like a placid beast, he was led through the southern gateway of the city. He heard its noise – wheels, the cries of vendors, the snort of a horse and the roar of a camel, girls giggling at the blind man, a bird twittering in a cage close to his right side. 'What is the city like?'

'Like any other city.'

'We must go to the house of Judas. On the Street that is Straight. You will have to ask where that is.'

'This one seems straight enough. He expects us?'

'A Jerusalem man. With lodgings for Jerusalem men.'

Saul stumbled. A cat, or other small beast, had darted between him and his leader. There was childish laughter as he stumbled. Seth seemed to shorten the cord, for Saul was aware of his bulk and warmth as much closer before him.

'Let's walk side by side,' Saul said, and he himself in a confident voice called to the darkness: 'The house of Judas on the Street that is Straight.' Judas the cobbler? someone wanted to know. He might well be a cobbler. And so soon Saul felt heat and noise exchanged for coolness and quiet, except for the distant hammering of, it could be, an apprentice making a sandal and the quiet introduction Seth was making to, it had to be, Judas of himself and his blind companion, the quietness being appropriate to a sickroom. But Saul was not sick, merely blind and very tired. He was led gently to, he could tell from the bounce of the voices against its walls, a small cell of a room and lowered to a hard pallet. There, foreknowing that sleep was a part of the act of transformation, he had a few seconds of drowsiness before being lowered into sleep's deep pit.

I can only guess at Saul's dreams, which must have been manifold and complex. Let us say that he saw the Temple, its main door blinding to his inner sight in the dawn, and that it dissolved gracefully, its angles softening to the arcs of the human form, and that the human form was that of a woman, naked and comely. The face was not clear, but the voluptuous contours of limbs and breasts aroused in him a lust which, though unsanctified by any legal contract of betrothal, seemed altogether wholesome, nay holy. He knew in his dream that his own body, formerly made tense by a zealous hatred, was relaxing to an acceptance of its functions, unbound by that fear of the body which had characterized his former comportment. The falling sickness, his dream told him, would not recur, and that disease had been the body's protest against rigidity of muscle and faith alike. What God had made was good. The human form was a miracle of workmanship and the whole of the human sensibility too precious an achievement to cast to the dust. God had accepted to be housed in it and return to the world of the pure spirit to will it to be modified by the nerves and blood. God had ascended to heaven as man, his human sensibility purified, true, but with that sensibility exalted to a new order that was not nameable under the terms of the ancient hierarchy. As man God had gone home, and man as man would follow him, not angelic, for angels were pure spirit, but in flesh transfigured to – a new word was needful. Sainthood?

The word love – *amor, agape, houb, ahavah, ai, upendo* – filled the fierce blue over the dissolved Temple, which now ran as liquid gold and ivory through the gutters of a transformed Jerusalem. Some of the languages in which the word was rendered he did not know, but meaning transcended the accidents of the tongue and teeth. Love was the proclamation of the unity of the divine creation, in which man was altogether at home, if only he could will it so. But, seen anew as a figure of God's cosmos, home in its humblest sense was holy and demanded a love that was more than mere comfortable habituation. The ants on the stone floor marching off with a fragment of bread smeared with honey, the slant of light from the casement and the motes in the shaft of sun, the old streetsinger with the cracked voice who passed his sister's house daily, the grey mouse that peered out from its cranny – all were part of the unity. Hearing the word one – *ena, wahid, echad* – he saw the gold and ivory that sang in the gutters flow back and the Temple fill the space that it had deserted, reconstituted in all its former beauty and strength. Nothing was to be destroyed or desecrated, since all was part of the unity of the Godhead. He heard various voices trying to call him, but their owners did not seem to know his name. Saul, he replied, but he was no longer Saul.

He woke and felt the raising of eyelids still heavy with sleep, but to his surprise and all too human disappointment he still could not see. He was aware of the groan of someone sitting by his bed, a man much disturbed. 'Seth?'

'Can you tell me yet?'

'You heard the voice?'

'I heard nothing save your cry when you fell.'

'It was *his* voice. He asked why I persecuted him. I will persecute no longer. You may go back to Jerusalem, Seth.'

'You mean – our work's over?'

'*My* work. You are your own man.'

'I stay with you. No more – of what we did to the Nazarenes?'

'I am to *become* a Nazarene. You may do what you wish.'

He heard a deep groan of pain and bewilderment.

'You're to join the Nazarenes – just like that?'

'I was fighting all along against what I had to be. I was trying to prove

123

to myself that the old way was fixed, immutable. Soon I must go back to Jerusalem – to put things right. Meanwhile – you remember the name of the chief of the Nazarenes here?'

'Ananias, the son of Ananias.'

'Find him. Bring him to me. Tell him of a change of heart.'

'He may not believe me.'

'He has to believe. I must put myself into his hands.'

'Very well. Will you take some food before you see him? You've fasted a long time.'

'How long have I been asleep?'

'Almost three days.'

Saul, as we must still call him, pondered on that. It had seemed no more than an hour. 'I can't eat,' he said. 'I must take water first.'

'I'll bring you water,' Seth's voice said eagerly.

'No. No. I meant in another sense.'

He was led, two hours later, to a stream called Mayim, which name, like the names of many streams and rivers, means no more than water. He could not see Ananias, the son of the Ananias dead of shame for his lying, but he could hear the gentle voice of a decent young man. He shuddered with the shock of his immersion. 'I baptize you, Saul, to the remission of your sins and in the plenitude of the grace of the Most High –'

'Saul no longer. Saul is the name of another man. Now dead.' He was becoming slowly aware of the remission of darkness as well as sin. He saw a dim vista of trees he could not yet name, a sheet of what must be water. He turned to take in the face of his baptizer, but he saw only a vague form with a raised arm, a generality called man. That generality would soon sharpen to the particular: soon he would be dealing with men. 'I am Paul,' he said.

So Paul, as we must now call him, sat later at the table of Ananias, eating with appetite. New bread, mutton somewhat overroasted, the tang of the wine of Damascus. A young woman, sister of one of the as yet nameless Nazarenes who sat at the table, poured him more of it. He felt the tingle of life in his groin as he saw the curve of her forearm, lightly flued. He said: 'I see now what should have been all too obvious but was not. What did Jesus say? "Because you are neither hot nor cold but are lukewarm I will vomit you out of my mouth." I was chosen for zeal, not for virtue.'

'And so,' Ananias said, 'you take over the work here?'

'Knowledge preceded hate. That same knowledge preceded love. But the knowledge is insufficient. May I learn more by teaching?' Seth sat at the table, but as far away from Paul as he could. His bewilderment still showed; he did not know at all what was best for him to do.

'Very often,' young Ananias said, 'the words come out of my mouth

124

unbidden. Only when I've spoken the words do I see what they mean. Yes, teach in our synagogue. We Nazarenes have to be cunning. Our cunning now lies in using you. Saul turned into Paul. Tell them your story.'

'Will they believe it?'

Some were all too willing to believe. Others would not have believed if that airless small synagogue had turned into the Damascus road, the roof into the vault filled with the thunder of divine Aramaic. Paul said to the crammed congregation, and this stench of sweat and garlic too had to be loved: 'I imprisoned, I whipped, I stoned, I put to death the followers of the Christ. Yet all the time, like yeast fermenting in the dark, the grace was working within me. Unwanted, unbidden. In a thunderflash the revelation came. The truth came not in a pale dawn when I was fuddled with sleep but in the effulgence of noonday –' The orthodox looked at each other, the pagan Godfearers listened. 'I was a horse disdainful of its rider, kicking against the spurs and the whip. Now I submit to the horseman –'

A heavy man stood, a leatherseller named Rechab. He said: 'You, Saul of Tarsus, known to all here and revered as the scourge of blasphemy and falsehood, were to come to Damascus to the joy of the faithful that the heretic and infidel might be seized and bound and taken before the chief priests of Jerusalem. But you are revealed as worthy yourself to be seized and judged and punished –'

'May not a man change?' Paul cried. 'Is it forbidden to the light to enter? What I was I was. What I am you see – a man reborn, refashioned, even renamed. In my flesh transfigured and in my soul irradiated I know that my redeemer lives and I know the name of my redeemer – Jesus the anointed, true Son of the Everlasting, slain and re-arisen. Believe as I believe –'

'Get out of Damascus,' Rechab countercried. 'You shame the faith. You defile the House of the Lord.'

'Oh, I will leave Damascus soon enough,' Paul said. 'The faith is strong enough here with no need of the buttress of words of mine. Do not fear, you faithless. My way lies where the word is still to come. I must tread strange roads and sail unknown seas.'

Transfigured within and yet the same, Saul or Paul showed no sign of transfiguration without. His hearers saw a young man growing untimely bald, his height below the ordinary, swarthy and with a sparse beard, the closeset dark brown eyes moist and luminous, though the luminosity might be as much from madness or disease as from inspiration. He dreamed of unity, but sometimes the body mocks the spirit. The frame was of one who seemed in prospect already chained and whipped, somewhat bowed, the movements of the body in speech as it were wincing from blows. It should not be so easy, the transformation from persecutor to evangelist; it should not be possible to snap away, with the hard thumb and fingers of a tentstitcher, so many martyrdoms. He had done much wrong, and the punishment had partly to be in the disguise of his own persecution for the teaching of the good. God is not mocked. Wrong is not negation of right but a positive quantum of great weight. Paul carried Saul on his back.

The Castra Praetoria lay to the northeast of the city, between the Via Nomentana and the Via Tiburtina, a structure of grim right angles with a great parade ground in its exact middle. Here one day the men and officers of the Guard, Marcus Julius Tranquillus with them, were forced to watch a display of gladiatorial skill. The taller and stronger of the two combatants was all too evidently holding back with the painted wooden sword he wielded. The other, shorter, fatter, clumsier, squealing with little breath as he thrust his own blunt toy at the guts of his opponent, did not observe the grace of permission with which this latter fell to the dust, clutching a makebelieve deathblow. When he fell the victor snapped his fingers at the uneasy referee, who at once handed over a real dagger that caught the noon sun. The squealer shoved the point in, tittering as the vanquished in surprise tried to get up, his two hands filling with the gush of red from his intestines. *'Plaudite, plaudite,'* Gaius Caligula cried. Those at the front did so with no enthusiasm; some at the back retched.

Gaius Caligula strutted in his little boots towards the gateway leading to the Via Tiburtina (Vetus), followed by staff, cushionbearers, sweetmeatcarriers. There was a shrine being erected not far from the guardroom by the gate, and the bust of the Emperor was already in its place, the cement affixing it not yet dry. The effigy, laurelled, held its modest eyes averted from the legend GAIUS CALIGULA DIVUS, but the mouth smirked. Gaius Caligula said:

'One god, one god. Well, the Jews have their one god and now so do we. Not an unwashed tribal deity but a lord of lands and oceans. Our holy mission is to bring this new belief in the single godhead to the barbarous places of the earth. Britain. Germany. Thrace. Other places.'

The tribune Cornelius Sabinus said: 'Palestine?' He had heard a loud contention between the Emperor and Herod Agrippa about this, the Emperor graciously yielding to the more serious view of monotheism, but the mad changed quickly. Gaius Caligula said:

'They already have their – You heard what I said. But still – logic, logic, there's a certain logic in it. All right, parade dismissed.' And he saluted his own bust before treading the purple carpet as far as his coach, a tasteless crusty gold affair. Some of the officers went off to bathe before the noon meal in the mess. The body of the dead Opsius was already being prepared for its obsequies. Nobody's appetite was much impaired; death was, after all, their playfellow. Marcus Julius Tranquillus stripped off his armour as though it were defiled and left it strewn for his servant to scour and polish. Then he hurried to the stables to the north of the barracks, there to saddle and mount the piebald mare Euphemia, who chewed the last of her meal and gave no whinny of greeting.

He rode west to the Viminal, turned on to the Vicus Patricius and with some difficulty trotted through the central streets of the city, which were thronged with noontime crowds. The Via Sacra. The Forum. The Palatine. He had right of entry into its grounds. Its slave quarters were thrust back to the northern limits of the estate, hidden by a grove of mixed planting – pine, poplar, cypress, chestnut. Marcus Julius found Sara waiting for him some yards away from the slave compound, in the territory of the masters where flowers grew. She was twisting a rose in nervous hands. Marcus Julius took her hands. The flower fell, depetalled. This situation was absurd, and both knew it. They spoke Greek; they were much on a level in Greek. Ruth? Ruth had died two days before, untended save by her sister, a nuisance, slave flesh no longer useful, give her to the compound incinerator alive. Sara had shown fire briefly respected, there is nothing like fire, and claimed burial in earth and the services of one of the rabbis of the city, the intoning of the *qaddish*. But slaves had no rights, much less in death. So Ruth had been buried like a dead dog. Sara was calm about it, with the calm of one who cannot bring with profit the rage of a known country to an unknown: rage here would be a useless language. But rage is liquid and calm is stone, and stone can break heads. Sara guarded her stone against a day, some day. 'I should not be here,' she said, meaning this zone a few footsteps beyond slave territory.

'Nor I. And I mean that in a wider sense. The madness grows worse.'

'You could go.'

'Go? Family tradition. Service to the Emperor. My father and my grandfather too. Their emperors were different. There were free men in those days.'

'How will it end?'

'It will end with someone sticking a dagger into the divine Gaius. As he stuck a dagger into Opsius this morning. No, don't ask me about that. It happens all the time.'

'Why are things as they are?'

'You need to ask why – when you saw what happened to your sister? Power divorced from reason. I call that madness. When I strike

127

there will be reason in the point of my dagger –'

'You?'

'Someone like me. It will be the army, certainly. He thinks the army loves him. Pathetic. The army may well be the striking arm of the people.'

'I don't understand these things. Rome isn't real.'

'The torture and death are real enough. So is the bankruptcy. Millions spent on temples and shrines to the divine Caligula. The people taxed to the limit. You've been sold into Roman madness. And we were always taught you Jews were the mad ones. You had to learn the virtues of Roman stability.'

'Oh, there's madness enough in Judaea. Agh – look who's coming.'

She referred to a middleaged woman once one of a family brought in chains from the Rhineland, gross, with greying strawy hair in plaits, in the blue gown of a slave overseer of slaves. This woman growled in bad Latin: 'You – whatever your name is – didn't you hear me call?'

'If you don't know my name, madam, how could I know you called?'

'There are a hundred fowls to pluck. Come on, get to it. You Jewesses are an idle lot.'

'You, whoever you are,' Marcus Julius said, 'are interrupting a private conversation.'

'Slaves don't have private conversations – whoever *you* are.'

'I am Marcus Julius Tranquillus, senior centurion of the Praetorian Guard. Learn your place, woman.'

'Don't,' Sara murmured in distress. 'I'll go.'

'And,' Marcus Julius said, 'mind your behaviour to this lady here. Yes, *lady*. *Slave* means nothing. Queens have been slaves before now.'

'It will do no good,' Sara said, going.

'Things will change. Things will have to change,' he said. 'I'll try to see you tomorrow.'

Tomorrow had a different meaning for Caleb, the brother of Sara, who was in training as a wrestler at the foot of the Palatine hill, in one of the gymnasia which fed the imperial games. 'Metellus,' he had said, mentioning also the name of that patrician sponsor whom he had impressed on the voyage hither. Strip off, he had been told by the games editor. Stripped off, he had been grinned at, though not unkindly, by all there present. *Nullum praeputium*. If you're Metellus, I'm the ghost of Julius Caesar. Let's see what you can do, lad. Aye, naked, balls all adangle. *Testibus ponderosis*, to quote Cicero. And Caleb had faced up to a lithe wiry oneeyed half-Greek half-Arab, whose body was already sleek with olive oil. Caleb knew that trick, an Arab one. He grabbed a towel and bade the man wipe himself unslippery and grippable. No, who was he, the Jew, to give orders? So

Metellus took him in his slipperiness by the long strangely ungreasy hair and flung him to the sand of the wrestling pit, rolling him over and over with his foot like fish for the frying in flour. Then, when the sandy Greek Arab rose protesting, Caleb showed some of his Palestinian holds. You'll do, lad. In time, that is. Style, grace are needed. You can't feed Roman audiences just anything. Come now, let the German giant knock you into shape. Or out of it. We all have to learn. This German giant was a Goliath with a wart in his brow like an embedded stone from a sling. He was strong but slow. His body was sown with sandy flue like a lawn, except for his wide chest, which was thick with hairs like three housebrooms. He tossed Caleb about like a mealsack and threw him down to grovel at his great flat German feet. Caleb sank his teeth in the left little toe and would have bitten it off had the giant not dealt him a nape chop, howling. The chop hurt Caleb sorely and lighted a rage which he knew must be subdued: rage was liquid, calm a stone. With the twin stones of his clenched fists Caleb leaped to smash the German's nose, whose thyrls sprouted hairferns like twin cornucopiae. The German went mad and flailed, shaking blood from his upper lip. Caleb leaped to gouge out his pale German eyes. Caleb was smashed in the jaw and felt bone seem, with surprise, to change its place. He took two seconds off, dancing away from the wind of new blows, to resmash his jaw back into position. He dove for the great mossy treetrunk of a right leg and held it in an embrace he refused to allow thwacks and fistthumps to dislodge. He would have him over, by the Lord God of Hosts he would. And did. He danced on the huge bare belly. Enough, lad, you've shown what you can do. Make reverence to your opponent. Move into barracks tomorrow.

Tomorrow in the other sense meant the day of reckoning, but with whom or what was not yet clear. Fire the palace. Arm the Jews. Hold the Emperor in an excruciating armlock and cry: Let my sisters go. One thing at a time. Tomorrow would come, though not tomorrow.

'Tomorrow?' Paul said. 'But he may be dead tomorrow. I say tonight, I say now.'

'I don't speak as a Nazarene,' Seth said, 'because I'm not a Nazarene, at least not yet. But I take it you still regard me as a friend.'

'Friend and brother. And you're concerned for my life. Well, I'm also concerned for it – I've much to do and I start late. But the cause isn't helped by cowardice.'

'The streets,' Ananias said, 'are always dangerous at night. It's madness to go out.'

'Who,' Paul asked, 'is the danger from? The Jews or the Arabs?'

'As far as you're concerned,' an old man sitting by the fire said, 'both.' Paul nodded: that seemed reasonable. He had been out of the city into Nabataean territory. He had even made a pilgrimage to Mount Horeb, thinking things out, but the God of Moses and Elijah had proffered no special signal, unless signally evil weather meant such: lightning had flashed about the summit like bad temper. The Nabataean Arabs he had preached at outside the town limits had understood his Aramaic but had responded rather viciously to his message about the Son of God. They wanted to be left alone with their bleating kids and cooking pots. They did not like baldheaded strangers dropping by and disturbing the decent monotonous day with new ideas. The ethnarch of the city, responsible to King Aretas, a most conservative man, was undoubtedly willing to side with the Damascene Jews when they shrieked against the turncoat blasphemer. The doctrine of love was highly subversive. Paul looked into the fire that Ananias's mother had lighted: it was a chill evening. In the fire, which spat like Nabataean Arabs and their camels, he saw no good auguries. He said:

'A fellow Nazarene lies dying because he was beaten by these thugs of the man Rechab. He needs my comfort. Am I to skulk here because of a few bravos with breadknives? Besides, I have a bodyguard. Have I not?' He smiled but got no answer from Seth, Ananias, and the burly but not notably brave twins Adbeel and Mibsam (if those were really their names). These last two were always biting their lips. Paul rose from the fire and said: 'I'm going.'

The house of the dying Nazarene lay not far from the city wall. The lane which skirted this wall was a narrow curve; labyrinthine alleys made twisted radii to it. The moon was near the full but had to fight with sluggish rainclouds. Paul strode, and his friends had to trot to reach him. They were in no position to guard him against daggers, being votaries of love and hence unarmed. But Seth, mercifully as yet unconverted, still had his knife. When three cutthroats sprang out of the shadows with foul cries that were oblique expressions of holiness, it was Seth who struck out. Paul saw Ananias, he was sure it was Ananias, go down gurgling. In the throat, true to their name. Paul stumbled against some stone steps to his right. At the top of them someone was swinging a lantern. By its light he saw Seth held struggling by two while the third swung his dagger back for a stroke in the belly. Then the lantern swung away. The one holding it called down: 'Paul! Paul! Here! Quick!' Paul mounted stumbling and found the steps led to an open door. A house whose walls were part of the wall of the city. 'In! Quick!' He heard a gasp below, which he assumed was Seth dying, and the feet of men running away, the lipbiting twins no doubt.

Paul panted and looked about him in the shadowy house. Its master,

130

whom his swinging lantern dramatized into red and gold facets with inky shadows, seemed to be a robust man in middle age. With his free hand he shot three screaming iron bolts. This house had been perhaps a sentinel's post in the days before Rome had pacified the region. Paul heard dagger hefts and ringed fists hammering at the tough wood of the bolted door. We want him, Saul the renegade, cut his throat, give him to God's good justice though summary. The householder yelled: 'Rebecca! Leah!' Two old women came from a dark hole of a room with one little lamp between them. The man came up to Paul and breathed on him the comfort of home and safety – goat's cheese and onions for supper. 'I'll have to open up to them. Come quick with me.' Leah and Rebecca went up to the door, nodded to each other, then began a loud gabbled curse on evil men who disturbed good women in their naked beds. Paul was led to an opening with shutters drawn back, beyond it the gloomy night, beneath it, the lantern showed, a precipice of stone wall, that of the city, with no toeholds. He shook his head. 'Wait,' the man said. He brought, yelling 'Wait wait' to the hammerers, a network bag of the kind called by the Greeks a *sagrane*, used for hoisting bales of hay. There was a rope already affixed to it. The two old women cursed heartily but with headshakes towards each other: this cursing was proving of little avail against godly persecutors. Paul got into the bag. 'Now,' the man said, 'easy does it.' And tugging on the rope while at the same time easing it free with the rhythmic giving of his hands, he watched Paul descend. Paul saw him high above, plying his tug and slack, and he waved when he felt earth bump benignly. The man could not see but he could feel the emptying of the bag. Paul got into the shadow of a buttress, listening. Where is he? Not here, your worships. Where do you have him hid? Very elusive these Nazarenes, slippery customers you might say. Grumbling and the slamming of a door, shouts and more grumbling and then silence on that peripheral lane. There was a whistled tune from above in the shape of a question. Paul whistled back the shape of an answer. Then he was left to the night and his tears of rage.

In the Hebrew manner these tears had to be deferred, along with the shouts to high heaven, until he had walked some way from the city. He rested, shivering also from the night wind, in the lee of some haystooks in a field. Cows lowed from their byre and an ass gave him a brief lesson in braying. He brayed an anger that no Nazarene could have taught him. What was the difference between the stoning of Stephen and the cutting into the flesh of Seth and Ananias? He had been responsible for both. He was the same man as always, a deathbringer, and the bringing of death had hardly begun. *Better not to have been born*, so clucked some far off fowls. Words of his own, spoken in bitterness during his studies under Gamaliel of the holy word. No man had ever been able to do right by that dyspeptic and capricious God. The smell of burned flesh pleased him, as well as the snipping of infant foreskins. He gave wholly irrelevant answers to the just plaints of suffering Job. How far had he changed under the humanizing influence of his blessed son? I have chosen you, Saulpaul, for your deathbringing rigour. Owls hooted, hunting for mice. The night world breathed the terror of pursuit. There was no unity, there was only a bitter division, and the division was the work of a creator who, secure in his own unity, was amused by the spectacle of pain, doubt, the law of eating and being eaten. The clouds had scudded off above the southwest road to Tyrus, leaving the moon full and veined like a bloodshot eye. The moon gave the flat fields and the hills beyond a mock blessing of silver.

Love. He would have given much to be in a woman's bed, she faceless as Eve and with Eve's body to comfort him, our first mother, our first mistress, her mind removed, impenetrable as God's, in the dreams of betrayal, her brain a maze of caprice. But the love of a woman's body was but God's cunning device to breed more creatures for suffering. He wished, of course, to be back in bed with his mother, comforted to sleep out of the bad dreams that had brought her to his cot, a mother's sleep ever quick to be disturbed by the cry, even the almost soundless whimper, of her child caught in the snares of nightmare, God's gift to the innocent. But he knew now he was totally alone with the burden of a very different and perhaps useless love. No woman's body would ever comfort him. That vision of acceptance had been the work of his nerves and muscles, announcing that the incubus of the falling sickness was at an end. Pain was henceforth to arrive from without. He was strong and girt and ready for teaching that all men have the falling sickness, a gift from Eve. He had a strange presentiment that it was against Eve that he must do battle. Eve stood silvered on that near hillock, her body sprouting breasts like monstrous warts. He dried his tears on the sleeve of his robe. Then, trying to fill his brain with love for the loveless world, he began to walk, staffless and scripless, the long road to Jerusalem.

In Caesarea early the previous day the first thing to be unladed from the merchant ship from Puteoli was a huge crate. Marcellus the procurator and the senior centurion Cornelius knew what it contained. They stood on the wharf and watched it dragged from the hold and set, with wholesome cursing from the *stipatores* or stevedores, beneath the hook of the crane which would lift it, swinging from its copper binding, to the shore. Marcellus said:

'What do I do, Cornelius?'

'Temporize,' Cornelius said. 'Delay. The true art of the ruler. On the other hand, if you want a general massacre – on both sides – obey the man, or the god as he thinks he is. I needn't point out to you the utter blasphemousness of this business.'

'Blasphemy,' Marcellus said. '*Blasphemos*. I hear this word all the time from the Jews. I don't understand it. It's not a Roman concept. I've had the wrong sort of education perhaps. If they believe in one god – well, why can't they have the image of this one god in their damned Temple?'

'Yes,' Cornelius said. 'A Roman education isn't much good here. Unless all Rome wants from them is money. You must often have considered the true meaning of the name of the rank you carry. A procurator is here to procure. So nothing else matters except their obols and shekels. They ought to be glad to pretend that the image of the deified Gaius Caligula is really the image of Jehovah. Bow down before it, worship. But God has no image. And God isn't a man.'

'You served here how long, Cornelius?'

'Long enough to learn about what they believe. Not long enough to learn to speak their language well enough to get their confidence. Not long enough to learn how to read their books. Now I've three years before retirement and a measure of spare time for getting down to it.'

'This, you know,' Marcellus said, 'is all wrong. You're not here to get their confidence or read their books. They're a colonized people. We're here to give orders.'

'They'd rather die than obey some of the Roman orders. Besides, it's laid down that their religion is inviolate.'

'Is what?'

'Mustn't be interfered with. Tell them that the Emperor is God and you're interfering with their religion.'

'But, damn it, they have to obey the Emperor.'

'They have to obey his taxgatherers. No more than that.'

Marcellus groaned. The vast crate was now on the quay. A slat of oak had loosened. There was a gleam of warm metal from within. He said: 'According to this new sect of the Jews God turned himself into a man. The slave called Chrestus.'

'A slight confusion there, procurator, as I've taken the liberty of mentioning before. Chrestus is, I grant you, a common enough name for a slave. What does it mean? Cheerful, helpful, useful. But the name you mean is Christus. This man was not a slave but a son of the royal House of David. If you have in mind pretending that this statue of the Emperor is really a statue of Christus, then you're in terrible trouble from both sides. You won't get it into the Temple. You won't get any image into the Temple. You're in a cleft stick. With respect, of course.'

The dawn wind sighed and Marcellus sighed with it. 'I must stop seeking information from you, Cornelius. You always give me too much. But I accept your advice. The divine Caligula must go into temporary storage. We make some excuse when or if that senatorial visit takes place. Or if the powers that be in Syria become inquisitive. The effigy badly cast or defaced by an angry mob, something of the kind. Our best workmen busy repairing it. We have enough trouble with these damned Jews without seeking more.'

But, as is too well known, good intentions, and this cunctatorial policy of the procurator might be regarded as good, are often foiled by the very people for whom they are implemented. It was in Rome that Judaea was put into peril of revolt. Philo Judaeus, leader of the Jewish community, demanded and obtained an interview with the Emperor himself. He wished to register a protest. He came to the gardens of the Palatine with a deputation of five of his race and faith, good Romans though heavily bearded and capped and robed in the style of their people. Gaius Caligula lounged in a garden chair, stroking the limbs of a Greek boy, taking wine but not offering it, half listening under the cypresses as Philo said:

'The concept of a single God – not of a pantheon – Jupiter, Saturn and the rest –' Philo looked at the pantheon of stone figures that lined a garden walk – bodies varying in musculature and implements of pseudodivine office, thunderbolt, trident, wings on heels, but all topped with the same smirking head. 'Well, Caesar – it has long been accepted by the Roman state that the Jewish concept is to receive the respect of the occupying power –'

'Only the Emperor,' the Emperor said, 'exacts respect. Your faith, which I know something about since it is the faith of my old friend Herod Agrippa, is certainly tolerated, and that should be enough. It is bizarre, exotic, amusing. It adds its own colour to the gorgeous tapestry of our Empire. It has even taught something to our Empire – this very notion of one god you talk of. The Emperor is this god, this god is the Emperor. What could be more satisfying?'

'It is not very satisfying to the Jews,' Philo said. 'God to us is a spirit – unborn, undying. Even the Emperor has to die.'

Gaius Caligula squeezed the thigh of the Greek boy and made him squeal. 'You will not speak to me of death, do you hear? A god is by definition immortal.'

'I beg Caesar's pardon,' Philo said. 'Let me confine the petition to this. Do not, we beg, for the sake of the tranquillity of your Palestinian possessions, insist that your statue be installed in the holy Temple of Solomon which is in Jerusalem.'

'It has already been installed. To the great satisfaction of the Jewish people. At least I hear no complaints. Now they can see their God. They have a solidity to bow down to.'

'I would be shaming the faith of our fathers if I said: yes, Caesar,

134

that is so. But it is not so. Your procurator Marcellus appears to be a man of sense and a credit to Caesar's capacity for choosing good administrators –'

'I did not choose him. The Emperor Tiberius chose him. I know nothing of him. Has he,' and he leaned forward gaping, 'has he disobeyed our orders?'

'Letters from Jerusalem inform our community here that he has very wisely delayed his obedience. But now orders from your governor in Syria force him into a situation of immediate compliance. I need not, I hope, stress the –'

But Gaius Caligula was on his feet, stamping with his little boots. He frowned viciously at Torquatus and Strabo, two state officers in attendance. 'Why,' he yelled, 'have I not been told of this? Why are things kept from me?' They could not answer. Philo said:

'To conclude, your procurator Marcellus has been forced to order that your statue – We beg of you to have the order rescinded – It is in the interests of peace and tranquillity –' Gaius Caligula frothed and danced, crying:

'Get out of here, you unwashed Jews. I shall be rid of your oh so friendly procurator. I shall have him recalled and punished. You shall have his head in your synagogue here to croon over, your one Roman friend, alas dead. You've always wanted a Jewish king over Jewry, have you not, eh? Well, you shall have King Herod Agrippa, a real friend of Rome. He will see that my image is installed. He will see that it is worshipped according to the sacred imperial rites. Take your unwashed bodies out of here.'

'With respect, Caesar,' Philo said calmly, 'it is you who are the unwashed people. You are also uncircumcised. It is the mission of the Jews to cleanse the world. You propose making it even more dirty. Much blood is going to flow, believe me –' But the Emperor got his whip to them. They padded down a walk of symmetrical arbutus with such dignity as speed would permit. Then the Emperor, dressed in a kirtle of skyblue embroidered with yellow crocuses which showed much of his hairless thighs, stormed at Torquatus and Strabo. Garotting, crucifixion, confiscation. They nodded sagely; they had heard such things before.

'Confiscation of goods,' Strabo eventually said. 'I am glad that Caesar has raised the matter. Whatever you wish to be done with the Jews, your other proposal is unacceptable.'

'What other proposal? What is unacceptable? To whom unacceptable? If a thing is acceptable to Caesar that is enough.'

'With respect,' Strabo said, 'it is against all our traditions to have Roman patricians arbitrarily executed in order that their estates may be confiscated.'

135

'It won't be arbitrary,' the Emperor said, calmer now, 'if you fasten crimes on to them. I need money. I intend to have money.'

'There are commodities,' Torquatus said, 'that may be sold at auction. Being of imperial provenance they will fetch good prices.'

'I,' the Emperor cried, 'selling his own goods and chattels?'

'Things Caesar has but does not use and will not miss,' Strabo said. 'There is, for example, the older of the golden chariots. The five hundred acres near Neapolis. The imperial household has more slaves than it can use.'

'Go away,' Gaius Caligula said. 'Go away. Your faces make me sick. A god selling off what he has by divine right. Some of your notions are of a headswimming lunacy.' And then he screamed: 'Damned Jews. You, Strabo, take ship to Palestine. See that that order is obeyed.'

'With respect, Caesar –'

'With respect respect respect. That's all I hear, that's what I never see. Am I the Emperor or am I not?'

For the moment, Torquatus said to himself.

Paul arrived hooded in Jerusalem. He also arrived at nightfall. But Joseph Barnabas recognized his gait. A rumour had come through from Damascus very hard to credit. But Saul was alone and not hooding himself against mere pacific Nazarenes. Joseph Barnabas watched him make for the street where the former house of Matthias lay. He took the chance and hailed him.

'Saul!' Saul turned.

'Joseph Barnabas? Yes. Has news come from Damascus?'

'News not easy to believe.'

'Nevertheless you must believe it. Will you accompany me to the brethren? You see me alone. I'm also unarmed.'

'A man,' Barnabas said, 'doesn't change from a hater of the faith to a preacher of the faith. Not like that, not overnight.'

'It was much less than overnight, Joseph Barnabas. Your faith tells you to accept miracles, after all. You see a man changed. Even my name is changed.'

'We heard that too.'

There were only Peter, Thomas and the two Jameses at home. The house was as unclean as it always had been since the Nazarene appropriation. The apostles sat around their dining table, on which a lamp sat spluttering like a poor substitute for dinner. They eyed Paul warily. Peter said:

'What I don't understand is this – if you're so frightened of arrest and retribution and the rest of it, why did you come back to Jerusalem? Damn it, man, it's right into the arms of your killers –'

'I came back for instructions.'

'Well,' Thomas said, 'that's honest, anyway. Tell the chief priest ye're pretending to be a Nazarene and what do I do now your holiness. Oh, very clever.'

'Don't be a fool, Thomas,' Peter said. 'He means instructions from us.'

'A swift change, I know,' Paul said. 'I'm still an instrument. But now for other hands. What do you wish me to do?' Thomas muttered something about a man that turns his coat once will turn it twice.

'Quiet, Thomas,' Peter said. 'What I say to you, Saul –'

'Paul.'

'– Is to get away from here. Think things over.'

'I've thought things over. Or shall I say it was done for me?'

'You're no use dead and it's dead you'll be if you stay. Go back home. You'll be safe there.'

'Home? Tarsus?'

'Get back to your father and your mother or whatever you have and your books and your tentmaking. Convert a little. Try it out.'

'I wish to try it out in Judaea. Not necessarily here in the city. But it's a kind of justice, preaching to the Greek Jews – that's what I have in mind.' His voice faltered. 'Talking of Greek Jews –'

'As soon as you'd left,' James the son of Zebedee said, 'they let your suffering lot out of the place where you'd had them put. It's been pretty quiet since you left. But if you start preaching here they'll chop you down and then bethink themselves of the rest of us. We've had enough trouble,' he added in his innocence.

'The Lord,' Paul said, 'told me what to do. He said nothing about running home to avoid persecution. I've a lot to make up for. I must take my chance.'

'Look,' Peter said, 'you come here all humble saying you want instructions. And then you start on about the Lord telling you what to do. The Lord told you nothing. You've never seen the Lord. *We* have. And the Lord was pretty clear about everything being in our hands. So will you be told by me or will you not?'

'What he could try,' James the Little said, 'is that concentration of Greeks down in Bethany. It's a powerful weapon, you see, the big whip becoming one of the faithful. It's a bit of a waste, sending him off home to think things over.'

'I've thought things over,' Paul said once more.

'Go on then,' Peter said resignedly. 'Stick to the fringe of the city. But as soon as they break your head with a stone come back here for your passage money. Barnabas and Thomas had better go with you. See how you get on. We don't just let anyone preach the word, you

137

know. You can't just suddenly know it all, just like that, with a twist of the wrist.'

'Leave me out,' Thomas said. 'I'm too old for yon stonethrowing.'

Marcus Julius Tranquillus breathed northern sea air, looking out in a chill dawn across bilious green waters to a ghost of white cliffs. He had a woollen cloak wrapped about him. He admired the steam of his breathing and that of his companion on guard, Rufus Calvus, who was neither bald nor haired reddish brown. 'Britannia Britannia Britannia,' Marcus Julius sang, stamping on the shingle near the long line of landing craft. 'What do the natives call it?'

'There's no one name. Each tribe has its own little region which it thinks to be the big world.'

'And now the real big world rushes in. The Roman eagle spreads its wings –' There was no need to complete the pleasantry, known, in many languages, all over the Empire. Rufus Calvus laughed guiltily. He said:

'This is known as building an empire. Ultima Thule. The edge of the world. And what do we bring?'

'Law. Order. Roads. Temples. For worship of the divine Caligula. A more pertinent question is: what do we take back?'

'Slaves. Tribute. Gold. Silver. To replenish,' Rufus Calvus spoke the words in a mockery of the senatorial rhetorical manner, 'depleted ah coffers. Britannia as a cure for imperial poverty.' A bucina brayed. There was soon a whole ringing consort of bucinae all over the camp that lay behind them. 'We'd better take post.'

Vast forces for the invasion. The camp sprawled far. Troops put on breastplates round fires that had been kept alight all night long, shivering. Piled shields and pila clashed and squeaked. Drums rolled. Tuba and bucina groaned in antiphony. Soldiers lined up by companies under barking under officers. Horses were dragged whinnying towards their sea transportation. They smelled cold and did not like it. There was a swish of swords removed for inspection and then sheathed. A forest of spears arose from the dunes. Officers bawled, faces red raw with the morning's razor. Tents were struck and loaded on to carts that were wheeled towards the boats. Waves crashed, gulls wailed. The tribune Cornelius Sabinus inspected in preparation for the imperial inspection. Trumpets. From his tent yawning came Gaius Caligula, queazy from the night's wine. He walked pompously, staff lined up behind him, to the inspection of the legions, to which had been attached a segment of the Praetorian Guard. The inspection was long, shivering, thorough. The Emperor complained bitterly of the cold, an affront to his divinity. The sun was well up by the time he was ready to be helped on to a cart in order to address the assembly. He addressed the assembly with due solemnity, though not well heard in the rear ranks:

'Soldiers of the Empire. Your brave hearts and fine bodies have come to the northern shore of our province of Gaul. From here you will embark and sail to the shores of Britannia. Britannia will fall to us and be ours. This is an exceptionally solemn occasion. The last province of the Roman Empire awaits our acquisition. But first – there is an important thing to do. You see these shells spread all along the shore as far as eye can reach? They are Roman property. Hence they must go back to Rome. Gather them.'

No one there could believe what he had heard. The Emperor repeated pettishly:

'Gather them. Gather them. Quickly. Put down your arms and gather them.'

Cornelius Sabinus's voice was near inaudible.

'All of them, Caesar?'

'Gather them. *Gather them.*'

Incredulous, trembling, the great disciplined force was reduced to a horde of children gathering seashells on the shore.

'Where – where shall they put them, Caesar?'

'Let them gather them in their helmets, which might have been made for the gathering of shells. And then empty their helmets into those transport wagons.'

'This will do it. This,' panted Marcus Julius faintly, gathering shells.

'What?' whitefaced Rufus Calvus asked.

'He can't survive it. The humiliation of the army. The shame of it. He can't he can't –' Gathering shells. All along the coast. Shells being gathered. The dry rustle of the shellfish market in Neapolis multiplied abominably. Gaius Caligula examined a single shell with minute attention, saying:

'Beautifully made, aren't they? Exquisite workmanship. That old god, whoever he was, had remarkable creative gifts. But the new god gets the benefit of them. That's as it should be.'

The knuckles of Cornelius Sabinus whitened and whitened as he gripped and gripped the hilt of his sword.

But Gaius Caligula was still a god. His effigy was being manhandled out of one of the dock warehouses, ready for dragging to Jerusalem, while Paul was stepping aboard the ship that would carry him to Tarsus in Cilicia. His head had, true to Peter's prophecy, been split, he had bruises on his jaw, and he limped. It was Peter and Thomas who had accompanied him to Caesarea, safe for the Nazarenizing mission

in the hands of Philip, this not being too far beyond Joppa, whither
Simon Peter had been summoned by another Simon, a tanner, who
had found some as yet undisclosed aspect of his evangelical work
beyond him. The wind already filled the sails and the tide was flowing.
Peter and Thomas saw the ship glide with pagan grace into the roads.
Peter said:

'I ought not to say this perhaps, but I say it.'

'Ye mean thank God we're done with him?'

'We ought not to think it let alone say it.' He took in some lungfuls of
sea air as though he would not again have the opportunity, though
Joppa was on the coast. 'He's a difficult sort of a man. Has his own
ideas too. Best to leave him in Tarsus, see what he can do there. I
certainly wouldn't want him back in Jerusalem.'

'Ye know what I think's the matter with him? He thinks too much.'

'Well, it's the place he comes from. I've heard tell plenty about
Tarsus. Big colleges there, people go there to study. And have done so
for a thousand years, so they tell me. He's read a lot of books and now
he'll have the time to read a lot more. We've not had much book-
ishness so far.'

'There was –' Thomas did not like to mention the name: it tasted
bad in his mouth. 'You know who I mean.'

'Yes yes, look where his booklearning got him.' Peter thought a
space. 'Poor lad, though. Too innocent to live.'

'So he died,' Thomas said brutally. 'Are we to go and call on the
Greek lad Philip?'

Paul paced the deck, his feet flat to its rolling, and savoured the
aches in his body. He had been punished, though not yet enough. He
foretasted the next punishment. For my sake a man must leave his
father and his mother. So be it. The neat house of a man grown
prosperous on sailcloth would be sullied by the very presence of the
sole son of the house. There had always been a bust of the Emperor set
on a voluted pedestal. Now it would be the bust of a god, perhaps with
a votive lamp before it. Don't talk to me of heresy, father. You've
joined the Roman pagans. You have your god in the sittingroom. And
his father blustering: That is no more than respect. I remain a good Jew
and a good Roman. And I, sir. Except that I accept the Jewish Messiah
and have too much respect for Roman order to wish to see it collapse
under a madman. *You speak thus of the Emperor?* I acknowledge only
one master now, father. I abjure the world's madness, whether of
Gaius Caligula or the man who was Saul of Tarsus.

Painful, painful. His mother, dressed as a Roman matron, crying:
To abandon your own name. The name you answered to when dinner
was ready or it was time for bed. Oh, Saul, Saul – *Sha'ul Sha'ul ma
'att radephinni?* (You always had to persecute someone.) I will not

140

believe it, will not, moans his father. You must, father. And you must be reconciled to it. Things change. History ordained it. An empire broken from within, the faith torn by its contradictions. *Double heresy, double*. Don't talk to me of heresy, father.

You must know there is no room for you here. *Paul*, as you now call yourself. *I expected that*. Disinherited and disowned. Your grandfather served Rome when Julius Caesar was in Egypt. I served the faith of our race from the very first day when I could recite the verses of the Torah. A good Jew and a good Roman gets his reward. And you will get yours some day perhaps soon – the headman's axe or the stones of the outraged faithful or the shame of the cross. *Not shame, father. Don't speak of shame*. And his mother: *Sha'ul, Sha'ul, lama sabachthani?*

He foresaw all. His homecoming and homeleaving for ever would be mere ritual. Well, Tarsus was as much his city as his father's. He would go to old Israel (entitled to the name, he would say, having been given the name of Jacob) who had taught him the tentmaker's trade. He would sit in the sun outside the shop and wrestle not with God but with tough canvas and bodkin. A man with a trade was a free man. He would not disrupt the gatherings at his father's synagogue. Filial piety was a vice with sharp claws. It would be, he thought, a matter of waiting. He could wait, stitching in the sun. He was, though bald, still young.

It is not, since Paul and he will some day be in close contact, as inapposite as it would appear to set down now the filioparental dialogue of Marcus Julius Tranquillus's imagining in the bath or on his hard military bed or, on the square of the barracks, awaiting a tribunal inspection. The sittingroom of a neat little house on the Janiculum, a bust of the Emperor on a voluted column, his father saying: 'This will be the end of your career. A career, I may remind you, that the family has followed since the days of the republic. It was always our intention that you marry into the family of Callidus Marcellus, a family with a fine tradition of loyalty to the Roman state. I have always hoped that you would beget sons who would carry on the tradition our families share.'

'A tradition, if I may say this, father, of trimming to the wind. Policy rather than conviction.'

'That is unseemly.'

'Oh, the world is changing, father. The world is breaking down in order that it may be remade. I wish to be involved in the remaking.'

'By marrying a Jewish girl,' his mother says, her face a well-made mask of suffering, 'a *slave*?'

'Slavery, dear mother, is a status decreed by tyranny, not by blood or lack of talent. Our civil service is in the hands of slaves, or freedmen with the ringpiercing of their ears hard to hide even by the most effeminate growing of the hair. If a girl of good Palestinian family is, thanks to the vindictiveness of a Roman official, turned into a slave, she is not by that act rendered contemptible. It is the Roman system that is made contemptible.'

'Strange words,' his father says, 'for a son of Rome.'

'Rome is not what it was. God knows when it will be what it was again.'

'What is this word *God*? Have you been learning something from the Jews?'

'The man who calls himself God is selling part of his household. The divine Caligula is heavily in debt and taxes can no more come to his rescue. I wish to buy a wellborn Jewish lady out of slavery. Have we the money to do it?'

'We? We? This is your own affair, son, not mine or your mother's.'

'There is such a thing as my patrimony.'

'When I'm dead, not before. And it doesn't amount to much. A professional soldier, as you're beginning to learn, doesn't become rich easily.'

Raising money to buy a bride. Talk about the world's madness. It would be necessary to talk quietly with the *tribunus militum* who, it seemed, was well enough disposed. For had not Gaius Caligula emptied whole strongboxes into the regimental funds at the time of his accession, one of his acts of sanity? Was not the freeing of an imperial chattel whose sister had been flogged to death by her demented master a legitimate employment of funds that were no longer a pledge of loyalty? Let his dirty money go back to him. Marcus Julius Tranquillus, stiff on parade or relaxed in the bath, saw hope in that sentimentality which the tough military carapace often hid. The senior centurion is in love with a slave. Read your Lucretius: Venus strikes where she will. Empty the coffers to buy him his bride. Talk about the world's madness.

Peter and Thomas rested outside a seaside inn in Joppa or Jeppa or Jeffa or Jaffa, the name was not at all clear when you heard the natives utter it. Thomas slipped off his sandals and flexed his stiff old toes in the sea's breeze. 'I'm getting too old for this foot travel,' he said. 'My bones creak.'

'You needn't have come,' Peter said. 'There's work enough back home.'

'Home. Aye, Jerusalem. I've a mind sometime to go back to real home. Across the big lake. Ye remember when we met there?'

'It's not so long ago, Thomas.' The serving girl brought cups, a jug of

142

wine and a small pitcher of water. Peter sadly watched her pert departing buttocks.

'There I was working in this garden for this family, and then the poor girl goes into a decline and the whole world thinks she's dead and then you come along, with *him*.'

'*Talitha cumi*,' Peter remembered. 'Rise up, girl. And by God she did. And the big meal afterwards, with you helping to wait on. We were always hungry in those days.'

'Still are. Not that an old man needs much. Good air is what I need and this is good sea air. They're not too bad of people either.'

'Simon's a good man, but he expects too much.' Peter looked into the winejug with a kind of sacerdotal concentration, as though inspecting entrails for auguries. His fingertip went in and brought out a fly. He dried the fly in the sun and then watched it wing off shakily into the blue sea air. The waves breathed like tired runners. 'He thinks he ought to be able to work miracles.'

'As I keep on saying,' Thomas said, 'it depends what ye mean by a miracle. It's the other business that's more worrying, especially after Philip's story about the big black without ballocks.'

'He can't do it,' Peter said. 'There's no argument about it. If the big black went off thinking he was saved, well, let him have his satisfaction till the day he gets disappointed. Because he will when the word gets through to him on his next Jerusalem trip. If I'm alive I'll watch out for him. A big black with a high voice shouldn't be easy to miss. That was Philip's one and only mistake. But friend Simon has been pouring whole gallons of good blessed water on Gentiles, and it won't do. There was never anything said about Gentiles. Nazarenes eating pork in their foreskins. No, it won't do. And this other thing won't do either, but we have to give them what comfort they expect.'

'How long has the body been kept there?'

'Too long, I'd say. But these women swear it's still – you know, in what they call a state of purification.'

'Meaning the opposite of putrefaction.'

'I may have heard wrong.' Peter took a good draught of wine and water, belched and said: 'Better.'

'Not stinking, to put it blunt and honest. More than can be said of Simon. He stinks of his trade. So does his house.'

'Tanning's a smelly trade,' Peter said. 'It's done with camel dung, did you know that?'

'Something I don't want to know. Well, there's plenty of camel dung around here. Look at that big roaring brute. I never cared much for camels. Well, we'd best get there and see if the stink's started. It ought to be a decent sort of ladylike stink.' They got up wearily and went off leaning on their staffs through a throng of fruit stalls and loud chaffering. Too much, I don't pay that much down the road there. Lady, I'm losing money charging you what I do. Outside the gate of a house with closed shutters two women in black were waiting for them. They went into darkness but no smell of putrefaction. There were a lot of lilies about in pots. Two more ladies in black were sitting drinking some kind of hot herbal decoction. Stay seated, ladies.

'Let's have that name again,' Peter said.

'Dorcas, Dorcas.'

'Or Tabitha.'

'Aye,' Thomas said. 'Both names mean that sort of animal that runs fast.'

'Gazelle.'

'Gazelle, aye. Run off to the next world, has she?'

This callousness started them all off weeping. One woman wept while sipping her brew.

'Discretion, Thomas,' Peter said. 'Where is the er –?' They led the two of them up a short flight of steps to a bedroom. The shutters were closed but the scent of nard was overpowering. Also (Thomas sniffed cautiously) camphor. A candle at her head and one at her feet. A quite young girl, a gazelle no longer footfleet, pretty too, not unlike that daughter of what was his name, Jairus.

'Aye, she seems dead all right, but ye can never tell.'

'What were his words? Yes, *Talitha cumi.*'

'And now ye have to say *Tabitha cumi*. Ye have to do what he did, Peter. He said we had to.'

'That's not for us.'

'Sometimes nature plays tricks like that Simon Magus did. *Seems* isn't the same as *is.*'

'I don't like it,' Peter said. 'But there's no harm in trying. *Tabitha cumi*. Rise up, girl.'

There was no response from the girl's body. 'It's a lot to expect,' Thomas said.

'Too much. He was him. We're just us.'

But Thomas, his eyes widening, put his hand on Peter's sleeve. He muttered something like a prayer that what seemed to be happening should not happen. Both looked with mouths stupidly opening at a mouth gently opening to let out what seemed a small store of breath kept shut in there. One of the candleflames flapped. That old breath once let out, new breath possessed the body, its rhythm as feeble as in a body about to die. Both men dreaded the opening of the eyes, with their message of light from a world nobody wanted to visit if he could help it. So falling over each other they got out of that room. Having fallen downstairs, Peter said to the women: 'You can go up there now.' The herb decoctions were spilt on the worn Greek carpet with its key pattern. Peter now saw for the first time a gaudy bird in a cage that looked at him, head cocked, as though from another world. A flight of heavy black birds went up those stairs with black wings flapping. In a minute, in the manner of women, they would start wailing joy that sounded like grief. The two men got out of that house with the speed of robbers.

At that moment the centurion Cornelius was holding a meeting of the senior under officers of his century. It was in his own house overlooking the bay of Caesarea. His wife was singing in the kitchen and his small son dribbled on to a toy centurion the garrison carpenter had kindly carved for him. 'Look, lads,' Cornelius was saying, 'the situation's not clear. No situation ever is these days as far as Rome's concerned. We stay but he goes.'

'No procurator?' said the decurion Fidelis. 'Ever again? Who are we responsible to?'

'You're responsible to me for the moment. And it looks as if I'm directly responsible to the man in Syria, Lippius.'

'Caius Lippius,' young Junius Rusticus said, a boy given to needless pedantry.

'But we also have to take orders from this Herod Agrippa who's on his way from Galilee. The King of Palestine, as he calls himself. Sort that out if you can.'

'So we get moved to Jerusalem?' Fidelis said.

'We'll be needed more in Jerusalem than in Caesarea,' Cornelius said. 'Especially if he has that statue moved in.'

'I can't see that,' the decurion Androgeus said, a half Greek and very oliveskinned, one who was on his third decurionate after two demotions for brawling. 'I can't see how a Jew can do that. Even if he calls himself like a king. The other Jews will cut his bleeding gorge for him,' proleptically. Cornelius said:

'It seems to be up to the Roman army to see that they don't. Meaning us. And the lads from Syria, a mean lot. The god Caligula, eh? For Jews and Romans alike. I don't think I can stand much more,' he said, singing in unconscious unison with another centurion many miles away, 'of the world's madness.' He went to his little balcony and looked out on the sea and the massed shipping. All that seemed sane enough. Then he turned and surveyed the room, not seeing his men. He was in his home, such as it was. Full of ornaments picked up in a variety of foreign bazaars, most of them cheap except for that bronze buffalo, all of them probably tasteless. He said: 'You know where sanity lies, don't you?'

'You've said something about it, centurion,' Junius Rusticus said.

'We need somebody to talk to us,' Cornelius said, eyes down. 'The man I have in mind was here a couple of days ago. The Greek man in the chandler's store, he said he'd gone off to Joppa or Jeffa, whatever they call it. He's a fisherman, this man Peter I mean. He's in charge. They say he's done strange things. A humble man for humble men, just the same.'

'Strange?' Fidelis said.

'Oh, you know what I mean. I don't know what word to use. Even words are losing their meaning in these days of the world's madness. Ask for the man Peter in Jappa or Juffa. Everybody's bound to know where he is. You, Rusticus and Androgeus, you two can volunteer.'

Where Peter was now was on the roof of his host Simon the tanner. He had got up there for two reasons. One was that the fumes of dinner cooking below could not easily overcome the stench of the trade that was carried on in the sheds at the back of the house. A hunk of elderly mutton was being turned on a spit by an elderly woman who turned the handle grousing, Simon the tanner's mother. You'll have to wait for it, she had said ungraciously. Time and tide wait for no man, irrelevantly. The other reason for being on the roof was to get away from the crowd that had heard about the sudden recovery of the gazelle girl, one who had been orphaned early and spent most of her very adequate inheritance on garments for the poor. A lot of these garmented poor were down there, exhibiting running sores and withered limbs and demanding to be healed by faith, not that many of them had any. There was a staircase leading to the roof and a door at its head that he, Peter, had bolted. He lay exhausted with the strain of feeling under a whitish canvas canopy that kept the sun off. His only company was cauldrons of sea water that Simon used, along with camel dung, in his unwholesome trade. There was a fist knock on this door.

'Who is it?'

'Me, Thomas. Your presence, sir, is requested for further miracles.'

'Tell them it's a blasphemy. Tell them to pray. Tell them I'm nothing. You too.'

'Aye, I know well I'm nothing. What I will tell them is that ye require a nap before your dinner and they'd best be away.'

'I need the dinner before the nap. You can bring it up here.'

'Ye're right, aye. The stench down here is no good for the appetite. But it's no ready as yet.'

Peter, not needing the nap, nevertheless dozed off. He had a dream almost immediately, and it was a dream that told him how hungry he was. The light of the dream was the light of this rooftop, and it shone on the right number of sea water cauldrons, or perhaps there was one fewer, as well as the two or three withered plants in pots that were there. A cat came on to the roof to stare at Peter and then, spotting an alighting sparrow, it lightninged after it and out of the dream. The whitish canvas canopy did not stay where it was. It flew off from over Peter's head and stretched itself very taut in the sky about nine feet in front of him. It began to fill up with the materials of one of these Roman banquets he had heard about. Haunches of deer, a whole roasted infant camel, writhing lobsters, crabs fighting each other though steaming from the pot, sucking pigs, pigmeat sausages (this he knew though his eyes could not penetrate their skins), a kid seethed in bubbling milk undoubtedly its mother's. Milk, of goat or cow, in crocks nudging the roast pork. In the dream all this was no abomination. A voice that filled the four corners of the world cried that it was all good. 'Eat, eat. Nothing is forbidden. All is from God.' Peter heard himself say: *I can't. It's unclean*. And the voice boomed: 'God has cleaned it. Eat.' Peter woke. The awning was back where it had been. He heard Thomas fisting the door, calling: 'Ye said ye wanted to eat. Eat.' Peter stumbled to the bolts and drew them. Thomas had a wooden tray with steaming meat on it, bread, a jug. Peter blearily said:

'Pig flesh. Washed down with goat's milk.'

'Urrrgh. Ye've been having a bad dream.'

'We can eat anything, Thomas. He just said so. We can be like the Gentiles.'

'Get yourself properly awake, man, then eat your dinner. All good *kasher* provender. Milk and roast pig. The devil's been at ye. Urrrgh.'

It was while Peter was tearing into the roast mutton that two men of the Italian *speira* arrived at Simon the tanner's house on horseback. 'You want *who*?' Simon's old mother asked. 'What's he done wrong, then?' No wrong. He's needed in Caesarea. 'Somebody dying?' You could say that somebody's dying for something.

Peter sat at the rear of Rusticus and Thomas at the rear of Androgeus. They had never before been on horseback. It was a jolting experience that did little good to their dinners. They had to hang on to the belts of the two riders and grip the hot flanks of the mounts with their thighs. Too many new things happening. Thomas yelled against the wind: 'It's no done. To enter the house of the uncircumcised. *He* never did it. It's again the law.'

'Which law? The law that's been persecuting us?'

'We're Jews, man. The followers are still Jews. We keep the law.'

'My dream broke the law. This voice from heaven broke the law about what to eat and what not to eat.'

'And ye'd take pig flesh? Lobsters out of the sea?'

'I know what the dream meant. If I hadn't been such a fool I'd have known when the new law began. When Philip baptized the black man –'

'He'd no right to. Not only an uncircumcised one but a eunuch too. For all we know, a damned cannibal.'

147

'Your brain creaks like your joints,' Peter yelled. 'The faith has to go to the Gentiles as well.'

'Who says so?' Thomas snarled over Androgeus's horse's snort. 'I'm no going in, anyway. On your own head be it.'

Cornelius had got a large company together to welcome Peter. He heard the octuple clop coming up the road and said: 'Right. We'll go out to meet him.' Alighting, Peter nearly fell. Thomas sat till he was helped down. They were in a small garden with a wide gateway. Thomas dissociated himself from the whole business and went to sit on a stone bench under a figtree. Peter stood uncertainly smiling and was shocked when this centurion got down on his knees. Others, anxious to do the right thing, also got down. Peter hurriedly raised Cornelius, saying:

'Up, up. I'm nothing special. I'm a man like yourself. Well,' with fisherman's honesty, 'there are certain differences. Law, I mean, if you know what I mean.'

'I know the law of your fathers, sir,' Cornelius said.

'Not sir, please please not sir –'

'That it's unlawful for you to mix with the uncircumcised. That you're defiled by association. And for me, us, you're going to break the law. You're coming into my house. That's why I knelt.'

'Into your house,' Peter said firmly. He heard Thomas groan from under the figtree. 'God seems to be no respecter of persons. Every nation that fears him and does right – well, it seems as if he accepts. You want baptism?'

Cornelius gave a solemn nod. He was in full uniform as if on parade. 'If you'd come inside –'

From the figtree a fig fell on to Thomas's lap. He picked it up and began to undress it. It was red and ripe. He started to eat it, shaking his head. 'A fig from a Roman tree in a Roman garden. Have I your permission, O Lord? Och, a bad business.'

The ceremony, performed by aspersion, took place in a small salt lake by the shore. Aspersion rather than immersion seemed in order. You did not ask men in uniform to get it all wet.

The name Cornelius had become common in Rome shortly after Publius Cornelius Sulla liberated ten thousand slaves and let them enrol in his own *gens Cornelia*. That had been some eighty years or so before Jesus was born. Things were different now. Slaves were property and only fools gave property away. For the seven-day sale of imperial property, which mingled slaves indifferently with golden chamber pots, Greek statuary, nags past their best, title deeds to distant fields of tare and hemlock, the Emperor, with an unwonted gust of shame, preferred to absent himself from the city. He witnessed some secondclass games near Neapolis and rather admired the wrestling displays. The Jew Caleb, who called himself Metellus though nobody was taken in, was coming to the end of a provincial tour and, it was said, was now ripe for Rome. Caleb Metellus sent a Pannonian giant to the dust and broke the arm of a sneering Athenian. Gaius Caligula commended his performance. If Caleb had been in Rome, along with his Emperor, he would have been able to see his own sister up for sale in the market off the Via Sacra by the Forum.

'Any advance on that?' the auctioneer cried. 'Good Syrian muscle there, not an ounce of fat.' He referred to a scowling slave woodcutter. 'Come, come, citizens, straight from the Emperor's own household. No rubbish here. You can do better than that – did I hear two thousand five hundred?' The Syrian's scowl could not compare with that of Sara, who had contrived also to make one leg appear shorter than the other and twist her shoulders into a pose of paralysis.

'A girl from Jerusalem, magic city of the East. Stand up straight, lass, wipe that dirty look off your face. A great joker, as you see, but speaks Latin and Greek, a real asset to any household. Broken in, if you gentlemen know what I mean. Who'll start the bidding at five hundred sesterces? Seven hundred and fifty that noble senator there. Good day, my lord Lepidus. Anyone make it a thousand? Fifteen hundred? Nobody? Sold to the citizen in the green toga for one thousand. Gold and silver, please. No promissory notes. Emperor's orders.' Sara was led off scratching by an unknown buyer. He said nothing. He led her to a small park near the Vicus Patricius. Then he took a small shears from a pocket under his robe and began to cut off Sara's chain. She looked down, astonished. Marcus Julius Tranquillus appeared from behind an umbrella pine. He said:

'Thanks, Gracchus. I'll see about getting the bangles off.'

Peter was considered by his colleagues in Jerusalem to have spent more time in Joppa than was necessary. They had a grave charge to raise against him, and he had reverted, they said, to being a fisher of fish and not of men. 'I fished enough men there,' he said, 'and women too. There was plenty of work, believe me, and if I went back to my old trade it was to earn enough to get the work done. I couldn't stay in the house of Simon the tanner any more, the stink was killing me, and I found my own lodgings. Lodgings cost money. I joined a kind of fish thing –'

'Syndicate?'

'Yes, that's the word they used. Then I bethought me that I'd better come back here, though I liked the sea, good air, not like here, better come back here to see how things are going. After all,' he said defensively, 'I'm in charge.'

James the son of Zebedee forbore to say that he had himself taken charge of the church in Jerusalem. 'Thomas,' he said, 'told us something rather disturbing.'

'Where *is* Thomas?'

'Thomas has gone south.'

'South? What does that mean?'

'He said he fancied travel before he was too old to take it. He left his good wishes. Whether he was to spread the word or not he wasn't all that sure. Meditation under the sun, he said, whatever that meant. We'll hear from him, he said.' Both the two Jameses looked gravely at Peter. There were only three of the disciples left now in Jerusalem. The others assembled in the house of Matthias were mostly new converts, Pharisees chiefly, one or two robed priests among them. They looked even graver than the two Jameses. James the Little said to his namesake:

'Shall I speak?'

'Speak.'

'Well, then. The story is that you've flown in the face of the law of Moses.' Peter frowned ferociously. 'Everything we practise is laid down in the scriptures, Peter. The law of Moses isn't changed by the new law.'

'What am I supposed to have done that flouts the law?'

'You've eaten unclean food for a start. And you said that there was no such thing as unclean food. You claimed to have heard the voice of the Lord saying that everything was equally good – pigs, lobsters, for all I know toads and spiders –'

'I had this dream,' Peter said, 'and it was a dream from God. You only have my word for it, but perhaps you've got beyond accepting the word of the rock on which the church is built. As for eating stuff with blood in it, yes, I did. It was in the house of this Roman that I baptized into the faith. What was I to do – scorn his hospitality?'

'Yes,' James son of Zebedee said. 'You shouldn't have been in his house in the first place. It was a Roman centurion, wasn't it?'

'It was,' Peter said. 'And he and his family and a lot of his men wanted to become Nazarenes. The grace of the Lord lit them up. I suppose the grace of the Lord had done wrong.'

'We understood,' a priest named Kish said, 'that the destiny of Israel was being fulfilled with the coming of the Messiah. A Roman centurion seems rather remote from Israel, except of course for helping to bleed Israel dry and sending blasphemous statues to desecrate the holy city.'

'What's all this about blasphemous statues?' Peter asked.

'We'll come to that later,' Little James said. 'One thing at a time.'

'Very well,' Peter said. 'So a man has to have his foreskin sliced off before he can have the baptismal waters –'

'That's a crude way of putting it,' Kish said. 'Circumcision is the pledge of God's choice of one people. That one people is redeemed by the coming of God's son.'

'So,' Peter said, 'I have to turn a Roman centurion into a Jew before I can turn him into a Nazarene?'

'You can't turn a man into a Jew,' another priest named Nathan said. 'You have to be born a Jew. And if you're born a Jew then you can become a Nazarene. It's as simple as that.'

'And so,' Peter said loudly, 'we ignore the Gentiles? As I remember, we were told to get out over the whole damned world and take the message to whoever would listen, and no question of lifting their kirtles up to see if they were circumcised. And we were told nothing about being made unclean if we went into the houses of Gentiles. Damn it, the Lord himself was ready enough to go into the house of another Roman centurion to cure his servant or whoever it was.'

'He didn't go,' James son of Zebedee said. 'The centurion said he was unworthy, which he was –'

'And the Lord,' Peter cried, 'said he hadn't met such faith among the damned Israelites.'

'We didn't have to be told,' Little James said, 'about going into the houses of the unclean. We knew it already. It's all laid down in the old law.'

'Right,' Peter said, breathing heavily. 'So I baptize a dozen Roman soldiers who believe Jesus is the Son of God and I do wrong. Is that it? And I eat a piece of Roman beef and wash it down with a cup of Roman goat's milk, and that's wrong too. Is that it?'

'Urrrgh,' went someone in the assembly.

'You gentry,' Peter said, 'seem to forget sometimes who was put in charge. He sends down a vision. And I accept the vision. And you say I'm wrong. I get the call to convert a gaggle of Romans. And that's wrong too. You're slow to learn. Poor young Stephen wasn't slow. That's why they killed him. Stephen saw that the old way was finished. Priests, synagogues, circumcision, the bill of fare laid down in Leviticus – the lot. We're not what we used to be.'

'I can't take it in,' James son of Zebedee moaned. 'I can't.'

'*Won't* is more like it. Some of this damned stubbornness has to be knocked out of you. And if the bloodstained Caligula himself saw the light and said he wanted to turn Nazarene – what do we do? Do we say no, your bloodstained majesty, you can't be a Jew so you can't be one of us, better go back to slicing heads off and having ten wives and buggering little boys? It strikes me you've all got a lot of rethinking to do.'

151

'And how about the Temple?' James the Little asked.

'What about the Temple?'

'Is it still our Temple? Do we join up with the Jews who aren't Nazarenes and die for the Temple?'

'Nobody,' Peter said, 'dies for a chunk of stone even though King Solomon himself raised it.' Peter saw that the devil was in him today, but it seemed a clean and salutary devil. 'When he could take time off from the Queen of Sheba and ten thousand concubines.'

'This is all very unseemly,' the priest Nathan said. 'We did not expect such frivolity. The matters under discussion are of a considerable gravity.'

'You don't seem to understand what I'm saying, Peter,' Little James said. 'We're still part of the history of the Jews. Which means we have to defend the Temple. *He* would have stood up there in the Temple with a whip – You know that.'

'Defend the Temple against what?' Peter was plainly bewildered. He had been away. All sighed.

'The statue of the Emperor Caligula,' John son of Zebedee said, 'is waiting on the outskirts of the city. Surely you must have seen that?'

'I saw a cart with troops and a load of Syrian slaves. There was something on the cart covered with a purple cloth. I didn't think more about it. Some new Roman nonsense, I thought. So it's the Emperor's statue. Ah. You don't mean –'

'The Emperor has declared himself to be God,' a priest named Nebat said, the rise and fall of his Galilean accent seeming to set the ghastly blasphemy to harmless music. 'He demands that his effigy be placed in the Holy of Holies. We await the arrival of King Herod Agrippa to arrange for its installation. Or, we pray and hope, to make some statement which will save Judaea from bloodshed. He will probably merely temporize, so we hope and pray. He has become a pagan Roman and has long been a friend of the Emperor. But he is also of the faith of our fathers. One thing will doubtless now be fighting against the other. The Zealots are arming. He will not want bloodshed.'

'Desecration, desecration, desecration,' the priest Kish intoned.

'Well,' Peter said, '*he* said, *he* said – *he* said it's not what goes in that makes a man dirty but what comes out. We've work to do. We can't afford to be knifed or strung up on a cross – not yet awhile. We've work to do. I'm not going to be sliced by a Roman sword because I –' He did not finish; he saw that he was going too far. 'The statue of Gaius Caligula in the Temple. We can't have that, oh no. What a filthy blasphemy.' And then: 'What's all this about Agrippa being king? You mean king of Judaea?'

'He's already king of the other places,' James son of Zebedee said. 'Now he says he's waiting for imperial confirmation of the greater

152

appointment. The Emperor sent the procurator off to Syria. It looks as if Judaea's going to have a king again. Not for long, though. He takes his choice of being butchered by the Romans or his own people.'

'We have to speak out,' Nebat sang. 'We even have to take the lead in speaking out. We have the responsibility of an Israel fulfilled by the redemption of the anointed one. We are Israel's true voice.'

'And,' Peter said, 'we have to deny the first of our martyrs. We have to die for the Temple. There's something wrong somewhere.'

'It may not come to that,' Little James said.

But next day, in the glare of noontime, a huge golden smirking effigy was unveiled before the eyes of a sullen people. It still stood on its cart, and it was insolently just outside the Temple precincts. It awaited a further brief and final journey. Troops from Caesarea had raised a forest of spears around it. None of the Zealots dared yet to strike. They only murmured or cursed.

Herod Agrippa, elegantly enrobed, was carried on a litter towards the holy city. At the city gates the senior members of the Sanhedrin awaited him, headed by Caiaphas. A choir sang one of the Lamentations of Jeremiah. The mournful melisma accompanied the slow procession to the palace built by Herod the Great, at present untenanted. Herod Agrippa deigned to mount the exterior marble steps, each step long as a short street, on foot. The throneroom was dusty, but the throne had been dusted. He did not seat himself on the throne. He chose a humbler seat some yards away from it. This seat was dusty. A chamberlain dusted it with the edge of his robe. Herod Agrippa sat. The members of the Sanhedrin remained standing. To Caiaphas Herod Agrippa said:

'I know the protocol, your eminence. Forgive my speaking Greek, by the way. My Aramaic needs – ah, dusting. I recognize,' and he twanged off the like terminations with sardonic relish, 'that my elevation requires imperial confirmation and the ratification of my coronation. You will know that I am king when I sit on that throne. I understand that a ship is just now putting in at Caesarea. It carries a particular document – with the imperial seal. In that document will be the imperial confirmation of Judaea's restoration, God be praised, to the company of the kingdoms.'

'A client kingdom,' Caiaphas said.

'The whole world acknowledges its clientage. Freedom has always been a relative term. Caesar is Caesar.'

'As you are not yet quite the king of Judaea,' Caiaphas said, 'I can speak without excessive humility. If the statue of Caesar goes inside the Holy Temple of Jerusalem –'

'The Jewish people will cut their throats. I know.'

'The Jewish people will cut Roman throats first. And then accept their annihilation.'

'Your eminence, be reasonable. The Emperor Gaius believes himself to be a god – indeed, to be the one and only god. You and I know that the Emperor is mad, but madmen have to be humoured. Place the statue within, as a gesture of acceptance of Roman rule, and no great harm is done. It can be regarded as a mere decoration.'

'You must know the answer to that.'

'I *do* know the answer. And therefore I temporize. Let the effigy stay where it is for a while. Put it about that it symbolizes the deference of Caesar to the God of the Jews. Gaius the god acknowledges the existence of a greater than he. His statue stands at the border of the Temple precincts as a symbol of his fealty to the Lord God of Hosts. Put this around. Your people, my people, will be content to believe it.'

'Put round a lie, you mean.'

'What is truth? Let the people grow used to the imperial image. The next step may be deferred.'

'For how long?'

'Who knows? The next step will be to move the statue into the Temple precincts themselves. One step at a time. Habituated to its presence, even the Zealots will forget to object. Besides –'

'Besides what?'

'Nothing. Nothing for the moment.'

What Herod Agrippa may have been thinking and yet, for superstitious reasons, unwilling to state outright was that Gaius Caligula's days might well be, as the saying has it, numbered. Caligula's own dreams were telling him this, but he would pay no heed to them. Some of these recorded phantoms of his sleeping brain have been confused with recorded fact, so that some believe that the statue of Olympian Jupiter, on being removed from its immemorial plinth for transportation to Rome (so that Gaius could have his own grinning head substituted for the grave bearded visage of the father of the gods), burst into giant laughter and shook the scaffolding to collapse, so that the workmen ran away in terror. This was undoubtedly a fantasy of a sleeping and fuddled brain, like the one that woke the Emperor during the night before his assassination: he dreamed that he was standing before Jupiter's celestial throne and the god kicked him with the great toe of his left foot (not his right, as some would have it) and sent him tumbling screaming back to earth. As for the assassination plot, this was contrived by Cassius Chaerea and Cornelius Sabinus, both military tribunes, and the chosen instrument for the act was none other than Marcus Julius Tranquillus, newly married, and deliriously happy in his bride, who was discovering that no man ever got anything for nothing. The three men had their conspiratorial meeting at the house of Cornelius Sabinus, in his study with its trellis shelves filled with

154

scrolls, for he was a reading man. Cassius Chaerea said bitterly:

'I could forgive the crimes. The crimes are nothing –'

'Nothing?' Sabinus said. 'Rape, incest, mutilation, confiscation of property, arbitrary executions, buggery. Have you seen the list of them?'

'You can't make,' Chaerea said, 'a quantitative judgment. Accept the evil of the man and you must accept his killing of the entire world. What I cannot accept is humiliation –'

'Your own humiliation?'

'Well, I will say this. I am sick of his taunting me with effeminacy in public, calling me Venus indeed. At my age too. Sticking his middle finger out for me to kiss but keeping that finger always at the level of his crotch. It is sometimes small things, endlessly repeated, that will drive a man to madness. But no, I think of the humiliation inflicted on the military in general –'

'The Guard or the legions?'

'Can you separate one from the other? I refer to the pretence of the invasion of Britain that he proposes. A raid or two. A few prisoners. Himself to stay snug in his tent and impose on the army the lie that he led it to battle, to victory in the southern tribal areas. A triumphal procession back to Rome. The gathering of the seashells was bad enough, but this –'

'And his successor?'

'Can you doubt who? A good man who drinks his wine in the Praetorian mess like a soldier but never loses the sense of a seemly humility in the presence of his military betters. A safe man given to study. Indeed, the only man.'

Sabinus chewed on that for a moment and then he addressed Marcus Julius Tranquillus. 'Centurion,' he said, 'you know now why I summoned you here.'

'You propose a terrible thing.'

'Oh yes, to kill a self-proclaimed god is undoubtedly terrible. Ask that charming bride of yours what she thinks of the *lex talionis*.'

'I do not think I –'

'Come, man, the law of retribution. You've told us all about her sister's being lashed to death. If the enormity of striking Caesar chills you, think of the referred satisfaction of familial revenge. Anyway, you won't be alone. Who killed the divine Julius your namesake? In effect, a whole perturbed and apprehensive nation. Your hand will not be your own hand. Besides, we shall have our daggers too.'

'But I,' Marcus Julius Tranquillus said, 'will be the only paid assassin. That sum, when I can save it, will be repaid with interest into the Praetorian funds –'

'Forget that, man. The freeing of a slave of Caesar's was itself a blow against Caesar.' He poured some wine for the three of them. 'So we drink to it then and bind ourselves with the pledge.'

'Where and when?' Chaerea asked.

Before the last banquet of Gaius Caligula a Jew named Caleb who called himself Metellus strode, in Roman tunic and leather wristbands, towards the imperial kitchens. He had at last arrived at the previously unattainable, namely the Palatine, because he was due to appear before the Emperor again, though this time at a private party, in a wrestling bout with a golden Greek of immense strength named Philemon. A whole troupe of imperial entertainers had assembled early in an antechamber to the banqueting hall – Parthian sword-swallowers, dancers from the island of Lesbos, Syrian musicians with gongs, shawms and zithers, a small pride of performing lions, a pair of young panthers, one of them a female on heat, which would copulate in public when their well separated cages were opened on the round tiled floor of performance. The human performers had been fed weak wine and kickshawses, and Caleb followed one of the servants back to the kitchens, first having asked him a question he was not well able to answer, having had his larynx removed. So he strode into the great fiery hell where innumerable fantastic dishes were being given their final touches of ornamentation. An undercook accosted Caleb at once and, lifting an iron skillet in threat, said *out*. 'You have two slaves here,' Caleb said. 'Girls from Palestine.' This he did not know, but it seemed a fair guess. *Get out. Here, Bubo, throw him out.* Bubo was a surly boily man who was scraping pans before washing them. He advanced on Caleb with a vast jellymould of copper. Caleb showed his muscle and Bubo growled. An old crone scouring a baking dish showed to Caleb an open mouth with few teeth. She said: *Palestine?* 'You know who I mean?' Caleb asked trembling now. *Well, it's a bit of a long story –*

Cassius Chaerea and Cornelius Sabinus were guests at the banquet. When he entered with his freedman Aufidius, who carried a leather bag with the imperial whip undoubtedly in it, Gaius Caesar, who had perhaps seen these two wading in blood in a dream, said: 'Fear not, gentlemen. I'll get you before you get me.' Then he giggled. He reclined without grace and bade the first course be served. It was some fantastic monstrosity – perhaps pastry moulded in the shape of newborn babies with minced lark brain protruding from the anus – and called on his uncle Claudius to recite something. Claudius rose with dignity, pushing his couch back to give standing room, and, with very little stuttering, announced that he would deliver a passage from an unknown philosopher. The passage was as follows.

'He who is all powerful is free to perform both good and evil acts. And because ggggood is harder to perform than evil, he will best show his ppppower in the enactment of good. He who pppperforms nothing but evil is clearly enslaved to evil and has forfeited his power of choice. The evil ruler is no ruler at all.'

He sat to an uneasy silence. Gaius Caligula said: 'Who wrote that? The fool Seneca? One of the bleating followers of the slave Chrestus? I hope I do not hear the ring of treason in it.'

Claudius, back on his feet, said calmly: 'An unknown philosopher, as I said. About fifty years of age with no wealth but a wealth of white hair.' And, having thus made the identification, he reclined with a certain grace on his couch. Gaius Caligula said:

'You've become quite agile with your tongue, Uncle Claudius. Are you as agile with your body? I've a mind to see you strip off and wrestle. I like an occasional bout of – what's the term? – ah yes, gerontomachia.'

'Alas, I'm a slow mover, Caesar,' Claudius said. 'I limp, nephew, I claudicate, as my name proclaims. I could afford you little sport.'

'Anyway,' Gaius Caligula said, 'old as you are, you're not quite old enough. Let's have the really old. You, sir – and you.' He addressed two ancient senators, bald, toothless, emaciated.

'We would rather not, Caesar,' the less ancient, though there was little in it, said.

'Dravernotsheezer,' the Emperor mocked. 'Come on, reverend sirs. Entertain your master. No prize for the winner. But for the loser an eternal crown. Eternal darkness, I mean. *Una nox dormienda*. Strip them, Aufidius.' So the two ancients were rudely rendered totally naked to only imperial laughter. They stood bewildered facing each other. 'Fight, come on, fight, you gerontomachoi. I demand sport.' They engaged in a show of earnest. The son of one of them, an importer of wild beasts named Licinius Calvinus, stood to protest but was swiftly dragged back to his couch by his burly wife. 'Must I get my whip to you?' called Gaius Caligula. 'Oh, signs of a misspent youth. Too much gloomy philosophy. Not enough cultivation of the pride of the flesh. *Fight*.' They grappled arthritically. The younger was blue at the lips. He fell with both hands on his heart. 'That looks to me like cheating, reverend sirs. That looks to me like natural death. Oh, take them away,' he cried petulantly. 'Bring on the professionals. I wish to see *blood*.' He was at least seeing a simulacrum of it, for the second course was an innominate crimson pudding containing heaven knew what. Licinius Calvinus came to drag his father away: he was not dead, merely feigning to be. It was now that the imperial master of ceremonies ordered on the Jew Caleb, somewhat dazed with the news he had heard, and the golden Greek Philemon. They made formal obeisance to the Emperor and then started to grapple. Hot butter squirted, by a quaint device, out of the bloodcoloured pudding. Gaius

Caligula laughed to see the exquisite Lollia Paulina's exquisite face embuttered. Then he watched the wrestling with critical care. He was not satisfied; he was seeing no blood. 'Take that golden giant away,' he called. 'Reserve him for my bed. It's a long time since I've been as it were punitively sodomized. Now, you, sir, your Emperor will show you how to fight. Aufidius – puss puss puss, miauuuu.' Aufidius took out of his leather bag a beautifully made catmask of Sicilian workmanship and a pair of catskin gloves with pointed claws. Gaius Caligula turned himself into an unagile cat, an overfed tom, left his couch and advanced on Caleb. Caleb was disconcerted. He stood and allowed the Emperor to gash his arms. He looked at the catmarks welling blood and wondered what to do. There was a rumble of talk from the couched watchers and he could not guess at its meaning. 'Come, boy. Miauuuuu. Grrrrr.' The Emperor struck at Caleb's left eye, missed, caught his left temple. Caleb saw with astonishment what looked like a falling curtain of blood, and then let his sister Ruth enter his body. He circled, wiping the blood off, and Gaius Caligula, complaining breathily of unfairness, found himself scratching at empty air. He caught Caleb's cheek with a lucky lunge, squealing in triumph, and then found himself pinioned from behind, flailing in impotence. 'Unfair,' he tried to yell. 'Let me go! Make him let me go ! Kill him!' Caleb had the vainly scratching Caligula off his feet in an easy lift, and the little boots kicked at nothing. Then he dropped him. The Emperor did not resume his catplay. Instead he called for Aufidius to kill, kill. Cornelius Sabinus stood and yelled:

'No!'

The tone of authority took even Gaius Caligula by surprise. Caleb ran off. The Emperor saw more inimical faces than had ever before dared to unmask. He tore his own mask off and grumbled: 'Spoilsports. No sense of humour. The banquet is finished.' He left with unimperial speed, his sycophants after, their hands making apologetic gestures to the statues, pillars with their garlands, uneaten dishes. Claudius looked at Cornelius Sabinus, his mouth open in a nervous rictus, desirous of saying something but his speech organs unable to engage.

Gaius Caligula would have been wise to remove to Antium that night. Masquerading as a cat gave him none of a cat's instincts. He went to the theatre the following morning to watch a mimed comedy entitled *Laureolus*, at the end of which the protagonist, a leader of a gang of highway robbers, died while vomiting copious blood. Following the custom of the time, the action was comically exaggerated by the performers in a kind of antimasque, who filled the stage with apparently regurgitated red syrup. Gaius Caligula, having prematurely brought the banquet to an end the previous night, had later declared himself hungry and had gorged on a cold grouse pie with pickled gherkins. The sight of stage blood now made him feel sick though unable to vomit. Perhaps he needed to settle his stomach with a light luncheon. He could not make up his mind. His uncle Claudius was with him on his orders: some instinct, not quite feline, was warning him not to let Claudius out of his sight for too long. Claudius last night had not behaved like a fool; the nephew had heard like an aureole round the uncle's voice the hollow echo of the senate chamber. Claudius now said to him: 'Give your stomach a rest. Come for a little walk.'

'It's too cold to walk.' It was too, a week from the end of the month of January.

'The ccccovered way.' Meaning the enclosed passage that led from the auditorium to the actors' greenroom. They walked – Gaius, Claudius, the actor Mnester, a handful of nameless effeminates. In the passage Gaius Caligula was charmed to see a rehearsal of a Trojan wardance by a group of noble youths who had recently come from one of the Asian provinces. 'Splendid,' he said. 'Most exquisitely done. We will have a special performance this afternoon.'

'I'm not at my best, Caesar,' one of the youths frankly said. 'I have a bad attack of the rheum. Rome is a cold city.'

'Sometimes at this season,' Gaius Caligula said kindly. 'You will see if you stay with us, and you are most welcome, a glorious spring and a summer whose heat is sometimes insupportable.' Chaerea and Sabinus now appeared from a passage set at right angles to the covered way, part of the first cohort of the Praetorian Guard behind them. This was led by a senior centurion whose face the Emperor knew well. He trembled, perhaps with ague, as he slapped his chest in salute. It was not cold enough to shiver. Sabinus said with deference:

'Caesar, what is today's watchword?'

'Oh, that. Let us say *Jupiter*.'

'By Jupiter, now!' Chaerea cried. Marcus Julius Tranquillus drew his dagger and struck his Emperor in the ribs. The point seemed to meet resistant bone, but Gaius Caligula staggered and turned. Chaerea struck out and split the imperial jawbone. Sabinus brought two conjoined fists down on the Emperor's head. The Emperor fell, yelling through blood: 'You can't do it! I'm immortal!' Then the entire cohort drew swords and fought each other to get their thrusts in, thirty all told, the thirtieth in the genitals. The imperial litter bearers struck out in loyalty though feebly with their litter poles. The German bodyguard came in running, slashing whoever was in their way. Cornelius Sabinus was slashed to the wristbone. The Germans, howling from the pits of their throats, were fought off. Caesar lay in his blood. Chaerea pulled away the imperial purple robe, sending the corpse

159

rolling. He looked for Claudius. All looked for Claudius. Claudius had taken shelter behind one of the painted drapes (the one of the rape of Lucrece) that lined the passageway. The Praetorians saw the drape that bulged tremulously and, violent impulses not yet abated, yanked it off its rod. It billowed about Claudius, who went kkkk. Chaerea went up to him with the purple.

The news took less than a month to reach Caesarea. An officer had been sent from Syria to act as a temporary procurator pending the confirmation of Herod Agrippa's elevation to monarch of Judaea. He, Junius Saturninus, stood on the quay with Cornelius and a maniple. They expected one or two messages: the confirmation, the renewal of the order to trundle that statue into the Holy of Holies, under pain of instant execution for – names need not be specified. What was not expected was news of Caligula's assassination. After all, it had been a rule of merely three years and ten months, and the Emperor was only twenty-nine years old, with a lot of villainy still in front of him. An officer courier or *frumentarius* could be seen as the ship eased in, clearly fretful at the delay in fitting the gangplank. He ran down it and handed a sealed scroll to Junius Saturninus. 'Here, you open it,' the temporary procurator said to Cornelius. Cornelius read trembling and said: 'Thank God. Four men to ride at once to Jerusalem. You, you, you, you.'

'What news?'

'No more trouble about that statue.'

Thirty miles from Caesarea to Jerusalem. At sunset the speared guard dispersed and left the smashing of the effigy to the Zealots. It crashed first into the dust and, when their hammers and cudgels got to work on it, it was found to be not pure gold but rather inferior stone with a beaten gold masking fitted on to it. This gold was melted into an ingot which was eventually turned into Temple money. That was no happy ending to a bad story, since there is no end to anything except doomsday. Zealotry became more watchful, better organized, spending Caesar's money on arms. The failure of the Jerusalem Nazarenes to betray more than a lukewarm concern about the proposed defiling of the Temple did them no good, and the appearance of Cornelius in the city, to bid farewell to Peter before his retirement from the service, signalled the growing separation of the new faith from the old. A dirty Roman, uncircumcised, kneeling for the blessing of one who had been born a good Galilean Jew. Herod Agrippa awaited a new Emperor's confirmation of his kingship and, having narrowly evaded one kind of blasphemy, learned that one of his tasks was to put down another.

THREE

To my shame I observe that it is just one year since I began this unhandy chronicle, and the new May is no better than the old. Rain, cold, rheum, and the grass too wet for scything. Of my bodily ailments I will say nothing, except to blame them for the long intermission of my task, for I had to travel to Mediolanum to consult a Sicilian physician reputed to have skill in healing diseases of the lower bowel, but he could do little for me except prescribe a blander diet than I am accustomed to and to advise that I not fight overmuch a chronic constipation which, he said, at least relieves through inaction the irritability of the nether tissues and – But what have you to do with this? You have your own troubles. Nevertheless, as body and mind are a unity, some deficiencies in my writing, and in the memory that serves it, have to be ascribed to an intestinal sluggishness that afflicts flesh and brain alike. I bring a headache daily to my desk, lowering myself delicately to the cushions of my chair, and the pain thrusts like a knife into my syntax. Also I suffer from failure to recall with the right precision the details of my multiple story, which is founded on what I have heard at one time and another and can hardly at all be checked through reference to documents of proven authenticity. And then I wonder about the utility of what I am doing, since I tell of a dead time and a dead faith and have no inner image of a possible readership. But, with a kind of hopelessness, I proceed.

I am now into the imperiate of Tiberius Claudius, who came to the purple at the advanced age of fifty and seemed to have little to recommend him except the referred glory of his brother Germanicus, for he was weak of body, shivered even in the heat, limped and stuttered and had cocooned his mind for too long in useless scholarship, as he cocooned his cold body in wool. What amazed the people and the Senate on his accession was the rigour of his sense of justice, which demanded open trial and subsequent execution for the assassins of his predecessor Gaius Caligula. Marcus Julius Tranquillus, who had struck the first blow, was for a time in mortal terror, but it was conceded that what he had done he had done under instruction, was a mere limb obedient to the controlling intelligence of his superiors, and

161

so punishment was not truly in order. But Julius suffered in other ways.

Many a night he dreamed of the terror stricken face of Gaius as the dagger was raised, of the stuck-pig scream as the point pierced and the blood oozed, and he sometimes awoke his wife with his yelling. He and Sara were living in a small rented house on the Janiculum, from whose tiny garden the whole of the city could be seen. It was on a January morning that he had his twentieth nightmare and was glad to awaken from it to the wintry light and the protective arms of Sara who, despite her unfailing sympathy, was growing a little sick of these dreams.

'The same?' she asked, and he nodded, scooping sweat from his forehead. 'But you had to do it,' she said.

'It had to be done. It was the only thing to do. So why should I have bad dreams? Perhaps I was never intended to be a killer.'

'Meaning a soldier.'

They lay quite naked, holding each other under the loosely woven wool coverlet. 'To kill barbarians isn't quite the same,' Julius said. 'Not that I've ever killed any. Part of Rome's civilizing mission.' He spoke with irony. She did not understand the Latin phrase he used. Though now a sort of Roman, the Roman tongue was still a foreign dress to her, like the belted long kirtle she wore out of doors and the upcombed hairstyle she disdained: her black hair flowed over the white wool. 'We have to discipline the lesser breeds.' Those words she understood: she had heard them in Jerusalem. She said:

'To kill is to kill. Life is supposed to be sacred.'

'All life? The life of a Gaius?'

'The Nazarenes would say that even Caligula's life was precious to God.' She thought about that and shrugged it away. Julius kissed her brown shoulder. He said:

'Soon I may have to kill Britons.'

'What are Britons?'

'Tribes who live in a northern land, twenty sea miles off Gaul. I saw its chalk cliffs. What Gaius wished to pretend to do Claudius says he will do in all truth. Men with yellow hair and long moustaches. Barbarians. Their speech is all bar bar bar. They have to be brought under Roman rule and made to take baths.'

'Palestine to the east and these people to the north. Everything under Rome.' She yawned. He had wakened her too early.

'This is your destiny, O Romans – put down the arrogant, spare the meek. Vergil wrote that. And yet the peoples we conquer and rule are sometimes less of children than we are. The Greeks have philosophy and you have a religion. All we have is troops, games, roads and orgies.'

'I trust you don't voice these ideas in the officers' mess.'

'I was never cut out to be a soldier perhaps. I just follow the family tradition. But what else can I do?'

'What time are you on duty?'

'Noon.'

'Today is our Sabbath. I'd forgotten. You make me forget too much. Another Roman conquest.'

'Hardly.'

For it was she who proffered the first embrace. Jesus Naggar was said to have sanctified the coupling of man and woman not only through the institution of what he termed holy matrimony but in the affirmation of its essential privacy: 'Even God himself,' he once said, 'turns his eyes away from the embraces of lovers.' Have I then the right to look on as these two kiss, stroke and moan beneath the coverlet? Yet I find that the contemplation of their ecstasy is, in a manner, therapeutic: it draws the blood away from my suffering zones and feeds glands too long sunk in hebetude. At it, then. Mingle your salivas, happy pair, feel the excitation of the membranes of your lips provoke, as in the sympathy of the unstruck lyre string for the string struck, the tingling of other membranes and soon a demented act of obedience to the goddess which culminates in a vocable of prayer in a universal language. This is religious enough: the fire of a sort of beneficent hell transformed into a heaven from which God is absent, and then the coolness of a limbo whose name is gratitude. Venus exists, whatever the rabbis say. This was as good a celebration of the Sabbath as any.

Those who took the Sabbath more seriously, that is to say devoted it to God, were at their synagogues, which were mostly decent edifices built in the Roman style out of the wealth of Jewish merchants and the pennies of the Jewish poor. In more than one synagogue that day there was trouble. The Nazarenes were at it, preaching the gospel of God's fleshly son and his doctrine of universal love. In the synagogue that stood not far from the Theatre of Marcellus there was a particularly eloquent votary of the Christ, probably that Matthew who had been a tax gatherer. There were the usual cries of blasphemy, stone him, this is an abomination before the Lord, but one distinguished and moderate Jew named Eliab bar Henon stood, prayed silence in a loud voice, and said:

'Brothers, what you call blasphemies and abominations are no new thing to us whom exile has driven to Rome. For we are surrounded by worse blasphemies and abominations than have been spoken. These are still, I would suggest, a matter for debate and cogitation, whereas the horrors of Roman paganism are the furniture of our daily lives. We tolerate them and, tolerating them, we ourselves are tolerated. But there have been instances lately of unseemly brawls and stonings outside our sacred edifices, of harm offered to what to many of the orthodox seem to be the diabolic agents of a heterodoxy so harmful that the very archangels must stuff wing-feathers in their ears so as not to hear. Now how must all this seem to the pagan Romans? It must seem that the Jews are become an unruly lot who have outlived their welcome. And how will the Romans respond to what they will term Jewish disorder? They will, at best, exact heavier taxes, at worst proscribe our faith as inimical to Roman order. Therefore I beg you to listen to these heretical doctrines, as you will name them, in calm of spirit and the desire to offer no more than intellectual or theological opposition. Let these men say their say, and let them be answered in a cool spirit of debate. Then let them depart in peace. I speak thus not to the end of saving their skins but rather to the end of saving ours. I have done.' Then he sat down again.

His reasonable words had little effect among the hotter and less tolerant of the assembled brethren. These resumed their vilifications and some of them went outside to gather stones. But Eliab bar Henon spoke sense and better truth than he knew. One thing he could not know was that a respectable pagan senator named Licinus Novatus, taking the air not far from the Ara Pacis on the Campus Martius, was shortly to be mobbed by a gang of young Jewish reprobates, who swore he was the heretic teacher Azaniah bar Jeshua. If there was a likeness it could only be most superficial, for Licinus Novatus was beardless and short-haired and wore no Jewish garment. But a number of Nazarenes had put off the habiliments of the Jewish people, and some of these renegade Jews were Greeks, who had been indifferent to matters of external distinction. The mob of bearded youth had been driven off and trounced, but Licinus Novatus, who had not been seriously hurt and despised the vindictiveness of the law, a Stoic too and a friend of Seneca, had not wished to take the matter further. But when, outside a synagogue at the foot of the Janiculum, there was an antinazarene riot that resulted in the accidental breaking of the head of a Roman child out walking with his nurse, this question of the unruliness of the Jews became a matter for senatorial debate.

The Emperor Claudius had his enemies in the Senate. One of them, a certain C. Silvius Rusticus, delivered a long speech against him in his presence, before a packed house, but his chief theme was more radical than the one of the obstreperousness of the Jewish community. He said:

'It is well known that the imperial designate has bribed the army into the sustention of his irregularly conferred status. The Senate has still to confirm it, and I doubt if the Senate will. Our recent experience with emperors leads many of us – and I would say a majority – to a wholly reasonable desire for the restoration of the republic. As a republic Rome flourished and will flourish again. As an imperial monarchy it has been disgraced, bathed in the blood of the innocent, and its slaughterous stink will not easily be expunged.'

There was loud applause, as also a noise of objection. The Emperor rose and was greeted with some boos, but the thrust-out jaws and bristling spears of his military escort silenced the more timid. Claudius said:

'Honourable senators. It is with ggggggreat ddddiffidence that I that I –'

His stutter set off farmyard noises from the whiterobed dignitaries farthest from the military escort. Claudius grew red and his neck swelled noticeably. By some temporary miracle his speech impediment was almost completely quelled and he spoke with clarity and vigour, saying:

'Yes – those among you who greeted with silence or even approbation the excesses of Tiberius Caesar and Gaius Caligula Caesar are quick enough to find schoolboy ppppleasure in my oratorical limitations. I address cowards, self-seekers, murderers, nonentities, ready enough to cringe at the tyrant's whip but not at all willing to see that the sickness of Rome can be cured only by a change of heart, not by a mere adjustment of its ppppolitical constitution. You see standing before you the physician, nay the surgeon who will administer the emetic and excise the ulcer. Rome will be what it was – a polity in which no man need fear injustice, its capital a city in which men may walk freely at night, its people united in a return to Roman virtue and the worship of the Roman gods, untainted by effeminacy or Oriental pollutions. And I call for a wider cccccconcept in the defining of the very term *Roman*. Those who subscribe to the Roman ethos – whether from Gaul or Germany or Asia – may call themselves true Romans –'

There was an outcry at that, but Claudius rode bravely over it.

'The Romanization of the Gauls has already begun, and with what consequence? That we have not had to raise the sword in Gaul against dissidence or rebellion. I look forward to seeing Gauls in this noble Senate –'

C. Silvius Rusticus got up, sneering. Claudius was not sorry for the interruption. His throat rasped and, without the swig of barley water he now took covertly from a flask, might collapse in grotesque cawings. He had more to say, but Rusticus was now saying:

'Take it further, Caesar. Fill the Senate with Oriental riffraff that despises the ancient Roman virtues and spits on the Roman gods. Make Rome the mongrel centre of a mongrel empire. Bring in the bearded Jews muttering prayers to their tribal deity. Conquer Britain only that the bluebottomed oystercrackers, covered with lice and stinking of the dogskins which barely conceal their nakedness, may mouth their barbarities in this noble house and defile its sempiternal marble.'

There were loud roars of approval. Claudius wiped his mouth with the back of his hand and cried:

'Like too many professional rhetoricians the noble senator emits more noise than sense. Britain will be conquered, yes, but it will be many years before it can be converted into more than a sullenly obedient tributary. As for the Jews – they are not wanted in Rome.'

At last he had the Senate's near total approbation. Not the least among those who fisted their palms and cried aye aye aye were the improvident who had mortgaged their estates to Jewish moneylenders.

'The Jews,' continued Claudius, 'cannot or will not assimilate to the Roman way of life. With their sectarian squabblings they are a disgrace to public order. They are a wandering race. Let them wander back to Palestine or to other of the barbarous places of the Orient. Whether they worship their own god or the deified slave Chrestus – both blasphemies against Rome – they will be content to find a Jewish king awaiting them. A king appointed by Rome. They will continue to belong to Rome but at a salutary distance. They will pay their taxes but will not nauseate us with their superstitious piety and their lack of discipline. And if that is not policy acceptable to the Senate, then the Senate is unworthy to advise its Emperor.'

On principle there were some catcalls, but there were also some cheers. Claudius turned to look at the leader of his bodyguard, in whose gripe the swordhilt had been relaxed. He nodded with quiet self-approval. The Jews were a useful people. An excellent device of loyal unification.

Herod Agrippa I, his unseemly fatness hidden in purple and gold, was borne on a litter towards the Temple. Before him walked the elders of the faith. Before them strode the discoursers of solemn festal music, the players of sackbuts and citherns and the thumpers of drums of various sizes. Alleluia. Judaea greeted its monarch. He was to ascend to the immemorial sacring place of millennia of kings, there to be endued with the robe and crown of rule. The people roared his name in jubilation. He acknowledged without smiles their plaudits, being, as he had to admit to himself, not well in his body, the salves and potions administered by his physicians having induced only a nausea and a thumping of the heart that was out of phase with the triumphant drums. He would have preferred to be in bed.

On the outer fringe of the crowd that filled the Temple precincts, whipped away from the path of the procession by guards in newly polished breastplates, Peter stood with James the son of Zebedee. James said: 'This should quieten the Zealots. They have what they want at last.'

But it was like a dissatisfied Zealot that Peter spoke. 'Don't you believe it. It's only Rome in fancy dress. The worst of both worlds, if you want my opinion. Roman arrogance and priestly intolerance. At last he gives our enemies an official whip.'

'Do we wait for the whip?' James asked. 'Or do we travel?'

'Some of us travel. Some of us stay where we are.'

The royal procession was mounting the streetwide steps to the great portal. The musicians had ceased to play. Voices of men and boys intoned an anthem within. Herod Agrippa I was carried to his crowning. He would be glad when it was all over.

The Jews had not yet been driven back from Rome to their royal homeland. The expected act had still to be promulgated. But those Jews who had official if lowly positions in the state – treasury accountants, municipal functionaries – were being summarily dismissed. Some of these had pretended to be indigenous Romans, ready to prove their respectable paganism by sacrificing to the gods, but there was much grim lifting of kirtles, certain things could not be dissimulated. In one of the imperial gymnasia Caleb alias Metellus looked sadly for the last time as he believed on wrestlers and gladiators in training. He snuffed the lively sweat and heard the thump of falling bodies as the games editor kindly broke the bad news.

'It's like this, Metellus – or do you want to be called by your real name?'

'There's no further point in pretence, is there?'

'If you were rich, like one of those fatbellied usurers, well, you know what you could do. Buy it. Not officially, of course. But it's being done. Her whorish majesty the Empress Messalina is making a quiet fortune. It's never been known before – citizenship for sale.'

'Well,' Caleb said, 'so much for a promising athletic career.'

'I'd keep you on, you know that – Greek, Jew or blackamoor makes no difference to me. You have the qualities, boy – but it's more than my job's worth. They've got it in for you people.'

'You know why I came to Rome,' Caleb said.

'To half-throttle the Emperor. Well, you did that. No, I know. Do you know the name of the man?'

'An army man, that's all they could tell me. Talk about – what's the word – pollution they'd call it back home. A Roman marrying a Jew.'

'That turns her into a Roman. *She's* safe anyway. And don't start this talk about clean and dirty blood with me, son. All blood's the same. I've seen enough of it to know. I'm as good a Sicilian Arab Roman as you'll find anywhere. There's nothing wrong with being a Roman. So there it is. Sorry. Good luck.'

He shook hands with Caleb, a decent nutbrown man with a nose like a beak, his former muscle settling to middleaged fat. Then he shuffled on his worn sandals through the sand towards the new Pannonian giant, seven feet if he was an inch, who was waiting to be taught how to gouge out eyes and break fingers. Caleb sadly left.

He walked sadly through the lively streets, set in the habit of hopelessly looking for her. Women. Roman matrons of the patrician class on curtained litters, beggars cawing for alms, the occasional white bangleted wrist revealed from the curtains, throwing a coin. Crones selling figs. Pert Roman girls giggling among themselves. He passed through one of the lesser markets, where mimosa was on sale and crocuses in small tubs, and lowly housewives did their own shopping for carcases of young lamb, wine-red joints of beef, little birds, palm grapes and fat gourds. There was a woman chaffering with a vendor much in the lively manner of Jerusalem. He could see her only from the back; her black hair flowed. A lump like hard bread filled his throat. He was ready to call 'Sara!' but it was not Sara. What was he to do now? Join the beggars? He was sturdy, young, employable, but he was a Jew. Perhaps outside the city, in the farmlands where a man could work as a daylabourer and nobody was interested in checking on the covenant with Jehovah, he might find dull work with plough or hoe. As well take ship for Palestine if he were to abandon his quest in the city. He saw and heard a tuneless streetsinger. Sing us one of the songs of Zion. He tried a limp: old soldier, lady, hacked at by dirty Jews in a far place, serving the Empire. But he was not old. He was hungry, though. When a loafseller turned his back to take two-pound loaves from his basket behind the stall, Caleb snatched a plain bun from the pile unattended. He shoved it beneath his Roman cloak. There was plenty of free water spurting from the Roman fountains. A few streets away he sat in the mild sun not far from a tentmaker who seemed to be of his own race, though neither spoke greeting to the other. Caleb munched his dry bun and later had a couple of mouthfuls of spring water. God knew what he was to do about the future.

Paul's future began. He sat in the sun stitching at his tentwork on the main street of Tarsus and saw a man he was sure he knew looking lost in the crowd. He sightlessly stepped into an ample mound of camel dung, cursed soundlessly, removed his sandal and hopped to the wall, where he began scraping off the ordure with a bit of shard. Paul thought the man had been thinner when he knew him in Jerusalem. He could not remember the name, but then the word *encouragement* swam into his head. That was it: son of encouragement. 'Barnabas,' he called. Barnabas smiled and hopped towards him, his sandal not yet wholly clean. 'I wondered,' Paul said, 'when somebody would come.'

'It's been a long time,' Barnabas said, shaking the proffered hand, the fingers hard from the pressing of the bone needle.

'Not too long to learn. Read. Think. Preach a little. But I have to confess to a certain impatience. Life is not long, even when it's everlasting.'

Barnabas nodded. Epigrams, subtleties, paradoxes. He would have to shed all that when he – 'I made the mistake of going to your parents' house. They turned the dog loose. I've come from Antioch. You and I are to work together there. You know the place?'

'I've been there twice. But not in my new incarnation. A town full of prostitutes.'

'They prefer to call themselves servants of the goddess. But believe it or not, it's the Gentile pagans who want conversion. Not the Jews.'

'I believe it. Pagans don't have prejudices.'

'Well, there's no trouble about preaching the coming of a messiah when they don't even know what a messiah is. They understand *Kyrios* and they understand *soter* and they understand *Christos*. They call us *Christianoi*. That's our name now, Christians.'

'You look well fed. I see no bruises. The work goes well, does it?'

'I need help.'

Paul made a vague noise of discontent. 'No arguments, no theological engagements. Clay, not stone. Like that, is it?'

'We preach to the Jews first. That's laid down. But there are a fair number of halfway Jews – you know, those who want God without having to have their prepuces torn off to get him. A lot of those come to the synagogue and when they hear about *Christos* they see that's the answer.'

'I never thought of the new way as a compromise,' Paul said. 'What do you preach – redemption from sin and the need for brotherly love?'

'I preach the essence of the faith,' Barnabas said. 'And love is the essence. Of course, you have to redefine the word. For a lot of them it's tied up with the goddess and what the Romans call *Daphnici mores*.'

'I don't think I know the expression.'

'The morality of Daphne, Daphne being this place about five miles out of the city where they worship Astarte or Artemis or Diana or whatever she's called. I can't see much difference between her and Venus or Aphrodite. You worship fertility and you have a bigbreasted earth mother, but then you leave fertility to nature and worship what they call the act of love. You'll see the place.'

169

'I've seen it already. Do you preach the resurrection?'

'The resurrection of *Christos*? Well, that's the cornerstone, isn't it?'

'I mean *our* resurrection. If he rose again we rise again. If he took his flesh to heaven we take ours. And I don't mean cart our bones and guts up to the sky. I've been thinking a lot about this, Barnabas. It's a subtle business. The flesh is transfigured. We don't join the angels, who've never known the flesh. We're a new order – those of us who are saved, of course.'

Barnabas sighed. 'They're simple people. They understood about sin and love and redemption. I don't think they're ready for anything deeper. Not yet.'

Paul had been stitching away, his eyes on his thoughts, his fingers displaying a skill independent of their master. 'When do we leave?' he asked.

'As soon as you're ready. I have passage money. It's a big city, Antioch, third biggest in the world. There's plenty of wealth there. No trouble about money.'

'We don't trudge overland then. A quick boat across the bay.'

'You're ready?'

'Spare sandals and a spare gown. I've been sleeping over the shop here. I must make my farewells. Pedaiah, the man I've been working for, he has a rather good young apprentice. I won't be missed.'

At Daphne, on the borders of the Syrian desert, there stood a pagan temple well endowed with pagan money. It was dedicated to the goddess Astarte, whose effigy in gold, an opulent bas-relief twenty feet high, was nailed to the brickwork of the façade. This effigy was fanciful, and the ample body of the deity was studded with breasts supernumerary to the bountiful pair which linked her to her mortal votaresses and, indeed, to the blessed virgin Mary mother of the Christ. All round the building, twelve feet above the eye of the beholder, were incised representations of the erotic act, man with woman but never man with man nor woman with woman. The holiness of the act in its generative aspects might seem thus to be proclaimed, but only one image showed the frank thrust of male sword into female scabbard, the others glorifying a variety of fancies whose end was not natural fructification – anal, buccal, axillary, intercrucial penetrations, kisses of gross ingenuity, appetites bordering on the cannibalistic. This was Greek and Syrian work, and it pointed the large difference between the Hebrew concept of the purpose of the divinely implanted sexual urge, which was to people the tribes and fill the land with soldiers and herdsmen, and the more sophisticated impulses of the cities of Asia and the Mediterranean, where the means was exalted over the end and the means was encouraged to exfoliate in a diversity of forms bounded only by the restrictions of anatomy. So that the goddess of many breasts, who had once stood for fertility, stood now instead for ecstasies unrelated thereto. She could not be Venus, who is, as Lucretius reminds us, the divinity of rutting beasts as well as of philoprogenitive humanity, and beasts know nothing of ecstasies which transcend the simple needs of biology. So the goddess was Astarte or Ashtaroth or was Hellenized to Artemis and Romanized to Diana. Diana, of course, was a virgin goddess, but virginity could be glossed as a state disdainful of the generative end of love. Love, as Barnabas had said, needed, in the Christian dispensation as Antioch now bids us call it, to be redefined. Paul, he thought, was just the man to redefine it.

One day, a month or so after the arrival of Paul and Barnabas in Antioch, a young physician named Luke, a pagan Greek, dismounted from the horse he named Thersites (perhaps because of its ugliness and bad temper) and entered the sacred edifice. He was dark, small, well knit, not unprosperous, and he wore a golden bangle or two to proclaim the modest success he had achieved in his profession. He entered the temple soberly, a doctor called to the treating of a patient, and he sniffed the perfumed air, on which nard and sandalwood smoked, without even the faintest stir of erotic enchantment. A priestess tended the fire from which delicious scents arose to a smiling ivory icon of the goddess. All about the temple, whose floor was cunningly embellished with Graeco-Syrian mosaic work depicting the coupling of Apollo and Artemis (for the cult of Astarte had arisen out of solar–lunar myths of western provenance, on which an Asiatic mysticism had been imposed), were booths closed for delicacy's sake with silken curtains, and the priestess, a handsome dark woman past her first youth, pointed to one of these. Luke nodded and entered the booth thus indicated. On a bed he found a young girl lying in some distress. She was a temple prostitute, her favours available to such as would or could pay a handsome tribute in gold to the goddess whose power she evoked: initially these favours had been available to all and freely, but complaints of the secular professionals of the town, as well as the healthy acquisitiveness of the ruling priesthood, had imposed a rational limitation of availability. This girl, whose name was Fengari, was ink-haired, pale as her lunar namesake, exquisitely shaped, straight-nosed and with her great black eyes set well apart. She was naked and unashamed. Luke treated her nakedness as a clinical necessity and examined closely the brown blotches that, like mushrooms about a tree, encircled her pudenda.

'They hurt when touched?'

'Like fire.'

'You've been in contact with a dirty man. This is not a clean occupation. Take this ointment, rub it in freely. Take this draught in water. And,' Luke added, 'give up this trade.'

'It's not a trade. I'm a servant of the goddess.' She was indignant.
'I'm not impressed. I call this no more than a highclass brothel.'
'The goddess will strike you down.'

'It's you she seems to have struck down.' She pointed, pouting, at a couple of silver pieces laid ready for him on a cedar press. He took these and empursed them. 'Your service to the goddess is temporarily intermitted,' he said with mock gruffness. 'I'll call again in a week's time.'

Riding back to town, he recited to the warm air the verses he had written that morning. Like many physicians, he desired to produce a book. He was not satisfied with what he had been writing: a kind of epic poem in Homeric hexameters about an Odyssean wanderer around the Greek islands who was searching for the Ithaca of philosophical truth. Where was reality? Did it lie in the invisible world of ideas or was it the crass tangibility of the natural order? He had read Plato. Plato would not have approved of the poem simply because it was literature, but could literature, meaning tales of wondering and strange adventures, properly encompass philosophy? Entering the town, he saw philosophy curl in the air like smoke and then get lost on the wind. For the material world shouted its primacy – traders and beggars and dirty naked children tumbling in the dust, above all women and girls with thrust breasts and haunches aware of their role in the world of pleasure, *Daphnici mores*. Juvenal had, in one of his satires, the third Luke thought it was, complained of the sewage of the Syrian Orontes, Antioch's river, polluting the Tiber. He read Latin as much as he read Greek. As though to provide a ready emblem of pollution, the horse Thersites stopped, as was his habit, to dung heavily on the cobbles. Finished, he responded again to the bit and clopped towards his stable. The stable was a rented one, two hundred yards from the little house which Luke also rented and where he lived alone. It was also on a lane at whose shady end, a four-storey warehouse leaning over it, stood the synagogue which Luke, an uncircumcised seeker of the truth, sometimes attended. Clutching his satchel, he walked to it, having spread hay for Thersites and locked the stable door, intrigued by the crowd outside it. They apparently wanted to get in but could not because of the many already congregated there. He knew the two Jews who complained to him. Amos, who had a hump like an ingrafted near empty mealsack, said:

'When a reverent believer can't get into his own place of worship – crammed with Gentiles – no offence, doctor – catchpenny eloquence – foreigners too.' The other, who was oneeyed, they were brothers in deformity, cackled:

'Keep out, you Greek heathen, if you don't want your innocence ruptured. Preaching resurrection and curing the sick. You'll be losing some of your patients.'

'Who is it?' Luke asked.

'The baldheaded runt from Cilicia.'

Luke pushed through politely and saw a bald pate and pair of waving hands. He heard: 'He leaves us the truth of his immortality and that of all who believe in him. Our spirits came to earth and joined with our bodies even at the moment of conception. The spirit cannot be extinguished as the body can, but when it departs this life with our death it leaves in a changed state. We live eternally through him, who took back to heaven the transformed lineaments of man. If he returned pure angelic spirit he would not be one with the father, his substance would be indistinguishable from that of the father and hence could he not properly be termed the son. It was through his taking on of flesh that he became the son, and the son he remains. But we too are the sons of heaven, of an unangelic substance. He has conquered death and we are his partners in that conquest. You seek renewal, we all seek it. The beginning of renewal is the acceptance of a covenant with the divine whose symbol shall be the act of baptism. And what is baptism? Let me explain.'

The oneeyed one was named Eliphaz. To Luke, leaving, he said: 'Impressed?'

'He's powerful.'

'Powerfully wrong. Why can't these people leave well alone? Why can't things stay as they are?'

Why, thought Luke to himself, cannot all the world be oneeyed? He went home to his simple meal of boiled beans and broiled riverfish. He took out his much punished manuscript from its press – all deletions, rescrawlings, interlineations. He studied it, sucking his teeth free of an enrobing beanskin. 'I sing the search of one who, despised of his fellows,/ Sought in the seas and islands, beneath an indifferent sun/ That gave no answers, answers to a single fevered question . . .' Perhaps he was not cut out to be a poet. Poetry was more than versification. Nor cut out to be a philosopher. And again, to write of a voyager when he himself had hardly moved ten miles from the Orontes. He needed to make the search himself. He was glued to a trade not over-respected in a city where magic and superstition paid better. He was growing stale.

It was by chance next day that he passed a baptism ceremony in brilliant sunlight on the left bank of the Orontes. He saw the little bald man at work, the drenching of the patient as he might be called, the announcement of the hope of a cure. Barnabas was with him; Barnabas he vaguely knew. Magic, a sort of. He rode on to the village where he had been treating a child ineffectually for a hydatid cyst. Larvae of tapeworms lodged in a swollen belly. They could not be purged. The child grew thinner. He saw the baptizers still busily at work when he rode back. There was, he supposed, no harm in it. A ceremony, a gesture of faith and hope, outward sign of inner grace, whatever that was.

An elderly man named Agabus came to Antioch. He was large and muscular and he had the exophthalmic gaze of the prophet. He wore a drab long shirt that left bare his hairy shins. Around his neck on a string he carried a cross, saying 'The emblem of shame is transformed to a sign of victory. Alleluia.' He sat with a Christian group in the house of the converted widow Agatha, a former pagan, where Barnabas and Paul shared a room, and ate heartily and, for the most part, silently of what was put before him. He smacked his lips over the sweetish Syrian wine, belched discreetly and said:

'He told you to feed the hungry and give drink to the thirsty. Am I not right? I am. Well, there are going to be enough of the hungry in Judaea, I can tell you. I never, to be honest, thought that this giving drink to the thirsty was more than a verbal flourish in a land where there is no shortage of water. Am I right? I think I am. Not only dreams, my friends, but factual reports. Three bad harvests in a row and corn already rising in price beyond the reach of the purses of the people.'

'Not only Judaea,' Barnabas said. 'Even Italy. The Emperor Claudius is going to have his hands full. Empty, rather.'

'Let him feed his own,' a middleaged man named Asaph said. 'And his own ought to include the people of Judaea. With the Romans it's all take and no give.'

'Judaea has her own king now,' Agabus said. 'But he is above such petty matters as the feeding of the people. Am I not right? I am.'

'What do you want?' Paul asked.

'Let your new Gentile Christians learn about corporal works of mercy. There's plenty of money here. Get it to Jerusalem. You and Barnabas here talk of going back there.'

'For fresh instructions, yes,' Barnabas said. 'But only when we've finished our work here in Antioch. We're still short of deacons.'

'You'll find no better work for the moment than taking money to Jerusalem. There's corn to be bought in Egypt and figs in Cyprus. The price is high, but what can you expect? It's going to get higher, get in there before it does. Am I not right? Let your Antioch faithful think of their Judaean brethren. This is a rich town.'

'How are the grain stores in Judaea?' Paul asked.

'Enough for two months if there was a just distribution. But the rich are hoarding and Herod Agrippa counts his gold. You've an urgent business on your hands. I'm right there about the priority, I think. I know I'm right.'

The brown blotches around the genitalia of the temple prostitute Fengari had yielded less to Luke's medicaments than to time and nature's own secret curative juices. Luke left the temple with his couple of silver pieces and was surprised to find bald Paul standing some ten yards away from the façade, looking up at the goddess in no posture of worship. Luke could not forbear to say:

'Drinking your fill of the enemy?'

Paul looked sharply at him. 'Those too many breasts make her a very unseductive one. Have we met?'

'Luke the physician. I heard you one day in the synagogue on Aish Lane, as they call it. Where the flour stores are.'

'I think I saw you one day on the riverbank, looking like a man who would like to swim but fears the water may be cold.'

'I wasn't too happy,' Luke said, 'about that thaumaturgical cure of yours, if I may call it that. The old man who believed he couldn't use his left arm. Then I thought: well, a cure is often a matter of confidence, which you would probably call faith.'

'And what is your faith, Luke the physician? You have just come out of where I would not for the life of me go in.'

'I was practising my skill, such as it is. One of the diseases of love.' Paul winced at that, but the term *eros* was distinct from *agape*: still, in marriage, which might be called the licensing of the gifts of that goddess up there, one was supposed to be expressed through the other. Luke said: 'You have walked all this way to frown at the polycolpous one? I rode and I ride back. There's my badtempered nag Thersites. You're welcome to ride behind me.'

'Thank you,' Paul said. 'As for the polycolpous one – a grotesque term but it has a kind of Homeric ring – she is both the enemy and not the enemy, if you understand me. I was thinking of our mother Eve, who brought us into the world and, with woman's curiosity, meddled where she should have not and made the discovery of sin. Fleshly embraces are here glorified in a manner that goes against nature. Eve is somewhere behind all this. I fear the enemy but I too had a mother.' He stood there brooding while Luke's horse, finding no grass here and fretting, gnawed at the hitching post in the temple's forecourt. 'I do not,' he said, in a manner somewhat defiant, as though countering an accusation, 'wish to make war on women. The goddess, however, is no wraith or fiction – she is real enough. She has to be fought. There is the desert all beyond her, as you can see. She presides over no grass or trees or cornfields.' He sighed. 'The goddess is a great nuisance.'

They rode together into town, Paul's hard tentmaking fingers digging into Luke to keep his balance. Paul said: 'You did not answer my question. About your faith.'

'I'm not yet ready to step into the water,' Luke said. 'It's still too cold.'

'Some need time to think. Others are very briskly assaulted and

175

thought hardly comes into it. Well, take your time. When I come back you may have taken it.'

'You're leaving Antioch?'

The moon was coming up, gibbous like the fractious Jew Amos. 'The goddess,' Paul said, 'is only dead metal. But dead metal buys food. Yes, leaving for Jerusalem with Antioch money. But I shall be back.' And then, entering the town, lively with the unregenerate, 'I wish to God that were true. About her being dead metal, I mean.'

Marcus Julius Tranquillus was transferred from the Praetorian Guard to the Ninth Legion; this could be interpreted as a sly gesture from the Emperor himself: if Julius wished to draw blood he had better do it with barbarians. For Claudius, whom the Senate had offered triumphant regalia, scorned such a bestowal without a genuine triumph, and he sought such a triumph in Britain. The Emperor whom Julius's family claimed to have been a kinsman, though on the patrician side, had invaded Britain but achieved no conquest. Of Caligula's sham you already know. Claudius sailed from Ostia, Julius with him in an officer cadre which would be assimilated into the Ninth Legion, at that time stationed in northern Gaul. It was not an easy voyage. They were twice nearly wrecked off the Ligurian coast, and there was a close shave when a storm suddenly broke off the Stoechades, but they made Massilia safely enough and then marched north to Gesoriacum. Thence, in clear weather, they crossed the water sleeve of the Channel and found the barbarians waiting for them. They were easily subdued.

Claudius set himself up in an ornate tent on rich downland and admired the agricultural potential of southern Britain. But the time for intensive colonization was not yet: now the simple aim was to collect barbaric loot and cart some yellow-locked prisoners back to Rome to grace an imperial triumph. Marcus Crassus Frugi, an experienced general officer, ordered the burning of a few native encampments and the slaughtering of their inhabitants, regardless of sex and age. On to Roman carts were loaded a great number of native artefacts which demonstrated that intricate art was not necessarily an index of high civilization. The shields, swords and vessels were of bronze and iron and most elaborately ornamented with curlicues.

Julius's active military career did not last long. Two miles from the coast he and his raiding party chained up a line of prisoners and started to march them to the boats. Out of a thicket a pair of lone British warriors peered, saw a barelegged Roman officer giving orders, then launched spears at him. One of the spears went nowhere; the other, razorsharp and well aimed, struck him deeply in the right leg. He cursed and tried to pull it out with both hands, but it was

176

profoundly embedded. He had to call a common soldier. This soldier clucked commiseration and wrenched out the shaft, leaving the point in. Julius fainted. He came to to find himself lying in a barge, at the prow, with a misty vista of chalk cliffs receding. Disdainful brawny British prisoners looked at his agony and expressed no satisfaction. There was an orderly there staunching the blood with white wool whose fibres stuck to the lips of the wound.

'Something seems to have got cut there, sir. Something inside. Have to leave it to nature, as they say. You won't be on the march for a long time.'

The imperial report spoke of no battles and no casualties, meaning Roman deaths. A great part of the southern section of the island had been subdued and garrisoned. The slow process of colonization could, some time in the near future, be undertaken with right Roman seriousness. There was a splendid triumph in Rome, in which Marcus Julius Tranquillus did not take part. He was at home with his wife, who had just given birth to a daughter. This girl Sara insisted on naming Ruth, though the father wished to commemorate a loved aunt by calling her Flavia. Flavia or Ruth – one or the other, depending on circumstances. Julius limped round their bedroom, rocking the howling child. Sara looked from the bed, expressing no emotion. The noise of the triumphal bucinae could be heard even here on the Janiculum.

Claudius beamed from his chariot, wearing the naval crown, which had a frieze of stylized ships' beaks on it; it symbolized his conquest of the ocean, meaning twenty-odd miles of channel. Behind his chariot rode the Empress Messalina, beautiful as the moon. She had demanded that morning from her uxorious husband the gift of a military escort. She had, she said, enemies. Claudius had said that he would see what he could do. The victorious generals marched behind her, trouncers of bare-arsed barbarians who smelled like old dogs, wearing togas with purple borders which signified the honour they had won. Marcus Crassus Frugi, having earned the right to wear such a garment in a previous campaign – one waged against a real enemy, redhaired Danubians – disdained to wear one again. He rode a horse richly caparisoned, dressed in a tunic embroidered with palms, trees not native to the misty northern island he claimed, on the Emperor's behalf, to have conquered.

Back in Jerusalem King Herod Agrippa I was supervising the torture of a young Nazarene or (we had better stay with the Antiochian term) Christian, Simon the son of Cleopas, whom we have already met and abandoned. He said to the torturers:

'Try again.'

The two robed men – it was proper for torturers to go halfnaked, but the royal cellars were cold – twisted the arms of Simon son of Cleopas round his back, upward till they neared breaking point. Simon yelled: 'I don't know, I tell you!'

'The man Peter,' Herod Agrippa demanded. 'For the last time – where is he?'

'They're not in Jerusalem – any of them.'

'Liar. They've gone to ground, haven't they? I want to know where.'

'I don't know.'

The king sat on a little stool and looked sternly at Simon. This was a historic cellar, and it still bore the marks of history – rusty bloodstains on the whitewashed walls. Here his grandfather, Herod the Great, had overseen the torture of servants of the Magi, those kings from the east who would not say where they were going. They knew, and the servants ought to have known too, but they had died of broken hearts or some such organ before disclosing their knowledge. What he, the grandson, was doing now had everything to do with Herod the Great's failure to elicit the right response to his bone-cracking. That child had got away to Egypt but was, in a sense, responsible for the brutal deaths of all those innocents. If he had not been born those murders would not have taken place. Herod Agrippa now proposed more politic murders. He said:

'You were seen with one of them yesterday. Who was it?'

'I wasn't – I didn't –'

'His name?' The boy fainted.

'Give him another baptism,' Herod Agrippa ordered jocularly. A wooden bucket of Hebron water drenched the lad and brought him shuddering to.

'Come on – his name.'

This time a bone snapped, not at all audible in that wide empty cellar. Before the breaking of another, exacted more punitively than in the cause of interrogation, Herod Agrippa got what he was after. Then he went to a meeting with old Caiaphas who, these days, had to be carried everywhere, his legs having lost all power of locomotion. As they sat together in one of the royal parlours – its furnishings distressingly pagan to the old priest's eyes – Herod Agrippa could see that Caiaphas was covertly disapproving of the swollen royal belly, which looked like a monstrous fruit of overindulgence rather than what it was – illness, illness, and grave illness. It would be cured, however. The chief physician was awaiting an infallible purge from Cyprus. Herod Agrippa thought much of death, but not for himself. He said now:

'This James is by way of being the resident leader of the Nazarenes. But it's Peter I'm really after. He's the head of the whole body. Lop him off and the whole movement will die.'

'You're sure of that?'

'Well, whether I am or not, it will please the people. And one of my royal tasks is to keep the people happy.'

'You could best please the people by giving them bread.'

'Things will come right. We're going to have a bumper harvest. To return to James. I've found out where he is. We could have a quick trial in which all the blame for the grain shortage could be laid at the Nazarene door. God's displeasure and so on.'

'James,' Caiaphas said, 'has not greatly offended against the Jewish law. Even in the conduct of Nazarene policy he's been scrupulous in avoiding talk about the equality of Jew and Gentile. Most take him to be a good orthodox Jew who believes that the Messiah has arrived and departed. He has no enemies that I know of.'

'All right,' the king said. 'But if it's Peter we want, and such of his confederates as are still here, the beheading of James will smoke him and them out. But it's him I have chiefly in mind. He's the true blasphemer. James is merely available.'

'I'm uneasy about this,' Caiaphas said. 'A little. The man about whom I have no scruple of conscience at all is the Saul who now calls himself by another name. There is a renegade self-confessed, and I understand he is now in Judaea.'

'But very cunning. And ready to plead the rights of a Roman citizen. Too dangerous, too difficult. And anyway it wouldn't be expedient to catch him even if we could. He's brought money from Antioch to buy bread for the people. The people are stupid. It would be hard to persuade them that such a man is a criminal.'

'Criminality is never expunged by good works.'

'Tell that to hungry Jerusalem. I prefer to tell them that the present shortages are the fault of the Nazarenes. God's displeasure at their heresy is visited on the whole of the Jewish people. The blood of James will gratify the Lord God. It will smell sweet in his nostrils.'

'And yet your majesty, if I may speak boldly, believes none of these things.'

'Oh, I believe in a single faith for a single people. That's policy. And, of course, I believe in the godhead. I even believe in those human attributes we attach to the godhead. The Emperor Gaius, now rotting in hell if there is a hell, taught me some things. The king is the Lord's anointed and therefore God's visible representative on earth. When does my effigy go into the Temple?'

'That cannot happen – this you know. The Sanhedrin is unanimously against it. For your majesty's own protection. And, whatever your majesty wishes, we have a faith to uphold.'

'Oh, yes. The sacred eternal Jewish faith in the great unloving loving merciful vindictive father of the tribes. Forgive my *private* scepticism. I've lived in the great world. Rome, I mean.'

179

James the son of Zebedee was picked up without much difficulty in the cellar of Cleopas. He was imprisoned without trial and led out to the forecourt of the Temple for his execution in the Roman manner – head on the block, decapitation by sword – a hefty broadsword sharpened on both its edges to an exquisite fineness. He came, hands bound before him, aware that he was the first of the apostles to meet a martyr's end and perversely content accordingly. With him was his personal guard Ezra. These two and the executioner marched to a soft drumbeat towards the block. The crowd was murmurous but not loud. Herod Agrippa sat on a portable throne. He raised his finger for the drumbeat to cease and then he addressed his subjects, crying, and each impulse of his voice caused a stab in his vitals: 'People of Judaea, brothers in the holy faith, we are met to witness a just act of execution. Our faith has been assailed by a noxious heresy. The heretics have met great tolerance, for the Jewish people are large of heart and unprejudiced of mind, but Gentile pollutions have sickened our stomachs and quelled our tolerance. Israel is a unity and must stand as a unity. We are one people and one faith and the strength of that faith must find expression not solely in passive piety but in the occasional flash of the sword of just punition. Especially, I may say, when the Lord God shows his displeasure. Has he not shown that displeasure by striking us with famine? The man James stands condemned. Executioner, do your work.'

Ezra the bodyguard now spoke clearly. 'King of Israel, if I may be allowed to speak, I have been the custodian of James since the moment of his arrest. I find nothing but good in him. I am become one of his faith. If he deserves to die I too deserve to die. But I will not die without denouncing the injustice of this butchery.'

Herod Agrippa yelled: 'If you seek the executioner's sword, lay your head on that block. You will serve to test the sharpness of the sword's edge. You add to your heresy the greater sin of disloyalty. Executioner!'

Not everybody watched the severing of Ezra's head. There were women who averted their eyes and the eyes of their children, and there were also Temple guards and secret policemen who had been ordered to keep a sharp watch for such members of the Nazarene faith as had slunk from their hidingplaces to witness the death of the first apostolic martyr. While Ezra's head, severed far from neatly, was being hurled to the dogs and the blood on the block was being wiped off with a wet rag, one of the guards pointed. An old man with a grey beard looking shiftily about him. This old man saw that he was being pointed at and he tried to lose himself in the crowd. James, waiting for the block to be thoroughly cleansed, looked about him and betrayed a sign of distress that his execution should be the occasion of one or more of his brethren's being put into danger. This sign was noted. But soon James was incapable of further innocent betrayal. He laid his head down without waiting for the executioner's assistant to do it for him, the cleansed sword was raised to the innocent sun, then it swept down and sliced through James's neck as through a cheese. Blood fountained, the crowd groaned and then began to disperse. The guards and policemen followed the path that was being pointed.

Peter was not arrested until the beginning of the week of the unleavened bread, that is on the eve of the fourteenth day of Nisan, also called Passover Eve. He was found almost by chance in a disused cellar under a burnt and abandoned house in the northwest of the city. A child's ball had rolled into it, the child went down to recover it, there being stone steps leading down but no door, and happened to come up when a couple of policemen were taking time off to eat a bit of bread. 'Man down there,' the child said. When taken, he admitted freely to being who he was, and was hauled at once to the fortress of Antonia, which was not far away. He was a valuable prisoner, and four relays of soldiers took turns in guarding him. On the first night, when a scullion brought food and water, with a guard standing behind him, Peter said:

'How long?' The guard said:

'Lucky, you are. You're kindly allowed to live till after Passover. Gives you a bit of time to brood over things, doesn't it? Eat your nice dinner.' The metal plate with its dry bread and a ragged chunk of nameless overboiled meat clanged on the stone floor; along with it thudded a clay pitcher. Then the door clashed shut. Peter ignored the food. He knelt on the cold stone and prayed aloud, saying:

'Lord, I heard you say that night that now seems a long time ago: not my will but your will be done. Those are my words now. Yet you made me head of the church, the first mortal father of the faithful. I have work to do, and I pray by your power I be allowed to do it. But everything is in your hands. Lord, I believe. Lord, I trust. Lord, above all I love. At least, I think I love. May our enemies be forgiven. May the faith live. May I see the kingdom. But not,' and he raised his voice as if addressing a fishing confederate hard of hearing, *'until I've finished the work*. Amen.' He sighed, drank some water and nibbled at the bread. Then he went over to the hard pallet and lay on it. Soon, prayer being the best of soporifics, he began to snore.

In his palace bedchamber Herod Agrippa brooded on the purge from Cyprus. It had so far done little except augment his pains. He considered, in that phase before sleep in which fantasy rows away from the shore of reason, that he deserved better of his body than this. He had caught and imprisoned the chief enemy of the state. He was not sorry that the time of the paschal celebrations forbade the spilling of blood. There was leisure to prepare for a full-dress trial in which the secular and the sacred would conjoin in the rhetoric of abomination, the case against the Nazarene faith could receive its most considered articulation, and the beheading of the father of lies who was also an ignorant fisherman could be presented as an act of piety shedding the ultimate credit on Israel's monarch. He would go down in history as the saviour of the race. He basked, just before sleep, in the contemplation of that ennoblement; it was almost as good as a medicine.

The Empress Messalina obtained her military escort, whose commander was Marcus Julius Tranquillus. The maniple of picked veterans, some of whom wore Britannic gashes like medals, marched before and behind her gilded litter, which had handles left and right as well as fore and aft and called for the brawn of eight carriers. These were all rather dull Germans, who had the look of men who thought, in so far as they thought at all, that they might as well be doing this work as any other. The covered litter had a couch in it, on which the Empress lay. Occasionally a chosen male friend would lie with her. It pleased her to copulate while being borne through the busy Roman streets; it made the act almost public. Marcus Julius Tranquillus did not lie with her; nor was he yet commanded to. He was somewhat severe of countenance and took his duties seriously. Moreover, he seemed to be in pain and, when he walked, he had to lean on a blackthorn stick. He did not walk much in the Empress's service; his place was with her in the covered and curtained litter, sitting primly at the foot of her couch. He intrigued her rather; he was handsome and evidently brave and had been in battle; he was serious and she liked seriousness for ten minutes of the day or thereabouts.

The undoubted beauty of Messalina and her immoral kind must always create problems for such philosophers as, discoursing on beauty, truth and goodness as related values, end with a mystical desire to promote the relation into an identity and even conjure a deity who possesses these values as attributes. God, say some philosophers, manifests himself in the sublunary world in particular beauties, truths and acts of benevolence; properly, the values should be conjoined to shadow their identity in the godhead, but this happens so infrequently that one must suppose divinity condones a kind of diabolic fracture or else, and perhaps my book is already giving some hint of this, he demonstrates his ineffable freedom through contriving at times a wanton inconsistency. If this is so, we need not wonder at Messalina's failure to match her beauty with a love of truth and goodness. She was a chronic liar and she was thoroughly bad. But her beauty, we are told, was a miracle. The symmetry of her body obeyed all the golden rules of the mystical architects, her skin was without even the most minuscule flaw and it glowed as though gold had been inlaid behind translucent ivory, her breasts were full and yet pertly disdained earth's pull, the nipples nearly always erect, and visibly so beneath her byssinos, as in a state of perpetual sexual excitation, the areolas delicately pigmented to a kind of russet. The sight of her weaving bare white arms was enough, it is said, to make a man grit his teeth with desire to be encircled by them; the smooth plain of her back, tapering to slenderness only to expand lusciously to the opulence of her perfect buttocks, demanded unending caresses. The face was the face of a virgin whose dedication to chastity transcended the mere forms of the Dianan cult, which is for the most part a pure hypocrisy: the brown eyes were wide and widely spaced, the nose disdained that excess, interpreted as strength of will, which disfigures most Mediterranean countenances, and the lips were less than perfect only perhaps in their excessive moistness, which seemed to argue a superfluity of saliva, and in their slightly thrust attitude suggesting a permanent pout of dissatisfaction. Her appetites, indeed, were not easy to satisfy, and they were seated not only, as with most women, in the crucial nerves that guard the centre of generation, but in outlying sectors of her body which might be thought too remote to catch fire. Her hair, Julius thought with a disloyalty which he was quick to quell, was of a richer and more odorous darkness even than that of his wife Sara. Messalina found only one man in her life capable of granting her the multiple satisfactions she craved, and her meeting with this man led to her undoing. Her imperial husband was old and as incompetent in bed as in other fora of activity, and their marriage had been sprung by Gaius who, knowing Messalina's proclivities, had thought to humiliate his stuttering uncle by the mismatch.

On their first journey together, Messalina engaged the captain of her guard in pleasant conversation with no hint of condescension in it. Her voice was as beautiful as her person, suggesting doves and honey and wallfruit reaching the highest pitch of ripeness. She said or sang: 'They tell me you did well in Britain, Junius.'

'Julius, madam.'

'Of course. The Caesar who was killed. But you have been killing the enemies of Caesar.'

'I would hardly call the Britons enemies of Caesar, madam. Tribes quite content to be left alone to get on with fishing and ploughing and fighting among themselves.'

'So,' she cooed, 'you disapprove of the great civilizing Roman mission, as my imperial husband calls it?'

'I didn't say quite that, madam.'

'Oh, you may speak freely with your Empress. After all, you and I are to be friends, isn't that so?'

'My Empress is too good. I am the least of my Empress's servants. But I have to confess – this is a little difficult to adjust. My trade was killing. And now – I sometimes wonder at my appointment.'

'Simple enough, my dear friend. The captain of my personal guard should be brave, honourable, discreet – presentable. I have it on your superior officer's testimony that you are the first three of these things. The other I am able to judge for myself. Tell me – are you a married man?'

'Yes, madam. And I recently became a father.'

'Good. Married men are more discreet than single ones. They have to be. They have something to lose. Tell me about your wife. Is she beautiful?'

'Very. But, of course,' (the courtier creaking to life) 'not so beautiful as –'

'Yes yes yes yes. And her name? Is that beautiful too?'

'Sara. A Jewish name. And our daughter's name is Ruth. Short sharp names.'

'Like birdcalls, yes. And why should a Roman officer of ancient Roman stock choose to marry a mere colonial?'

'Love, madam.'

'Oh then I approve. I approve of love, Junius I mean Julius. Love is the whole of life. Life is nothing without love. Love cuts across all our barriers, our formalities, our vows, our duties. Tell these slaves we're here,' she added, pulling the curtain aside the width of three fingers. Julius knocked with his stick against the outside of the litter. And then, with some pain and difficulty, he got up and got out. 'Poor boy,' Messalina cooed. They had arrived at an estate beyond the Servilian Gardens, in the thirteenth district of the city, just north of the Ostian Gate. Julius thought he knew whose estate this was. Discretion, he told himself. Messalina said: 'I shall be here for an hour or so. You'd better dispose the guard around the house, in the grounds, very discreetly. You know whose house this is?'

'No, madam,' discreetly.

'Good, very good. Full marks for discretion.' She smiled bewitchingly and then swayed towards the gate. When she was lost to view, one of Julius's men, not known for his subservience, looked his captain full in the eyes and made a throat-cutting gesture. He said:

'If she was mine –'

And so the work went on, if you could call it work. There was also the question of Julius's glandular responses to the almost daily propinquity of his Empress, so naked under her lawn. The body followed nature, blind goddess, sister of Fortuna, and knew nothing of words like love and fidelity. What precisely *was* his work? This Sara, giving the breast to Ruth, had asked often enough. Oh, I have to

184

guard the Empress's quarters. Do you see much of the Empress? Hardly anything. She's pretty remote from us common soldiers. I've heard different. From whom, Sara? Everybody knows about her. One of these days, Julius feared, she would issue a command while they swayed towards a discreet indiscretion of hers on the Esquiline or near the Naumachia Augusti, the Marine Theatre not far from his own rented house, or beyond the Gardens of Lucullus on the Via Pinciana. So, Junius I mean Julius, you find your Empress unattractive, I have had men whipped for such ingratitude. Come over, put your hand here. His nights in bed with Sara were, thanks to blind nature, becoming riotous. Women were not fools, women always knew what was going on. He could well imagine Sara confronting the Empress, woman to woman, with 'Leave my husband alone or I'll scratch your eyes out.' Eyes would be out, certainly, but no woman would do the scratching. There were cruel Syrians and Pannonians on the imperial payroll, adept at that manner of punishment for *laesa maiestas*.

Julius rose early one morning in country air, hearing the crowing of cocks and the snuffle of pigs. He and his men had slept soldierly rough in farm quarters. The farm bordered the estate of a certain Laturnus, just south of the gate which opened on to the Via Asinaria. In the manor house the Empress was staying the night with – Julius knew who, but was discreet even with himself. He had taken a rough breakfast of bubbling warm milk fresh from the cow and a piece of yesterday's bread with conserve of blackberries. Now he sniffed the good air and foresaw a damnable future for himself. She would be found out one of these days, and he would be indicted for disloyalty to the Emperor. It was his duty, always discreetly, to drop a word to one of the Greek functionaries on the Palatine. But Messalina's private intelligence service would have him discreetly stabbed before he got so far. The misery on the face of the young man with a growth of black beard who now came from the direction of one of the barns, scratching as from an uneasy sleep in straw, was, he was sure, a mirror of his own. The young man looked at the uniformed and sworded Julius somewhat fearfully and strode in the direction of the Via Asinaria with a speed that could be termed furtive. Julius called cheerfully:

'A moment. All right, you're in no danger. Haven't we met?'

The young man paused and frowned: had they?

'A wrestling match. You were one of the wrestlers. The other one wore cat's claws. He is no longer with us.'

The young man spoke. His Latin was not good and it contained gutturals that might be Greek. He said: 'Yes. I remember the occasion. But I didn't have time to look at the spectators. It seems as though I've been sleeping where I shouldn't. I didn't know they had military guards on farms.'

185

'I'm part of an imperial escort, awaiting the morning's orders.'

'I want nothing to do with imperial escorts.'

'You're no longer wrestling?'

'Wrestling to live but not doing very well at it. Some of us are barred from making a living. An imperial decree.'

'Are you a Jew?'

'I didn't say that.'

'Jews shouldn't be here at all. Don't worry, I shan't report you to the police. I'm married to one of the daughters of Israel.'

'Her name her name?' the young man panted with great urgency, opening and closing his fists.

'Sara.'

'No. No. It's not possible. Does she ever speak of a man named Caleb?'

'Frequently.'

Caleb nearly collapsed with the relief of his discovery. Julius took him to the farm quarters and gave him a cup of milk, cooler now than it had been.

There was a couple in a bedroom of the manor house of Laturnus, now away in Sardinia, not yet ready for breakfast. It was not a luxuriously appointed bedroom; it had something rustic about its furnishings. But the bed was huge and deep. The naked Messalina lay with her lovely arms entwined about the nakedness of Gaius Silius, a patrician young man of rather empty handsomeness. He said:

'Why do those soldiers have to tramp around outside? I feel – well, watched.'

'The Empress requires protection. From her numerous enemies. Don't worry, dear Gaius. They say nothing. They daren't. For that matter, they *see* nothing. The Empress Messalina pays her social visits. Business visits too. They're quite in order. There's nothing to feel frightened or guilty about.'

'You, my love,' Gaius Silius said, more at ease, 'are one of the eternally innocent. You don't know what guilt feels like. Your skin's untouched by the lines of – oh, you know, remorse, compassion –'

'Cruelty? *Am* I cruel?'

'Sometimes.'

'Cruelty,' she said, having read this somewhere and at once recognized the truth of it, 'is one of the sharp sauces of *love*. All the rest is just – well, policy, self-protection, being the Empress.'

'The Emperor too,' Gaius Silius said somewhat primly, 'he has his right to self-protection. How would the Emperor feel if he knew he was being cuckolded?'

'At least,' she said, catching something of his primness, 'I don't *flaunt* it, do I? Claudius makes sheep's eyes at his own niece, puts his

186

gouty fingers in her bosom when he thinks no one's looking. Ugh, an old man's lust. The Emperor is above taboos like incest. I think Agrippina will have to drink something that disagrees with her. And perhaps her dribbling uncle could share the cup.'

'Sometimes, *meum mel*, you – what can I say –?'

'Revolt you? Frighten you? Never be frightened of clear thinking, Gaius. And never enter on anything you're unwilling to pursue to the end. I sometimes think that you thought you could get into the Empress's bed without having to pay for it. Messalina is a whore, but she's different from all the other whores. She costs nothing. The stupidest slut of a village and the first lady of the Empire have that in common. But the Empress Messalina, my dearest heart, costs everything. As you're to find out. How is the beauteous Lollia Paulina these days?'

'I don't know. She's at Herculaneum. She lives her own life. I say nothing. She says nothing.'

'If she ever were to say anything,' Messalina said tenderly into his right cheek, 'her jewels would be stuffed down her throat. She'd be crammed like a goose with them. I'd have her before me covered with them, like starlight as that stupid poet said, and then she'd be stripped to her buff, link by link of pearls and amethysts, and they'd be rammed down her throat.' Gaius Silius could sense the excitement in her hot breath. She then said: 'Certain things have to be done, dearest Gaius. You and I are to be together for ever and ever, or as near that as makes no difference. This is one bed you don't steal away from with a couple of coins on the coverlet and your fingers to your lips. I want you for myself, and by Castor and Pollux –' (she grasped with sharp nails that part of his body which they had so jocularly named) – 'I don't let you go.'

Gaius Silius held back a sigh and said: 'I'm flattered but, forgive me, *cor cordium*, somewhat sceptical. Tell me, how many men have you had in your short life?'

'How many? I can't count. Their names would make a book, I suppose, even just those I remember. A woman,' she said fiercely, 'is entitled to her pleasures. Few men can do more than touch the fringes of a woman's satisfaction. You, honeycomb, are quite exceptional. You are *tireless*. I think that's your only talent. You're far from bright in many ways, but you have that. As well as fantasy and ingenuity. You know how important the life of the body is. That's rare. I'm not going to let you get away. You and I are going to be married.'

He nearly leapt out of the bed at that. '*Married?* You mean – divorce from Claudius, divorce from Paulina? That's impossible.'

'Two long dark divorces. With no actuaries or notaries or whatever those legal gentlemen are called. Don't ask me any more about it now.

There's much to be done, dear Gaius, but there's no great hurry. As you see, the sun's a slow climber.'

She seized him with inordinate appetite. The next hour was consumed in a remarkable variety of embraces and penetrations.She was succuba and incuba, mare and rider. They left the bed for the floor, the wall, even for the edge of the open casement, and even then she was not satisfied, though Gaius Silius thought she must grow hoarse with her screams of attainment. Back on the bed, she achieved at last the consummation of her need and her lovely face glowed with a rapture only to be described as saintly. This is, all of it, quite disgusting.

Peter, on his prison pallet, had, though proleptically a saint, no such glow. He slept well, though this night had been announced to him as the last before his execution. He had been brought out of jail daily during the last week for a slow trial whose conclusion had never been in doubt. He had been interested to note that the heretical aspects of his master's messiahship had been dwelt on rather less than the opening up of the new faith (which some of the deposing priests had been prepared to regard, for argument's sake, as an almost legitimate expansion of orthodoxy) to the uncircumcised Gentile. The conversion of the centurion Cornelius had been presented as an unauthorized act of pollution; the willingness to relax the basic hygienic and dietary regulations of the Jewish faith in deference to Gentile prejudice was presented as a brutal act of deracination, not, as with the imputation of messiahship, a tearing off of bark or a lopping of branches. The arboreal similitude persisted: the Judaic tree must be pruned by its own designated tenders, which meant getting rid of Peter and depriving the upstart sect of its head. It was in vain for Peter to protest that his innovations had come directly from God: that only made matters worse. In the closing speeches the vigorous piety of Israel's monarch, absent during the trial, confined to his bed with atrocious stomach pains, had been commended; his high place in the history of Israel's struggle to sustain the ancient purity of the faith was assured. Peter was then solemnly condemned to death. In his innocence he requested crucifixion in a form not identical with that of his master, for which he professed himself unworthy: let him be nailed to a Greek *chi* or on a regular Roman T inverted. Roman, he was told, Roman, he was demanding a Roman punishment when Rome no longer ruled the land. Properly he should be stoned to death, like the Greek heresiarch Stephen, but the precedent of the sword for the execution of James was acceptable as a clean, easy and somewhat apposite mode of dispatch: there had been much talk of symbolic lopping; let there be a literal

188

and, it was hoped, final lopping. With the cutting off of Peter's head the limbs of the detestable new faith would lose all power of locomotion. Amen and alleluia.

Peter slept well because he had been given a cup of drugged wine. He snored heartily, but an angelic visitant might have noted a pallor as of sickness: in spite of his acquiescence in the death sentence and even a demand that the mode of death be excruciating, he was still something of a coward, and his sleeping colour showed this. A light passed the window and a cock, thinking the dawn had come, sang loudly. This woke Peter: even his deeply sleeping mind was sensitive to the crowing of cocks. He smacked a dry mouth. The crowing had ceased. Now a dog somewhere bayed at the moon. Peter was surprised to see that the two guards appointed to his person lay on the stone floor asleep. He felt a certain indignation at this: men should do what they are paid for. And then he saw that the cell door was open. This was more than warders' carelessness. There was a trap here somewhere. The sleeping guards snored loudly and not in unison. Had they drunk too of the drugged wine, thinking it to be undrugged? When a door was open it represented an invitation to go through it. He took the old cloak he had used as a coverlet and wrapped himself warmly. Then he cautiously peered out into the corridor, which was illuminated with two wall torches, and found it empty. There was something terribly irregular here, unless, of course, he was still really asleep and dreaming of escape. But a glance back into the cell showed him that his pallet was empty. Someone was engineering his escape, but who and how?

He then saw, scrawled on the outside of the cell door, the name Ioannis Markos or John Mark in yellow chalk. That was the name of the cousin of Barnabas, who was supposed to be lying low, along with Saul or Paul as he now was, in Caesarea. A right instinct told him to wipe off this name from the door with his cloak. Then, with little confidence, he went on soft feet along the corridor and came to another open door. This opened on to another corridor, right-angled to the one he had left, and a few yards down it, on the left, he heard the noise of what he took to be boisterous drunkenness. There was an open door and light, the only light of that corridor, beamed out of it. Guards having a party. Something told him that furtiveness would not be in order now, so he trod with some confidence and even a loud chest-clearing cough towards the light. Someone inside, hearing him, called 'Everything all right then?' in bad Aramaic and he replied, taking care to use Judaean and not Galilean tonalities, that everything was. Then he passed the light and came to a gate of rather thin metal, open as he had expected and, in a part of his brain, not really wanted to expect, and found that this led to a narrow stairway going down.

He then found himself in the open air in an ill-tended garden with stunted shrubs and a young Judas tree. At the end of a weedy path there was a very massive iron gate. He walked towards it under the moon, which more than one hound now howled at, fully expecting to be picked up at any moment by boisterous troops and perhaps even a thin intellectual officer saying 'Thought we'd let you have a last taste of hope, old man. Fine thing, hope. I've had lots of it in my time. Never came to anything, though. All right, boys, bundle him back in.' There was indeed a presence, but only of a rising wind. This rose so violently that it clanged open the left half of the gate. Peter hurried through and came to the seven steps he had often observed from below and only once before, looking back to lost freedom, from above. He now went down them and found himself in the deserted street. Herod Agrippa's police would be waiting round that corner. The game was up, and a cruel one it was, so he walked staunchly towards their hidden arms. They were not there. There was nobody there. His liberty was the real thing. He ran into it, meaning in the direction of John Mark's mother's house.

He turned into a dark alley. He heard drunken singing begin to resound down it: two late revellers taking a shortcut home. He found a back door open and got into a yard in which cats intent on a courting ritual took little notice of him. The singers passed: their song was a banal popular one that had recently taken the fancy of the Jerusalem young, something about a girl being as straight as a *dikla* tree. He was out again just as the cantorial part of the feline courtship, perhaps encouraged by the human caterwauling, began to wake the sleeping household above it: a male groan, the threat of the throwing of an old boot. He left the alley and got on to a wider street, then he turned right to a treelined residential quarter where, he knew, the house of John Mark's mother lay. There were lights on in that house: perhaps there was a prayer meeting concerned with the repose of his soul; more likely they, having contrived his escape in a manner still inexplicable, were waiting for him to come there.

But the outer gate which led to the forecourt of shrubs and flowers, well tended, was locked. A little bell on a chain was affixed to an iron staple on the wall. This he shook. Its tintinnabulation was tiny, but it seemed to him likely to wake the street. Light still blazed from an upper casement. He rang again, deafeningly it seemed. This time the front door of the house opened and a young fat girl appeared. He knew her; her name was Rhoda. 'Rhoda,' he called in a loud whisper, 'it's me, Peter. Let me in.' Rhoda's response was to shriek and slam the door shut. Stupid fool of a damned girl. He rang the bell again and this time did not care if he woke the whole damned street. Damned idiotic imbecile of a stupid girl. The front door opened again and he saw

John Mark's mother come down the path with a key. She let him in. She relocked the gate. They entered the house together.

John Mark lay in bed. He was supposed to be a genuine imbecile immune from the probings of the law which, at the time of Saul's persecutions, had been interested in the Nazarene philanthropy of his father, now dead of starvation in one of the camps that Saul had set up. His imbecility was now so taken for granted in the city that he could drool around the market, steal apples unmolested, and giggle obscenities like 'Jesus lives'. He was supposed to have picked up the slogan from his father without knowing its meaning. In fact he was a learned young man who said now, as Rhoda hugged the wall, fearful of the thing that said its name was Peter: 'She still takes you for a *fravashi.*'

'A what?'

'It's a Zoroastrian term I find useful. Not quite an angel, not quite a ghost. A *fravashi.* Touch her, go on, hug her, kiss her, show her you're real.' Peter made for her grimly and she screamed and ran out, falling over things. 'A good girl but silly. Her name means rose but she doesn't smell like one. Welcome to liberty.'

Peter sat down heavily and was given, by John Mark's mother, a cup of wine, not drugged. 'What I want to know is,' he said, 'how did you do it?'

'Do what?'

'Get me out of that place.'

'I had nothing to do with it.'

'The cell door was open and your name was chalked on it.'

'There's more than one John Mark in the world.'

'Perhaps,' his mother said, 'there'd been another prisoner there with the name John Mark.'

'Well, then,' Peter said through his winewet beard, 'somebody must have bribed somebody or killed somebody. Not that I saw any corpses around.'

'Friends of the faith have no money,' John Mark said, 'and they don't kill. It's divine intervention or some such thing.'

'I'll believe that when I see it.'

'How do you know you haven't seen it?'

'It's a damned mystery, that's all I can say.'

'Not damned, surely?'

John Mark's mother was a cunning woman reputed to be a devout daughter of the strict faith; she was known for her loud denunciations of the Nazarene heresy and her rich choice of epithets in the regard of its adherents. She would call them desert dogs, whelps of dugless bitches, walking chunks of maggoty cheese, corrosive pilgarlicks, costive beggars, ambulant diseases and the like. Some of her terms of

191

opprobrium were, even by members of the Sanhedrin, considered to go too far, particularly those which attributed sexual perversion to the Nazarenes, such as stuffers of their lousy heads up their mothers' cunts, defilers of the arses of the unblemished sons and daughters of Jerusalem and so on. Still, nobody could ever be sure of being wholly safe from the investigations of the religious police: her excesses of objurgation might one of these days be seen through. She said now: 'I hope to God you wiped the name off the door.'

'Do you take me altogether for a fool?'

'Well, then,' she said. 'Even so, we have to be careful. You'll have to stay in the cellar here for a while. It's cold but it's safe. We've plenty of blankets. James is down there.'

'Little James?'

'There's no other, is there, since your old fishing friend was done in by his majesty. God knows how long it will have to be, but we'll get you away in time. James is stubborn, though. He says his place is here and here he stays.'

'James doesn't know yet?'

'About you getting out? How can he know? Unless, of course, that stupid Rhoda is down there now trying to shake him awake to tell him. A heavy sleeper is James the Little. That girl's stupid and she blabs. She'll have to go.'

'If she blabs, mother, that's all the more reason why she ought to stay. Anyway, she's one of us.'

'So she says. But she doesn't know her backside from her little finger, forgive my language. You can never tell with young girls these days. Their heads are stuffed with a load of nonsense, love stories and young men and popular songs. She doesn't know *what* she is.'

Peter, according to a falsified record later unfalsified, was duly beheaded the following morning. It was not, of course, the real Peter who laid his head on the block but a substitute Peter, a greybearded criminal long incarcerated on a purely secular charge (killing his son-in-law in a drunken quarrel about the ownership of a small silver cow made by one of the fine workmen of Ephesus, itself stolen by one or the other from someone or other) and now given a delayed quietus drunk and heavily blindfolded. The king was, it was already known, incapable of attending the execution, groaning in his bed as he was, and it was not thought necessary to have a speech delivered on the Nazarene horror and the justice of the dispatch of its leading exponent, since all this had been exhaustively and exhaustingly taken care of at Peter's trial. Head and body were speedily buried and all concerned – guards, captain of guards, prison governor and his assistants – breathed huge relief. If news of Peter's baffling release were ever to get outside the prison and, through the channels of the department of internal security, to the ears of Herod Agrippa, then the *Codex Criminalis* would be invoked, this being one of the king's Romish importations, and the entire prison staff would suffer beheading. There were a few quiet lashings, with tongue and thong, within the prison precincts, and then everybody agreed to forget the matter, though attempts to explicate the inexplicable went on for some time in the guards' wet canteen.

King Herod Agrippa, feeling a little better, forced himself out of bed to travel to Caesarea, there to preside in his new silver robes over the festival held every five years on the anniversary of the founding of that city, in honour of the living Caesar whose title shone from the city's name. A few Roman officials came down from Syria and one or two senators on a travelling commission attended the games which bloodily attested the spread of Roman culture. There would not have been such games in Jerusalem, but Caesarea was a Roman city, meaning that it was full of Greeks, and considered to be the true capital of the province. As well as Romans there were Phoenicians present, a couple of fearful emissaries of princely rank from Tyre and Sidon, towns on the Phoenician seaboard which, though prosperous enough ports, were slow in paying for recent grain imports from Galilee. The amount of grain sent was much smaller than was usual, and there were Galilean grumbles about grain being sent at all, since this was a time of severe shortage and the feeding of Palestine came first. But Tyre and Sidon had depended on these imports ever since the time of Hiram and Solomon, and the royal treasury in Judaea received a sizable commission from both the Galilean factors and the Phoenician agents. The emissaries from Tyre and Sidon desired an opportunity to explain to Herod Agrippa why payment had not yet been rendered and why it could not be rendered for some time (a long story which could not be expected to interest the king, something about peculations, the failure of a docking project, a mining investment that had gone wrong) and they had a word with the king's chamberlain Blastus the evening before the ceremony in which Caesar and Caesar's city were to be honoured and the king to declare the opening of the games.

'He's sick,' Blastus said, 'and in a perpetual foul temper. Soft words and promises aren't going to do any good. He's not been too happy about you people for a long time.' He spoke slow Aramaic which, cognate with the tongue of Phoenicia, the emissaries understood well enough.

'We've brought presents.'

'Good presents?'

'The best. Fine Phoenician workmanship. Gold and silver bangles and breastplates and the rest of the nonsense.'

'The rest of the –?'

'Well, he'll still demand heavy interest on the unpaid bill, and we like to deal with businessmen not monarchs weighed down with jewels and the rest of the nonsense. Flattery's not in our line.'

'You'll have to flatter him just the same. It's meat and drink to him these days, practically his only meat and drink.'

'How much interest do you think he's going to charge?'

'He'll go to the limit. If I were you people I'd start thinking about getting grain from Egypt. They understand business there better than he does. He's lived too long in Rome.'

It was while Herod Agrippa was writhing in bed with an intolerable resumption of his pains that his daughter Bernice lightheartedly gave him bad news. 'That man's still alive,' she said.

'Which man, child?'

'The man that was supposed to have his *rosch* cut off.' She had the habit of mixing her nurse's Aramaic into her Greek. 'The one who used to catch *dagim* and then preached, the one with the white *sakan*,' stroking her pretty smooth chin.

'Speak plainly, child.' Her father was up on his elbow, looking at her fiercely.

'Well, they were all talking about it in the *schuk*, so old Miriam said, they knew the old *yeled* whose *rosch* was really cut off, some of them saw it after it was done, the *rosch* I mean, and said that's old whatsisname. And the other one, he got away, and he's alive in somebody's cellar, there was a *naarah* who saw him, she thought it was his ghost at first but it wasn't. There's been a bit of trickery, old Miriam said, and it's a king's job not to be tricked, she said. That's what I heard in the kitchen,' Bernice said.

The king furiously rang the bell by his bed and at length Blastus came in. Blastus looked at the king without deference: it was plain to him that Herod Agrippa I was not long for this world; Blastus was only thirty and he had a non-monarchical future to think about. The king let his daughter tell the story again. 'Have you heard the like from anyone?' Herod Agrippa asked, fierce and wincing. Blastus had to admit that he had. 'Get back to Jerusalem,' the king ordered; 'get the police on to this. I want that man's head on the block and everybody else's head who covered up the truth from their king. I want blood, and by God I'm going to have it.'

'After the ceremony? The opening of the games, that is?'

'Now. Take horse now.'

When Herod Agrippa appeared amid clamouring Caesareans and distinguished visitors and the clangour of sounding brass and thumped drums he looked not only in robust health but unutterably majestic, for he wore his glittering gown of silver that the early sun caught, he shone like a planet. His face had been farded and he had been fed an energizing drug and, when he spoke, it was with the deliberate articulation of one who is slightly drunk. He met his Roman visitors in the gaudy anteroom to the royal box of the circus, saying: 'We welcome the honourable senators Auspicius and Cinnus to our royal port of Caesarea. We trust that they will find their entertainment satisfactory. We have arranged – what have we arranged, Blastus?' But Blastus was on his way to Jerusalem. The under chamberlain said:

'Wild beasts, majesty. Gladiators.' One of the two emissaries from Phoenicia got in quickly then with an open box of bright jewels and the cynical language of courtiership, saying:

'Majesty – I say majesty inadvertently – deity, I would say. Your holy personage glows like a god. Your people need no god but Herod Agrippa. And here, holy one, are gifts unfit for a god but all that humble and erring humanity could contrive for the decking of one who already outshines the sun, the moon and a myriad constellations.' Herod Agrippa greedily dipped his heavily ringed right hand into the casket and raised a particularly finely wrought wristband to the light. Then he saw something fluttering in from the open casement. A bird. It settled on one of the ropes on which fresh flowers of the season had been festooned in the king's honour. A little white owl. It looked at him without deference. Then Herod Agrippa remembered something. Many years ago, when he had incurred the displeasure of the Emperor Tiberius, he had been put briefly into chains and made to share an openair prison with criminals of the common sort. He had been leaning against the bole of a tree, and in the branches of that tree were twittering birds. But one did not twitter; it hooted. A white owl, more mature than this. He had been frightened at first, believing owls to be birds of ill omen. But a prisoner from the Rhineland had laughed and gutturally said that this bird meant Herod Agrippa would be released soon, which he was. But the German had also, without laughing, said that next time Herod Agrippa saw a white owl it would mean that he had only five days more to live. 'Take that bird away,' he now shouted, then collapsed.

He howled in agony and was borne swiftly away on a litter to the palace. Should not, muttered some of the bearded councillors, have accepted the Phoenician blasphemy as his due. He elevates himself to the divine, and the divine responds by striking him down. But Luke, had he been present and not awaiting the return of Paul to Antioch, there to baptize him into the faith, would have delivered a less fanciful diagnosis: the rupturing of a hydatid cyst, the writhing of tapeworms in the final royal stool confirming it.

The death of Herod Agrippa I was nowhere regretted. Even his funeral lacked the extravagant gestures of mourning which the eastern territories are so cynically adept at furnishing. He was shoved into the tomb of his royal ancestors with minimal ceremony. He had blasphemed, though passively, and he had, after five days of condign suffering, given up the ghost with a cry that had sounded like a curse. The party of the Zealots, after a dissatisfied intermission of their plans for liberation from a foreign yoke, were now able to resume their secret meetings and their amassing of arms in secret places: things had reverted to the only situation most of them had known before the three-year reign (in Judaea that is; he had had rule of the neighbouring territories for seven) of one who, despite the gestures of autonomy, had been no more than a Roman puppet. Now they awaited the appointment of a procurator and some years of renewed but impotent disaffection, the only state in which they were really happy.

The law promulgated at last by Claudius and the Senate by which no Jews, except those who had been able to purchase full Roman citizenship from the Empress Messalina, were permitted to remain in Rome brought shiploads of refugees to Caesarea, refuge being glossable as repatriation, but few of these Jews had ever seen Palestine or even wanted to see it. There were a great number of Nazarenes among them, and the Jerusalem church gloried in expansion. The high priests of the Jewish faith, sickened by Herod Agrippa's vindictiveness, which had no roots in genuine piety, guilty also at the execution of James, in which they had acquiesced uneasily, left the Nazarenes alone. Some converted Pharisees, speedily apostasizing under the brief monarchy, now dusted off the intermitted faith they brought out of the cupboard, and they were loud in their demands that its essential Jewishness be proclaimed and regularized.

Peter, no longer in hiding, presided over a great meeting of Nazarenes in the open air on the Mount of Olives. He had carefully prepared his inaugural speech with the help of John Mark, and he spoke as follows:

'Members of the faith, friends of the faithful, we are assembled in a time when little would seem to hinder the growth of this church in Jerusalem and the daughter churches of Asia. The rule of Judaea is, as you know, reverting to Rome after the unregretted death of its king. We expect a procurator appointed by the Emperor Claudius, and we anticipate a measure of Roman justice and a measure of Roman indifference. My brother and colleague James – whose name none of us can utter without sad but triumphant memories of his martyred namesake – has been granted the authority of head of the Jerusalem church. We may call him the overseer or *episcopos* or bishop of Jerusalem. My work lies elsewhere, as does that of so many of my colleagues – such as Paul and Barnabas, who are busily bringing the word to the Gentiles. We are met here to consider a particular problem – that of the relationship between these same Gentiles and those followers of the Lord Jesus Christ who, brought up in the Jewish faith, consider themselves still, despite so many radical changes, to profess that faith. The word is with Matthias.'

Matthias got up from the grass, spitting out an olive pit first, and spoke thus:

'Father Peter, as I must call him, and brothers in the faith – I put the matter plainly. We followers of the Lord Jesus, blessed be his name, came to his teaching not as a new thing but as the fulfilment of a very old thing. His coming was foretold by the prophets, his lineage is of the House of David, his messiahship came as a salvation to the Jewish people. If I may put it simply – the Jews first, the Gentiles after. This sums up the mission of our brother Paul, who first enters the synagogue of any town he visits, addressing Jews who may or may not accept the word, but also those Gentile Godfearers, as they are called, who, in his experience, have been quicker than the Jews to follow and absorb the new teaching. Now a Gentile who follows Christ follows also the law which preceded Christ. He is bound to the law of Moses. He is bound to the acceptance of circumcision, to the abhorrence of unclean food, to the avoidance of fornication and the forbidden degrees of marriage –'

Peter cut in here, saying: 'You mean he must conform as a Jew before he can conform as a Nazarene. I sense in Matthias's words a certain rebuke of myself as the one who baptized the Roman centurion Cornelius into the faith without demanding that he change his eating habits or have his foreskin cut. But we have no ordinance which compels the baptized Gentile to accept the laws of Jewry. That must be made clear. The faith is for all. Foreskin-cutting does not come into it.'

A priest of low rank stood up to say: 'I am not yet a follower of Christ, though I – and many of my brothers here present – am inclined to his way. Indeed, we Pharisees, who accept the resurrection of the body, are halfway there. But you cannot expect us, who call ourselves Jews and, though ready for the act of baptism, must always call ourselves such, to accept the modes of the Gentiles. More, you cannot even expect us to mingle with Gentiles and call them our brothers, since, according to our prior beliefs, they are an unclean people.'

Peter cried out angrily at that, having that vision to support him: 'Nothing that God has created can be called *unclean*. That too must be made clear. Jesus Christ enjoins brotherhood on all who follow him. Circumcision and food laws do not come into it. Brothers, listen.' For there were some belligerent mutterings going on there on the Mount of Olives, an olive being, as you may know, an emblem of peace. 'Listen, I tell you.' They listened, most of them. 'A good while away God made choice among you, that by my mouth the Gentiles should hear the word of the gospel and believe. And God, who knows the hearts of men, gave the Gentiles the Holy Spirit, even as he did to us. And he made no distinction between us and them, cleansing their hearts by faith. Now why do you make a trial of God, that you should try to put a yoke on the necks of Christ's disciples which neither our fathers nor ourselves were able to bear? What we believe is this: that we shall all be saved through the grace of the Lord Jesus – Jew and Gentile alike.'

There were more murmurings and one or two shouts from the back. Another man in priest's robes got up, older than the other, and spoke reasonably. He said: 'We get reports of the evangelizing work of the man whom we remember as Saul, and of the others. We hear that the Gentile converts to your faith, not yet mine, regard themselves as a special and privileged people who follow their own laws, or the lack of them. They shout out about being saved by the Lord Jesus, who has cleansed them of all sin, past, present and to come. So they can behave as they wish, jumping into bed with their mothers and grandmothers and nieces and daughters, nephews and sons too for all we know. Outside any decent law, do you follow me? Love one another, and we all know what that can mean. Only the Jewish faith lays down what you may and may not do. Eat a bit of pork and you'll end up eating dogshit and saying how good it is with a little mustard. Fornicate freely and you'll start buggering sheep. What I'm saying is this: this story of universal love and everlasting life isn't enough. People have to behave. People have to have clean genitals and not carry the muck of the towns and the sand of the desert inside their prepuces. Nazarenes have to be Jews first. I propose that that be laid down as a fundamental law.' And he sat again on the grass, applauded by many. James the Little, who no longer needed the distinguishing sobriquet, James the only James, James stood and said:

'Brothers, listen. We know that long centuries ago God went first to the Gentiles, looking among them for a people who would follow his law. He found the Jews instead, but he said that the rest of mankind may seek the Lord, and, and now I quote sacred scripture, "all the Gentiles upon whom my name is called". What I conclude from this is that we stop troubling the Gentiles about these matters, but that we write letters to our new churches in Asia, telling them not to worship idols, not to commit fornication, not to bugger and sodomize, not to eat food that's been strangled and contains blood. Will not this serve our need? Compromise is always to be followed. And that compromise weds the word of Moses to the word of Christ.'

'They have to be circumcised,' somebody shouted, and others took up the cry. Peter, angry, yelled:

'Is the spread of our faith wholly to be tied to – What's the word, John Mark?'

'Coition. The organs of generation.'

198

'What I say is that a good deal of the work of our men in the Asian provinces is spent fighting goddesses who stand for –'

'Coition.'

'Coition. People fornicating around and getting blessed by a goddess for doing it. In those places of the Gentiles you could say that the big enemy is the female genitals. And here in Jerusalem some of you people are making the genitals of men into a kind of rod forbidding entry into the Lord's congregation. What we're supposed to be concerned with is the soul and love and salvation. You make all that of less importance than having a piece of skin snipped off your –'

'Organ of generation.'

'Organ of generation.'

But the demand for Nazarene Gentile circumcision went on. 'We'll mention it in a letter,' James called. Somehow he had not thought that the spread of the faith and its organization would entail the writing of letters. Christ had never written any. None of them were letterwriters. Paul was different, of course. He represented the new way. On his brief visit to Caesarea with the famine relief money he had been writing letters all day long. They had never had anything in writing before.

Marcus Julius Tranquillus received a letter, a note rather, telling him to watch his step and signed *Quidam amicus*. He had destroyed the note on receiving it, but he sat now in the diningroom of the little rented house on the Janiculum brooding about it. He was not watching his step. He was taking action. Tonight he had an appointment. Why night? Narcissus, the Greek freedman, had said night and he had his reasons. The trouble was that it was dangerous to have enemies at night. During the day you could avoid them. Night was different.

Sara was clearing the table after their evening meal, and Julius's brother-in-law Caleb sat at the table trying to force a white grape into the mouth of little Ruth, who resented being weaned and spat out solidities. But she sucked the scant juice of the grape.

'Time for her bed,' Sara told her brother, taking the child.

'I must get work,' Caleb said. 'Get married. Set up a family of my own.'

'If by that,' Sara said, 'you mean you've outstayed your welcome here –'

'No. Just restless. And whatever the work is, it won't be my real work.'

'Killing the Romans. Not very complimentary to your Roman brother-in-law.'

'Oh,' Caleb said, 'Julius thinks as I do. The Roman Empire is a great sham. Foul with corruption and yet it thinks it has this mission to clean up the world. I don't want to kill Romans. Not ordinary ones. They're just human beings. The Roman state is something else.'

'Julius gets paid by the Roman state,' Sara said, rocking the baby in her arms. 'But thank Jupiter or somebody he's no longer serving the wife of the Roman state.'

'I didn't know that,' Caleb said. 'When did that happen?'

'Eh? What? When did what happen?'

'He wasn't listening,' Sara said. 'He was brooding about being removed from the beauteous company of the divine Messalina.'

'I have to go out,' Julius said.

'Tonight? Why?'

'I have to go to the Palatine.'

'Walk? It's a long way.'

'Only a mile or so. Downhill. Something to do with being given a new commission perhaps.'

'And yet you look gloomy. I do honestly believe,' Sara said, 'that you miss the divine Messalina.'

'Don't tease me,' Julius said. 'I never felt safe. And don't use words like *divine*. There ought to be an opposite to that word, but I don't know what it is.'

'There's an opposite in Hebrew,' Caleb said.

'She gave off a kind of – I don't know how to describe it.'

'She looked like ice,' Sara said.

'You've never seen ice.'

'I've seen *her*. Admittedly only from a distance. Beautiful like ice.'

'No ice there, I can tell you. Sizzling imperial smiles. When she – Never mind.'

'When she what?' Caleb asked.

'When she asked for *discretion*. That was her big word. But now I have to be indiscreet. Caleb – I mean, Metellus – We have to be discreet there, don't we? There's something – Never mind.'

'The Jews are coming back to Rome,' Caleb said. 'The Romans can't do without us. The synagogues will be opening up soon. With Roman troops outside to stop riots.'

When Sara took little Ruth to her cradle in the main bedroom, Julius said: 'What I wanted to say was – will you walk with me as far as the Palatine?'

'Gladly. But is it – '

'No, it's not safe. Nothing's ever safe these days. Especially at night.'

'Shall I bring my –?'

'Yes, bring that. I may be foolish, but a married man has to be – well, cautious. You'll understand that one of these days.'

'I've learned to understand about caution.'

He put a shine on his dagger while Sara sang little Ruth to sleep:

'When the wolf howls
    Feel no fear.
Romulus and Remus
    Dropped no tear
When they heard the wolf's howl
    Drawing near.
Mamma is coming.
Mamma is here.'

Julius went first down the hill, limping still, cloaked, sword gripped under his cloak. Caleb, dressed like a Roman citizen, followed after. The Via Aurelia was empty of traffic. When they had passed the Marine Theatre three men jumped on Julius from some arbutus shrubs. Caleb ran thirty paces and was athletic with his dagger. He struck down one of the assailants. This assailant tried to crawl back to the bushes in his blood. The other two ran off. 'Not very efficient,' Caleb said. 'We'd better question this one. Looks as though it's too late, though. See that gash. At last I've killed a Roman.'

'No need for questioning. I expected something like this.'

Julius felt safe after passing the Palatine sentries. He was known, there was no password to utter. He stated his business and was taken a long way to a room with a desk and a lot of scrolls on it. He had to wait a while before Narcissus appeared. He told Narcissus what had happened on his way there.

'There's no need,' Narcissus said, 'to stand stiffly to attention. You're not on parade.' He was very Greek, and he wore his curled hair long and over his ears to obscure the piercings that had accommodated earrings, badges of slavery long done. Manumission. A freedman. The Greeks were best at the higher administration. There were a lot of pierced ears on the Palatine. He was much shorter than Julius. He invited him to be seated. They sat. Narcissus said: 'You have reason to believe that you were set upon for a special reason? I mean, these were not just common footpads?'

'I was expecting that some way would be sought of – keeping my mouth closed. If my brother-in-law had not been with me this mouth would have been closed for ever.'

'Yes yes yes. Your brother-in-law, whoever he is, deserves well of you and, I suppose, of the state. A brave Roman of the kind we're always hearing about but rarely see.'

'He happens to be a Jew.'

'A Jew? Oh yes, they're coming back, aren't they? I said to Caesar that you couldn't really keep them out. A sop to senators who owed the Jews money. Well, now you must come and talk to the Emperor.'

'I hadn't expected –' Julius was startled. 'What I mean is –'

'He's only just back from Ostia. The new harbour, you know. One of his pet schemes. And tomorrow morning he's off to Neapolis. Tonight seemed the best time. Come with me.'

Narcissus led him down many corridors and towards the imperial suite, which was guarded. The guard was being changed, though without the bark of orders. Julius knew the captain of the guard, one Flaccus. They nodded at each other. Narcissus said, as they trod carpeting, soft to Claudius's ailing feet: 'The Emperor knows you and thinks well of you. That you were wounded in the British campaign is enough to gain his affection. You have little need to be concerned about the future of your career if – well, all goes as we pray it will.'

'Amen.'

'What's that word?'

'I'm sorry, sir, it just slipped out. A word I learned. From my wife. Hebrew.'

'You know Hebrew?'

'Not much.'

'But some. I see, I see.' Narcissus knocked on a door and at once entered. 'I beg the Emperor's pardon,' he said, though with no tone of sincerity. The Emperor had been nursing in his lap a personable young woman whom Julius recognized as the imperial niece Agrippina. She ran out very rapidly by a side door. Claudius, somewhat embarrassed, said:

'A display of avuncular afffffection, no more.' He did not look well: the hair pure snow, the face lined, the stammer bad. 'So this is the young man I hear well of? So now I bbbbbrace myself and you tell me tell me aaaaall.' He spoke the last word on a rising intonation. Julius gulped and began.

'You will understand, sir, that there has been a certain division in my mind, what may be termed a conflict of loyalties. I was given a post in which discretion was enjoined on me. I was to be loyal to the Empress, but this loyalty entailed being disloyal to the Emperor. You understand my difficulties.'

He and Narcissus had been standing; the Emperor, in a dressing gown which parted to show glimpses of a slugwhite fat body, was sitting on a wide chair loaded with yellow cushions. The Emperor said: 'I think you had better sit down. I think we had bbbbbetter have some wine. You're a soldier and I've done my share of wine-bbbbbibbing with soldiers. You may relax as in your own mess. Will you, Narcissus –?' Narcissus brought a plain winejug and cups from a table in a far corner of the room, not overlarge, its quality intimate and domestic. Julius was glad of the wine: his mouth was dry. 'Pppproceed,' the Emperor said. Julius proceeded:

'The Empress made many visits about the city and its environs, with myself in charge of her armed escort. Most of these visits were to the same individual – often in one or other of his houses, sometimes in a farm or villa not owned by him. Occasionally in an inn on the road to Ostia. The individual in question was Gaius Silius, though I heard the Empress address him by name only once. That was when I was on patrol round the house of a kinsman of his former wife, the Lady Lollia Paulina.'

'Ffffformer –?'

'Yesterday, before I was dismissed her imperial majesty's service, I heard her address the consul Gaius Silius as *husband*, and the – gentleman in question responded with *wife*. I thought at first this was a kind of facetiousness. But one of my last assignments had been to provide a military guard for a – I do not know whether to call it a party or a religious celebration or an orgy –'

'You mean,' Claudius said, very pallid, 'one of these Oriental – the slave Ccccchrestus or whoever it is –'

'No, sir, not religious in that sense. On the estate of a certain Silanus there was what was termed a homage to the god of wine, appropriate for the time of the wine harvest. Grapes and vineleaves and much wine and a fat naked man impersonating Bacchus. There was a good deal of drunkenness –' Julius heard the primness of his tone and felt, paradoxically, soiled by it. 'The consul Silanus, perhaps inevitably, turned himself into Silenus. There was – lechery, nakedness. It was a warm afternoon,' he added, as if to excuse the nakedness.

'Cccccc –'

He did as he was bid and continued. 'Then a man in priest's robes appeared to conduct a marriage ceremony. Perhaps I saw more than I should. I was supposed to stay in a sort of grove. But I saw this ceremony between the Empress and Gaius Silius and I assumed it was all a game. There was a great deal of laughter and little solemnity. Then the marriage or mock marriage was – It is hard to continue –'

'You must,' Narcissus said.

'It was – consummated at once and in public. And, in sympathy as it were, the other guests – A great mass of naked bodies. Men and women. Fornication for them. There were boys there too, Ganymedes. For the Empress and Gaius Silius it was termed a consummation.'

Claudius said, with calm and without stammering much: 'You were right after all, Narcissus. I owe you many apologies. A bigamous marriage to show her ccccontempt not only for her husband but for the law of Rome – a signal to the world of ggggglory in depravity. And when does Gaius Silius think he can strike the blow that will seccccure him the imperial cccc –'

'I do not think,' Narcissus said, 'that Gaius Silius has such an ambition. He is a weak man besotted by the erotic, no more.' To Julius he said: 'Where are they now?'

'I was told there would be no further need of my services and that I must report back for reassignment. Also that I must be *discreet* in my reporting back. The word was uttered in a tone which I interpreted as one of menace. I heard brief talk of a journey to Neapolis.'

'And perhaps,' Narcissus asked, 'of taking ship there for the island of Capri? The Villa Jovis? That,' he said to the now shaking Claudius, 'was by a deed of gift assigned to the Empress.'

'Do not refer to her as the Empress. You may, if you wish, allude to the late Empress. Immediate arrest and almost immediate execution.' His tones were clear and pedantic, as though he were referring to peccant personages in his own historical writings. 'As for a trial – all Rome must know already of a depravity too foul for its very sewers to discharge. All except its Emperor. I've been weak, Narcissus.'

'Tolerant, Caesar. Distracted by multifarious duties.'

'Young man,' the Emperor said to Julius, 'the world is more evil than any man can know. Every day there is some new foul surprise, some new pppputrid revelation. The times need to be washed, scoured, to become the tttttablet for the writing of a new age. A great pppppurging and a fresh beginning. But none gives the word. None none none.' And with an astonishing and totally unexpected howl of animal terror he dashed his wine to the floor and tottered out.

There was a pause. During it Julius stood. He had done his duty and was ready to be dismissed. Narcissus looked up at him from his chair.

'How much more can you tell me?'

'Only of the road to Neapolis. Wait – some talk of Gemini, the heavenly twins. I did not attend much to that. It seemed to be some private joke.'

'There's a ship of that name. It plies between Neapolis and Capri. Or used to. Tell me – do you fancy following your purgative mission to the end? Apprehending the – criminal couple?'

'Do I have a choice in the matter, sir?'

'Oh, I think so. I can understand your wishing to be done with the business. I'll have some bully from the Praetorian Guard assigned. You've done well. You've also, to be candid with you, restored my own credibility with the Emperor. I warned him of this, but he was not prepared to listen. He even, at one point, made sounds indicative of great rising anger, as though I were speaking a kind of referred treason. And now – I think a wholesome week or so in the bosom of your family would be in order. And a little bonus from the treasury perhaps. So be it, or – What was that Hebrew word?'

'Amen.'

'Yes. You have some connection with the Jews, you said.'

'Through marriage, sir.'

'Do you fancy service in Palestine?'

'I think of myself as a good servant of the Empire. But I've lost my taste for blood.'

'One of our tasks is to stop people shedding it. Perhaps you'd better work on your Hebrew.'

'Aramaic, sir.'

It would, I think, be wearisome to recount the details of the many voyages that the tireless Paul undertook in the service of the new word, for wherever he went he said much the same thing and met much the same mixed response. He went back, after the delivery of money for the famine relief in Judaea, to the city of Antioch, where he baptized Luke the physician, saw that the Christian community was in good hands, and then prepared to go to Cyprus. Of the church leaders in Antioch it is perhaps interesting to note that one of them must have been black (else why should he be called Symeon Niger?) and one of them, named Manaen, meaning the comforter, was the foster-brother of Herod the tetrarch. Apparently his grandfather, who had the same name, pleased the infanticidal Herod the Great by prophesying great things for him, and Herod had the whole family accommodated in the royal household, so that the young Manaen became a sort of adoptive prince. This gives us an image of two boys playing together with golden balls and so on, one of them destined to be a church leader and the other to have the head of John the Baptist shorn off as a gift for a dancing girl named Salome. This should mean something, but I do not know what.

Paul took ship with Barnabas at Seleucia, five miles north of the mouth of the Orontes, and later the learned John Mark joined them at Salamis, on the east coast of Cyprus, where some saw the light and others hurled bricks. In the provincial governmental town of Paphos, where the proconsul Sergius Paullus ruled on behalf of the Roman Senate, Paul prayed that the blasphemous sorcerer Elymas be blinded, and his prayer was heard and implemented promptly. Sergius Paullus was impressed and agreed to consider the possibility of his joining the new faith, but I think he was merely being polite to his near namesake. Paphos had its many-breasted goddess, closer to Aphrodite than to Artemis, and Paul thundered against fornication. Many listened with pleasure, but most continued to fornicate.

The party then sailed for Perga, or rather for Attalia, taking a riverboat down the Cestus to the inland city, and Paul in the synagogue gave a long seamless account of the search of the Jewish people for a Messiah and the fulfilment of that search. Little, bald, thundering, though shaking with malaria, he impressed the Gentiles more than the Jews. He also seemed to take it for granted that he was the leader of the mission, although Barnabas had the priority of longer service and hence greater authority in the mother church of Antioch. John Mark resented this relegation of his cousin to second place. He told Paul so and Paul said:

'I do not see that this is any business of yours. Barnabas does not complain. He is too busy preaching the word to consider such a thing as being of any importance. Get on with some preaching yourself and cease this pettiness.'

'I think you are growing puffed up. I think your eloquence is inflating more than your lungs. You speak to the congregations as though you were the inventor of the faith. A lot of what you are preaching does not seem to me to be all that orthodox.'

'Who is to say, except presumably yourself, who have read too many books and meditated on the faith too little?'

'Jesus made friends with prostitutes, and you howl at them as though they were the devil.'

'And so they are.'

'I think I shall go back to Jerusalem.'

'How will you get there? Work your passage?'

'A week's lessons in Greek to the daughters of that man Nabal will earn me enough. And I was asked to give a lecture on Zoroastrianism. No trouble about money, O father of the faithful.'

'What did you call me then?'

'Never mind. Good luck with your preaching.'

'I call you a traitor and a deserter.'

'Call me what you like. I could call you some things.'

So John Mark went back to Jerusalem, and Paul and Barnabas caused trouble by filling up the synagogues with Gentiles, who were forewarned to get there before the regular time for the arrival of the Jews. Stones were hurled as they took the eastern road to Iconium. In that city they had trouble too, but an Iconian resident named Onesiphorus gave them notice of coming mob violence initiated by some of the civic leaders, so they were able to get away unscathed. Onesiphorus was much impressed by Paul, and he has left us a little poem in Greek which fixes his appearance for all time:

Strongly built, though small in size,
Large-nosed, with penetrating eyes,
Omega made by leg and leg,
His eyebrows meet, bald as an egg,
A man, yes, but angelic grace
Shines sometimes from that ugly face.

So on to Lystra and then to Derbe, then back to Antioch. Here Paul and Barnabas quarrelled. Paul said:

'Things go well enough here. Now I suggest we take the same trip as we did before and see how things go there.'

'Now?'

'Soon.'

Barnabas gave an apologetic cough. He said: 'There's somebody here in Antioch who's sorry for his sins. He keeps out of your way. I tell him to come and beg forgiveness, but he's frightened.'

'You mean your damned cousin?'

'Yes, and I trust you use *damned* as a mere conventional expression of displeasure. John Mark is good and useful. True, he sulked in Jerusalem for a time, but he realized at last where his place is. So I think we ought to give him another chance.'

'He's a traitor and a defector and I'm not having him.'

Barnabas sighed. 'But if I want him?' he said.

'Look, Barnabas, there's family sentiment at work here. You want him because he's your first cousin. I don't want him because he's disloyal and, to speak candidly, his conception of our faith is not orthodox. He's more trouble than he's worth.'

'It seems to me, if I may say so, that you're taking too much on yourself. Nobody denies your eloquence and intellectuality and your success as an evangelist. But you assume precedence over me, and that without cause. You were sitting on your arse making tents in Tarsus when I summoned you. It was I who set up a church here in Antioch and I called on you as a helper not as one free to usurp my primacy when he felt like doing it. That's plain speaking but you asked for it. John Mark goes with us.'

'Oh no he does not.'

'Oh yes he does.'

'You're pigheaded, Barnabas, and you don't have the cause at heart. We can't afford to have mere passengers, especially carping ones like John Mark who, moreover, trembles on the edge of the heterodox in too many of his views. He doesn't come, and that's an end of it.'

'Very well then, I don't come either.'

'Oh yes you do.'

'Oh no I do not.'

'So,' Paul said, 'this is very regrettable, but it looks like the parting of the ways. You go where you will, since you proclaim the authority of primacy as you call it, taking that damned cousin with you. I'll have to look for another helper.'

'You see? That's all I was to you, a mere helper, not a colleague working on the level of equality. John Mark and I will go as brothers in the faith.'

'Cousins, and distant ones too. Where do you propose to go?'

'To Cyprus to begin with.'

'To undo the good work already begun? To have John Mark converting temple prostitutes?'

'The way of the Lord is open to all.'

'Get on with it, then. Anyway,' he now said brutally, 'I need somebody who's a Roman citizen like myself. It's always been awkward going round with someone who can't claim those rights that belong to the Roman citizen. I haven't claimed them yet and why not? Out of loyalty to you, Barnabas. There's that young Silas who's on a visit here. He has the ancestral privileges, or so he says and he's no reason for lying. Well, so it's come to this, and we preach a doctrine of love.'

'My love for you, Paul,' Barnabas said primly, 'is in no way impaired by our altercation.'

'I'm glad to hear it,' Paul said.

So he and Silas, a young man proud of his Latin, which he spoke with Ciceronian rotundities, so that native speakers of the tongue had difficulty in understanding him, went back to Paul's own Cilicia, then crossed the Taurus range through the pass known as the Cilician Gates, entered the kingdom of Antiochus, king of Commagene, who had had part of Cilicia and the whole of eastern Lycaonia added to his territories some years back, and performed church inspections in Galatia. The mission of Paul and Barnabas had borne reasonable fruit there, and many asked with affection after Paul's former partner in the work. Paul said blandly: 'The egg has divided, and there are two travelling teams where there was but one before, praise be to God.' The church at Lystra highly commended a young man named Timothy as one well fitted to learn the evangelizing craft from Paul, and Paul, having inspected the church, inspected him. He was young, like Silas, and shy-eyed but not secretive. Paul said: 'Tell me about yourself. Everything.'

'My mother,' Timothy said with a slight Galatian lisp, 'is named Eunice, and she is Jewish. My father was a Greek Gentile. I carry his name.'

'Ah. That makes you a Jew.'

'The Jews don't think so. They call me the uncircumcised son of a Greek. They make it sound like an insult.'

'No trouble about getting you circumcised.'

Timothy was appalled. 'At my age? Besides, you wrote a letter, didn't you, about there being no need. It was read out in the Galatian churches.'

'Yes, but that was before we received this letter from Jerusalem. The one about Gentiles trying to conform to the Jewish law as much as they can. For the sake,' smiling kindly, 'of quietening dissension.

Circumcision. You're just the man for it. They'll be pleased in Jerusalem.'

'But,' Timothy frowned, 'it's painful and it's dangerous.'

'Nonsense. You'll feel like a new man after it. We'll see about having it done this afternoon.'

So poor Timothy had his foreskin tweaked and pulled by the strong hard fingers of the *mohel*, whose primary trade was that of blacksmith, closed his eyes, felt the bite of the razor, opened his eyes to see a part of his body lying on a white cloth, bled, recovered, and sorely walked off with Paul and Silas to places Paul already knew in Galatic Phrygia, went north to Philomelium, and then northwest through Asian Phrygia, where Paul did no preaching. This area was not yet ready for the word of the Lord. At Dorylaeum or Cotiaeum (my informants are not sure which) they ventured west and smelled the sea at Troas. This was a Roman colony but it remembered that it was a Greek town. Paul breathed deeply of the ozone and said: '*Thalassa*.' Then he heard a voice behind him say:

'Or *thalatta*, according to the dialect you prefer.' Paul turned and saw Luke the physician. They were at a small openair wineshop on the main quay. Luke smiled at Paul, swinging his small leather bag of medicines. 'I said I'd be here. It's better than Antioch. More sickness. Well. Introduce me.' He sat down and another cup was brought. 'Sore is it still?' he said eventually to Timothy. 'It's the swinging against the legs as you walk. Try this ointment.'

'Macedonia,' Paul suddenly said. 'Plenty of ships going there, I see. Philip of Macedonia. Alexander the Great. The land of the conqueror conquered. You're coming with us?' he said to Luke.

'As your medical consultant? I can't preach. I'm in the faith but I'm not learned in it.'

'How does your poem go?'

'I abandoned it. I'm not cut out for verse.'

'Try prose.'

In the lodgings of Luke, where Paul was granted the privilege of the bed and the rest lay on the floor, Paul slept heavily and had several dreams, some of them trivial but one of them, he thought on waking, significant, indicative, authoritative. He saw Alexander coming into his tent and taking his armour off. He sat at a table and conferred unintelligibly with his commanders. Then he looked out of the picture straight at the observing dreamer and said: 'I've drunk everybody else's blood. I may as well drink his.'

So the four of them took ship next day across the north Aegean, got to Samothrace at sundown, felt the waves of the immemorial cult of the Cabiri beat out at them from its mountain, and the next day arrived at Neapolis on the Macedonian shore. 'Philippi,' Paul said, having discovered from one of the sailors that it was ten miles away from the coast, give or take a furlong. 'You realize,' Silas said as they walked, 'that we're now in Europe? We're on the Roman continent. Antony and Augustus, Octavian as he was then, beat Brutus and Cassius at Philippi. We're into Roman history now.' Interesting, Paul said, though distractedly. More interesting was their failure to discover a synagogue in Philippi. No Jews? 'Augustus settled his veterans here,' Silas said, 'not only after his defeat of Brutus and Cassius but after the battle of Actium when he trounced Antony and Cleopatra.' Interesting: all Gentiles, not a Jew to be seen. Ten men the *minyan* for a synagogue, so there must be at most nine. The four of them sat down by the river Gangites and ate the bread they had bought on the way. Some women were washing clothes, beating them against stones in a manner too vigorous to conduce to their longevity, as Silas put it. Timothy suggested that he go and look for Jews, though without much enthusiasm. Paul said:

'No. Gentiles will do for the moment. Leave this to me.' And he raised his voice at the women. 'You've heard of the Christians? We're here to speak for them. Carry on with your linen-thumping, ladies, and listen or not, as you please.' Some listened. One woman, who was not washing clothes but enjoying the cool of the willows, listened very attentively. Her name was Lydia, she said, and she was from Thyatira, part of the old province of Lydia which had given her her name. She knew the Jews of Thyatira, where was a Jewish colony, and she was by way of being what was known as something of a Godfearer. In Lydia they fished up the murex, a spiky creature out of which they made purple dye. She was unmarried, and she made her living by importing the dye from Thyatira. Interesting. Did she wish to be baptized? Later, she said, let us not rush things. Have you gentlemen anywhere to stay? Just arrived, they said. I sometimes take in lodgers, she said. I have two spare rooms.

So they stayed with Lydia, who seemed to have done rather well out of the business of importing purple dye, and they sat at a table where a servant brought in broiled riverfish with a sharp sauce, after the manner of the Philippine kitchen, in a ceramic pourer. While they were eating (the sauce was of crushed garlic and mustard seeds in wine), they heard outside the casement which gave on to the main street a girl's voice yelling what sounded like nonsense. Lydia sighed a sigh of habituation and said: 'I consider this a sin and a shame. That poor girl is not right in the head, and a couple of men have got hold of her, her being an orphan, and they use her as a kind of fortune teller. She says such nonsense that it's taken by some to be the voice of the god Apollo, and they ask questions and these men say what her mad answers mean. They take plenty of money and keep the girl locked up

210

in a cellar like a prisoner, feeding her nothing but stale bread. I call it a crying shame. Have some more fish.' While she was serving all except Paul, who said thank you he had had enough, the house shook and the earth rumbled. An interesting place, Philippi. 'We often get tremors,' Lydia said. 'Those two men who have that poor girl say it's the anger of the god Apollo not being paid enough for his prophecies. Some people will say anything for their own profit.' Silas said that there had been an earthquake during the battle of Philippi and that it had discomfited Brutus and Cassius though not Octavian.

Paul and Silas went out alone the following morning, leaving Luke and Timothy, who had no Roman citizenship and had best be prudent in a Roman town, to recover from the sharp sauce in the house of Lydia. They saw the poor demented girl at her imposed trade in the market place, crying out nonsense like *alaba alaba arkkekk* and having this translated as 'The god says you may make the journey but do not be away longer than three days'. The earth trembled. 'There is the voice of the god himself confirming that statement and ordering you to be generous to his servants.' The two men were middleaged and wore greasy robes, shifty-eyed; Paul guessed that they took more than pecuniary advantage of the girl. The girl herself had eyes too widely set apart and had filthy hair but a clean blue priestess's garment. Paul and she looked at each other; if she was feebleminded then so was he, Paul. He said to her very clearly:

'What is your name, girl?'

'*Arg werb forkrartok.*'

'I'm not having this nonsense. You're frightened of these two men who are your jailors and exploiters and they've turned you into a voice that speaks gibberish under the guise of prophetic truth. Even by the standards of pagan Rome this is an abomination. Come with us and we'll look after you. We serve the true God, which is to say truth and kindness and decency. Leave these vile men and we'll take you to a place of comfort and safety.' The girl began to weep bitterly, and the two men hurled abuse at Paul, calling on the bystanders to witness the blasphemy of these two foreigners, though Silas had as yet said nothing. The weeping girl responded differently. She got up from the threelegged stool on which she had been sitting, a Pythonian tripod, and cried:

'It's right enough. I'm sick and tired of it all. *They* make me do it. This one's right when he says it's all nonsense.' And she joined herself to Paul and Silas, who hurried her away towards the house of Lydia. They did this with some difficulty, for the common sort do not like to lose contact with what they consider the numinous and some of them threw pebbles. Lydia was pleased to have the girl, who permitted herself to be embraced by the older woman and sobbed and howled as though her heart would break. Paul nodded and said:

'Let her. She's discharging the foul stuff within. Ah, we have visitors.' These were the masters of the girl, who now hammered on the front door and yelled that they had brought the lictors with them. Paul opened and nodded pleasantly at the uniformed officials, who carried rods which were both a symbol of authority and a device of punition. One said:

'Foreigners? You've got a charge to answer. Come with us.'

Paul and Silas shrugged and suffered themselves to be led off to the courthouse, where the duumvirs or praetors were called out to examine them. One of the plaintiffs said:

'It's like this, your worships. These two are foreigners and Jews by the look of them, and they're here interfering with good Roman religious practices as well as good Roman trade.'

One of the praetors, a man with crumbs on his jowls from a meal interrupted, said to Paul: 'Are you the men who were preaching some outlandish superstitious mumbojumbo contrary to the laws of Rome yesterday by the riverbank?'

'If by that you mean the Christian faith, yes. That, however, does not seem to be the charge. These men have brought my colleague and myself here to answer a plaint which they have not yet preferred.'

'Never mind about that for the moment. You're Jews, are you?'

'Jews, yes.'

'And also –' Silas began, but Paul kicked him to enjoin silence. 'Why?' Silas frowned, puzzled.

'We don't like foreigners coming here,' the crumbed praetor said, 'causing disturbances and interfering with the Roman way of life. You lictors,' he said, 'use those rods of yours to some purpose and then shove these two bignosed gentry into jail.'

'But,' one of the mountebanks said, 'they've been interfering with our business, which is the holy invocation of the oracle of the god Apollo. That girl we have, your worships, they've interfered with her so she can't do the holy work any more.'

'As I said,' the praetor said, getting up from the bench, 'lay the rods on hard and not only shove them into jail but fix them in the stocks so they can't move for a bit. That will cool their foreign hotblooded interferingness. Go on, get on with it.' The other praetor, following the first, added: 'You heard what we said.'

So the lictors, who were out of whipping practice, kicked and shoved Paul and Silas to the marketplace, where they added to the day's entertainment by stripping them down to their clouts and thwacking them with the rods. 'They can't do this,' Silas gasped, 'not to – It's against the law.'

'Let them put themselves in the wrong,' Paul winced. 'That sort of thing can be – ow – useful sometimes.' Lydia witnessed the flogging,

212

leaving the girl, whose name appeared to be Eusebia, back home to have her hair washed and protected by Luke and Timothy against the reappearance of the men who alleged they owned her. Lydia was respected in the town and got some of the women to join her in her cry of 'It's a disgrace to Roman justice, as they call it.'

There was an earth tremor, variously to be interpreted as the god Apollo's approval of the flogging or else the disapprobation of the god of those two who were being flogged. The flogging over, Paul and Silas refused to put back on their robes, saying sensibly that they did not wish to have these glued to their backs with blood and that the heat of the sun (or the blessed god Apollo) was good for their wounds. And so they were led off to a cell where incarceration was compounded with the immobilization of their limbs in an ingenious Roman machine called the stocks. Lydia and another woman bullied the guards into letting the prisoners be fed by hand, which the two women took care of, shovelling in broiled fish and bread. 'None of that sharp sauce, please,' Silas stipulated. And pouring wine down. Then Paul and Silas were left. The earth tremors resumed and made a bourdon to the loud psalms that they sang, interspersed with the odd ode of Horace recited by Silas. They were not alone in the cell. There were a couple of thieves to whom Lydia and her companion had fed the remains of the fish and wine, plenty left over. They were appreciative of the psalms, both Paul and Silas having loud but melodious voices, and they liked the erotic Horace, a poet they had to confess to not having heard of before. 'Here we are, proper Romans, and we have to learn about one of our own from a couple of Jews. You don't have to be in those things,' said the burlier of the two thieves, whose name seemed to be Parvulus, examining the mechanism of the stocks. 'I mean, you're not going to get out of here in a hurry, are you. Injury to insult, I call it. Here Calvinus, give us a hand.' These two hard men, used to breaking into houses, wrenched slat from slat, though with difficulty, and not helped by the earth tremor, which made the stone floor as unsteady as a ship's deck at times. 'There,' Parvulus said in triumph, and Paul and Silas rubbed wrists and ankles with relief. 'Not well made that thing. Foreign workmanship.' And then the tremor, like a strong man underground who had been trying to break a set of stocks and merely exhibiting the strains of his exertion, now achieved what it was after, which was to disrupt the smug stasis of Philippi's architecture. 'Castor and bleeding Pollux,' went Parvulus with awe, as the cell seemed to descend into an ocean trough and the door was detached from its hinges. Then, the tellurian message having been delivered, the earth settled to the sleep denied to its immediate dwellers. 'We're gettng out of here,' Parvulus said, making for the welcoming doorway. But Paul said:

213

'Wait. If you do that the guards will be in trouble. They'll have to fall on their swords. You know the law.'

'Let the guards be shagged to death by Pluto and his wife for all I care. I don't give a rat's turd for the law, it's the law that put us here.' But at that moment two guards came in in relief, seeing their charges present and intact. Paul said:

'You see how it is. Our God looks after his own. He's released us from our bonds and opened the door to our freedom. But we thought of what your plight might be and declined the proffer. Now you see the strength of our religion. Join the line of converts we're going to have when we get out of here.'

As it happened, it was not long before Paul and Silas were released, though the two good thieves, whom Paul duly taught that men of their kind had special niches reserved to them in the Christian heaven, had to see out their term. Paul and Silas were brought up once more before the praetors who, in a pose of Roman magnanimity, said they trusted they had learned their lesson and they were now to be booted out of town. But Paul said:

'Wait. My colleague and I are Roman citizens. *Cives Romani sumus.* Yes, easy enough to make the claim without being able to substantiate it, but our status is on record in, respectively, Tarsus in Cilicia and Caesarea in Palestine. We demand that you seek confirmation of our claim. We are prepared to wait. We have much to do here in the way of teaching the new faith. You know the penalty for (a) whipping Roman citizens, (b) imprisoning them without trial and (c) making them leave Roman territory under constraint. You will be removed from your praetorships and punished according to the provisions of the Valerian and Porcian laws. Very well. We will say no more about it. But if you do not accord proper tolerance to the discreet practice of the faith we profess, you, gentlemen both, to say nothing of your lictors, will be in grave trouble. Good morning.'

Thus a church was established at Philippi with little opposition either from the Jews, of whom there were fewer than ten, or from the Romans, who saw the value of discretion. Luke elected to stay on at the house of Lydia, allegedly for the purpose of medicating the girl Eusebia, who was covered in sores and vilely undernourished. Also, he said, the town was not rich in physicians and he wished to set down in the cool comfort of the room he had been given some details – in prose – of Paul's missionary journeys. Paul, Silas and Timothy set out west along the Egnatian Way which linked the Aegean to the Adriatic. They came at length to Thessalonica, the Macedonian capital, where there were plenty of Jews, mostly with Hellenized names, and a thriving synagogue. A hired mob tried to have Paul, Silas and Timothy brought up before the politarchs, or city magistrates, on a charge of setting up one Jesus Chrestos, a Palestinian criminal who became a Greek slave, as a rival to Claudius. But Paul, Silas and Timothy were speeded out of the town at night, and the only adherent of the treasonous conspiracy they could get hold of was a Jewish merchant named Jason (his real name was Joshua), who was acquitted by the politarchs for lack of evidence. This infuriated those who had hired the mob, and the mob turned up in the town of Beroea, whither the evangelists had travelled. Silas and Timothy went into hiding, but some of the Beroean converts got Paul to Methone or Dium, or some other port, and so he took ship alone to Athens.

Athens. Here now Paul faced the most difficult task of his career, that of persuading intellectuals learned in the philosophy of Plato and of Aristotle, Zeno and Epicurus to give ear to a religion not well founded in reason. The Greeks were under the Romans, a proud people colonized, but the inventors of the science of government were, for the most part, allowed to go their own way. Thus Paul met no opposition to his preaching, either from the Jews, who were too rational to be bigoted, or from the governing body, which tolerated every kind of intellectual or religious novelty. To Paul, who lodged in an inn under the Acropolis, the whole city was a seductive affront to his faith, whether as Jew or Nazarene. For here were all the gods and goddesses which, under changed names, the Romans had appropriated, limned in fine marble with a skill and sophistication the Jews, whose only art was literature, could never hope, if they ever took their horny paws from plough or nannygoat's udder to assume the chisel, to touch. The temples to these demons, as he considered them to be, were of a superb elegance. These people had everything but God. And, he almost added, good wine, for the resinous urine they sold ensoured his stomach. He was lonely: Silas and Timothy were supposed to follow him here but they had not yet arrived and he feared somewhat for their safety. They would be safe enough in Athens, where the new faith provoked not opposition but yawns.

He went daily to the Agora, a kind of marketplace west of the Acropolis, where he met Stoics and Epicureans. They did not deny that there might be a God or world soul, but this being was too lofty to concern himself with the affairs of men. The Stoics went in for morality and duty without eschatological sanctions, the Epicureans believed in pleasure and tranquillity and the conquest of the fear of death. 'But,' Paul said, 'there is nothing to fear in death. Death is the gateway to the fuller life. Duty and the moral life have their reward, and terms like pleasure and tranquillity hardly suffice to describe the eternal elation of unity with God.' How do you know this? Who told you? Where is the evidence? 'In the appearance of God made flesh in the world, in the resurrection of his fleshly Son after death.' Many misheard the name

Jesus as *iasis*, meaning healing, and *Ieso*, the name of the goddess of healing in the Ionic dialect. They interpreted *anastasis*, which signifies resurrection, as a restoration of health, and *soter*, meaning saviour, as the physician who so restores. They were not impressed. Nothing new here. No rationality in it. They called Paul a *spermologos* or seed picker, a pecking gutter sparrow, a purveyor of scraps and trifles. 'But look here,' said a serious teacher of rhetoric named Cratippus, whose homonymous father the peripatetic philosopher had obtained a professorial post in Athens through the influence of Cicero and was less inclined than many to scoff at what was not Athenian, 'this Cilician Jew has come a long way, he's evidently intelligent and learned in his own theology, and his Greek isn't bad. He's wasting his time here in the Agora. He ought to go before the Areopagus.'

'The Areopagus?' Paul repeated. 'But I haven't committed any crime that I know of.'

'Oh, they're not justices in the Roman way. They're supposed to look after our religion and morals. The best way of getting these ideas of yours over to Athens is to speak to the Areopagus. They'll listen. They're not like the Romans, who won't listen to anybody, as my father always used to say. And they'll pronounce on what you tell them. They'll let you know whether there's anything in it or not.'

'But I don't need this Areopagus to confirm what I know to be true in my very blood and bones and guts.'

'There speaks the Jew. You're a very physical people. We go in more for the soul. Prepare your brief carefully. I'll arrange things for you. Shall we say this time tomorrow?'

The Areopagus had used formerly to meet on the hill of Ares, which is what Areopagus means, but now they met in the Royal Portico northeast of the Agora. Paul, brought thither by Cratippus, found a number of grave men, some very old, all of magisterial appearance. Cratippus said: 'I bring before you one Paul, who has come all the way from Palestine to propound the principles of a new religion very active in that province and, indeed, well beyond it. Athens has still to hear of it. Here is the man who bids you hear.'

So, in a clean Greek free of the pollutions of Cilicia, Paul spoke. He said: 'Citizens of Athens, in my brief stay in your noble city I have observed your concern with matters of religion, even though it may be termed a negative concern, for I have seen many altars inscribed *to an unknown god*. This implies a willingness to worship a negativity, which neither grammar nor theology will properly permit. Now I would ask you to consider a singular and unique God, not one of many but the only one, who created the world and all things in it, who, having made man as well as the earth and the heavens, is much concerned with the ways of man. He is especially concerned that men

216

seek him. He is not remote from us, he is easily found. Why, even one of your own poets, Epimenides the Cretan, says that in him we live and move and have our being. We are the offspring of God, creatures made of his substance, and it is absurd to think of him as a mere thing, an object of silver or gold or stone, which occurs when his unity is split into mere personifications of human needs and motives. For a personified quality is no more than a lump of metal. Now, God has been tolerant towards human ignorance of him, but now he commands that men repent of this ignorance. That this ignorance be no longer excused by the sense of his remoteness, which encouraged his conversion on the part of men either to a thought or to a thing, he came to earth himself, and that recently, to a particular place, Palestine, and in a particular time, that of my own generation, in the form of a human being. We may use the metaphor of the father sending down to the son, so long as we regard this as a mere similitude. So the Son of God taught the way of righteousness, showing human goodness as an aspect of eternal goodness enshrined in the godhead, and taught also that righteousness would lead men to dwell eternally with the fountain of righteousness, or, to change the metaphor, that human water should at the last be shown to be part of the divine ocean. I teach *anastasis*, which signifies not the survival of the soul, which any of your Platonists could demonstrate at least as a logical possibility, but as the survival of the sensorium also, though in a transfigured form. For God the Son himself rose from the dead and, in that filial or human aspect, returned to the eternal home of the Father. This, learned men of Athens, is the gist of my message.'

There was a kind of rumbling and squeaking silence. Then a very old man squeaked: 'You quote a minor poet, or rather you make a very doubtful attribution to a minor poet. I would quote a major poet, our own Aeschylus, who, in his *Eumenides*, says there is no *anastasis*. The man dies, he says, and the earth drinks his blood, and there is an end of things. Words attributed to the god Apollo himself, alleged to have been spoken when this very Areopagus was founded by our patroness Athene. The Epicureans, true, speak of the indestructibility of the atoms of which we are made, along with all things in the universe, but the notion of *physical* human survival is a mere undemonstrable supposition.' Another, younger, man boomed out boredly:

'We require that a proposition be reduced to its first principles. We Athenians do not take things on trust.'

'The first premise of a logical statement,' Paul said, 'has always to be taken on trust. We all have to begin with the evidence of our senses.'

'You actually *saw* this man rise from the dead?' a man so emaciated as fancifully to seem pared down to pure thought said.

217

'I have lived with those who did and are still living to recount the experience,' Paul said.

'Well, then, send them to us. Not that their testimony would necessarily be credible. The world is full of madmen and liars. I think we have heard enough.'

The president of the Areopagus, a discreet legal-looking man in late middle age named Demetrios, said: 'We will hear you again, if you wish. Not tomorrow, nor the next day, but sometime. It interests us to know what new fantasies are being entertained in the great world outside Athens.' He lightly hammered *great* with irony. 'For the moment, thank you for your attendance and the evident sincerity of your discourse.' Then the Areopagus rose, leaving Paul alone save for an old man who announced his name as Dionysius. Dionysius said:

'Interesting. And it has the charm of the exotic. Are there books on the subject?'

'Not yet, alas. It is too new to have settled itself into books.'

'Yes, a novelty. Well, you must come to dinner and tell me more.'

The invitation was vague, but Paul, sensing that he was about to drown in a *thalassa* of unconcern, determined to hold on to this flotsam of possible persuasibility and persuaded Dionysius to fix a date and a time. Thus, three days later, Silas and Timothy not yet having arrived, Paul dined with him, very frugally, and met at the table a *hetæra*, as he took her to be, named Damaris. She was a little too enthusiastic about the new doctrines, and Paul's heart sank into his stomach, where it met a wave of acidity induced by the resinous urine. Athens, he knew, was a failure. He received a message the next day from Silas and Timothy, brought by a travelling Beroean, which said they were staying in Macedonia a little longer, pursuing the good work already initiated. He was very much alone.

On his journey to Corinth he pondered the problem of spreading the word to the rational and educated. The Jews, most of them, opposed it because they were satisfied with what they had, and the pagans drank deep of it because they had nothing else. First principles. Credibility. Seeing, on the outskirts of Corinth, a temple with a many-breasted goddess transfixed on its façade, he felt the resurgence of hope. *Eros* once more to be transformed into *agape*. He greeted Astarte or whoever she was almost as an old friend. He went, after a light meal bought with his remaining coins of the Empire (he must find work soon), to a corner of the marketplace where, like any cheerful mountebank, he offered the secret of eternal life. It cost nothing, he eventually said, except everything. One man at the front of the crowd, loaded with larder provisions, maintained a faint smile of appreciation for the clarity and rhetoric but said nothing. Paul said he would say more at the synagogue in two days' time, where pagans would be welcome to usurp the seats of the regular attenders, and, as he had no money for a night's lodging, he slept in a public park, under a bronze effigy of the goddess, who held a detached phallus over him in, he thought he might fancifully think, a gesture of protection. This goddess must have put erotic images into his sleeping mind, for he woke polluted with a nocturnal emission. Not his fault, though he prayed that God might protect even the untracked regions of his brain in this city so well known for its erotism that it had given the verb *korinthiazo* as a synonym for *I fornicate* to the Greek language. For breakfast he drank fountain water and, without shame, begged a bit of bread from one of the gardeners. Then he walked towards the marketplace again. On the main street, however, a voice hailed him with a welcome. It was the faintly smiling man he had seen yesterday, sitting before a shop in the morning sun and stitching at what seemed to be a tent. Paul stopped and, with a nostalgia for that work, sat down next to him. The man said:

'I heard you yesterday. I look forward to hearing you on the Sabbath. Not that I'll be easy to convince. This is my wife, Priscilla.' A smiling woman with a superior air about her, rinsing a cloth on to the pavement. 'This is Paul, who preaches the Nazarene gospel. Oh, my name's Aquila. That means eagle. The nose, see. Some wine, or is it too early?'

'Some water, if I may. This is thirsty weather.'

'And you're off to do that thirsty business again?'

'Corinth seems promising.'

'A very fleshly lot, if you catch my meaning.'

'I catch it. *Korinthiazo* – I fornicate.'

Aquila looked shocked. 'Surely not.'

'No, no, the word. As though fornication had been invented in Corinth.' He looked at some women passing, perhaps temple prostitutes off duty; they seemed specially bred in some erotic stable that their rotundities of seduction should painfully provoke. But there was no pain in it save for Paul: they provoked only that they might satisfy. And the walk: undulant, the buttocks awag, the breasts thrust upward by some ingenuity of corsetage. The mouths very red, the hair crackling black from recent washing. Paul sighed, recognizing that the impulse in himself could not be evil, not unless one admitted the dualism of John Mark's Zoroastrians. What did one do about it? One turned Christ into one's bride, which produced its own complications; one married. He, the preaching tentmaker, married. It was not possible. His groin whimpered resentment. But Aquila was saying something about the stress of work, the city full and rich, partly because of the inflow of Jews exiled from Rome, though some were going back. A trading town this, big port, rival to Athens. Paul did not want to hear the name Athens. He said, looking at Aquila's stitching fingers: 'I don't think I ever saw that double-over lock in Tarsus.'

'It's the Roman way. Though it's more awnings and bed hangers in Italy. You seem to know about the trade, knowing the double-over.'

'It's mine. My only living, except for charity. A man has to make a living somehow.'

'You plan to stay long in Corinth?'

'There's a lot to do.'

'So you wouldn't mind practising the trade here?'

'Making tents? Are you offering me something?'

'There's enough work for two. And there's a little room at the back of the shop. Very little.'

'I'm grateful.'

'Of course, we shan't be staying here for ever. My wife's of a better class than I am. A good Jewish girl but a true Roman. She wants to get back. So do I, for that matter. But we thought of training some grown men, not young apprentices, and putting a manager in charge. Both here and in Ephesus. There's money in the east. But Rome's the place for spending it. You don't know Rome, do you?'

'No, but I will.'

So, fortified by good meals from Priscilla, Paul smote vigorously at Corinthian fornication, grew visibly elated in his invocation of the new faith, angered the Jews, baptized the pagans, and opened a chapel which was a kind of rival synagogue. A certain Titus or Titius Justus, an Italian who had been in the trade of exporting dried raisins, called currants after Corinth, and now a retired widower, owned a large house quite near to the synagogue, too large for his own use, and offered it to Paul for his preaching and the ceremony of the supper of the Lord. The Church is the body of the faithful, but a church is where the faithful may meet. This was the first of the brick-and-mortar churches. To it one day came the Jew who was in charge of the synagogue, much troubled. His name was Crispus. He said to Paul:

'I'm convinced. God help me. I say that because it puts me in dire peril. Physical, that is. My former fellows – what are they going to think, do? My own feet have started to take charge. I walk towards the synagogue and then they make me bear left and I finish here. For God's sake, what am I going to do?'

'Some of us Christians remain Jewish,' Paul said. 'It's only the bigots who insist on the *schisma*. Take your baptism in secret – it can be done here in that kind of fountain in the back garden – continue your synagogue duties. I'm still a good enough Jew to wish to go to Jerusalem for Passover – this year, next. The new faith is only the fulfilment of the old.'

'I wish to God I could make some of the others see that.'

'I've tried. You know I've tried. One can't try for ever. Life is short and there's the whole known world to cover. Will you be blessed now with the baptismal water?'

'Yes, God help me.'

Paul sat in the evenings in the living room of Aquila and Priscilla. She sewed delicate fabrics; he drank wine, his due after a hard day, and chewed currants out of a silver dish. Paul recounted his adventures. Priscilla laughed at some of them, and he could not see why. He was saying one evening: 'Silas and I were at Lystra – Silas should be here soon, by the way – and a man in our congregation was a cripple more in mind than in body. His limbs were unshrivelled, they looked sound enough to me. He was not difficult to cure. The people were ecstatic, they said it was divine magic, and then – ah, they insisted on identifying Silas and myself with two of the pagan demons – he was Jupiter and I was Mercury. They even brought in a couple of white oxen garlanded with flowers. Of course, Lystra is the centre of the Zeus and Hermes cult – why are you laughing? You find this blasphemy comic? I work in the Lord's name and they hail me in the name of Mercury –'

'The god of thieves,' Priscilla said with wet eyes, 'but also of fine speech. I find the story has humour in it. Like the other one you told – of being put in prison and then having an earthquake open the door for you. I always knew that God had a fine sense of the comic.'

'I don't see it,' said Paul.

'Perhaps you will when the stories are written down. They mustn't be lost to the future, they're too good.'

'Precisely the words of Luke,' Paul said grimly.

'Who's Luke?'

'A Greek physician I converted in Antioch. He has a taste for writing. And also for what you would call the comic. I see. I become a character in a Greek tale.'

'But who,' Aquila said, 'is more real than some of the Greek heroes? Why should the pagans have the best heroes for themselves?'

'*The Pauliad*.' Priscilla laughed again.

'No, no, no, no.' Then there was a thunder of knocking at the shop door.

'They're here again,' Aquila sighed. 'I wish they'd leave us alone.'

'My apologies,' Paul said. 'It isn't you they're after. It never is, I'll go.' He went and unbolted. Three Jewish elders were there, frowning in the mild light of early evening. The chief of them, Amoz, said:

'Saul or Paul or whatever your name is, the governor is ready to see you.'

'But I,' Paul answered, 'am not ready to see the governor. Can the matter not wait, whatever it is? A man has a right to rest after a long day.'

'A teacher of blasphemies has no right to rest. Gallio is just come from Achaia and is anxious to try your case.'

'Meaning that you people are anxious for him to try it. Not that you have a case.'

'Under Roman law ours is a lawful faith. Yours is not. From the mouth of a Roman consul –'

'Proconsul,' Priscilla corrected. She had come to listen. She was smiling broadly.

'I don't need to be put right by foreign women who give lodgings to heretics,' Amoz growled. 'All right. From a Roman proconsul you will hear the judgment. Come.' Paul went. Priscilla laughed very merrily. All this fuss. And all because men were concerned about the cutting of their foreskins.

Gallio's real name was Marcus Annaeus Novatus. Born in Cordova and educated in Rome, he was adopted by the great expert on rhetoric Mucius Junius Gallio and so took his name. He was a man of charm, wit and some tolerance, tolerance meaning that he considered religion to be an inconsiderable toy. Tired from his journey and his chronic lung weakness, which he had saved from turning to phthisis by winter sojourns in Egypt, he was yet goodhumoured enough when his deputy reported the arrival of a gang of Jews who wanted judgment on something or someone. He sat in his library, looking over a scroll of new verse that had come from Rome. *Furfur caelestis*. Heavenly dandruff. Why couldn't these moderns say *snow* and have done with it? 'They won't be heard in here? No, of course, the house of the infidel. Ah well, I must bow my head in my impurity. I see they have brought their own torches.' Their light could be seen through the casement, marching under the oleanders. He went out to his garden which, being God's and not a Gentile's, was pure. The gang was there with a small bald man with calm eyes. The rest stamped and neighed around him. The old Jew named Amoz spoke loud words:

'Gallio, proconsul, greetings and long life. This is the man Paul we have spoken and written of. He continues to persuade men to worship God contrary to the Jewish law. Now the Jewish law is decreed by the Emperor to be *religio licita* –'

'Has he spoken some villainy? Theft – murder – treason – has he committed any of those? Has he spoken against the Emperor?'

'No, but he blasphemes by saying the new heresy supersedes the law of Moses –'

'I have,' Gallio said, 'no concern with the law of Moses. That is your own affair. Your religion, as you rightly say, is under Roman protection. And so are all variants of your religion, heretical and otherwise. We Romans therefore have no right to meddle with their inner workings or dissensions between them. That would be breaking the law. And so I will not be a judge of these matters.'

'Think carefully, Gallio,' Amoz said, insolently it seemed to the proconsul. 'What decision you make here establishes legal precedent in the Roman provinces and must be upheld in Rome itself. If the man Paul is made free to preach his doctrine as he calls it, that doctrine or abominable perversion of a doctrine becomes allowable under Roman law.'

'I have thought as carefully as the matter seems to warrant,' Gallio said. 'Which means I have thought for twenty seconds or so. And I say with the Roman weight you seem to demand: So be it.'

Naturally a number of Nazarenes had followed the torchbearing orthodox into Gallio's garden. These now let out whoops of glee and began to beat the sour vanquished as they left. There was one decent elder named Sosthenes who was taking over the leadership of the synagogue in succession to Crispus (who had resigned discreetly on grounds of ill health), and he came in for most of the battering. Paul used his authority, calling: 'Stop that. Brotherly love. Tolerance.' But the batterers went on battering as the company, loud in its discomfiture, passed down the garden walk and out of the gates. Gallio said to Paul:

'I've heard of your religion. Through my brother. He's a philosopher. Lucius Annaeus Seneca. Do you know of him?'

'I see. You're a son of the elder Seneca. My father spoke once of meeting him. That would be in Spain.'

'We're a Spanish family. And what was a Jew doing in Spain?'

'You're Spanish and Roman. We're Jewish and Roman. It was a matter of trade. The wings of the eagle are wide, as they say. What have you heard of Christianity?'

'That it comes close to the philosophy my brother teaches. The philosophy of the stoic. Do right, even when the state counsels wrong. Be prepared to suffer for the right. Be proud in your knowledge that right prevails, even when the state crushes it.'

'I don't teach pride.'

'It's a proud man who dies for his faith – like this man of yours.'

'He went like a lamb to the slaughter. We follow him. The Stoic has no God, so he himself has to be the guardian of virtue. The Christian's virtue is all in God. He can afford to be humble.'

'Which God? The God of those ravening elders out there?'

'There's only one. He loves mankind. He sent down his only son to suffer in the flesh. That's the measure of his love.'

'You don't seem to me to be a madman.'

'You'll find no saner faith than the one I preach. Love, forbearance, forgiveness – sane virtues. The world won't survive without them. Ask your brother what *he* thinks.'

*   *   *

We have been absent from Rome some little time, and now that the name of Lucius Annaeus Seneca has been sounded we may as well look on the owner of the name, seated firmly in the Palatine as the confidant and adviser of Agrippina and the tutor of her son. He has haunted eyes and a mouth as it were set in suffering, his lank hair falls carelessly over his forehead as if he scorned the combed order of the world, but he is shrewd enough in the ordering of his estates, and the look of the ascetic is delusory. He is acting one of the characters of his own closet tragedies, surviving voice of virtue in the face of wrongs done not only by men but by the gods. But what wrongs have been done him? The Emperor Claudius banished him, true, for an impudent mock in one of his moral essays, but Agrippina soon had him recalled. His wealth is enormous. His influence in the state will, if he is discreet and prudent, be considerable. We see him for the moment seated in one of the schoolrooms of the palace, a spare room with maps and scrolls and the scent of a pinetree outside the casement reminding the moral philosopher of the wild grace of the natural world. His pupil lounges next to him, interrupting a discourse on the philosophy of Zeno by saying that he has had enough of this skeletal unreality and it is time for his music lesson.

'You will need philosophy more than you will need music.'

'In what?'

'In whatever position in the state you are to hold. You must prepare for responsibility.'

'I want to be a great actor, dancer, singer. Isn't there such a thing as responsibility to art?'

'It is not a moral responsibility.'

The pupil's name is Lucius Domitius Ahenobarbus, and Agrippina, daughter of Germanicus the brother of the Emperor Claudius, is his mother. His father, Cn. Domitius Ahenobarbus, died in suspicious circumstances into which the son, though aware that his mother may have had something to do with it, has never too closely inquired. Morality does not interest him. He says now:

'You talk too much of morality. And by morality you mean – I forget the words –'

'The repression of impulse.'

'Yes, you repressed my natural impulse to see life. The execution of the Empress Messalina, for instance.'

'That was hardly life.'

'But she was very beautiful. To see her beautiful head severed and the golden blood flowing, no spurting, over her ivory skin. A living poem. Wouldn't you say that it was immoral to avert a young man's eyes from the sight of the beauty of the world?'

'There is no beauty in death, even when it is encompassed in the name of justice. Death is a necessity – which we ought to spend our whole lives learning to embrace without fear. As for the deaths of others, there is something shocking, I could almost say seismic, in the sight of human dissolution. To speak of the beauty of golden blood on ivory skin might be considered immoral. You must not subvert an organism, whether living or dying, into a mere arrangement of shapes and colours.'

'But I do that all the time. You wouldn't understand, Seneca. You're not an artist.'

'I am considered,' and the grim mouth relaxes into a complacency which the pupil is quick to notice, 'to be an efficient poet of tragedy. Tomorrow we shall read together my *Hercules Furens*. There you will find an exquisite ordering of words and rhythms serving a stoic end.'

'I know the play, and I find it too violent. Not in what it shows but in its language. You have no ear for words. And if, as you say, you serve *a stoic end*, you are committing a gross immorality against the ethics of art, whose end is not the inculcation of a moral lesson but beauty for its own sake. Beauty, beauty, *beauty*.'

'Who has been telling you this nonsense?'

'Never you mind who's been telling me. Whoever he is, he's right. Beauty and morality may be considered deadly enemies, he also says, and you would say that goes ridiculously far. There is also the question of beauty and sexuality, and that poses a very difficult problem.'

'A problem,' Seneca says, 'which you seem to have solved quite satisfactorily. The headless corpse of a beautiful object of sexual desire is reduced to mere shape and colour. You see where a concentration on what you call beauty will lead you. It will lead you beyond the limits of compassion and, I may say, all moral feeling. But man is defined as a moral creature. Beauty is a matter only of the senses. Let us continue with our study of the moral system of Zeno.'

'Oh, Seneca, Seneca,' the precocious youth said, leaning on his arm, which was flat to the table, 'you have no subtlety. It's useless discussing these high aesthetic matters with you. Very well, if we're to study morality, tell me why you and other moralists look with such horror on incest.'

'Why do you raise this question?'

'You know very well why. The Emperor Claudius proposes to marry his own niece, who is my revered mother. You are shocked and Pallas and Narcissus are shocked, or say they are. And the Senate refuses to pass an act permitting it. And yet the kingdom of Egypt insisted on the royal house being sustained by brothers marrying sisters. Incest there was not merely permitted, it was regarded as desirable and holy, and I believe it still is. So why is it so terrible for Romans?'

'If you read my play on Oedipus or, your aversion to my style being so great, the play by Sophocles on which it is based, you will see that the two gravest crimes against morality have always been in our western culture the act of parricide and the act of incest. You kill the father, you impregnate mother or daughter or sister or niece, and the whole structure of society is menaced. There is an instinctive abhorrence of these acts which is based on an instinctive knowledge of what makes for the stability of society. The family collapses and along with it the authority of the priests and the governors. The products of incest are very frequently monsters.'

'You have seen such?'

'I have read about such.'

'So my revered mother will bring forth a monster?' Lucius Domitius Ahenobarbus smiled contemptuously at his tutor. The family cognomen meant *bronze beard*, and, though Lucius Domitius was beardless, his curly hair had the sheen of bronze and glowed gold in the sunlight. His eyes were blue and his features well formed: he was a pretty boy more than a handsome one. He was somewhat pustular, a condition not uncommon in adolescents, but maturity would calm the eruptions in his skin. Seneca said:

'The Emperor will not be permitted to commit incest. There are limits even to the imperial power. The Senate has the duty of imposing these limits. Your mother will not become Empress.'

'Will you bet on that – say, a hundred sesterces?'

'I am not a betting man. To bet is to place yourself in the hands of chance, unseemly in a Stoic.'

'You're an old fool, Seneca.'

'That is more than unseemly. You will apologize in fifty lines of hendecasyllables and deliver them tomorrow.'

'And if not?'

'I shall report you to your mother.'

'May I sing the hendecasyllables?'

Paul was now in Ephesus. Aquila and Priscilla had travelled thither with him, considered the prospect of setting up business there, thought better of it, then, Priscilla's homesickness prevailing, took ship for Italy. Silas appeared but not Timothy, who was conducting his own ministry in Macedonia. Luke arrived with some pages of neat Greek documentation of Paul's work, more or less accurate but, in Paul's view, disfigured with Greek humour. 'Cross that out. That too. Unseemly. And that, there, is more than unseemly.' Very well, sighing. Then Paul went to the synagogue and spoke as follows:

'Men of Ephesus, I came to you after many journeys – from Jerusalem

226

to Tarsus and from Tarsus to Antioch. I have brought the good news to Cyprus, to the other Antioch in Pisidia, to Iconium, Lystra and Derbe, to Philippi, to Thessalonica, to Athens, to Corinth. I have seen and suffered many things and have been as sick from the waves of the sea as I have from men with hard hearts in the towns of my travels. It has been no easy work to bring the good news, yet the hardship is softened by God's grace, for God's love permits the working of the yeast of his word through signs and wonders. When you say the man Paul has cured the sick, given sight to the blind, driven out the frenzy of the devil in men's souls, you say wrong: it is the power of God working through Paul, for the man Paul has no power. Take heed, for this city of Ephesus is too well known in the world for its jugglers and magicians. I am come not to compete with them but to bring the divine word. And when I say now the power of the name Jesus makes you whole, I indulge in no petty mountebank's cantrips. For man is made whole only by faith in Jesus the Son of God.'

A man in the congregation stood and held up for all to see a piece of worn leather. He cried to Paul: 'Do you know what this is?'

'No,' Paul said.

'It's a piece cut off one of the aprons you use when you sit to your morning tent work. I got it from my handyman. He admitted stealing it. He's been going round trying to cure the halt and the blind with it. If that's not magic, what is?'

'I can't be blamed,' Paul said, 'for the superstitions of others. Not only my *semicinctia* but my *sudaria* –'

'We don't speak Latin here.'

'Sweatrags. There's neither unholy magic nor holy power in these things. Neither in me nor in my shadow nor in the miserable things belonging to me. Mark this well. Only the name Jesus possesses the power.'

A man named Sceva took this too literally. He called himself a chief priest, but this was an imposture assumed because only chief priests were supposed to know the correct pronunciation of the Ineffable Name, a cantrip omnipotent in magic. He did not know it, though he had tried *Iao* and *Iae* and *Iaoue* and other approximations. He sat now with some of his magician colleagues in his stuffy study with its smell of assafoetida and other noxious gums reputed to be useful in exorcism. He rolled absently between his hands the sad dry skull of a little child, saying: 'They won't pay any more, they tell me, without seeing results.'

'You can't command *perierga*,' a man who called himself Antipholus said.

'Perhaps not, but it's *perierga* they're paying for. We've tried everything. We've even fallen back on *Sabaoth* and *Abraham*, a fat lot of

227

good such names have always been. You've seen what the new one can do. Is it safe to try it?'

'It worked with old baldhead and that one with the palsy.'

'You miss the point. He believes in what lies behind the name. We don't. It's foreign to us and maybe dangerous. It could kick back.'

'Now you're being superstitious.'

'The strength lies in the name,' a man called Trophuz, very dark and small, of God knew what provenance, said. 'And the name's anybody's property, the way I see it.'

'I suppose the worst that can happen is that nothing will happen,' Antipholus said.

'All right,' Sceva sighed. 'We'll go.'

They went, seven of them, to the house of the widow Sameach, a sad woman despite her name (meaning glad) and the wealth left by her husband, who had been in the Lebanese timber export business. She was sad because of her son Bohen (so called because the Lord had pressed his thumb into his neck before birth and left a deep depression), who lay on his bed all day in a kind of stupor enlivened with occasional fierce writhings of the limbs and unintelligible shouts, also with fits of upright violence in which he smashed vases. She had taken to locking his bedroom door, upon which he now and then hammered. He ate little, spewed much and nauseatingly, and was impervious to medicines and cantrips. When Sceva and his colleagues arrived, Sameach's brother-in-law was there, a sceptic who was sick of the mumbo jumbo. 'Good money thrown away,' he said. 'Not a penny more.'

'This time,' Sceva promised, 'you'll see results.'

The seven of them went into the little bedroom, a close fit, and heard the widow lock the door behind them. This they never liked, but there had been an occasion when the boy had responded vigorously to the intonation of a deformed version of the Ineffable Name and rushed out to smash things. The rest of the day he had been quiet. The seven looked at him, no pretty sight, for he dribbled some yellow viscosity from nose and mouth and his eyes rolled independently of each other. From his mouth there issued voices of contention in no known language, like the later stages of a drinking party, and in one passage a bass voice argued simultaneously with a treble, while the other voices maintained a kind of listening silence. Trophuz nudged Sceva and said: 'Now.' Sceva took a large breath and sang:

'Evil spirits that dwell within our brother here, I conjure you in the name of Jesus whom Paul preaches – leave him.'

The response was immediate and terrifying. A single voice spoke from the dribbling mouth in clear Greek, saying: 'Jesus I know. Paul I know. But who are you?' Then the youth leapt from his bed and waded into the seven with horrible energy, yanking at beards, gouging eyes, twisting ears, stamping on feet, tearing robes. Sceva hammered on the door, yelling. Two of the bolder and brawnier of the seven hit back at their patient, who did not seem to feel the blows. When at length the door was opened, the seven rushed out with energetic Bohen in the midst of them, kicking back as well as forward. The widow Sameach screamed, and her brother-in-law shook his head sadly, saying: 'More harm than good. Not a penny.'

I tell the story that I was told, leaving it to my readers to reject or accept. Bohen in the street was a wonder of ferocity that set the dogs barking and then scurrying off yelping, while children and women rent the air with their yells of fright. He roared, stripped a poor old woman near naked, overturned a market stall full of gourds, and finally he lay exhausted in a puddle, whimpering and faintly howling. Paul at this time had been forbidden the use of the synagogue and was arguing a knotty point about the physical resurrection with some of his new plants or neophytes in the schoolroom lent to him by the teacher popularly known as Tyrannus (no relative of the father of the protomartyr). He was called out, saw poor Bohen, had him carried back to his mother's house, and there induced a deep natural sleep from which the boy emerged cured. Or so I am told.

Certainly some such thaumaturgy must be invoked to explain the amazing scene which ensued that evening in the marketplace, when books of magical cantrips, treatises on the *perierga*, crudely illustrated guides to the winning of love, amulets, ikons, beads, flasks of unwholesome decoctions (dogturds, wolfsbane, menses) were thrown on to a fire. There were attempts to throw on it also Sceva and his fellows, but this was, Paul said, going too far. Silas and Luke, both bookish men, were uneasy about the incineration of some very fine volumes bound in leather with gold locks, but Paul said: 'Look at that obscenity. And that.' Dog pedicating man. Man pedicating dog.

'They could be sold.'

'To other magical charlatans.'

'But see the workmanship.'

'On to the fire with it, Luke.'

An old woman brought a small silver figurine to Paul. 'What do I do about this, sir?' Paul examined it squinting. It was an effigy of the goddess sprouting breasts like warts. 'Me and my family – we don't worship her any more.' Paul said:

'The effigy is evil. The silver is out of the rock that God made. Melt it down and give the silver to the poor.' Then he raised his voice: 'It is well know that this city of Ephesus is the shrine of the false goddess Artemis, whom some call Diana. You who give homage to her – repent. You silversmiths whose wealth is in the making of her image – change your business to the making of candlesticks. Have done with false idols.' A silversmith named Demetrius heard these words and was very unhappy.

Now this was the time in spring when night and day are about equal, the beginning of the month called Artemision, when the eunuch priests and their priestesses presided over rituals to Artemis or Diana in the Ephesian temple. This temple was, and still is, one of the wonders of the world, being some four hundred feet long and two hundred feet wide and beautifully embellished with images of copulation. There had been a previous temple destroyed through the incendiarism of a young man named Herostratus, who did the deed to make a reputation for himself, successfully, for he is still remembered. (He performed the act, we are told, on the night when Alexander the Great was born.) The image of the goddess in the temple was not destroyed and indeed was indestructible, being a thunderstone or chunk of a star fallen to earth. It was, by celestial chance, formed in the image of a many-breasted female, and even the educated and sceptical were easily persuaded that the gods had sent down a crude representation, perhaps hammered by Vulcan, of one of their own. Certainly, Ephesus gained a great reputation as a town highly favoured by the goddess and, indeed, became the centre of her cult. To hear this cult assailed by a baldheaded Jew with a taste for bookburning was too much for the silversmith Demetrius and others of his trade, who made much money out of making and selling figurines of Artemis or Diana. Especially at this season.

So Demetrius and some of his fellow craftsmen held a meeting in Demetrius's workshop the following morning. This was a large shed full of fires, where some men poured molten metal into moulds and others cracked cold moulds open to reveal the smirking godlingess. Demetrius said:

'Look, friends, this is our trade. This is how we make our money.'

'In your instance, a lot of money.'

Demetrius ignored that. 'We're all involved in the worship of the goddess, blessed be her holy name and sacred influence. This man Paul is telling everybody that there's no such thing as gods made by hand. Before we know where we are he'll have the damned temple pulled down and the traffic stopped.'

'Traffic?'

'You know what I mean. The holy pilgrimages from all over Greece and Asia. This is our bread, friends.'

'He's blaspheming against precious metal. So we – ?'

'Stop him.'

Thus it was that Paul and some of his fellow Christians were dragged to the Ephesian temple by the militant guild of silversmiths, aided by a rabble that did not need to be hired, for the gratuitous manhandling of foreigners is always both a virtue and a pleasure in provincial towns where, anyway, there is little to do in the evenings. Silas, fearful in the ruddy flare of the torches, seeing the mound of the goddess's huge belly threatening twenty feet above his eyes, panicked in the belief that they were to be sacrificed to her, Christian blood to be smeared laboriously over her polymastic or multimammial rotundity. He began to hit out, and Paul hit out with him. The mob, always suggestible, hit out too in the same directions, and one brawny lad shouted to Paul: 'That's right, give it to these impietous Cretans or whatever they do be called.' A surprising and very Greek instinct for a kind of civic regularity then took over, and what seemed to be the entire male population of Ephesus pushed two recent Christian converts, both foreigners, Gaius of Derbe and Aristarchus of Thessalonica, who had followed Paul hither, towards the huge open-air theatre. Paul and Silas and Luke shoved against the current without opposition, for everybody was absorbed in a rhythmical yell of 'Long live Artemis of Ephesus!' So while Gaius and Aristarchus and other, nameless, converts were driven up the hill towards Pion, the converters got down to the inner harbour and hid behind some corded bales, panting.

It has to be noted that the chief citizens of Ephesus, known as Asiarchs, were not inimical to Paul's activities. The decision of Gallio had established a precedent in the Roman provinces, and Paul had broken no law. When, a little later, he and his fellows sat, Silas still fearful, in the schoolroom of Tyrannus in the dark, a friendly Asiarch came to report on what was proceeding in the theatre. 'Threequarters of them,' he said, 'have no idea why they're there, but the notion has arisen that this is an anti-Jewish demonstration and there's a Jew called Alexander telling them that the Jews love Artemis as much as anybody, a damned lie but you can't blame him. Anything to quieten them down.'

'As for quietening them down,' Paul said, 'I'd better go and address a few words myself. It's not often we get the whole town assembled.'

'Are you mad?' Silas said. 'Are you completely and irrevocably stark staring demented? They'll tear you to pieces, man.'

Luke said: 'I'll go and see what's happening. On the fringe, so to speak, with my little notebook. After all, it's a kind of literary duty.' So they let Luke go. Luke stood at the back of the mob which had been transformed into an audience, marvelling at the thousands making their own entertainment with the monotonous choral chant of 'Diana of Ephesus for ever!' while an old man with a long beard whom he took to be Alexander mouthed and gesticulated inaudibly from the *theatron*. Then a man strode on to the stage whom Luke knew: he was the *grammateus* or city secretary, a functionary responsible for the publication of civic decrees and a link between the municipal council and the provincial government. Thus he was responsible to the Roman authorities for good order in the city, and when he spoke he spoke with an urgency that quietened the assembly and made them listen.

'Men of Ephesus,' he cried, 'there is no need of your protestations. We all know Artemis is great. We all know that Ephesus is the keeper of her temple. We know that her image fell out of the skies from the hands of the god Jupiter himself. Why waste your breath on a truth too well known? Why not assume the dignity of quiet and the avoidance of rash acts? These men you have brought here are neither robbers of the temple nor blasphemers against the goddess. If Demetrius there, and others of his craft, have anything against these men who are called Christians – well, the law courts are open, the proconsuls ready to sit. Let everything be settled in the regular assemblies. Riot and civic pride do not sit well together. Go home.'

If the grumbling assembly now broke up and went home, it was partly out of a Greek sense of dramatic form. They had been there two hours, long enough for a play, and the final speech had the capping quality of well-shaped dramaturgy. When Paul heard Luke's report, he nodded in approval of the good sense of the *grammateus*, though naturally deploring his paganism, and he said: 'No bigot. In him you see the great change coming. Men will not fight for the old gods unless there is profit in them. If there is good sense in holiness, there may well be holiness in good sense. You will live to see that silver melted down and the goddess become a memory. She is already no more than dead metal.'

Dead metal, indeed. He had said that before but he would not say it again. What I have now to recount is extremely painful, but Paul should have known that everything has to be paid for. Demetrius and his fellows were not by nature men of violence, except against defenceless silver, and they were half content to wait to put their case to the proconsul (there was only one at that time, despite the town secretary's habituated pluralizing: Marcus Junius Silanus, proconsul for Asia, had been murdered on Agrippina's orders, but that is another story). Nevertheless, they felt it was only just that Paul should have a taste of the goddess and that that would much modify his rantings about purity. They arranged for a temple prostitute to be introduced into the bedchamber where Paul, the due of his status, slept alone while Luke and Silas had to share a cell: this was in the house of the convert Pyrrhus, where they lodged free. The girl was ready enough for the game, and she was helped up to the ground floor casement by smirking Demetrius and a dwarfish colleague named

Achilles. Paul slept heavily after a morning of stitching canvas and an afternoon and evening of shouting the word. She stripped herself naked and slid into the narrow bed, encountering bare hairiness and a flaccid rod which she swiftly whipped into life. Paul thought he was dreaming. Then he awoke shocked to find himself held in the posture of succubus by a smooth female body which knew every trick. He yelled, and the laughing girl leapt off and to the window, without which the two confederates were waiting. Paul, to his shame, found himself pumping seed on to his blanket. Dead metal indeed.

The finger was much pointed at him the following day. He boiled, composing in his head eloquent letters to all the churches about the deadliness of the sin of fornication. For himself, he required ritual purification, and there was no provision for that in the new order. He needed Jerusalem, he needed the Temple of Solomon. As for the temple of Artemis, this stood solid and mocking, and the huge effigy of the goddess leered at him in a kind of triumph. She was going to be hard to melt away.

You have heard something of Agrippina but you have not yet met her. She was a woman, at this point in our story, in the prime of her beauty, presenting the same philosophical problem as her predecessor Messalina, namely the apparent reconcilability of a celestial virtue, for beauty is that and always that and must always be that, and a capacity for unutterable vice. But whereas the vices of Messalina were in themselves venial, being mostly a passion for sensual gratification and only dangerous, as you have seen, in the lack of moral scruple which subordinated all things to its encompassing, Agrippina lived solely for power, frightening enough in a man but terrifying in a woman. She had countered the Senate's opposition to her marriage to Claudius by personal threats to the more vociferous senators, and some of these threats were, with the aid of Pallas, the Emperor's financial minister, whom she had efficiently seduced, very ruthlessly fulfilled. It was eventually decided that Claudius might be permitted to break the law which forbade incest, since (a) marriage with a niece was not much different from marriage to a cousin, which was lawful, and the degrees of marital prohibition properly applied only to immediate blood – maternal, sororal, filial, and (b) Claudius seemed beyond not merely the begetting of a child (who would, of course, be a monster) but too old and feeble for the marital act itself. As for Agrippina, she would sleep with anyone, though not for physical pleasure, only for political advantage. She was cursed or blessed with a certain sexual coldness, knowing as much as a temple prostitute about the arousing of male passion and the procurement of its ecstatic

233

release but keeping herself aloof, despite an occasional simulation of desire and the odd false orgiastic shudder and scream of fulfilment, from a process she found distressingly bestial when it was not frankly comic. She had initiated her own son, L. Domitius Ahenobarbus, into the transports of physical love at a quite early age. It was a device for keeping him under. Even when married to Claudius she softfooted in the night to the boy's bedroom and lashed his pustular body to loud transports a waking servant would interpret as a nightmare. This son, by the way, had been adopted by Claudius and now bore the new name Nero Claudius Drusus Germanicus.

Let us now softfoot into the imperial bedchamber, which is shaded against the intrusive sun of the late afternoon, for Claudius has a headache and wears a wet bandage over his eyes. Agrippina, gorgeous in her thin lawn, her bare arms a miracle of shapeliness, her hair the hue of an Egyptian midnight spread over her delicate shoulders, strokes his brow and says: 'Better?'

'Bbbbbetter. But only in the sense of not as bbbbbad as yesterday. And not as bbbbad as ttttomorrow.'

'Nobody knows about tomorrow.'

'An ageing man knows that ttttomorrow he will not be any younger.'

'Oh, these shining platitudes. Gems of imperial wisdom. Golden rays of the obvious. I hope the book you're dictating isn't full of aphorisms like that.'

'I write history. Moral ppppplatitudes I leave to Seneca.'

'Get rid of that man.'

'Eh?' Claudius raised himself from the pillow an instant in surprise, then fell back. 'It was I, as I seem to remember, who got rid of him some time bbbback. It was at your request that I released him from exile.'

'I've changed my mind about him. He teaches my son treason in the guise of philosophy.'

'Ttttreason to the Emperor?'

'The Empress.'

'Meaning bbboth of us. I've heard of this. Morality is morality. There are no moral exceptions for Seneca. We are living in a state of incestuous ppppollution, whatever the Emperor and the Senate say. He has probably been telling your son that. Not to upset him or to ddddenigrate our imperial selves, but to remind him that there are no moral exceptions.'

'I was taught as a girl that the whole point of power was to be able to break the rules.'

'I've certainly bbbbroken one rule.'

He spoke wistfully and she answered sharply: 'You regret it?'

'You taught me new raptures of the body. Raptures which not even Messalina – Ah no, I don't regret it. But sometimes I feel – well, ccccculpable. Chiefly when I look at your son. There's something wrong about having a grandnephew who calls me fffffather. He calls me it rather more than Britannicus does. He seems to be trying to impppplant an idea in my mind.'

'The idea,' Agrippina said frankly, 'that he's fitter for the purple than Britannicus. Britannicus is a fool.'

'I don't think I'd have tttttolerated that from you when you were merely my niece. Britannicus may be the son of Messalina but he's inherited surprisingly fffffew vices. He's even something of a thinker. And he did well as a soldier in Britain. It was he who ccccaptured Ccccccaracttttacus.'

'Which we're not allowed to forget. But which I personally don't believe. When you say *Britannicus* I feel we're always expected to stop what we're doing and drink his health.'

'I shut from my mind, dear niece–wife,' he said wearily, 'a ppparticular thought – that you love your son more than you love me, that your love for him is great enough to have surmounted various barriers, the least of which is incest. Now let me sleep. My head throbs.'

'Marriage is a gateway to legitimate progeny, *dear* Claudius. That gateway is always open. You're always too tired or too sick to – I say no more, fffffather of all the Romans.' He sat up and looked at her without affection. He said:

'That mockery is unseemly. It is also unseemly to pretend a situation that does not exist in the ppppresence of one who knows it does not exist. The physicians pronounced you barren shortly after the death of your revered second husband. Do not ppppretend to be more of a fffffool than you already are.' He thought better of that. 'No, no fffool. But a liar, as she was. And, I begin to suspect, much more vicious.'

'You have something particular in mind?' she said in a voice that oozed Hybla honey.

'Yes. What has happened to Sttttatttttilius Ttttaurus?'

'The old bull? You sometimes forget who you have and have not had put to silence, to use that delightful state euphemism. The old bull has been slaughtered.'

Claudius nearly got out of bed. 'Not on my orders.'

'On the orders of Pallas. It's the same thing, isn't it?'

'What was the charge against him? Pallas said nothing to me about this, gave me no pppppapers to to –'

'He said,' she said in a voice modulating to the innocently childish, 'that he'd hand his gardens over to me. He knew I wanted them. Then he changed his mind.'

'What?'

235

'Wealthy Roman citizens should sometimes show their gratitude for being allowed to remain wealthy. And they certainly should not insult their Empress by reneging on their promises. The gardens are very beautiful. You must walk them with me sometime. The pinescented air will be good for your weak chest.'

He breathed very deeply the closer air of his sickroom. 'Pallas,' he said and then, more characteristically, 'Ppppppallas. I see. The efficient minister of finance is more your servant than mine. Are you exerting your witchcraft on him?'

'What do you mean – witchcraft?' she said, not without a faint note of anxiety that Claudius would be too deaf to catch.

'Your charms. That ppppungent odour of sensuality which ccccaptivated your old uncle and tttturned him into the ffffool he is.'

'Pallas is devoted to you. He takes as much off your hands as he can to leave you free for your higher concerns. He consults me, as is right. I am the Emperor's helpmeet.'

'It was Pallas who urged my ttttransferring the impppperial inheritance from my son to yours.'

'He had only the welfare of the state at heart. Britannicus is a good solid soldier, which means a bit of a fool. My son is ready even now for high office. He studies hard, and with the best teachers. He is intelligent, sensitive –'

'Insufffficiently so to the sound of his own sccccrannelpipe voice. Your son may sing and dance his way round the Empppppire for all I ccccare, bbbbuying appppplause, but he is not going to wear the ppppurple if I have anything to do with it.' He tried getting out of bed, but his migraine issued contrary orders. He collapsed on his pillows again. Agrippina nodded kindly.

'Sleep,' she almost sang. He had mentioned witchcraft, too much the enlightened intellectual to apply the term other than metaphorically. But real witches existed, and they practised a real craft. There was one who lived in the Suburra, her name Locusta. Agrippina had used her services before. *Sudden, you say? It must not be too sudden. The art of the sleepbringer lies in the imitation of nature. You know how to – administer?* Sleep, silence: admirable euphemisms. She made a derisive gesture at Claudius's groaning bulk and then left.

Paul came to Caesarea not only with Luke but with a convert of Ephesus named Trophimus. This Trophimus was a fairhaired youth, son of a goldsmith slower to be converted: his final words to Paul as he saw his son off were that he would think about it. He believed young men should see the world, preferably in the company of older men who would keep them out of taverns and brothels, and of Paul's continence and sobriety he was in little doubt. In Caesarea they went to call on Philip, the Greek who had converted a black eunuch and still felt uneasy about it. He had four chattering daughters who were always prophesying the end of the world and seemed to have little time for the work of the household. Still, Philip's fat wife cooked well and they would all have eaten a pleasant meal together – the daughters, when not prophesying, were good silent trencherwomen – if another regular prophesier had not called, well remembered from Antioch, his name Agabus. He began prophesying about Paul while they were still eating. He said:

'I was right about the famine in Palestine, was I not, yes I was. So watch me carefully now and listen with both your ears. Give me that girdle you have round your middle.' Paul, mystified, unknotted it and handed it over. Agabus said, taking it: 'I follow Holy Writ in miming what I prophesy. Did not Ahijah the Shilonite foretell the disruption of Solomon's kingdom by rending his new cloak? Yes, he did. Did not Isaiah walk naked to prophesy the Assyrian captivity of the Egyptians? Most certainly. So now Agabus ties his feet and hands together – with some little difficulty, I confess – to signify that the Jews of Jerusalem will take the owner of this girdle, bind him hand and foot, and deliver him into the hands of the Gentiles. The only Gentiles in Judaea are the Romans, am I not right, so stay away from Jerusalem. Enough.' He handed the girdle back. Regirding himself, Paul said:

'I have to go.' The four daughters of Philip started to wail in unison. 'Quiet, girls,' Paul said sharply. 'I beg your pardon, Philip, I should have left that to you, but I am growing a little sick of people consulting my safety. I had a similar prophecy delivered to me in Tyre, less cogent perhaps than Agabus's, for it was purely verbal. Much more to the point is the question of a safe lodging in Jerusalem for these two Gentiles who have come so far with me. I know hardly anybody there now, except my sister, and she has no love for me any more. Any Jewish lodging house will be dubious about letting the uncircumcised in. Where can we go?'

'There's this man Mnason,' Philip said. 'A Cypriot Greek, one of the first Jerusalem converts. He's here in Caesarea now, but he'll want to be back in Jerusalem for Passover. A matter of trade only. He sells unfermented grape juice, very popular with the children.'

Mnason was agreeable to taking in three temporary lodgers. He was a sharp soldierly old man who rode a white horse. 'I'll be there well before you,' he said. 'Anybody will tell you where the house is. It's a pity you all have to walk. Sixty-odd miles and in this heat. As for you, sir,' he said to Luke, 'I'll be happy to sit down with you any evening and tell you all I know about the early days of the faith here. I always said someone should make a book out of it. Bloody reading it will be, though, a lot of it. Well, Jerusalem then, gentlemen. Look after your feet.'

With sore feet Paul went alone to see James, once called the Little, now named, with some justice, the Just. He was the only one of the original disciples left in Jerusalem, the others dispersed about the world, some of them dead. He presided over a number of new Jewish converts who, somewhat timid and stayathome, looked on the great missionary traveller with awe. James, as on the other brief occasions of meeting him, felt his intellectual inferiority to Paul weigh on him like his own fat, for the muscle of his younger days, when he had emerged from country wrestling to follow the faith, had decayed to an unbecoming adiposity. It was absurd, he often felt, that such a one as he should have become the bishop of Jerusalem, but he had the right qualifications, which might be glossed as the wrong ones for an active mission: he preferred to stay where he was and, not wanting too much trouble either, compromised all he could with the orthodox Jews, seeming to present a new and revolutionary faith as a mere harmless annexe to the old. He paid his Temple dues, fulfilled the requirements of seasonal ritual, and gave Nazarene money to even such of the Jerusalem poor as said that rightly was that one hanged between two thieves. He was glad to see Paul hand over a small bag of coins of the Empire for the disbursement of the Mother Church. 'Go on remembering the poor' was a slogan that Paul seemed to have remembered. James said to him:

'We're glad to see you well and safe. We shall be more glad to hear of your adventures and successes, though perhaps in the form of a formal discourse to all our elders. This house of poor Matthias is hardly big enough to accommodate them and you. Perhaps in the open air, on the Mount of Olives.' Paul looked round him: the house had grown shabby and seemed to have shrunk, and spiders, like little black Romans, were at the work of structural engineering in dark corners. Paul said:

'You say poor Matthias.'

'He's at work on the Italian mainland and has had, from what we hear, little luck and many buffets. Italy, I would say, needs a man like yourself.'

'I have every intention of going to Rome. The dagger to the heart, so to speak.'

'Yes. Good. Now there is something disturbing which these gentlemen here will confirm. There are some wicked stories going around, none of them, naturally, based on truth, which you will have to do something about confuting. I think you know what the stories are.'

Paul shrugged. 'I take it that the Jewish converts are at it again. Alleging that I've said that circumcision is a lot of unnecessary nonsense. Well, so it is, in comparison with what we may term the circumcision of the spirit. There are some grumblings too about the new Sabbath – Dies Solis instead of Yom Rischon. That had to be. Now they're saying, according to Philip up there in Caesarea, that I'm turning Jesus into the sun god. Let them say what they wish.'

James was unhappy about that. He shifted his bulk and made his chair creak. 'I've always been against rapid innovation.'

'Rapid? I think we've been damnably slow. Life may be eternal, but it's not very long.'

James had heard that before, perhaps too often. He said: 'There are thousands of Jews here in Judaea who've been converted to the faith, but they don't want to give up their zeal for the old law. Too many of them have been told that you've been persuading the Jewish Nazarenes who live among the Gentiles to give up Moses, which means chiefly to stop circumcising their sons. And then there's the matter of the food laws. A little song's been going the rounds. What is it, Remaliah?'

A scarcebearded convert in a too clean white robe cleared his throat and warbled:

'Paul's Sunday services are not all talk.
They start with lobster and end with pork.'

'A mere stupid song,' Paul grinned. He doused the grin and said: 'One of the big complaints of the Christians in Ephesus is that meat doesn't taste good any more. No blood in it. I've done my best to enforce dietary laws, but few of the Gentiles see what they mean. That dream that Peter had in Joppa seemed to me to be a very sound one, but I hear now that Peter's been denying that he ever had it. A great one for denying,' he added somewhat viciously.

'The point is,' James said uncomfortably, 'that you've some explaining to do.'

'Doing is better than explaining. I'll shave my hair off, not that there's much left, and go to the Temple with the mandatory menagerie. You'll have to give me some of that money back.'

'A ram, two lambs, a quart of wine, white flour – I forget how much, I'll find out. You mean the purification rite.'

'I need it, believe me.'

'That will work with our own people.' And then: 'Need it? Why?'

'Defilement. I say no more.'

'I ask no more. The real trouble is the Jews who've come from the provinces – Antioch and so on. They didn't feel free in the lands of the Gentile. Now they'll feel all too free. Shadow of the Temple. Consecration of hate. You see what I mean? It won't do any of us any good if they start on you.'

239

'You're sorry I came, James? Upsetting your cosy stability, am I? Shall I wait for night and take the road back?'

'No no no no no. All I'm saying is that you have to watch out.'

Before totally bald Paul went to the Temple for his purificatory rites, he took young Trophimus into its outer courts. Trophimus was awed by the magnificence but found it hard to reconcile with the noises of a meat market. There was a notice whose key words were *Thanatos* and *Mors* and *Mavet*. 'Thus far, no further,' Paul said. 'You see – death by execution to all nonbelievers who enter the inner Temple. An old law – not even the Romans can touch it. Indeed, a Roman was once misguided enough to disregard the warning. He was stoned to death on the orders of the priests. The Roman law couldn't save him. We'll turn back now.'

Paul and his friend were closely watched. A couple from Antioch, Job and Amos, squinted through the sunlight with especial care. 'See him?' Amos said to a knot of strollers from the same town. 'Remember him? He's there, see, large as life, taking one of those fairhaired bastards with a hat on his prick into the Holy of Holies.'

'No, he's not. He knows the rules. There, they're away now.'

'Filthy defiler of the Most High, the bastard.'

'You're going too far.'

'Wait.'

Paul's enemies got him when he was completing his ritual obligations in the Court of Israel. This was that part of the inner precincts reserved for lay sons of the faith: priests and Levites could go in to the limit, or nearly. *To those under the law I became as one under the law though not being myself under the law that I might win those under the law.* He tasted the phrase: it would go well in a letter to Corinth. He was surprised, looking up, to see what seemed to be a great portion of the Jewish population of Corinth glowering at him. Then somebody pointed a finger at somebody and said: 'There he is.' This latter stood in a shaft of light and was momentarily all gold. Then, seeing himself pointed at and probably having some reason to feel guilt, he moved into darkness and then out. 'Bringing Gentiles into the Temple of the Most High.' Paul made himself limp as he was grasped: he had expected this, though not yet and not here. Someone harmlessly slapped his bald head with a shoe. He was dragged down the steps into the outer court. He heard the gates of the sanctuary clanging to. There were some trying to get up there to grasp the absent Trophimus: the police of the Temple wanted no riot and did their own beating. A ready crowd poured into the outer court. A man recognized by Paul as a known troublemaker in Ephesus yelled: 'Come on, help smash him to pulp, men of Israel. He's defiled this place. He brought Greeks in,' pluralizing easily. 'He preaches against the law and the people and the

240

Temple. Law and order. Justice. Knock his teeth in.' Paul was being kicked and thumped. One gross sweating man in old robes fisted him on the crown before saying: 'What's he done, then?' Then Roman troops arrived and stopped the riot.

There was a cohort of armed Romans up there to the northwest in the fortress of Antonia. The military tribune had been quick. Two hundred men with their centurions poured in, happily beating the Jews with the flats of their daggers. They handcuffed Paul and were ready to drag him up the steps to the castle, criminal, thief, pickpocket, something, but he was ready to mount with dignity. The rearguard fought off the mob with kicks. This was a great day.

Panting, Paul stood before the tribune in the guardroom. This officer, close to retirement, weary, too much fat on his jowls, said:

'Causing a riot, eh? Stirring up trouble. I know you. You're that Egyptian we had trouble with three years ago. Found you out, have they? Saying the wall would come down if you told it to and then you'd march in and take over. Well, they got what was coming to them, but you got away, Egyptian swine, didn't you? Well, now you're for it.'

'Do I look like an Egyptian? Do I sound like one? I'm a Jew, of Tarsus in Cilicia, citizen of no mean –'

'Only got your word for it.'

'If you want that crowd quietened down let me speak to them. In the language of the Jews.'

'That's right, get them to attack this tower. All right, centurion, take him away.'

'Did it look as if I was ready to lead a mob? It was my blood they were after, not yours. Let me say a few words in Aramaic.'

'Let him, sir,' the centurion said. 'Seeing what they were doing to him he's got a right to. Let's get that crowd cleared.'

They led Paul back to the stairs leading up to the tower. He had troops above him and troops below him. The crowd yelled and then grew tired of yelling. They would be glad of inflammatory words; they wanted to be further incensed, being a mob. Paul did not shout. He pitched his voice high and forward and said: 'Men of Jerusalem, listen to me. I am a Jew, born in Tarsus in Cilicia but brought up in this city – instructed according to the strict manner of the faith and the law of our fathers, being zealous for God – just as you are, all of you. I sat at the feet of none other than Gamaliel, the glory of the law. I am a Jew then, but one who heard the voice of the Lord telling me to cease persecuting his saints, the followers of Jesus of Nazareth who is the Christ. For it was said to me: "The God of our fathers has appointed you to know his will, and to see the Righteous One, and to hear a voice from his mouth. Arise, be baptized, wash away your sins, calling on

241

his name." Again, it was said to me: "Depart, for I will send you to bring the word to the Gentiles." I have obeyed the voice of the Lord of our fathers. In what way have I done wrong?'

It was the word *Gentiles* that threw oil on to flames become briefly quiescent. It was a filthy word. The mob responded not merely by yelling. They followed some of the more devout of their number and began tearing their clothes, throwing their cloaks in the air, kicking up dust. Paul saw that he had not been discreet; this would not have happened to James. The howl that the Roman troops heard was one they knew well but had not heard lately: it was the growl of colonial disaffection screwed to a rage insentient of blows and the sword. The centurion himself, who stood on the tread beneath Paul, started punching him in the ribs and then kicking him upstairs.

'This makes no sense,' the tribune said. Paul had no breath. He looked at the blood dripping on to his right hand from a cut from a ringed fist on his right cheek. 'What you said, what I could follow of it, and what they're yelling makes no sense. You'll have to be examined according to Roman law. You know what that means?' Paul shook his head. 'All right. Take him down to the courtyard.'

In the courtyard they began fixing his wrists with thongs to a chain hanging from a kind of gallows. He saw a couple of soldiers appear lashing the air with *flagella*, lengths of leather studded with spikes and bits of bone affixed to a wooden handle. To the centurion he said: 'May I speak?'

'No. Not till after this lot. That's the only way to get at the truth of this business.'

'I *will* speak. Is it lawful for you to scourge a man who is uncondemned and is, moreover, a Roman?'

'You,' the centurion gawped, 'a Roman?'

'A Roman.'

The centurion saw his tribune in the far corner of the courtyard, looking at an amendment of standing orders that a clerk had brought. 'Wait here.' Paul humorously indicated his bonds. The two flagellators practised flagellating Paul's still-clothed back, standing well away and letting the boned tip peck at the garment, enjoying the whistle of the leather in the air. The centurion came back with the tribune. The tribune said:

'The centurion here says that you say you're a Roman.'

'I *am* a Roman. The records are in the procuratorial headquarters at Caesarea. You can check. Meanwhile you're breaking the law by binding my hands in this manner. This you will know.'

'Look, friend,' the tribune said. 'It cost me a pretty penny to buy my Roman citizenship. All right, I know, you can tell I'm a Greek, have I ever denied it? You don't look to me all that rich.'

242

'I didn't have to be one of Messalina's customers. I'm Roman born. As I say, check up on it. Meanwhile don't do anything you may regret.'

The tribune stroked his two blue chins. Then he said to the centurion: 'Untie him. Lock him up for the night. We'll have their priests on to this business in the morning. You know the penalty for beating up a Roman citizen?'

'I do, sir, I do.' So Paul was untied and led into the castle. The flagellators, thwarted, tried to flagellate a pair of alighting sparrows. Unharmed, they flew off. Paul, from his cell, watched other birds homing to eaves as night fell quickly. They brought him a soldier's meal: dark bread and a piece of rank goatmeat with blood in it. Also wine. He drank the wine, composing letters in his head. It was by virtue of the Roman courier system that they got to their readers, heads of congregations who read them aloud at the love feast or eucharistic service. Put to death therefore whatever belongs to your earthly nature: sexual immorality, impurity, lust, evil desires, greed, idolatry. Because of these, the wrath of God is coming . . . Husbands, love your wives and do not be harsh with them . . . Fathers, do not embitter your children, or they will become discouraged . . . He saw a whole sunlit world of white stone, the odour of camel dung and of decaying figs on the air, and the words were perhaps no more than shaped air. He was growing into middle age, the night air was chill on his total baldness, and he felt that his words were heard but not well understood, that Christ had grown into a legend, that he had been wasting his time. His tents would outlive his preaching. Then he smiled, recognizing certain familiar devils of discouragement which negatively proved that there had been no waste: the devils knew if men did not.

He thought of his own death, which might not be much longer delayed. If he believed, if he truly believed, then he would carry into a world beyond time the gifts of time, which he sleepily envisaged as an earthenware dish of the dried raisins of Corinth. Not an angel, any more than Christ was. Human but immortal with a kind of purged sensorium. So the pleasures of the next world would be, in a manner, of the senses. Meaning a barrier to the experience of pure spirit, which meant denial of the ultimate vision. Meaning that Christ, also a creature of sense, was barred from merging with the Father. That explained why Father and Son, though consubstantial, were distinct persons. Theology. Life was too short for it, but he foresaw before sleeping men writing long books about the personality of Christ and neglecting the multiple message. The point was that the thing had rooted, message or metaphysics. It could not be willed away, not even by God the Father himself. And God the Father was closer to that damnable unknown god of the Athenians than to the Jehovah to whom he had dedicated his ram and his lambs. He slept.

He was awakened at dawn to be taken to an emergency session of the Sanhedrin. There was already an energetic crowd around, spitting through the steel cage of his Roman military escort. He was handed over to Temple guards who gratuitously thumped him into the council chamber. The Roman escort waited without, grumbling. Paul looked at the yawning priests and holy laymen as they assembled. He recognized few of them, but he could tell the Sadducees from the Pharisees. The latter had red farmers' faces and gnarled hands; the former had a Roman look. All stood when the chief priest came in. He was new, the successor of Caiaphas, thin and with a look of inner torment, perhaps intestinal. He was given a paper by a clerk. He glanced at it and said:

'You, Saul of Tarsus, are charged with a serious breach of the Jewish law.' Before he could say more, Paul said:

'My name is Paul. I admit no breach. Brothers, I have lived before God in all good conscience until this day.' He prepared to say more but the chief priest, to the surprise not only of Paul, struck him with a ringed right hand on the mouth. Paul bled. He was sick of having to bleed all the time. He heard with anger the priest's words:

'You blasphemer, you have the gall to claim purity of conscience before this holy assembly here met?' Paul snarled:

'God shall strike *you*, you whitewashed wall. You stand in judgment on me according to the law and you smite me contrary to the law.'

A Sadducee arose and said: 'Fellow, you address Ananias the high priest of God. Watch your mouth.' So. A forked name. To the Christians an Ananias was no more than a liar. Paul said:

'I know what is written: you shall not speak evil of a ruler of the people. But nobody told me he was the high priest. Nor did he behave in a manner befitting a high priest.' Somebody at the back of the assembly guffawed briefly and Ananias looked daggers. Paul gathered that there was little reverence for him except among the wealthier Sadducees. He said boldly: 'I see the disposition of your council. I see Sadducees. I see Zealots. I see Pharisees. What do the Sadducees believe? That there is no resurrection, that death ends all. But the Pharisees accept the hope of the resurrection of the dead. Brothers, I am a Pharisee and the son of a Pharisee. The dead rise as Jesus of Nazareth rose –'

There was some commotion among the Sadducees. The Zealots spat, and one cried: 'Resurrection of the free Jewish state under God.' A Pharisee somewhat younger than Paul banged on the marble floor with his staff and raised dust. He shouted: 'I smell conspiracy.' Paul did not understand. 'What fault do you find in this man? Go carefully. You cannot always know who you are dealing with.' Then the dissension grew very loud. Another Pharisee arose and yelled over all:

'We are met to deal with a mere frivolity. I am sick of the hypocrite and the timeserver. He was right when he spoke of a whitewashed wall. Profaner of the sacred office. Greed and rapacity. While we are met let us condemn who should be condemned. Ananias, son of Nedebaeus, admit you take the tithes that should go to the *low* priests. Friend of the Romans, licker of the Emperor's arse.' There was now some very unseemly punching. Ananias trembled, white as a whitewashed wall. Then the outer doors were battered open and the centurion who had accompanied Paul hither came in with troops behind him. He was surprised to see Paul standing aloof from the noise and unhandy fisting. Ananias glowered at the centurion and cried:

'This is a holy place.'

'It sounded like it. Come on, you, sir, back to headquarters.' This was to Paul, who nodded and submitted to being caged in by barelegged troops with drawn steel for the march back to the tower. He was howled at by many who did not know why they were howling. He saw Luke and Trophimus, mueh disturbed and shouting what sounded like *Courage*. James he did not see. Paul was marched back to his cell.

In a tavern later that day a group of Zealots listened to Amos and Job, the illfavoured visitors from Antioch. The leader of the Zealots was named Jotham, and his hard young face was much scarred with a pox picked up in Samaria. 'So,' Jotham said, 'that's his story, is it? To hell with the kingdom of this world and forget you're a Jew. Get rid of him and that's one enemy out of the way. We have to make a start somewhere. If he's a Roman, as he says he is, then it's a beautiful situation. They won't react, they daren't. Sons of the kingdom kill a Roman citizen. And that's the end of the Nazarenes.'

'How?' asked a Zealot named Jehoash, a lad of few words.

'Get the Sanhedrin to have him brought in for another examination. Not the full council, no Pharisees, that can be worked. Stick the knife in then.'

'Difficult.'

'Look,' Jotham said fiercely as the serving boy put fresh wine on the table. 'I'm ready to propose an oath on this business. No eating or drinking till it's done. Tell the priests. We curse ourselves till we do it.'

'Tell Ananias?'

'Not that lump of goat's dung. Yochanan the disciple of Pinqai.' The Zealots guffawed, but the visitors from Antioch did not understand. If they had thought about the writing of the name they would have seen that Hananiah spelt backwards gave Yochanan. The twenty-fourth psalm of David had the line: 'The temple court cried out "Lift up your heads, O ye gates and let Yochanan the son of Narbai and the disciple of Pinqai enter and fill his belly with the divine sacrifices." ' Ananias was noted for his greed. Pinqai suggested pinka, a dish of stewed meat with onions to which the high priest was partial. In some ways the Jews were a subtle people. The boy setting the wine down on the table heard that business about not eating and drinking and was prepared to take it away again, but Jehoash clamped his heavy hand on the crock handle. Presumably the oath was to go into effect tomorrow or the next day. The boy went off.

The boy left the tavern and ran all the way to the Tower of Antonia. He started to run up the outer stairs but was stopped by a soldier. The soldier was ready at first to push him away, but the lad was very earnest. You had to be careful since that Jew being a Roman citizen business. Best leave decisions to the higher command. The soldier let the boy climb up to the centurion, who had just finished guard inspection on the middle terrace. The boy spoke to the centurion. The centurion took the boy kindly by the hand and led him in to see the military tribune.

Later that day the military tribune dictated a letter. It took a long time, he had difficulty with the Ciceronian kind of Latin. His amanuensis put his grammar right silently. 'Claudius Lysias, tribune in Jerusalem, to the most excellent governor Felix in Caesarea, greetings and long life. This man was seized by the Jews and was about to be killed by them. I rescued him, having learnt that he is a Roman citizen. Anxious – no, desirous to know the grounds of their accusations, I had their council examine him. He was accused about certain questions of their law, but nothing was laid to his charge worthy of death or even imprisonment. Now it has come to my notice that there is a murderous plot against this man, therefore I send him to you forthwith. I am charging his accusers also to speak against him in your presence. Got that? Usual flowery stuff to end it.'

This Greek Lysias, who had taken on the name of the Emperor when buying citizenship from the Empress, had his own good reasons for getting Paul off his hands. If the Jews killed him there would be a lengthy inquiry, and it would certainly come out that he had in his time taken bribes from Jews. Everybody did it. A perquisite of colonial service. Best to throw the whole business into the lap of the procurator up there in Caesarea with his Jewish princess of a wife. He ordered a horse for Paul, a mounted squadron and a platoon of infantry. That should be enough. Set off at nine in the evening, when these noisy Jewish bastards would be in bed with their daggers under the pillow, and march steady, five minutes' break in the hour, be at Antipatris before dawn, not Jewish territory so safe, send the bulk of the escort back to Jerusalem, a handful of cavalry enough to take him to Caesarea, there let Felix, miserable sort of a swine, strange how a man's name is always a kind of joke, take over. There it was, then.

Paul, his rear sore, was lodged in a neutral kind of chamber, locked but not a prison cell, until the Sanhedrin had its case against him prepared and a counsel for the prosecution appointed. He was fed regularly on bread, beans and watered wine, and he was allowed writing materials. There were always letters to write. After five days he was permitted warm water for washing and a new robe. Somebody in the palace, clearly, had not unfriendly feelings towards him. Probably the wife of the procurator, daughter of the unlamented Herod Agrippa I. Washed and enrobed, he was led by a couple of Syrian private soldiers to the hall set aside for the hearing. Ananias was there, glowering, with three assistant priests, and there was a portly man puffing over his papers, introduced as Tertullus, a Greek Jew from the look of him. The procurator came in with his personal escort and sat resignedly on a kind of throne. He irritably waved a flywhisk. Paul took him to be of lowly origin, a civil servant who had worked his way up by threats and bribery. He was to learn later that he was a freedman who had served Claudius's mother Antonia and added the forename Antonius to the servile Felix. Also that his brother was Pallas, financial minister to Claudius. Felix's wife Drusilla was to tell him this. The procurator frowned at Paul and asked where he was from. From Tarsus in Cilicia, no mean – Let this business begin. Tertullus bowed portlily and started:

'Seeing, O illustrious Felix, that under your governance we enjoy much peace, and that by your providence many evils have been corrected in this territory, we accept the judgment you shall be pleased to make, most excellent Felix, with all due gratitude in the matter now laid before you. I will be brief and put off all tediousness and say merely that here we have a most pestilential fellow, a mover of insurrections among all the Jews throughout the world, and a ringleader of the sect called by some Nazarenes and by others Christians. Another matter, and the one immediately at issue: he tried to profane the Temple in Jerusalem by leading thither a man of Gentile persuasion contrary to the sacred law of the Jews. By your own examination, O illustrious one, you will see these things to be so. I will not presume to put into your honourable mouth the judgment meet to be meted out, but would merely at this time emphasize the gravity of his crime.' While he drew breath to continue, the procurator shook his flywhisk and then pointed it at Paul, saying:

'Let the accused speak.' Paul smiled and spoke suavely, saying:

'I know, sir, you have been a judge of this nation for many years, and therefore I make my disposition to you cheerfully and with confidence. Briefly, then. I have spent no more than twelve days in Jerusalem. In that time I have stirred up no crowds, neither in the synagogues nor in the city. I have not even been involved in any religious disputation. Nothing I am accused of can be upheld. The Jews of Asia who initiated my accusation are, I see, not present. Those of Jerusalem can find me guilty of one thing only, and that a thing confidently accepted by the sect called the Pharisees, who are of right and tradition represented in the religious councils of Israel –'

'What thing?'

'That after death there is resurrection. Believing this, I do not offend against the ancestral creeds of the Jews. Wherein then am I guilty?'

'And the other matter?'

'Taking a Gentile into the Temple? This is expressly forbidden. Would I knowingly lead a friend who has come far with me to his condign death? I note that there are none here present who can bear witness to this allegation.'

Claudius Felix grunted. There then entered a very young lady of exquisite dark beauty who smiled at Paul and kissed Felix on the crown of his head. This would be the lady Drusilla, his wife. She stood behind the chair, smiling now more generally. Felix said: 'I know the ways of the Jews. I will consider the matter at greater length with the accused himself. Clear the court.'

The priests were not happy about this, but Tertullus bowed and bowed his way out backwards. Felix summoned with his flywhisk Paul at the decent distance of a prisoner at the bar to approach the procuratorial chair. Paul did so, catching a whiff of the procuratorial consort's perfume. Felix said: 'I have ratified from the records that you're a Roman citizen. This means you have money.'

'A Roman born. I have no money.'

'A pity. Money can often resolve things that legal wranglings make more and more – well, knotty. You are acquainted with the lady Drusilla?'

'Honoured. Daughter of a king of Israel.'

'She prefers to be known as the consort of a Roman procurator. Listen. I hate nonsense. I hate hypocrisy. I hate petty kings. I hate law. I love expediency.'

Drusilla began to speak to Paul in Aramaic but then changed to charming Greek with a strong rasp on the *chi*. 'My father, I regret to say, did things not easily forgivable. Neither to you Christians nor to Roman justice. Will it surprise you that his daughter is anxious to hear something of the new belief?'

'And,' Paul smiled, 'her husband – who hates law but loves expediency?'

'Paul, I'll be candid with you,' Felix said. 'I don't want to judge your case. I'm not sure that I even understand it. Moreover, I've been recalled to Rome. Some nonsense about undue harshness in putting down an insurrection in Samaria. You know the sort of thing. While I wait for a ship to arrive you're welcome to expound your doctrine. But you're in custody. The custody may be long. Your case will be heard by my successor, and Castor and Pollux alone know when he'll be here.'

'With respect, as there seems to be no case to answer, might it not be expedient to let me go?'

'Ah, you're a Jew but you don't seem to know the Jews. That's the Roman in you, I suppose. They won't be satisfied with an acquittal. If I dismissed the whole business and let you take ship from Caesarea to Tarsus or wherever you want to go, those gentry in Jerusalem would find out quickly enough and tear the place to shreds. I don't want to leave here in the middle of a fresh insurrection. These damned *sicarii* – you've heard of them?'

'I've heard of them.'

'No, I've enough on my plate as it is. This Nero is something of a new broom. Only a boy, but he knows all about cleaning the provinces up, or so he thinks.'

'What was that name?' Paul frowned.

'Of course, you won't have heard, will you? We have a new Emperor. Claudius has been turned into a god.'

'Custody, then,' Paul sighed. 'I submit.'

'You have to, don't you? All right, Drusilla, ask him your questions.'

Time. Time. We have been living, with Paul, in Claudian time. Now we shift to Neronian time. Time is not, as some say, a universal waterclock but a submissive consort of place. But the chronicler, servant of Chronos, has to forget that place is the reality and time a phantom hovering over it like the smoke from a stewpan. Whipped by his master, he goes back in time, which is absurd. What is now to happen has already happened.

Claudius lay in uneasy sleep. Agrippina shook him gently awake.

'I'm ttttired. I have this ppppp –'

'I know. *Dear* Claudius.' She embraced his ageing bulk with a show of love, even of desire. Sick as he was, he began creakingly to respond. 'No, dearest, not now,' she crooned, then deliciously laughed. 'Time to eat. Supper's ready. You've been starving yourself. Silly Seneca and his stoical self-denial. You must eat to be healthy. I've ordered your favourite dish – wild mushrooms.'

'Wild mmmmmm –'

They were already on the table when Claudius came in. His daughter was absent with a migraine, a physical endowment from her father. She had none of his mental endowments. Britannicus, his sturdy son, stood at attention. Agrippina, all smiles, helped her husband on to his couch. The three were reclined when Claudius took in the empty place. 'Late again. Not on the hour but five minutes bbbbefore the hour. Isn't that military ppppunctuality, my son?'

'A family dinner isn't a parade, father.'

'No. Well, at least ccccommon ppppoliteness. An empire ought to be run like the ffffusion of a ffffamily and an army. If that's ppppossible.'

The mushrooms in their thick brown sauce steamed less urgently 'Eat, Claudius dear. We won't wait for Domitius.'

'I've little appppetite, my dear. Still, the odour is – seductive.'

Agrippina's son now rushed in, unclasping his cloak, crying:

'My profoundest apologies. An appointment in Suburra. One of the litter-carrying slaves broke his ankle. I do most sincerely regret my unpunctuality, dear father. I beat the fool, of course, and borrowed a slave from somebody, I forget whom – Ah, mushrooms, delicious –'

He was ready to put his fingers unceremoniously in the dish, but Claudius proffered his own full plate. 'Take these. I can't eat.'

Agrippina coughed violently. She then, preoccupied with the feigned paroxysm, overturned her goblet blindly and let wine cascade on to her dress. Her son took Britannicus's napkin and wiped her down. Claudius said:

'Well, since you ordered them, my dear –'

He fingered in three of the fungi whole. Agrippina exhaled in relief and cried: 'Oh, I'm so pleased. Let's drink to the Emperor's restored health and appetite. May the Emperor Claudius live for ever.'

'Not even you, my dear, can prevent me from turning into a gggg –'
He turned pale. He sweated. 'Greed. Always one of my failings. The virtues of ttttemperance. Seneca is very good on that subj – Oh, no.'
His round face under the snow thatch passed from colour to colour like a chameleon. He gaped and tried to drink in all the air of the world. He clutched his big belly with both hands. Quick to act. That witch in the Suburba knew her craft. Nor, it was hoped, had suspected who her veiled client might be. But, to be on the safe side, have her put, operative word, to silence. Agrippina clapped her hands, her eating son thought, for a moment, in applause, but it was that servants might come. Claudius, moaning, was helped out. One servant performed a more important act – the removal of the mushrooms and their consignment to silence. Domitius tore white meat from a bone. Britannicus stood to attention, waiting for orders that did not arrive.

Pallas and Agrippina stood in the imperial bedchamber and

watched Claudius turn painfully into a god. He had vomited, but she had been ready with what she alleged to be a healing aperient well watered. She openly embraced Pallas when Claudius opened his eyes wide for a last gulp of the world. Gaping to the limit to take it all in to take below to the bloodless land of the shades. She made a rutting motion in Pallas's arms as the rattle began. 'Goodbye, uncle Ccccclaudius,' she jeered. Then, affronted by the audible collapse of nether muscles, she strode to the one lamp and blew it out.

When the Roman dawn was gorgeous over the pines beyond the terrace, Narcissus paced, waiting for the commander of the Praetorian Guard to appear. He at length strode in, Afranius Burrus, a decent moral man, though chosen for the office by Agrippina. 'The news?' he asked.

'All over. It was a failure of the heart. To be expected at his age after unwonted gorging.'

'What had he eaten?'

'Mushrooms.'

'Mushrooms can always be dangerous. He proclaimed the succession?'

'Pallas and the Empress report that he proclaimed it.'

'Be so good,' Burrus said weightily, 'as to assure the Emperor designate that the Praetorian Guard is ready to serve him with all the devotion it accorded his father.'

'Adoptive father I take it you mean. The Emperor designate is *not* Britannicus.'

'Not Britannicus?' Burrus seemed to take all of ninety seconds to perform an act of simple subtraction. Then he heard the voice of a mere boy, though a precocious one, up early to practise his music, moaning a song to the accompaniment of a cithern:

'Troy is destroyed,
But a greater Troy
Will rise in the void
None shall destroy.'

If I have neglected for many pages the minor personages of this chronicle, it is because they have done little worthy of your attention. Who can compare a mother's wiping of her child's nose with the spreading of the word? If you reply that the word will not last but noses will always drip you are doubtless speaking a profound truth, but chronicles are not compiled that the obvious may be eternized. When the great men are gone it will be time to give ear and eye to the little ones. However, let us go briefly to a gymnasium in Rome where Caleb alias Metellus no longer trains himself to perform skilled acts of aggression

251

and defence in the circus but instead trains others. He has lost his youth but is in robust maturity, health glowing from him like oil, or it may be oil. 'Break now,' he says to two Greek wrestlers. 'Rub down. Then to the baths. Ah, Julius.'

For Marcus Julius Tranquillus the senior centurion has trodden sand and made a circuitous way past sweating gougers and punchers to say a word of farewell to his brother-in-law. During the past years he has done nothing notable. His leg was long in healing, he put on some weight and lost some hair and is clearly no longer a young officer of whom much may be expected. His sole triumph was the confirmation of Messalina's villainy, but he took no pleasure in witnessing her execution, seeing that glorious body rendered into proleptically putrescent morphology or worm's food. The Emperor Claudius was not as grateful as he might have been: he probably associated Julius with a phase of pain and humiliation, and Narcissus, in his concentration on amassing wealth before his retirement, forgot the humble soldier who had lent the weight of a witness to a most dangerous accusation. He served briefly in Syria but was stricken with fever and sent home. He grew weary with duties in barracks. But now, with a new Emperor, and with a new procurator in Palestine, he is to be given a chance to serve Rome with his Aramaic, not that he has much of it. Caleb says:

'How does Sara feel about it?'

'She won't come. She never wants to see Palestine again. She's happy in Rome, she says.'

'You're going with the new procurator?'

'Yes. Poncius Festus. But I retire in a year. I'm given this short tour as they call it, and then – a pension, a garden, boring reminiscences to make Sara yawn. Sara thinks she can bear a year's separation.'

'Can you?'

'She has Ruth. Do you think of going back?'

Caleb rubbed his chin as if to remind himself that there was no beard there, he was no longer a real Jew. 'To start insurrections? Kill Poncius Festus and you in the name of a free Israel? I'm a married man now, with a child on the way. First things first. I'm seduced. I've succumbed.'

'Grown up.'

'Oh, I still believe. But I think Israel will get her independence through negotiation. Break the link through a new client monarch. I have a feeling that Rome will want to be rid of Palestine. Costs too much in taxes. Too poor to pay taxes. I don't know. But Hannah comes first now. And the child on his way.'

'You're sure it's going to be a son?'

'I take what God sends. When do you sail?'

'The day after tomorrow if the wind's good. From Puteoli. And if the Emperor's performance at Neapolis ends on time.'

'What performance is that?'

'Shameful, really. He sings and dances before an invited audience. Conscripted, I mean. I'm one of the conscripted. Bad luck. We lodge the night with the garrison at Puteoli and the entire garrison has to attend.'

'God help you.'

This was the well-remembered occasion on which the gods or the chthonian demons responded with displeasure to a Roman emperor's making a fool of himself in public. It was in an indoor theatre outside Neapolis. The entire Puteoli garrison, a number of patricians, knights, consuls and their wives sat dismally on stone benches while a certain Gaius Petronius, a simpering aesthete in a violet robe carrying a bunch of hyacinths, danced on to the stage and announced:

'Honoured guests. Imperial entertainment. His Grace the Emperor Tiberius Claudius Nero Caesar.' He tucked his hyacinths under his arms and led the applause. There were dutiful shouts of 'Ave!' The Emperor, looking like the silly though precocious boy he was, came on smirking. He was in frilled purple and florally crowned. With him were a number of shamefaced lute and flute players who had nothing to do but hold him to the simple tune he had composed to bear words he had composed. The tune was this:

The players preluded with it while the Emperor announced: 'The Siege of Troy.' Under the loyal or sycophantic applause there were deeper rumblings from below ground. Some of the ladies showed reasonable fear, but the lynx eyes of the Emperor were on everybody, and the husbands quietened their spouses. The Emperor began:

'Richly enrobed with the flames of her funeral,
Ilium yielded her limbs to the fingers of fire,
Lovingly, lustingly, cooing like columbines,
Roaring like lions and howling like wolves of the wood.
See how the citizens, screaming and scurrying,
Scamper like woodlice from logs freshly thrown on the fire . . .'

253

One of the audience inadvertently yawned, a young soldier unused to high art and happier with the dirty songs of the taverns. The Emperor cried: 'I demand not only attention. I demand appreciation. Take that man away.' The wretched fellow was dragged off by two of his comrades, a little too eagerly thought Marcus Julius Tranquillus, who sat next to Poncius Festus. The Emperor resumed:

'Ancient Anchises, caught sleeping, awakening
Now to the flames that devour his ancestral abode,
Calls to his son, young Aeneas, to rescue him,
Pious Aeneas, our father, the builder of Rome . . .'

The underground rumblings grew and the pillars of the *theatron* visibly shook. Women now screamed. The Emperor cried:

'Stay! Stay! Nobody is to leave! The Emperor's orders!' The nervous musicians resumed fluting and thrumming, though not all at the same time. The Emperor sang loudly but not loudly enough to drown the treasonous noise of something crashing outside:

'Pious Aeneas, our father, the builder of Rome,
Bore on his shoulders, so handsome and muscular,
Anchises, the father of all of the fathers of Rome . . .'

He gave up. There was no applause. The shaking earth seemed to be applauding enough. Brave or stupid, the Emperor watched part of the roof giving way. Gaius Petronius came on and led him gawping off. Julius to Poncius Festus said:

'Well, that's one way to stop him singing.'

There was no smile in response. The procurator designate was pushing his way through the frantic pushing audience. The earthquake continued its performance.

FOUR

The month of the oxeyed goddess and, round about its ides, the weather has improved sufficiently for me to move my chair out of doors and admire the fat thrushes or enjoy the wink of the sun in the leaves of the planetrees. I have been reading in a rather rare book which appeared during the imperiate of Galba, brief and perhaps apocryphal, its title *A Dialogue Between the Emperor Nero and His Friend Gaius Petronius*. Petronius you will know from his scurrilous but witty *Satyricon*, which I sometimes think to be a mockery of Luke's 'Pauliad', but this dialogue, more of a monologue, for Nero interjects only phrases of wonder or agreement, has been recognized as a dangerous work and copies have probably been privily burnt by censorial decree. It presents a philosophy which I have already made the young Nero adumbrate in a discussion with Seneca. This philosophy is said to have been derived from Gaius Petronius's youthful indoctrinations by a poet exiled for blatant sodomy in the unequivocally heterosexual Claudius's reign, his real name unknown but his sobriquet Selvaticus. Briefly, the philosophy states that everything must bow down to beauty, and that the artist is above the regular moral concerns of ordinary humanity. As the laws of the state are hardly likely to concede such a transcendence, it follows that only the individual whom rank has raised above the law is free to pursue beauty to the limit. Beauty in nature is admirable but too sensuous to satisfy the totality of man's aesthetic nature. The beauty of art is far higher, and art is permitted to rearrange the forms of nature into new and often intricate patterns, entailing – and this is the point where moral freedom enters – a curtailment or a perversion of what may be thought of as natural rights. The basic natural right of all living things is to subsist and to fulfil what is sometimes termed their vital cycle. In Petronius's aesthetic, which became Nero's, this right was denied, and human life was to be regarded by the imperial artist as living wood is regarded by the carpenter – namely, fissile and susceptible of new shapes. It was necessary, in cultivating this aesthetic philosophy, to nullify such natural sympathetic responses as make the ordinary anaesthetic man wish to avoid giving pain to others, especially those close to him, and to regard what ordinary humanity calls cruelty as a morally neutral means of procuring new aesthetic transports. To understand this philosophy of beauty is partly to understand the enormities of Nero's imperiate, which, by Petronian standards, were not enormities at all but wholly legitimate devices for flushing the imagination with a hint of a higher reality. As Petronius's own skill as a verbal artist lay in the creation of imaginary personages who could be manipulated freely and freely annihilated, so Nero's special artistic achievements lay in acts of manipulation which operated in the realm of actuality, not imagination. In one sense he was the finest artist of his time, in another, and this was partly due to the enforced absence of salutary criticism, he was not the worst but merely one of many mediocrities. His verse was bad, his music tuneless, his singing deplorable, his dancing ridiculous, his acting painful. Petronius, who could have been a useful critic, was so enthralled by the Emperor's total moral freedom, one of the Petronian requisites for high art, that he tended to ignore the wretched results of this freedom in the creative realm.

I mentioned above a certain higher reality invoked by art. Petronius, following the tradition of Plato and indeed of Aristotle, accepted the notion of a supreme being, though one remote from the Hebraic and Christian concepts. This being was amoral, and hence he did not acquaint mankind with his essence through acts of justice or the inspirations of the natural philosophers. A whisper of his quality was heard in manmade works of beauty. The more cultivated Romans of the time accepted with good humour, and even sometimes with vindictive persecution of their rejectors, the gods of the state as useful and perhaps diverting personifications of social virtues and natural processes. But, like the Athenians whom Paul failed to convince, they took a mystical pleasure in brooding on an unknown god whose greatness lay in his capability of definition through negative means. Beauty, said Petronius, was his one sure attribute, and the pursuit of beauty was the highest of human activities. Nero believed this too, since Petronius had taught him when his young mind was blank and open to eloquent influences. Seneca, who taught only moral obligations, found him either contentious or deaf.

Being young and concupiscent, Nero naturally found the orthodox outlets of sexuality quite as important as art during the first five years of his reign. Indeed, having read Ovid, he accepted that there was an art of love and assiduously cultivated it. A young and eager ruler without frustrations, he arose from his multiple orgasms to acquiesce in the just running of the state and the efficient administration of the provinces. His mother, who was primarily concerned with ridding herself of her enemies, actual, potential or purely imaginary, did not at first greatly interfere with either his duties or his pleasures. Soon, though, she had leisure to consider how best to assume the control of the Empire herself behind the mask of her son. Her son, whom she had considered wholly controllable, she discovered to have a will of his own.

One sunny afternoon Nero disported himself in the imperial bed-chamber with his latest love, a freed slave named Acte. She was vulgar but her limbs were supple and her skin gave off a maddening odour. Nero, naked, still sadly pustular, breathed like a runner at the finishing tape as he relaxed in the convalescence of achieved orgasm. Acte admired the furnishings, which were all Greek, the hangings, the Pompeian pictures of human and bestial dalliance, and said:

'Well. Just think. I'm here.'

'And why not? Isn't the Emperor's bed the only place for the most beautiful woman in Rome?'

'I'm not that beautiful,' she said conventionally. 'But I know things, don't I? Don't I know things?'

'You're a mine of wisdom. There's more wisdom in your left buttock than in the entire gloomy library of Seneca.'

'Who's Seneca?'

'An old man who thinks he knows everything. He used to teach me. Virtue, selfcontrol, what they call the stoic qualities. What he didn't tell me is that true wisdom lies in the nerves and in the arousing of the imagination.'

'Did I teach you that?'

'You give me practical demonstrations. And now I have to go to the Senate.'

'Have to go? You?'

'Courtesy. Discretion. Pretend you're letting them have their own way. Lower taxes. Make yourself popular. Tricks, really.'

There was then a knock at the great double door. Acte covered her delicious breasts with the coverlet and said: 'Would that be your wife? The Empress, I mean.'

'My wife is reading Seneca with Seneca. I don't know who it is. Yes, I do. Get dressed. Go out that way.' He pointed to the new egress he had had knocked out of the wall, a plain doorway covered with a tapestry of Odysseus multiply assaulting the screaming Sirens.

'The other Empress, is it? Your mother?' She dressed far more quickly than she had undressed.

'Go on – come tomorrow. The same time. You have the ring to show the guard at the gate?'

She thrust out a winking finger and thrust and thrust, blew a kiss and left. Nero put on a fringed gown, went to the double door and unbarred it. Agrippina came, neck stretched forward like a hen, into the bedroom, sniffing. 'Has that slave been here?'

'She's not a slave. Not now. What if she has?'

'You're slow to learn. The whole household knows. If you must conduct these unsavoury affairs, get out of the city.'

'Like you and Pallas, you mean? You have to go *very* far out of the city to conduct *that* unsavoury affair.'

'You will not,' Agrippina said, 'speak to your mother in that way.'

He picked up a flute and blew three derisive notes on it. 'The Emperor will speak to anyone in any way he wishes. The Emperor will *do* what he wishes – within reason, and subject to the gloomy advice of Sextus Afranius Burrus and Lucius Annaeus Seneca. The sending away of Pallas was not such gloomy advice. The Emperor's mother should conduct herself like a respectable matron.' He blew three more notes, lower but still derisive. She said:

'Put that thing down. Listen to me.' He sat petulantly on the bed. She sat beside him. 'This woman Acte is not so stupid as she looks. Nor is she as enamoured of you as you seem to think. She plays a slow game. She'll drag you into situations and places where your title and status won't help you. She's in the pay,' she suddenly decided to invent, 'of Britannicus.'

'I don't believe that. I don't. Oh, no. You're making that up. Britannicus is not that kind of stepbrother. Britannicus accepts the situation.'

'Britannicus has friends who *don't* accept the situation. Britannicus was publicly named as his father's successor. Rome has only the word of Pallas and myself that Claudius nominated you. I see something in your eye that bodes no good to Pallas, but be careful. I'm not above speaking out whenever the time comes. If you don't ride the imperial horse like a real horseman you'll be thrown.'

'That sounds like something from one of Seneca's plays,' he said, examining the nails of his right hand and pushing cuticles back with the thumb of his left. 'By the way, you know that place on the Rhine that the divine Claudius named for you? Well, I've decided to rename it. Not Colonia Agrippinensis but Colonia Actensis. Less of a mouthful, don't you agree?'

He was biting a bit of scarfskin off his right little finger. She struck him on the face. He was surprised. He said: 'You'd better not do that again, oh no.' She struck him again. He struck back, though with an instinctive filial diffidence. 'No boy,' he said, 'likes hitting his mother. Except, that is, in those bouts of loveplay one particular mother taught her son. I think you're jealous of Acte. A younger body and she knows more. But you may be right about her being dangerous. I sometimes trust your judgment, the judgment of an *older woman*. You're not jealous, I notice, of dear Octavia.'

'I'm jealous of no one. I'm jealous only for your reputation. Get rid of that slave.'

'I'm young,' he pouted. 'I'm entitled to live my life.'

'Meaning, to use Seneca's words, to indulge in flagrant promiscuity.'

'Did he say that? About me?' The pout grew ugly.

'I don't doubt he says it. Though not to me. Part of your claim to the purple, remember, rests on your marriage. Humiliate Octavia with this slave of yours and her brother will take action. Britannicus adores his sister.'

'You mean,' he said with wide eyes of innocence, 'that they go to bed together? I don't think I'd mind that really. It would show that there's a bit of life in them. And it would be useful to have the charge of incest hanging over them. As, dear mother, it hangs over you.'

'You can be a filthy little brat, can't you?' she said. 'No capacity for love, for the natural expression of love. The extent of my love has been shown sufficiently by the danger I've put myself into to secure the title for you. And the thanks I get, the thanks?'

'Yes,' he said blandly, 'you poisoned Claudius. You poisoned several people, good people. You made the faithful Narcissus commit suicide. With impunity, total impunity. Protected by the Emperor, dear mother. Still, it's another thing you've taught me. The first and best imperial lesson. Get rid of those who flaw the artistic pattern of one's life. Rub them out like bad drawings with breadcrumbs. Quickly. Thoroughly. I think I must get rid of Pallas. Exile isn't enough. A son has a right to protect his mother's reputation for virtue. Hasn't he? Hasn't he?' And acting a panting beast in rut he thrust his left hand into his mother's deepcut gown and fondled her right breast. 'The greatest of all virtues, isn't it? A boy's love for his mother.' She struck the hand away. She got up and looked down at him. She said:

'I sometimes think I was wrong. I think that more and more.'

'So stuttering limping old Claudius should have turned into a god at a ripe old age? And dear decent virtuous Britannicus should have put on the purple? Or have you some idea of his putting on the purple now? Poisoned mushrooms for your son. Get your stepson into bed and teach him all the lambent and ictal joys. You'd overwhelm him, mother. He'd be wax. I see I must go very very carefully.'

'You're a loathsome little boy, aren't you?' Agrippina said, gasping in her distaste.

'You're a beautiful woman, mother, though not quite so beautiful as my Acte. She has youth on her side. I plunge into honey with her, I writhe in a snow of petals.'

Her hand itched to strike him again, but she merely said: 'The character of a slave and the manners of a snotnosed urchin. The

Senate awaits you, Caesar. Try to behave like an emperor.'

'Oh, I will, I can. I can act anything, dear mother. A considerable artist, you know. Leave me while I dress the part. I don't think I want you to see me naked any more.' But then, in a kind of unbidden poem, he saw himself lying naked before her, stabbed in his choicest parts, and the poem said something about if a mother could seduce her son she could kill him as well. Looking at him now, she seemed to disengage the seed of some fruit from her teeth and spit it in his direction. Then she left, and he performed a short savage dance in her dishonour.

A week or so later he saw her sitting with Britannicus in the audience ordered to attend his performance of the rôle of the soldier Pyrgopolnices in Plautus's comedy *Miles Gloriosus*. The imperial dining room had been turned into a theatre for the occasion, with a platform of wooden slabs as a stage, and curtains swagging at the sides to cover entrances and exits. Gaius Petronius played the part of the parasite Artotrogus. He said, sycophantically:

'*Novisse mores me tuos meditate decet*
Curamque adhibere, ut praeolat mihi quod tu velis.'

Nero–Pyrgopolnices asked: '*Ecquid meministi?*' He was got up in armour of pulped papyrus and a little helmet. He was trying to make his voice fruitily pompous like that of Britannicus, a *miles*, yes, but not at all *gloriosus*. He saw Burrus and Seneca sitting at the back, looking and listening with little show of pleasure. Gaius Petronius–Artotrogus listed the killings of Pyrgopolnices:

'*Memini: centum in Cilicia*
Et quinquaginta, centum in Scytholatronia,
Triginta Sardis, sexaginta Macedones
Sunt homines quos tu occidisti uno die.'

But how many altogether? '*Quanta istaec hominum summast?*' And Artotrogus gave the total: '*Septem milia.*' Some of the audience loyally laughed; Agrippina, Britannicus, Seneca and Burrus were stonyfaced. A very old man whispered to another:

'If I pretend to die will you carry me out?'

At the end of the play Nero said to Petronius: 'I forgot some lines. Did you notice? I had to improvise.'

'So that's what it was. I thought old Plautus had inadvertently let the spirit of poetry in. You must forget more lines, Caesar.'

'You're too good, my dear. It's not terribly good comedy, is it? Some of the laughs sounded a little, well, dutiful. I have a fancy for doing something tragic. A real *Oedipus*, with nothing hidden. Incest on stage, and real suicide and self-blinding. Britannicus in the lead and the Dowager Empress as Jocasta. I could be Creon.'

'I appreciate your joke,' Petronius said doubtfully, seeing little spirit of fun in Nero's spotty pretty face. 'As for the kind of realistic approach you suggest, you or I will have to write something with real deaths in it, so you could bring on condemned criminals and have them beheaded as part of the action. You have unlimited artistic scope, dearest Caesar.'

'They wouldn't have to be speaking parts. I mean, you can't tell a man to learn lines to speak before he's chopped.'

'Oh, you underestimate your own ingenuity. Give him a free pardon and exalt him by letting him perform in one of Caesar's own tragedies, and then the chop, as you so exquisitely term it, could come as a complete surprise.'

'I must think about it, dear Gaius.'

When Nero, demilitarized and dressed in a green robe with artificial gladioli sewn on it, sat later chewing sweetmeats and wiping his sticky hands on the plentiful hair of a Greek slave, his praetorian prefect and his former tutor spoke serious words at him. Burrus said:

'I must, forgive me, employ what authority I possess to beg you not to make such an exhibition of yourself in public.'

'You think I act badly? Sing badly? Dance badly?'

'Aesthetic judgments hardly apply, my boy,' Seneca said. 'It's a matter of the dignity of your office –'

Nero said, acting the part of a dangerous tyrant: '*My boy?* You call me *your boy?*'

'I beg Caesar's pardon,' Seneca said. 'Force of habit. You're not long out of the schoolroom. Forgive me. And forgive me for pointing out that actors, singers and dancers are a low breed, and Caesar should not associate with them, let alone practise their craft.'

'You know nothing, you old fool,' chewing Caesar said. 'You've seen nothing of the *real* world.'

'With respect, Caesar, I've seen a little too much of it. That's what has turned me into a Stoic. With respect again, do I have to remind you that I'm considered a competent playwright myself and that I can have nothing against a private reading of one of my tragedies, say, to a limited audience? It's these public performances that worry myself and your praetorian prefect. And your proposal to ride in chariot races – that, surely – well, apart from putting your inestimable life in danger –'

'Caesar,' Caesar said with well-enacted weight, 'will think about depriving his people of wholesome and uplifting entertainment when he is ready to do so. At the moment, I merely require your advice on a matter of state.'

'Caesar,' Burrus said cautiously, 'sincerely seeks our advice?'

'Yes. But two questions first. First, did this reign begin in murder

261

and terror and a return to the horrors of the imperiate of the undeified Caligula?'

Seneca said carefully: 'There were too many people summarily removed, if I may say so, Caesar.'

'You may say so,' with right condescension. 'I like your euphemism. You mean murdered. Second question. Who was responsible? Come on, don't be afraid to answer. You know well enough. Very well, I'll answer for you. My mother. The Dowager Empress Agrippina. Come on, what do you say, Burrus?'

'You expect some advice from me, Caesar?'

'Not exactly. I merely seek your approval, as the mentors of a *boy* who has just begun to shave, approval of a course of action. My revered mother must go into exile – Tusculum or Antium, she has estates in both places. Do you endorse my decision?'

'The decision,' Seneca said, 'must be delicately worded. Retirement from Rome on grounds of ill health – something of the sort.'

'Ill health, I like that,' unfilial Caesar said. 'She's as healthy as a sow. But her ill health could, of course, be arranged. She knows that. She knows my feelings. Yesterday I took her guard of honour away.'

'Something of an insult, if I may say so, Caesar.'

'You may say so, Burrus. She knows the situation. There's not one sword that can be drawn in her defence. Seneca, I remember something you made me read once. Let me see. Yes. "Nothing in human affairs is so –" '

' "Transitory and precarious –" '

'My pause was not a signal of bad memory, you old idiot. It was for dramatic effect. Let me conclude. " – As the reputation for power without the ability to support it." There, am I not a good pupil? So, a fond farewell to the Dowager Empress Agrippina, the bloodthirsty old bitch –'

'Your mother, Caesar,' Seneca reproved.

'I don't have to be reminded she's my mother. The former suckling is now weaned. That reverend womb has served its purpose. Out of the way with her, cross her lines out of the comedy, let her rot alone in Antium or Tusculum. I say, that's not bad, that has a reasonable dramaturgical rhythm. All right, you're dismissed.'

Few of the chroniclers of Nero's reign have been accurate when relating the situation that obtained between the Emperor and his mother from the time when, reft of her German and Pannonian guards, she lived in a more or less solitary rage on one estate or another. Nobody knew what had happened to her lover Pallas, but she feared the worst. She was no nymphomaniac and summoned no slave or bought incubus or succubus to her bed. She merely brooded on her son's infamy and sent the story about that he had tried to

262

murder her by arranging for the roof of her bedchamber in the mansion at Antium to fall in on her. That the roof had fallen in was no lie and she kept the room for all to see in its wrecked condition, dust and plaster and bricks lying on the bed and the imprint of her body, which she had providentially removed to the privy a few moments before, on the dusty mattress. An old elm had in fact collapsed on to the roof, but there was no sign of artful sawing to incriminate either her son or any other of such of her enemies as she had still kindly allowed to survive. When Gaius Petronius heard of the incident he had no doubt that his imperial master and colleague in the arts had tried to arrange an ingenious quietus, and he deplored the failure of the attempt, saying: 'Very frequently the best thought out of our dramatic devices come to nothing. That is not the fault of the scheme itself but rather of the interposition of the mischievous goddess Chance. But one tries again.'

'Do you,' Nero said wideeyed, 'honestly believe these stories that are going around – that I would wish to kill my own mother, bitch though she is?'

'Oh, dear Caesar, some of us kill our mothers when we are born. I killed mine, you know, she died of having me. A comic situation in a way, a chance that women take in their lust for maternity.'

'You say comic?'

'Well, it can hardly be tragic, can it, if we hold by the Aristotelian rules? In a sense, you know, dearest Caesar, you rather disappoint me with this conventional posture of shock at the mention of matricide. Caesar is not as free as he ought to be. You're always complaining, loudly and often very beautifully, of maternal persecution. Dramatic soliloquies unresolved in action. Still, Caesar knows best. Your mother may be the necessary irritant that produces the poetic pearl.'

'Do you think I *ought* to kill my mother?'

'Ought? Ought? What are you invoking now, dearest one? Moral duty, peace of mind, some law of artistic economy?'

'I don't understand.'

'If we are thinking of life as a drama we cannot overcrowd our stage, can we? Enough of that for the moment, though this aphorism of dear dead Selvaticus is worth imprinting on the imperial brain – *True freedom begins only when we have slain the gods of biology*. I have a boy for you.'

'A boy? What do I want with a boy?'

'What you want with a boy is what you want with the removal of a mother – release from the biological tyrants. To put it bluntly, liberation from the womb.'

'But I like girls. And I adore dear Acte.'

'Liberation, dearest Caesar. Come with me.'

They had been sitting together in one of the imperial gardens, among winking leaves, speaking loudly as though on the stage, surrounded by undeferential birdsong. Now they were carried in the wide litter that had once belonged to Messalina to a little house just north of the Theatre of Pompey. Here Gaius Petronius knocked thrice and was welcomed by an old Greek satyr who cordially embraced him. When the Emperor was introduced he went down on the marble and kissed the imperial feet until Nero grew embarrassed by the sight of a bald crown turned into a lateral pendulum. Then it was the best of the host's Falernian with little snacks of toasted cheese on fried bread, and the boys were brought in. Exquisite, this one, a German lad, all the way from Colonia Agrippinensis. Take the little horror away. Or this, Greek of course, or this Syrian beauty. Finally the Emperor went to an airy cubicle, exquisitely clean and delicately scented, with a blond boy named Sporus. It was, really, a revelation.

If his mother was not permitted to come to Rome, nothing prevented her from using the internal courier service and berating her son for unnatural practices (of these, presumably, incest was not one):

> . . . I am almost tempted to start believing in one of these crackpot religions of Asia which posit an eternal struggle between the forces of light and those of darkness and show plausible enough evidence that evil beings get into human brains and force them to perform filthy things. Do not think that Rome does not hear of the abominable perversions you and your friend Gaius Petronius the dirty poet are getting up to. If Rome hears I hear too, and, more pertinently, the faction that supports Britannicus hears very clearly and plots measures to cleanse the imperiate of monstrosities that were thought to be done for with the death of Gaius Caligula. Your stepfather the divine Claudius, one of the finest men who ever breathed, and not one ounce of perversity in him, must be turning in his grave or weeping on the shoulders of his fellow gods to think that the Roman Empire has been delivered into the hands of such a monster. Yes, I have begotten a monster and do not know in what way I have offended that such a shame and a misery should fall upon me in my exile and loneliness. If a mother's curse carry any weight with you know that a mother's curse is radiating from Tusculum. You have disgraced the Empire and yours, etc.

Nero was reading this when Gaius Petronius, the dirty poet, was carried to him on an open litter by his slaves, genuinely dirty from the mud of the Roman gutters, with cuts and bruises untreated on his face and limbs and, in his hand, a large carrot that he alleged had not merely been stuffed but *hammered* up his anus. His exquisite robe was torn and his hair, which he wore long and over whose dressing he spent an hour at least every morning, was hacked off in places by, apparently, a butcher's knife. Nero nodded as he listened to the loud plaints. More than mother's curses were radiating from Tusculum (probably Antium; his mother was a foul liar): she was sending a slave secretary to Rome with ready gold to pay nocturnal bravoes. 'Yes, yes, dearest Gaius,' the Emperor soothed. 'It is time to put on a comedy of the kind you have frequently suggested. Let us celebrate the feast of Minerva at Baiae and arrange something really *exquisite* to crown it all. My poor dear friend.' Then he wrote a letter and had two copies made, one for Antium and the other for Tusculum. In it he said:

Dearest mother, your words strike to my very heart. I see all too clearly now how I have been led astray by unscrupulous companions who, while professing both friendship and loyalty, have been in the pay of Britannicus and other enemies of the state. I have been a fool and beat my breast for my folly. The Empire needs your wisdom and political gifts; your wayward but repentant son desperately needs his mother. Let us be reconciled under the aegis of the goddess of wisdom and celebrate our reconciliation with wine, kisses and the public self-abasement of your always loving, etc.

Petronius had been made responsible for the arrangements of the entertainment at Baiae, but it was deemed prudent to keep him out of the way when Agrippina (as she did, as she was bound to do) arrived on her hired galley from Bauli, beautiful as ever, dressed as Minerva with a live owl on her shoulder. There was an unfortunate accident as her craft pulled into the shore: one of the decorative barges, on which nymphs and satyrs swayed demurely, singing a song of the Emperor's own composition on the beauty and wisdom of the honoured guest, rammed the galley, and a boatman with a boathook, trying to push the galley away, made a hole in its flimsy side. Underwater swimmers, some of them from the choral party of satyrs, made further holes in the hulk and the vessel, visibly letting in water, was towed away rapidly for repairs. 'It is as well, dearest mother,' Nero said, embracing her. 'I have a boat more in keeping with your status waiting to take you back.' She suspected nothing; her long dull exile had made her wish not to be suspicious; she genuinely wished reconciliation and the commencement of new intrigues in the centre of imperial civilization.

It was a fine party, with no ephebes or catamites, only decent adulterous matrons and staid senators who got quickly drunk. There were boars roasted whole on spits, the members of swans and peacocks in sharp sauces, tarts and flummeries and much wine. The company begged Nero to sing, but he said: 'Ah no, my friends, totally unseemly in an emperor. I have learned my lesson, ah yes, and am ready to join the grave and judicious, submitting once more to my blessed mother's influence.' And he kissed Agrippina lovingly. At nightfall lanterns were lighted in the trees, and a host of owls were loosed from cages. Agrippina's own owl, frightened by the collision, had flown away to roost and did not reappear: at least nobody came across a bird with little golden anklets and tiny bells. When it was time for Agrippina to leave, Nero escorted her with trumpets to the landing stage, where he prepared to hand her into the barge he had provided, its superstructure hung with gold curtains. 'Dearest mother, it was a joy to have you. We've been apart too long,' he said.

'No doing of mine, my son. You made it clear that I was not welcome in Rome.'

'All over, all all over. Make your arrangements for return. I need you.' Quite how these words were meant was not clear, for the son kissed his mother not only on the lips but on the breasts, gently pulling her robe from her shoulders to do so the more sincerely or intimately. Then she got aboard, and the rowers pushed the land away before settling to their strokes. Agrippina lay on the couch thoughtfully placed under the canopy, a couple of servingwomen and her freedman Lucius Agerinus with her. It was Agerinus who first noticed something irregular about the canopy: two of its wooden supports were beginning to crack under the weight of something hidden under the golden cloth; moreover, the craft was lower in the water than it ought to be. He said: 'Somebody's been playing tricks with this boat. Let me – Oh, no. Out, madam, quick.' And he pushed her into the water as a lump of what looked like lead came down, braining one of the two servingwomen. The struts of the canopy broke entirely and more lead hurtled. The rowers dove overboard, but few of them could swim. The Dowager Empress, however, disclosed an athleticism Lucius Agerinus had never suspected, and, himself swimming, watched her ply lustily, hands joined and then circling away in a steady rhythm, strong legs paddling, towards the shore. He looked back, spewing water, to see the boat sink and desperate arms weave at the air before going under. Touching the shore at last, he found Agrippina sitting in her wet and dredging for breath.

Lucius Agerinus splashed along the coast to Baiae, where he found the festive lanterns doused but lights still on in the canvas pavilion where the imperial party had got drunk and done honour to the name of Minerva. There he found Nero fondling rather absently the limbs of a Syrian catamite. Gaius Petronius, whom Lucius Agerinus had thought to be banished, was also there, wearing a yellow wig. 'Caesar,' the freedman said, 'I come to report an accident. The vessel in which the Empress Agrippina was being conveyed –'

'Yes? Sunk, has it? My poor mother. My beloved wretched mother.'

'The gods be praised, Caesar. Your mother and myself are the only survivors. We swam ashore together.'

'Where is she?' Nero asked, with an excessive show of relief.

'In a workman's hut three miles down the coast.'

266

'Brave mother. *Lucky* mother. And you – what is your name?'

'Lucius –'

'Never mind. She sent you to kill me, didn't she? Thinks it's my fault. Vindictiveness to the last. Aufidius! Crespus!' Two bodyguards came running into the pavilion. 'An assassin among us. You know what to do.'

In the workman's hut Agrippina sat wrapped in a rough blanket, sipping hot wine. The old man who lived in it had built a small fire in a brazier. He was lonely and garrulous, saying: 'A question of workmanship, lady. Things are not half so well made as they were in the glorious days of the Emperor Augustus. A falling off, if you catch my meaning. And now they have this mere lad as an emperor, up to all sorts of tricks. Encourages a falling off in everything – bad behaviour, dishonesty, rotten workmanship. Sorry I can't give you better hospitality, lady – you see how things are. A poor labourer not used to receiving visits from the gentry.'

'You'll get your reward.'

'Oh, what I say is ordinary decency is its own reward. Not that I wouldn't be grateful for a good word put in for me with the Office of Works. A good worker – look at these hands – tough like leather and hard like horn. I get on with the work and no fooling –'

It was then that Aufidius and Crespus came in, daggers drawn. She looked at them and nodded. 'A charge of conspiracy,' Aufidius said, 'with the pretender Britannicus. Your attempt at assassination failed. Come as you are. Don't resist arrest. We have orders to take appropriate action in the case of –' What she was doing now: leaping for the door with her blanket around her. Crespus struck and she lay moaning. Aufidius finished her off with two more stabs. The workman, terrified, said:

'See – I did nothing. I know nothing about who she is or anything. Just took her in halfdrowned, that's all. I don't meddle in high matters. I won't say anything, honest.'

'True,' Aufidius said. He held him and Crespus cut his throat.

Later the son, drunk, had the body of his mother brought to him. He looked at it, naked, the wounds cleansed and dry. 'I think of that time when Messalina had the axe,' he said. 'A beautiful body. What, Gaius, should be the aesthetic approach to the corpse of one's mother? It's only a matter of form, colour, isn't it? She's dissolved into – what's the term?'

'Morphology.'

'Beautifully proportioned. Fine skin. What do I do now to prove my conquest of the gods of biology, as you call them? Rape the corpse? No. Prepare a eulogy, I suppose. Or do I mean an elegy?'

The histrionic grief, Gaius Petronius thought later, deceived nobody. Nero stood in deep but highly decorative mourning. Acte smirked behind him; the Empress Octavia looked embarrassed. The Emperor cried: 'I will write an elegiac poem and perform it publicly, whatever my learned mentors think. Has a son no right to lament the loss of his mother and present to an unfeeling world a salutary model of filial grief? She was everything to me – the womb that bore me, the breasts that nourished me, the care and wisdom that watched over my growth. There will never be another like her. Dearest mother, consigned to the shades, look down on your son, bring him guidance in dreams, watch with shadowy pride the progress of his reign and the growing glory of the Rome you loved. I would that the dead rose again, but alas – cities are destroyed and rebuilt to a newer glory, empires perish and rise again – but, once gone, we mere human creatures become dust, ash, nothing. Dear mother, live on in memory. A mother's love is eternal. So is the love of a son. I weep, I weep – and nothing can console me. *Vale, mater.*'

Somebody at the back ironically applauded. It was suspected to be Burrus, but nobody could be sure.

This, then, was the Emperor whom Marcus Julius Tranquillus was serving in Palestine and to whose justice Paul was to appeal. Julius was not long in becoming unhappy with his assignment. He had no confidence in Poncius Festus, who was inexperienced and infested with a number of prejudices, the chief of which was against the Jews. 'Caesarea,' Festus said, as the ship eased in. 'Felix told me to stay here, to go to Jerusalem as little as possible. At least we breathe the wholesome air of the ocean at Caesarea. Not the stifling stink of Jewish superstition. They're bad enough in Rome. What they're like here – I shudder to think of it.'

'So you start off with a prejudice.'

'Oh, there'll be no nonsense while I'm procurator. Keep them down. Remind them who's master. No, I don't like the Jews.'

'You know I'm married to one?'

'Yes. Of course. I'd forgotten. Well – the women may be all right. They probably don't take this religious nonsense seriously. I've nothing against Jewish women. Very seductive, some of them. Good in bed, they say. You'd know more about that than me, of course.'

'Procurator, with all respect, I don't like your tone.'

'No? Well, with all respect, you'll have to put up with it. As long as we work together. I notice you didn't seem keen to bring your wife with you.'

'She prefers to stay in Rome. A year is not for ever.'

'Better that way. She'd bring you too close to these people, get you absorbed. You have to stay aloof, that's important. Know the language, do you?'

'Enough.'

'Avoid speaking it too well. Keep your distance. Make them speak Greek or Latin. I suppose Felix has left a lot of unfinished business behind him. Jewish law, Jewish taboos, trials that go on for ever. Why can't they learn to think like Romans? That's what we're here for, anyway. Bring Roman clarity of thought, Roman reason, Roman manners. A civilizing mission.'

'And, of course, we collect taxes.'

'That too. After all, civilization has to be paid for.'

Paul was still at Caesarea, waiting for Poncius Festus to deliver judgment. His cell was commodious and he was permitted visitors. The chief of these was Luke. To Luke Paul dictated a letter about 'Charity, which is another name for love. If I speak with the tongues of men – and of angels – and I have no charity, I'm nothing more than a cracked trumpet or a bit of struck metal. I may be able to prophesy, to understand mysteries, to have immense knowledge of all things, be able to move mountains indeed, but if I have no charity I have nothing. Nothing. I may sell all my property to feed the poor. I may submit to execution, burning, martyrdom. But if I have no charity it means nothing at all. Let me tell you what charity is like. It's ready to suffer. There's no envy in it. It isn't – puffed up. It's never unseemly, never selfish, thinks no evil, isn't easily provoked. It submits, believes more than doubts, hopes more than despairs. It never fails – not in the way that prophecies fail, or words fail, or even knowledge fails. We know a little, we prophesy a little. But when the perfect thing comes – and that is charity – we don't need even that little. When I was a child, I spoke like a child, but when I became a man I put off childish things. So the business of knowing more goes on. Now we see through a curtain, darkly and imprecisely. But some day we'll see reality face to face. Now I know in part, but some day I shall know thoroughly – even as I'm known. And all this will come about through the power of love. There are three things as you know, all great – faith and hope and charity. But the greatest of these is charity. Got all that?'

'Greatest of these is –' Luke put down his tablet. 'You believe all that?'

'They'd better believe it, the ones who are going to have it read out to them. Yes, of course I believe it. You're not staying to eat something?'

'I have to see this new man again. Trouble in the belly. Cramps. Diarrhoea. Newcomers just will not leave the fruit alone.'

'You're his official physician?'

'No. Just called in. I ply the trade. A man has to live. We can't all enjoy the hospitality of a Roman prison.'

'Rather excessive hospitality. Two years.'

'As long as that? Everybody must have forgotten what the case is about.'

'I don't think so, Luke.'

He was right. Festus and Julius met the leaders of the Sanhedrin at the confines of the Temple, which the two Romans duly admired. Ananias said: 'We appreciate the courtesy visit, procurator. We're glad that Roman law is in operation again. It's been asleep for too long.'

'Blame the functionaries of Rome for that,' Festus said. 'A change of Emperor, a reorganization of the civil service. If you have cases for me to judge, bring them to Caesarea.'

'There is one particular case that has slept since the departure of the procurator Felix. The man Paul. He lies in jail in Caesarea, as you will know. We humbly request that he be sent here to Jerusalem for the further investigation of his crimes.'

'Crimes? Somebody mentioned these crimes to me, but I still don't know what they are. Anyway, it's the task of the judiciary to determine whether there are crimes or not.'

'Oh, we're sure.' Festus looked at them, and he saw one of them lick his lips. The physician Luke had fed the procurator more than a white medicine. Festus said:

'Did you have summary justice in mind? An accident on the road to Jerusalem? I've heard of these tricks before.'

'We do not perform *tricks*, procurator. We leave those to the Nazarene enemies of the Roman state. We are at one with you in our love of justice.'

'He'll get justice. And he'll get it in Caesarea.'

In the open courtyard outside the praetorium in Caesarea Marcus Julius Tranquillus looked with great curiosity at Paul, whose wrists were chained together at the back, who was bald, ugly, ageing but, it seemed, much at peace with himself. He knew all about Paul, or rather Saul, fellow student of his brother-in-law, murderer turned Nazarene fanatic, traveller, religious orator, Roman citizen. He had read the file on Paul in the praetorial office. He did not at all understand the charge which the pompous Greek Jew Tertullus was enflowering with compliments to a Roman official who had as yet done nothing to deserve either praise or blame.

'So, to conclude, most illustrious Felix –'

'Festus is the name. Porcius Festus.'

'I apologize. I've been speaking from the original brief. Most illustrious Festus, this man not only profaned the sacred Temple of our fathers but persisted in teaching false doctrine to the scandal of all true worshippers.'

'This,' Festus said, 'is an internal and local matter and does not concern Rome.'

'But, illustrious one, his acts and words have been much to the detriment of public order and tranquillity, and those are very much the concern of Rome.'

'What,' said Festus, 'does the defendant say?'

To Julius's ear what the defendant now said was spoken in admirable if provincial Greek with a rise of the voice at the end of each phrase, doubtless a device to ensure clarity but conveying the lilt of a question. 'I have done nothing amiss – neither sin under the laws of religion nor crime under the laws of Rome.'

'It's that second part that concerns this court. You say that you've committed no crime against Caesar?'

'I repeat: neither against the law of the Jews, nor against the Temple, nor against Caesar –'

'Will you,' Festus asked, 'go up to Jerusalem and be judged there – before me – of the things of which you are accused?'

Julius thought he saw a glint of complicity in the glance that the procurator cast at the man in black robes who was called the high priest. He certainly saw one of his own troops make a thumb-rolling gesture at a colleague; the colleague sagely nodded. Paul saw too. Paul said:

'I'm standing before Caesar's judgment seat, where I have a right to be judged. I have done no wrong to the Jews – this you know well. If I'm a wrongdoer and have committed some crime worthy of death – well, I resist neither the charge nor the execution. But if none of these things of which I'm accused are true – then no man can hand me over to these accusers. My appeal is to Caesar.'

'You say you're a Roman citizen. Centurion, is that confirmed in the records?'

'It is.'

'Very well. You've appealed to Caesar. To Caesar you shall go. Wait,' as the Jews started crying to heaven. 'Less noise there. This is a court of justice. I hadn't finished, had I? You shall go to Caesar when it's sufficiently clear to me what precisely this whole case is about.' The Jews relaxed: there was still a chance of putting the knife in. 'Take him away. Clear the court.'

What image of Caesar possessed Paul's still provincial mind is not at all clear: probably some gaunt figure cruel but constant as the north star, lifting a judicial finger towards Olympus, in billowing toga and

271

goldsmith's laurel crown, unaware that conspirators were ready to strike. The real Caesar, pretty but pimpled, was, in that Neronian time which does not quite correspond with Pauline time, marauding in mask and green wig with some of his old schoolfellows in the Suburra district of Rome, among the shops and brothels that lay between the Vicus Longus and the Vicus Patricius. He was, in a sense, trying to escape into a happy adolescence from a matricidal guilt which would not leave him. Rome congratulated itself on the removal of a figure made more rather than less sinister by her undoubted beauty, and Rome guessed where responsibility for that removal lay. Eventually Rome would, when it was convenient, speak of the second most abhorrent crime in the calendar; at present it rejoiced in the liquidation of a monster whose monstrous enactments had been unmitigated by masculine compassion, masculine lethargy, masculine rationality. Rome's citizens slept sound, but Rome's ruler woke sweating. He heard her voice calling him at night; by day he saw her momentarily resurrected in audiences at the theatre, making him forget his lines when acting or, when singing, croak. He was beginning to learn also that one murder always leads to others: her assassins had, in their turn, to be assassinated and the new knifers knifed. He saw that murder could not properly be delegated unless he wanted the whole world to be killed. He was led, which was tiresome, to the study of poisons and the acquaintance of that Locusta (here in this very district of Suburra) whom his mother had vicariously employed to his own ungrateful aggrandizement.

Gaius Petronius, of course, had praised the device of the leaden galley as most artistic, deplored its failure, accepted the subterfuge of an imagined treason as inferior drama but legitimate, if banal, improvisation. He dismissed the bad dreams and waking apparitions as what he termed, in his refined Greek, mere *epiphenomena*, comparing them with the tiresome ghosts that encumbered the tragedies of Seneca. He chattered too much and Nero had sent him away on a long paid holiday to Athens, there to prepare the way for his master's participation in the singing contests. In the meantime, nightly raids on shops and brothels in the company of the yelping friends of his youth. Panting after the beating-up of a grocer who had just been shutting up his emporium for the night, they turned a corner and found a closed fish market still open. They had an enjoyable time running after the shop assistants with their own knives for gutting and scaling, flailing each other with sea bass and octopus, slipping and recovering on the slimy floor, whooping and roaring. When the apparent owner of the market appeared, calm, indulgent, even smiling, a huge flounder in his arms like a sleeping child, they paused in their play: they were meeting a reaction past experience had not led

272

them to expect. The man, dark, broad, in early middle age, went up to the disguised Nero and tried to hand the flounder to him, saying:

'Hail, Caesar. A gift from Neptune to the ruling divinity of Rome.'

'How do you know who I am?'

'The imperial light shines, despite that elegant mask, from your worship's countenance. You smell of divinity as this flounder smells of – whatever it smells of. On second thoughts, it's past its first youth. I have fresher fish within. Already in the pan, with garlic, sweet butter, cloves and capers.'

'You dare to invite the Emperor to supper?'

'Humble duty, sir. The pride of a subject. I can bring in dancing girls. Or boys, if you prefer. Naked.'

Wigged Nero smirked at the man. 'So there's money in fish-mongering, is there?'

'Money in a lot of things, your celestial goodness. I've come back to what I started as out of a certain nostalgia. I plan to make a monopoly of the Roman fish trade – fresh fish, rushed from the coast in cool tanks, sold cheap and hence sold quickly. I already have a monopoly of the Sicilian horse trade. Money, yes. But to be spent, sir. I hate hoarding. I like life. Strong flavours, if your Olympian sagacity knows what I mean. Fish blood is thin, but some blood is as thick as cassia honey. The juices of life, sir – blood and semen. Let them flow.'

'The Emperor,' Nero said with mock dignity, 'is pleased to consider you a man after his own heart. Your name?'

'Ofonius Tigellinus, at the Emperor's service. A euphonious name, would your holiness not agree? Euphonious Ofonius. Tigellinus the little tiger. Ever ready to give your supreme imperial divinity most earthly pleasures. An Epicurean is what I am, if I may put this business on a philosophical level.'

'With no love for the Stoics?'

'Stoics? Seneca and his crew? I spit on this fishy sawdust. Hypocrites, I'd say. Pretending to virtue and practising secret vices. I hate the hole in the corner. Let's laugh in the sun.'

'Ofonius Tigellinus, I can smell that frying fish from here.'

'Good, isn't it, sir? It's the garlic. Nothing like garlic.'

It was on the Vicus Longus that Aquila had his shop and, behind the shop, the living quarters where, with his wife Priscilla as hostess, he sometimes gave hospitality to fellow Jews. They had made money in Corinth but were glad to be back in Rome. Except that these days, nights rather, it was unwise to go out much. They could hear the loud bravoing of the youthful wreckers and wondered when their turn would come. But there was nothing to wreck except a bare workshop, and the shutters Aquila put up were of hard pine with metal bars. Aquila said now, hearing whoops and smashing:

273

'The times we're living in, eh? You need somebody to shout out against it. Like your old friend, Caleb.' For Caleb was there with his wife Hannah and their son Yacob, also Sara, who had that day received a letter from her Roman husband telling her about Caleb's old friend, and Ruth, who was now ripe enough for a husband. They were a handsome party. Hannah, who in Gentile company sometimes gave her name as Fannia, was the orphan daughter of a moneylender whom one of his senatorial clients had indicted and convicted on a charge of defiling a statue of Vesta. She had been quick to learn cynicism from Sara, who trusted neither God nor man and had a slight ancestral contempt for the pretensions of Rome: for all that, both ladies could pass as Roman patricians whom a sun more southerly than Rome's had touched. Caleb, whom Rome's sun had made swarthier with the years, caught Aquila's reference and said:

'Preaching wouldn't get him far here. When there's a bad smell you run away from it, you don't try to hide it with civet.'

'You can get used to a bad smell and call it roses.' They had both somehow got off the point. 'Like you with blood.'

'Blood honestly spilt. Nobody orders a gladiator to open his veins. Blood's his trade.'

'How about the Britons?'

'Yes. That's giving me a few bad dreams. Untrained men and boys being hacked to pieces. But the crowd loves it.'

'Because,' Priscilla said, bringing out some of their store of Corinth raisins which seemed to last for ever, 'the Emperor does. Corruption always starts at the top. Why don't you get out of it?'

'And do what? I've a living to earn.'

'You see how it works out, Caleb,' Aquila said. 'You start off by thirsting for Roman blood – oh, in a good cause, may God bless the Zealots. You end up by accepting the shedding of any blood at all – Roman, British, Syrian, anything.'

'We're fed full of blood,' Priscilla said.

'Saul's people,' Caleb said. 'Paul's, I mean – they drink it. And they eat flesh.'

'That's horrible,' Hannah said. 'Let's change the subject.'

'Now you talk like a scandalmongering Roman,' Aquila said. 'Look, neither Priscilla nor I is a Christian yet. But I made a bargain with Paul. If ever he got to the Tiber, I said, he can plunge us into it. Both of us. What I'm trying to say is that it's the body and blood of Christ they eat, but it's in a different form. Bread and wine. It's a very subtle and intelligent idea. You eat the *soter* and he becomes part of yourself.'

'And then,' Caleb said coarsely, 'you void him.'

'You're not with your circus friends now,' Hannah said. 'Can't we talk about Octavia's new hairstyle or something?'

274

'Religion,' Sara said, 'is not merely useless. Religion is dangerous.' Aquila comically groaned, having heard this from her before. 'To get through the day without a headache is the important thing and to breathe a sigh of relief that you've made the long journey to your pillow.' The noise of juvenile disruption had been still for some short time. Now it began again.

'It sounds as though they're –' Priscilla began. 'Oh, no.' For there was loud fisting on the shutters of the shop, yells to open up, a grinding that suggested that crowbars were at work on the iron binding of the stout pinewood. Caleb's neck seemed to have thickened by a good two inches. He said:

'You and I, Aquila, are going up on the roof. I get very tired of the Romans sometimes.'

'And what do you propose we do on the roof?'

'That tub of yours should be full of rainwater by now.'

'Oh, no. It won't stop them, you know, what you seem to have in mind. They'll only come back again.'

'I think I can manage that tub by myself.' And Caleb made for the stairway, more of a fixed ladder, that led to the loft. 'You stay there, Yacob.' He raised the hatch and found himself under Roman stars. Below, to the right, the yells and hammering continued. The wooden tub was only half full, but his muscles strained to the lifting of it. He carried it to the parapet, panted, paused, looked below. Stupid boys of the patrician class, one of them in a green wig. He tilted the tub on to them with care. There were screams and threats, round holes of mouths howling up at him. He picked up the emptied tub and raised it. He threw it down at the green wig and struck. The wig came off and its owner circled like a drunk howling before he fell. His companions, much concerned, bent over him. One of them looked up at the roof and cried:

'Do you know what you've done? You fool, do you realize what you've done?' Caleb made a coarse noise with the back of his throat much used by gladiators to express contempt and loathing, wiped his wet hands on his buttocks, and then went down back to the company. He did not hear his victim, who had merely been stunned, emerge from blackness crying 'Hic et ubique, mater?'

Nor, some weeks later, did he recognize that recovered victim in the Emperor who paid a courtesy visit to the performers in the games. Caleb, calling himself Metellus, stood to attention with the men he had helped to train when the pretty pimpled young man, no longer a boy, came down from the imperial box in his purple to the performers' well which debouched into the arena. From the arena came the noise of Rome seated, chewing sausages, waiting for blood. A number of exotic captives, not yet fully aware that they were to shed blood to

275

please Rome, lay and sat around, paleskinned and fairer of hair than the Emperor, unresponsive to the games editor's barks that they should jump to their filthy feet in Caesar's presence. Caesar was much taken with a freckled boy of about fourteen years who stood bewildered by noise, fuss and his own ignorance; he embraced him lovingly. 'What do you think, Tigellinus?' he said. 'Much too pretty to be turned into mincemeat, wouldn't you say?'

Where, Caleb wondered, was the prefect Burrus? Another one sent into exile for yawning during an imperial recitation? The man addressed as Tigellinus wore no uniform but he seemed to have come into a kind of praetorian authority.

'Caesar is too softhearted. Caesar's subjects like to see young flesh torn to tatters. You,' he said to Caleb, 'what's your name?'

'Metellus.'

'If you're Metellus I'm Cleopatra. Does this one know enough daggerwork to make it look like a fight?'

'He's a child. He doesn't stand a chance.'

'He'll have armour on, won't he?'

'They don't understand what armour is. And what chance is he going to have with Tibulus there?' Nero beamed at Tibulus, a chunk of handsome stone from Liguria, more massive than supple, ponderous to kill and too stupid to feel pain. The games editor said:

'He'll hold back, Caesar. At least five feints before he comes in for the kill.'

'Just like that,' Caleb said hotly. 'The kill. And this boy doesn't understand what's happening. He can't speak Latin and we can't speak British.' He made a coarse noise at the back of his throat much used by gladiators to express contempt and loathing. The Emperor was charmed by the sound, which he did not seem to have heard before.

'They're only animals,' the games editor said. 'Great Caesar, we wait on your pleasure.' So the Emperor and his entourage climbed back to the imperial box and air unpolluted by rage, sweat, fear and kindred emanations. The Empress, stupid bitch, was there. She rose on Nero's entrance and, as he did, remained standing to bow to the loyal roar of the crowd. The crowd was huge: sure sign of a prosperous Empire, this massive afternoon leisure. The *hydraulis* or water organ was footed and growled chthonian thunder. It was the voice of a coarse and pampered citizenry wearing the collective blue cap of a flawless placid heaven. The weak voice of Vergil's ghost called them to collective virtue, but they wondered what team Curgil or Purvil had played for. Nero smirked and bobbed and said aloud but unheard of them: 'Filthy inartistic lot, what do they know of the agony of forging flawless hendecasyllables?' Then he sat. Britannicus came in late, mildly drunk from his complexion. Nero frowned, Britannicus beamed. When the bewildered Britons came on, hefting unfamiliar weapons against (at first) prancing playful professional opponents, he beamed less. He had a kind of proprietorial concern with these pallid naked northerners. 'A mockery,' he was heard to cry. 'They fought well in their own way. They're still fighting well and rightly after we've raped and beaten and burned them.' Nero heard all this treasonous talk with pleasure. He saw bare Britons hack unhandily, hacked back efficiently when the general howl for blood grew loud. Bare bloody Britons lay in blood and sand. Then the freckled boy of fourteen was pushed on, looking at his dagger with the puzzlement of one who handles his first lizard. Tibulus gave stolid acknowledgement of the crowd's welcome, which was to say he looked at the crowd much as the boy looked at his dagger. The boy, assuming he had to use his dagger against this one here, stuck it into his arm. A trickle of Roman blood primed a roar of patriotic affront, dirty little foreign bastard, even babes in arms in that northern mound of dogturds are trained to be treacherous to our brave boys. Tibulus watched the red drops trickle with the sincere interest the elder Pliny might bring to a march of fire ants, then he swished his sword terribly to the mob's delight. The boy now performed what this mob took to be a barbaric filthy wardance round and round the brave Roman and, which was totally against the rules of fair play, nicked him in the buttocks not once but twice. Nero was surprised not to hear Britannicus crying against the current; he looked round and saw that Britannicus was no longer there. Tibulus stood blinking at the dancing boy, then he downed with his sword at the lad's dagger. The lad seemed happy to be rid of it but seemed also to wonder whether, in the rules of a sport he was beginning dimly to understand with the crowd's help, he ought not perhaps to pick it up from where it lay at Tibulus's feet. He decided instead to run away from Tibulus's sword, which flashed unpleasantly in the sun at him, but this, according to the crowd's rage, was not in the rules either. Running, anyway, he stumbled over a British corpse, disclosed a tearful and impotent anger, and appeared ready to be hacked, that was the crowd's evident but mysterious need, best get it over. It was then that Britannicus appeared in the arena and stopped the fight. At first the crowd did not know who he was and they howled down what he was trying to say. Then, to the horrid amazement of the Emperor, Britannicus sang.

Sang. *Sang.* Opened his throat and sang, in a clear and altogether audible and apparently trained tenor, two or three wordless measures which had the effect on the crowd of a minatory trumpet. The crowd hushed and heard what followed. 'I am Britannicus, son of the divine Claudius. Where, I ask, is the ancient Roman spirit of mercy to a brave enemy? I fought the Britons. I helped conquer them. It is enough. Let them not be humiliated as well.' And, as Nero had done previously but in the impulse of a very different velleity, he took the boy in his arms. The fickle mob howled its joy. You could never trust the mob. Caligula, Nero thought, was right in wishing the Roman people to have but one throat and himself the satisfaction of cutting it. After, that was, the duty of slashing more particular throats.

Any mob likes to howl, though it does not always know why it is howling, any more than a dog knows why it bays at the moon. The Jewish mob, away in Jerusalem or, having transferred itself seg-mentally to the mainly Gentile port, as near as it could get to his cell in Caesarea, still howled at Paul, having forgotten or never having known precisely why. It was time for the new procurator to be himself sure why this baldheaded one in chains had incurred both high and low displeasure, and what relevance this had to Roman governance.

He was lucky to receive about this time a courtesy visit from King Herod Agrippa II and his sister Bernice. For this son of the dead and unlamented monarch of Judaea knew all about the Jewish law, so it was said. He had been ruler of Chalcis, which lay between Lebanon and Antilebanon, and afterwards took over the tetrarchies which Gaius Caligula had granted to his father before his elevation to the greater throne. Nero, in his early conscientious days, had added a few scraps of territory around the Galilean lake and, in gratitude, the little king had changed the name of his capital from Caesarea Philippi to Neronias. Bernice, or Berenice (that being the original or Macedonian form of the name), was a pretty young widow who had been married to her uncle Herod of Chalcis. There was a fair number of avuncular espousals in the Herod family, and it is curious that nobody thundered against them, the Jews being hot against violations of allowable mari-tal limits, while the Roman Senate, not a notably moral body, had howled against Claudius's proposal to marry his niece, until, that is, his niece had stopped their howling with an assassination or two.

The neatly bearded little monarch, in his fine black and gold thread, sat with his sister, recently groomed and coiffed in Alexandria, on little thrones set up on the procuratorial rostrum. It was a blue and gold day, and Bernice's sharp little ears were concerned with analysing the components of the birdsong about them more than with attending to the harsh Greek of the procurator's exordium.

'We are met in order to clarify the issue yet again of the accusation brought by the Jewish people against the man Paul. The Roman law operates in the sphere of secular action. It is fitting that a monarch greatly experienced in the Jewish law should, of his graciousness, assist the Roman arm in the elucidation of the issue. King Herod

Agrippa, here is the man.' There indeed was chained Paul, bowing slightly in the direction of Hebraic royalty. 'The Jews of Judaea have made suit to me, protesting that he must live no longer. I myself have found in him nothing worthy of death. He has requested appeal to the Emperor in Rome, and this has been granted. But the question is this: what must we write to Rome? Perhaps, at last, we shall find out. Let the prisoner speak.'

The Jewish prosecution then clamoured to put their case in Aramaic, since probably the situation had not been made sufficiently clear in Greek, a pagan tongue, but Festus said that he was satisfied that the accused would make the accusation as clear as the defence. So Paul set sail on a wide sea of self-justification with an eloquence honed by enforced repetition. Marcus Julius Tranquillus listened with great care and, though he had made a Jewish marriage, his head swam with the Oriental subtlety of it all. That business of Paul's having desecrated the Temple no longer seemed to come into it. He was being set upon by the Jews for preaching heretical doctrine, and the Jews hoped to bring the Romans into it by laying at his door the disruption of public order which they themselves, rejecting the logic of what was not at all heretical, had caused. Paul appeared to give an elegantly concise history of the Jewish nation, their hope of a redeemer, the fulfilment of that hope in a form which, since they had got used to hope and did not particularly want its fulfilment, they stubbornly rejected. Paul quoted massively, and names like Ezra, Nehemiah, Ecclesiastes, Jeremiah, Ezekiel, Daniel, Hosea, Joel, Amos, Obadiah, Micah, Nahum, Habakkuk, Zephaniah, Haggai and Zechariah evidently registered as mere uncouth noise with Festus, who stared stonily in a Roman intellectual sleep. Paul ended by saying:

'I have taken my mission to Greece and to Asia, to Jew and Gentile alike. For this cause I was seized in the Temple and men made attempt to kill me. Having obtained the help that is from God, I stand to testify to all, small and great, saying that I have preached nothing but what Moses and the prophets said would surely come: how that the Christ must suffer and by his resurrection from the dead proclaim light to both the Jews and the Gentiles.'

Both Festus and Herod Agrippa began to speak at the same time.

'I beg your pardon –'

'No, please –'

'All I was going to say was that he's mad. He's read too much. Too much brooding on things makes a man go mad.' Julius felt a reluctant sympathy. Life was hard enough without bringing Habakkuk into it. All the Romans wanted to do was to make life simpler for everyone: a sufficiency of meat and drink, the odd afternoon at the games, taxes, a few memorized tags from the classical authors, *una nox dormienda*.

'Seen a lot of it in my time,' Festus added, untruthfully. Paul, good-humoured, said:

'I'm not mad. I speak the truth in all sobriety. The king here knows of these things. Nothing's been hidden from him. Nothing of what has been done has been done in a corner. King Agrippa, you believe in the prophets. I say no more.'

Herod Agrippa said: 'If you're right, and you preach the Jewish fulfilment, what have the Gentiles to do with it?' Very shrewd, Julius thought.

'Would you have the word caged?' Paul answered. 'Would you have a limitation on it? God made more than the Jews. He may even be said to have made the Romans.'

Festus did not quite like his race to be bundled into the same creative arena as subject peoples, but he contented himself with muttering that Paul was mad. Agrippa grinned at Paul and said:

'You're persuasive enough to make me see the road if not to follow it. You've persuaded yourself into a particular situation and I can quite see how you've persuaded others.'

'Yes. I would to God everybody could take the stand I take, standing here as I stand. Except, of course, for these chains.' And he shook them. Julius laughed and Festus looked at him, wondering why.

'I would say those chains should come off,' Agrippa said. 'If the defendant would be good enough to retire and have them removed, the procurator and I have a word to say to each other.'

So Paul was rattled off, and Festus said to Agrippa:

'It seems a lot of nonsense to me.'

'Not Roman, you mean. No, it makes good enough sense. The point is that he's done nothing wrong. He can be set at liberty.'

'Then he's torn to pieces. A pleasant start for my term of office. A Roman citizen torn to pieces, and then I have to have one of those massacres to quieten the tearers down, troops brought in from Syria, oh no. Besides, there's the question of his appeal to Caesar. That's gone through, that's on record, that can't be rescinded.'

'If he hadn't made the appeal you could have put him on a boat going to Corinth or somewhere. Now you have to send him to Rome. I have the feeling that he wants Rome more than he wants Caesar. A chance to spread the doctrine in the imperial capital. At Roman expense. The man's no fool.'

'Not mad, then?'

'Far from it.' Bernice now unexpectedly spoke. She had a lovely low voice, and both its trained resonance and the information she imparted reminded her brother that that school in Alexandria had been a good school. She said:

'In Rome, of course, he'd be preaching a *religio licita*.'

'A what?' Festus said, as though he did not know Latin.

'The Nazarene faith is permitted on Roman territory. Gallio established that precedent.'

'Who is or was Gallio?'

'Come, procurator,' Herod Agrippa said, 'he's the brother of the Emperor's tutor and speech writer. You know, Seneca.'

'Spanish, aren't they?' He knew that Seneca was, it followed therefore that –

'My sister's right,' Herod Agrippa said. 'Of course, the priests won't accept the precedent, and this man Paul knows it. What he's after is imperial confirmation, which might make the Sanhedrin grumble but think twice about throwing stones. I think he might well get it. Rome takes kindly to new things. Anyway, my advice is that you get him aboard a ship as soon as you can. With a military escort, naturally. He'll still officially be a prisoner. Then he ceases to be your responsibility. He belongs to Rome.'

This seemed to imply that he, Porcius Festus, was not Rome. But he saw the point: *real* Rome.

Tigellinus, so Nero had discovered, was a blunt and somewhat brutal man but not lacking in a philosophy. He listened to his imperial master expound the doctrine of art learnt from Gaius Petronius, who was still away in Greece, and he grunted and nodded, though in no gesture of affirmation, before saying: 'I see the point – an image of reality and so on, but what do you want with an image when you, so to speak, *are* the reality?'

'I don't quite see the –'

'Oh come, Caesar, art is for the impotent. Dreams of manipulation are dreams of power. Why dream when it's more satisfactory to be awake? The reality is *potestas*.'

'Of course, but *potestas* to create *pulchritudo*.'

'The *pulchritudo*, as you term it, lies in the *potestas*. There's nothing beyond that.'

'How strange. Just what my mother said.'

'In one of your dreams, Caesar?'

'Don't despise dreams, Tigellinus. Dreams are a fantastic way of putting things into focus, sharpening them, showing you what you've been thinking without really knowing it. I've had a lot of nightmares with my mother in them. I wasn't all that good a son, I suppose. But what happened only the other morning just before I woke was that my mother stood there, very beautiful as she always was, even when she was nagging at me, and smiling and saying: "Everything is right in the name of *potestas*. I forced that lesson on you, son, and became a *martus* to it." '

'Became a what?'

'She meant a witness, I think, it's a Greek word. Then I woke up and felt very well and no longer a bad son.' He smiled in complacency and leaned back on his cushions. The two were sitting together in a loggia that caught the dying light, sipping a drink that Tigellinus had imported: wine fortified with bitter herbs, a sharpener of the appetite. Tigellinus said:

'You must clean up your life.'

'Morally, you mean? You sound like Seneca.'

'No, no, no. There's too much of the last imperiate still hanging about. You can smell its stuffiness. And I don't mean Seneca. Not yet.'

'Will you invite us to dinner, Tigellinus?'

'Us?'

'Oh, me and the Empress, and, yes, Seneca, and, of course, my stepbrother. Perhaps,' he said bitterly, 'he could be persuaded to sing for us.'

'Swanlike.' It was not a question. And then: 'Honoured, naturally. At the villa, of course?'

'Oh, none of them could tolerate the stink of the Suburra. You know this woman who lives there, Locusta?'

'I'll know her before the dinner takes place.'

The villa was, as Nero had expected, somewhat vulgar in its opulence: the selfmade rich man showing off. But dinner was served away from the clutter of ornaments in a paved court next to the piscina. On the table, which was heavily cluttered with flowers of a heavy sweetness, there was a real piscina or fishtank. In it swam little fishes. Tigellinus had served his bitter appetizer before dinner, but only his chief guest was drunk. Tigellinus was aware of the artist's weakness in him: he had to be drunk for what was to come. The host, he was permitted to chatter away, saying:

'Brought up by barge this morning from Ostia. I supervised the cooking myself. And there, you see, are some live fish. It is a pleasant sensation to feel them slide down your throat raw and alive. They nibble as they go down. Would Caesar like to essay the painful pleasure?'

'Try it on old Seneca first. He *needs* pleasures. A man who's lived a long life without them.'

'I doubt that, Caesar,' Tigellinus grinned. Seneca did not feel especially uncomfortable, though he ate little. His stoicism served him well. The butler brought in wine. The wine steamed. Nero said:

'Our host has considerately remembered that the lord Britannicus was, on his British campaign, introduced to the comfort of mulled wine. Try some of this. You too, Seneca, cold fish as you are.'

'This cold fish prefers cold water, Caesar.'

'Oh, clever. Water's a dangerous drink. Try this delicious hot brew, Britannicus. Garnished with rare herbs. Come, it's a cool night. Oh, I see your problem. How terribly insulting. He fears the Emperor may poison him, Tigellinus. But Tigellinus has no such fear, see.' And indeed their host took a few sips. 'You see, harmless, wholesome. But perhaps you would prefer to wait a while, Britannicus. Tigellinus may be a kind of Socrates, and some poisons are slow to act.' Without changing his tone he added: 'Octavia, you're an adulteress.' There was shock. Octavia stammered:

'I beg the Emperor's pardon?'

'That's right, do beg it, not that you'll get it. Closeted with old Seneca there, pretending to study philosophy. Scratch a Stoic and you find a lecher, isn't that so, Tigellinus?'

'That,' Seneca said, 'is a joke in very bad taste, sir.'

'Bad taste? That sounds like an aesthetic judgment. Leave such judgments to an artist, Seneca, like your lord and master. *Artifex, artifex.* Very well, Octavia, I know you wouldn't touch old Seneca with a ten-foot strigil. Hot in the blood calls for hot in the blood. I'll find him out yet, never fear.'

'Bbbbritannicus,' Octavia stammered, 'at least have the ccccourage to pppprotect your sister.'

'Oh, that would be dangerous, wouldn't it?' Nero jeered. 'That might offend the Emperor. The good kind Emperor who persuaded our kind host to prepare some mulled wine for the conqueror of the Britons. Taste it. Our host has done so and smiles unharmed.'

Britannicus obeyed, rage trembling in his forearms. 'Too hot.'

'Easily put right. Add some cold water, somebody.'

Tigellinus was quick to obey, using the blue jug by his plate. Britannicus drank more copiously, though with little pleasure. Tigellinus said: 'Because you are neither hot nor cold but merely lukewarm you shall be vomited out of my mouth.'

'That's rather good,' Nero said. 'That's very good. Who made that up?'

'It's attributed to the unkillable slave Chrestus. Around whom a cannibalistic cult now centres. They eat each other, you know. And they swive each other with no concern for lawful relationships. Sister with brother, mother with son, father with daughter –'

'I'm afraid that's a libel,' Seneca said. 'I know differently.'

'You always do, don't you,' Nero jeered, 'old Senna Pods? Whenever a thing sounds moderately interesting, as this Chrestus business does, you have to throw cold water on it.' Britannicus retched. 'What's the matter, you sweet singer and lover of British boys? Is a little live fish nibbling your little grape? Heavens, not at all well.' For Britannicus tried to speak, but could not. Tried to breathe, but could not. Tried to rise, but. Tigellinus said:

'Perhaps a little cold water?'

'Too late. Choked on a fishbone. A shame. Not much of a singer but a fine soldier.' Octavia and Seneca got up from their couches, their hands flapping in useless concern. Britannicus gasped like a landed sea bass, then stopped gasping. 'Sit down, both of you. Seneca, I thought the Stoics took this sort of thing in their stride. Vomitorium on the left, I think,' as Octavia blindly staggered. Tigellinus looked closely at Nero, though keeping his distance. He clicked fingers for one servant to clear the plates, four to remove the body. Nero, he thought, was acting well the part of the amoral monster. But he did not really have the stuff of the murderer in him. He would not sleep well tonight. He would have bad dreams. The artist's hysteria without much artistic talent. But he, Tigellinus, would look after him.

The wind blew fair at Caesarea. The sails bellied. The ship was a coastal vessel that had put in from Adramyttium, not far from the island of Lesbos. Commodious enough, but needed a lick of paint, some of its lines frayed. Cranes creaked as bales were hoisted aboard. Porcius Festus said: 'You'll be seeing Rome sooner than you thought.'

'I'd be seeing it sooner if we waited for a ship bound straight.'

The procurator, eyes slit to the sunlight, looked at the mob held off by the entire Caesarean garrison. 'You'll pick something up at Sidon. Or Cyprus. Or Myra.' The owner–captain yelled at two new crew members in an obscure Greek dialect and cuffed the ship's boy. 'We have to get him out of here. I'm sick of stones being thrown and gibes about Roman friendship for heretics, whatever heretics are. I wish I understood what it was all about. Or perhaps I don't. Whatever it is, it's well – dirty, not Roman. You have that letter safely stowed?' Marcus Julius Tranquillus tapped his breast. 'My thanks for writing it. Of course, you understand these things better, what with having a Jew wife. You'll be in bed with her soon. Well, not too soon, of course.' More affable with his senior centurion, knowing that he was now rid of him. Transferred him, with permission from Syria, to the corps of couriers or *frumentarii*, but still in command of troops, also responsible for prisoners.

Paul was already below. Luke was with him, gladly posing as a personal slave. That would make a difference. There were other prisoners, riffraff but Roman citizens, a soldier who had attacked his decurion in drink, a captured deserter, a Tiberside murderer who had escaped to Syria, picked up in Damascus. Paul was an appellant, not a prisoner, but you could not expect the troops aboard to see the difference. Give him a slave going yes master no master and it might get into their thick heads that here was a bald and hooknosed *gentleman*. A gift of new robes had come through from Bernice in Neronias. He often impressed women of the higher class. The officer in charge, who had introduced himself as plain Julius, had allotted Paul and himself, Luke, a two-bunked cabin next to the one, privilege of rank, he occupied alone. This Julius had, unheard of deference but he made all clear, apologized to Paul for what looked like being a lengthy voyage.

'I fear it's very roundabout. Rome by way of little Asia.'

'A mad voyage for a mad man. Not so mad a man, not so mad a voyage. The procurator was eager to get me away, but doesn't seem so eager to get me to Rome. A procurator's relations with Rome should be very simple – taxes delivered on time, nothing more. Now he has to get involved with the legal department. I'm afraid I'm an embarrassment to the procurator. I have a feeling that he'd be happier if we were shipwrecked somewhere.'

'We'll be sailing into the season for shipwrecks.' Julius smiled. Paul smiled. Seagulls crarked. Paul said:

'Tell me, do *you* understand my situation? Do *you* understand what I've been preaching and teaching and doing? Your superior officer clearly doesn't.'

'I have a certain advantage over him. My wife is Jewish. My brother-in-law claims to have known you. You were students together. In those days they called you Saul.'

'Who is he?'

'His name's Caleb. In his revolutionary moods he calls himself Caleb the Zealot.'

'Oh, I remember. But what's a Zealot doing in Rome?'

'Finished with revolutionary politics – for the time being, he says. Married with a son. A trainer of wrestlers and gladiators. I look forward to your reunion.'

'I look forward to a number of reunions. Including one at Sidon – if you'll permit me to go ashore. Ironic. I persecuted the Greek Nazarenes of Jerusalem, and some of them flew off to found a church at Sidon. In a sense, I founded that church. The ways of God. You don't think me mad when I say *God* and not *the gods*?'

'Sara says *God* too.'

'Sara? Caleb's sister. I can't remember their parents. I remember an uncle, though. The twelfth disciple.'

'The name Matthias is sometimes mentioned.'

'And there was another girl –'

'Ruth. A name that lives on in our daughter. Ruth died. Oh, why hide what happened? Ruth was slaughtered. Rome was vicious under Gaius.'

'And under your new Emperor? The one I'm petitioning?'

'Too soon to say. He's young. But he has Seneca to keep him on the right road.'

'Seneca, yes.'

Seneca, yes. Nero was at breakfast and already tipsy when Seneca achieved at last a long-requested interview with him. Tigellinus sat apart from the Emperor's table, a small one befitting a small meal, though it was covered with silver dishes – crayfish stewed with saffron, plover's eggs hardboiled, a piece of cold braised beef in a crust, cold water he did not touch, warmed wine he did. 'I would prefer to make my request in private, Caesar.'

'No secrets from the praetorian prefect.'

'I – don't understand.' But he did.

'The lord Burrus has unaccountably vanished. I was in need of a replacement. What better man to fill the post –'

'Than a fishmonger. I see.' Tigellinus took no offence, grinned comfortably rather. 'And when you say that Burrus has vanished –'

'I mean that Burrus was not well. Was not happy. Was dissatisfied. Was not greatly efficient in his office of praetorian prefect. Don't disparage fishmongers, Seneca. They know how to sell fish. What you and Burrus tried to sell found no market. Not here.'

'My request comes opportunely then. I'm growing old. I have books to write – ideas to contemplate. I need to go into retirement.'

'To which of your many estates? See, Tigellinus, this egg is undercooked.'

'I don't doubt that I've accumulated more property than is perhaps fitting for a – Stoic philosopher. I'm beholden to Caesar for his gifts. Now I wish to return them.'

'So at last you become *really* a Stoic. You were right, Tigellinus. They're all damned hypocrites. Preaching the virtues of the simple life and cramming their chests with gold and silver and title deeds. I don't think I want to let you go, dear Seneca. You write me good speeches. They impress the Senate.'

'Yes, Caesar. You're right to talk of hypocrisy.'

'And what,' sucking a marrow bone, 'precisely,' blowing a hoarse note through it, 'do you mean by that?'

'I've discovered that politics and morality have little to do with each other. I beg you to let me go into retirement. I can't cleanse the Empire, not with mere words. But I can do something for myself.'

'Shall we let him go, Tigellinus?'

'It would be useful,' the new praetorian prefect said, 'if Caesar knew precisely where he is going. A man as talented as Seneca ought not just to vanish – as Burrus did.'

'So stay in Rome, Seneca, or on its immediate outskirts. I may call on you to write me the occasional speech. And, of course, it would be pleasant if you would say a few words at my forthcoming marriage. Something about the virtues of marital love and the glory of a woman's fidelity to her husband.'

'Marriage? I don't understand.'

'You never seem to understand anything, do you? For a philosopher you've precious little understanding of the real world. Your protégée the Empress Octavia learned nothing of virtue, for all your lessons in moral philosophy. Adultery is always a crime. When the Emperor is cuckolded it becomes the crime of treason. To which, of course, there is only one answer.'

'You mean,' Seneca said, appalled, 'you propose to marry that – I assumed that – I thought that was –'

'Get it out, man. You're as bad as that clown Claudius. No, not Acte, delectable as she was. Acte's finished with. A lady, sir. The Emperor is to marry a lady.' He belched in finality. 'All right, go.'

They sailed north, hugging the coast, to the old Phoenician capital named Sidon, seventy miles of calm. Two bales of Galilean grain were unladed, and a rift in the rigging had to be repaired. Paul and Luke were permitted to go ashore, with Julius accompanying them. There were two harbours here, and they anchored briefly in the one called Leucippe. Here members of the local church assembled to meet Paul, under a screaming sanhedrin of gulls. It has been Luke's task to get the message through. Some of the Sidonese Christians believed that Paul was long dead, and they fingered his limbs as in a meat market. There were tearful embraces badly interpreted by some of the low soldiers at the taffrail, who knew all about the Christians as cannibals and perverts, and then Paul spoke urgent words he had already dictated to Luke in their cabin:

'The Holy Spirit has made you overseers or bishops of a flock always in danger from wolves. This flock, this church, he bought with his blood, he who, in conjunction with the Father, maintains this Spirit to guide you. I know that already the enemy is at work, trying to draw Christ's followers in the direction of lewdness and bad habits and spitting at what they formerly reverenced. Work hard, help the weak, give of your strength and love, remembering that it is more blessed to give than to receive.'

Then they had to get back on board. But, following Julius, Paul suddenly turned and cried words to the faithful not, it seemed, previously meditated. 'I know how things are. You think Christ's blood has bought you from sin for all time and that you're free to sin without

287

reproach or punishment. But Christ's ransom works only retrospectively. You think you're special, rightly aloof from the sanctions of both Jewish and Roman law. You think you can sleep with whoever you wish and eat garbage if you want to. Well, you can't. You've seen a light which others haven't, and that gives you a moral responsibility the rest don't possess. I shan't be around here again, and you'll hear my voice only in the ghostly form of letters I shall write, but remember what I want from you, what Christ wants – purity, purity and again purity.'

'We have to get aboard,' Julius said apologetically.

'All right. I've said my say.' Some of the troops at the taffrail were making a little song about *purity*, a word that had clearly carried. Paul grinned at them, but his eyes were angry. Julius gained the notion that he was angry with himself: work not well done, mission not well understood, the voyage a voyage towards the realization of failure. But he could not be sure.

They sailed east and north of Cyprus. This was summer, and the prevailing winds were from the west, so they kept to the lee of the island. Paul lay on his bunk, hands joined behind his head on the filthy straw pillow. Luke sat on the edge of his bunk, looking at him. Nothing to dictate? Nothing. How is your stomach? Well enough. On the deck some of the troops were playing the game of trying to ring a peg with rope quoits. Their coarse shouts rang in, the cabin door being open for the breeze. *Pone in culum. Fili scortorum.* Luke went out and saw they were letting the west wind carry them to the Asian coast. It would be a matter of creeping north, embracing the land, dropping anchor in inlets when the wind defeated the coastal current and the little breezes from the Asian landmass. A slow long journey. By the rights of it Paul should get up from that bunk and start preaching the word to the troops or those genuine prisoners who lay in the dark brig in chains. Somehow God seemed landlocked, a thin voice high in the rigging, slave to tide and winds, overawed by the sea he had made. What did the God who hammered the universe together have to do with virtue, redemption, the strange doctrine of hypostasis?

Everybody except the chained was up on deck to see the port of Myra dance sedately towards them. Here they were to change ship. 'That,' Julius said, pointing, 'will be ours. One of the grain fleet.'

'From Alexandria.' Paul had reduced himself to the mere knowledgable traveller; he had sailed more than anyone here, except for the captain–owner. 'They all put in at Myra. Due north. A good bay.' Their ship danced towards dancing Myra, unpestered by bumboats; these flimsy craft, laden with fruit, small idols, gaudy trinkets, yelling vendors and a rowing boy, swarmed about the grainship. Prostitutes, their faces modestly veiled, languidly pulled up their skirts to tempt the jeering troops. The gangplank went down. The chained prisoners came up painfully blinking. The sun was a hot bath; slave breezes shook cooling towels. The soldiers, making finger gestures at the whores and crying bad Aramaic, humped their gear to the land. Civilian passengers in robes, who had remained nameless even on the communal messdeck, shouldered nameless goods in sacks and waved at greeting knots by the godowns. Paul and Luke stood patiently by bales for loading, under the eye of a soldier who spat out datestones like dirty words. Marcus Julius Tranquillus handed money over to the captain–owner, who wailed to heaven about Roman sharp practice. Then he went to look for the master of the grainship. Sacks were being craned on board. 'Look out,' Luke cried, as one of them split and discharged its content. Paul dodged. It was yellow, a very fine and quite unknown grain. Luke let some run through his fingers.

'Sand?' he said.

'Sand for Rome,' the foreman said, 'believe it or not. It's a mad world.'

A pair of wrestlers stirred up sand as they fought. One of them was Caleb, muscular still but carrying too much weight round the middle. The crowd swallowed sausage gristle and roared and booed. All Rome was there, as ever, doing no work. Wheat from Egypt and sand from Myra. The world paid tribute and granted leisure to watch blood being spilled, less precious than sand. Not that blood would be spilled now. A mere interlude. The Emperor had asked to see Jewish wrestlers. Well, here was one, somewhat past it. His opponent, whom he had trained, was Sicilian and knew when to hold back. Caleb would yield when he felt tired.

The Emperor sat chewing dates and spitting out the stones petulantly. Behind him stood Tigellinus in uniform. Next to him sat his new wife, whose husband had been banished to Lusitania. I note that in this chronicle I have not mentioned one ugly woman. I would, for variety's sake, make Poppea Sabina ugly if I could, but I cannot. She was of the jet and ivory race of Messalina and Agrippina, her perfection of face and body rendering description a bore, but she was, unlike those ladies, good. She was also clever, but not in matters of intrigue. She read the poets and philosophers. She had even read the Septuagint. Nero frowned at Caleb's performance and said:

'Too old. I like to see young bodies.'

'That man,' Poppea said, 'has a reputation. He nearly strangled the late Gaius Caligula. In a wrestling bout like this. Caligula challenged him. It was his own fault. The Jews fight well when they have to.'

'You admire the Jews, don't you? An intransigent people. Riots

289

again last week outside one of their what do you call them –'

'Synagogues.'

'Something to do with this crowd that worships Chrestus. I think that Claudius's idea was a reasonable one. One of his few ideas that were. Throw the Jews out. They're a nuisance. They spit on the gods of Rome. And that's a way of spitting on Caesar.'

'Such Jews as I know are respectable and intelligent. They read books instead of going to the games. They regard the games as bloodthirsty and childish.'

'Do, do they? They're also too rich. I think the imperial exchequer might do a little dipping there. Oh, that was well done.' Meaning that the pseudo-Jew had caught the real one in an excruciating armlock, and the real one hammered the sand to show he yielded. They stood, bowed, ran off quickly for fear the Emperor might order the diversion of throatcutting, and then Nero said: 'What's next, Tigellinus?'

'Elephants, Caesar.'

'Ah, elephants. "Proud with his pachyderms piling the perilous passes." Part of a poem I once started on Hannibal. Never finished it. Poppea, dearest, I think I could profitably use your friendship with these people. Find out how much they're storing up. Rifle their whatdoyoucallthem synagogues. Rome needs money. I have the most gorgeous plan for Rome. Art. I can't finish my poems. I sing, I act, I dance, and it's all spent, gone, impermanent, smoke on the wind. "Do not expect again a phoenix hour." I couldn't finish that poem either. I dream of a lasting work of art.'

'I'm not adept at using friendships. The Jews trust me.'

'Do, do they? Ah, marvellous beasts. And so intelligent.'

The elephants had come lumbering on, grey, wrinkled, clumsy. They began to dance very heavily, whipped and cursed by their mahauts, as they are called, to the elephantine music of the *hydraulis*. The Romans chewed their sausages. Grain, sand, elephants.

It was slow going from Myra. The smell of the grain from the hold was sickening, but not so much as the ship's roll. The sea, Luke thought, when he had given breakfast to the waves, was like dissolving marble, as though Rome had melted in Tiber. Still something of the poet. Paul lay groaning on his bunk. They shared the cabin with a certain Aristarchus from Thessalonica, who had embarked at Myra and proposed leaving the ship at Cnidus on the Carian promontory of Tropium, if they ever reached there. He was a man of strong stomach who talked much of the kitchen of Tropium, which was said to be exceptional. He also had the grace to be curious about his messmates, and was ready, when Paul's stomach allowed him to be rational, to

hear all about the great Christianizing mission. The eating and drinking of the *soter* seemed to him to be excellent doctrine. 'A good religion,' he pronounced, 'itself eats and drinks of what it supersedes.' He
seemed to have no religion. 'I've heard from certain travellers about
what is called anthropophagy in certain primitive places which the
Romans have still to colonize. People eat people. Crunch their bones,
chew their flesh. Cooked, of course, probably with herbs of the country.'

'Please. Not now.'

'My belief is that it's the salt they're after. The human body contains
salt. If you're far from the salt of the sea the corpses of your friends and
relations, enemies too of course, may well be the only source of that
vital mineral.' He felt he himself at that time had no particular need of
a religion. 'What I need now is cheaper labour and higher profits.' But
he would, when he retired, take a close look at the claims of this new
faith. He had the impression that it was popular among slaves, which
was no recommendation to free men. While he snored and Luke tossed
out of phase with the ship, Paul lay on his back and heard the timbers
creak and the waves lurch and wash. He tried to conduct a colloquy
with Christ, but Christ was coy and would not come. Only when at
length he slept fitfully did answers flow out of a kind of inner marine
phosphorescence.

'What will happen to me in Rome?'

'Unseemly to ask. Time is a road that is all high gates. Even I had to
engage them.'

'Are you satisfied with what I've so far done?'

'You chose the easier way. You have not sufficiently hammered at
the Jews. Seeing me turned into a Lord of the Gentiles, they will the
more readily reject my messianic function. It is all a great pity.'

'Do you still consider me to be a murderer?'

'Of course. That will not be forgotten. But your murderous energy
was needed.'

'I think I am going to be sick.'

'You will find a canvas bucket hanging on a peg at the foot of the
companionway.'

It took several queasy days to reach Cnidus. Here, hale and crackling with energy, Aristarchus of Thessalonica descended by a net to
one of the passenger boats that bobbed in the roads. His packages
were hurled down at him; one went into the water and was
boathooked out. Then he waved his way to shore. The captain, who
had the simple and engaging but not altogether suitable name Philos,
for he was misanthropic and had a vile temper, debated with Julius the
advisability of putting into one of the two harbours, the eastern one
being the larger, among the massed Egyptian shipping, there to await

291

a change of wind. Julius, though a soldier, was granted a certain authority by virtue of his representing the Roman state, while Philos was a mere concessionary, and he prevailed when he said: 'I see what you mean. Cythera lies due west, but it may take weeks for the wind to veer. My instructions are to consult speed more than safety.'

'And how about my ship? And my crew? And the cargo? And the passengers who pay out of their own purses not the almighty Roman state? I know how it is, you want to get those bits of jailmeat off your hands and into bed with your everloving. In this trade you go careful.'

Julius jabbed his forefinger on the chart and slid it to the right. 'We make for the eastern end of Crete.'

'Cape Salmone.'

'Is that what it's called?'

'I don't like this one little bit.'

Philos grumbled that he had been right, that the damned north-wester was going to crack them like a walnut against those rocks there as they crept south of the thin wide island. By dint of yelling and appealing to thirty years of seamanship, fifteen of them as owner-master, he got his way and steered into Limeonas Kalous or Fair Havens, the first sheltered bay they came to after rounding the cape, there to wait till the wind changed. Julius said:

'It's not going to change in a hurry.' They stood on deck, watching the crew bring skins of fresh water in the launch from the little quay with its highcharging chandlers. The ship laboured at anchor. Paul said:

'Centurion, captain, if I may speak. The bad time for sailing's already begun. This is the month of Tishri.'

'Of what?'

'October. I may be a landsman, but I'm not unfamiliar with the seas of these parts. You'll have to winter here.'

Philos grew redly truculent. 'Look,' he said, 'I don't need the advice of a lump of Jewish jailfodder –'

'You'll take that back,' Luke said.

'I think you'd better take that back,' Julius suggested. 'You're speaking of a Roman citizen appellant to Caesar.'

'All right, I take it back. What none of you gentry seem to know is that this is a bad winter port.'

Julius surveyed the small islands that half ringed the harbour. 'Those break the wind, don't they?'

'It's more open than you think. Broadside on, smack – look at those rocks, all teeth. What we're going to do is make for Phoenix, or Phineka as some call it. See it there on the chart.' He sniffed as at a good dinner cooking. 'There's a change on the way, I'm getting it in both nostrils. With a decent southerly we'll make Phoenix with no trouble. One step at a time. We'll think what to do next when I'm anchored safe at Phoenix.' And without waiting for the approval of the Roman state he gave his orders and the boatswain whistled them. Paul smelt the softness of the south wind. Soon they were coasting gently westwards, and the sailors sang to the wind as to a fickle woman, spoke tenderly to it, prayed that it waft them safe across the mouth of the Gulf of Messara. And, Paul asked himself, was the prayer idolatrous? God was up there, the wind here; you had to pray to something that behaved with the capriciousness of a god and a woman but was palpably *down here*. Monotheism was not for the anxious daily woodtouching business of the world. A luxury like art?

Then the wind changed. Swiftly, without advance notice. East by northeast – *anemos typhonikos*, typhon, typhoon. He heard a sailor curse the woman that had changed into a beast called Eurakylon. Greek *Euros* and Roman *Aquilo* conjoined into a hybrid like a centaur, though this one winged. They could not head up to the gale. Clouds rolled against each other from opposed quarters of the sky and lightning wrote a brief signature. For those who could not read thunder gave hollow voice some instants after. They went scud before Euraquilo twenty or more sea miles, under ink clouds and the rain's first bucketloads. He held to the rigging with Julius; Luke fumbled his drunken way below. That island dimly descried to leeward? Cauda. Some called it Gavdho. Thank God or the gods for the shelter of the lee. All hands to the securing of the dinghy. This they had still been towing astern, full of water. The forward sloping foremast served as a derrick; all hauled the lines and helped with the belaying of the boat. Then came the undergirding with the frapping cables.

Paul watched fascinated as the work was done. The cables were dragged out of their locker, *hypozomata*, a word he had not heard before. Hardy sailors dived overboard and passed the cables under the garboard strake and up again, binding the timbers like a magistrate's fascis. That wind would smash spars and hull and all if left unbraced. The captain said seriously to Julius: 'This wind's going to drive us to Big Syrtis. You know what that is? No. Well, it's those quicksands west of Cyrene. We're going to drop the tophamper and set the stormsails. Then we'll lay to on the starboard tack and do a slow drift northwest.' He looked fiercely at Paul and said: 'You a religious man?'

'You mean a praying man, I suppose. I'll pray.'

'Pray to the right gods. Poseidon and Aeolus and the rest of them. We don't want that Jewish one. He never did the Jews any good and he won't do us any either. We're going to need all the help we can get from up there. And,' he flapped his hands helplessly, 'all round here.'

Next day Philos ordered the jettisoning of the cargo. The gale was fierce and vindictive. Nobody's gods had been listening, or perhaps they had. The first thing to go was the bags of sand for the Roman arena. These were dragged from the hold and hurled into the wind, whose cunning fingers picked holes in the sacks and threw the sand back. The grain went over ungrudgingly. The day after the spare gear had to go. 'Spare gear?' asked Paul. He soon discovered what that was: the mainyard, a spar as long as the ship. All hands, crew, passengers, prisoners all united to cast it over. There was no more that they could do. The storm did not abate in days. There was no east nor west nor north star, the whole firmament blacked out as with coarse sackcloth, and the sea sloggering and churning and buffeting the bound oaken staves of the ship. The entire company was assembled on the messdeck, battened down but leaks in the bulkheads showing the sea's impatient intention to establish full possession, a sloshing mate first, then master, god, all. Philos was hopeless about their situation:

'If I knew where land was, I'd run us ashore, wouldn't I? But I don't know where land is. If this goes on we founder, so make up your minds as to that.' Some of the passengers wailed. Paul said:

'Forgive my saying I told you so, but if we'd wintered in Fair Havens –' Philos would have raged thoroughly at that had he not been exhausted. 'As things stand,' Paul said, 'I think we all ought to eat something. It's been days now, and if we have to meet God we'd better do it on full stomachs.' Julius would have smiled if his risor muscles had been capable of action: this ageing baldheaded man had been sick in what would pass now for fair weather; he seemed now, near the limit of their desperation, to be in good health and humour. Paul said: 'One thing I know is this – that I shall reach Rome. You may scoff at dreams, but experience teaches me that dreams are God's way of breaching the wall. If I am to reach Rome the rest of you will certainly see land. We are, so to speak, all in the same boat. Let's see now what provisions the sea has left us.' The ship's cook, a greatnosed Phoenician, rolled in nausea like the rest of them, but there was nothing more to come up. Two of the company tried to heal the leaks in the starboard bulkhead with bits of soaked sacking. Another baled incoming water into a cask which sloshed over the deck.

Paul and Julius found in the store next to the adjoining galley a sack of wheaten flour whose top half was unsoaked though infested with weavils, a sealed tub of stale water, dried beans no longer dry. The livestock – poultry and two sheep – had long been washed overboard. With flint, dry tinder and green wood they got a fire going. Rough dry unleavened bread and boiled beans. The pitchsealed amphorae of wine were broached. With many the food stayed down, the wine enlivened to more lively fear of what was to come. Paul sang a cheerful hymn in Aramaic. The comfort of the Lord's love, his infinite goodness: it was all an outlandish metaphor of men's obdurate will to survive. 'Oh, shut up,' the captain moaned when Paul got to his fifth verse.

Some friends I have had knowledgeable in sea matters have told me that the mean rate of drift of vessels laid to in such weather is something like thirty-six miles in a day and night. Thirteen days and something over an hour would take this ship from Clauda to Koura, which is a point on the east coast of Melita or Malta. With a slight abating of the gale, Philos and his boatswain opened the battens to find scudding cloud and the roaring song of shore breakers. They were drifting in to rock, the breakers told them. Philos ordered a sounding.

'Twenty fathom.' Very faint on the contending winds.

Paul and Julius had followed the captain up to night wind which was sweeter than the closed-in odours below. Julius said: 'I think I believe. If we get through this water I'll be ready for a drop more.'

'Baptized? You? But you know nothing of what you have to believe.'

'Oh, yes, I do. A God who accepts pagans as well as Jews. A fellowship of all people caught in a storm. You broke the bread and poured the wine and said what they'd become. I believed. What more must I do?' He howled the question over the gale.

It was not a true question. Paul said nothing and listened to the new sounding:

'Fifteen fathom.'

That meant they were closing in to the unseen rocks. They could smell stale driftweed. The captain shouted for the dropping of four anchors from the stern. Clutching the taffrail, Paul saw the two cables pour from the port hawseholes: they would keep the prow pointing shorewards. Four of the crew then began furtively to cut the lines holding the launch to the deck. He called: 'What are you doing?'

'Laying out anchors from the bow.'

'I didn't hear the order.'

'Never you mind about orders.' They were clearly intending to make for that shore in a safe company. Paul called Julius. Julius called his troops. The troops grappled with the sailors and sent the dinghy splashing overboard to go adrift. That was unwise: they would need that dinghy. For the moment the ship would hold by its stern anchors. They tried to get some sleep, but it was difficult.

At dawn Paul brought out not only the remains of the hard unleavened bread but a basket of hard tack he had discovered nestling behind the last of the amphorae.

'You're going to need your strength. Eat. Drink.' In the sick light, the rocky shore ahead of them, the wind anxious for its morning work of pushing the ship to its last disaster, he broke his own bread and said: 'Thanks, God, for this gift. Lord, we are children in your hands. We trust, we love, we hope. Amen.'

'Amen,' Julius repeated.

Now they saw the shore more clearly. It was the western side of the bay that was rocky, and to this they had been driven. To the east was a creek with a sandy beach. Philos called his orders: 'Slip your anchors. Jettison what's left of the cargo. Foresail up to the wind. Unlash the steering paddles. I'm going to run her aground.'

Julius's under officer said: 'The prisoners, sir. They'll get away. We'll have to kill them.'

'Kill?'

'The prisoners, sir. Starting with this one here.' And he nodded at Paul without menace.

'What sort of a man are you?'

'It's the regular thing, sir.'

'Get out of my sight.'

The man was puzzled. 'Sir?'

'No, wait. Pass on this order. Prisoners and troops alike. Let those who can swim get overboard now. The rest – Ah. It's happening.'

They struck. The foreship hit not rock but a bottom of thick mud which grasped it fast. The stern was left to the pounding of the green dragons with the wind riding their scaly backs, salivating rabid foam in the rancour of the kill. Paul leaped, Julius, Luke, stout as Julius Caesar with his chronicles encased in a leather roll lashed to his waist with part of a ship's line. Others screamed soundlessly, grabbing at splintering beams. *Rari nantes*. Vergil's phrase. Strange, Julius thought swimming, how the brain can remain aloof and pick at the past, the boring schoolroom, coolly testing old useless knowledge in the light or dark of crisis. The rare swimmers fought for the shore. Those who could not swim and thought they were drowning were borne with rough care loving and vicious to the beach, offered couches from which, panting, they could watch the spine and entrails of their ship torn by the sea's teeth and go into the green maw, while the foreship burrowed deeper and deeper into deep clay. All were saved.

Pauline time, Neronian time – they will not come together, not yet. No matter. That company of stricken voyagers may not even have seen the marine disintegration of marble below or about or above them at the time when Nero was addressing the Senate about enduring monuments of marble. 'What I seek I seek for Rome only. The city as it is affronts my artistic soul. I would leave behind me – you know what. The expenditure can be furnished from many sources. The people are ready for an increase in taxation after so long a period of fiscal clemency. There is gold lying unused in the city temples. That fine device of the late Empress Messalina, of offering Roman citizenship for sale, could be revived with even larger profit – to the state, I say, to Rome, to Rome, I must make that clear. Moreover, there are communities within our cities that reject Rome, its virtues, its gods. I refer to the Jews and the sect that follows Chrestus or Christus. It would be a gesture of Roman clemency to permit these groups to continue with their barbarous rituals and insolent beliefs – but, of course, to make them pay for such permission with heavy imposts. There are various ways in which the financing of the building of a new city worthy of its citizens could be effected. I put them to you as a matter of imperial courtesy – reminding you that power rests where it is meet that it should rest but that, as a good son of Rome, I acknowledge senatorial wisdom and experience without necessarily having to abide by senatorial advice.'

Gaius Calpurnius Piso stood, a young steely man breasting the muffled response to imperial insolence without fear. 'The Emperor's artistic ambitions are well known to this assembly. To rebuild Rome in his own image is an ultimate ambition some of us have long expected. But I would remind the Emperor that there are greater urgencies which cry for his attention. I refer particularly to the situation in Gaul and Spain, where the loyalty of our armies is now being openly attached to their provincial commanders and being removed from Rome. The situation in Britain is appalling, with seventy thousand of our Roman citizens slaughtered by the barbarians and no punitive act yet undertaken –'

Nero was outraged. 'No! No! It is not for this august body to act as the Emperor's conscience. The Roman provinces are mere discardable extensions of Rome which may drop off, for all we care, like lizards' tails. Rome first, Rome last –'

An ancient senator, C. Lepidus Calvus, stood to say: 'Rome *is* the provinces. Rome is her Empire. Rome is the imperial world peace and the great flower of order. Rome is not sickly songs and obscene dances and degrading spectacles and a city rebuilt according to the emetic tastes of a mediocre would-be artist. I speak out, Caesar, without fear of the consequences. An old man whose physicians have granted him short time to live has little to fear. But for once the Emperor shall listen to the truth and not the sycophancies of toadies and catamites.'

'I will accept many affronts,' Nero said indulgently. 'But I will not tolerate an attack on the divine spirit of beauty which in my short life I have ever endeavoured to honour. You will see your new Rome whether you will or not. Greybeards, tottering imbecilities, impotent hypocrites – who needs you? I speak for Rome. You speak for outworn notions of civic and imperial virtue grey and tattered like old sackcloth. I speak for the new age. Gentlemen – you're dead – all of you.' He swept out in his frilled purple between his two lines of guards, Tigellinus after him. Part of his retinue stayed behind to perform the dumbshow drama of frowning menacingly at the assembly.

'Refuge,' Paul said. 'Nothing to do with honey.' He was referring to the name of the island that had given them shelter – Phoenician or Canaanite with a Hebrew cognate. They watched from the deck of an Alexandrian ship called *Dioscuri* or *The Heavenly Twins* as it nosed out of the harbour. Golden rock in the sunlight, golden buildings. Publius, the Roman governor, stood with his old father and waved *vale* from the quay. Luke and Paul together had cured that old man of a fever. All the Roman help imaginable in the brisk conversion of a good part of the island. And Julius himself converted in an inland pool of salt water, Paul explaining: 'A symbol of cleansing, no more. But symbols are important. The human spirit lives in the world of water and fire and bread and wine. We must not be cut off from the world. The world of things. But things are sanctified by faith. The water of the sea is sanctified by your baptism.' He waved at a waving group of Maltese or Phoenician converts, squat brown people, quick with their gifts of fire and *hobz* and *ilma*.

In calm weather they reached Syracuse after a day's sailing. The southerly wind which had carried them now fell. They tacked in a northwester towards Rhegium, Italy's toe. Julius said:

'I had a strange thought last night. Here stands a soldier who never expected to be converted to the faith. What could happen to one pagan Roman could happen to many. And Rome, without knowing it, makes things easy with her roads and her sealanes between province and province. We never know the true purpose of what we do. An empire maintained without swords. I suppose it's a preposterous idea.'

Paul said: 'We're all instruments. My great desire was to go to Rome – voluntarily, a free instrument of the faith. Yet I come to Rome in chains.' He did not mean that literally, though he knew that real chains were waiting for him, a kind of decorative symbol of an appellant's bondage to the law.

'They mean nothing. You're still a free voice. A prisoner who converted his jailor. Could anything be more improbable?'

'What will happen in Rome? How will my case be judged? How long must I wait? What will be the outcome?'

'If you want my opinion, the case will go by default for absence of accusers. You'll be a sort of prisoner still. But then the courts will wash their hands of you.'

'Yes. That happened before. Very ominous, this talk of judges washing their hands.' Julius did not understand. A south wind rose after one day in Rhegium and bore them towards Puteoli, the main port of the south, well sheltered in the bay of Neapolis. Their ship was one of the Alexandrian grain fleet. It had precedence in the crowd of mercantile vessels that crammed the roads. They had to strike their topsails or *suppara*, the wheat ships not. It was a sign watched for from the quays. *The Heavenly Twins* eased into its moorings. 'Italy,' Paul said, unnecessarily. Luke too looked at Italy, less impressed: he was a provincial Greek but still a Greek. The quay was busy, and the work of the loaders and unloaders, the port officials with their manifests, seemed somehow obstructed by the great statue of the Emperor as the seagod, pointing his trident out at the bay. But the plinth of the high bronze edifice was home to the beggars and the women who sold bruised fruit. The gangplank was lowered. Julius's troop waited for his orders. Julius said:

'I have to report to the office of the *frumentarii*. Then we have a long march.'

'Is there time to contact the local Christians?'

Julius was apologetic. 'I'm afraid you have to stay with the rest of the prisoners. We march you in chains and the march starts soon. You can't go into the town, I'm afraid.'

'I can,' Luke said. Whereas most of his fellow voyagers had lost weight, Luke seemed to have put on quiet muscle and his neck had grown somehow taurine. It was as if he had to show these Romans what a Greek kin of Odysseus, who had also been shipwrecked, was supposed to look like. 'There's a bunch of Jews over there. They'll know.' There was indeed a group of bearded men in striped robes, flashing rings in the sun as they chaffered over carpets and ingots.

Elders of the Neapolitan faithful took the Appian Way with Paul, his fellow prisoners, the military escort. Paul said: 'One must always question motives. A slave becomes a Christian because he has no hope from this life. He dreams of a heavenly kingdom, a kind of perpetual soothing bath with somebody handing him grapes. He has nothing to lose, everything to gain. I'm more encouraged to hear of the rich giving all to the poor, men in high places risking all, even the Emperor's displeasure. What's the official attitude?'

Old Simon, whose family had come to Neapolis from Galilee at a time unrecorded, stroked his brown beard and said: 'The faith is tolerated. Chiefly because it's mainly a faith of the poor. There are absurd stories about our cannibalism and incest. We set ourselves free from the constraints of civilized society – so men like to believe. I foresee danger.'

'When?'

'Every society has to have an outcast minority to blame – for floods, famine, low wages, the rheumatism of the praetorian prefect. The priests of Rome don't like to see defectors from the worship of the old gods. Conservative senators grumble about unroman activities. It's still a faith of upper rooms, cellars, dark corners. But it germinates.' They had reached Appii Forum. 'Those look like members of the Roman church. The message got to them – how, God knows.' There was indeed a knot with welcoming arms, and not all Jews by the look of them. And there, their agedness a mirror of his own ageing, were Aquila and his wife Priscilla. They had come in a cart drawn by an old donkey. Aquila said:

'In the Tiber, you remember? God, man, you're in chains. Why?'

The Roman faithful, being, after all, of the metropolis, were greeted with both deference and resentment by the Neapolitan faithful. It was after all, to the Romans that Paul had written three years back, promising a fiery and loving visit sometime, not to the Neapolitans. But Simon and his contingent, politely taking wine with them all and Paul at a waterside tavern, the soldiers standing aloof and wondering with their wondering jailmeat, affirmed Italian Christian unity before being glad to take the road back. The road forward brought Paul and the Romans to the place called Tres Tabernae where, in fact, there were five taverns and more joyous Christian Romans waiting. Julius was divided: what was he – an official of the state or one of this exuberant party, mostly Jewish, extravagant in gesture, full of jocular buffetings and smacking kisses? He decided that he would not properly be a Christian until he had told his wife, and that would not be until the morning after their reunion. She might be annoyed, derisive, indifferent. It made no difference: a man's soul was not his wife's property as his body was.

They entered Rome by the Porta Capena, and Julius marched his prisoners to the Caelian hill, headquarters of the *stratopedarch* or *princeps peregrinorum*, who was in charge of the imperial couriers. The criminals were sent to jail pending trial; Paul, pending his hearing, had a young soldier literally attached to him by means of a thin long chain and then was told to find his own lodgings. He knew where he was going to stay: with Aquila and Priscilla in the Suburra district. Julius saluted him, Paul sketched a blessing. They would see each other again soon. Meanwhile Julius would himself, on the orders of the princeps, deposit the procuratorial papers concerning Paul with the imperial legal department. Paul dragged his soldier to the Vicus Longus and introduced him to his host and hostess:

'This young man is Sabinus. He finds this chain as embarrassing as I do, but the law is the law. I understand that you'll receive a lodging allowance if you'll take him in. Sabinus, these are Jews. Do you have any objection?'

'All one to me,' in the Greek of Calabria. 'But I don't like Jewish cooking. I'll cook my own rations.'

'Back to the old trade,' Paul said.

'Not tents here,' Aquila said. 'Canopies. Much more delicate.'

The elders of the unreformed faith were quick to visit him. He sat chained to gawping Sabinus, who understood not one word of Aramaic, while he told them his situation: 'Brothers, I did nothing against the Jewish faith or the Jewish people, yet I was delivered a prisoner from Jerusalem into the hands of the Romans at Caesarea. The Romans set me free because they found no cause of death in me. But the chief men of Jerusalem were against me, and I was forced to appeal to Caesar. I have to make it clear that I have nothing against my nation. I'm in chains, as you see, or rather bound with a chain because of the hope of Israel.'

The rabbi Ishmael said: 'We hear nothing against you. We received no letters from Jerusalem. None of the brethren has come to me with reports or accusations. All I know is that the sect you lead is spoken against. From your own mouth we would wish to hear why this is so.'

'Or rather – why it should *not* be spoken against. Very well. Listen.'

While still chained to Sabinus, Paul performed a number of baptisms in the Tiber, the river not running strong at that season. Luke, who had set himself up in the physicians' quarter off the Via Lata, came to help. Good pagan Roman citizens watched the ceremony and spoke bad words: *Cannibals, motherswivers, defiling Father Tiber with their uncleanliness, disgusting I call it.* Sabinus said: 'Listen, friends. I'm his official escort, got that? Imperial orders. Interfere with him and you interfere with me. Now bugger off.'

'I baptize you, Aquila, in the name of the Most High, the Son who proceeds from him, the Holy Spirit that proceeds from both. To the new life of that Spirit you are now admitted.'

Argument was hot most evenings in the house of Aquila. Sara, who had accepted her husband's conversion with a shrug, was nevertheless curious to see Paul, as was her brother, who still called him Saul. She shocked the Christians if not the Jews by saying:

'God forgives all sins, you tell us. What I want to know is – who forgives God?' Neither Luke nor Julius had read the Book of Job. 'A good God wouldn't have allowed what happened to my sister. An innocent girl torn to pieces by a madman while all stood by and saw it. I stood by, Julius stood by, but, most of all, God stood by. God looks after his own, does he? God has never yet looked after his own. The Israelites call him *abba* – father – only to be kicked in the teeth.' Paul said:

'God gave man freedom – for evil or good. A terrible gift but also a glorious gift. God will not interfere with the freedom of his creatures. For good or ill. There is much suffering still to come – for Jews, for Christians, for those who profess no faith. History is a record of human suffering. God knows it, and yet God will not interfere.'

'But,' the rabbi Ishmael said, 'according to your belief he *did* interfere. He sent down his son – blasphemy, blasphemy – to enter the stream of human life – meaning (oh, blasphemy) that he came down himself.'

'To die, to suffer, but to rise again. Human evil does not prevail for ever. Death at the hands of human evil is itself a victory, for if a thing does not die it cannot rise again. We share birth with the animal creation. Resurrection we share with God.'

'I cannot accept it. None of us can.'

Paul spoke up. The parting of the ways. 'The Holy Spirit spoke through the prophet Isaiah, and the Spirit spoke well. "Go to this people, and say: By hearing you shall hear, and shall in no wise understand. And seeing you shall see, and shall in no wise perceive. For this people's heart is gross, and their eyes are shut, and their ears stuffed with wax. They do not wish to perceive with their eyes and hear with their ears and understand with their hearts. Be it known therefore that this salvation of God is sent to the Gentiles: the Gentiles will hear." Brothers, strangers rather, the Gentiles have already heard.'

'I think,' the rabbi said, '*we* have heard enough. I think there is little point in staying to hear more.' Courteously enough they bade the company good night, these courteous honest Jews set in their way of living in a state of unfulfillable expectation. Paul felt deeply depressed.

Julius was summoned, still in his uniform but in a state of official suspension, waiting for discharge, terminal leave and the piece of land that could be converted into cash, to the office of the jurists Holconius Priscus and Vettius Proculus. These were old men learned in Roman law and they were brisk to elucidate the legal position of Lucius Shoel Paulus or Paullus.

'That Shoel has a fine exotic ring. Where is he now?'

'Under a kind of house arrest,' Julius said. 'A chain on his wrist. Awaiting your lordships' pleasure.'

'The Emperor's pleasure. The pleasure of the people of Rome. Already detained at that pleasure for – how many years?'

'Two and a half. That goes beyond the statutory period for bringing an action.'

'No. His status has changed. He's an appellant to the state. The period begins from the moment of his appeal – when was it lodged?'

'Over a year ago.'

'No record of any accusation being brought here in Rome. Not yet. One more month. If nothing happens we file a writ of *Liberetur*.'

We come now to an episode possibly apocryphal, though my informants were very circumstantial and most corroborative in their accounts of it. It seems that the Emperor Nero was in the district of Suburra in daylight and in disguise – that is to say bewigged – having called on the sorceress Locusta (still flourishing and too discreet not to be so) about a matter of giving an immediate and painless quietus to the Empress's ailing pet panther (this story you need not, of course, elieve). His guardsmen were also in disguise, meaning cloaked and their daggerhands cloaked too, and they kept their distance from their master five yards behind and ahead. Tigellinus was not with his master, nor was Gaius Petronius who, fearing Tigellinus for some reason, was writing on his estate ten miles down the Via Ostiensis. Nero seemed to remember a particular shop: surely water had been poured on him from that roof there? Who had had the effrontery to do it? It had given him a slight chill and he had not forgotten. He did not propose punishment, which would be an unworthy thing as, after all, he had been dissimulating his status at the time and accepted what came in the way of buffets (a citizen of the equestrian order had beaten him for molesting his wife and with total impunity) as part of the game. Indeed, he looked at the shop with some respect and then with some curiosity. A very old man was stitching away at what looked like sailcloth, and an oldish bald one was working on a recognizable bed canopy. Chained to this one was a Roman soldier. 'What is this?' he wished to know.

'Who asks?' asked the bald stitcher. Nero said:

'No ceremony, please. Caesar sometimes likes to walk among his people.' And he doffed his wig. The two workers recognized a face omnipresent on coins and medallions and started to rise. 'I said no ceremony. Be seated. Though that soldier there may remain on his feet. Have you a cup of something cooling for your Emperor?' Thus it was that Paul, who was still an appellant to an abstraction called Caesar, met Caesar face to face and was encouraged to talk to him.

'A Christian, you say, a Christian? A dangerous sect and an unnatural one, so I'm led to believe.'

'A *religio licita*, Caesar. You will find that in the imperial records.'

'Cannibals, indulgers in unnatural acts of love, is that not so?'

'Unnatural love is expressly forbidden. As for cannibalism, we do not eat little children, as is too often alleged. We eat merely the body and blood of the Son of God under the disguise of bread and wine. A harmless ceremony which promotes solidarity and has a wholesome mystical meaning.'

'The son of which god?'

'There is only one God, Caesar. His simple nature is fracted and diversified under various forms that pass for divine among the Greeks and the Romans. When you think of Zeus or Jupiter you are trying to grasp one aspect only of this single simple God's essence. The God we believe in made the world and loves it, made man and loves him. He is

303

a highly moral God, detesting evil and approving the good.'

'What should morality have to do with divinity?'

'God is of a radiant purity who wishes his creation to attain to a like purity. The smallest sin makes his purity scream out with pain.'

'That is absurd.'

'No, Caesar. His infinite perfection must of necessity be appalled by evil.'

'What do you mean by evil?'

'Acts of destruction, of corruption, of selfishness.'

'And by good?'

'Love of our fellows, even of our enemies, acts which demonstrate that love.'

'But it's impossible to love one's enemies.'

'Difficult, Caesar, but we have to try. It's a way of turning our enemies into friends.'

'A way of life, then, rather like that ridiculous stoical one the illstarred Seneca taught me.'

'No, Caesar. We live the virtuous life in order that we may be worthy of standing in the presence of God.'

'How?'

'In the next world. After death. The good attain the divine vision and the evil are cast away from it. Their pain consists in knowing what they miss. It is like a million fires burning them for ever and ever.'

'And all this was taught you by a slave?'

'No, Caesar, that is another error. God so loves his creation that he was willing to come to earth and live like a man. He taught us, yes, and he was punished for teaching us, strange as that must seem. He was nailed to a tree in Judaea and died. But he rose again from the tomb.'

'Stuff and nonsense. Dead men don't rise again. Or women.' Having affirmed that he nevertheless shuddered.

'There were too many witnesses, some of them still living, Caesar. He was seen after death. His resurrection bids us believe in our own. The righteous rise again after death. So do the wicked. Both are judged. The sheep are separated from the goats. Eternal bliss or eternal fire. We take our choice. We are free to do so.'

'So you people see death as a gateway to a better life. If you have been good.'

'Caesar puts it simply and well.'

'The destruction of the body is nothing?'

'Painful perhaps, but acceptable – more than acceptable to the just.'

'*Una nox dormienda*. We're taught to believe that. That is what I believe.'

'Catullus was wrong, Caesar. The being destroyed rises to a greater beauty. The pagan legend of the phoenix is an apt illustration. The thing must die in order to rise again. We sow in death, we reap in life. Death is no problem.'

'All you tell me – what is your name?'

'Paul, Caesar.'

'All you tell me, Paul, sounds like a negation of life. No wonder there are some who fear you and even more who despise you.'

'We accept that, Caesar. To be vilified, to suffer execution for the sake of the faith – what happened to the Son of God is not to be feared by mere men and women.'

'The phoenix, eh? To perish and to rise again. To burn grey, then to burn gold. And what does this Son of God you speak of decree for Caesar, who is not like ordinary men?'

'Caesar as flesh, blood, bone and spirit must face divine judgment like the rest. Caesar as a ruler must be obeyed. "Render unto Caesar the things that are Caesar's, and to God the things that are God's." '

'And if it be considered that Caesar is above God?'

'The made cannot be greater than the maker. There is nothing above God.'

'If,' Nero said, 'there is what you call an eternal maker, there ought to be an eternal destroyer.'

'God has his enemy, Caesar. What you say is well said. The story goes that God's most beautiful angel Lucifer the lightbringer rebelled against God's rule and was cast from God's presence. God could not destroy him, because God is committed to creation. God could not prevent this evil one from being committed to destruction, because God made his creatures totally free. So evil stalks the world, but evil cannot eventually win. Good is too powerful.'

'This sounds as if your God wills himself to impotence.'

'A measure of his love, Caesar.'

'Interesting.' Nero got up to go. 'If I accepted your religion – No, please remain seated – I would have to be good. But an emperor cannot always afford to be good. He cannot love his enemies. It is regrettable but unavoidable that he should have to destroy them. A ruler is forced into what you would call the commission of evil.'

'There's always forgiveness, Caesar. God forgives everything. God responds at once to the least gesture of repentance. God, as I told you, is good.'

'And yet he throws people into fire and emptiness or whatever it was you said?'

'No. The sinner throws himself into the fire. Choice, Caesar, is free to all. To slaves and to Caesar alike. Even Caesar is free to live the good life. A life that is no more than a shadowy preparation for the true life which begins with the death of the righteous. But,' and now it was as if he were thumping away at the Ephesians, 'if we identify ourselves with the fallen forces of destruction, then be in no doubt as to the nature of that ultimate punishment. For, though the body dies, the body rises in a transfigured form for bliss or for punishment, whichever we ourselves choose. Punishment, Caesar – loss, darkness, emptiness filled with pain greater than the pain of fire for ever and ever. Not even an emperor is exempt from the logic of his own acts. As a man sows –' And he bent to a different sewing. Nero felt himself to be dismissed. He said:

'And the first step to the faith?'

'Baptism, Caesar. The washing away of past sins.'

'Washing?'

'In water, water transfigured into a sign of redemption.'

'Ordinary water?'

The old man who had been stitching canvas looked uncomfortable. Nero nodded, put on his wig, sketched a kind of confused imperial blessing, then left. He walked rather shakily towards the Imperial Forum, his cloaked guards before and behind. An old woman in a shawl turned and grinned at him. It was Agrippina with blackened teeth, her hair scorched, back from that place. Hell. And then it was not. There was no need for his mother to come back in brief visitations from the outer blackness. Nor Britannicus. Nor Octavia. Nor all the others whose names he had forgotten. The vision of fiery emptiness was probably enough. Stain the illimitable candour of eternal beauty or goodness or whatever it was with splashes of crimson. The pure white screams aloud in pure white pain.

It might be said that Paul sowed certain notions in the mind of his Emperor. That there was an ultimate creator seemed totally logical, maker of Jupiter and Apollo and Mars and Priapus and the rest of the comic pseudopantheon: it always had seemed so, having much to do with the deathless principle of beauty. But that there should be an eternal principle of goodness and an everlasting system of reward and punishment was not so acceptable. Seneca had droned on about it or something like it, but he had never propounded the possibility of an elected damnation. Nero found it easy enough to see this as eternal fire. He saw it: an eternally blazing city full of the screams of the blazing. But the property of destruction which did not destroy was hard to accept. It seemed more logical to pass from earthly time to a region which might be termed parachronic but not achronic: the fire could burn out guilt and the purged being rise from it to the purity of the eternal vision: beauty, the Platonic idea of it personalized, deified into a kind of work of art that moved and breathed as a deathless organic being, never ending music that offered also a never ending act of love. Absurd perhaps. Certainly indeed absurd. There was time and there was not time. In not time you went to bliss or to eternal punishment. Nero did not at all like the notion that there were in his Empire perhaps thousands who already had an image of him, the Emperor, burning in hell. For ever and ever. While slaves with names like Felix and Chrestus leered down at his fiery screaming from a cool abode that was all poetry and music. It was not right, it was not just, it was a situation of *laesa maiestas* and he was not going to have it. Rid yourself of the believers and you were rid of the belief. He saw the fire and then, through the grace granted only to the artist, he saw the phoenix rising from it. That was different, that was encompassable. And then again he saw the pure illimitable candour. It was offended. It screamed and its scream filled eternity. It was all nonsense.

Tigellinus thought so too. 'Goodness. The *summum bonum*. Each man has his own. Each living thing has its own. There is no single *summum bonum*. What is the *summum bonum* of the hungry lion? The lunge at the throat of the helpless hind. Goodness as divine order? Balderdash. Order is expediency. Order is a dead body. For the common people it means tomorrow being no worse than today. The exceptional *break* order in order to see the blinding light. You don't understand me? The sharp truth of pleasure in the act of outrage. Tonight, say, we deflower the Vestal Virgins –'

'Oh no.'

'Oh no? A new thing and a shocking thing. The fires of another power breaking out of the destructive act. A door into a reality the generality of men cannot know. Only through certain modes of destruction can the new visions be attained.' He paused, then he said: 'We didn't build the Empire on notions of tolerance and brotherly love. And yet is not the Empire the greatest good the world has ever seen? There are forces ready to break it not through action but through inaction. Love one another, and that means those unwashed tribes on the Rhine and the Danube. Let's have them in, taking Rome, toppling the gods. The Jews, the Chrestus people – they'd let it happen.' And then: 'The Empress is too friendly with the Jews.'

'She'll get money out of them yet. Rome needs Jewish money.'

'She doesn't want Jewish money. She's fascinated by their dark eyes and olive skin and their sexual knowledge and magic handed down by their desert prophets. The child she is carrying is certainly not yours.'

Nero, enraged, hit out and left red ringmarks on Tigellinus's left leathery cheek. 'That's outrageous. That's treasonable.' Tigellinus always found it a good thing to see how far he could go. Then, as now, he prudently drew back.

'I'm probably wrong. My devotion to Caesar is such that I sometimes see harm where there is none. Think no more of it. She's an estimable lady. I beg pardon for my unworthy suspicions.'

That night Nero's dreams were, as so often, of the next world, whose geography, climate and social organization had been clearly defined by the epic poets. A thin place that lacked blood. He, Caesar, joined the thin phantoms. There was no rancour among ancient enemies. It was not a question of love or forgiveness. There was just not enough blood to feed the violent emotions of the living. Then he saw another next world and there was nothing thin or bloodless about it. Fire. Nerves strung like lyrestrings to the snapping point but unable to snap. Pain. The snow, maddened by its defilement, screamed. Nero screamed and liberated himself from the dream. That damned Christian.

That damned Christian was informed that the writ of *Liberetur* had gone through. He and Sabinus were no longer chained to each other. Paul, having spoken to the faithful, many of them newly created in Tiber water, on the Esquiline, Caelian, Viminal, Aventine and Quirinal hills, and even on the Campus Martius, made ready to sail for Spain, ample travel money clanking at his girdle. A large crowd attended him on the quay at Puteoli – Jews, Gentiles, patricians, slaves, the *miles* Sabinus – and some wept, emotional lability being a property of the temperament of the peninsula. Luke told Paul he had come to the end of his story and had had ten copies made by professional scriveners. He needed a dedicatee, some fictional personage who might be imagined as requiring elementary instruction in the faith and the spread of the faith. 'Any lover of God,' Paul said. He grinned. 'To the Emperor? No.'

'I've become rather friendly with one of my patients – a poet named Gaius Petronius. Sincerely interested. He's read my little book with flattering avidity. A former friend of Caesar's, looking for the light he says. Call me Theophilus.'

'Theophilus will do. Theophilus could be anyone.'

Embraces, kisses, tears, women's wailings. A song, pagan but appropriate: 'Come back again, come back.' Paul waved from the deck as his ship, bound for the Spanish port built by Hamilcar Barca, nudged its way out of the throng of shipping. He noted distractedly another ship easing its way in. An old gnarled man with an unkempt beard sat on a coil of rope on that ship, distractedly watching Paul's ship ease its way out. 'And where would that be off to?' A sailor told him. 'Aye, it's a big empire they have. A big world altogether. I've seen little enough of it.'

'I thought you'd been in this line yourself. You know the knots and the tackle.'

'Boats on Galilee lake. Mending nets. Fish. My line.'

So Peter came hesitantly down the gangplank, a knotted bundle on his shoulder and in his gripe a roughly cut stick of blackthorn. He was old and unwell and he had to get to Rome, wherever that was. There were a lot of people around, Jews, Gentiles, who seemed as though they might be Nazarenes, but they chattered in Latin or Greek, languages he had never learnt, and it was too late now. But *'Rum?'* he asked a lounging dockworker, who pointed vaguely. All roads led to, they said. After an aching mile or so he came to what was called the Appian Way. Much traffic passed him – nobility or gentry in litters, slaves carrying bundles under the lash, maniples of sweating troops under barked orders. Covered in dust, he hobbled to the roadside and sat under a tree of a kind he did not know – beech, pine, plane? He ached, his joints creaked. He should have stayed in Joppa but James was urgent about this mission. The man he had to see in Rome was named Linus, a Graeco-Roman or something, a real foreigner but a Nazarene. Had to see him, and they didn't speak each other's language. Peter whimpered to himself. There was a ship leaving for Caesarea in a few days, and he had the money for the fare: the Jerusalem brethren had given him more than he needed. There was a curious sense in Jerusalem of things moving away, closing down, of the faith losing ground, of apostasies and a general slackness. It was all a matter of the Jews and the Romans now. The Nazarenes were outside it all, preaching peace when all the talk was of an impending struggle. Peter hungered for Joppa, where he combined leadership of the local church with membership of a fishing syndicate. But he was head of the *whole* church: he had been told that a long time ago. Not James. The man Saul who became Paul had been given no real instructions, and it was he who, with his fine Hebrew and Greek and Latin, had seemed to regard himself as in charge. He, Peter, was the rock, scared of cocks crowing, scared of his own dreams, his limbs weak and his head fuddled. From his scrip he drew the comfort of some dried fish and bread and a little flask he had filled at the fountain near the docks, spring water gushing from the grinning gob of a creature with horns in dull metal. He had to go on and would when he was rested. The dream he had had on shipboard had been as clear and as sunlit as that old one about goatmilk and pigs and lobsters which had caused so much trouble. He dreamed he sat under a tree like this and then made up his mind to go back to the port and wait for the ship back to Caesarea. Good summer weather and plain sailing. And then *he* appeared, *he*, jauntily carrying a crosspiece on his immense shoulders, smiling at Peter and shaking his head as if at his foolishness, crowing briefly like a cock and jauntily lightfooting it Romewards. That meant that he, Peter, had to go too, though on heavier feet. He sighed, rose, set himself to trudging north, seeing a foreign sun go down and a dangerous foreign night coming on with strange slowness, then he settled himself under trees, wrapped in his cloak, hearing owls and other

309

tsiporim of the *laylah*, including one that poured out song as if its heart would break. He saw known stars but felt desperately homesick. The wrong man. He had always felt that.

But he trudged another day and another. Nobody spoke to him. He bought food at stalls by pointing. At the place where the taverns stood he heard what sounded at first like Aramaic but turned out to be some other tongue, Phoenician probably. On his brain he had imprinted a name and a vague location. Linus. A fountain on a street near the Via Labicana to the east of the city. At length he saw the outskirts of a great town, bigger than Jerusalem, playing hide and seek with him through a grove of what he took to be pines. He asked a donkeydriver at once for the Via Labicana, but the man laughed at him and made wide arm gestures. A long long way away. He slept another night under trees. Hot dry weather, perfect for sailing home. In a morning that began faint green and oystershell with eventual gilding, he ate the breakfast he had bought of an overyeasted loaf and a half pint of thin and acid wine. He took breath and, under a company of quarrelling crows, limped towards the city.

Breathtaking. Not a place for him. There was the faint smell of the brutality of nobody caring for anybody else. Via Labicana? An old woman emptying a bucket into the gutter of a street that was a dark valley to toppling tenements could not at first understand him. She pointed. He was no wiser. So people lived here, climbing stair after stair in order to dry their wet garments on the sills. And hurrying down, chewing hasty bread, to go to work. Everybody had to work.

He walked squinting towards a sun still low on the horizon. He looked for fountains, finding one in every piazza, Rome's benison of spring water to its citizens. Women were up early washing clothes, filling buckets to carry up all those stairs, though some ingenious families hoisted them by rope and pulley to the windowsills. There was quarrelling, very Jewish, with arms raised to heaven, over the price of the fish that a vendor slapped on his handbarrow. Peter asked a woman with a dribbling child on her hip his one-word question. She understood, a small morning miracle, and pointed.

The same question again as he mounted in pain the many worn steps of the tenement. Linus? *Sum Linus, ego.* A youngish swarthy man, beardless, rather bald, looked down the stairwell. *Petrus*, Peter said panting, at least knowing his own name. He went up. Petrus the piscator in Rome, entering a single room seven storeys up, seeing a bed and a table and a dead oilstove. The two Nazarenes or Christiani looked at each other, a faith in common but no tongue. But Linus offered yesterday's bread, watered wine, some cold thin slices of veal, garlic. He remembered something belatedly: he went down on his knees for Peter's blessing. Then he went out for an interpreter. Peter was left looking at a tableload of scrolls, all in Latin. He looked for a place to void water, not fancying a trip down (and a struggle up again) to look for a public latrine. He found a bucket behind a curtain and emptied, with some little pain but more relief, his old bladder. Soon Linus came back with a young Roman Jew who was popularly known as Canis because of his bark. His real name was Shadrach ben Hananiah but he was used to Canis, call me Canis. It comforted Peter to hear his own speech again, the accent not far off the Galilean. He said:

'Peter, head of the faithful, appointed by Christ. You are the man I was sent to see. What, by the way, is your trade?'

'I work for a publisher of pagan books. Poetry, history. I copy. I am a good copyist. Why am I the man?'

'James in Jerusalem showed me your letters. I couldn't read them, nor could he, but there were some who could and they made translations. Rome is to be the mother. A mother, James said, hiding behind the skirts of a whore.'

'Why me?'

'Right, I come to Rome, appointed father of the faithful but a fool who knows neither Greek nor Latin. But I'm old and it won't be long for me. Age or the axe will do for me. I have dreams just as James does. He sees it all over there, and I think he's right. The man Paul saw it too and he's right, though I fought against it. But you won't know this man Paul.'

'Oh yes. He wrote a letter to Rome then he came to Rome. He's been gone less than a week. Oh yes, I met Paul. Remarkable man.'

'But not one of the twelve,' Peter said. 'A Jew who found no luck with the Jews. Well, so he was here. And now he's gone.'

'He'll be back, he promised. What you say disturbs me. We look to the mother church in Jerusalem. Rome is just another pagan city.'

'Two faiths in Jerusalem,' Peter said, 'and they can't live together. It was a faith for the Jews we taught, but it wasn't a faith that taught rebellion and bloodshed. The Romans have played into the hands of the Zealots. Slack, corrupt, cruel. There has to come a breaking point. This Nero you have here has let things collapse all over. Now the Jerusalem Jews want to get in and drive out the Romans. They think Rome will do nothing about it, and they may be right. But they don't want the Nazarenes with their peace and love and strike the other cheek. Look, it's obvious when you come to think of it. The faith has become a faith for the Gentiles. Some day the Gentiles will teach the Jews, but not yet. None of us ever thought it would be like that. And here you have the centre of the big Gentile Empire. This is where the mother church has to be. And you its first true father.'

'I'm totally unworthy.'

311

'No. You're a Roman. You know Rome. It's your city.'

'A Greek in fact. But long in Rome.'

'Right, you know the Rome of the streets and the squares and the fountains. And the Rome of the cellars and the dark places.'

'We practise the faith in the sunlight. We've no need of the dark places.'

Peter shook his head several times. 'No. You'll be glad of the dark places. I can feel it coming. Smash the Jews for revolting and smash the Nazarenes while you're about it, the Nazarenes being only a kind of Jews.'

'That's not true any more.'

'I know it's not true. I know only too well it's not true. Something went wrong somewhere.'

'This is a great moment for us, your coming here. You must speak to the church.'

'In Aramaic?'

'The language of the master, the authentic voice. Heavens, it's still hard to take in. You knew him, worked with him, saw him crucified in that place, on that hill –'

'Golgotha. No, I wasn't there. God help me, I wasn't there.'

The meeting was held in a disused gymnasium, not far from the Garden of Maecenas and the Mansion of Aulus, at the corner of the Via Labicana and the Via Tiburtina. Some of the Roman Christians were Jews and remembered their Aramaic; most of them were uncircumcised, some fairhaired; some were of the patrician class. The Gentiles looked with a little awe and a certain contempt hard to hide on this unkempt ancient, a pioneer from the mists, unable to explicate the mystery of the Trinity or relate the coming of the Messiah to an obscure prophecy in Vergil's *Eclogues*, talking about the genesis of the Paternoster in a remote and uncouth tongue: 'For Jesus himself taught me this prayer, me and my companions, common fisherfolk, when we were fishing in the lake of Galilee. A storm arose and we were afraid, but he told us never to feel fear. We must trust in the father who keeps us in his care, praying: 'Our father, who are in heaven, may your name be blessed . . .' They joined in, some in Greek, most in Latin. But the Gentiles were all a little embarrassed.

When the meeting broke up after the blessing and munching of the sacramental bread, those whose sense of smell was well developed sniffed at smoke coming from the south on a hot dry wind from the south. Peter could smell nothing.

Nobody knows how the fire began, but there are still some who swear they saw Tigellinus setting a brand to an oilshop all of dry wood just north of the Servilian Gardens on the Aventine. Nearly all the dwellings there were of wood and, in that dry summer's night heat, it was pure tinder. Accius owned the oilshop but did not live in it. Seeing it blaze from his door fifty yards away, he yelled for men to draw buckets from the fountain, to form a bucketempying chain, but the yellow and blue tongues licked the water and asked for more. The heat brought sweat and the sweat blinded. Black flinders gyrated in the fiery air like bats. The fire climbed the hill and crunched the pines, ate the wooden summer house of Lucius Aemilius and grew fat on it. The family of C. Aeserninus was trapped in its small brick mansion when the fire entered and climbed the stairs, eating as it went. A child was thrown in mother's panic from an upper casement and was brained on the stone surround. In District XI on the borders of the Tiber the tenements near the Circus Maximus sang a blazing song to high heaven, invisible in the smoke, and the hundred families within fought each other with claws out, coughing more than screaming, as they blocked the stairwell. Those who survived the desperate tearing saw the fire coming in for them at the main tenement entrance. Some yelled their way through it and then ran till they dropped, having turned into fire. The black flakes danced and rode on the wind and dissolved like black snowflakes into the river, what time men waded in the river with their canvas buckets and passed up water which was a mere dandelion in the jaws of a cow. A warehouse near the crossing of the Via Ostiensis and the Via Latina was crammed with jars of olive oil which burst their stoppers or cracked in the flames and sent out a fiery aromatic river with squeaking rats swimming on it, tails little torches, pelts singed. The library of the Aequiculi on the Aventine was housed in marble, but fire was puffed in through a casement whose wooden shutters were speedily devoured, and then a treasury of Greek and Roman history was a swift meal like frozen fruit juice to the thirsty jaws of the gang of flame. The librarian Bogudes made a longer snack, but he joined his manuscripts in ashes.

The fire spread east as well as north, as far as the Caelian. The Temple of the Divine Claudius was the core of a terrible conflagration in which the houses of priests and augurs went up in spite of prayers that the flapping of the flames drowned. Men and women in undress or full dress blackened and smoking at the hems ran the streets moaning, carrying household treasures of no value. The Temple of Isis seemed to put out a hand of Egyptian magic to forbid the passage of fire further to the east; it was obeyed. To the north of the city, in the area enclosed by the Pantheon, the Mausoleum of Augustus and the Castra Urbana, fire raged that seemed to owe nothing to the colonizing zeal of the scarlet empire to the south, for the Baths of Agrippa, the Temple of Jupiter, and the headquarters of the city vigiles were a zone untouched by even the tips of the fingers of the terror.

Pagan Romans, those who had sat with their gristly sausages and skins of watered wine howling for the real red at the games, stacked and ranked in a semblance of mock civic order, were now thousands of ants scurrying from the fist dinged and dinged and dinged again on their hills. What do we care about them, Canus and Capys and the Casca brothers, Cestius and Crassus and Domitilla and Fausta and Augusta and the dancing girls just in from Alexandria, Polla and Vettius, the brothel madam Omphale, Macro and Marius, the Salnatores and Livius and Livilla and? Little, since we do not know them. But Caleb and his wife Hannah and their son Yacob we have at least met. They were tenement dwellers in the north of District XII, with two rooms on the fifth floor. They were in bed, and they woke to strange light and heat and noise. 'The skies are on fire!' Hannah screamed, and she grasped the sleeping boy. In their night attire they fell over each other to the door and saw men and women scampering, all tangled hair and bare legs, down the stairway, children clutched and howling. Caleb ordered his wife to stay behind him, clutching his robe with one hand and their son with the other, as he proceeded brutally to fist his way through the gasping and coughing throng that grew thicker at each new landing of the stairway, all eager to crush each other and be crushed and then to be eaten by the flames that waited at the great door of the tenement building. 'Now!' Caleb cried, and they thrust down to the second landing, clawed back at, clutched, bleeding. In the wall was an open casement and beneath it a clutch of young arbutus well lighted by flames from the left but itself as yet untouched. 'Now!' he yellcoughed, then he leapt out to the air. The bush broke his fall and he stood barefoot on hot earth. 'Throw him!' She threw the child blindly, and Caleb as he caught him had no time to be puzzled that the boy was not a yelling wheel of limbs but strangely still as though sleeping through it all. He placed the child on the ground while Hannah hurled herself at his arms from the high window. He caught her. She picked up Yacob. The boy bled heavily from the head. Was that bare bone showing through? She could not scream, only cough her heart out at the hidden heavens. They ran with the body south and hardly stopped till they reached the triple junction of the Via Ardeatina, the Via Latina and the Via Appia. Here there was no fire, only a huddle of moaning mourning bereft.

Marcus Julius Tranquillus and his wife and daughter were safe on the Janiculum, as most of the Christians were safe on the Viminal and Esquiline. The Jews had suffered down there in Districts XII and XIII, their shops ruined, cheap wooden houses charcoal fringed with fire sated. Those on the outskirts of the fire on the Caelian saw Rome burn to the northwest, the Palatine too. Some, looting, were drunk and saw more. Julius Caesar marched a flaming legion through the streets,

Romulus and Remus sucked fire from the dugs of a wolf that was all fire, it was rumoured that the Tiber was all aflame with the oil that had rolled heavily into it from the store south of the Circus Flaminius. Jupiter rode a flaming winged bull over the flames, picking up gobbets of flame in his hands and hurling them high in joy. The Vestal Virgins held up flaming skirts to show flaming pudenda. Over the bridge that led from the Capitoline to the Naumachia Augusti the screaming ants scurried, with no eyes for the imperial barge moored to the Tiburine island just to their north. There the Emperor and his entourage watched the fire march and blare over the Circus Maximus to the Palatine, indifferently crunching and swallowing the fine parkland and the gorgeous palaces. Tigellinus said, deeply moved by the purple and gold majesty of the invading army of flame, that there was virtue in catastrophe, that now Rome, or Neropolis if that was to be its new name, had to be remade, even the Senate must see that. Nero said, trembling as if on the brief road to orgasm:

'There's no art like this. No music or lyric verse or tragedy like this. At last I see what I've only sung before. End of the second Troy, birthpangs of the third and last.' And he sang:

'Richly enrobed in the flames of her funeral,
Ilium yielded her limbs to the fingers of fire,
Lovingly, lustingly, cooing like columbines,
Roaring like lions and howling like wolves of the wood . . .'

But he felt the despair of even the major artist at the inadequacy of words. The huge smoke pall had blotted out stars and moon, the tiny smut bats flew in massive disorganized hordes, smoke choked, Rome was eaten steadily, the blackened marble not yielding but the hidden supports of wood chewed to nothing, the metal struts buckling in their white heat. And all the time, across the river, the screams and groans and manic coughing of a city that had suffered before as all cities must suffer but never before like this. Rome had had her fire watch for two hundred years, trained men with waterpumps in their station just west of the Via Lata, but the strong dry wind blew fire up at them from the south and they retreated hopeless. Only with the sudden shift of the wind to the northwest did it seem possible to shove the fire back from the threatened Forum and the northern edge of the Palatine. But it was too late for the rescue ladders and the damp blankets huge as fields in the stricken streets of the tenements. The citizens of Suburra, the Quirinal and the Esquiline came down with slow timidity to the Gardens of Maecenas and the fringe of what was to be the Domus Aurea to see those who had flung themselves north of the horror with a kind of sick wonder but also the desire to help, but they felt helpless in the face of maddened women with charred hair screaming over the charred bodies of their children. The smell of Rome had become the smell of a barber's singeing multiplied a manic millionfold.

Peter, whose new home was the shop of Aquila, since he could no longer face the climb to Linus's apartment, spoke of Sodom and Gomorrah, but the Gentiles did not comprehend the reference. It was the task of Christians to give aid to the stricken, but what help could they give except prayer? Those who lay stricken in the Gardens of Maecenas or in the streets in the triangle whose base was the Via Praenestina looked up in weak bewilderment to see an old bearded man with a staff raise spread fingers over them and mutter magic spells in an uncouth language. Luke the physician brought his scrip of ointments but stood impotent over hard dry blackened flesh beyond mere soothing. There was terrible thirst about and it could be slaked, but too often it was a viaticum before a sleep from which there was no rousing. Catullus strode glowing like a cinder muttering about *una nox dormienda*.

Dawn fought its way through the pall, which was drifting to the southeast. It would have been better if the night had continued, hiding the poor blackened corpses, the timbers whose dying glow could be roused to a brief curse of flame in the dawn breeze. The stench was insupportable, the black flinders flew languidly, burnt-out groves sent, in the stronger wind of full morning, flurries of skeletal leaves, substance eaten but veins miraculously whole. The nakedness brought a new obscenity: the city had cast off the clothes of its foliage to glory in the visible horror of its mutilation. For two days corpses lay untended for the rats to gnaw. In the dying smoke a smoky figure or two could be seen stumbling bowed over and through the ruins, searching and not finding or else, in crazed automatism, affirming life through aimless locomotion. On the third day the Senate called itself together and found some of its members missing. None knew where the Emperor was: it was rumoured that he had transferred himself and the remnant of his court to quarters in the Castra Praetoria. Gaius Calpurnius Piso was elected head of a small body of inquiry into the causes of the fire which still smouldered and occasionally flared. The group glumly trod rubble, jumped away from sudden disclosures of healthy flame beneath it, put togas over noses in the presence of black cadavers. On the Aventine they met, as they thought they might, Tigellinus and a maniple of Praetorians. He was waiting for Caesar. Who arrived in a litter. With him was the Empress, clearly pregnant. Piso introduced himself, stating the Senate's business.

' – And, of course, to supervise the provision of places of refuge for the unfortunate victims.'

'I know you, Piso, don't think I don't. You rebuked me in the Senate for various derelictions whose nature I can't clearly remember. Can nobody do anything about this stench? See, the Empress is being made sick by it all.' A senator made a token gesture of waving the stink away. 'Well,' Nero said, 'as to the homeless, poor souls, your Emperor has already made certain arrangements. The imperial gardens are at their disposal, and carpenters and tentmakers are already providing temporary shelters. Also, of course, the Campus Martius is being made ready for housing what I fear must be an incomputable number of sick and homeless. Messengers have been sent to Ostia to bring in emergency supplies. Things are being taken care of. Did you anticipate otherwise?'

'We marvel at the speed with which Caesar has put things into operation.'

'Reverend senators, we shall meet tomorrow to discuss the raising of finances for the rebuilding of the city. There is not a moment to be lost.'

'Has Caesar,' Piso asked, 'any notion of how this disaster may have started?'

'Oh, Rome has always been a terrible place for fires. These wooden shops and tenements, oil lamps, sudden strong winds. On this occasion we have been more unfortunate than usual.' But he could not help seeming to smile. 'But think of the phoenix, the resurrection, that sort of thing. We must always look on the bright side. One of these days, and it may be soon, you will look on a Rome to be proud of.'

'The trouble is,' Tigellinus said to his master, walking beside the northward-jolting litter, 'they will want to fix the blame somewhere.'

'Why? An act of the gods, an accident. Rome has known it before.'

'May I put it another way. They will feel happier, if you can talk of such an emotion, if they have someone to blame. If I may say so, Caesar, you've talked too much about the great phoenix Neropolis.'

'Every emperor has talked, and freely too, of finding brick and leaving marble.'

'This Emperor is no darling of the Senate. It is the Senate that will want to fix the blame in one particular direction. Your trouble will begin with the finance bills. The Senate will talk of starving the legions in the provinces to pay for Caesar's folly.'

'It is no folly. You have seen the plans. The plans are a masterpiece of ah planning.'

'I've seen the plans. You have not been backward in showing the plans. Everybody has seen the plans. They have not been rushed into being to meet an emergency. Those plans have been around for more than a year.'

'Oh, longer, longer, Tigellinus. I've had the dream a long time.'

'I think Caesar will have to pay a little money out of his own purse before he can even dream of putting those plans into operation.'

'Money? To whom?'

Tigellinus sighed deeply, then coughed: there was still acrid smoke about. 'Well, I would suggest a certain senator named Vettius Caprasius. Quite an orator. He will implant some of the right ideas.'

'Where?'

'Leave all this to me.'

It was a week later that a demure Nero sat in the senate house, listening to an eloquent Vettius Caprasius, a lean man in early middle age, who told Caesar and the Senate who were the people who started the fire.

'Caesar, reverend senators, I rise to report on the findings of the special commission appointed to inquire into the causes of the recent devastating conflagration that struck and crippled our city. Documents, letters, depositions – all of which the Senate is encouraged to examine at its leisure – point to an inescapable conclusion. The fire was an outrage perpetrated by a dissident group of this city, one that despises Rome, flouts the gods, regards the traditional Roman virtues – including those military virtues which built and sustain an empire – as totally derisory. Not the Jews, oh no. The Jews have suffered as much as any yet have been quick to contribute lavishly to the reconstruction fund. I refer to the Christians or Chrestians, a sect favoured by slaves, plebeians, perverts and foreigners, to whom vice is virtue and virtue vice. Well known for such hideous secret practices as cannibalism and incest, for refusing patriotic service of all kinds, including the taking of arms against Rome's enemies, they are at last revealed as terrorists and incendiaries. It is proposed that a new commission be formed to drag these loathsome reptiles out of their holes and to deal with them not according to the dictates of the law but in obedience to our impulses of disgust and outrage. We do not try mad dogs in courts of justice; we kill them outright. They bade our city suffer. They must suffer themselves.'

'Oh, surely if we fined them,' Nero put in over the growls and murmurs, 'heavily that is, justice would be satisfied?'

'As always, Caesar is too softhearted. Let just indignation take its inexorable course.'

Not all the Senate agreed. Many of the Senate had a fair idea of what was going on. But there was no harm in letting the suffering people get at the Christians; it stopped them from clawing at the senators, who had already been inveighed against by mob orators as defective fathers and coldhearted selfservers with villas untouched by the fire. Why, even Caesar himself had suffered: he wept bitterly over the ruined Palatine. Tigellinus quietly paid a mob to howl against the Christians and augment itself in a march on a house insolently near to the Imperial Forum. They knew the day to choose – Dies solis, when this atheistic lot got together to stew babies and eat them. The house belonged to a Greek master tailor named Lemos because he was goitrous, and the mob was delighted to find him presiding over a meal of white meat and Greek wine with others, men, women and children, of his filthy persuasion. The white meat, they swore, was really bread: taste it. It tasted like bread but the mob knew it was really meat. They spat it on the floor then went into the kitchen, where they made brands out of firewood and then began to inflame the house. Let these bastards get burnt like poor decent Romans did. They went further; they made a fire in front of the house, feeding it with furniture, books and bedclothes. Then they threw on it the smallest Christian child they could find, save the poor little swine from these bastards' cannibalism. The adult Christians, who were supposed to turn the other cheek of the arse they'd been battered on, turned very nasty and clawed the righteous mob. They were thrown on the fire too, some of them.

It was then that the military took over. Christians had deliberately burnt this house which belonged to a decent Greek Roman named Lemos, who had a contract for making uniforms for the Praetorian Guard. Ergo they were incendiarists. Ergo they had set the city on fire. The soldiers set up under orders ten-foot stakes at six-foot intervals in the charred earth of the residential areas that had suffered most, and to these they bound Christians, men, women and children, soaked them in pitch and set light to them with torches. It was not hard to find the Christians. They did not deny what they were and they made a cabbalistic sign in the form of a cross when they were arrested. But of course they did not get all the Christians: there were too many of them.

They did not get Marcus Julius Tranquillus, for instance. As they packed, Sara scolded him. 'I said from the first, you should never have got mixed up with them.'

'Nonsense. Paul warned us we'd be scapegoats for something. Thank God we got the warning in time.'

'Paul – Paul – First he's responsible for a shipwreck, now for a fire. I didn't like the look of the man.'

'You're talking foolishly, woman. There'll be time to knock the nonsense out of you when we're safe in Pompeii.'

'How do you know we'll be safe in Pompeii, wherever that is?'

'Because my uncle will make sure we're safe. Respected, discreet, a reader of books, kind, lonely – I own him a visit. The story will be I incurred Nero's displeasure for something trivial. He'll be glad to shelter us. He believes in the old republic.'

'Disaster, nothing but disaster. God makes the fire, God makes the wind blow. Blessed be the name of the Lord. All through our history. Escape, exile, wandering in the desert.'

'For once the Jews are nobody's enemy. It's the Christians this time. You know, preachers of love and tolerance. We're the enemy.'

Aquila had an urgent order for tents to be pitched in the Campus Martius and had to take on more help. Nobody thought of him as a Christian. Luke, leaving copies of his 'Pauliad' with his patient Gaius Petronius, left for the Adriatic coast. Linus was just discreetly no more around. But Peter, beard stirring in the wet wind, staff in hand, went weeping round the corpses of those he must think of as his butchered flock. Linus could postpone his paternity, papa of Rome to be, but Peter owed God a death and defied the morning cockcrow as he went about the city blessing and mourning. He was taken at first for an old foreign madman and left alone.

Tigellinus said: 'If Caesar would care to read the report. Here is a list of some of the more unexpected members of the ah sect.'

They were seated on that northwestern segment of the Palatine which had missed the fire. Here were living quarters enough, though not for an emperor. The work of reconstruction had started: engineers consulted their plans and foremen bellowed at sweating slaves. 'I'd no idea,' Nero said, 'there were so many of our pureborn aristocrats. Lucius Popidius Secundus – he was one, and I never knew. A fine eater and drinker.'

'Well, of course – some of the enemies of the state have been listed as Chrestians. That makes things a lot easier. But most of them are the real thing.'

'The term is *Christians*, Tigellinus. And I'm rather sick of these allegations of anthropophagy and so on. I can't bear ignorance. I learned a lot, you know, from that man.'

'And *that man*, unfortunately, has left Italy. But I'm assured that he'll be back. These people talk very freely. They don't lie, or they don't seem to. They seem rather pleased at being arrested, some of them. They're mad, even the Romans have lost their Roman qualities. It's a debilitating sort of superstition.'

'You don't understand, do you, Tigellinus? They don't mind dying. To them death is the gate to eternal life, if they've done right. If they've done wrong they go to a place where the fire burns without consuming. And that goes on for ever. But if they're executed because of their faith, then that turns them into witnesses for the faith, and all the wrong things they've done are cancelled out.'

'You speak, Caesar, with a certain wistfulness. Not a pleasant thought, is it – eternal fire for having murdered and raped and tried to castrate a boy to turn him into a woman and turned yourself into a bride losing her maidenhood and thrust at the Vestal Virgins? Not a pleasant religion to have about the place. We're better without them. And the dear Roman people are having the time of their lives burning and robbing. Ah, policy, policy. We'll get them all, including the bald Jew who took your fancy.'

320

'It won't do, though,' Nero frowned, 'all this burning. I'm sick of the stench of fire. It's not aesthetic. It's disordered. Gaius Petronius thinks so too. His sense of beauty and order is deeply offended.'

'I thought you'd banished that waterlily.'

'That waterlily, as you so rudely term him, has more sense of beauty in his little toes than you have in all your burly fishfed carcase. You're a coarse man, Tigellinus.'

'Caesar, of course, knows all about coarseness.'

'Caesar knows a lot of things, Tigellinus. That's why he's Caesar.'

One thing Caesar knew was a little book written by a Greek physician which described the early struggles and triumphs of the Christian faith. Gaius Petronius had been enthusiastic about the strength of the narrative line, the almost Homeric terseness of the phraseology, though he regretted what the Greek language had lost since the time of the great ancients: it had, as the second language of the Empire, become a medium tending to the utilitarian, commercial, political, sentimental. It lacked the old marble and fire. The book was addressed, see, to a certain Theophilus, lover of God. Gaius Petronius had it on the word of the author himself that it was assumed some day Caesar would be Theophilus: what man better endowed with the insight to be washed in the pure light of the emergent truth? Nero knew Gaius Petronius was about his old game of extravagant flattery, but he was complaisant. Nero the darling of the ultimate god of truth and beauty and goodness: it was a pleasant idea. Unfortunately there was this doctrine of eternal fire. Given time, he might repent of his dastardly acts, acts thrust upon him by the destiny of the imperiate, but there was no guarantee of that. It was best to have the *una nox dormienda*, after all, and this meant having no Christianity in his realm. He burned the little book with his own hands, not knowing there were other copies. He would kill the upstart faith and all its adherents, so that none could prate to him of eternal fire, yet he would enable those adherents to believe they were going to eternal bliss. It would cost him nothing. But the whole business had to be carried out *aesthetically*. He conferred with Gaius Petronius as to how this might best be done.

'You're so right, Caesar. It offends one's senses to see and smell all those corpses along the Appian Way and, indeed, the streets of the city.' Nero was with Petronius on a garden seat in an arbour of Petronius's leafy estate, whither the stench of smouldering Rome had never travelled. 'Refine the taste of the people – has not that always been our aim? Confine the deaths of these fanatics to the arena but in no brutal manner. Let them be drawn into representations of Roman myth and history. Greek too. It's a marvellous opportunity. Will you leave it to your humble friend and coadjutor to sketch a programme?'

When the Roman people filed in from their temporary shelters to sit with their garlic sausages and children and wives, twenty thousand strong under awnings to hold off the sun, having become most sensitive to burning, they did not quite know what they were going to be given. The *hydraulis* boomed at them the usual purple music which conveyed vague emotions of death and glory, but then it abruptly ceased as a hundredfold of men and women marched proudly into the arena singing. The auditors were prepared to applaud the chorus, which resounded with what sounded like the poetic expression of the good old Roman virtues, but when the name Christus came into it the crowd reacted very unfavourably. Indeed, the brains of the less intelligent whirled with the terrible notion that things had become inverted, that the Emperor had gone suddenly mad and wished to present the Christians not as Rome-hating fireraisers but as a sect to be admired for their fireraising courage (always said the bastard wanted the city burned, didn't I, but he won't get away with this). But everything came right when a portcullis whizzed up and a pride of starved lions was thrust into the arena by men in Etruscan masks with five-thonged whips. The lions snarled back at their keepers, but then the portcullis clashed down and the lions began to show a vague interest in the Christian chorus. There were very hungry and they sniffed human sweat. They crept forward on their furry bellies, expecting resistance from their prey. All that happened was that the Christians, at a signal from a brawny young man who seemed to be their leader, went down on their knees with total unanimity and began to recite what sounded like a poem in Latin to their father in the skies. The phrase *panem quotidianum* raised some laughs among the vulgar; no more daily bread for this lot. When a lioness, with the instinct of a mother needing flesh for her cubs, made a leap on the *Amen*, a fighting spirit arose among the Christians, some of whom leapt on the lioness, to her apparent surprise, and rolled on top of her, pinning her to the sand with her paws up, roaring. Some of the lions looked languidly at this, but then one of them seemed to resent this human attack on one of the pride and walked, not too quickly, towards an old woman still on her knees. She screamed but remained immobile while the lion licked her left arm with his rough tongue. He clawed off the sleeve to get at the flesh and then blood started. It was enough. He had that old woman down on her back, lay on her and began to tear her throat out. A couple of young men who might have been her sons beat at the lion's rump and pulled his mane, but he kept to his meal, impervious.

And now a number of the predestined victims ran away from the knot of feeding lions, rebuked by the crowd for poor sportsmanship and a failure of solidarity. But, clearly, the lions could not eat everybody. They were doing well enough with their concentrated bone crushing and limb tearing, though most had the wit to get at the softer parts first – a good clawing of the belly and the spilling of the guts and an easy meal of bloody puddings. The limbs could come later. But this was not art. This was no gladiatorial display. It was only butchery. Gaius Petronius in the imperial box shook his head: the overture had gone on too long; it was time for the aesthetic part to begin. The master of the games must have thought so too, for the masked keepers with their whips reappeared, lashing the beasts back to their enclosure. Most of them objected, being engaged still in heavy feeding, and they snarled, raising one paw while the other held down their meat. At length they were per-suaded, having tasted the whip, to go to their den, some of them carrying chunks of Christian in their jaws, while the rest of the mess, blood, bones, skin, flesh, sand, was pushed with them by men handling wooden pushers on long poles. The uneaten Christians were lashed towards the gate opposite. They had no need of the whip, for they marched firmly, singing as before, some of them waving to the sausagechewers. The cheers they got were not all ironic. Things were not going quite as they should.

Gaius Petronius had found little useful Roman myth or history to dra-matize: it was all conquering people or betraying them, and to dress up Christians as Etruscans or Carthaginians and to put swords and spears into their grips was not necessarily to make them fight. Very clear round yawns were to be heard from some of the gristlefed mob. There was wheeled on a catapult, of the massive kind for hurling stones at enemy fortifications, and male Christians were shot into the air, it having been explained to the four corners of the arena by a bullvoiced announcer that Christians expected to fly to heaven: well, see them fly. So the steel bow was bent by means of a windlass, the cord was released by a spring, and Christians went flying into the audience without the permission of the audience having been obtained. This resulted in the grave injury of cer-tain good Roman plebeians, who rightly grumbled that they had been hurt enough by the damned Christians without having to be hurt more. The Greek myths would perhaps go down better.

Caleb, very sour and vindictive, explained to a young Christian what was now to happen to him. 'You know the story, do you? Dædalus was the first man to make wings and fly. He made wings for his son, too. His son's name was Icarus. But Icarus flew too near the sun and the wax on his wings melted. So he fell. You're Icarus. You're going to fall. You're going to have your skull split open. And that goes for the rest of you,' he said, raising his voice to a group of other potential Icaruses.

'You're a Jew, aren't you? You speak to a fellow Jew.'

'No, you're a Christian. A killer. You killed my son. Blast you to hell.'

'So you believe what you're told?'

'As you do. Get out there, blast you.'

323

In the centre of the arena a very high wooden tower had been placed, eight strutted feet holding it firm to the ground. There was a ladder to the top, and at the top was a platform on which Dædalus stood, having, by an acceptable fiction, flown there by means of his wooden and sackcloth wings. His task was to grasp each Icarus as he arrived at the top of the ladder and then hurl him off. To ensure that the skullcracking would be effectual, a scree of rocks lay at the bottom. The game did not go well. Some of the Icaruses refused to mount: if they were going to die anyway, why should they have to suffer physical exhaustion and humiliation first? When they had their heads clubbed at the foot of the ladder, Gaius Petronius wrung his hands: these Christians had no sense of art; how could their god be a god of beauty? But it was with relief that he saw a muscular Christian Jew, heavily bearded and bullnecked, gladly climb the ladder in his thin wings of wire and cloth. On the high platform he nodded at the sight of a skin of water to relieve the thirst of the circus performer who played Dædalus, took it, grabbed Dædalus by the neck, then solemnly baptized him. With one hand on nape and the other on fat arse, he sent the father of flight yelling into the air and to a messy, though presumably holy, death below. Gaius Petronius chewed his nails: that was a lie, that was not the ancient legend, it was a perversion, no sense of art – Circus hands mounted the ladder to get at unfallen Icarus, but he kicked them easily down or hit them with the club Dædalus had intended to launch the more reluctant fliers. Eventually the tower itself was, through the combined muscles of a dozen circus hands, toppled into the dust, and the young Jewish Christian, having blessed the populace, spilt his brains for its delectation. A spectacular ending to the act, but, even the dullest could tell, it had not quite followed the devisers' intention: a lack of sportive justice in it, somehow.

Various naked Christian women were made, successively, to ride a vigorous white bull. If that bull was meant to be Zeus, then this was a blasphemous parody. When the Europas fell into the dust screaming and were duly tossed and gored, the blasphemy was somewhat mitigated. 'Watch. *Watch*,' Nero ordered Poppea. She had been hiding her eyes in her veil. She dropped it now only to bunch her lovely face in nausea. Then she left the imperial box, vomiting on Tigellinus as she went. Some noticed this and a faint wave of approval arose from, it was supposed, the plebeians of her sex. Nero was angry and spat viciously at Gaius Petronius.

As an amythic interlude, several Christians were brought on dressed in animal skins. Then wild dogs, their jaws adrip with hydrophobia, were loosed on to them. These creatures were frightened by the sudden unleashing of a confident Christian hymn, and they were confused when some of the Christians tore off their skins and threw

324

them at the snarling teeth. The dogs assumed that it was these skins they were intended to devour, and they did so for a time despite the crowd's remonstrance. Then, finding no nourishment in the aromatic pelts, they leapt at the Christian throats, of which there were enough to go round. Finally there came a carefully organized setpiece, in which Roman troops were dressed as barbarous Britons, complete with stuck-on yellow moustaches and yellow wigs. The male Christians were comically dressed as Roman troops, armed with wooden swords and spears. The pseudobarbarians had bows and arrows and, with fine style and accurate aim, they transfixed at their leisure the pseudoromans. Now the crowd was placed in something of a dilemma. It appreciated that the show was intended to remind them of the recent British revolt against well-meaning Roman colonialism; it understood that the Christians were, in a sense, being butchered for mocking stalwart Roman troops; it knew that the arrow-aiming display demonstrated Roman skill even with barbaric weapons; but they were confused because the final image – warwhooping of bowmen with moustaches coming unstuck and wigs awry under the dying sun – was not really one creditable to the Roman Empire. Gaius Petronius's patriotism, it seemed to Nero, was of a highly qualified kind: it let art, and mediocre art at that, get in the way. It was to be hoped that the second day of the games would go better than this.

The duty officer at the city council offices, which stood at the junction of the Via Tiburtina and the Vicus Longus, was puzzled that evening when an old man who spoke neither Greek nor Latin seemed to demand to be arrested. The officer searched for an interpreter, having at least established that the old man was Jewish, and found a wounded soldier who had served in Palestine, now working for the municipality as a limping messenger between departments, who understood the old man well enough.

'He says he's Petrus, sir, and that he's not only a Christian but the head of the Christians. He says he got that appointment from the man himself, Christus that is.'

'What does he want?'

'He says he doesn't see why he should go on living while so many of his friends are being seen off, so to speak.'

'He wants to *die*, you mean?'

'Well, it's reasonable, sir. He's a Christian, he says.'

'This isn't a military headquarters, Crassus. It's nothing to do with us. He'd better be sent to the Castra Praetoria. They're in charge of rounding up Christians. Strange, though. *Wants* it, does he?'

'You can see his point in a way, sir. He's had his time, he says. When mere children are getting the knife stuck in, he says, why should the father of the whatdoyoucallit go free. He's done his best to attract

325

attention, he says, shouting the odds in the street, but nobody's taken a blind bit of notice.'

'He seems harmless enough. Take him there. You don't need any help, do you?'

'Well, it's not really in the way of duty, is it? And me with this bad leg. We could get somebody from the Vigiles to take him. That's only round the corner.'

'All right, get somebody.'

There was no shortage of speakers of bad Aramaic at the Castra Praetoria. The interrogating officer was as puzzled as the functionary at the municipal offices by what sounded like a calm acceptance of a sort of collective guilt on the part of the old man. But guilty of exactly what? Of burning Rome or of belonging to a superstitious sect which had been declared illegal? All the old man would speak of was two outlandish places called Sodom and Gomorrah, which had been burnt by the Lord God for their sins, and he said that Rome was worse than Sodom and Gomorrah. That sounded very much like an admission of Christian responsibility for massive incendiarism, and the old man was asked if he would sign a statement to that effect. No, he would sign nothing. He had never signed anything in his life. Crucify me and get it all over with. Crucify? Who are you to specify your mode of dispatch? I've given myself up, haven't I? I have certain rights, don't I? I want to be crucified, but not in the usual way. I want it to be done upside down. The old man was clearly crazy. Perhaps they ought to discharge him with a caution. Upside down, indeed. That made the whole thing vaguely comic. Well, they could wash their hands of the business by sending him to the master of the games. Christians had become material for popular entertainment. Undignified, somehow. Rome was losing its reputation for punitive dignity.

Peter was locked in a cell for the night and taken to the games master early next day. The games master saw possibilities in the inverted crucifixion. It was comic, yes, but that was in order. The carpenters had better start work right away on a gallows that could be affixed inverted to a kind of cart. The remaining Christians at the end of the day's sport could drag the cart in, with this old fellow upside down on the cross, they could sing a hymn, and then they could meet, as planned, the gladiators and be mown down. Meanwhile the old fellow could be set alight and the announcer could announce that the burning of Rome had finally been avenged. And that that was the end of the Christians.

Gaius Petronius had contrived very complicated setpieces for the day's entertainment. But, again, the Christians did not seem to recognize their duty to art. A ship on wheels was dragged on to confront an artificial island of singing sirens – men, or properly half-men, in fair long wigs with melon breasts stuck on their chests. They wore gloves with honed razor talons, and they were to tear to pieces the naked seamen who were really Christians, these to be thrust off the boat to their doom with very sharp spears. The siren music was provided by a chorus of genuine women hidden beneath the wooden rocks. Some of the Christians preferred the spears to the claws, and others fought the sirens very viciously with their fists until, their eyes mostly torn out, they could fight no more. But many of the spectators objected strongly to seeing men dressed up as sirens. There was enough effeminacy in the city without making a public glorification of it. The Cretan labyrinth went down rather better, with the more massive gladiators in Minotaur disguise clubbing the Christian wanderers through the wooden maze. And the Trojan horse, into whose door in the flank two hundred Christians were impelled, there to be burnt alive, was considered ingenious. But the penultimate item of the day was thought to be in very bad taste.

All the Christian children that were left, some hundred of them, were clothed in lambskins. The very young ones thought this a fine sport and gambolled gleefully into the arena among others, less young, more doubtful, led by a prancing shepherd. This shepherd was quick to make his comic exit when the wild dogs, their heavy meal of the previous day long digested, leapt out and savaged the lambs. There were murmurs from the more reasonable of the audience: these youngsters had committed neither cannibalism nor incest and it was doubtful if they had had any part in the burning of the city. This was, not to mince matters, gratuitous cruelty. Many left. It was to a half-empty arena that the final show of Christians sang their song of faith and courage, dragging on the cart which displayed the nailed and bleeding old man who looked like anybody's grandfather, absurdly inverted, seeing, if he could still see, the world fading as the world was not. This man, the announcer bellowed, had ordered the burning of the city. Few believed it. When burning pitch was applied to the poor old devil he was clearly already dead. The Christians had not responded with any zest to the swordsmen: they let themselves be cut down. No sport and a weak ending to two days of entertainment which could not properly be called games at all. The audience left murmuring.

That night Nero, in his lonely bed as big as a barge, dreamed of hell. He woke screaming and spent the rest of the night awake, gloomily drinking warm wine without water. He was in a foul temper when he met his Empress at the breakfast table, and she herself inflamed and concentrated his diffused rage by inveighing against the brutality of the games, a brutality, she would point out, which would have an effect the reverse of the imperial intention. 'You and the Roman

327

people. Spasming under your togas to see men and women and children torn to shreds. So easy, is it not, to give way to the beast inside us. History is supposed to record the taming of the beast. The Roman Empire takes over history and trumpets the victory of reason. But it's the trumpeting of a rogue elephant. The beasts are with us, and they have names, but mine shall not be among them.'

'It was your duty as imperial consort to cry out for the blood of the criminals like any good Roman, do you hear me?'

'For the blood of Tigellinus and his accomplices, you mean. My lord, I have performed the last office of an imperial consort. I carry in my womb what may be the next Emperor. I can only pray to whatever god there is that he shall have more of the blood of my family than of yours.'

'Your family and what other? That of a Jewish athlete running to fat? Some bearded mumbler of Hebrew mumbo jumbo? You've tasted of uncircumcised meat and I presume you like it. I cry the cry of all fathers – how can I know, how can I know?'

'This child, to my shame, is yours. I would to God it were some other's.'

'God, eh? Which god? You whore, you loathsome hilding. You've named the beast, you say. Go on naming him, go on –' And with this he knocked the Empress to the hard floor and viciously kicked her belly. She writhed and screamed and then she stopped screaming. Nero gave her one last kick. There was no response of fear or pain, and he grew frightened. And then he was not frightened, recognizing that, being on the side of the destroyer, anything was permitted him except fear or compassion. There was dignity in destruction when that urge to destroy was seen in the context of a kind of cosmic struggle. The religion of the Romans failed there. There was a kind of holiness in fighting God.

We must not be surprised if the sufferings and courage of the dead Christians and, indeed, one element in their eschatology furnished images in the furtive talk of virtuous Romans who were heartily sick of their Emperor and wished to be rid of him. Gaius Calpurnius Piso had picked up the word *martyr* and, in the view of Subrius Flavus of the Guard, overused it. 'Very well,' Flavus said, 'some of us will have to die, but to dwell on that is morbid and not in the Roman tradition. Stick to solid positive action and forget the refinements. If we die, we die, and it's damned bad luck. But we go into battle to win.' The two of them sat in Piso's house, one of the many senatorial mansions untouched by fire. From the terrace one could see the work of reconstruction proceed, slave labour unlimited, the fiscs of the provinces heavily ransacked for the quarrying and transportation of the marble, the precious stones, the gold, the filched statues of Greece. Piso said:

'How are things with the Guard?'

'The Guard's behind you. Those who aren't scared.'

'There are too many scared.'

'You have the look of one of them, Piso.'

'For me it's in order. To denounce Tigellinus publicly was not the most discreet of acts. Nero has grown accustomed to being denounced and takes little notice. Tigellinus knows that I know certain things. I have sworn affidavits from some who saw him on the night of – No matter. The question's very simple – who? And, of course, when and where?'

'You mean the head and not the right arm?'

'Root and branch.'

A slave named Felix heard all this while he was serving wine. That night, in the sordid quarters he shared with other slaves, he lay awake meditating on what the nature of the reward might be – manumission, of course, but what besides? – while two fellow slaves, male and female, groaned in the act of love. He waited until the transport had finished, then he got up and put on his single simple garment and his sandals.

'Where are you going?'

'The cloaca. Ate something I shouldn't.'

He went into the city, seeing in moonlight mountains of marble slabs, cranes, cement mixers. He ran and walked alternately to the town villa of Tigellinus, which lay south of the Castra Praetoria.

Tigellinus was in bed with a boy. Lamps glowed on either side of the bed: Tigellinus liked to see what he was doing or having done. There was a knock at his door. At this hour?

'Gnaeus, sir.'

'What do you want?'

'It's something urgent, sir.'

'It's always something urgent. Come in, blast you.'

He motioned to the naked boy to leave by another door. He yawned, settled himself on his pillows. Gnaeus, a portly bald freedman, came in. 'There's this slave here, sir. He's got information. He wants a reward for it.'

'A slave? Whip him and stuff his information up his. Whose slave?'

'He says he's the slave of the senator Piso.'

'Piso? Send the scoundrel in.'

The scoundrel came in, trembling. 'Every day, sir. They mention different names. People they'd like to have in on it but aren't sure about.'

'Such as?'

'One name was Seneca, sir.'

'I see. And you say Subrius Flavus was there. Are you sure? Think

329

carefully. Subrius Flavus is a high officer in the Praetorian Guard.'

'It was he did most of the talking, sir.'

'You're a good boy,' Tigellinus said, 'and a fine patriot, not, of course, that you have any of the rights of even an unpatriotic citizen. But a slave should always be loyal to his master. Go and see Gnaeus out there. He's got the whip ready.'

'But, sir, I thought –'

'Slaves aren't paid to think. Slaves aren't paid at all, are they? Get out.'

Get out was what he wished to say next day to Gaius Petronius, seated in his exquisite violet robe and soft leather boots with Caesar in an arbour from which one could hear the heartening din, sufficiently muted by distance and greenery, of Rome's rebuilding, the creation of Neropolis. Petronius was talking of Nero's voice – 'a poignant sword that strikes to the very *pia mater*, that impales the centres of love like an almost intolerably potent aphrodisiac.' And Athens: the Athenian judges had given the award to their Emperor *in absentia*: they knew, with their Greek subtlety, the invincible excellence of Caesar's voice without having to hear it.

'Some day,' Nero said, 'they *shall* hear it. They shall have *The Burning of Troy*.'

'But not, I trust, with the pyrotechnical accompaniment that distinguished your last performance of that immortal work.' Petronius saw from his master's scowl that he had been indiscreet. 'I refer, naturally, to the burning of the aesthetic passions of those who heard you.'

Tigellinus could stand no more of this. Besides, there were urgencies. He strode from the leafy flowery trellised entrance to the arbour into Caesar's presence and said:

'News. Urgent. Does this waterlily have to stay while I give it?'

'My butterfly? If I let him flit away I may not be able to catch him. You're rude, Tigellinus, you're coarse. Oh, I'll come over there if you have things to whisper.'

They spoke together, and Petronius could not hear, nor did he wish to. A spot of birdlime had disfigured the toe of his left boot. He wiped it off with a sycamore leaf. Nero called: 'Petronius!'

'*Dear* Caesar?'

'You know elegant ways to live. Do you also know elegant ways to die?'

'Oh, suicide,' Petronius said promptly. 'In a hot bath preferably. A gentle slashing of the wrists. The water reddens to a delicate rose and deepens to a royal purple. One fades out as in a dream.'

Tigellinus said: 'This you know?'

'This I imagine.'

Tigellinus nodded. 'That will do for Seneca. But no delicate rose and royal purple for Flavus. Not for Flavus.'

When, some days later, Flavus stood with his hands bound, ready for the axe, which was ostentatiously being sharpened on a whetstone, he insisted on speaking. A word.

'You will say no word,' Tigellinus told him.

'I wish to address the Emperor. I have nothing more to say to you, except that you were more acceptable when you smelt of fish than now, when you smell of blood.'

'Oh, let him speak,' Nero said. 'He has a certain rough talent for rhetoric.'

'Caesar, I was loyal to you when you deserved loyalty. When you ceased to deserve it, I gave it still. But I began to hate you when you murdered your mother and your wife, when you paraded yourself as a secondrate singer and actor, and my hate brimmed to overflowing its cup when you turned yourself into an incendiary. You have ruined the Empire, and that Empire is now withdrawing its loyalty from Rome. The provincial governors proclaim their independence from Caesar. The barbarians revolt. We needed a ruler, and all we were given was a slovenly singer and dancer, a slovenly murderer, a matricide, an uxoricide, a sodomite, and a fireraiser.'

His grave, six feet away, was still being dug.

'A slovenly job, like everything perpetrated under your rule. I shall be glad to be released from that rule. Strike, when you're ready.' Nero and Tigellinus watched. Nero said:

'One stroke. Half a stroke. Hm. Slovenly, he said. Very nasty, Tigellinus.'

Seneca received his orders for suicide, and the precise mode in which that act should be performed, with little surprise. He had been mentioned as one asked to conspire, and he had refused. But the mere mention was enough. It was typical and wholly fitting. He lowered himself into his warm bath with arthritic care: his slaves wept to see his shrunken body. There was not much blood in it, and the arteries were reluctant to flow. 'Don't weep,' he said. 'Life is a hard burden, even for free men and women. Leave me now.' He used the razor again, but the blood flowed sluggishly. Soon it responded to the heat of the water and Seneca faded into sleep. *Medea superest. Seneca superest.* It was not true: nothing remained.

When Gaius Petronius's orders came, he protested that he had done no wrong. He was Caesar's friend, was he not? But therein danger had always lain: Tigellinus did not like Caesar to have friends, especially friends of the exquisite ability of Gaius Petronius. He put off the act until he heard that the praetorian prefect was impatient, that armed troops would come to dispatch him more brutally than a mere razor could. Petronius was no Stoic. He had been charmed by some of the more poetic aspects of the new faith but disappointed in its adherents, who had a brutal concern with morality that overrode the delight in beauty which was civilized man's most characteristic trait. They worshipped a god whose visage was still to be revealed to the brutish world. Ah, well.

Petronius duly cut his wrists, admired the rich red flow, but then ordered his new medical man to bind them up for a time. He had lost Luke, who had exquisite Greek hands and some remarkable Asiatic potions and salves. Ah, well. His suicide, exquisitely prolonged, was to be in public, that was to say among his friends, who drank and ate and made love all about him. Life, he was leaving life. This admirable chamber, marble, hung with flowers of the season. This beautifully set table, at whose head he lay encouched. To his friend the young poet Hortensius he said:

'Those exquisite lines of Catullus.'

'Of course.

'Soles occidere et redire possunt:
Nobis cum semel occidit brevis lux
Nox est perpetua una dormienda.'

'Exquisite. Suns rise and set. When our brief light has sunk and died, there remains only a long long night to be slept through. Do you believe that to be true, Hortensius?'

'A thin life whimpering for human blood. Hardly worth having. Or else nothing. Nothing is best.'

'Life was sweet, you know. And I did no wrong.'

'I think it's time now, Petronius. There are soldiers waiting outside. They will want to ride back to Rome with the news.'

'Keep them out of here. *Rough* soldiers. Will you do it for me?'

'You know I can't.'

'Very well, then. We will unbind the mortal wounds and see the blood flow. I will even cut again. I will pretend that I am going to shave this delicate golden flue on my forearms and render them as naked of hair as a eunuch's. Oh, but a little more wine. Some more Catullus.'

'No. Now.'

'Louder music, please.'

It was soft music that Nero was plucking from a lyre ineptly tuned. Tigellinus said: 'He's gone.'

'Who?'

'The waterlily that had a snake hiding under it.'

'The only man who *truly* appreciated my singing. And you had to have him killed. You've had everybody killed, haven't you? You turned Rome into a prison and then into a bath of blood –'

'A rather banal metaphor, wouldn't you say?'

'I didn't foresee that things would be like that at all. All I wanted was to make people happy. I never wanted to be an emperor. A great artist, that's all. And I *was* a great artist – *am*.'

'With no audience. I leave you now, Caesar.'

'*You* leave me? *You*?'

'The games are finished. The slaves sweep fruitpeel and nutshells out of the empty arena. I have to go. The Senate wants my head.'

'Your head, yours? Who's master here? What is the Senate that it should want – Does it want my head too? Does it?'

'Get out of Rome is my advice. Now.'

'Why does the palace seem so empty? I can hear my voice echoing. Where is everybody?'

Tigellinus grinned sadly and said: '*Vale*.' He left quickly.

'Where are you all? Lepidus! Myrtilla! Phaon!'

Phaon, a freedman, neither insolent nor deferential, came in, saying: 'Caesar called?'

'Oh, thank heaven you're still with me. Where are the others?'

'Gone. And it's time for *us* to go. The villa. Only four miles. There aren't enough slaves to carry a litter. I might find a couple of horses.'

'Leave Rome? *My* Rome? My great gift to the world? Oh, very well. My cloak, Phaon, my riding boots.'

'Caesar knows where they are. I have my own arrangements to make.' He went out. Nero cried to an invisible auditorium:

'Phaon! Phaon! I'll have your head for this!'

In the Senate the leader of the house had given the latest news. 'Vindex, the legate of Gaul, has declared his allegiance to only the Senate and the people of Rome. The legate of Spain, Servius Sulpicius Galba, has made a similar declaration. The Emperor is left without allegiance, either civil or military. The revolt has begun in the provinces. Galba, old as he is, stands as the only reasonable imperial candidate. But first things first. Is it resolved by this august body that the present incumbent of the imperial chair be declared a public enemy and an outlaw and most meet for apprehension, trial and execution?' Piso should have been there, it would have been a great moment for him. But Piso was not anywhere.

Nero was very much in the scarcely used villa four miles out of the city, breaking jars and tearing curtains. His only audience was Phaon, who sat on a stool, chewed nuts, and watched and listened with no visible reaction as his master ran up and down, calling for people long dead, screaming. Then Nero said: 'They won't dream of looking in the slaves' quarters, will they? They'll find this place empty, then they'll leave. Isn't that so, Phaon? Isn't it? Show me where the slaves' quarters are, Phaon. Quickly, quickly.'

Phaon got up at his leisure. His sharp ear caught a sound outside, some way away, horses. 'Come with me then, take a torch.'

He went out, not too hurriedly, and his master followed eagerly, stumbling, till they came to a dark and dusty area beyond the kitchens. Those kitchens had cooked no food in a long time. 'Safe here then, you think, Phaon? Quite safe?' His torch showed him a wallsconce. He fitted the torch in. He did not like all these shadows. He did not like Phaon's shaking his head and taking a dagger from his kirtle. He handed it to his master, with a slight bow. 'I do that? Never, never. It's a coward's act, Phaon.' But Phaon insisted. 'Show me, then. Show me how to do it. You do it first, Phaon, then I'll follow.' But Phaon wrapped Nero's fist around the hilt and guided it towards his throat. So great an artist and he had to die. No, not so great: this was not the time for self-deception. If there had been the chance to learn, and to learn humbly. A martyr to the art in a sense: testifying to the future that one had to give up all for art and he had not been permitted to give up all. As he began to choke on his blood he saw a page of perfect sapphics not now to be written. He heard them sung in some phoenix version of his own voice, but the voice did not get beyond the first line and a half. Up to the caesura. The arriving squadron was loud about the house.

There is irony in the fact that Paul's death came after that of Nero. He arrived from Spain in an interregnum, but the law still ran, like a mad horse beyond curbing. He was unaware of this. Christianity was a *religio licita*. The ship came in at Puteoli, a grainship that had docking precedence. It was unladed of its bales and passengers. A couple of port officials asked the ship's master to show them the manifest of these latter.

'Leave men from Spain. Private passengers. Who's this Paul?'

'Roman citizen.'

'That doesn't look like a Roman name.'

'He's just known as Paul. A Christian preacher. Made a lot of converts in Spain. Including some of these leave men. Why, anything wrong?'

'How long have you been away from Italy?'

'I've been doing the run from the Spanish mainland to the Balearics for three years. Why?'

'Christianity's a proscribed religion. Punishable by death. Where is this Paul?'

The ship's master pointed to a very brown, very bald, very lean but quite old man in a brown habit, shouldering his pack and preparing to leave the dock area. The port official who had spoken spoke again:

'And he doesn't know either?'

334

'No more than I did. What are you going to do?'

'We have our orders.' A maniple was summoned; it moved in to arrest Paul; he could not understand why. He tried to resist, but strong arms grasped him. He was taken to the offices of the quaestor in Neapolis. Paul spoke first.

'I seem to be under arrest. Is it permitted to ask why?'

'I suppose you're entitled to an explanation. The religion you preach has been proscribed. You oughtn't really to be surprised.'

'Why?'

'It's an antiroman activity. You're cannibals, buggers, incendiarists and Jupiter knows what.'

'Very good. And I personally am to be tried on those charges?'

'No. The state dispenses with the formality of a trial.'

'Even for a Roman citizen?'

'There were plenty of Roman citizens who burnt down their own city.'

'So what happens to me?'

'I have to order your instant execution. That's the way it's done these days. Look,' the quaestor said, a man as bald and brown as Paul but much younger, 'I don't like this. I don't even believe all those stories. It's not the way we did things before. But we have our orders.'

It was always a matter of orders. Rome would choke itself on orders. Paul said: 'Crucifixion?'

'No. The axe. It's quicker.'

Paul had an unworthy thought. Crucifixion ruptured nothing. Nails ran through the wrists, sometimes without even breaking the bones. A corpse could be taken down from a cross and be seen later to be not a corpse. Pockets of air in the lungs. Resuscitation. If Christ had been beheaded, would the disciples have noticed a thin red band, like a delicate necklace, marking the miraculous rejoining? But Christ had not been beheaded. 'When?' he asked.

'Now. Best get it over. We've had to set up a block in that yard there. I'll have to call the axeman. Sorry about this.'

It was proper that Paul should meet his end in a seaport. Rome had never been his city, and it is irrational to search for his bones there. He died in the seawind. For the official record he made a statement:

'I must make one final protest against a flagrant miscarriage of justice. I am a Roman citizen. I am guilty of no charge. I was exonerated by the state of what previous charges were held against me. I am a Jew and I am a Christian and hence profess beliefs acceptable to the Roman state. I have a right to demand justice.' These words were not taken down. He was taken to the block and, before laying his bald head on it, he prayed: 'Father, forgive them for they know not what they do. Now to God the Father, God the Son and God the Holy Spirit

335

I commend my soul and the souls of my enemies. Amen.' He prayed in Aramaic. Then the axe fell.

In Rome, despite the death of its imperial architect, the work of rebuilding went on. Caleb, who had left behind the butchery of the arena, worked as a foreman responsible for the carting of blocks of marble and travertine. A jagged wall was being demolished to make way for something thicker, higher, nobler. Something seemed to have been carved on the wall, near obliterated by dust. He brushed the dust away and saw a crude drawing of a fish. He nodded: he knew the sign. That man Peter had been a fisherman, but Tigellinus had merely sold fish. Now Christ had actually turned into a fish. Caleb had no great love for fish: his muscles had been built on meat. But he looked at the crude drawing with a certain tenderness. These people were not going to give up in a hurry. The faith they practised was, after all, of Jewish provenance. The Jews were not going to give up in a hurry either.

FIVE

This is the last time you will have to hear of my bodily infirmities, which have been somewhat soothed by the continuing good weather of the month named for Gaius Julius, no mean Caesar. But I cannot deny, nor do my physicians attempt to, that I have little time left. A crab crawls in my belly and its claws nip more perniciously every day. Of the condition of my bowels I dare hardly speak. I see now, however, that there has been more relevance in imposing my pains on you than I formerly thought. The decay of one small body is a metaphor of the organic corruption of the Roman Empire.

I remember very well the death of the father of one of my friends. The old man had been named Kederah for his rotundity, but the name was now a mockery. His was a death which his ailing organs were only too ready to hasten, but his indomitable mind held it back. Or rather it was the seductive power of a particular book which rendered his mind at least temporarily indomitable. He had worked hard all his life at trade, and only in his retirement was he able to return to the love of his boyhood, which was reading. He had never read the *Odyssey* in his youth and was unable to find a copy until his last illness. Then he became determined to finish his bedrid reading of it before yielding to the arms of the dark. So he reached the final lines, read them, put aside the book, then composed himself for his pagan end. He died at peace. He had done one thing he had wanted to do, and now let the shades enclose him.

I feel myself to be in something of the same situation. I too have a book to finish – the writing of it (I fear there may be no time to read it through, correct the style, banish inconsistencies, adjust my portrayals of great men evil and good) – and then I shall be content to leave this beautiful and damnable world (last night there were fireflies in my bedroom, and I could see Sirius poised on the tip of one of my Alps), of which I hoped so much and received so little. My friend's father could at least rejoice vicariously in Odysseus's final triumph – the defestation of his island kingdom, the lying in sleep and love with patient Penelope – but I can record little but failure. A faith was born and then died. It was slaughtered by Jews and Romans alike. The hopeful words of Linus to his flock, much diminished by martyrdom and defection, ring pathetically.

'Children in Christ, we have celebrated the supper of the Lord, taking in love and amity the consecrated bread and wine which, by the daily miracle, become his flesh and blood. The body of the Lord was torn and rent and crucified that we might live. But the hard task of proclaiming the word and suffering that it might be proclaimed remains one which we share with him and are proud to share. The Christians of the city of Rome have suffered. They have been a bloody show to gratify a depraved mob and an even more depraved emperor. But their deaths have not been in vain. They have proved to a pagan world that if a faith is strong enough men and women are willing to die for it. The church of Rome is in constant peril, and yet it is in no danger of extinction. Alas, the great men, the founders of the faith in far places, are disappearing from sight and may soon disappear from memory. Peter was crucified in Rome, Paul was beheaded in Neapolis. I, Linus, your bishop, follow very humbly in their wake. I present to you now our brother Cletus, my successor when the time comes for my death at the hands of the executioner or in the jaws of the beasts. I would say now and say strongly that the Church will prevail. The Church is indeed stronger than the empire which assails it. That empire casts around for a Caesar. It is in confusion and may soon be in a state of civil war. We who profess peace have nothing to fear from it but the death of the body. We who profess love may yet see this agonized empire transformed into a vehicle of the universal expression of divine and human charity. Be strong in your weakness and proud in your humility. In the name of the Father –'

Pathetic, yes. Damnably so. We have to imagine Linus and his congregation as a huddle of fearful people meeting, by an irony, in those groves some four miles from Rome where the tomb of Nero was already overrun by coarse grass and bindweed. Prayers were often gabbled, and the accidents of the sacrament all too frequently gulped. The end of Nero was not the end of intolerance. It was a weed that flourished rankly and still does.

Consider Servus Sulpicius Galba in his camp not far from Cordova, the town where Seneca and Gallio were born. The governor of Spain, he hobbled out on aged twisted feet which could hardly bear sandals to the occasional harrying of dissident Iberians. As now. He looked up in satisfaction at three men leaping and gasping like landed fish on three crosses on a little hill. Seventy, hairless, his joints twisted but his spirit vigorous, he had let old age harden a native brutality and bring no glimmer of compassion. His aide Porcellus had some of this last quality and he spoke, albeit nervously, of the Senate's possible displeasure at the crucifixion of Roman citizens.

'Look carefully, man, and you'll see that our delinquent Roman hangs a little higher than our delinquent Iberians. Roman citizens may claim no special leniency. Justice is justice. As for the Senate, the Senate has been loud in its denunciation of the Christians. I am only pleasing a Senate I am called upon to serve and yet not serve. I wish I could have caught that Jew Paul before he took ship. He too was a Roman citizen.'

'Our Christians,' Porcellus said stoutly, 'have been no worse soldiers than the rest.'

'Careful, Porcellus, go very carefully. Keep your sympathy from my ears and eyes. The Christians are by definition followers of a slave cult, scornful of our virtues and of our gods, haters of blood, unless it is the infantile blood they drink disgustingly at their incestuous feasts. There will be no living Christians in *my* Rome.'

They had come to Galba's tent, an elaborate contrivance with a wingspreading eagle high above its central pole on a sort of canvas cupola, out-tents attached to the main body, twelve soldiers on perpetual guard around it. Blue Spanish hills, haunted by real eagles, lay beyond, misted in the dull hot day. Galba paused before going in.

'You read the letter, Porcellus?'

'I even studied it, sir.'

'Oh, very conscientious. You agree that this is the only course? Nero orders my death because our Spanish army proclaims me – though the gods alone know how he thinks my execution is to be arranged. I countermand the order. And there's only one way to do that.'

'I must get used to calling you Caesar, Caesar.'

'Servus Sulpicius Galba Caesar.' He grinned with few teeth. 'It rings well enough. Pity I'm old, Porcellus. How many years am I given to clear up the mess left by Nero? Oh, send in a woman for me, will you? Not too young. I'm no longer athletic.'

'These Iberian women are dirty, Caesar. Shall I have some bathed and then Caesar can take his choice?'

'Have one of them bathed. I leave the choice to you. Will you be like me at seventy, Porcellus? Asking for a woman to be sent in?'

'I doubt if I'll reach seventy, Caesar.'

'Very true. You won't even reach forty if you go on telling me that Christians make good soldiers. All right, dismiss.'

The truth is that Galba cared little for the embraces of women, clean or dirty. But the heterosexual gesture worked well in a province which associated homosexuality with a burnt and dirty Rome which it was the destiny of the provincial governor to go and clean up. Galba loved his little boys like all our pagan magnates except Claudius, and one must wonder at this sickness of inversion which was not just an imported Greek cult but a satisfaction deeply rooted in the male glands and psyche of the Roman governing class. They begot children distractedly but had, perhaps, a deep fear of those magical caverns of the female body which had their counterpart in the female mind. They feared women more than they durst admit, and they were content to allow the infantile loveplay of the boys' gymnasium or the school baths to be prolonged even into old age. When Galba landed with his legion at Ostia, he was, twisted and toothless as he was, eager to engage the perversions of the imperial life that, a grave fault in Nero but, to be truthful, one he had at first resisted, his mother having helped there, had to be associated with other perversities – gratuitous cruelty, arbitrary power. Galba did not cleanse Rome; Rome would never be clean.

A clean-looking Roman met Galba at Ostia. During the complicated disembarkation of troops and war engines, he accosted the new Caesar with a pleasant smile but no servile obeisance, saying: 'Marcus Salvius Otho, if you remember.'

'I remember your wife.'

'Yes,' Otho said sadly. 'Caesar's wife. As she became. You never met her, if I may contradict you. She was not in Lusitania with me. My transfer to the governorship in Lusitania was my official divorce.'

'I don't remember ever having called on you in Lusitania. But I remember meeting Poppea Sabina in Rome. Whither I march tomorrow. I suppose it is useless asking if she is well, or even still alive.'

'Useless. And unnecessary to ask where my loyalties lie.'

'Yes, I can see where they might lie. So you join me in cutting Nero's throat?'

'Of course, you've heard no news. Nero performed that necessary task himself. Last week. The Senate approves your nomination. Your march will be a triumphal one, Caesar.'

'Thank you. You have the privilege of being the first to call me that on Italian soil. Where do I lodge tonight?'

'Rough lodgings for the Emperor, I fear. The confiscated mansion of an import merchant who was imprudent enough to have himself converted to this new faith.'

'Imprudent indeed.'

'But we soldiers are used to rough lodgings, are we not?'

'You call yourself a soldier?'

'Oh, I've done my share of leading troops. Against Rome's enemies. Caesar,' he added. They looked very steadily at each other. Slaves ran up, carrying a litter. Otho smiled at Galba and then looked down, not smiling, at his Emperor's twisted feet. 'A painful condition?' he asked.

'Old, Otho, old, old, old.' He confirmed the statement by opening his ravaged mouth in a grin hard to interpret but certainly ugly. 'I must do something very rapidly, mustn't I, about proclaiming my successor

340

to the purple? An old man without a wife and without heirs of his body. How old are *you*, Otho?'

'Thirty-seven, Caesar.'

'Ah, youth, youth. And a man of good connections. Very close to two emperors.'

'My closeness to Nero was, as you may guess, a matter of policy, which may be interpreted as a question of survival. The divine Claudius was very good to me, Caesar, and to my family.'

'Well connected, as I say. Is it far to my lodgings?'

'Less than a thousand paces.'

'So we'll march together, shall we, Otho? Yes yes, march together.'

The march to Rome that followed the following day should have partaken of the quality of a holy procession in which priests hymned their deliverer and little children strewed flowers of the season in Galba's way. But the tuba and bucina brayed harshly in opposed tonalities, big drums were thumped and little ones spanked, and a bald old man with twisted feet rode a fine bay and grinned horribly at the crowds which greeted him and his bronzed troops. There were some in the crowd who mysteriously objected to Galba's succession though they shouted no worthier name, and the new Emperor was very quick to dispense what he called justice. The dissidents were nailed roughly to trees or summarily beheaded. When he entered Rome by the Via Ostiensis he was somewhat disappointed that the ravages of the famous fire should so speedily have been repaired: Nero had left Rome looking rather better than he remembered it. The Palatine was still in process of being made more beautiful than ever before, and the palace which Galba entered on his hideous bare feet, leaving flat damp footprints on the marble, was of a magnificence not, naturally, to be paralleled in Spain. Galba had hoped to create a kind of Galbapolis, but Neropolis bloomed all about him. He called the court together quickly: remnants of the old palace administration including Tigellinus the great survivor. He would see the Senate later. He said:

'Servus Sulpicius Galba. Caesar. New purple on an old body, but do not be deceived by the signs of natural decrepitude. I am here to rule, not to sing, dance, cavort on the stage.' Tigellinus seemed to grin at some inner image of Galba dancing on those ghastly feet, and Galba said: 'Who are you?'

'Ottonius Tigellinus, Caesar, at Caesar's service. Praetorian prefect under the late Emperor.'

'I appoint my own praetorian prefect,' Galba said. 'I make my own appointments. But I do not necessarily consider that the servitors of the late unlamented butcher are unemployable. Listen, all of you whom I must consider to be the imperial court. You have lived through bad times and some of you have helped to engineer them. We must forget those bad times and look forward to a future which, in the nature of things, can hardly be a long one for me. I crown my provincial career with Rome's highest honour, a widower whose wife is long dead and his sons, alas alas, are dead also. I appoint as my heir in my first imperial act the noble Piso Licinianus.'

Galba looked carefully at Otho when making this announcement. Otho reacted only with apparent satisfaction. Piso Licinianus, a handsome emptyfaced young man in military uniform, stepped forward to be inspected by the court. None knew him, few had heard of him before, all wondered how Galba happened to know him. He did not know him; he had picked him out rather arbitrarily from the squad of young nobility which had been presented to him in Ostia. Anyone would do for the succession. Galba addressed the army prefects present, saying:

'To the imperial forces I say this. Look for justice but do not look for special favours. I am all too well aware that the army considers itself to be a maker of emperors and a sustainer of emperors in office. I, with my own decree, make the next emperor. It is my custom to levy troops, not to buy them. I demand loyalty from you all, I do not seek it. Titellonus, stay with me a while. The rest of you may dismiss.'

The court padded or marched out. The two villains, one in advanced old age, the other certainly greying his way towards it, looked at each other. 'So, Titilinus –'

'Tigellinus, Caesar.'

'Whatever your name is, was all that well said?'

'In what capacity do you ask me, Caesar?'

'I can see that you're something of a rogue. Responsible for the burning down of Rome, weren't you?'

'That was solely the responsibility of the late unlamented, Caesar. He was an artist. He loved bright colours.'

'Well, I'm no artist. A plain man. They tell me you were once a fishmonger.'

'An honest occupation, Caesar. I was seduced into the imperial office I still officially hold by the wiles of the late Emperor. It was an unhappy time for me, but I did my duty.'

'So you want no more of the imperial service? You'd rather go back to selling fish?'

'I would wish to serve a true Emperor with every ounce of blood and sinew I possess.'

'Very well. I'm appointing a new praetorian prefect, never mind who for the moment. A matter of a promise. Call it a matter of honour. But I need the Praetorian Guard well watched. Perhaps you can understand why.'

'You levy troops, Caesar, you do not buy them. At Caesar's service.

I am to spy on the Guard I once had the honour of commanding.'

'Somewhat crudely put. You're a crude man.'

'I am anything that Caesar says I am.' Galba chuckled.

When it seemed certain that Galba's appointment of Piso Licinianus as his successor was to be officially confirmed, Otho gave a party for the senior officers of the Praetorian Guard at his estate on the river. He did not at first produce the cates and vintages they expected; they looked, most of them, puzzled at the lack of the materials of revelry. They were puzzled also at the smiling presence of Tigellinus and the absence of their new prefect Cornelius Laco, but the latter was excused by his being ill of a toothache and the former explained in terms of a nostalgic desire to be with old friends. Otho had severe things to say before his guests became fuddled and lecherous. 'Gentlemen,' he told them in a flowery bower where undisciplined thrushes sang merrily, 'I've done enough soldiering to know that it's a hard life and that the material rewards are nugatory. As a lifelong friend of the Empire's most distinguished soldiery I blush at Caesar's ingratitude and, indeed, ineptitude. I think, to be charitable, we may speak of senility.' Many of the officers looked at each other: this was bold language. 'Seneca, a great man slain, said something very wise, as I seem to recall. He spoke of the danger of authority without power. Dangerous to the one in authority, he meant. Such a man cuts his own throat.' He beamed at them. That was, as they all all too vividly recalled, no mere metaphor. 'Too many promises made. Too few fulfilled. Gentlemen, I keep my promises.'

'What exactly do you mean, sir?' a grave senior officer asked.

'I think, with the help of my good friend Tigellinus here, I'm in the happy position of being able to compensate you for the Emperor's deficiencies.' He clapped his hands in the Oriental manner and the whole roast boars were wheeled on. Flitting through the green groves which were part of the estate, white naked bodies seemed to be seen and tinkling laughter to be heard. 'I do not, of course, speak of bribery.' Of course not, most dangerous word. His guests, being sharpset, fell to.

Somewhat later, Galba went to address the Senate. Followed by his foolish followers Titus Vinius, who had served him in Spain, Cornelius Laco, an arrogant idiot, and the freedman Icelus Marcianus, who was after Laco's post, he made for the curule chair. He found it turned to the wall. He was furious as the attendants hurriedly put it into its right orientation. 'Who did this?' he called. 'Who had the effrontery to arrange this act of ill omen?' None spoke. Galba said: 'I'm well aware, reverend senators, of your attitude to your Emperor. Inured to bribery, you are unused to justice. I hear murmurs of promises unkept, sums unpaid. You will hear from me this this *this* – that there are steps to authority, and they make for heavy climbing, but if the climbing is helped and eased by ready hands and arms, then such aid is rightly rewarded with soft words. But at the head of the stairway stands the plateau of power, and power lies in the very name of the office, its very history and mystical resonance. I will not buy the sustention of my office. Caesar is Caesar.'

The reverend senators recollected that they had heard similar words before, composed by Seneca, intoned by Nero, now presumably passed on to the new man by that damnable Tigellinus, who had been rendered immune to senatorial vindictiveness, or justice, by an imperial fiat. They looked with little confidence on the old toothless baldhead, in whom only sharp blue eyes burned with a promise of imperial vitality, pitying and despising the gouty hands that could not even unroll a parchment unaided, wondering how many more weeks he had to go.

Tigellinus said to Galba later in the gardens of the Palatine: 'It's as you surmised, Caesar. The Guards were ready for mutiny. They're a bad lot. Venal.'

'Like the whole city. What made them change their minds?'

'A little talk from your humble servitor. A little bribery.'

'Whose money?'

'My own.'

'That takes loyalty very far. What do you want?'

'Caesar knows what I want.'

'I don't sell offices, Tigellinus. Not usually. We'll see. You say ah the ah disaffection has been damped?'

'Caesar may walk abroad in perfect safety.'

Caesar walked abroad towards the Temple of Saturn. Icelus Marcianus told him that Otho had seized the camp of the Guards. 'The legionaries,' Galba panted. 'Where are the legionaries? Immediate orders that the legionaries rally to my standard.' He saw with panic that his entourage was, singly and at various degrees of speed, running towards the Forum.

'The cavalry, Caesar, see.' An unnecessary notification. Armed horsemen were galloping in from the eastern end of the city. 'Caesar, I humbly take my leave.' Galba found himself facing, under a hot sun, a reined-in squadron that raised much dust. To his relief, he heard and then saw behind him a running platoon of German troops. Then there was no relief because they ran too slowly and the swords were out and bright.

'What is all this? What do you want of me? I don't like those looks. Come, aren't we comrades? You belong to me, I belong to you.' It sounded like a popular song that would have been despised for its banality by Galba's predecessor. The leader of the troop made a rough

344

vocal signal, then it was all hooves and blood. Struck down. He was left there by the ornamental pool named for Curtius. The German troops about turned and marched back. The cavalry galloped back east to the Guards barracks, where Otho was being proclaimed. The bleeding body was left to the phagocytes. A common soldier knew whose it was and had a vague notion that he might be paid for the head. He sawed it off without difficulty, the neck being thin, all strings, and then he cursed it because there was no hair to carry it by. He stuck his thumb in the toothless mouth and hooked it against the hard palate. Then he bore it aloft and swaying towards the head-quarters of the Praetorian Guard. He heard cheers. Otho was being borne on stout shoulders. A new Caesar. How long would he last?

Aulus Vitellius, a long man in his fifties, on whom a dispropor-tionately gross paunch seemed to have been plastered, received the news of Otho's accession in his camp on the lower Rhine. He chewed fibrous gobbets of overboiled boarmeat with strong brown teeth as he read and reread the letter in which Otho asked for the hand of his daughter and invited him to share the rule of the Empire. Vitellius's slow brain, inveterately clogged with the fat of gross feeding, pondered this and pondered also his present gubernatorial appoint-ment, which had been made by Galba. Evidently these upstart Caesars feared him. One had wanted him out of the way; the other craved an alliance. It was as good as an invitation to take over. His aide Severus agreed. Picking delicately at the bone Vitellius had offered, he said: 'The fact is that times have changed. The Praetorian Guard thinks it makes the emperor. The days of the power of the military in the capital are done. This province of Germany speaks for the future. The Empire is its provinces.'

'How long since Otho seized power?'

'A few weeks.'

'Who helped him to it?'

'You know Tigellinus?'

'I know the bastard. A few weeks, eh? It seems hardly fair to allow him to get settled in.'

And so Vitellius disclosed to his troops an affability he had not previously shown, embracing odd common soldiers as far as his belly would permit, showering gold pieces on them, inviting even centurions to share his breakfast, a meal which tended to be prolonged until it could be fairly called dinner, and obtaining a cheering procla-mation without much difficulty. How sordid all this is. When Otho got the news that the legions of Vitellius had already been sighted in northern Italy, he reluctantly marched at the head of the Thirteenth, ready to parley, and was suicidally depressed when he found he was committed to battle. He was not a fighting man. In his tent outside

Brixellum he spoke harshly to Tigellinus, who had unexpectedly changed from uniform into the garb of a civilian traveller:

'Did not expect it? What do you mean – you did not expect it?'

'I did not,' Tigellinus smoothly said, 'expect such a state of unpreparedness. I gave you my support on a different understanding. Even under my first master Nero there was a sort of stability. Which, I must admit, Nero at length totally liquidated. After all, my loyalty is to Rome.'

'Meaning whoever is capable of taking Rome?'

'You can put it like that, yes. It's no unpatriotic act to leave you now, Otho.'

'I'm still called Caesar,' Otho said, loudly though with little conviction.

'So briefly. So terribly briefly. Still, you're entitled to the honorific. *Vale*, Caesar.' He gave the ancient European salute and left the tent. One of Otho's senior officers came in and looked inquiringly at his master. Otho said:

'No, I know what you're going to suggest. Leave all that to Vitellius.'

'Do we fight, Caesar?'

'Well, we certainly don't surrender. But I've no real taste for civil war. I think I'd better get my papers in order.'

This took a long time. To his secretary Britannus he gave certain simple signed instructions. No punishment of deserters. All manifests of Otho's supporters to be burnt, along with all private letters which might incriminate his friends. No records, in other words. Though an exception could be made for Tigellinus. 'I'll retire now. I don't want to be disturbed till dawn. I recommend that you go into retirement. Somewhere remote and safe. You know you're provided for.'

'I'm grateful, Caesar.'

Otho, like so many of the personages of my story, was completely bald, but he had always worn a well sculpted toupee that dissimulated his condition even to friends and concubines. Now he took this off. In a mood of total serenity he ate a light supper and then went to bed. By his bed a good sharp dagger was waiting. At dawn the army of Vitellius roared into the camp, pillaging in a fierce red light that was the shepherd's warning. In the tent of Otho they found the body of Otho, neatly pierced, the face above the wound relaxing from the contortion of death into a deep peace. The hair above the face was very neatly disposed. It was what was known as a Roman end.

Vitellius ate his way into Rome, crunching the votive bunches of grapes that peasants humbly handed him, digging his blunt fingers into watermelons, calling for grilled meat from the stalls by the road-side. The first ceremonial banquet would be of three days' duration.

Tigellinus was wallowing in a bath of bubbling mud in the establishment of a certain Laetus on the outskirts of Rome when he heard the news that his days were numbered, indeed his hours. One naked handmaiden was kneading hot red mud into his groin while another shaved him. He embraced the kneader with hungry fervour before politely saying to the shaver: 'Give me that razor. Then leave me, both of you. A gentleman sometimes has to be alone. There are certain things a gentleman can only do for himself.' The girls snatched up bathrobes and giggled their way out. Tigellinus grasped the razor by its white bone handle, mumbling to himself.

'Well, little Nero, it was a good run. True to one's nature. I was always true to mine. Well, until recently. A gentleman should never scheme to obtain power. Power comes to those who can use it – for whatever end. I was a bad man, Nero. Totally bad. That in itself ought to be pleasing to some god or other. But I don't know his name. I rose out of the mud. And here I am. At the last.' He scored both forearms very deeply and watched with a kind of admiration the rich red flow. 'Sleepy, a little sleepy. Back to the mud, Tigellinus.' He sank into it.

A man like Tigellinus could be regarded as a supererogatory element in the reign of an emperor like Vitellius, whose main distinctions were gluttony and cruelty and a willingness to indulge both at the same time. There was, for instance, the time when he sat alone at table, gorging brains, livers and pancreases seethed in cream and honey, having already taken a morning snack of the sacrificial meats offered to the gods and additional bevers of sturgeon, oysters, pies made of small wild birds and sickeningly sweet pastries, what time he gloated over the forthcoming dessert of the execution of a good citizen named Octavius. Octavius stood near the block, far enough away from the dining table to ensure that no blood would stain its napery, while the axeman waited to his left and his wife, Livia, wept and pleaded on his right. With courtesy Vitellius said:

'You will forgive my dining at this solemn moment in your life, Octavius. I have a busy day. I must eat when I can. Have you anything to say before the carver ah carves?'

'I die deservedly, Caesar,' Octavius said. 'There is no worse crime than being a fool. You should write a treatise called *A Short Way with Creditors.*'

'Oh, Caesar,' Livia sobbed, 'he did only good to you, sir. He sold his mother's house to get you the money you said you needed. Be merciful. He won't do it again.'

Vitellius choked on that, spraying the air with fragments of stewed milt. Octavius said to his wife: 'Go now, Livia. Remember me as I was.' Vitellius said to her:

'No, don't go, Oliva or Lavia or whatever your name is. You can still remember him as he was for a second or so. A capitate husband, so to speak. You realize, of course, that your crime is rather greater than his. You pleaded for his life. You said in effect that the imperial verdict was unjust. Headsman, try out your blade on an *easy* neck – delicate, swanlike I think the poets would say.'

'I congratulate you, Vitellius,' Octavius said. 'I thought Gaius and Nero were the ultimate monsters. You do better than both. And you'll meet the same end. If you don't burst first like a poisoned dog.'

The screaming Livia was carried to the block while Vitellius ate with relish. This was no exceptional day for him. The exceptional days were marked by consumption of the great Minerva pie, which was compounded, under a thick crust of flour and eggwhite, of the organs of pikes, carp, pheasants, quails, partridges, peacocks, flamingoes and lampreys and the execution not merely of creditors but of close friends who came to the banquet smiling. There was always plenty to eat for Vitellius.

What can one say of this Rome except that it was in great need of moral redemption and that it had missed its chance? And what can one say of the corruption of the present writer, who admits to a gross fascination in the recording of bloody misrule and a certain reluctance to return to the lives of small people who sweep, bake bread, make decent marital love, perform their humble duties to the community but raise yawns more than admiration when they become matter for a book? God, if he exists and does not recognize Petronius, may think differently, but you are not God.

Marcus Julius Tranquillus and his wife and daughter left Rome at an opportune time. Julius's uncle, who was ageing and lonely, made them welcome in his villa in Pompeii, which lay not far from the fertile slopes of Mons Summanus, a mountain which had erupted recently and would not, so the astrologers decreed, erupt again for at least a century. Julius, a retired soldier, took to what many veterans did for health and pleasure in those days: he cultivated a garden. But he tended his uncle's grounds, which had been neglected, for profit also. He added to the garden two acres of unused paddock: the soil was so rich here with the past effusions of the volcano that it cried aloud to be planted and harvested. So Julius grew salad greens, cucumbers, melons and marrows, plucked plums and cherries, and tended vines which produced wine so miraculous that it was called the tears of the gods; the few quiet Christians around (of whom Julius was no longer one) went further and called it the tears of Christ. When Julius's uncle died, full of years and still dreaming of the return of the republic, the property went to the nephew. Julius prospered, employing two boys and his own son-in-law in the planting, tending and marketing. Ruth had married the son of a Greek bridging engineer named – like his father – Demetrios, who had migrated hither as a child with his family from western Cyprus. While the Roman Empire was setting to history the worst possible examples of morality and rule, it was also, distractedly as it were, proclaiming the virtues of intermarriage, which I have always held to be one of the hopes of a humanity which has tried to thrive too long on divisiveness.

Julius was growing old now, irongrey but not bald, muscular and sunburnt but given to shooting pains in the back and thighs. Sara was less old, but she too was greying and her body, which had been slender as a sword, had rounded to an acceptable matronliness. She retained her old cynicism about the ways of God and empires. The day was enough and whatever the day brought – the kitchen tasks, the laying of the red dust, the feeding of the hens and pigeons, the evening gossip over the tears of the gods, the stroll with her married daughter through a town grown soft in its cultivation of pleasure, well planned however, full of ridiculous statues and refreshing fountains. It was a town of baths and brothels, fantastic fashions in dress and hair for the patrician women, lavish dinner parties for the rich, a general tolerance of Oriental faiths though not of Christianity, games and plays and singing contests, a balmy climate, Mons Summanus recovered from his sickness and puffing slackly and benignly.

One day Sara's brother Caleb and his wife Hannah came unexpectedly, leading a grey donkey on which their household gods were bundled and corded. They were travelstained and weary but swiftly revived after a warm sluice and a cup of the divine lacrimation. They unloaded their beast and sent it to graze in the orchard among the plum windfalls.

'How long are you staying?' Sara asked.

'Myself not at all. Hannah, until I get back. If I ever do.' Hannah was thin with a grief she could not lose nor seemed to wish to. Caleb was hardy enough but looked older than Julius. His nose seemed more assertive than before, his cheeks had shrunken. They had had no further child; they had settled to an unphilosophical resentment of the death of their son.

'There's room for her.'

'She's a good hand with the needle. And her cooking isn't bad.'

'And you go where?'

'Well, it's a long story,' Caleb said to Julius and Sara, as they sat over the cool jug. 'I'm going back to Jerusalem. I take ship from Puteoli. I've waited how many years for this? And it comes when I'm too old, an old married man with no son to promise a future to.'

'What future?' Julius asked. 'What's going on?'

'You get no news here?'

'News of what?'

Caleb sighed heavily, sitting on his ornate little chair nursing his cup, his shoulders hunched. 'The Romans always ran Palestine badly. Our people put up with a lot but there had to be a limit. The procurator Florus has forced this on the people. Robbing the Temple, God help us. What do the Jews do? Sit back and let him do it? They hit, at least the Zealots did. There've been some Roman deaths. Florus ordered a massacre and some woman there tried to stop it. Daughter of Caligula's puppet – I forget her name.'

'Bernice or Berenice,' Julius said. 'I saw her in Caesarea. A pretty little woman. No fool.'

'Now she's gone on to the Roman side,' Caleb said. 'Perhaps she can't be blamed. The Jews burned down her palace in Jerusalem. The Jews can sometimes be very ungrateful. But the Jews at the moment are mad, and who can blame them?'

'Where did you learn all this?' Sara asked.

'It's come through to Rome. There are prayers in the synagogues. It's the war at last. The Romans brought this on themselves. I've got to get out there.'

'To be killed,' Hannah started to sob. 'They won't win, they can't. It's going to be butchery.'

'Oh, yes,' Caleb admitted. 'They've got the legions coming in from Syria. And we, they, the Zealots, have stones and a few knives and no organization. No unity, no control. The Sadducees want to keep out of it and the Pharisees aren't sure. As for the Nazarenes –' He looked straight at Julius. 'It's the end of the Nazarenes.'

'I thought it would be, some day,' Julius said. 'God hasn't been helpful to the Nazarenes. Or to the Jews. I lost faith. I see now it was Paul I had faith in.'

'You're no longer one of them?'

'No longer. I attached my faith to something else. Something more in keeping with the needs of a retired centurion.'

'He means,' Sara said with some scorn, 'he's been washed in the blood of the white bull. Nonsense like the other thing. But more fanciful nonsense. Mithraism, they call it.'

'In what way,' Julius asked, 'is it the end of the Nazarenes?' He felt a lump like hard cake in his mouth.

'How could the Nazarenes be trusted? They don't believe in war. They turn the other cheek. They won't die for the Temple.'

'And quite right too,' Sara said. 'Why should anyone want to die for a chunk of stone?'

'*He's* ready to die for it,' Hannah sobbed. 'Men are fools.'

'Suicidal idiots,' Sara expanded. Caleb looked sheepish. Julius said: 'What happened to the Nazarenes?'

'Nothing much. They were given a warning. They were asked to show where their loyalties lay. And when their *episcopos* as they call him had the stones thrown –' He gulped, remembering Stephen.

'Who?' Julius asked.

'James. Head of the Nazarenes in Jerusalem. The last of those who saw Jesus Naggar. The Zealots said it wasn't safe to have him around.'

'I never met him,' Julius said. 'But I heard about him. He did well. He kept the balance. I thought the Jews loved him.'

'Oh, they were ready enough to tolerate him before this Florus raided the Temple. Then he talked about forgiveness and the Temple not made by hands. So the high priest Ananus permitted the stoning. He knew what would happen if he didn't. They killed the high priest Ananias. Cleaning up the Jewish camp before the great war. The pure clean blade of the sword of Israel.' He began himself to sob like his wife but he soon gave over and then showed proud wet eyes to the company. 'I know it's hopeless, but what can I do? Could I live with myself? I take ship from Puteoli.'

'The war will be over by the time you get to Caesarea,' Julius said.

'It will never be over,' Caleb said. 'It will take the Romans for ever and ever to kill all the Jews of the world. The Temple may be destroyed, but the Jews carried the Ark of the Covenant through the desert places and will carry it again.'

'Go,' his sister said, 'to the desert places and wait for them. You're following a bad dream.'

'A good dream. I had it when I was a boy, you remember. I have to be true to my boyhood. It's as simple as that.'

Caleb marched to the port on a rainy day, with the cone of the great mountain masked in grey moving mist. He kissed his wife and sister and niece and he wept. Julius shook his hand hopelessly and went to the weekly service at a temple less glorious than Solomon's. The altar was a simple stone table, and on the wall behind it was a painting in Pompeian blues and russets of the god Mithras as a beautiful youth driving his sword into the neck of a white bull which was, for good measure, being devoured simultaneously by a scorpion, a crab and a dog. He found himself praying to the severed head of Paul for the safety of his brother-in-law, then he shook off the blasphemy. The masked priest stood near a tethered white bullock, knife in hand. Julius too was masked and, like so many of his fellow worshippers, he wore a military uniform worn, too small, somewhat mildewed. There were five young postulants, unmasked. The priest said:

'Worshippers of Mithras, lovers of Mithras, god of the sun, lord of life, hearken well to his story. The god of light was conceived to be our saviour from the god of darkness Ahriman, prince of evil. The struggle continues until the death of time, and we participate in the

351

struggle. Behold the solemnity of his mystery. The swift sword of light saves the force of generation from being devoured by the force of evil. The killing sword is also the sword of rebirth. For from the blood of the slain new life springs. For those postulates assembled today with the initiates, a most solemn moment is at hand. For they shall be bathed in the blood of the slain and be given new life.' He raised the sacrificial knife and Julius closed his eyes. On the roof of the temple the rain beat. He remembered another bathing on the shore of the island of Melita. Sacrament meant soldier's oath. Broken, broken. Cowardice. No, realism. Were they not all the same? Isis and Osiris, at whose ceremonies his daughter Ruth wept and rejoiced for the death and rebirth of the god of fertility, taking her new pregnancy to the priestess of Isis to be blessed. All the same under different names. He opened his eyes as the heavy bulk of the bleeding bullock fell to knees, to flank, bellowed in fear, died with blaring eyes. The postulants went forward to the altar to be smeared with the blood of the slain. 'For at his last supper the Lord spoke and said take ye and eat for this is my body. Take ye and drink for this is my blood.' Julius was hearing the wrong words. The priest was saying: 'Bring low the armies of Ahriman. Saviour, accept our love.' Rain continued its rebuke, Julius beat his breast.

Titus Flavius Sabinus Vespasianus, whom we will call simply Vespasian, hale in his fifties, once *legatus legionis* in Britain, hated by Nero but indispensable to him as an efficient, tireless and incorruptible general, sat with his son, who had the identical name but whom we will call simply Titus, in their military headquarters near the Syrian border. 'The Tenth Fretensis,' Titus said. 'The Twelfth Fulminata. The Fifteenth Apollinaris. The Fifth Macedonian.' Regimental orders were sealed and stacked for delivery. Vespasian said:
'I leave it to you.'
'But surely there's no urgency. These Jews come first.'
'Rome comes first.' Vespasian read once more the dispatches. The Moesian and Pannonian legions had repudiated Vitellius. The legions in Syria and Judaea also. Their allegiance to Vespasian had not been sought and certainly not paid for. Vespasianus Caesar. Titus said:
'If you leave it to me you leave to me also the fulfilling of the Antonian dream.'
'Listen,' his father said urgently, 'things never happen twice. The Eastern Empire was an impossibility, and Antony would have seen that if he hadn't been besotted.'
'Bernice is no Cleopatra. Bernice accepts the *pax Romana*.'
'Which is administered from Rome. Where, when I die, you will be

352

Emperor. Another thing, Jerusalem is not Alexandria. I know what you have in mind, young as you are.' Titus was in his middle twenties. 'It's a Neronian idea in the sense that it's an artist's dream. The fusion of Roman discipline and Oriental glamour. Well, there's no glamour in the Jews. They don't have the decadent softness of the Egyptians. I can understand your being bewitched by this Galilean princess of yours, but that's just a young man succumbing to Asiatic languor. You'll get over it.'

'I propose marrying her.'

'Ah, no. When your time comes the Romans will never accept a foreign empress. You won't even have time now to use her as a mistress. You're in total charge of the Palestinian campaign from now on. It won't take long. Show no mercy. They deserve no mercy. Pound it to dust and sow salt in the ruins. Spare nobody. Spare nothing. Not even their damned temple.'

'There are certain things not even a conqueror ought to do.'

'Oh, I know – fine architecture, sacred to an ancient people. But batter it, desecrate it, don't be seduced by the tears of your Galilean mistress. There's no room for strange gods in the Empire. Cover the body of the Jewish faith with quicklime.'

'And the Christian faith?'

'That's already finished.'

I have not much to say about this Jewish campaign: the story has been exhaustively, if sometimes inaccurately, told by a man named Joseph ben Mattias, who turned his coat and, in devotion to the dynasty initiated by Vespasian, renamed himself Josephus Flavius. It was after the massacre at Jotapata in Galilee that he, a rare survivor and a competent captain of infantry, sought Titus in his tent. 'He comes under a truce flag,' the centurion Liberalis told his general. 'He wants to come over to our side, he says. He has valuable information, he says.'

'I don't like defectors. Why didn't he die with the rest of the – What's this place called?'

'Jottapatata or something. Shall I let him in?'

Titus tiredly nodded. A young man in armour, heavily bearded, came in, his brown eyes sharp as though feverish. He gave his present name and what he trusted might be his future name. 'The Jewish cause was always hopeless,' he said. 'Why have you crucified some and not others?'

'We ran out of wood.'

Josephus sighed. 'I fought but saw that fighting was a mode of selfslaughter. I wish to join the Roman cause.'

'And what do you hope to gain from the Roman cause?

'For myself, nothing. Except my life. Rome I know. I pleaded the

353

cause of the Jews there once. The Empress Poppea Sabina was generous enough to say that she was impressed. She proposed joining the
Godfearers. No, irrelevant. I'm a writer of histories. As such, I know
that no man can fight against history. It is a strong tide and a man
must float with it. History lies, for the next few hundred years or so,
indubitably and ineluctably with the Roman Empire.'

'And how many of your fellow countrymen feel the same?'

'Not many. We Jews are a stubborn people. When I come to the
writing of the history of this war I shall not deny either the stubbornness or the courage or the faith. The way things are going, all that
will be left of the Jewish people is what will be in my book. But that
must be so with all peoples, even the ones who establish their empires
for eternity.'

'I'm a patient man,' Titus said. 'I've listened. But I'm not greatly
interested. Why do you tell me all this?'

'I tell it you because, without realizing it yet, you are desperately
interested. Every victorious general needs the palms of the poet or the
historian. Otherwise he becomes only a garbled tale for children. But I
do not come primarily to tell you this. I come to tell you of the rifts in
the fortifications of the holy city.'

Titus showed brief revulsion. 'You come here to betray your own
people?'

'Hardly. I do not wish Jerusalem to suffer a great siege. Let Jerusalem be taken with the minimum of bloodshed. I will show you the
surest way to the citadel. I think you may find me useful in other
ways. Your Aramaic hardly exists. Aramaic is my mother tongue.'

'What prevents my treating you as a captive and as a slave?'

'Your good sense. Your victorious generosity. The fact that I am
what I am. A man who has the right view of history. As for captivity
and slavery – these, of course, I will not accept. I can always fly at
your throat with my teeth and then be struck down. All death is
captivity. Living, we have a choice.'

'Highly philosophical. You'd better tell me about the rifts in the
Jerusalem fortifications.'

It was not intelligence of any great utility. The battering rams found
their own weak places in the city walls. The catapults hurled rocks at
the battlements. When Titus's forces entered they found a wailing
population white with dust, arms raised to heaven, women howling
over the dead children they still carried tightly in their arms, Jew
fighting with Jew. Odd troops of Zealots armed with the slingshot
David had found efficacious against Goliath, sworded and daggered
too, opened fierce mouths at the invading Romans and rushed on
them to no great effect. Those who were caught were nailed in
cruciform postures to the city walls. The weak and old had already

354

found refuge in the Temple, which had its protective garrison of young warriors. The Tower of Antonia was in Jewish hands. Arrows and stones rained on the vanguard that Titus himself led to the Temple gates. Titus, marching through the inner courts, saw with interest a notice in the three languages of the province, promising death to the Gentile intruder. That in itself was a challenge. He ordered the rams to be dragged to the massy doors, marvelling at their gold and ivory, fighting a sickness that was a mere transitory disease of his impressionable youth.

'Steady, there. Watch that offside wheel. Come on, move.'

Wails came through the clouds of white dust. The Romans completed their forcing of the doors, finding it no easy task. Within the Temple they found howling women raising babies like weapons or shields. The old were on their knees, though not to the Romans. A noisy lot, the centurion Liberalis thought. There was now battle in the Temple. Young men with beards fought for the Holy of Holies. Priests cried prayers to their all highest. Sweating Roman troops, awed distractedly at the magnificence of gold and onyx and carbuncle and amethyst, stuck their spears in and seemed to hear the blood gush in cries about the horror of the ultimate desecration.

In the morning glory of birdsong, Titus surveyed the multiple crucified bodies that were crammed on the skyline. There were no trees left in the environs for further crucifixions. He walked with Josephus through smoke, dust and broken stone, stumbling over corpses. One corpse came alive and spoke:

'Yusef ben Mattias. Traitor.'

'Josephus Flavius. Roman citizen.'

The corpse, briskly speared, rejoined its fellows.

'One thing I would not wish to be recorded in my history,' Josephus said calmly. 'The desecration of the Temple through pillage and demolition. Posterity will never forget that.'

'Even though it's been used as a military fort?'

'Necessity, necessity. The citadel of the faith and the faith means the city. I will tell you the true reason why I accept the Roman mastership of the lands of the Mediterranean. The future can never lie with theocracy.'

'Explain that big word to a simple soldier.'

'The Christians are right when they render unto Caesar and unto God but keep the two tributes apart. All rule must be secular. When God enters politics he turns into his opposite. Always has. Always will.' Titus did not well understand.

The troops stumbled over the bodies of men, women and children in the forecourts. 'Heathen muck,' Liberalis said, as the pillaging began. The veil of the Temple was rent. The great menorah was taken away.

355

One young soldier shook his head sadly. 'A bit doubtful, are you, lad? No direct orders, is that what you're thinking? Haven't you ever heard the word *discretion*? No general officer likes to *order* this kind of thing. But he knows it has to be done.'

The destruction of the ransacked Temple called for all the engineering skill the invading legions possessed. Huge metal balls swung from chains on derricks: the outer walls were stubborn, but they yielded at last in torments of dust and smoke. The pillars cracked, there was a scramble for safety as the great ornate ceilings began to bow. There were few Jews left to wail. After two or three weeks of steady destructive energy there was only a great heap of rubble, sending up dust to an invisible sun.

When Caleb landed at Caesarea he looked like a Roman growing old in the service of ships' cooking galleys. To any who asked he gave his pseudonym Metellus. He felt a stranger in this port where there was hardly a Jew to be seen or heard. Roman patrols clanked through the streets; a homegoing legion paraded on the dockside. Caleb saw an old blind man sitting on a bollard, clanking a cup, crying for alms. He put a coin in the cup.

'Todah, ach, achot.'

'What news from Jerusalem, *av*?'

'You don't want to know the news from Jerusalem, *ben*. Jerusalem is no more, *ben*. Get you to Masada.'

'Why Masada?'

'All that will be left of Israel will be the young men of Masada. Until the Romans get there. They will come and starve you out. But the faith will prevail, *ben*.'

'But tell me of Jerusalem, *av*.'

'Thank the great Lord of Creation I never saw Jerusalem. And even had I the sight I would not see it. For Jerusalem will be no more. The trees cut for crucifying by the forestload. And the grass of the pasture outside the city burnt and the soil of the richness of the land sown with salt that no more life shall henceforth spring. Get you to Masada, *tsair*.'

Caleb trembled and sought the road. He met with a ragged column of Zealots who were seeking to join up with the forces of Eleazar.

Vitellius felt great fear when he heard the news, and the fear promoted massive appetite. He gnawed meat, trembling. He stuffed pie into his mouth, trembling, with two hands. Fight. Start recruiting campaign immediate discharge bounty regular pension after victory. Troops assembled in Palatine. Never wanted to be Emperor, never asked for it, forced against will. Give us the money now and we'll stand by you.

Call on Flavius Sabinus, brother of invading Vespasian: won't have you put to death for disloyalty, instead offer five hundred thousand no a whole million gold pieces if hold off brother. Peace, I want peace. Tell Senate send envoys for armistice, Vestal Virgins in front cooing peeeeeeace.

'Who are you?' he asked, eating.

'*Explorator*, Caesar. First detachments of Vespasian's legions close at hand. Recommend immediate evacuation of palace.'

He called for a closed litter for himself and one for his chief cook and Arab expert in flaky pastry. Mouth stuffed, chicken drumstick in fist, he stuffed himself in. Quick, my father's house on the Aventine. Soldiers outside the palace, relaxed, cooing of peeeeace, no need to worry, Vespasian is still busy in Judaea. But the palace was empty. Vitellius took from a cupboard a belt with pockets already stuffed with gold pieces and strapped it on. Not starve, limp away anonymous, unnoticed, cloak and hood. Then he heard noise. He ran, clinking, chewing, to the quarters of the janitor. The janitor's dog, chained outside, snarled bitterly. Vitellius fed it a piece of meat and went in, jamming the bed with its mattress against the door. The vanguard could be heard tramping, smashing, looting. They broke in.

'Who are you?'

'Only one left. Look after palace. What have you done to my poor dog?' The centurion and his troops eyed Vitellius's paunch and nodded. 'Important message for Vespasian. Demand safe custody till he arrives.' They tied his hands behind him, tightened a noose about his neck, dragged him out of the palace whimpering, desperate for food, tore his clothes off him, sliced off his leather moneybag and threw the gold to the mob. Then they kicked him along the Via Sacra towards the Forum. He tried to bury his wineflushed face in his chest, but they stuck a sword under his chin and made him squint in the sun. The mob cried fatbellied old bastard. The troops played the game of the little cuts with him, a swordjab here, a daggerthrust there, then, on the Stairs of Mourning, they stuck into his belly and watched the guts flood out. Then they threw his body into the Tiber. He floated some time before he glugged to the bottom.

When Vespasian entered the palace he found it fully staffed and a banquet prepared for himself and his entourage. He looked at the loaded table with loathing.

'Take this filth away.'

'Filth, Caesar? It was specially prepared –'

'Remember my name. It is Vespasianus Caesar and not Vitellius Pseudocaesar. Vespasianus Caesar would appreciate an imperial luncheon of bread, goat's cheese and raw onions. And, to drink, some *cervisia*.'

'Ccccervisia, Caesar?'

'Yes. It is not wine. It is a fermented beverage made from malted barley. It foams. It is bitter and invigorating. Rome needs its salutary acerbity and an infusion of its salubrious vigour. Things are going to change around here.'

So, with the whole of Israel subdued except for the fortress of Masada, the final task of the Romans was to break the resistance of Eleazar, leader of those most zealous of the Zealots called the *sicarii*, who had gathered his forces and led them toiling up the steepness of the rock on which Masada stood. There were two ways up, both precipitous, one to the east above the lake Asphaltitis, the other a serpentine pass to the west. Herod had built a kind of palace at the summit, with a wall about it all of white stone, thirty-eight watchtowers set upon it, equidistant on the circumference. The new procurator, Flavius Silva, marched from broken Jerusalem with siege engines, setting them up on the so-called white promontory three hundred cubits beneath the highest part of the fortress. Forgive me, I am not well able to set down the details of siege engineering, lacking the knowledge, being also in pain and somewhat drunk, but it is sufficient to say that Eleazar was able to look down on the smoke of a vast camp of ready Romans in the knowledge that the supplies of the fortress had run out, except for the water in the natural wells, that the enemy was confident none of the· Jews could escape, and tomorrow or the next day a stream of Roman armour would file up by the two passes, breach the walls and commence the work of systematic, God help us, slaughter.

'I know what some of you are thinking,' he said to the men of the garrison (there were wives and children there too, also to be systematically slaughtered). 'Best to be taken prisoner and fed. But they won't take prisoners.'

The man they called old Caleb muttered something about the leeks and onions the Israelites had eaten in Egypt, that captivity was no burden.

'You don't seem to understand, Caleb. The Romans are not going to behave like the Egyptians. Nor like the Babylonians. This is the modern age. History is in the hands of the Romans and the new pattern of history is based not on the humanity of enslavement but on the ferocity of liquidation.' Eleazar, though he called himself primarily a fighting man, loved to hear himself speak. He spoke now at great length about the beauty of death, how it was no more than a sleep, and was not sleep to be considered a great benison after the long day of work and thirst and heat and aching muscles? No, they were not to be killed by the Romans; the Romans would make their laborious ascent in vain; they would find the fortress filled with the corpses of brave men (and not so brave women and children who, in terms of the morality of a holy war, were neither one thing nor the other). Cheated of their prey. One man was chewing something; Caleb squinted at it: it looked like the corpse of a rat. Forbidden, of course. Mass suicide also was presumably forbidden. To manifest the glory of the law you had to break the law. 'You men who have wives and children moaning in the quarters of the mothers,' Eleazar said, 'ought not to apprise them of what you propose to do. Do not afford them the time of protest, but do what has to be done without a word, though, and this is fitting, on a valedictory kiss.'

'You mean,' said a slowwitted man named Yigael, 'we have to stick the knife in our nearest and dearest?'

'Crudely put, but that is precisely what I mean. Look at the Romans down there, eating the meat of our country by their campfires, polishing their swords and slavering over the prospect of mass slaughter. I know what the law of Moses says about murder, but what I propose and indeed command does not come into the category of homicide in anger or in lust or greed. In killing each other we still fight a just war. You, old Caleb, I see shaking your head. You have been too much softened by a sybaritic Roman life and, I don't doubt, by the watery creed of conduct of the Nazarenes. Be a Jew, be brave, set the younger ones an example.'

Coldblooded slaughter is never easy, even in a good cause. It was found better to dispose of the children first, and this was mostly done by hurling them down the rocks so that their skulls might be fractured on the flinty prongs or solid surfaces. The Romans looked up from eating, laundering or polishing to see white things falling through the rare air of the height: tokens of surrender or what? The slaughtering of the mothers was more difficult, though some threw themselves weeping or cursing after their children. Two male friends had usually to hold down a yelling wife while the trembling husband thrust a dagger under her breast. These widowers were among the first to be willing to stand bravely against the wall, throat bared to the dagger, murmuring *Israel* as the blood spurted.

Caleb confronted Yigael, standing over the corpses. Eleazar, still orating about the beauty of death, had said that he would see his friends bedded down for the long night before taking the knife to himself. Yigael said to Caleb: 'Who first? Yacob there will do in which one of us two is left.' Caleb thought of his own Yacob, dead and buried in Rome, and felt the acid of a great despair rise to his gullet. Without voicing an answer, he walked round Yigael, who stared out to the hills of Israel, and struck him in the bone of his back with his borrowed dagger. Then he struck in the flesh and saw blood well. Yigael said: 'Not so bad as you'd think after all.'

'Loss of blood,' Eleazar said, 'induces a desire for sleep. And sleep is a benison and to be sought for.'

'Ah, be quiet,' Yigael said, tottering. Yacob, a brawny man in early middle age with few facial expressions, suddenly grabbed Caleb by the collar of his filthy tunic and, with a wide arm arc, let the dagger's point fly to his throat. So that was it. What was life all about? What were we sent for? Caleb saw and heard the red tide gallop all down his tunic front, Hannah would be annoyed, have to wash it, always wash out blood in cold water, then, which was not pleasant, began to choke in it. Blow to the heart best, centre of the scarlet city, not the outlying streets. *Israel*, he heard someone say and remembered, choking, that the name meant a struggle with God.

Struggle with God, indeed. I am drunk enough to proclaim to the whole world, meaning these trees and that prospect of Alps beyond the lake, these nesting thrushes and the quietly though busily growing grass, that, despite all the depositions of the sceptics, God exists. There has to be an explanation for man's unwilled misery. Yet God is above human morality and, in the arena of morals, knows not what he does. He is no more than a gamester. Was not this all a game? He played the game of bringing a fleshly son into the world, whose task it was to cry the salvation of Israel. He ensured that Israel should either shut its ears to the cry or puzzle over it as if it were in a foreign tongue, and then reject it. To ensure that Jerusalem should not be the centre of the creed of its own redemption, he smashed the church in Jerusalem and sent its father to Rome, there, before his ludicrous death, to establish the spiritual lineage of its insubstantial paternity. What worse centre for a doctrine of love could well be imagined? Oh, a great game of unquestionably divine provenance, and the game goes on. That it makes men suffer does not come into the sphere of God's supposed omniscience: the flesh is a curious substance he does not well understand, not himself possessing it, and, since he does not possess it, it must be deemed to be of a negative quiddity. I am drunk on sour wine, so forgive me. He does not see my pain and is certainly incapable of feeling it. He does not see the deep wound in the body of Israel, the ruined Temple, the streets where dogs bark and whine in the ruins, the fields where crows caw, pecking at the eyes of the countless crucified. Trumpets shrill in Rome as the menorah is borne in the victorious procession of Titus. The woman called Israel weeps under the willows. Let me out of it, I have had enough.

In Pompeii the Israelite widow Hannah wept and Sara gave little comfort. Sardonically she recited:

'If I forget thee, O Jerusalem, let my right hand lose her cunning. Let my tongue cleave to the roof of my mouth if I remember not Jerusalem above my chief joy.'

'You're – heartless. He was your brother.'

'I don't think I approve of martyrs. Life's hard, and we have to get through it somehow. We don't have to make it harder by inventing gods and causes and holy cities. Cities are only stones and bricks and thatch. Easily burned. Rome was burned, Jerusalem was burned. What does it matter? Living is what matters, such as it is, keeping alive in spite of all of them – the hard faces, the men full of their own authority, the big causes, God, Deus, Zeus, Jehovah –'

'It's a comfort,' Hannah sniffed, 'to know he died for what he believed in.'

'Nonsense. You are what he should have believed in. But you'll find somebody else to believe in you. A man who gets on with earning his daily bread and doesn't make his eyes big with dreams of big causes.'

'You're heartless, you just have no heart. I don't want another husband. I just want to die.'

'Yes, you say that now. In a few weeks' time you'll wake in the night, alone and cold, and want the comfort of somebody or something. Forgive the truism, but life has to go on.'

'You keep saying that. It doesn't mean anything.'

'It isn't meant to mean anything. I'm going to make you some chicken soup. Eat, girl. Keep going. Live, if you can call it living.'

She ate, and she kept going, and she lived, if you could call it living, and she accepted the courtly advances of the widower Isidorus who, despite his name, was no cynic. And Sara's daughter Ruth, who gave birth to a daughter named Miriam in the year of the death of Nero, was happy enough in the little house at the end of the Street of the Smiths, and Julius grew old in his work, ruddy and healthy in the air, though his back creaked. This is not the stuff out of which history is made. History pretends to be a straight road with a mapped destination at the unseen end, whereas ordinary life is a circle. Miriam grew, slender as a wand, proud of her black hair with a curl in it, and she became friendly at thirteen with a lad of sixteen named Ferrex. Ferrex, as the name will tell you, was a Briton. His father had come as a captive with Caractacus and, because of his fighting skill, had lived to be a freedman gladiator at Neapolis, dying in the arena at Pompeii when visiting Galba had given the thumbs down. Young Ferrex was in training in the same trade when he first met Miriam.

I leap ahead in my narration to these two because I have to find hope somewhere, and only in these young can I find it. They were living under a reasonable Emperor whose elder son would carry on his reasonable father's business; of the other son, the Emperor who sends the taxman to me, I will say nothing as yet. Life and the world lay

361

before them. The Empire was at its old distracted business of mingling bloods. Ferrex loved Miriam. They sat on the lower slopes of benignly puffing Vesuvius and talked. Ferrex's red poll became gold in the sun. Miriam's grandmother's brother had not yet been wholly forgotten. Ferrex believed that he done a stupid thing, going to a foreign country to let himself be killed.

'But he believed.'

'Well, I believe. And you believe too, don't you? In the god Osiris. But I wouldn't die for my belief.'

'Perhaps that's what's wrong with the god Osiris. Nobody would die for him. He's only a kind of poem about the winter and spring.'

'You'd better not let the priests hear you say that.'

'He didn't make heaven and earth and the sea and everything in them.'

'Now you're talking like a Jew.'

'I *am* a Jew.'

'That's something else you'd better not talk about too loud. The Jews are supposed to go into slavery or feed the beasts at the games.'

'Only the Jews who fought the Romans in Judaea. Why did you say what you said?'

'What did I say?'

' "Now you're talking like a Jew." As though there was something wrong with being a Jew.'

'There's nothing wrong, except – Well, you take everything so seriously. About the God who made everything. And he looks down on you all the time, growling if we kiss or – well –'

'Yes?'

'We *ought* to get married.'

'You're starting again. Round and round and round. Like the god Osiris. And I say we're too young.'

'We're not. We're not too young to – Well, if you knew how I felt about you –'

'Oh, I know how you feel. Perhaps we ought to stop seeing each other. Perhaps you ought to go out with that Greek girl who rolls her eyes at you when she's not pretending to pray to the divine Osiris. What's her name? Daphne or something. You wouldn't have to marry *her*.'

'That's not a very pleasant thing to say. I'm not – well, like some men, boys. I believe in love.'

'*Amor, eros, agape, ahavah*. Look at the mountain. Fire. It's gone now.'

'It's your God getting angry.'

'That's stupid and – you know –'

'Blasphemous. Would it help if I became a Jew? Would you marry me then?'

'That's stupid too. You can't become one. You just *are*.'

362

'A Christian, then. That's serious too. With a God who made every-thing and even had a son of flesh and blood that people eat every Sunday.'

'They don't now. It's not allowed. It's death to be a Christian.'

'Is that why your mother's father gave it up? Because he was scared of being thrown to the beasts? If you're frightened of that I suppose it's right to give it up. But it's not very brave.'

'He was *very* brave.'

'Yes, when he had the Roman army behind him and in front of him. Not so brave now. Going to worship this god who killed the white bull. With the rest of the old soldiers, making him feel as if he's a fighting man again.'

'Ferrex, if you say another word against my grandfather I'll get up and leave. Do you hear me?'

'I hear you. Vesuvius hears you too. And he's sticking out his big red tongue at you. Now it's gone in again. I love you, Miriam.'

'I love you too, Ferrex.'

And they kissed with closed mouths, arms entwined. The great mountain, unseen of them, vomited a little spit trail of lava.

Charming, are they not? Young love. Oh, I know the bubbling of the juices of the glands comes into it, but I think if there were a God who understood love he would put down his paper games for a moment and bless. His son knew all about it, but Paul was not too sure. And the rest of the disciples? It would not have been possible at this time, seventy-nine years after the birth of their master, to ask any of them, for they were all gone under. Barbarous deaths for most in outlandish places. But stay.

One afternoon while Julius was deploring the depredations of the birds in his orchard, an old man, older than Julius, came timidly to the gate. He said: 'Is it Julius? Is that your name?'

'At your service. What can I sell you – a fine melon, some cherries, some squashes, a cucumber?'

'May I come in? May we talk?'

'Yes.' A very old man, infirm, ragged, with a knotty stick to help him hobble. 'Let's sit under this beech tree here. Would you like some of this wine and water? How did you know my name? Did someone send you to me?' They sat on the rough wooden bench Julius had knocked together. The wine and water had been married in a leather skin. The old man drank shakily but with gratitude. He said, wiping his mouth on his ragged grey sleeve:

'Yes and no. I'd better give you *my* name. It's not fair to have the advantage of you. Matthias. From Jerusalem. I was called the new twelfth apostle of the Christ. Does this make any sense to you?'

'But,' Julius said, 'you're Sara's uncle.'

'Sara,' Matthias said. 'Is she alive?'

'Very much so. She's in the house now. Let's go to her. She'll be amazed.'

'But perhaps not happy. She held things against me – well, one thing. It was in the old days of Pontius Pilatus. Her brother, my nephew, condemned. There was a possibility of bribery. But the new Nazarenes didn't believe a man should do what he wished with his own money. Besides, I mean no offence, women talk. This is a very secret visit.'

'You're a Jew,' Julius said, 'and a Christian. Those are both deadly things to be – with the way things are. I take it you fled from Rome.'

'I fled from Rome. I came to Pompeii because I was told there was more tolerance here – tolerance, indeed, for too many things – strange faiths from the Euphrates, brothels as a major industry, drunkenness, adultery. And is my nephew Caleb alive?'

'He went to the Judaean war. He never came back.'

'Yes. That was to be expected. Fought for the Temple. And Stephen and James died because they thought nothing of the Temple. Mostly dead I believe, my colleagues, companions. I grow near to death. According to a man's just expectations, I'm well past it. But, as you see, I'm hale though stringy. My voice still carries. I have work to do in this city.'

'No,' Julius shook his old head with vigour. 'There's no work for you here.'

'Yes. There's a grove near the foot of that mountain. Fit for meeting. Fit for the breaking of the bread. But you must tell me where the Christians are.'

'This I don't know and don't wish to know. I think you're under some misapprehension. I was a Christian, baptized by the apostle Paul himself, but I repudiate the faith. I follow the cult of Mithras.'

'A very inadequate substitute, if I may say so. You worship a myth instead of a flesh and blood reality. God walks into human history and you turn your back.'

'I must warn you,' Julius said harshly, 'to keep out of our way. Sara must know nothing of your coming here. A man has a certain responsibility to his family.'

'I understand. Clearly. That's why I come to you here under the trees, not to your house. Is that your house – where the chimney is smoking?' It was a good mile off from these converted paddocks. Julius nodded. 'It's easier for a single man to follow the path of martyrdom. But you can help me in another way. Give me work. I can gather fruit, sweep, tug out weeds. Old but hale, as I say. And I have to earn my bread.'

'My son-in-law works here. Today he's at the games. The Pompeians pride themselves on their amphitheatre – big as the one Vespasian's building in Rome. Work? Well, you're welcome to your bread. As for shelter –'

'Oh, I see your problem. Some day I'm arrested and you're arrested for harbouring a criminal. Surely you have a shed, stable – where I can creep in at night and you can disclaim all knowledge of my being there. Or am I proposing to make life too difficult for you?'

'I give under the pretence of your taking. I leave food and you take it. But soon you'll find Christian friends with deep cellars.'

'It grieves me that you yourself are not a Christian friend. But I regard your – apostasy as a temporary lapse. You'll be back.'

'I think not.'

'Julius,' Matthias said, grinning with few teeth, 'you're better known that you think. You knew a man called Luke, a Greek physician with a talent for writing? He turned up briefly in Rome again when I was there, looking for Paul, and then disappeared – God knows where to. Perhaps to Athens, where they have a bishop named Dionysius and the Romans leave Christianity alone. They seem to regard the faith there as a harmless form of Platonism, if that's the right term.'

'I knew Luke, yes. He and I and Paul were – close. We suffered shipwreck together. In what way better known than I think?'

'Luke kept the record of the bright days for the dark future. His writing is copied and read. The name Julius is there. A humane and helpful Roman centurion.'

'And how did you know I was here?'

'A very old couple in Rome told me about you and your wife Sara. A tentmaker, very old. He's survived and his wife too. I think you will survive. You have the look of a survivor.'

'One who *has* survived. What does it matter now? I have to worry about other survivals.'

'I can say that also of myself, I suppose. But I don't matter, nor really do the others. The great battles are remembered, but who recalls the names of the soldiers who fought in them?'

In Rome things went well for the Romans who did due, if cynical, reverence to the Roman gods. But a return to the bad times was in preparation. Titus Flavius Domitianus, second son of the Emperor, whom I shall call simply Domitian, was, though in his late twenties, not inclined to follow paths of virtue and wisdom. He drank, gambled, whored, paraded the streets with a flock of badmouthed cronies and a bloodthirsty wolfhound from Neapolis called, with no onomastic originality, Lupus. He had no skill as a soldier nor even as a sportsman, though he showed a certain aptitude for archery. When, one day, a slave came out of the imperial apartments to the walled garden on the Palatine where Domitian and his friends were pelting each other with fallen fruit, Lupus emptily barking the while, he would not allow the man to deliver his message without making him submit first to a sportive torture. The slave had to stand against a whitepainted board set against the wall, his right arm extended laterally and the fingers spread. Then Domitian took his arrows and his bow and, from a distance of many yards, aimed at the fingergaps. He hit no flesh and was duly if wearily applauded by his friends. The slave said:

'My lord Domitian –'

'I know, I know. My imperial father awaits. Come, Lupus, let the two beasts march together to the sacred presence. Why does he want us?'

'You, my lord, not the dog. He gave strict instructions which were passed on to me to pass on to you. He doesn't want to see your dog. You alone, sir. Why, I don't know.'

'Stand there. Don't move.'

Domitian shot a final arrow which parted the slave's hair

'Some day,' he said, 'I'll shoot lower. Much lower. You know where. You talk too much.'

When he had gone, one friend said to another: 'Exeunt the beasts.'

'You're not being fair to his wolfhound.'

Vespasian was taking his frugal luncheon alone in the small dining room of the very limited, but, he said, entirely sufficient, imperial apartments. Bread, cheese, garlic, ale imported from Alexandria. He could hear the dog whining outside, tied to a post, so he lifted his head in the expectation of seeing his second son. Domitian, sleek, stocky, insolent, came in with a mock salute, crying: 'Hail, Caesar.' Then he took a wedge of cheese for himself and chewed it noisily.

'I don't like your manners, son. If you behave like this with me, the gods alone know how you behave with your slaves. You may sit down.' Domitian sat chewing, grinning, showing what he chewed. 'You don't have much knowledge of imperial history, do you? Indeed, you don't have much knowledge of anything except dice and whoring.'

'Fair shot with the bow.'

'You don't know how I, with the help of your brother, have brought this Empire back on the road to sanity after decades of total disaster. Titus follows me. You follow Titus.'

'If I live. If Titus lives.'

'We assume you both will. Only I wouldn't blame any slave who strangled you in your sleep. Or any whore who secreted a razor – never mind, I say no more. I know it wearies you to be reminded of your future responsibilities. I propose granting you a provincial quaestorship. I want you out of Rome. You do the Flavian reputation no good.'

'But I don't want to be a provincial quaestor. I want to stay here and help you, father. As I've done already. Help with the collecting of the taxes.'

'The tax on the Jews is useful, I never doubted it. Any tax is useful. But listen to me –'

'A tax is useful when it doesn't involve loss of imperial dignity, I would say, father. People going to the public urinals have started to call them vespasians. That impairs your dignity.'

'I don't mind. It's a wholesome tax. Money doesn't smell. But at least men going to a urinal uncover their private parts privately. You, I'm told, make men prove that they're not Jews by doing that publicly. It's unseemly.'

'But the Jews are the enemy. They're lucky not to get worse.'

'The Jews are the conquered enemy, which is slightly different. The only salt we rub in their wounds is the salt of exorbitant taxation. The Christians are a different matter. The Christians defy our gods and spit on the new temples I've built. And you can't uncover a Christian by uncovering his genitalia. You have my permission to persecute whatever Christians you can find out. But not in Rome. We can take care of the Christians without your help. I'm sending you to Pompeii.'

'But I want to stay in Rome. My friends are in Rome.'

'You'll make new friends in Pompeii. Decent retired centurions and Greek businessmen. And you'll find a decent city council that will keep you in your place. On my orders. I'm asking for monthly reports. If you do more than usually badly I'll send you off somewhere savage and remote. Britain, for instance. Now, get ready.'

Domitian rose, took a crumb of cheese, mocksaluted and gave his father *vale*. Then he left. Vespasian could hear the dog barking now, not whining. Then the noise receded in the direction of whatever mischief Domitian had arranged for the afternoon.

He spent the afternoon, like most, including his last one in Rome before assuming his commission, in a low gambling den, playing dice with a oneeyed man named Scrupulus, while Lupus sat panting at his feet ('Bring your master luck, boy') and whores sat around drinking wine fortified with grape syrup, ingesting at the same time the lead of the bowl, which was conceivably a factor contributing to Roman madness. Scrupulus said:

'Got you there, your lordship. I make it three hundred sesterces.'

'Roll you for double. No, wait – double and double and double.'

'Six hundred and sixty-six, the holy number. Good, my lord.'

Domitian lost and said: 'Loaded.'

'You wouldn't have said that if you'd won, your lordship. Six six six sesterces.'

'Don't spit at me. On to him, Lupus. Bite him.' The dog obligingly snarled and made for Scrupulus, who retired to a dark corner where the dripping fangs held him. Domitian chalked the sum on the wall: DCLXVI, saying: 'Very well, that's what I owe. I'll pay you when I get back from Pompeii. But I still say those dice are loaded. Come, Lupus.' And he left. This number has ever since been the mark of the beast, expanded in the secret writings of the Christians to an abbreviation of *Domitianus Caesar Legatos Xsti Violenter Interfacit*, meaning that the Emperor Domitian is violently killing the legates or representatives of Christ. The collocation of office and act was still to come and is proceeding as I write, but Domitian, as I shall show, was brisk enough in persecution while still merely a prince.

He rode to the assumption of his office in Pompeii with the dog Lupus in a saddle basket, followed by his personal slaves and the dour Greek Amilon, a very starchlike man, whom Domitian called his secretary. He was fed and wined amply by the town officials, installed in the rarely used imperial lodging on the Street of the Flowers, and he spent his first few days and nights in pursuing the ample pleasures of the town. He whored, gambled, drank, attended the games in the imperial box, became well known as a roaring boy on whom a dangerous authority had been plastered. One day he pursued a young man named Keravnos, so called for his loud voice, with a party of lictors: he wanted the young man to raise his robe and show the end of his penis, but Keravnos, who thought this to be merely a heavy joke in bad taste, ran away very quickly, Lupus lolloping after him, and entered the house of Marcus Julius Tranquillus, whose door was ever open. He slammed and bolted this door, hearing the scratching and whining of the dog and then the thunder of the lictors' fasces on the wood, demanding admittance. The widow Hannah was sitting there with a new suitor named Achilles. This had been their conversation:

'I mean, I know.'

'You know?'

'About loneliness, I mean. When my second wife died – well, I drank you know. Drank. It doesn't do a man any good.'

'Drink, no.'

'Loneliness. Or a woman either. I got over the drink. My business suffered. But I've never got over the other thing. So I ask you to think.'

'Oh, I think all the time.'

'Think. We're all entitled to our little comforts.'

'Spoken like a Greek.'

'I *am* a Greek.'

'Well, that's why you speak like one. Now I'm being – what's the word? – pert. I'm being pert. I apologize. I'm grateful you should ask.'

'Well, I haven't asked yet, to be truthful. But, with your permission, I *will* ask. There's no need to give an answer now. Tomorrow, say.'

'Or the day after.'

It was at this moment that Keravnos ran in and bolted the door. 'The lictors,' he panted, 'asking for something ridiculous. And the new man, Dom something –'

'Domitian,' Achilles said, going pale. 'That's the Emperor's son.' There seemed to be an attempt to tear the door from its hinges while a kind of wolfhowl, representing authority derived from Romulus and Remus, combined with loud male shouts to open up. 'We'd better –' Then Sara came in from the kitchen. She went straight to the door, frowning, and unbarred it. Domitian and his dog tumbled in. She looked at Keravnos, still frowning, asking:

'Is this a friend of yours?'

'Never saw him before in my life.' The lictors, who knew no harm of this family, stayed outside, somewhat embarrassed, unhappy under orders. Domitian and his dog strode about the room, Domitian saying:

'Domitian, son of the Emperor, performing an imperial duty. Is this a Jewish household? Are you,' to Achilles, 'a Jew?'

'I'm a Greek. I'm also a mere visitor here.'

'We'll consider the taxing of Greeks later. At the moment we're not concerned with the uncircumcised brethren. Is one of these women your mother?' he asked Keravnos. He shook his head. Sara said:

'The head of this household is away on business. He is a Roman citizen and a retired centurion of the imperial forces. I think that should be enough for you, whoever you are.'

'I've told you who I am, woman.'

'We have only your word for it. Whoever you are, remember that Roman citizens have certain rights. One of these rights is privacy. Kindly stop your dog or wolf or whatever it is lifting its leg against my furniture. And now, leave. Whoever you are.'

'Whoever I am. You'll see. Good day to you.'

He left, Lupus dribbling on the floor in valediction. Achilles said: 'Unwise. Very.'

Sara said a foul word in Aramaic and went looking for a mop.

Matthias, whose native Aramaic had given way to Greek, which he spoke with elongated vowels and rasping *chis*, was at this moment talking to a number of Pompeian Christians in a grove near the foot of Vesuvius, which was today quiescent, merely sighing out odd wisps of vapour. 'Marriage,' he said, 'that is to say holy matrimony, is a sacrament or holy oath of allegiance that one breaks at one's peril. With us Christians, it is an act of grace which binds us to God and his blessed

369

son. When a man and a woman enter into the holy state of matrimony, they place themselves before the throne of God, binding themselves to eternal fidelity. They beget children and thus help to people heaven with new souls –'

Ferrex and Miriam, hand in hand, were wandering near the grove. Miriam was surprised to find her grandfather sitting alone on a long-congealed lump of lava. Julius knew Ferrex. He grinned at them both and said: 'Keeping watch. A secret meeting.'

'What kind of a meeting?' Miriam asked.

'If you want to see a man who actually knew Jesus Christ, he's in that grove talking to some Christians. I think you can both be trusted, can't you? I'm here to come out with a wolfhowl if anybody suspicious starts hovering. You know what happens to Christians?'

The nodded. They knew. They wandered, hand in hand still, into the grove and saw a very old man talking to fifteen or so citizens of Pompeii. The old man was saying:

'The ceremony is a very holy one. It is not a matter of making a civil contract. It is a heavenly contract, and over it presides one of God's deacons or bishops. I must consider myself the bishop of Pompeii and empowered by the Lord himself to preside and tie the holy knot. Jesus Christ said certain words I would ask you to remember: "What God has joined together let no man put asunder." An eternal contract between the man, the woman and God himself. Unbreakable by the laws of the state or the will of man –'

'You saw Jesus?' a woman asked.

'I am the only man now living who did. I had just been elected to the discipleship. There were two candidates for the office – myself and poor dead Barnabas, and it was decided on the throwing of dice. The Lord appeared to us, wounds in his hands and feet, but truly raised from the dead, and bade us preach the word. But I stray from the point –'

A wolfhowl came from further down the slope. The party disbanded. Matthias smiled briefly on the two children, one Jewish, one Celtic, as he hobbled away. Ferrex said to Miriam:

'Well, there you are – marriage.'

'Christian marriage.'

'They take it seriously, anyway.' And then Ferrex said: 'They say I'm ready. They say I can appear in one of the minor bouts at the next games. They say I can call myself a gladiator. My probation's over. I can move into the main barracks. I asked about married quarters.'

'Oh no.'

'That's what *they* said – I mean, they laughed and said gladiators don't marry, they have a different woman every night, and the women fight for the privilege, ladies too, some of them, very high born.'

'But that's terrible.'

'That's what I said. I said I loved somebody, and not all of them laughed. One of them said there's no harm in loving somebody so long as it doesn't interfere with your training, but he said being married is a different thing altogether.'

'What did he mean?'

'And one of the gladiators made sort of sucking noises at me. I didn't understand that either.'

Domitian did not understand the signs which one of the lictors charcoaled for him on the white wall outside the civic offices. 'A cross,' Domitian said, 'I thought they had a cross.'

'You mean a Greek *chi*? No, that's a beggar's touch sign. They mark the houses where they hand something out. Food or money. It's the first letter of *cheire*, meaning a hand. They hand something out, see? No, what you used to see, more in Neapolis than here, was a drawing of a shepherd, not easy to do, or an anchor, or else a fish.'

'Why a fish?'

'Because the Greek for fish is *ichthus*, and that gives the initials of *Iesous Christos Theou Uios Soter*. See, sir? I first saw that outside the ichthic market, which the ignorant call the ichthic fish market. In Neapolis, I mean. Here there aren't many left. You won't find those signs much about.'

'I saw that fish thing today.'

'Where, sir?'

'We're going to dig them out.'

Sara was looking for her husband Julius. There was a shed near the ramshackle gate of the orchard where the donkey, Hannah's and Caleb's, young then, growing old now, was lodged. Sometimes Julius sat there whittling stakes for his plants. She found the donkey chewing straw and, sitting in straw, a very old man trying to bind two lengths of rough wood together to make a cross. They looked at each other, he smiling uncertainly.

'Who are you? What are you doing here?'

'You don't know me, Sara?' She frowned, puzzled. 'I know you. I knew you as soon as I saw you in the market the other day. But I didn't say anything.'

'Uncle Matthias? But it's not possible. Uncle Matthias joined the Nazarenes. He's dead, they're all dead.'

'I should be dead. I've been lucky, I suppose. But I'm still in the faith. That's why it's better for you not to know me, Sara. An old man doing odd scraps of work, sleeping in this stable. I don't want to cause trouble. But I wondered how long it would be –'

'Good God,' Sara said, with force and decision, 'must we spend all our lives being frightened, being cautious when we're not hunted? Is there no place in this world where people can be free to think and do

371

what they want without men with laws and swords and axes and crosses interfering? You come to the house, Uncle Matthias. No flesh and blood of mine has to sleep in a dirty manger.'

'No, leave me here. Don't put yourself or Julius in more danger than you may be in already.'

'Julius? How do you know Julius? Did Julius tell you to stay here? In what way is Julius in danger?'

'He keeps guard when we Christians have our meetings. It's good and brave of him.'

'Julius,' she smiled sourly, 'washed in the blood of the white bull. You've dragged him back among the Nazarenes?'

'No. He's not with us. It just happens that he's on the side of the hunted, that's all. I used no persuasion.'

'Come to the house at once.'

'Let me think about it. I have a meeting arranged here. A young couple. They want to get married. I have to tell them that they can't have Christian matrimony without the Christian faith. And I feel like using persuasion there. Negative. I don't want them to be baptized. They're too young to be martyrs.'

It was not until the next day that Matthias took courage, really a vicarious courage, and went to the house of his niece. He admired the signs of very modest property, the swept and scoured very Jewish cleanliness. He found in the house not only Sara and Julius but the widow of his nephew Caleb and his great-niece Ruth with her husband Demetrios, a ruddy young man with soil under his nails. The table was laid with platters, winecups, sliced bread, a Pompeian jug with the contorted body of a young athlete as its handle, vegetable soap steaming in its tureen. 'Sit,' Julius said. 'You, Uncle Matthias as I ought to call you, at the head.' They sat. Matthias said:

'So I, a Christian, sit in a house of very mixed beliefs. Hannah and Sara, who believe little –'

'Nothing,' Sara said. 'Except in what's so simple and what we can't have. To go our own way.'

'Will this company be offended,' Matthias said, 'if I offer this bread and wine in the way I was taught?'

There was a silence of some embarrassment. Sara said: 'If it pleases you, Uncle Matthias. It can do the rest of us no harm.'

'So, then. The night before he died, the Lord took bread and broke it, saying: This is my body, eat in remembrance of me.' He passed the bread round. Sara would not eat it. Hannah nibbled. Ruth said:

'The broken body of Osiris. I take it.'

Julius could not eat. When the wine came Sara said:

'I take this as wine. Wine is wine.'

'The shed blood of Osiris.'

Julius muttered: 'My Lord and my God.'

There was a fierce barking outside. The door crashed open. This time the lictors entered, preceded by Domitian in princely raiment. Domitian said: 'This is imperial Rome, my children. Searching for Jews who evade the payment of taxes. You, old man. I've had my eye on you. Do you know anything about fish?' Julius, standing, said:

'This is a Roman household, my lord. We give shelter briefly to an old man workless, breadless, homeless. We break no law.'

'What's your name, old man?'

'Matthias.'

'Not a very Roman name. Take him. And you, whatever your name is –'

'Marcus Julius Tranquillus, former centurion, citizen of Rome.'

'You have some explaining to do. The rest I can deal with later. Come, let's go.' Matthias, batted to the door by the fasces, forbore to bless the company. Sara spat. Domitian ignored her.

Domitian ignored Matthias and Julius until the following day, which was also the day of Ferrex's first appearance at the games. Ferrex vomited in the morning but recovered at noon. Matthias and Julius starved in a cell until they were summoned to an interrogation room in the quaestorial offices. Domitian sat languidly with his short bow and his quiver of short arrows. The prefect Rusticanus was ready to follow the regular interrogatorial procedure; he waited for Domitian to tell him to –

'Proceed.'

'Your name?'

'Matthias bar Yacob.'

'Born where?'

'Jerusalem in the province of Judaea.'

'You admit you are a Jew?'

'I was born a Jew. But I do not practise the Jewish faith.'

'What sort of life do you lead?'

'Hurry,' Domitian said. 'I have to attend the games.'

'What sort of life?' Matthias said. 'Blameless, I think. And without condemnation in the eyes of anyone I know.'

'You say you were born a Jew but are no longer a Jew. What are you then?'

'A Christian.'

'My lord,' Rusticanus said, 'the situation has changed. The interrogation now is not in respect of this man's being a Jew.'

'He stands doubly condemned, doesn't he?' Domitian said. 'We proceed in respect of his holding a faith condemned by the Roman state. But hurry.'

'What are the doctrines that you practise?'

373

'I've tried to become acquainted with all doctrines that men hold. But I've committed myself to the true doctrines of the Christians, even though these may not please those who hold false beliefs.'

'Are there other Christians in this city of Pompeii?'

'There are.'

'You meet with them?'

'I do.'

'Where do you meet with them?'

'In various places.'

The sharp ears of Domitian caught the noise of citizens proceeding to the amphitheatre. 'Hurry, man. The games are beginning.'

'What is that thing in your hand?'

'A wooden cross. The symbol of my belief. My master died on the cross.'

'What is that writing on it?'

'Pater Noster. Our Father. Meaning my God.'

'You believe that when you die you will rise again?'

'I do.'

'And if you are scourged and beheaded do you believe that you will ascend into a place called heaven?'

'I know this. That for those who lead a just life here below the divine gift of eternal life is waiting.'

'So you think that you'll ascend into heaven?'

'I don't think it. I know it.'

'Will you sacrifice to the gods of Rome in accordance with the laws of Rome?'

'I cannot. Those gods were made by human hands. I cannot worship gods of stone and wood and metal. There is only one true God.'

'Those who refuse to sacrifice to the gods are to be scourged and executed in accordance with the laws. You stand condemned.'

'So be it.'

Domitian stood. He said: 'Matthias, which is your lucky hand?'

'Lucky? I don't understand you.'

'I see that you hold that cross thing in your left hand. Is that the hand you use for holding things?'

'Yes.'

'Good. Are you a sporting man?'

'Again, I don't understand.'

'Do you have luck with the dice?'

Matthew smiled briefly at that before replying. 'Many years ago I had luck with the dice.'

'Good. I will give you a chance, Matthias. Take these dice and roll them.' From his beltpurse he took the carved white bones with black dots on them. He threw them on to the table. 'If the number you roll is higher than five you shall take the chance of my marksmanship with these arrows. If the number is lower than five then you die at once – with a point straight to your old *cor cordium.'*

'A man doesn't play games with his – well, call it destiny.'

'Take them. Roll.'

Matthias saw Peter and the others watching, Barnabas watching most of all. He took the dice. There was a perceptible trembling below their feet and a faint smell of brimstone came in through the unshuttered window. 'Nothing, sir,' Rusticanus said. 'We sometimes get these tremors. It will pass.'

'Roll.' Matthias rolled. Six. 'Spread your hand against the wall there. Your *lucky* hand.'

'This,' Matthias said, 'is madness.' But he obeyed. Standing his good three yards back Domitian let his arrows fly. Two of them refused to impale the wall but all missed flesh.

'Your luck, Matthias – amazing. But sometimes luck isn't enough.' And he shot an arrow straight at the old man's heart. It went deep: crimson welled on to Matthias's old grey robe. As he fell Julius ran to him. 'You – Roman centurion – are you too a Christian?'

'I am.'

'So. We'll leave your interrogation till after the games. Shove him in a cell somewhere.' The floor trembled again; brimstone fumes sailed in. Domitian went out into the courtyard. Vesuvius belched golden fire and dribbled red lava. The dog Lupus, tethered to a post, howled bitterly and retracted his tail. 'Take your chance,' Domitian said, patting him as he unleashed him. The dog ran with limbs ill coordinated, whimpering. Domitian strode to the stables, where ostlers were wideeyed with fear and stood as if paralysed. *It's coming.* The horses stamped, their manes atoss, their eyes blaring, snorting and sweating. 'Quick, the piebald.' Domitian galloped alone eastwards. He had to live to become Emperor; there were many hearts to be transfixed before he died.

Smoke, fire and lava. Lungs filled, choked. A black pall began to be pulled over the day's serenity. In the amphitheatre ten thousand Pompeians felt the ground heave, heard the thunder, saw the black pall drawn over. They screamed, yelled, crushed each other. Ferrex dropped his sword and ran. The mountain vomited endlessly. Air thick, defiled, a pale sun sometimes trying to shove through. The road of scorching lava down the mountainside spread to the streets and divided.

I please myself, in as much as I am capable of being pleased, with an image through the smoke of Ferrex and Miriam together, scrambling through fallen bricks that raised high dust. A donkey has raced from its stable and missed being brained by a crumbling wall. Ferrex and

Miriam find the donkey, Miriam mounts, perhaps Miriam and Ferrex have anticipated their knot and she is already with child. For good measure let them also find the wooden cross of Matthias, with Pater Noster upon it. Then they race off away from the disaster, carrying hope. I do not think this happened. One hopes in a sense without hope. If only that mountain could be my body, flooding out its life. But I have to wait.

They have all gone. Accius and Acerronius Proculus and Achilles choked and crushed by a fallen roof. Gaius Acilius and Aviola Acilius and Glabrio Acilius trampled upon. Paulus Aemilius meeting Aeneas dragging Laertes from tumbling ruins. Afranius and Agrippa and Titus Ampius running, their arms held up, outlined in fire. The Aequiculi falling into hot lava. Annona and Antistius in bed together, brained by falling timbers. Aponius and Antillus and Anicetus caught in their cups, toasting each other, forced to drink fire. Epicadus Asinius straddling the body of Asillius, his back broken by the fall of a pediment. A priest calling on Osiris, another on Mithras, a deacon on the Lord Jesus. Dying Julius saying *My Lord and my*. Hannah and Sara choked on the floating poisons of the air. Balbillus and Bibulus and Blossus not able to get the name of the *Bona Dea* out of mouths silting up fast. Caesonius Priscus trampled by Cassius Longinus. Cornelius Fuscus and Corvinus and Cremutius and Clodius and Salvito and Licinius and Marcus Curtius caught naked in the baths seeing with surprise a smoking solid river lurch into the water and contrive a temperature they have not before known. Drusilla about to deliver with Domitia helping, the child ready to emerge into hell. Ennia Naeva suffocating in black and golden air. Flavia Domitilla – no, she is in Rome, safe daughter of Vespasian. Furius Maximus with his leg broken, crawling in pain to a safer place that is unsafer. Fonteius and Gabinius reading poetry while Vesuvius bellows its own and thuds with its feet to mark the rhythm. Gallius, Quintus or Marcus, stumbling with a torch through an underground tunnel to see bricks collapse at both ends, the poison meanwhile seeping in. Halotus and Hasdrubal and Hecuba and the Helvetian visitors swimming a burning tide, one last breaststroke into final fire. Hortensius and Hermogenes safe in a deep cell except for the thud of stone blocking the way out from which, to their delight, the door had fallen from its hinges. Isidorus perpetrating his final cynicism. Janus Quirinus not knowing which way to turn. Julius Marathus and Julius Saturninus and Julius Vestinus Atticus and Julius Vindex and Junia Calvina scalped by hot raking fingers, burning claws snatching out mouthfuls of teeth. Laberius and Labienus and Lactus and Livius and Lollia and Lollius and Lucceius eating on the leaf in a pleasance of poplars hearing the rattle of pebbles and then seeing the pebbles as rocks, and the rocks burning and crushing. Macro and Marcia Furnilla running to child and nurse left at home, finding the home dust, then dust themselves. Mummia and Mucia passing straight into death during an afternoon nap. Nonius and Norbanus and Novius Niger and the elder Nymphidius eating hot lava, seeing the red blast of volcanic triumph through the darkness suddenly swept off by the hot wind, not seeing the outer darkness any more. The Oculata sisters resigned, stiff in each other's arms as the blundering flood comes. Odysseus and Oedipus and Oenone turned to fire in the sky, enormous, burnt on to clouds shroudlike in their stiffness, crying for wife, wifemother, Paris. Orestes pursued. Paconius and Pacuvius and Paetus and Palfurius and Pallas hearing loud flutes of Pan in the innermost chambers of the brain as they gasp in the last air of pitch and sulphur. Pedius pleasuring both Phoebe and Phyllis sodomized by the huge splinter of a wooden pillar in a downtown brothel. Pitholaus hearing the voice of Plato saying only ideas are reality. Try this pain, Plato, and then no pain. Plautius and Pollux and Pompeius and the Psylli with their charmed snakes writhing in blasts of a wind pumped from the terrene viscera. Priapus dephallified. Proserpina cool in hell. Ptolemy recalling a prophecy of an end by fire but only for Alexandria. Pyrrhus the victim, Romulus screaming as he sucks at a firedug, Rubria a red body before the final charring. Rustius and Rutilius embalmed screaming, their quarrel cut off. Salus praying in his last nightmare to Saturn, god of health in old age procured by liberal use of seasalt, while he raped Sabines to the approval of the Salli, singing priests. Salvidienus tearing the skin of his own face off. Scipio eaten by an igneous Africa heaving with scorpions. Selene failing to drag Semiramis moonwards. Spiculus stoned by Stephanus, both stoned by ultimate firestones. Statilius set upon by a bull as big as an island. Sulpicius on a gallows of molten marble. Theogenes seeing no heavens, all burnt, the stars flying sparks, for his scrying. To say nothing of the Thessalians, Trioptolemus, the Vinii, the visiting Vonones. The lights out, time's ruination, our mother our killer, an uncaring deity, so everything ends, a figure of the finality and nothing done.

And Sadoc the son of Azor in great agony among the cropping goats, manybreasted, with nothing to pray to, a great idea having burgeoned, having flowered, having died, the sun over the circumcised alps and the Helvetian thrushes opening their throats, waiting for another end.

Author's Note

It is fitting that I acknowledge my various debts. My fictitious narrator sometimes muddles up, sometimes gets right, authorities we take for granted but he, presumably, cannot know. The major ones are Tacitus, Suetonius, Josephus and the Acts of the Apostles. I thought it best to consult these in the original tongues and, for the last, I make special acknowledgment of the Graeco-Latin edition of the New Testament published in Graz and furnished with an apparatus criticus by Augustinus Merk SJ. My lesser authorities are numerous and include the exegesis of the Acts by F. F. Bruce, which forms a volume in *The New International Commentary on the New Testament*; *Paul* by M. Dibelius; *St Paul the Traveller* by A. M. Ramsay; *Die Romfahrt des Apostels Paulus und die Seefahrtskunde in römischen Kaiseralter* by H. Balmer; *Jerusalem zur Zeit Jesu* by Joachim Jeremias; the second volume of the New Testament Apocrypha in Edgar Hennecke's edition; *The Acts of the Christian Martyrs* in the Oxford Early Christian Texts. I wish also to acknowledge the help of my friend Dr Vincenzo Labella, with whom I have worked on the scenarios for three television series, *Moses the Lawgiver*, *Jesus of Nazareth* and *A.D.* I prepared for the writing of all three by composing literary works first – the poem *Moses* and the novels *Man of Nazareth* and this present one. The amount of research that goes into a popular television series is not clearly to be seen in the finished product, which has to aim at great narrative simplicity and the conscious elimination of elements which would appeal only to the scholar or the reader of fiction. Thus, *The Kingdom of the Wicked*, which was partly written for its own sake, partly in anticipation of *A.D.*, may be regarded both as an expansion of the latter and a literary diversion in its own right. The opinions, interpretations, errors, falsifications and ultimate pessimism of the supposed author (whom I supposedly translate from the supposed demotic Greek) are not always mine. The main thing we have in common is a location: he wrote in Helvetia, outside Lucanum, in the reign of Domitian; I write in Lugano in Switzerland under the democratic wings of I am not quite sure whom.